# The Sea Ain't Mine Alone

## C.L. BEAUMONT

# Contents

*For my dad, who surfed off Cam Ranh Bay*
*And for K, who is my marvel*

# 1

The love affair began with salt.

Thick salt. The kind that coated shivering skin in chalky warmth and crusted like splintering glass in between tiny strands of hair, seeking the water, seeking the sun, seeking the froth.

Salt that crackled across his tongue and burned in the corners of his tear ducts. That whipped through the valleys of his pruny fingertips and nestled thickly in the thin hair on his arms, the tiny crevices of his big toe nails, the hidden curve just behind his ear. That dried and slithered in shrinking flakes across the skin of his forearms under the baking sun.

"Jesus, stop licking your skin, Jimmy," his mom said to him. "You crusty old shrimp." She had a warm smile on her lips and one hip propped against the metal doorframe of their little red and white seaside mobile home. Cotton balls stuck between her freshly painted coral toenails, hairnet over curlers, and a languishing Lucky Strike perched between her fingers.

She always called him a crusty old shrimp when she was happy—when her Friday night date after her shift at Lou's Diner went well, and she came home to James already tucked in his bed with the bowl from his cornflakes washed and drying in the sink. She'd step out of her mint green Baby Doll shoes, her pink and white frilled waitress cap still bobby pinned to her curls, and press a kiss to his salt-free forehead, drowning out the sound of the waves. And James would pretend to be asleep while she rummaged through the hamper of their clothes, all fresh and dry from the laundry line in the sun. She'd search until she found his little pale blue swimming shorts and set them on the bed for him to find as a surprise when he woke up to the clanging of his Bugs Bunny alarm clock—the promise of a full Saturday's worth of daylight spent waist-deep in salt water and sand.

When James was ten years and four months old, he shut off the radio during the final credits of Cisco Kid and stood up on his tiptoes to wash his cornflakes bowl in the sink. He checked that the screen door was shut tight and sucked a little toothpaste onto his tongue so his mom would think he brushed his teeth. Then he climbed into his little couch bed, dreaming of the salt that crested and fizzled in the white froth of the waves. Of the way his pale blue swimming shorts floated and swished around his legs in the soft, wet swells and crusted in the hot and heavy Long Beach sun.

He waited and waited for the bubblegum kiss to his salt-free forehead. Waited and slept and dreamed. Until he woke up in the morning to a blaring Bugs Bunny clock and an empty trailer and no pale blue swimming shorts laid out on his bed. No frilly waitress cap hanging off the metal doorknob.

James' aunt took him in after his mom looked the wrong way stepping off the moonlit curb at the end of the pier and met with the hood of a cherry red Chrysler speeding on its way to catch Teddy Edwards at the Lighthouse Café up in Hermosa Beach.

Auntie Cath lived way out in the San Fernando Valley in some chicken ranch desert called Reseda. Her house wasn't made of metal and didn't sit on wheels with a screen door that rattled in the breeze. Her kids Ron and Susan ate Kix instead of cornflakes and didn't listen to Cisco Kid on Friday evenings. When James asked them if they liked to lick the salt off their skin too after playing sunup to sundown out in the waves, they told him they'd only ever been to the beach once. It had apparently taken Auntie Cath and Uncle Ron almost two hours to navigate the old station wagon through the Las Virgenes pass to make it all the way out to Zuma Beach, and by the time they got there they'd had just enough time to suck on some popsicles, dip their toes in the icy water, pack up, and leave again.

James didn't taste the salt again for years. His forehead stayed clean and fresh, salt-free. The little crevice behind his ear was as sterile as a freshly washed palm.

When he turned seventeen, he hopped in the passenger seat of Billy Madden's dad's old Buick and handed him a wad of money he saved bagging groceries to use for gas. They drove and drove until they reached the fizzling licks of salty waves lapping at the Santa Monica sand, baking in pools of golden sunset light.

There was a bonfire and chilled bottles of Pabst. Girls in little white swimsuits and the same four chords played over and over again on an old cheap guitar. And when James took Lisa Kerny's hand and lead her away into the quiet, pristine bed of velvet sand and tide pools, and let her drag her coral pink nails across his bare chest, chasing little droplets of sandy water, he licked the salt off her skin at the place where her neck met her shoulder, and it tasted like a crusty old shrimp.

# 2

The air pierces James' lungs as he gulps it down in heaving gasps, head bursting up out of the water like a rocket. His legs scramble below him, trying to find purchase in the ripping currents as another wave washes over his face, cutting off his lungs from the oxygen with a sharp clash. He needs to find up. Needs to find his board. Needs air.

His body is hurtling through a churning void, ripped and thrashed by the water's gripping fingers while the seaweed drags his shins deeper and deeper into the black depths. He has the vivid sensation of an iron black hand tugging his ankle down away from the air, and he fights against it, struggles with all his might, until he realizes it's the yank of his own ankle strap and board pulling him up to the surface, to life.

Weathered fingers finally find rough, waxy fiberglass, and the sun and breeze burst across his face in a great blast. They beat away the waves and froth still clinging to his skin and lungs until all that's left is the salt on his grinning cheeks.

"Shitty luck, Jimmy!" he hears Rob call out. "Next time you get yourself pitched over, at least have the courtesy not to look like you're drowning. I missed a fucking primo barrel waiting for you to surface."

James hauls himself up onto his board and then collapses on his back, chest heaving.

"I'll try to be more considerate next time," he says. The hot sun feels like a kiss on his chapped lips.

"Hang ten on a wave like that without getting your ass kicked next week and you'll be looking at a nice pocket of cash, courtesy of the ISF."

James turns his head to look over at Rob sitting idly on his surfboard, wet spine swaying with the rocking waves as they wait for the next swell. The truth of his friend's words sits like a weight on his chest, cutting him off from the cool sea breeze.

He knows as well as he knows his own name that the International Surf Festival next weekend up in Hermosa Beach is his last chance to finally earn enough points to make it out of the damn qualifiers and up into the pro's. If he makes it, it means a whole new year's worth of competitions. Extra cash in his pockets, traveling up and down the coast, sleeping in the back of Uncle Ron's old station wagon, waking up each morning before the sun with the only care on his mind being how many minutes'll pass until he drops in on his first barrel of the day.

If he wipes out, however, it's back to the Long Beach dockyard until he can pay his way back into a qualifying membership. James' body goes limp onto the fiberglass-coated wood beneath him as his mind clouds.

"Hey man, mellow out," Rob says, cutting through his thoughts. "I can hear your brain flipping out from all the way over here."

James yelps when a handful of seawater gets dumped on his face.

"Buzz off! Can't mellow out if you're drowning me all over again, asshole," he laughs. He moves to sit up on his board and rolls the kinks out of his neck in a long, slow circle. The endless blue stretches out in front of him, a question and an answer all at once. He sighs and runs his fingers through the wet tangles of his hair, brushing back his overlong bangs that've turned almost white from the blinding sun. He revels in the way the little droplets of water trickle down his sides and back in a salty race.

"For real, though, man," James goes on. "I can't go back to that dockyard full time. Gotta make at least a grand or two riding this year or. . ." He trails off. Rob hums.

James leans forward onto his elbows and watches Rob retie his long, curly hair into a loose bun out of the corner of his eye. The wavy, salt-slicked strands look like black silk in the waking sun, and Rob's chest rises and falls in tandem with the gentle rocking of his board. His stomach muscles clench to keep his balance as he tucks in the last loose lock of wet hair. The sight makes James feel warm and dry in the back of his throat, just like it has every early morning for the past two years, drifting side by side out on the velvet waves.

"Jimmy," Rob finally says, staring straight ahead. "You know those guys over at Val's have been banging on your door since you first turned up on this beach telling you they'll sponsor you once you're pro."

"They tell every new young punk that," James interrupts, but Rob fixes him with a hard stare.

"Been riding the waves on this stretch of beach since I was eight, man, and they've never given me a phone call, I'll tell you that much. And you're not a young punk either, you old geezer."

James forces a laugh and splashes some water Rob's direction.

Rob's right. He isn't young anymore—not really. Not when nearly every guy in his heats at the competition last month was younger than he was way back when he even first set foot onto a Navy ship.

"Sorry," he says, shaking his head once and speaking down to the water. "You know how I get."

Rob knows. After two years of constant friendship and near daily pre-work surfs out along the sleepy Los Angeles coast, James knows that Rob has trained himself to look out for the faraway dark stare he sometimes gets in his eyes. The blackness that pulls him down away from the jokes and laughter and joy of flying off the ocean spray on a shiny waxed board, and instead entombs him in its deep, sightless depths.

Rob sees it, and he doesn't ask how or why, and he pulls him back up gently, slowly. He offers James his hand without pity. James knows that's perhaps the only reason Rob Depaul has become his longest lasting friend to date.

And yet, what Rob doesn't know could fill an ocean. They're both well aware that Rob's only ever tiptoed across the very tip of the iceberg that is James Campbell. Rob never asks, never pries. He tells James the story of his life and his parents, the places he's been on vacation and the way his girlfriend Lori tilts her head when she drinks a milkshake. He talks steadier than the firm breeze in the patient calms in between sets while they perch on their boards to wait, and he never once asks James a question in return. He fills in the histories for them both, and for that James is eternally grateful. But this—the darkness, the void, the inequality—it's there all the same.

Rob doesn't know that the reason James was sleeping down alongside the beach in the back of a station wagon when they first met was because he'd stepped off a Navy vessel fresh from the Vietnam coast just a few months before with nowhere to go and nothing to do. He doesn't know that James never once set foot back in the little Long Beach trailer park where his mom's frilly waitress cap hung off the metal doorknob each night. He doesn't know that James shot a man face to face at point-blank range and then looked down at the dying body to see that the kid was too young to even have a driver's license. He doesn't know that James thinks about the way Rob's thighs hug the smooth fiberglass and wood of his board. Thinks in the middle of a fourteen-hour shift down at the dockyards of the precise, unchanging process Rob uses to tie up his hair in a bun.

Rob grins, a little smirk at the corner of his thin lips, and rolls onto his stomach to start paddling out into the smooth vast blue.

"Yeah, I know how you get, old man," he calls back over his shoulder. "Crotchety old hodad shit sitting out here on your wrinkly ass, wishing us young kids weren't putting you to shame on every wave."

James rolls his eyes and shakes his head down at his board, then flings himself down onto his stomach to try and catch up to Rob, cutting through the sharp, clear water with his arms as they race out to the rolling horizon.

Rob's gone and done it again—pulled him up and out. James' back feels open and assured, pushing back up against the weight of the world and drying, inch by inch, in the shimmering sun.

"Gotta head in after this set," he yells up to the bottom of Rob's feet. "Shift starts at 9."

"Show me what you can do then before you're late to your fucking bingo game and Odd Couple reruns."

James feels the familiar slow burn start to build in his shoulder sockets, spreading out from his core and threading through every vein in his body. It rushes his blood so fast and hard that his body melts seamlessly in with the coursing blue water beneath him. He duck-dives under a nice barrel and smiles as he shoots a stream of bubbles out his nose through the thick churning salt. Then he sucks in a deep breath before turning to watch the very top of Rob's loose, wet bun bob up and down as he rips down along the glassy shoulder of the wave until his strong, sturdy legs are swallowed up by whitewater along the shore.

Rob's victorious whoop echoes out to him across the waver. "Behind you, old man!" he cries, palms cupped around his mouth where he stands next to his board stuck in the sand. "Bomb coming—got your name on it!"

James' heart beats double time in his chest as he turns back out towards the endless blue. He spots it immediately. A rolling, rumbling crack of a wave forcing its way across the surface, pushing up from the murky ocean floor to form the biggest set they've seen all morning.

His brain shuts down, and his muscles take over. The low, humming tremble of the wave rocks against his board and wraps around his bones. Crisp air slaps his face as he whips his arms through the water, paddling through the churn and racing against the rushing force of the wave. He can feel it starting to crest behind him, lifting up the tail of his board towards the heavens, towards the take-off, up and away and out of the sightless black depths.

The froth rockets him forward, bursting off the spray. His hands grip the waxy board as his legs and feet scramble for purchase, fighting against the ocean's strength. This is his light. His therapy. This is his sitting in a circle in a small beige room and sharing in a monotone voice the horror of shooting a little boy point-blank in the face, leaving his body to rot in the jungle with James' military-issue bullet in his skull. This is his walking halfway up to the little brown box that Auntie Cath told him was holding his mom while she slept and not being able to walk all the way up to it to peek inside. This is his sleeping alone in the back of a station wagon and wishing Rob's hand was the one softly pressing between his legs.

James opens his mouth to let out his own victorious cry as he tips his board for the take-off down the crushing face of the barrel, and the sun-warmed salt whips and crackles across his tongue as he soars.

## 3

James' nose draws in a deep breath of body-warmed bed sheets and salt-scented air as his eyes slowly blink open into the golden haze. It's James' favorite thing about this shitty, hole-in-the-wall, one room apartment—the windows. Ever since Rob helped him enter his first surf competition and the prize money meant no more sleeping in the back of Uncle Ron's old station wagon, James has blinked awake before dawn to a view through a thin, rattling window of the great vast blue, a deep velvet glass cupping the earth in its wet palms and beckoning James out to its depths with the soft, rolling, even crush of the waves against the shore.

He props himself up on his elbow and turns to look out of them now, expecting to see the barest hints of dawn peaking up lazily over the sharp horizon. A beach quietly preparing to host a competition in a few short hours. James' sleep-crusted eyes blink slowly awake against the unexpected glare, and he squints and holds up a palm to shield his eyes from the sun. It's not the milky darkness hovering over the waters that he sees. Instead, it's a white-hot beach bathed in sunlight and swarming like an anthill in people, a forest of surfboards sticking up in the sand waiting to be waxed and glinting in the sun, a parking lot full of beat up Winnebagos and Corvettes alike, waiting to bake in the California heat.

"Shit shit fucking shit!"

James hurls himself from bed and snatches up his alarm clock in a shaking hand. The dead battery light blinks back at him like a taunt.

"Shit!"

He zooms about the tiny apartment haphazardly getting ready, throwing on board shorts and a torn Quicksilver t-shirt he's pretty sure is

15

Rob's from when he went on vacation with Lori to Australia before he and James even met. He shoves deodorant under his arms and splashes water on his face, grimacing at the stubble on his cheeks and knowing there's jack shit he can do about it now.

James sends up a quick prayer of thanks to whatever god is up there watching him flail around from above that he thought to pack his gear bag the night before, with some semblance of prepared responsibility. He inexplicably throws a banana and an entire loaf of bread into the already full bag, then slings it across his shoulders and onto his back.

The sound of the crowd already cheering from down on the beach rushes to his ears as he flings open the crooked apartment door. He jams on a scratched pair of Ray Bans and shoves his feet into flip flops before tucking his surfboard under one arm. He drops his skateboard down in front of him with the other as he jogs down the driveway and out to Hermosa Avenue.

James tries to calm his hammering heart and lets himself smile at the feeling of the warm wind whipping through his hair as he bobs and weaves down the windy slope of road that will get him down to the sand. Palm trees, patio coffee shops, and ramshackle surf bars zoom past him as his body leans and sways with the movement of the skateboard, hurtling over blinding pavement and hot asphalt. Sweat starts to tingle down the back of his neck and under his arms, and James curses under his breath when he realizes the only damn thing he forgot to bring from his entire apartment was sunscreen.

The beach, when he gets there, is a zoo. A giant hand painted sign boasting the "International Surf Competition 1976—Hermosa Beach, California" hangs fluttering in the breeze between two palm trees, while across the sand, a churning throng of people battle against the sun with hats, sunglasses, umbrellas, and tiny bathing suits. They're straining their necks to watch the first surf heat already out in the water and trying to listen to the commentary going on over a large, crackling loud speaker set up in the back of a pickup truck next to a purring generator.

James leaps off his skateboard at a run and swoops it up under his other arm, knowing full well he looks ridiculous with a board under each arm, crooked sunglasses, and a frazzled sweat already pouring down his forehead so early in the day. He weaves through the crowd as best he can, making his way towards the white competitors' tent off to the side and hoping against all hope that they'll still let him surf.

"Well looks like fucking Sleeping Beauty decided to actually show up! And in my own goddamn shirt!" he hears a voice call from the tent's shade. James breathes a sigh of relief, then feels that damn irritating flutter in the pit of his stomach when he spots Rob jogging out to meet him, already ready for competition in his wetsuit bottoms with a small damp towel draped around his neck. His brown curls hang down long over his shoulders, still half-wet from when he must have taken a warm-up dip in the waves.

James shoves the tail of his surfboard down into the sand and drops his gear next to Rob's before running his hands over his sweaty face. "Damn alarm clock battery died," he sighs between his fingers.

"More like up too late last night doing something far more interesting than resting before a competition, you fucking juicer," Rob says as he jams a sandy fist into the top of James' head and messes up his hair.

"Aw, fuck off!" James laughs as he shoves Rob away from him. He tries hard to make sure the smile reaches his eyes as he smooths his hair back down into its usual swoop. It's times like these he jarringly remembers that Rob has absolutely no idea that he's his one and only friend in the world.

He walks beside Rob up to the check-in table and almost whoops for joy when he sees that it's Lori behind the little fold-up table. She greets them with a flip of her long brown ponytail and a deep eye roll.

"Well thank God you decided to show up. I almost had to put this one in a corner; he was whining so much about why you weren't here yet to play in the sandbox with him," she says, pointing her thumb towards Rob and pretending to resist as he wraps her in a hug from the side and tries to press a sloppy kiss to her cheek. James chuckles down at the sand, unsure as to whether his laughter is real or forced.

"Look, Lor," he says, once Rob's pulled away, "Any way you can do me a solid and pretend I was here an hour ago in that paperwork of yours?"

She smirks and wipes the sand off her chest from Rob's arms. James can see Rob staring almost open-mouthed at her little red bikini out of the corner of his eye as Lori stands and leans across the table towards him.

"Already told them you were here," she whispers into his ear, subtly passing him his heat number.

"Far out, Lor. I owe you one." He kisses her cheek and takes the heat number in his hands before following Rob back over to their boards.

"I've still gotta wax. My heat's two groups away," Rob says as he bends down over his backpack and rifles through for the bar of wax. James forces himself to look away from the long curve of his spine.

"Yeah, I'll join you."

They receive a fair amount of attention as they make their way through the sea of competitors stretched out on beach towels and lounging in the sand. Rob's been a staple of this beach for his entire life, and, as much as he doesn't feel like it deep down, James has made somewhat of a name for himself on the SoCal scene over the past two years of local competitions.

"Shit, man, beach is crawling with groms and kooks today. Can barely pick out the competition," Rob says as he lifts his board above his head to avoid a group of onlookers spread out in the sand.

"Don't see you complaining about the chicks, though," James quips with a sly grin, and Rob looks back to flip him the bird.

"Gonna go pro today, dude, I can feel it!" someone calls out to him from the crowd. James rubs his hand over the back of his neck and barely jumbles out a thankful reply, already starting to feel the crushing pressure bearing down upon his shoulders. He hears a similar sentiment four or five more times as he and Rob make their way past groups of young high schoolers smuggling Budweisers onto the beach in brown paper bags, sprawled next to some of the most distinguished names in Hermosa, most with a platinum blonde beach chick hanging off their arms, passing a cigarette back and forth with lazy fingers.

Rob smirks back at him as he continues to stutter over his replies to the well-wishers, and James is inordinately grateful when someone starts blasting Earth Wind and Fire on a nearby boombox loud enough that anything more than a smile and nod becomes impossible. He feels like he's been dropped onto a goddamn Hollywood film set, with a costume thrown on his body and a fake surfboard shoved under his arm and a director yelling, *"Hey there, sonny, just walk down the beach and pretend you're one of the boys!"*

He feels one hundred years old, and he struggles not to limp in the sand. The last week's worth of shifts sweating down at the docks sit like icy lead in every muscle of his body, leaving him frustrated and already out of breath as they trudge through the deep, hot sand.

Rob leads them out to a more secluded spot, up just high enough on a bluff that they can see the whole event stretched out before them like a colorful mirage. James marvels again at the sheer volume of it all. It seems to him like this whole surf scene suddenly appeared overnight. One day he was catching his last wave on a completely empty stretch of beach before boarding a Navy vessel, and the next day he was stepping off that same boat and waking up in the back of a station wagon to see an entire beach plastered with people wanting to watch a real, organized surfing competition. It had seemed absolutely insane to him then, and it still feels surreal even now.

"We are lucky sons of bitches, aren't we?" Rob says, reading his thoughts.

James hums in agreement as he gets out his wax. They don't say anything more.

He settles his knees deep in the sand and feels the burn in his tight hamstrings, then grimaces at the thought of stretching them out later before his heat. Gradually, he loses himself in the hypnotic ritual of waxing his board, listening to the steady waves call out to him as they pound against the sand in time with Rob's deep, focused breathing beside him. James pretends that his already anxious, racing heart doesn't speed up even more when he sees Rob eventually sit back on his heels to tie up his hair into a bun.

"You don't believe them, do you?" Rob asks in a quiet voice, once he's finished.

James startles out of his zen and looks up from his board with a frown. "Believe who?"

Rob pockets his wax and leans back in the sand on his elbows. "Anybody. When they tell you that you can really go pro with this, that you can make it up to the Championship Tour and make a living."

James shrugs, avoiding Rob's gaze. "Guess I'd rather be pleasantly surprised than hope, you know? Works better that way."

He flinches when Rob's hand is suddenly right in front of his eyes, slowly dragging the Ray Ban's down off James' face before leaning over to look him in the eye. James' breath catches in his throat as those deep brown eyes latch on to his.

"You know what? Fucking win this, Jimmy," Rob whispers, holding his gaze. "For all that shit you've seen that you keep bottled up in there. Go out there and fucking blow this thing out of the water."

James' throat closes up, and he quickly looks away, embarrassed, as he blinks the moisture out of his eyes.

Rob's never said anything like that before, never acknowledged out loud the secret past that James keeps hidden from him, from everyone. Rob's seen the scar, of course. And the tightness James gets in his shoulder when his body hasn't fully woken up yet. He's seen the way James jumps if a car suddenly honks back up on the road. He's seen it all hundreds of times in the pre-dawn light as they perch side by side on their boards and quietly wait for the next set.

James remembers the first day he decided to go without his wetsuit top in front of him. It was one month after they'd met, and it was terrifying. The whole night before he'd been sick to his stomach just thinking about it. Lying in the back of the station wagon listening to the crickets and the waves, convincing himself to just suck it up and do it like a man, then talking himself back down from making the biggest mistake of his life and pushing away the only true friend he'd made since Billy Madden. He didn't know then how Rob felt about it all—about the war and the politics and the soldiers coming home to tree trunks without yellow ribbons and brains that thought cars backfiring were machine guns in the middle of Sunset Boulevard.

The next morning, he'd risen before the sun like normal and brushed his teeth from bottled water over the gutter on the side of the Pacific Coast Highway. The seagulls cawed down to him, mocking his uncertainty. He made his way on shaky legs down to the shore with his board tucked under his arm and a bulky sweatshirt thrown over his thinning frame. And he'd watched as Rob jogged down to him from where he parked his beat-up Chevy with a smile on his face in the cool grey sand, and taken his hand and thumped him on the back like usual. And then James had forced himself not to vomit as he pulled the sweatshirt up over his head and left himself bare chested in the slowly warming virgin air, waiting to hear the gasp he knew would come from Rob's lips.

Except it hadn't come. Instead, Rob had simply pulled off his own sweatshirt, cursed and shivered at the cold, and then run forward into the fresh waves to start the day, calling back over his shoulder for James to get his shit together and join him before he had a birthday waiting for him to come.

James sees now that it probably wasn't really as much of a surprise as he'd thought it would be. Thousands of boys his age were being shipped off to Vietnam every month, and almost just as many thousands came limping back one year, two years later. If they made it back at all. It didn't matter if anyone disagreed with why they were over there in the first place. The soldiers still got shipped back all the same.

Even now, sitting up on a perfect sunny stretch of sand and looking down at the grand spectacle of the International Surf Competition, thousands of miles away from the little stretch of beach in Da Nang, James knows there has to be at least a solid handful of secret soldiers hiding amongst the surfers and spectators in the vast crowd. They all hide in plain sight. Laughing over beers down at the surfer bar or smiling around the bonfire after a day out on the waves. And then they wait for the crowd of friends to pack up and leave, they wait until they're truly alone, and then they let the haunted darkness seep back into their eyes.

They see each other in the crowd. James looks at them, and they look back at James, and they know. They *know*. There's a nod sometimes, or even just a blink. James received two just now following Rob through the crowd with his board under one arm and his wax in his pocket. The haunted darkness isn't welcome on this sunny California beach, brimming over with cheers and smiles as young, unmarked men rip their way across the waves and spray. As pretty little girls cheer them on while sipping on Pepsi and the kids studying over at UCLA make plans to grab fish tacos before studying in the back of someone's station wagon by the shore.

And now Rob's gone and told him to fucking win it all anyways. To stick it to the haunted darkness and take the prize money and make a living doing the only thing in the world that keeps him from walking out into the sea and ending it all.

And he can't think of a single way to thank him.

James swallows hard and blinks out of his thoughts. Rob's still watching him calmly, patiently, sitting back on his heels in the hot sand, knowing he should be getting ready to paddle out and surf.

"Okay," James finally chokes out, and Rob just smiles once and winks before nodding back to the crowd.

"Time to get back and stretch so you don't break a hip, old man," he says. "And also, the stubble on your face looks like shit."

And James laughs, breathless. Nods once, hard, and slips his sunglasses back down over his wet eyes.

It's time.

# 4

*"Right on! And with a wild first wave score of 8.1, our own local boy Jimmy Campbell clears his first qualifiers heat with three waves all over 7.5. I think we all know that he's gunning for those last couple thousand points today to push him up into the coveted pro circuit. We'll see if he can pull it off in the second round of heats, coming up next just after lunch. And speaking of lunch, dudes, why don't you head on over to Dave's down on the pier for a bitchin' burger and fries..."*

James sweeps his first heat. Annihilates it, in fact. The other three surfers didn't even stand a chance.

He's walking calmly back up towards the competitors' tent, listening to the chorus of applause and shaking the salty water from his hair, when he's barraged by a swarm of other surfers congratulating him. He laughs and tastes the salt on the inside of his lips.

"Alright, alright, ladies, form a line," he gets out.

The other surfers laugh along and slap him on the back, reaching out to touch his board like it's some kind of trophy. James looks around and realizes he barely knows not even half these guys—some of them not even just by name or face. A mixture of elation and dread fills his gut. He's known now. He's becoming one of them. No longer just a local guy who some of the ex-surfers down at the Alcove Bar talk about as a little guy to keep your eye on as they nurse along a fourth beer and groan over the good ol' days.

He needs to live up to something now, to prove that he's worthy of surfers from all over the entire goddamn world patting him on the back and unknowingly clapping their palms over the ropy scar on the back of his shoulder. He needs to hold his head high and act chill and pretend he's used to having his five minutes of fame on the hot sand.

He also needs to get the hell away from them all. Needs to find a quiet corner to unzip the top half of his wetsuit and throw on a t-shirt before anyone sees that he's a worn-out Vietnam sailor who's nine years older than the rest of them, not some hot new kid climbing up the ranks of the Hermosa Beach waves like surfing's just the greatest fun game in the world.

Rob breaks through the crowd and grabs James gently around the neck, rubbing his fist into his hair to mess it up again. He leans down and whispers, "You did it, old man," in James' ear before telling the other surfers to fuck off back to their girls and leave the poor guy alone to relax. James shoots him a grateful smile. The side of his neck feels cold when Rob takes his arm away.

James watches Rob jog back to his circle of friends in the sand, the warmth in the pit of his gut slowly fading with each step Rob takes away from him, then he keeps his head low and slinks through the crowds up towards the bluff by the pier so he can change in the shade of a palm tree trunk. He leaves the top half of his wetsuit hanging down around his waist beneath his t-shirt, shivering once at the scratch of the cotton over the layer of wet sand still plastered to his chest. On a whim, he aimlessly wanders over to the packed boardwalk once he's done. His feet just lead him there, towards the thronging chaos; he has no idea why.

Dave's burger shack has a line snaking down almost the whole length of the pier. James dodges skateboarders and families, fishermen and groups of bikini-clad girls as he makes his way barefoot down the rough wooden planks, seeking out a bathroom or a lemonade or whichever comes first.

A woman about his age with waist-length straight brown hair and a bikini top with cut-off jeans roller skates past him out of the crowd. She shoots him a knowing look and a wink, popping her lips around her pink bubblegum. She skates by too quickly for James to fully respond. For a fleeting moment, James imagines if Rob looked at him that way, all sultry desire and radiating flirtatious confidence, and now he needs to find a cold drink to get rid of the warm flush on his sunburned cheeks. A Beach Boys song from back before James even got drafted blares from a little ice cream stand he passes in search of a soda, and James feels a sudden pang of nostalgia in the pit of his chest for the times he would hop in Billy Madden's dad's Buick and race down along Pacific Coast Highway with an ice chest of beers in the trunk and nowhere to be but the sunset sand.

Just when he almost reaches the end of the crowded pier, it happens.

James is scanning the pier one last time, in desperate need of a drink, when he catches the eyes of a single man through the sea of bodies. They're piercing and clear, nearly hidden by half-wet locks of brown curls.

Time stops.

James senses the crowd continue to swarm and move around him while he stands frozen on the pier, eyes riveted and breath throbbing right at the back of his throat. The other man is staring, too. He holds his gaze as people continue to pass obliviously between them, as the air horn sounding the end of the current surf heat blasts across the beach followed by a wave of fresh cheers down on the sand.

James feels the dryness in the back of his throat, feels the aching flush spread up through his neck and onto his face. The man is looking at him like he's surprised by James' very existence. Like he's slowly blinking out of a fog, and James is his lighthouse in the storm. James has never been looked at like that in his entire life. He sucks in a breath of air and moves to step towards the stranger, licks his lips to speak—to say what, he has absolutely no idea.

Then it's over. The spell broken.

After what could only have been three seconds, the other man is gone, absorbed back into the crowd and leaving James adrift in a weaving swarm of people. He lets out a shaky breath and fights the urge to rub his hand over his scar. His eyes trace the splintered boardwalk railing, the distant mirage-like sand, the glass sea.

For the life of him, he can't remember the color of those eyes.

Half an hour later finds him back on the beach, frosty bottle of Coke in hand as he spots Rob in the middle of a circle of his oldest surfing buddies—guys James knows by name but barely anything more. He plops down on the sidelines of their group to a more mellow chorus of well wishes and pats on the back, ready to sit back and take a deep breath for the first time since he shot up from bed that morning. He looks out over the roaring waters as the sun slowly bakes the saltwater off his skin. The top of his wetsuit still hangs limp down by his hips, and he burrows his toes under the first layer of hot sand to reach the cool, wet mud underneath.

A group of French surfers walk by, followed by two from Mexico. They all look at James with mild acknowledgement, even appraisal. It makes his skin itch to realize he's no longer anonymous. He's almost up there with them. Almost.

"Tough luck on your draw for the final heat, Jimmy," one of Rob's friends, Kip, calls over to him.

"Shit, I haven't even had time to look. Who is it?"

A snicker passes over the group beside him, and a strange warning tingle zips down James' spine.

"Facing off against that fucking fairy," says Dean, as he runs his fingers through his long beard and sneers.

*Fairy.*

James' heart stops beating in his chest. It takes everything in his power not to look over at Rob, to find solace in the shape of his broad shoulders, or in the way his shorter hairs curl softly at the nape of his neck. He wills his body to stay neutral, digging his heels a bit harder into the earth. The air horn starting the next heat echoes across the beach, and James wishes desperately he could just sit silently and listen to the commentary on his competitors.

Instead, he takes an invisible, slow breath and faces Kip. "Who?" he asks.

Kip finishes taking a swig of cold Budweiser and sticks the frosty bottle down into the sand.

"Don't tell me you haven't seen him here yet. That kid from over in Hawaii—Danny Moore."

A small chorus of girly, high-pitched voices echo the words "Danny Moore" after Kip speaks, causing another round of laughter from the group.

James prickles as a cold sweat breaks out over his skin. His heart's beating faster now than it had been when the horn sounded at the start of his last heat. He takes a deep breath and stares straight ahead at the waves, eyes unseeing.

26

He knows exactly who Danny Moore is.

Who doesn't? The second day James had ever surfed with Rob, Rob got stars in his eyes and told him how he read in *Surfer's Journal* that last month a nineteen-year-old kid stole someone's board, ran straight out into the water in the middle of the First Annual Billabong Masters without even registering to surf, and took on the biggest fucking wave anyone had seen all day like it was just business as usual. Then he'd simply untied the ankle strap, left the board floating in the whitewater, spat his name over to the judges' table, and disappeared off into the palm trees. It had taken almost six months to track him down to mail him the prize money.

James decides to play aloof. If he doesn't, he'll go and sink right down into the sand, small and forgotten.

"Ah yeah, him," he says, falsely casual. "He actually that good?"

Dean snickers. "Oh, he's good alright. Not some fucking kook or anything. Won the Billabong Masters in Oahu the first two years they ran it, and they say he didn't even break a damn sweat to do it. Kid barely leaves Hawaii, only seen him out here once before. Son of a bitch goes after the huge ass surf they got over there in Waimea. Word is he's going for the world big wave record—"

"But man he's a miserable asshole, Jimmy," Kip cuts in. "Thinks he's Jesus Christ or something looking down on all of us poor losers. And keep fucking far away from him out there unless you want him checking out your ass as you paddle out, sick fucker."

James swallows hard and slips his shades back over his eyes to hide the panic he knows is showing. He thinks, with an alarm of quiet terror building in his chest, of how careless he's gotten with his looks at Rob over the years. His stomach fights against the banana and slice of bread he ate earlier before his heat as he agonizes over whether Rob's ever noticed him checking out his ass as he paddles out in front of him in the early morning waves day after day.

He feels sick. "I'll keep my ass thoroughly out of sight," he says with a forced smile after a beat.

James goes to look back out over the waves, studying the lines the other surfers' boards are cutting through the surf, when he feels his curiosity start to boil over within him. He barely stops from wincing even as his mouth forms the question, "Wait, what makes you say he's a queer?"

Another friend, Jeff, chuckles deep and ironic in his chest. "Shit, you never heard? Not sure what you'd've called it, Jimmy, if you'd been the one to walk in on him with his tongue down some whore's throat last year in a bar toilet after the Laguna Beach competition. Harry said he almost upchucked all his beer when he saw it," Jeff finishes with a dramatic shiver.

"He's lucky we all still even let him surf, isn't he?" Kip adds.

James' mind flashes back to the memory of his own hand between his legs just the night before, and the images that had been running through his mind as he tried to stifle his own moans. Miles of sand-covered tan skin rolling through the waves. Long curtains of soft hair falling across his own muscled chest. Deep brown eyes and a stubbled jaw.

His skin burns hot with shame.

Then it occurs to him. "Wait, if he's such a big shot, what the hell am I doing in his heat?"

"Matt Randley twisted his ankle on his last wave," Rob explains casually, as if his voice hadn't groaned other words in the deepest corners of James' mind last night as he came. "Would've been you against him, based on your rankings, but—"

"But that miserable fucker jumped in and *volunteered* to surf against someone still in the qualifiers," Kip interrupts. "Like some surfing Mother Theresa. If that doesn't scream hidden goddamn motive, I don't know what does. Probably just wants to see someone get crushed."

James swallows hard over the ice at the back of his throat. Five minutes of fame after his first heat aside, he's still just a nobody. A local boy getting too old for all of this with a forgettable face, who only got people talking because he seemed to materialize out of thin air two years ago and wasn't a complete limp noodle on a board.

He has absolutely no business in hell going up against someone who won the Billabong Masters not just once, but twice. The inevitable humiliation feels like someone pouring thick, wet sand over his face, closing off his lungs from the brilliant clear sun and sky and dragging him back down slowly to the depths. Back to the dockyard.

He startles when a hand with glossy, bright red fingernails clamps down on his shoulder.

"Jimmy, dammit I've been looking for you!"

Lori looks flushed, as if she just ran to him across the beach. "You know you're up in fifteen minutes?"

James curses under his breath and leaps to his feet, almost head butting Lori in the process.

"Lor, you're an angel!" he calls over his shoulder as he sprints through the crowds to his board, a chorus of "Good luck, you'll need it"s hitting his back.

The sand falls off the legs of his wetsuit in wet clumps, and he fruitlessly runs a hand through his bangs to try and get out the crunchy tangles. He really needs to wax his board a second time. To stretch and condition a little bit, go for a jog or chug some water or find some damn sunscreen or just sit down and breathe. But instead he's just sat and listened to everyone tell him all the ways Danny fucking Moore is going to demolish him without doing anything to even try to set himself up for a chance at success.

He flies through his preparations on autopilot, ducking behind a tent to rip off his shirt and zip up his wetsuit top before nearly sprinting to the starting area of shore near the judges' tent.

He breathes a sigh of relief when his competitor isn't even there yet. James isn't ready to face him, to see him face-to-face knowing that every wave out there during the next thirty minutes will have the other man's name written all over it. There's no way he can compare the monolithic terror of a man—no, *kid*—that he's built up in his mind over the past hour with a real human being.

James stares straight ahead, taking the final minutes before the air horn to study the rises and falls of the water. Trying to plot out the surf breaks and find the best pathways to catch the smoothest barrels. Trying desperately *not* to think about his competitor's tongue down another man's throat in a dirty bar restroom. His hand between another man's gripping thighs.

James forces air slowly into his lungs and gradually settles into his pre-surf calm. The familiar meditative state of watching the lungs of the ocean rise and fall in beat with the earth.

He considers his actual chances: it'll just be the two of them in this heat—no fighting with a whole group of other surfers for the best waves. Whoever wins gets 10,000 more circuit points, a reasonably fat pocket of cash, and the ability to say they made it to a second-round qualifying heat of a major international surf competition.

James Campbell would go pro.

Except why the hell a fucking two-time Billabong Masters champion would ever want to boast about making it to a second-round qualifying heat of a major international surf competition makes absolutely no sense. And so James' careful contemplation of the water turns once again into churning anxiety, his eyes fighting with him to start glancing around frantically for the man who should be next to him in the sand.

*"And here we have a special treat down on the shore today, folks. Those of you arriving just now for the afternoon's Championship heats, you're in luck, because first here we have Jimmy Campbell, fresh from a primo first qualifying heat and ready to face off in a chance encounter with Oahu's own champion of big wave surfing—Danny Moore—"*

James nearly winces at the sound of his own name booming from the crackling loudspeaker. It feels like being stripped naked in front of the giant, surging crowd. Like he's in a dream where he looks down after surfing for three hours and only then realizes he's completely naked.

The announcer sounds like he's had one too many beers already that day, and not a little bit of heatstroke. The buzzing murmur of the spectators mixes with the static of the loudspeaker and songs from three different boomboxes to create a wave of pulsing sound at James' back, pushing him forward inch by inch towards the calm of the waves. He grips his long, waxed board harder under his arm and curls his toes into the sand. Sweat trickles down his sides beneath his wetsuit, and his heart pounds blood through his legs.

Suddenly, like a mirage appearing above the sand, someone materializes to his right.

In one calm, smooth movement, the empty space next to James becomes inhabited by a man in long black wetsuit bottoms and, of all ridiculous things, a skin-tight light grey hoodie. The crowd at their backs draws in a collective breath of silent awe and anticipation as the infamous young surfer plants the tip of his board down into the sand. James wants to laugh as he stands there trembling with nerves and sweating in his wetsuit. He must be ten years older than this kid, he learned to surf before this kid was even alive,  he's seen *war*. James turns his head sideways to get a better look.

It's him.

James nearly gasps. The man from the pier stands next to him utterly transformed. Gone is the shocked curiosity, the vulnerable, searching stare covered by loose curls and locked on to James' eyes from the center of a swarming crowd.

In its place is a statue. A God. James knows his mouth is hanging open as the man next to him slowly strips off the hoodie to reveal tanned bare skin, his entire muscled back covered in an intricate tattoo that James can't quite fully glimpse from where he stands off to the side. He stops himself just in time from dashing over to get a better look.

Danny Moore is no fucking kid.

The loose curls from before are now slicked back hard against his skull, harsh and sleek like the lines of a jet-black Porsche. He has gleaming aviators on over his eyes, and suddenly James would bet anything that the man has no plans of taking them off, even in order to surf. The wetsuit bottoms are so tight they seem to melt into his skin, hugging the sharp curves of his hips and clinging to every muscle.

James' heart beats double time in his chest as his eyes guiltily roam over the warm, tan skin. The rippling strength as the man bends to pick up his board and tighten his ankle strap. The way a dusting of hot sand drips down his ankles like honey, clinging to the bottoms of his calves. The pure, unadulterated focus that beams out of him like a laser. The slow rise and fall of lungs that have no reason in the world to be nervous.

And James has always known, deep down, years before he ever first shook Rob Depaul's hand, that men were always gonna be what did it for him, but- *Christ*. He can barely breathe. The sheer presence of the man next to him dazzles into the air and aches across his skin. He forces himself to look back towards the water, but not before Danny quickly turns his head to look at James.

Even behind the sunglasses, there's no recognition there. No acknowledgement of the pier. There's only competition in the harsh lines of his face. The sharp, fierce focus layered over a sizzling burn of adrenaline and competency. Full, pink lips pressed into a harsh line of determination.

That one glance is all James needs to know that he's about to be absolutely pummeled. He might as well set his board down now, strip off his wetsuit for good, and hop on his skateboard right back down to his thankless job at the docks. Go back to earning paychecks and paying rent and buying groceries instead of playing around in the sand, convincing himself he's still allowed to be carefree in the waves.

He distantly realizes the two announcers are still babbling about their predictions for the waves and the heat when the air horn blares unexpectedly, starting the heat with an awkward anticlimax.

James flinches at the horn, startled, then quickly regains his wits as the caught-off-guard crowd hesitantly starts to applaud. An invisible relief floods through his chest when he realizes his flinch was too small for anyone to have seen.

He thinks he hears his competitor mutter, "Idiots," under his breath as they both jog towards the waves and throw their boards down into the water to a fresh roar of cheers, pushing and pulling at the small shoreline swells until they reach the wide open blue.

James tips the nose of his board down and duck dives under an incoming wave, losing himself to the sensation of the current ripping and writhing at his body. When he surfaces, though, he nearly curses out loud. The ocean looks like smooth glass—not a ripple in sight. The sounds of the crowd have long since faded, even the booming of the announcers disappearing up into the clouds. All James can hear is the soft trickle of water droplets falling off his arms as he paddles. That and the smooth, even breathing of the man ten feet to his right.

"Well shit," James breathes as he looks out at the waveless water. He perches on his board and tries to count the minutes in his head. Each second that ticks by without a swell feels like another chance at going pro is slipping effortlessly out to sea, just out of the reach of his fingertips, gone for good. The only benefit of waiting there like a sitting duck is the fact that *the* Danny Moore can't knock him on his metaphorical ass if the ocean isn't giving him jack shit to surf on either.

It's awkward, sitting perfectly still just ten feet away from each other with absolutely nothing to do and hundreds of people watching them not do it.

James clears his throat. "We haven't met yet. I'm Jimmy," he says.

His competitor doesn't even turn his head. "Obviously."

His voice is rough and deep, like he hasn't used it in days. The sound of it makes James clench his stomach muscles as his board rocks beneath him. He'd honestly half expected Danny's voice to be effeminate. A perfect embodiment of the walking stereotype Kip and Dean and the rest all painted so vividly for James back in the sand. He wasn't expecting melted dark chocolate. The sound of a rich, thick wave slapping hard against a rocky shore.

The water beneath them continues to ripple and roll in soft, slow curves. No waves in sight. James licks his lips against the sun and runs a hand through his drying hair.

"You're a big deal," James tries again. "I feel I'm lucky to even get to surf against you here. So thanks, I guess, for volunteering to—"

"We're not even surfing, for God's sake," he cuts in.

James takes a deep breath and prays with every fiber of his being for a swell to come in. He taps his fingertips on his board and swishes his ankles impatiently in the water below.

When the ocean stays mockingly flat, James realizes that apparently the only way to let the excess adrenaline out of his limbs is to take on the challenge of talking to the man next to him. He takes another breath—feels it press out against his ribcage that's still sore from an eleven hour shift the day before.

"Well, gotta say it's pretty amazing what you did in Oahu two years ago. I read about it, that piece in the *Journal.* And you were just a kid—"

"Yes, yes, I'm the young prodigy and you're the old washed out vet trying to go pro before your knees or your wallet give out. Glad we've got those tedious details out of the way."

"How the fuck do you know about–?" James stops himself before he really lets loose. Righteous anger or no, he's smart enough to know that the middle of the ocean next to a no doubt champion swimmer is not exactly the best place to go and lose his head.

Danny's words, *old washed out vet,* drape over him like heavy ice as his ribs clench.

It's then that his patience—for the lack of waves, for the man next to him, for the sunburn forming on his cheeks, for the hours and hours of extra shifts he'll have to work to afford to enter his next qualifying competition—runs out.

"Well, crucify me for trying to have a conversation," he spits out.

The man finally turns to look at him, pure incredulity plastered across his face, spreading out from underneath the aviators still covering his eyes and cheeks.

"You sat surrounded by so-called friends for an hour before this heat hearing about what an asshole fag I am, and then you walked up to the shore expecting to be absolutely humiliated in front of everyone and having the chance at going pro taken from you by a dickhead who volunteered to annihilate you, and your first instinct when we got out here to this flat water was that you wanted to *converse* with me? Who the hell are you?"

James bristles. He fights down the urge to slam his fist down onto his board in front of him like a five-year-old who was just reminded of the fact that they're irrelevant and irrational and small.

"Well who the hell are you?" James shoots back. "What the fuck do you know about me?"

Danny lifts a hand and gestures out before them at the sea, casually, as if the answer to James' question is written on the horizon line, plain as day for anyone to read.

"I know that you're considering taking this little swell that's coming towards us as your first wave in a last-ditch attempt to end this horrible conversation—which, incidentally, was your idea in the first place—and I know that when I tell you that that wave's gonna be closed out because of a rip current and isn't even worth paddling out for, you're going to look at me and go ahead and do it anyway just to spite me and admit to yourself that you don't have to try and be civil to me anymore because I've now proven myself as a verified asshole. And also, tough luck about your alarm clock battery."

"Jesus Christ, they weren't exaggerating," James mutters as he shakes his head out at the flat horizon. He keeps his eyes trained on the little swell Danny mentioned. He's no idiot. He can see as well as anyone that it's gonna be closed out. It would be embarrassing to chase after it in front of the finest surfers in the world. It would be mad.

James starts paddling.

He nearly laughs to himself when he hears Danny's incredulous huff behind him as he cuts through the water towards the oncoming wave, feeling a thrill down his spine as he watches it slowly gain speed to reveal a perfect swell coming in right behind it. The muscles in his shoulder start to groan and spike under the heavy wet blanket of his wetsuit as he pulls his body through the water, and the muscles across his back and sides clench to keep him balanced on the waxy board.

James lets his mind slip away and his body take over as he leaves Danny farther behind with every paddle. He can feel the rushing surge of the wave just behind him now, scooping up the tail of his board and lifting him up towards the sky. It's going to be a full barrel. He can feel it. With a grunt down in his gut, James grips the sides of his board with trembling fingers and hoists his feet up behind him, toes gripping to find purchase over the power of the wave.

It's his favorite part—the lift off. The treacherous moment between lying flat against the belly of the earth and being lifted up into the heavens on the wings of the spray. James' tired legs find a second wind and pump him down the face of the barrel just as it folds into the perfect pipeline, cocooning him in a swirl of water and echoing the sound of his heavy breathing. He reaches the opening of the barrel and clenches his core to turn his board up towards the lip of the wave, tapping the crest twice before cutting back and leaving a rocket of spray.

Just as the whitewater starts to swallow up his legs, James shoots a glance back to Danny Moore perched nonchalantly on his board with his fucking aviators still pulled down over his eyes. James smirks as the sound of the wild applause begins to fill his ears, and he does a full soul arch, face lifted up to the sky as the churning foam swells around his calves.

Danny isn't even looking his direction.

James falls back into the shallows to end his ride, letting his body melt into the water. His muscles surge with excess adrenaline, lactic acid from holding himself tight on the board during the cutbacks starting to leak its fiery way through his veins. For a tiny moment, he stares straight up at the open sky, cloudless and blue as the waves cradle his back. The same sky he'd closed his eyes against that afternoon in Vietnam. The sky he thought would be the last thing he ever saw on earth.

Foam slaps across his face, cutting off his view.

By the time he clambers back up on his board and cracks his neck, he can hear the distant booming crackle of the announcers going wild. One glance out at the pathetic waves coming in tells James that that ride will be his first and last one of the set. His chance at going pro, his chance at everything, resting on the previous thirty seconds of his life. That and whatever Danny Moore is able to accomplish in the next four minutes between now and the airhorn.

James' breath catches in his throat as he turns in the glassy shallows to watch Danny chase after his own incoming swell—small, but with promise. The long, lean lines of his body cut through the water like silk. James desperately wants to turn away, but he's frozen. Riveted as he stares at the way the inky tendrils of the tattoo shift and ripple across the muscles as Danny paddles. He turns to catch the wave, aviators reflecting the glinting sun. He paddles once more, then shoots up all at once to a gasp from the crowd. James convinces himself the burning in his cheeks is just from the sun as he watches Danny's long, sinewy arms extend for balance, ripping down along the face of the wave and throwing up spray with each half turn up along the lip.

James' heart sinks deep in his chest.

It's over. It's all gone. There's no way in hell, even with his perfect pipeline, that he could ever compete with this. With the pure muscle and grace and elegance that glides along the water as if gravity doesn't even exist. As if the waves were begging Danny to ride them. He's just resigned himself to turn back towards the shore and escape the beach as quickly as possible when Danny looks over to him, mid-way through his perfect ride.

James' heart beats once, twice, stops.

Danny stares, and he pulls the aviators down off his face as he continues to surf along the crest, all while looking straight at James.

Then he wipes out.

The crowd goes insane. Gasps and wails and cheers and there's no fucking way that James is really hearing people chanting his name across the hot sand. He wades towards the shore on shaky legs and pulls his board alongside him, floating on the water, when suddenly Rob is on top of him, tackling him down into the froth with two warm, soft hands on either side of his face.

For one heart-stopping moment, James thinks he's going to kiss him. That Rob will pull James into his body and press those perfect, chapped lips to his in front of hundreds of people on the shore. Will let a curtain of long, soft hair fall across James' chest.

But then Rob's pulling his hands back and roughing up James' hair just like he always does, the grin on his face threatening to leap off his freckled cheeks.

"Jimmy, you professional surfing son of a bitch, you just left Danny Moore in the fucking whitewater!"

And James wants to cry. At the saltwater stinging his eyes, and the way Rob is looking at him with his hair falling into his eyes like he just went and hung the sun, and the swell of cheers he can still hear pouring over him from the beach, and the way the sheer thrill of his ride has shocked the scar on his shoulder into being too numb to hurt yet.

It's all just overwhelming enough to make him wish he was walking up onto a deserted beach instead, just after dawn and a Los Angeles sunrise with only Rob by his side. James looks back once more towards the sea and sees Danny standing in the shallows, pulling his aviators back down over his eyes and running his hands through his hair to smooth down the curls.

James freezes. He swallows hard as a shiver of realization runs through his core, turning his joy into ice.

He's standing there on the Hermosa Beach shore, having just defeated a two-time Billabong Masters champion. Having just stuck it to the haunted darkness and fucking won it all anyways. And now James Campbell can't even stop and enjoy it all, because he suddenly realizes two very important things:

One, that the way the tattoo rippled across Danny's back made James dry in the back of his throat in an achingly familiar way.

And two, that this Hawaii-big-wave-surfing-champion son of a bitch just went and wiped out on purpose.

# 5

The love affair began with physics.

With crinkled graph paper stolen from the cupboard of a $4^{th}$ grade classroom in Iowa, covered in sharpened red crayon. Wavelength charts and gravity pull calculations and the effect of wave peel angle versus wave break intensity based on the size and composition of the sand hidden in the water's depths.

Physics that started with accidentally getting his small, sticky hands on a full color advertisement photograph of a wave breaking fresh and clean on the Hawaiian shore, found on the last page of a copy of Playboy magazine buried deep in a wet rubbish bin just off the little dirt road in the middle of landlocked Kentucky.

That stayed folded up in the back pocket of Sydney Daniel Moore's only pair of khaki pants until his khakis became three inches too short for his legs, and until Lieutenant Moore announced that after moving eight times in the last five years, they were finally gonna settle down and have a house of their very own. A little slice of paradise on the military base way out at Pearl Harbor, where rumor had it the ocean was bluer than the crayon in the box.

And Danny sat sweating and cramped in the back of their beat-up pickup as they drove across the desert headed straight for the Los Angeles airport, trying to tune out the rattling old cassette tape of a Sunday sermon that his father had made them listen to eighteen times already. Something about fire and brimstone. Something about needing to be saved.

He held the torn and faded photograph in his quiet ten-year-old hands as they drove while his younger brother asked every fifteen minutes whether they could stop to find a Dairy Queen for a frostee and some fries. He closed his eyes and leaned back against the hot leather seat and imagined what the water near Pearl Harbor would sound like crashing against the shore, with the wind in the palm trees and the crystal blue waves and the way the soft, warm sand would feel different than prairie dust against his bare toes. Imagined a velvet beach covered in a blanket of shiny white pearls.

It was almost enough to help him forget that his momma wasn't in the car with them. That she was still back crying on an Arizona porch with a liquor bottle in her hand and no wedding ring on her finger. With her beloved cross necklace lying on the rough wooden floorboards of the kitchen after she broke it, trying to hold Danny close into her chest, snot covered lips groaning out, *"Not Sydney, please not Sydney,"* the only voice he'd ever heard call him that name, and his father's firm grip tugging him clear the opposite direction towards the Chevy, piled high with their packed bags.

It was physics that filled his head and drowned out the sound of the sweating preacher every early Sunday morning, where they bowed and knelt and prayed in the sticky, hot, humid air of the Oahu church, his father's starched formal uniform on one side of him and his father's new wife's traditional muumuu on the other. And it was physics on his mind when he tuned out his dad saying grace for fifteen minutes before each meal while his brother snuck early bites off his plate and chewed soft enough that only Danny ever noticed. Physics that he thought about late on the night of his fourteenth birthday lying on the bunk bed underneath his brother, after he had asked their father if he could have a surfboard for his gift, and instead he'd gotten a lecture and a brand new, too-small necktie.

The day after Danny's fourteenth birthday, he took apart an old fax machine he found dumped behind the high school where everybody laughed and called him Egg-white, on account of the fact he had the palest skin any of them had ever seen, and he'd committed the social crime of eating an egg salad sandwich packed by his father's wife on his first day of school there. A sandwich she'd had to ask Danny how his other mom used to make.

Danny tinkered for a week and finally put the fax machine back together so that it only ever printed out Led Zeppelin lyrics. And it was then that he realized that a whole lot of people would pay good money to get a kid to fix their televisions and calculators and radios for half the price it would cost them at a Radio Shack.

On his fifteenth birthday, Danny Moore walked up to the counter of the local surf shop with bulging pockets and purchased his first very own surfboard, just like the ones he watched the older guys ride across the neighborhood beach. He stayed up all night memorizing the rises and falls of the waves—the perfect stance to have on the board in order to surf a smooth barrel. Practiced paddling and popping up on the worn carpet of his small bedroom floor as sweat pooled in the small of his back. Nine years' worth of handwritten notes on wave physics. Nine years' worth of observations on the clear, vast blue. The way the ocean breathes and the force of the spray. Angles of the wind and the thick black pull of the deep.

And on the day after his fifteenth birthday, he planted his new board proudly in the sand on the empty local beach right at sunrise. He ran down to the shore just to give himself a first fresh dip in the virgin waves, and, when he eventually walked back up to his precious board, he nearly fell to his knees in the sand when he saw someone had spray painted "faggot" across the face of it in angry red.

He stood there frozen with the icy, curdling realization that Chet Morgan must have caught a glimpse of the photo of a half-dressed sailor he kept hidden in the back of his beloved notebook. Must have somehow seen it after Chet stole it from him in the hallway last week and made him hand over his lunch money to get it back. Something straight out of a cheesy high school bad boy film. And he'd just stood there like a dumb statue thinking of the winking sailor hidden in the notebook's pages currently clutched between Chet's thick and sweaty fingers, feeling like some stupid idiot just waiting to get caught and hanged.

And he also realized, kneeling in the sand on the sunrise after his fifteenth birthday, that a group of other just-turned fifteen-year-old's were currently hiding in the bushes laughing their asses off at him.

In the end, it was impressively efficient how little time it took his father to pack up his entire life for him in trash bags left on the doorstep, with a few yelled parting words and a shocked and embarrassed snicker coming from his little brother half-crouching at the top of the stairs. It was even more surprising to hear the sound of bare feet running after him down the sidewalk three minutes later. To turn and see his father's wife Lahela with tears in her eyes begging him to let her know whether he was alright. To not disappear forever. To not turn his back on the Lord.

So Danny found new places to sleep, as far from Pearl Harbor as he could possibly get on the tiny island of Oahu. Quit high school and instead devoured every science book he could get his hands on. He studied the ocean with romantic obsession, chronicling her every quiver and breath. He fixed people's broken clocks and telephones and primitive computing machines in his little trailer for cash under the table, and he wrote a secret letter to Lahela once a month.

He scrubbed the spray paint off the face of his surfboard. Went out every morning before the sun and stayed out until he barely had the strength to still stand upright on the waxed wood.

And he realized that, since the first time he ever picked up a sharpened red crayon and worked out a physics equation in vibrating, shaky scrawl, he had finally found something he was actually good at.

He was really fucking good at surfing.

# 6

It's all very unexpected.

Sydney pauses after throwing his sunglasses back on over his saltwater-stung eyes and running his hands through his soaked hair, still thigh-deep in the waves, with his board floating restlessly by his side. It bobs and presses against his leg, like an anxious pet dog waiting for a pat on the head or a scolding.

The swelling roar of the crowd spills out to him over the surface of the water, mixing with the harsh slap of the waves against the shore. They're cheering for his competitor. Surrounding him and reaching out to touch his board like a talisman. Clapping their hands all over his wetsuit across his shoulder, where Sydney would be more than prepared to bet, based on the way Jimmy had paddled out to the wave, that there's a hidden war scar, aching in the Pacific's icy cold.

*"Danny Moore wipes out to give Jimmy Campbell his Championship Tour ticket on a golden platter! Right on, Jimmy!"* the announcers cry.

No one is looking at him. No one is watching him be pushed around by the waves in the shallows, mocking the fact that none of those cheers are for him.

He breathes slowly through the emotions brimming up inside of him, crawling out through his skin. There's surprise, for one thing. Surprise at himself that after just 1.8 seconds of staring straight at Jimmy Campbell while ripping across the surface of a wave, he had apparently decided to go and fling himself off his own board on purpose. He can't even remember the last time he wiped out on accident, let alone because he chose to. The potential memory feels false and fleeting in his mind.

There's also resentment. Irritation and misplaced humiliation and a pit-of-his-gut desire to rewind time and absolutely crush Jimmy Campbell the way he had intended to when they first threw their boards down side by side and paddled out into the smooth glass sea.

Sydney keeps his head down as he emerges from the foam and walks as fast as he can along the sand away from the crowds, still-dripping board clutched hard under his arm. Someone's blasting the latest irritating mishmash of sound by The Doors across the beach. Sydney feels it in his bones like a personal insult—the little keyboard mocking him as he stumbles in the sand. People fall uncomfortably silent as he walks past, shocked that "Oahu's own champion of big wave surfing" just got literally knocked on his ass by a local boy without a reputation and a wave barely taller than a ten-year-old kid.

Except they don't know. None of them stop and think and just *realize* that of course "Oahu's own champion of big wave surfing" didn't suddenly forget how to surf like he hasn't done it literally every day since he turned fifteen.

No one notices when he stops at the edge of the swarming crowd and looks back. They light up new cigarettes and snap open new cans of Coors and fawn over the local underdog like sheep following a new prophet. Sydney wants to scoff at them. To laugh at how ridiculous it is that they all think worn-out Jimmy Campbell somehow had the skill and the strength to actually, in fair contest, beat *the* Danny Moore. He wants to cross his arms and smirk that Jimmy's probably basking in the glory with no idea whatsoever that of course Sydney knew there would be a good wave hiding behind that little closed-out dud of a barrel. He didn't obsessively study the ocean for his entire life for nothing.

He wants to think these things and mentally pat himself on the back for a job well done fooling them all, and then escape back to his little motel room by the sea. Wait until the sun sets and the beach clears so he can whip his board back out and surf alone through the quiet calm of midnight under the stars.

But then he looks at Jimmy Campbell one last time before turning to leave, catches a glimpse of golden sunlit hair through the crowd, a hint of a warm smile tinged with a fleeting and invisible melancholy, and suddenly the idea of going back to a motel room alone sounds goddamn miserable.

Sydney grips a handful of frizzy curls with his fingers and huffs. He feels unsettled, betrayed by his own body and mind, because while he may be the only person on that beach that knows he wiped out on purpose, even he doesn't fucking know *why*.

And then there were those ten seconds. Splintered, rotting wood beneath his feet and the hot sun on the back of his neck. Ice-cream licking crowds. The parting of the sea.

Jimmy clearly thinks Sydney doesn't remember what happened on the pier. No human being has ever been more wrong in their life. Sydney remembers exactly what happened on the pier. He remembers the way his breath caught in his throat, and his bottom lip dropped open, and his heart felt like it would explode on the spot. Remembers Jimmy emerging from the crowd like a lighthouse through the fog, for no discernable reason other than that he existed, flesh and bone.

The way he bolted before Jimmy could open his mouth to ask him what the hell he was staring at. The way he hadn't been wearing his shades.

Sydney scoffs at his own thoughts and forces himself to look away from the perfect picture of Jimmy giving a last wave to the still cheering crowd. His little best friend with the ridiculous bun hangs by his side like a puppy, and the girls in bikinis practically line up to kiss his stubbled cheek. It looks straight out of a cheesy 1950's Los Angeles advertisement: *Come to the City of Angels, where the waves and the women never run dry!*

It's not until he's a fifteen-minute walk away from the beach, thoroughly enjoying his self-imposed sulk and trying desperately not to think of why in hell his body willingly fell off his own board, that Sydney suddenly realizes he forgot his bag back at the competition, including his wallet and motel room key. He groans and reluctantly turns back towards the crowded chaos, still avoiding the eyes of shocked fans and strangers alike, willing himself to look as if doubling back to the beach was all part of the plan. He tunes out the blaring music and the roar of the crowd, slinking through so silently his tall form is rendered nearly invisible, even with an 8-foot-long surfboard tucked under one arm.

His bag is right where he left it—back up behind the crowd a ways and perched in between two palm trees, just on the outskirts of the big dirt parking lot. He double checks that his wallet and motel key are still in there, slings it over his shoulder, goes to pick up his surfboard again, and freezes.

It can't be, but it is.

Jimmy Campbell has absolutely no idea that Sydney's standing barely fifteen feet away, perfectly concealed between the two palm tree trunks, face hidden in their shade. Sydney can't move. He stares silently, watching with a clenched jaw as Jimmy leans against the back of the lifeguard stand and breathes slow and deep, face gazing up at the cloudless sky, utterly alone on a beach filled with hundreds of people. Jimmy runs a hand through his long, sun-bleached bangs to sweep them back up off his forehead, and Sydney's chest clenches tightly when he sees Jimmy's fingers move to the zipper of his wetsuit.

It's his signal to leave. A blaring red siren screaming: *private, private, private!*

Sydney stays. He pulls the aviators off his eyes.

He unconsciously licks his chapped lips as Jimmy peels the wetsuit off slowly, inch by inch, to reveal broad, tan shoulders, sharp collar bones covered in a dusting of freckles, hot sand clinging to the muscles on his chest, toned arms hiding a quietly commanding strength. Sweat and saltwater glisten over the firm lines of his stomach, clinging to the muscles on his back and dripping down the curve of his spine like honey. A fat drop of seawater falls from a loose lock of Jimmy's hair and drips onto his firm chest, lazily rolling over a peaked nipple in the chill of the shade.

Sydney sucks in a quick breath and bites his bottom lip. Sweat prickles hot and sticky at the back of his neck, down his sides and under his arms. His eyes are riveted, drinking in every new inch of revealed skin like a dying man in a desert come upon an oasis. It's impossible to believe, unimaginable, that Sydney sat perched just ten feet away from this body not even hour ago, back when it was covered up and unassuming. An irritating inconvenience sitting in Sydney's way from catching another winning wave.

Jimmy slowly rolls his neck to crack it, and the quiet groan he lets out sends a shiver down the skin of Sydney's forearms. He can feel his own feet shifting restlessly in the sand—the unwanted clenching of his thighs. Before he can inwardly curse himself into turning to go, Jimmy lets the top of his wetsuit hang down by his sides and stretches his arms behind him, suddenly revealing the blasted skin of a gnarled scar across his shoulder.

Sydney gasps. It's horrific—marring the sturdy, smooth, powerful lines of Jimmy's body with a firework of raised, pink tissue.

It's also the most beautiful thing Sydney has ever seen. He thinks of a crumpled-up magazine page with a Hawaiian wave crashing onto a perfect shore. He thinks of a topless sailor winking at him from a photograph bought under the table at the back of a record store back on Oahu. And he suddenly thinks of what it would feel like to draw Jimmy Campbell into his arms, letting him rest his weary skin against his own too-tall, too-bizarre body, feeling the quiet strength and competence in his forearms, his shoulder blades, his kneecaps, the little salty sliver of skin behind his ear. Fingertips which had gripped a smoking gun, touched blood, and paddled furiously on a surfboard out onto a flat sea. Which had pulled down a wetsuit zipper.

And it's then, with the crashing force of one of Waimea's biggest waves, that it finally hits Sydney why his body decided to fall off his own damn surfboard when he could have just left Jimmy Campbell behind, defeated in the whitewater. Why he opened his big mouth out on the lifeless, smooth sea and goaded him into chasing after that closed-out barrel knowing he would catch the perfect wave hiding just behind it.

The answer is so blindingly simple in retrospect that Sydney wants to kick himself. He gazes through the palm trees at this hidden sailor, currently standing alone behind a lifeguard stand and smiling down at his feet like he just had his dreams handed to him from the wet palms of the sea herself. This man who stared death in the face and said, "Not today."

Sydney sees now that he had two options when he popped up on his board to catch his first and only wave of the set, following in Jimmy's wake.

In the first option, he absolutely crushes Jimmy Campbell as intended, boards a plane back to Oahu the next day with a pocket full of prize money, and moves on with his preparations to win the Billabong Masters for the third consecutive year. And Jimmy Campbell picks his board up out of the water, shakes his head with a sheepish smile, and goes back full-time to a Long Beach dockyard with no future surf competitions in sight and a sore shoulder.

In the second option, Sydney embarrasses himself, lets Jimmy Campbell win the heat and go pro, and sees those deep blue eyes again in two weeks in Oahu.

He wonders if he ever even really had a choice.

Sydney is still frozen, clutching his aviators in a sweaty hand, breathless with this revelation and almost choking under the weight of it, when he suddenly feels a pair of eyes hot against his skin.

Jimmy Campbell's staring at him through the trees like he can't even decide what emotion to begin to express.

Sydney panics. With a sharp intake of breath, he jams on his aviators, bolts from behind the palm trees less than a second after those eyes first locked onto his, then purposefully loses himself in the chaos of the crowd for ten minutes before finally breaking free to make his way back to his motel room down Hermosa Avenue.

Sydney Moore doesn't wait until the beach quiets down. Doesn't take his board out into the quiet midnight waters to surf free and open in the moonlight under the stars.

Instead, he stares at the ceiling of the motel room for a long time. Thinks of all his earthly belongings in a trash bag on the front porch, his momma's broken cross necklace lying lonely on the rough floorboards, Chet Morgan's gritty fingers clutching a photograph of a winking sailor.

Thinks of Jimmy Campbell's blond hair under a sailor's cap. Of his thighs dripping with wet sand and glistening with sweat, tan and firm against his own shivering skin. Thinks of the sinking, desperate look on Jimmy's face when Sydney had taken off his sunglasses and looked over at him halfway through his own ride across the face of the barrel, right when he was on the cusp of taking Jimmy's dream away. Thinks of Jimmy's stunned face on a crowded pier.

He slowly, achingly lets his hand slip down between his legs for the first time in years, ears tingling at the unexpected moan that escapes his salty lips. Sydney sighs as he feels himself harden in his hand, hips moving slowly in a pool of warmth that spreads down his legs to his toes. His breath stutters in his chest as he pumps his long, smooth fingers over his cock, cradling himself in the palm of his hand and trembling at the coiling tension in his groin.

His body feels oversensitive. Exposed, like the skin's been peeled back from his bones, revealing his veins to the air. He tries not to make a sound as he remembers the way Jimmy Campbell practically growled as he hunkered down and paddled with all his might, chasing after a wave out of pure, muscled spite. He hears the memory of that deep, quiet grunt echo softly in his ears.

When he finally lets go and comes, he sees Jimmy's face, fierce and set and determined as they waited for the air horn for their heat, a soldier preparing for battle. A man who's seen war.

And Sydney lies there in the silent, dark aftermath, still buzzing between his thighs, feeling slow and dirty and utterly, ridiculously dull.

Just before midnight, Sydney finds himself back down at the shore, walking slowly along the water's foaming edge. The muted yellow street lights along Hermosa Avenue cast ghostly shadows across the cool sand, flickering off the water like a layer of liquid gold covering the swells of the sea. The ocean roars just as loudly in the dark of night. The sound of it never fails to calm him.

Just up ahead, the road cuts closer to the water, revealing a strip of seaside bars and surf shops. The sound of laughter and self-important talking gradually gets louder as Sydney approaches. Even if he was back at his home in Oahu, he knows he has absolutely no business at a crowded, popular surf bar the night after a major competition. He's the absolute last person anyone would want to see during their social hour. Still his feet drag him closer, drawn towards the flickering light like a moth. He sits in the shadows down by the water, half hidden by a craggy outcrop of rocks, and listens to the hum of people talking too loud as the music pulses against his back.

After only a few minutes, a cheer erupts behind him, and he turns to see a crowd of surfers part to reveal Jimmy Campbell at the center, basking in the glow of his newly professional status with a calm, embarrassed pride. He's shaved since that morning. Showered and changed into jean shorts and a navy and white striped long sleeve shirt rolled up over his forearms.

Sydney watches out of the corner of his eye as Jimmy's handed a beer and gradually moves out to the rickety patio, his brunette friend with the long hair beside him. They stand shoulder to shoulder, leaning out on the wooden fence, talking softly in each other's ears to be heard over the din of the crowd.

Sydney feels absolutely ridiculous watching them as closely as he is. Somehow, in the past twenty-four hours, Jimmy Campbell has reduced him from Oahu's untouchable, unbeatable champion to a brainless, predictable high-schooler, tripping over his own toes in the hallways and clutching a notebook to his chest with a secret photograph tucked inside. An egg-salad sandwich growing warm in his locker.

The friend laughs at something Jimmy just said, and Jimmy takes another long sip of beer before reaching up and tucking a lock of loose hair behind the friend's ear.

Sydney's heart pounds as his mouth goes dry. He couldn't be . . . could he?

The friend doesn't react, but keeps looking out over the water as if nothing even happened. Sydney wants to scream at him. How can he stand there with absolutely no reaction when Jimmy Campbell has just casually run his fingers through his hair? He watches through his eyelashes, rapt with attention, as Jimmy leans even closer to whisper in the friend's ear, face turned serious. Sydney desperately reads the lines of his body for clues. The hard rod of his spine, the grip of his hand along the railing, the firm set of his shoulders all signal new territory, subjects long left untouched finally being spoken aloud. Jimmy's free hand rubs unconsciously at a spot under his left shoulder. Sydney can practically feel the tiny warm puffs of breath against his own ear, can almost hear the smooth, warm voice spilling over with secrets.

"Rob, stop flirting and get your ass back in here! We finally got the pool table free!"

Jimmy practically leaps back from the friend—Rob—as Rob smiles and calls back an answer to the friend inside the bar. Jimmy's not smiling. He shoves his hands down into his pockets and flinches as Rob claps a hand down on his shoulder in some sort of apology. No doubt some sort of "finish this talk another time" nonsense while he nods towards the pool table. Sydney watches Jimmy resolutely stare down at the sand as Rob walks back into the bar, still softly shaking his head 'no' in response to Rob's probable offer to join, as if he was still there to see his reaction.

Suddenly Jimmy's tearing across the sand, half-full beer left back on the patio. Sydney stupidly thinks of laying down to hide like a child behind the rocks before he realizes it's too late. He's going to be seen. It's inevitable.

He smoothes out the front of his tank top and grits his teeth. He's Danny fucking Moore, not some starstruck little kid, even if Jimmy did catch him watching him through the palm trees earlier that afternoon. He feels his face settle into his familiar mask of untouchable, intimidating indifference.

Right when Jimmy is five feet from his hiding place, practically running now in the sand, Sydney speaks.

"Bit late for a jog, isn't it?"

Jimmy startles and curses under his breath as he whips around.

"Christ, you startled—wait a minute, *you.*"

Jimmy points an accusing finger at him, brow fiercely set, and Sydney rises warily to his feet. It isn't exactly the reaction he was expecting.

Jimmy stalks towards him in the moonlight. "You. What the fuck was that today? Huh? The hell are you playing at?"

His voice is a harsh whisper, and Sydney feels it like ice down his spine. He'd been expecting some good-natured gloating, maybe a "too bad" or two, or an "are you alright." After all, Jimmy Campbell was the first surfer in three years who'd taken it upon himself to try to have a goddamn conversation with him.

Instead he looks furious. Sydney clears his throat to buy a second of time, and the corners of his mouth tighten. "I believe the correct term, in case you forgot, is 'wiped out,'" he spits back.

Jimmy practically growls. "No you don't. No you fucking don't. How big of an idiot do you think I am? Danny Moore magically wipes out on his only wave of the day after three years of a near-perfect record? Wiped out my ass."

Sydney feels like Jimmy Campbell is twenty feet tall. He barely stops himself from cowering. He opens his mouth to retort, but Jimmy beats him to it.

"Tell me, what's your game, Moore? What is it? You want to help me go pro just so you can watch me get my ass handed to me by you and everyone else on the circuit for the next year? Was it pity? Do I look so fucking depressing you felt like I needed a free meal from your blessed hands?"

"Oh cool it and spare me the theatrics. You're hardly the first broken sailor I've come across on the waves."

Sydney hates himself even as the words leave his mouth, but the rage he expects to see on Jimmy's face is quickly overtaken by . . . irritation? Curiosity?

"How can you possibly know that? Earlier, when you said . . . Fucking tell me how you knew that about me," Jimmy demands.

Sydney physically stops himself from leaning closer into Jimmy's space. The man is looking up at him with a challenge, daring him to continue to prove himself as a know-it-all asshole so that Jimmy can keep up with his righteous anger in the cool sand. Sydney decides to play along. He files away for later the fact that seeing the furious glare in Jimmy's deep blue eyes sends a completely unfamiliar thrill up his own spine.

"Oh please," he scoffs, trying to hold himself upright, "how many people do you think you're fooling? There are thousands of you. Who in hell wears a full wetsuit at a surf competition in Los Angeles in July? Someone with something to hide. Can't be an embarrassing tattoo— you're sure as hell not the type, and probably even too terrified of commitment to get one. You may be short, but it can't be anything to do with your physique. You rub at your weak shoulder every chance you get when you think no one's looking. You magically arrived here sleeping in a van two years ago with absolutely nothing to say about how you spent the last five years of your life. You stand up straight like you're at inspection when you wait on the start line. The Navy was just a lucky guess—some sentimental bullshit having to do with your childhood spent in the waves I'd guess. Combine all of that with the fact you keep even your apparently closest friend a twenty-foot pole's length away from your actual thoughts and that you change your shirt in secret alone behind a lifeguard station after just winning the competition of your life, and I'd say I'd have to be an absolute airhead not to have worked it out before, *Seaman*."

51

Sydney blushes hot across his cheeks as his mouth spits out the last part about seeing Jimmy change on the beach. The admission hangs between them like a lead weight in the air. He tries to control his breathing so it doesn't rasp even louder than the waves.

Jimmy stares him straight in the eyes and takes a deep, grunting breath. "Swear to God I've never wanted to say 'fuck you' to anyone as much as I want to say it to you right now, and I've seen people do some terrifying shit."

Sydney's mouth goes dry at the sheer rage, the vibrating, barely contained power radiating out from the fiercely controlled man in front of him. "Well, what's stopping you then? Your delicate sensibilities? Getting soft in your old age?"

Jimmy huffs out at the water before looking back at Sydney with a sharp danger glinting in his eyes. "Watch yourself. I'm not that fucking old."

"No? If you'd asked me that five minutes ago, I'd have said the exact opposite."

"Oh yeah?" Jimmy growls. "Says who?"

He puffs up his chest and steps into Sydney's space, face just inches from his.

Sydney's mind flashes through images of Jimmy Campbell looking alone and lost in the middle of a crowded pier—slumped shoulders and tired legs and shadowed eyes just moments after absolutely annihilating his first heat over surfers a decade younger than him.

Sydney laughs, a harsh, shallow breath. "Says you!" he cries. His arms flail out to the sides like a dramatic idiot on a daytime soap. "You walk around this beach like you've got a noose around your neck and you're five steps away from the gallows. If you hadn't won, I don't think I would have even seen you smile all fucking day. We're *surfing*, for God's sake. It's muscle and adrenaline and physics. It's just a game. We're not standing on the brink of World War three."

Sydney feels like he could fly with all the energy pumping through his body. He hasn't had a conversation this long with someone in years, even if it has just devolved into a shouting match. Being less than a foot away from Jimmy's heaving chest, pectorals rising under his thin cotton shirt, is causing his brain to short circuit. Spitting out anything and everything and not even able to pause for breath.

He stands breathless and waits as Jimmy lets out a long sigh through his nose. Suddenly, before his very eyes, the fight leaves Jimmy's eyes, completely snuffed out. Sydney's heart hammers in alarm within his chest. He clenches his fists to keep from reaching out and shaking Jimmy—from trying to shake the life and the anger back into him to keep his eyes from pooling dull black like they are now.

"So it was pity, then," Jimmy finally says, holding his gaze. "I'm pathetic, to you."

Sydney's mind practically screams at him to say, "*Anything but.*" He simply doesn't understand. They're on a fucking beach in one of the most beautiful places on earth, getting paid money to fling themselves across the surface of the ocean and rip through the spray. But Jimmy's eyes look like they're still facing down the barrel of a gun on a beach in Hanoi.

Sydney realizes he's been silent for far too long, and when he opens his mouth to respond, Jimmy holds up a hand to stop him.

"Shut it. I don't want to hear it," he hisses, but it sounds weary. Jimmy takes a step back and runs a hand through his hair. He looks out at the crashing waves and breathes slow and deep. Sydney wishes he knew what Jimmy was looking at—what he was really seeing out in the moonlit sea.

"They warned me about you," Jimmy eventually says. Sydney can barely hear him over the roar of the oblivious water.

He drums up the last of his energy, forcing himself to spit out the words he thinks Jimmy's expecting. "Let me guess—that I'll check out your ass? Force myself on you when you aren't looking?" he sneers back. He suddenly thinks of his hand down his pants earlier that evening in his dingy motel room and forces himself not to visibly shiver with shame.

Jimmy hesitates, then looks straight at him. His body goes absolutely still. It's terrifying.

"No," he says. "That you're a miserable asshole who thinks he's the Jesus Christ of surfing."

Sydney scoffs. "That's the most ridiculous insult I've ever heard. It's not even clever!" He doesn't realize he's closing the gap between him and Jimmy again until Jimmy's hand is on his shoulder, pushing him away so roughly that they both stumble in the sand.

"Stay the fuck away from me," he growls. "I'm telling you now, Moore. I don't fucking care about whatever grand plans you have to humiliate me. Whatever shit you pulled in the water today, I fucking earned my place here. I *earned* it. You can look down on me from your high horse all you want, but I know what I want, and—"

"And what do you want?" Sydney interrupts. "Besides just lounging around on a beach all day with chicks lining up to wish you good luck, huh?"

"*God,* you are something else."

"Just *tell* me, then!"

"I don't need to tell you shit," Jimmy snaps as he starts backing away quickly. "But, for a start, I want you to stay the hell away from me!" With that, he turns and begins to storm down the beach, kicking up sand behind him.

Sydney's gut clenches. The reason for his wipeout earlier hits him so hard in the face again he feels dizzy with it, his vision blacking out everything but the man practically running away from him now in the sand.

"Well tough shit!" he yells after him, "Because your precious pro status means you'll see me again in two weeks at the Billabong!"

Jimmy doesn't even turn back to look at him as he flips him off.

Sydney watches him go, chest still heaving. He finally forces himself to roll his eyes, without exactly knowing why, and turns to leave when he spots something glinting in the sand. He reaches down in the moonlight and picks up a bullet casing, dropped a few inches from where Jimmy had shoved Sydney back from him. He doesn't have to think hard to know exactly where the bullet casing is from. He looks quickly bath and forth, for some reason needing to make sure he's alone, then pockets the smooth metal.

In a daze, Sydney walks down the beach in the opposite direction of the bar and his motel. The opposite direction of Jimmy Campbell. His fingers rub the worn metal casing in his pocket until the sun starts peeking up over the mountains at his right, sending puffs of slowly warming salty air across his skin. His body is exhausted, begging him for rest and water. He pats his other pocket to reach for cash for a cab and realizes he left his wallet back in his motel the night before like an absolute moron.

And when he finally drops down limp onto his motel bed almost three hours later, sweating and dehydrated and spent, he lies there and tries very hard to hate Jimmy Campbell with every fiber of his being. To hate him for staring straight into his eyes in the middle of a crowded pier, and for stubbornly insisting on introducing himself while they waited for the waves, and for emerging from the whitewater as the winner, and for making Sydney's throat tighten when he placed his warm, rough hand on his shoulder and pushed him away, and for being so damned unpredictable.

He tries to hate him for hours, listening to the cars zoom down the busy street outside his motel window, filling his mind with the grating hum of urban white noise.

He fails.

# 7

The last hour before a meal break always drags by like an eternity. James can feel every muscle he used the day before in the competition screaming out at him now, exacerbated by getting only a couple hours of sleep after he'd stood staring out the window of his apartment all night fuming, Danny Moore's choicest phrases repeating through his head on an endless loop, smothering the excitement of his win.

*You're hardly the first broken sailor I've come across out on the waves.*

*Who do you think you're fooling?*

*It's just a game.*

They're doing maintenance on a shipping ramp today, welding and soldering metal with bursts of flame cutting through the heavy late morning sun. James' skin feels like his own personal humidifier, and his button-up work shirt is plastered to his back and sides with sweat.

His coworkers are distracting themselves with stories of their exploits from the night before—girls and booze and Sunset Boulevard antics. The older guys are arguing over last night's Dodgers' 9th inning upset, distinctly leaving out any mention of wives or children.

James remains characteristically silent. After over two years, none of them even know that the reason his hair is still damp when he gets to work each morning is because it's ocean water from surfing, not a shower at home with a fake wife and kids. No one wears a wedding ring on the job; it would just get lost. It makes it easier to lie.

He thinks briefly back to those times on the Navy ship in between missions, playing cards late into the night in a cloud of cigarette smoke, on shore leave in Ha Long in a seedy bar with Christmas lights hanging from the ceiling and warm beers covering the rickety wooden table. It's a hard thing to realize about himself, and he recoils from the thought like he always does. Hard to know he only ever really gets close to people if the threat of death is hanging over his shoulder, creeping beneath his skin.

And here, now, on this sunny Long Beach dock with four hundred and seventy-two accident-free workdays in a row, and counting, he grimaces and shakes his head against the unwanted thought that he wishes he was back in a camouflage dinghy motorboat hovering off an exploding jungle coast, surrounded by bright, freckled faces with adventure and fear in their eyes, smears of blood and mud on their cheeks, looking over at James like he's been their best friend since the womb, knowing that one of them will be dead by nightfall.

James stands up straight from his crouch, hauling a stack of new wood over to the building site, and winces as his back pops and groans. About half of the men sweating and grunting around him are older than him, some by a lot. Their spines creak and sag as their calloused, gloved hands reach for the next shipping container, the next thick cable, the next lukewarm beer. It's like working surrounded by ghosts of his future self.

A quick look into his finances that morning at the bank before his shift had showed James that even if he won a small amount of money at every major professional competition that year, he'd still have to keep the dockyard job part time to make ends meet—at least to cover plane tickets until he could rope together a sponsor. As much as Rob tries to convince him otherwise, he's under no delusions that the call from Val's will ever actually come through. The thought of it feels like suffocating in slow motion. Stuck on an unmoving surfboard as the water heaves and rises around him, trickling down into his lungs.

The whistle eventually blows for lunch, and the entire dock lets out a collective groan of relief. James wastes no time booking it over to his water canteen in a tiny block of shade against a fence, ripping off his work shirt so that the breeze can cool his skin through his sweat-soaked undershirt. His work boots feel worn and heavy on his feet, and the thick leather gloves covering his hands are quickly torn off and thrown to the ground. Finally he removes his hard hat and swipes a hand through his dripping hair, shivering as rivulets of sweat drip down the back and sides of his neck.

He's just about to take a sip of water and let his brain shut off for his thirty-minute break when he stops, frozen in his tracks, mouth half open.

Danny Moore looks like a Hollywood film star accidentally wandered onto the grimy, salt- and rust-stained set of a maritime horror movie. A perfectly cut white shirt hugs his lean body, shirt collar left open to reveal the long, smooth lines of his neck. His legs look a mile long in crisp, ironed slacks, hot sun glowing on his brown suede shoes. His hair is tamed in perfect curls—a night and day difference from the frizzy halo he was sporting the night before when he had caught James unawares in the sand.

He looks like a completely different person. As if someone straight out of that Star Trek show Rob's always bugging him to watch made a magic clone of Danny Moore, where the original man is just a young kid in a tank top with frizzy hair, and the clone's a top-level Hollywood executive just stepping off a private jet at LAX. James' eyes flicker over the barest hint of collarbone, and he swallows over a dry throat.

Danny stops walking once James notices him and stands there waiting, eyes squinting hard against the harsh noon sun. James still can't even believe what he's seeing. For a terrifying moment, he thinks he must have heat stroke and is seeing a mirage. Because there is absolutely no fucking way that not even twelve hours after thoroughly chewing him out (and being chewed out) on the moonlit sand, and being explicitly told to stay the hell away, that Danny Moore has donned a suit, found out where James works, and come here to . . . what? Humiliate him some more? Gloat? Tell him that all of yesterday was really just a lucid dream, that James was slipped some mushrooms or some shit by a co-conspirator and never actually made pro in the first place?

James realizes Danny is waiting for him to approach and finally does so, wary eyes watching him with a mixture of apprehension and irritation. The tiny part of James that's excited at the thrill of this unexpected turn of events is thoroughly clamped down.

He runs his forearm over his sweaty forehead as he approaches and wipes his dirt- and grease-stained hands on his work pants. He sees

Danny's eyes roam once quickly up his body, probably self-righteously disgusted at the stark difference in their current states. James finds he can't even blame him one bit. No one he knows has ever seen him at work before, in this dripping, tired mess—not even Rob.

He decides not even to give him the benefit of a "hello" or a "what the fuck are you doing here." He stops before Danny and waits, brow furrowed, shoulders back, eyes narrowed.

Danny licks his lips and clears his throat, hastily looking down at the ground before meeting James' gaze. It has the unexpected effect of making him look startlingly young. James tries not to get lost in his cool, grey eyes. Little droplets of fresh ocean water in the middle of the dirt, sweat, and grime. He wonders what happened to the aviators.

"I believe you dropped this," Danny says calmly, holding out his palm from his pocket.

James' blood turns to ice. He hadn't even realized it was missing. He shoots out his hand and quickly grabs the bullet casing from Danny's long fingers, shoving it down in a zippered pocket in his pants before looking up and giving one brief nod. The metal is still warm from Danny's skin. James' heart is thumping so hard he's sure Danny can see it through his thin, dripping undershirt.

James waits expectantly for Danny to turn on his heel and book it out of there as fast as possible in his perfectly shined shoes. Humiliation accomplished. Mission completed. 'Holier than thou' gloating quite successfully achieved. When he doesn't, James starts to grow wary.

He can practically feel the weight of Danny's gaze on him—judging, scoffing, pitying. James' defenses rise, prickling the hairs on the back of his neck and his arms.

"You got anything else to say or can you leave?" he spits out.

Danny blinks slowly. His eyes widen a fraction, then stare unfocused at the ground before looking back up at James. His face is soft and unguarded. The man from the pier.

"No, I—I don't," he says. James crosses his arms and puffs out his chest as Danny's eyes roam quickly over him once more. James stares back, daring him with just a look to say something more. Practically begging for a fight.

Instead, Danny simply backs two steps away, hands slumped in his pockets. He gives James a ghost of a tight smile, then turns on his heel to walk away, long legs graceful on the rough, uneven dock.

James' brain flashes back to the image of Danny the day before, fresh out of the water from his defeat and walking, utterly alone, away from him down the sand, head slumped and avoiding everyone else's shocked gaze. James' mouth opens before he even realizes what he's doing.

"Wait!"

Danny freezes in his tracks, and James jogs to catch up with him, running his fingers through his hair once more to buy time as they stand face to face.

"You—you didn't have to do that." He swallows roughly, staring just over Danny's shoulder. "Thank you."

Danny shrugs one shoulder. He couldn't look more bored if he tried. "Yeah, well, can't have a fish choke on it and die or something, or the environmental hippies'll be all over your ass."

James huffs out a startled laugh despite himself, and Danny's lips quirk up just at the corner.

"How the hell did you find out where I work?" James asks, not bothering to hide the undertone of a dark challenge in his voice.

"Wasn't that hard," Danny says calmly with another shrug. "Calluses on your fingers consistent with some type of manual labor. Tan lines on your wrists from the gloves, scars on your forearm from stray sparks from welding, articles in all the local papers about the controversy over expanding the dock ramps down here. Might have overheard another surfer or two mention you in connection with the maritime industry. Would've been tempted to guess you worked out on the lobster trap boats or an oil rig, but I suspect you haven't stepped foot on a boat since you last stepped off one in uniform. And you wouldn't be near enough to the shore to surf."

James purses his lips and stares Danny down.

"That's unbelievable," he says tightly.

Danny furrows his brow. "But I just walked you through it all, told you my reasonin—"

"No, no, I mean that's fucking amazing," James says.

60

Danny looks at him steadily for a second, his body completely still. It looks like he's a robot who's just been unplugged. James tells himself his heart is still racing because of the work he did all morning, even if his break started over ten minutes ago.

Finally Danny responds. "You still look like you're angry."

James hums, crosses his arms once more. "I don't know a single soul besides Rob that would ever casually mention I work in the 'maritime industry,'" he says.

Danny casually bites the inside of his cheek. "Perhaps not."

"You asked about me. Snooped around so you could find out where I worked."

Danny squints, staring off over James' head, and quirks his head to the side. "I'd call it more . . . happened to pass by when people were discussing relevant information this morning on the shore. You know—right place, right time."

James shuts his eyes and shakes his head, pressing his lips together in a firm line to hold back the retort that's right on the tip of his tongue. He takes a steadying breath and wills his voice to come out steady, calming the surprising amount anger inside of him.

"You're a real fucking creep, you know that?"

Danny does that irritating shrug again. "Been called worse."

When James doesn't immediately shoot a retort back, the air between them turns tense and fragile, and James' blood thrums hard through his veins. They stand in a silent stalemate, both staring at the ground.

Finally James clears his throat. It's hard to breathe right with Danny Moore standing tall and gleaming and untouchable just inches away from his own sweating, grimy chest. He takes a step back and gestures his head towards the crew lounging in the shade of the dock with their lunches, hating the fact that he suddenly doesn't want to leave.

"Right, well, gotta get back to—"

Danny's arm darts out and catches James' upper arm, stealing the breath and the words from his mouth.

"You want to win in Oahu. Pick up a sponsor there so you can quit working in this hell hole."

His voice is smooth and clear. Urgent. James' skin prickles beneath Danny's long fingers, still snugly gripping his upper arm to keep him close. Danny's eyes are dazzling, staring straight into James' like his face is the only thing on earth that's visible to see. James forces himself to breathe and shakes his head.

"No way I can win there," he says.

Danny takes a step closer, invading his space so that James has to crane his neck to see him. From this close he can feel the heat radiating off his chest.

"But you want to. You told me you know what you want, and this is what you want. To get out of here."

James sighs, then lifts his hands in a helpless gesture at his sides, encompassing the punishing heat of the dock, the blood and sweat, the stooping, rough ghosts at his back. "Yeah. I—yeah. Who wouldn't?"

Danny seems to realize for the first time that his hand is still on James' bicep. He snatches it back quickly, fluttering his fingers by his side. James' arm invisibly twitches at the absence.

"I'm staying here another week before flying back to Oahu," Danny goes on, as if nothing happened. "Train with me."

James freezes, repeating those last words in his head, then groans and shoots him an icy glare. His odd, giddy breathlessness falls away in a split second, replaced by solid, familiar anger. "God, you're unbelievable. You didn't get the picture enough last night when I told you I didn't need a fucking handout?"

"I've studied the waves in Hawaii most of my life. I know how to win there. I can show you."

"And what? And come competition time you'll just stand back and let me win?"

"Obviously not. I won't be surfing."

"You . . . *you* aren't going to surf in the Billabong?"

Danny stands up even taller, puffing out his chest. It strains against the buttons on his gleaming white shirt. James stops himself just in time from licking his lips.

"Couple of surfers are holding a big wave surf contest at Waimea the week after the Billabong—one I fully intend to win. Weather's supposed to make for some prime conditions that day—chance that only comes around every few years. I'd be an idiot to waste all my strength trying to get a prize I've already won twice."

James huffs. "Oh yeah, right, wouldn't want to look greedy. How fucking humble of you."

Danny puts his hands on his hips and stretches impossibly taller. He looks like a businessman late for an important meeting, and James is just the valet taking too long to retrieve his car. "Look, you're wasting time pretending to feel offended. I'm serious about this, James. Train with me."

James stops in his tracks, eyes searching Danny's exasperated face for any sign that this is all some sick and elaborate joke. The sound of his name, his proper name, in that voice runs slowly through his body with an unsettling, fizzling warmth.

"Nobody calls me James," he finally responds.

Danny rolls his eyes and huffs. "Well we can't both go by names that end in 'y' if we're going to be around each other," he bites back. "It'd be like some horrible sequel to a 'Dick and Jane' children's book. See Jimmy swim. See Danny surf."

James feels the spark of irritation start to boil over again inside him.

"You're an infuriating dick. Change your own damn name if it's so important to you. You do realize Danny is a nickname for Daniel, unless your parents just gave up."

Danny rakes his fingers through his hair and pulls, so comically exasperated that James almost laughs.

"Look, this isn't the point," he groans. "You need to win. I need to train for Waimea. You need someone to tell you about the surf out there, and I need something to keep my mind from imploding over the next week stuck in this boring, hot, shithole of a city until my flight. The way I see it, you'd be an absolute idiot to say no."

"You already think I'm an idiot. There is absolutely nothing about me that you even like!" James shoots back. He laughs once, harsh and incredulous as he looks up at the sky. "Man, I wish I knew what game you were playing at here. What you could possibly want from me."

Danny is silent, hands hanging limp by his sides and still waiting for an answer. James finally looks up and sees that Danny's eyes have gone soft. For the first time since Danny Moore ever stepped up next to him in the sand, James fully remembers how young he actually is. How, underneath the toned physique and the sunglasses-while-he-surfs and the biting remarks, he's just about the same age James himself was when he took his first trembling step onto a Navy ship, wishing his mom had still been there to hand him a sacked lunch and kiss his cheek goodbye.

It makes him want to reach out and take Danny's hand and lead him—to where, he doesn't even know. He can practically see the thoughts warring in Danny's mind as they stand there staring each other down, deciding whether to continue being a haughty asshole or whether the silence will eventually guilt-trip James into agreeing.

James takes a deep breath and licks his lips against the hot sun. He feels like he's just made a decision, and he doesn't even know what it is.

"You need to know," he starts. His breath tightens on the words, and he clears his throat and starts again. "You need to know this isn't just a game for me."

Danny's soft, grey eyes dart down quickly to the pocket where they both know the bullet casing is hidden. He breathes out quickly through his nose and dips his head. "I know. I—I'm realizing that."

A silent moment passes. Out of nowhere, a thought hits James with sudden, breathtaking clarity. "You knew there would be a great wave hiding behind that closed-out one yesterday, didn't you?"

Danny's eyes go wide with surprise, quickly masked again by a calm indifference.

"Didn't study the ocean all these years for nothing," he says back, sounding bored.

James wants to ask a thousand questions—mainly what the hell was Danny Moore thinking when he took advantage of James' stubbornness and goaded him into riding the best wave of the set. He stands there staring up at him in disbelief, painfully aware that they're still standing far too close for two acquaintances in the middle of a dockyard, one covered in blue collar sweat and grime and the other one just stepped off a fashion show runway.

Suddenly, the alarm signaling the end of lunch blares harshly across the dock, and James startles and flinches down. He blinks hard against the familiar haunting boom in his mind that makes him want to duck and find the nearest cover after a loud noise, and his aching heart pounds the blood through his veins, preparing his limbs for the imaginary fight.

Except he's in Long Beach. He's at his job with four hundred and seventy-two accident-free workdays, and counting.

He takes a deep breath and tries to shake it off while he stares hard at the ground, feeling tense and hot and embarrassed. Danny silently waits. James tries to read pity or impatience in the still lines of his body, but, surprisingly, all he finds is an anchoring calm.

Finally James looks back up to sheepishly meet his eyes and turns his head back towards the dock in a silent excuse, a cold sweat breaking out over his neck as the pent-up tension starts to leak out through his limbs. Danny nods, understanding, eyes slightly narrowed in thought.

James wipes his hand once more on his work pants and extends it out in front of him. His hand is steady.

"You infuriate me," he says softly, lips set in a harsh line.

Danny's mouth twitches as he takes James' hand, his fingers long and warm. "As do you," he replies.

"Six-thirty tomorrow morning? Hermosa?" James asks as he rubs the back of his neck with his other hand.

"Alright."

James shivers once as the tips of Danny's fingers lightly trace at the tip of his wrist, and suddenly the hot air around them crackles with anticipation. They've been shaking hands for far too long. James stares spellbound as Danny looks down at their joined hands, then back up at him through his eyelashes, eyes quietly wide with uncertainty.

James swallows hard, making a soft noise in his throat. They're back on the swarming pier, drawn into each other like magnets, likes waves to the shore. He's going to take a step forward. He's going to reach out his other hand and press his dirty, calloused fingers against the perfect, clean white shirt. He's going to trace the tan, lean muscles of Danny's chest, feel his heart rate quicken under his palm, lean forward and smell the leftover salt on his skin–

"Campbell, the fuck you doing over there? Stop being a flat leaver and get your ass back here before The Man sees you!"

James flinches back at the sound of his coworker's booming, raunchy voice. He snatches his hand away and, after a sharp nod at the silent Danny, turns and jogs back to the work site and his crew. He feels cool eyes on his back. His palm tingles by his side, and he fights the urge to wipe it off on his pants when it starts to sweat. He doesn't turn around to look until he's all the way back at the ramp, with his work shirt pulled on and his hard hat and gloves jammed back onto damp, tired skin.

When he finally does take a breath and look back across the dock, Danny's long gone. James hates himself for the sinking feeling in his chest when he sees that Danny didn't stay there long enough to watch him get back to work.

He shakes his head angrily as he grips a wrench in his gloved hand. He's a grown man. One who's lived a full life, and fought a war on the other side of the world, and come back to absolutely nothing only to rebuild himself from the ashes. He isn't some clueless, trigger-happy surfer dude getting into pointless, macho turf wars. Isn't a nervous, hormonal teenager who's never met anyone in his life before who happens to be attractive.

James purposefully pushes away the thoughts threatening to drown him and focuses on the steady ebb and flow of work, the push and pull of working muscles, the breath and pulse of the docks. He lets the memory of Danny Moore's fingertips on his wrist fade into a distant memory, melding with his pointless dreams from the night before into the thick opacity of the unreal.

It isn't until nearly three hours later, as he hoists one end of a steel rod over his shoulder and heaves it across the dock, following the man in front of him, that James suddenly realizes that tomorrow morning will be the first morning in over two years where the person he meets down in the pre-dawn sand won't be Rob Depaul.

James is awake, dressed, and gazing out his window with a cup of instant coffee in his hand a full thirty minutes before he even needs to skateboard down to the beach to meet Danny.

*To meet Danny.*

The sentence sounds ridiculous in his head. If someone had told him a week ago that he'd be waiting to go for a private surf and training session with *the* Danny Moore just two days after winning his pro status in front of the crowds at the International Surf Festival, James would have thought that all the POW training in the Navy had finally caught up with him and absolutely fried his brain. Left him just a hallucinating vegetable.

And yet, here he is.

He'd stopped by Rob and Lori's place after his shift ended last night—the little house in Redondo that Rob bought for them with the savings he'd built up over the last couple years, working his way up from being a fresh recruit in the LAPD.

James had only really been there a handful of times to drop Rob off in their driveway after a surf session on days when Lori was using their truck. One of those rare times, there'd been a young kid playing in the front yard sprinkler just down the street, laughing as he drank the icy water with little pale blue swimming shorts on his freckled legs. The kid had looked up at James and madly waved, as if the entire neighborhood was his own pool, and James the best friend he'd been waiting to meet. But James had quickly looked the other way without even a nod, just as the kid's mom called him inside for an early lunch.

And then there had been the party. James still remembers Rob and Lori's housewarming party with a shudder, for multiple reasons. The main one being the fact that he'd taken one look around the place after he arrived and realized that he was somehow by far the oldest person in the room. That people were avoiding him like the dreaded older brother, and that he had absolutely no business being there intruding on all of their good time by standing ominously in the corner with a warm beer in his hand, waiting for Rob or Lori to come over and talk to him. He'd left after just twenty minutes, the on-sale toaster he'd gotten them as a lame gift shoved in an unpacked room.

But last night it had just been Lori and Rob barbequing some hot dogs on their patio, surrounded by overgrown, hopeful potted plants. James hadn't mean to stay any longer than it took to tell him that he needed to cancel their surf plans for the next morning, hoping Rob wouldn't question why he hadn't just gone home and called instead of driving all the way out to their place in rush hour traffic. But Lori had taken one look at him and said that if he went home alone to his apartment and ate a plain sandwich when he could have stayed with them and had bratwurst and homemade potato salad, Rob would have to arrest him on the spot for stupidity.

So James had stayed, and jokingly rolled his eyes with Rob behind Lori's back when she insisted on only listening to Jefferson Airplane records, and laughed at how unexpectedly hilarious Lori's stories from her Vet school classes at El Camino College were.

James had noted with hidden curiosity that their little home was all fully decorated now. A photograph of the two of them taken in Australia hanging on the wall above a secondhand bright red couch, Lori's college beach volleyball trophy sitting proudly on the coffee table next to Rob's police academy medal, both recently buffed clean.

The sight of it all had made James feel like a little kid visiting a friend's house who got stuck talking to the parents. He'd thought of his own undecorated, barely furnished, one room apartment near the beach with his hard hat hanging on the back of the door and felt like his life was moving in slow motion, stuck forever at the age he'd been when he first put on his sailor's cap and picked up a gun.

He'd helped Lori clean up the dishes after dinner while Rob played with their yellow lab Josie out in the warm backyard of dead grass. He'd listened to Lori ruminate over what to get Rob for his birthday while the two of them watched him through the kitchen window, arms elbow-deep in the sink, and he'd prided himself that he wasn't fiercely, ragingly jealous over it all. At one point, Rob had looked up at the two of them from the yard and smiled, tucking a strand of loose hair back behind his ear, and James had flushed at the memory of his brainless slip up the night before—reaching out and doing the same exact thing on the patio of the beach bar without even the excuse of too much alcohol to hide behind.

Now, in his silent apartment without any photographs or trophies or medals, James smirks again to himself, sipping his coffee as he remembers the look on Rob's face when he'd told him why he couldn't meet up with him to surf in the morning.

"Fucking hell, Jimmy, I told you to beat him, not date his sorry ass," Rob had joked, eyeballs popping out of his head.

James had swallowed down his panic and laughed along, explaining Danny's warped reasoning for why they should train together and decidedly leaving out the part of the story where Danny had picked up his most treasured possession from the moonlit sand, black magic figured out where he worked, and then followed him to his job a forty-five-minute drive away from Hermosa just to return it in person.

Rob said he had early morning shifts over in Torrance anyway that whole week to train with the beat there on freeway pursuits down the notorious 405, and so after a few more jokes about how Jimmy needed to knock some sense into Danny Moore and not let him be too much of an asshole, James had hugged Lori goodbye and clapped Rob on the back and driven back to his dark and empty room by the shore.

James is startled from his thoughts of the night before when a tall, dark form appears down on the grey sand, hair blowing in the misty fog that the slowly rising sun hasn't burned off yet.

James fights back a smile and ignores the thrill down his spine as he grabs his skateboard and surfboard and hurtles out the door. The pre-dawn streets are sleepy and quiet, suspended in the hazy fog like a breath waiting to be exhaled come rush hour. Palm trees sag limply in the grey light, fronds hushing by him in the breeze as he weaves his way down the sloping avenue to the shore.

Danny doesn't even look his way five minutes later when James finally walks up next to him and sets his board down in the sand. He's standing perfectly still, gazing out over the water, eyes soft and unfocused. James stands frozen at his side and breathes in the sharp, cool air, slowly filling his lungs. He silently marvels at how comfortable it is, standing there next to this man who he's spent the majority of the past two days either yelling at or inwardly gritting his teeth over.

Here, with their backs to the world, it feels like they're the last two people at the edge of the earth, being beckoned side by side out to the sea. The reverent, foggy air melds with the steady roll and thrum of the waves lapping at the shore. James gazes out at the first hints of sunlight reflecting on the water as it rolls towards the flat horizon, and he has a sudden, panging thought that some people go their entire lives without ever seeing the ocean.

He thinks back to Harold Carmichael, one of the Army recruits sent to share Intel with James' ship docked off the outskirts of Hanoi, who'd never seen a body of water bigger than a Kansas pond in front of him until the Army jeep carrying him from the southern base camp near Saigon dropped him off at the Navy ship dock, and who'd wept in secret in his bunk under James that night over the fact that he'd never seen so much water up close in his whole damn life.

After a moment, Danny kneels beside James in the cold sand and gets out his wax, settling into an age-old routine in silence. James follows. He lets his toes curl up in the dry grains of sand, breathing deep at the stretch in his thighs.

James thinks as he waxes in slow, steady circles that the man next to him seems to be able to transform into an entirely new person at will. That this contemplative, peaceful presence next to him is anything but the pushy runway model from the day before, or the hesitant man who eventually held out the bullet, or the frizzy-haired kid splaying him open in the moonlit sand, or the statuesque god who scoffed at him out on the waves from behind a pair of aviators. The man beside him now isn't even the man from the pier.

Something warm flutters in the pit of James' chest when he thinks that maybe only certain people get to see Danny Moore this way—unadorned and wiped clean, kneeling silently in the sand to the sound of the waves. The prospect that James has somehow been chosen to witness it shouldn't feel as exciting as it does.

Eventually, Danny sits back and rolls his neck to stretch, then pulls his grey hoodie up over his head. James goes to follow and hesitates, fingers tightening over the zipper of his jacket. He realizes in a moment of panic that he completely forgot to don his full wetsuit while he spent the morning lost in his thoughts. He'd simply gone on muscle memory, pulling on the board shorts and jacket he would normally wear to the beach with Rob.

Danny's eyes are on him as he stands and brushes the layer of sand off his sweatpants. James stands on shaky legs beside him as Danny shucks off the sweatpants to reveal a pair of short black boardshorts rippling in the breeze. He bends down next to James to secure his ankle strap, and James can't stop himself from turning his head to finally gaze at the tattoo covering Danny's back.

He sucks in a breath and stares.

A giant black and white jellyfish radiates out from Danny's shoulder, its billowing, translucent tendrils winding their way across his spine as if his back is made of water. It looks like a crisp, clean photograph painted onto Danny's smooth skin.

James has seen plenty of tattoos. The other sailors in the Navy had their arms practically covered in anchors and koi fish, pinup girls and American eagles. But he's never, never seen anything like this. It's oddly beautiful, unsettling and precise. The inked lines look poised to swim away at any moment, threatening to leap off Danny's back and disappear into the sea. James is lost in it—eyes drowning in the swirls of translucent tentacles. He leaps back startled when Danny chuckles softly from where he's bent over his ankle strap before standing tall again.

"Were you expecting a koi fish? A giant heart that says 'mom' in it surrounded by an anchor?"

It's the first thing either one of them has said all morning. James shakes his head and looks back to the water, embarrassed, swallowing over the dryness in his throat. He doesn't answer the question.

"Can the rule of today be 'you don't get to be an annoying dick all the time just to get a rise out of me'?"

Danny picks up his board and starts walking towards the water. He looks back over his shoulder at James and smirks. "Sure. But only if your rule of the day is 'don't be a killjoy and stand there for ten minutes wasting time debating whether or not to take your jacket off'."

James huffs and mutters an "unbelievable" under his breath as he watches Danny casually jog into the waves. The jellyfish glistens on his back in the sunrise light, hesitantly peeking out through the cool, grey fog. James takes a deep breath of salty air and listens to the seagulls start to make their way across the sky. The beach is quiet, save for the gentle roar of the waves on the sand, the smooth hiss of foam spreading out across the shore. They're utterly alone—nothing but the craggy mountains at their backs.

James unzips his jacket and reveals bare skin with shaking fingers. He feels brazen and reckless. It took him months to get to this point with Rob, to trust him to see the darkest, blackest part of him etched permanently into his skin in an ugly snarl—a reminder that he was sent back broken, unwanted on either soil.

And now, after just a handful of tense lines and two days, he's shedding his jacket and running breathlessly towards the waves where Danny Moore waits perched on his board for him, the barest hints of a smile at the corners of his mouth as he watches James shiver at his first dip in the icy water.

James braces himself for more sarcastic comments when he finally paddles out to Danny's side, mentally preparing for a day of irritation and wasted time that will inevitably lead to both of them agreeing never to do this ever again.

Instead, Danny angles his board so that he's right next to James, shins gently butting against each other beneath the ocean's surface, and he points out to the distant horizon tinged with gold, and, in a smooth, velvet voice, he tells James everything he knows about the waves off Oahu.

And just like that, James is sucked up into a hurricane, utterly at the mercy of a force of nature. Danny's lips move a mile a minute, spouting facts and statistics, studies and observations. His eyes rapidly scan James and the horizon and the swells and back to James again. Tracking the waves, the wind, the currents, the correct and incorrect lines of James' body as he hunkers down across a rumbling wave.

Danny drops in with him on barrels, calls out his corrections, tells him how Hawaiian water would be different from the Los Angeles swells. He makes James laugh and scoff, shake his head and listen with such focus that every cell of his body is zeroed in on the rich sound of his voice over the churn of the waves. He's an encyclopedia, and he's ruthless. Fierce and awkward and ridiculous and terrifying and *charming*. James finds himself following in Danny's wake like a breathless disciple, amazed and indignant as he tries to hold on for dear life just to stay afloat in the sheer onslaught that is surfing with Danny Moore.

They surf for almost three hours. By the last wave, James is aching and sore, arms trembling with exhaustion as he paddles after the largest wave yet of the set.

"Come in at a southeast angle!" Danny yells between cupped palms from his board. "This will have a perfect face for cutbacks, so gather your momentum from the drop-in and gain a little air up at the crest. Judges love that!"

James bites his lip over a cutting remark that *obviously* judges love that—that he didn't just wake up one day and get to where he is by sheer luck— and then does exactly what Danny says nevertheless. If the past three hours have shown him anything, it's that Danny can read the ocean like a damn book. Every current, every force, every swell—he maddeningly plots out the ride in perfect sequence and practically hands it to James on a platter. It feels like flying and cheating all at once. Like James has somehow never once known how to really surf, like all of his wins up until now have been nothing but luck since he never before had this kid to barrel in and show him how.

James digs deep and pops up in one clean motion to catch his final wave of the morning, legs shaking with the rushing force of the water beneath him. It's not a full pipeline, just a towering face with plenty of spray flying off the top, exactly as Danny predicted. James squats his legs like he knows how to do and pumps down the face of the wave, shooting towards the very bottom before twisting his core and rocketing back up to the crest, shooting off a wall of spray and whooping at the top of his lungs at the sheer speed beneath his board.

When he finally falls back into the whitewater and surfaces to gulp down air, he half-expects to hear, "Far out, old man!" echo across the waves in Rob's familiar, even voice.

Instead, he hears, "Not horrible, but you could have easily fit in two more cutbacks. You're convinced your legs will give out on you sooner than they will."

James' elation dies. He practically crawls back to shore, dragging his board behind him, his fingers clasped behind the back of his sore neck. He glares at Danny waiting for him in the sand, with his head high and arms crossed like a petulant teenager.

"You couldn't have just trusted yourself to fit in two more turns?" Danny asks, voice haughty. "The wave was only just beginning to crest and you didn't have any wind resistance. If you'd only just trusted your instincts, the wave wasn't gonna cave on you before you could –"

"And you couldn't let me just have one moment of victory, could you?" James bites back, cutting him off and inexplicably tingling with fresh rage. "I just surfed for three fucking hours while you mostly just sat there and talked at me. You couldn't just let me have fun on my last ride?"

Danny huffs and turns to head back to their bags, squeezing the saltwater from his curls to dry them out as he walks.

"I'm sorry," he mutters under his breath, infuriatingly soft enough that James has to strain to hear it. "I was under the impression you actually wanted to win, not be 'given charity' as you so kindly put it."

James groans and rolls his neck slowly to crack it. What happened out on the water, their easy silences, the startlingly familiar camaraderie, suddenly feels like a lifetime ago. As if the moment they both set foot on the dry land, the past three hours became just an odd dream, and the air too thin and dry.

Now, as James bends over to undo his ankle strap, all he feels is weariness and contempt flood through his chest. It's only been thirty seconds since Danny chastised him for ducking out of that wave early, and James fucking damn well knows that he should have fit in those last two turns, and already he's completely exhausted. He feels like an old dog, and Danny's the young kid, irritated and resentful that his pet can't learn any new tricks.

And James *knows* how to surf, goddammit. Knows how to live and surf and survive. He knows how to be shot at, and he wonders if Danny Moore is even old enough to legally drink at a bar.

He rubs a palm over his shoulder and grimaces, studiously avoiding Danny's gaze. His work shift is going to feel like absolute hell. He shakes his head finally, not even answering Danny back, and walks towards his bag to pack up and leave.

It's just that Danny is so goddamn unpredictable. One moment he's calmly, patiently explaining a brand new technique to James, one tailored to the Hawaiian water. His eyes soft but alight with excitement, body so close that James can practically feel the heat from his dripping skin. Then the next moment he's an untouchable genius, telling James everything he did wrong and not even bothering to pay attention long enough to hear James' retort.

It's absolutely nothing like surfing with Rob—all soft comfort and warmth pooling in the pit of his gut and spreading out through the tips of his fingers, smiling across the spray and whooping together for joy.

Surfing with Danny is more like trying not to fly and drown all at once.

James can hear Danny following him, breathing slightly hard from the morning's worth of surfing. Aside from that, the man had hardly broken a damn sweat.

"I don't understand," Danny says, voice barely concealing his frustration, fighting to meet James' gaze. "You want me to tell you what to do to win, you agree that that's what you want, and then you hate it when I actually tell you."

James sighs and turns to face him, desperately wanting to avoid this conversation. "Look, Danny, I appreciate everything you've done for me today. I really do. But I can't—I just . . ."

"You want me to be a surf buddy, not a coach," Danny says, eyes narrowed.

James thinks of their shins brushing against each other as they perched side by side on their boards, Danny's eyes soft and bright and focused on nothing but James and the water. He hates the odd shiver that the thought causes to run along his arms.

"Something like that," James replies. "And I know that's your idea of a worst nightmare, so we'll just—"

"Run with me tomorrow."

James freezes with his jacket half-zipped up. Danny's looking at him so intensely it's like James will disappear if he blinks. James looks at Danny's impatient, frustrated face, eyebrows furrowed in irritation, and wonders why he could ever possibly want to spend two more minutes in James' company. Danny couldn't look more exasperated with him if he tried.

"But you hated this," James finally says.

"No, *you* hated this, because our age difference and my tone of voice made you think that I don't already believe you're an excellent surfer. Which is why we'll do something different tomorrow. Run with me."

James shakes his head, zips his jacket the rest of the way up. He ignores the first half of Danny's response, and the way it had sparked something hot in his throat. "Look, Danny, I don't know if that's—"

"God, what ever happened to you to make you so afraid of success? It's the most goddamn irritating thing I've ever seen. You already want to agree; don't lie to me and say you don't. You're probably a good runner, possibly even better at it than me, which should excite you. So agree to run with me and you can get your little personal victory in and then we can surf the day after without all of this emotional nonsense."

"You know what?" James huffs as he shoulders his bag and scoops up his skateboard. "You are something else. Fuck you."

"So same time tomorrow?" Danny replies, still standing by his board in the sand.

"I said fuck you!" James calls back over his shoulder.

He barely hears the "Six-thirty, then," called after him as he reaches the pavement beyond the sand and does a running step onto his skateboard. The wind whips away the last droplets of water clinging to his hair, clearing the salt and sand from his skin.

He tries desperately to think about anything but Danny fucking Moore, standing back there in the sand like the know-it-all asshat James had been warned about over and over. Danny Moore who has the goddamn gall to strip away all of James' secrets, and witness his scar, and then comment on his technique as if James hasn't been surfing for almost as long as Danny's even been alive.

Danny Moore who handed back the bullet in his palm, and spent three hours telling James everything he knows about the waves in Oahu just so that James can win, and who wants to spend even more time with him tomorrow even after James walked away from him with two impressively fierce "fuck you's" lobbed at his face.

James sighs as he glides back up Hermosa Avenue on his skateboard, tightening his grip on his surfboard under his arm. He already knows, without a shadow of a doubt, what he's going to do tomorrow morning.

He's going to run beside Danny Moore along the shoreline at 6:30.

# 8

Sydney paces in the sand, sinking his bare feet deep into the soft, cool grains while he wills his hands to stay still by his sides. His mind is on fire. Since yesterday morning, he hasn't stopped going over every detail of his morning surf with Jimmy Campbell—trying to figure out where he went wrong, where he went right.

Out of all the snippets of yesterday playing on an endless loop in his mind—Jimmy's surprised, soft eyes when Sydney started telling him about the ocean, Jimmy's quietly indrawn breath when their shins brushed against each other beneath the water, his gritted-teeth determination as he tirelessly surfed wave after wave, his fierce look of burning resentment that he lobbed at Sydney as he finally walked away—one thought rises above the rest:

*If he comes today, don't fuck it up.*

Sydney knows it is nothing short of a miracle, an absolute miracle, that he even got Jimmy to go out surfing with him yesterday after that train wreck at the dockyard. Sydney still doesn't even quite know what went wrong.

Here he'd kept Jimmy's possession safe, and driven all the way to his work, and dressed up nicely so he wouldn't embarrass Jimmy in front of his coworkers with them thinking he was talking to some young, naïve surfer punk. He'd handed back the bullet without a word—no judgement, no questions. Sydney isn't sure what he'd even been expecting in return. Not anything too grand, certainly, not after what happened that night on the beach. Not even a smile, really. Just . . . *something.*

And instead he'd stood there feeling like a dumb kid while Jimmy pushed back his shoulders and glinted hard at Sydney in defiance, seemingly completely unaware of the way Sydney had to control his breathing just looking at him all drenched in sweat with tan muscles bulging and chest heaving and a little smear of grease right along his freckled cheekbone. Instead he'd been left completely unmoored by Jimmy's quiet admission, coupled with a fleeting, black pain in his deep blue eyes—"*This isn't just a game for me.*"

But for a moment, one shining, glorious moment, Jimmy had given him that look of wonder that he gave Sydney on the pier, even while his lips had formed the words, "*You infuriate me.*"

Their hands had joined. They'd touched each other in the palm for far too long, and Sydney knows he can't be the only one who'd felt the electric current run through the thick, salty air around them.

And then Jimmy had come back the next morning, exactly like he said he would. And he hadn't made fun of Sydney's bizarre tattoo like so many people had before him, or asked a thousand questions about it. And he'd unzipped his jacket and bared himself before Sydney in the soft dawn air, scars and all, and run breathlessly after him into the waves.

So now he's pacing on the shore at 6:25 am and running a hand through his curls on repeat, hoping against hope that Jimmy's final "fuck you" the day before hadn't been quite as permanent as it had sounded.

Something moves out of the corner of his eye, and his breath catches in his chest when he turns to see Jimmy Campbell walking calmly toward him across the sand, perfectly on time. Sydney immediately stands up straight and rolls back his shoulders, trying to school the surprise off his face.

Jimmy's hair ripples softly in the breeze, glinting in the shimmering, grey light of sunrise. His legs underneath a short pair of red running shorts are steady and loose, completely devoid of all their usual thick tension. Sydney clenches his fist against the imaginary urge to run his fingers through the soft, blonde hair covering sturdy, tan skin.

The breeze picks up, blowing locks of frizzy curls over Sydney's eyes. By the time he successfully sweeps his hair back from his face, Jimmy's standing beside him, looking out at the ocean.

"You came," Sydney says. He prides himself that his voice doesn't come out breathless and giddy.

Jimmy shrugs his shoulders underneath his pullover and crosses his arms over his chest. "Yeah, well—figured you'd have nothing to do today if you didn't have me yelling at you for something, so I thought I'd save Los Angeles from the carnage you'd wreak on it if you were left to yourself."

It's an apology for the end of yesterday, Sydney sees. A guilt-ridden admission cloaked in a poor joke. Sydney tears his eyes away from the tips of Jimmy's eyelashes and gazes out at the water while clearing his throat, forcing the corners of his lips not to smile too widely.

"A solid plan. Wouldn't want that policeman friend of yours to arrest me before I can impart all my surfing wisdom to you."

Jimmy looks up at him with his arms still crossed, a look of exasperated bafflement in his eyes. "How the fuck do you know Rob's a cop?"

Sydney doesn't meet his gaze and shrugs. "Can't force me to give away all my secrets, can you? Anyway, we're wasting time. You have the day off today, judging by the general lack of 'dead man walking' about you this morning, but I imagine you're still hoping to spend the afternoon with him after he gets off his shift, and I'm hoping we can fit in this run before we bake in the sun and smog. So, ready?"

Jimmy's shaking his head slowly and groaning under his breath. He doesn't respond. Finally he turns and starts walking in the direction of the nearby lifeguard tower, pulling his sweatshirt over his head as he goes to reveal a white tank top. He balls up the sweatshirt and throws it up in the tower, then, without a glance back at Sydney, starts running at a brisk pace down the beach, bare feet kicking up loose sand until he turns down towards the wet, compact sand of the shoreline.

Sydney bolts after him, already left behind. He breathes a secret sigh of relief that Jimmy started running south towards Redondo instead of north towards the insanity that is Venice Beach. Something about this run already feels private, even though Jimmy's just run off and started it without him, and the thought of sharing it with swarms and hordes of muscle men and sideshow carnies makes him feel a bit nauseous. No—Redondo beach will be almost empty this early. It's perfect. Jimmy's a genius.

Jimmy runs smooth and steady along the shore, head barely bobbing up and down as he glides. He's a natural runner, calm and loose and easy. His shorts fly up with every step to reveal thick thigh muscles, pale above his tan line. Sydney's eyes slowly trace down his legs to his calves, already dripping in clinging, wet sand being kicked up by his toes. Sydney feels ridiculous chasing after him with his halting, gangly stride, and then scoffs at himself for even caring in the first place. Jimmy shoots a glance his way when Sydney finally catches up, already breathing a bit hard from his initial sprint. Sydney gives a quick nod.

They run in easy silence for a mile. A quiet calm settles over Sydney's body as they breathe side by side. It's as if the only thing his mind can think about is one foot in front of the other, timing his lungs with the man beside him. He feels a thousand pounds lighter. It's glorious.

"You're unbelievable, you know," Jimmy finally says over his steady, even breaths. "Do you actively try to be a smug know-it-all all the time or does it just come naturally to you?"

There's a hint of a smile behind his words, and Sydney unexpectedly huffs a laugh. The sound of his own chuckle catches him off guard, and it takes him a few strides to catch his breath again.

"Ah, you know," he says, exaggeratedly serious, "I've got a reputation to maintain, haven't I?"

Jimmy doesn't laugh back. Instead he hums distractedly and cocks his head to the side, frowning a bit at the stretch of untouched sand ahead of them.

Sydney doesn't need to work too hard to guess what he's thinking about—probably repeating the choicest phrases from his circle of so-called friends the other day before their round at the competition, warning him of the dangers of Danny Moore. Sydney didn't even have to be close enough to hear them talking to know what was probably said. He's heard it all plenty of times before. The knowledge of this makes him feel strangely desperate.

Here, now, running on the beach next to Jimmy Campbell with nobody else to see, he wants to do something different, to prove to Jimmy that he isn't like *that*. Not really. Not all the time. To tell him that he likes Coca-Cola better than Pepsi, and can play the ukulele, and that he once wiped out into some coral and barely missed shredding his knee—words that he's never before strung together into sentences even in the depths of his mind.

But then the prospect of revealing himself so thoroughly feels like being stripped naked in front of a crowd, and he nearly shivers at even the thought of opening his mouth.

The silence settles over them again, thick and heavy as they pass by a narrower stretch of beach, abutted on their left by a high, rocky cliff leading up to a portion of the coastline highway and lined with swaying palm trees. A plane on its way to LAX flies low overhead, momentarily drowning out the sound of the waves. When it finally passes, Jimmy speaks.

"Rob told me the other night that the sunglasses are kind of your thing," he says out of nowhere. "Never seen without 'em."

Sydney frowns. It's the last thing he expected Jimmy to say. It sounds like an accusation, yet another thing to have to defend against, and his skin starts to prickle under under what feels a lot like poorly-masked scrutiny.

"Well I have to keep something private if every competition I turn up at I'm always going to be such a topic of *discussion*," he responds, voice hard. It's a pointed dig at Jimmy's earlier recollections of his pre-heat talk with his friends, and they both know it.

"Keep what private—your eye color?" Jimmy huffs out.

"No. My expressions, reactions." The implied "obviously" hangs heavily in the air.

Jimmy looks over at him, and Sydney forces himself to meet his gaze as they continue to stride across the wet sand. He startles when he sees that Jimmy's eyes are soft.

"Sorry, I—I didn't mean it like that," Jimmy says. "Guess I just meant . . . or I was gonna ask. . . you don't wear them around me."

Sydney's heart pounds in his chest, even harder than it already is. That sensation of being stripped naked returns, prickling hotly across his skin.

"That's completely untrue," he says, forcing a casualness into his voice. "You saw me wear them at the ISF, and then you can hardly have expected me to be wearing them at night like some idiot."

Sydney trails off, knowing that any other points he could make are useless. He hasn't been wearing them, and he hadn't even fucking noticed. He feels flayed open and raw. It's maddening that such a simple thing as a pair of goddamn sunglasses is turning him into a deer in headlights, somehow caught and exposed.

His mind races, aborted sentences dying on his lips as he struggles to come up with a better, cleverer, less immature response when he suddenly feels Jimmy's warm hand briefly grip his upper arm. It knocks the wind out of him. The soft, anchoring pads of his fingers.

"I wear full wetsuits in July. I get it," Jimmy says quietly, a self-deprecating smile drooping on his lips. He slows down a little to get the words out without gasping.

Sydney holds his breath for three strides and swallows. All he can do is nod.

Jimmy slows further to a jog and then finally stops as they come around another bend, opening up onto an enclosed stretch of pristine beach. He crosses his hands behind his neck in a gesture that Sydney now finds oddly familiar as they both pant for breath.

Sydney stops and leans over his legs, cursing himself for being so out of shape when it comes to just straight running. He wipes his forearm over the early morning sweat forming across his brow, blocking his sight so he can't watch Jimmy's shorts cling to the backs of his thighs as he bends to stretch his hamstrings. He stares at his feet until Jimmy stands upright again. He can feel Jimmy's deep blue eyes on him, furrowed in thought.

"I can't seem to shake the habit of wanting to fight with you every moment," Jimmy finally says to the sky. The truth of the statement pings Sydney deep in his gut, but he forces himself to huff out a sharp laugh as he straightens his spine.

"I'm sure you're not alone in that sentiment," he replies. He swings his arms once behind his back before continuing, "And besides, you're a soldier. You're supposed to fight."

Sydney expects a chuckle, but James lets out a harsh sigh. "I'm just a sailor," he says, nearly whispering. "Well, was a sailor."

Sydney hears the sudden darkness in Jimmy's voice and turns to look at him, shocked at how the energy of their run, the vibrant life in his eyes, could fade away so quickly. Now, Jimmy looks limp and small, staring out at the waves while his body sways gently with the wind. Sydney can feel deep in his veins that this moment is important somehow. That his response to this is the most important thing he'll ever say.

"Look," Sydney clears his throat. "The way I see it, you flew halfway around the world, put on a uniform, and got shot at," he says. His breath catches in his throat when Jimmy's eyes meet his, full and desperate like he's dying to hear what else he'll say. Sydney presses his own thumbnail into his palm and looks out at the horizon. "I'd say that makes you a soldier."

Jimmy blinks hard and bends down to sit in the sand, scooting once to the side in a silent offer for Sydney to sit beside him. The breeze brushes gently against their sweaty backs, mixing with the fresh salt air coming off the waves. The scent of Jimmy and the salt of the sea fills Sydney's nose as he continues to recover from the run. He feels on edge, fragile and tense and waiting with bated breath—for what, he has absolutely no idea. Just when the silence becomes unbearable, when Sydney thinks that he's gone and said all the wrong things, Jimmy speaks.

"I've never talked to anyone about the war. Ever," he whispers.

Sydney can hardly breathe. He can feel the heat radiating out from the man beside him, can feel as the tops of their arms brush together when they shift and move in the soft, warm sand.

It's almost unbearably intimate, sitting here side by side at the edge of the earth—as if every breath coming from Jimmy's lips is traveling straight to his own, like he can taste Jimmy's words on the tip of his own tongue. He forces himself to be patient, not to interrupt. Jimmy's voice when he speaks again is low and trembling, like warm, amber honey filling all the silence in Sydney's ears.

"They warned us about that," Jimmy goes on. "At the Navy hospital, when they were coming around getting people ready to be discharged. Said that people wouldn't be . . . receptive, when we came back here to the States. All those war protests and shit people are doing up in 'Frisco and D.C. and places."

Sydney glaringly notices he didn't say, "*when we came home*".

Jimmy licks his lips and lets out a shaky breath, running his fingers through his sweat-damp hair as he stares blankly into the distance, seeing something out there in the swelling froths of water that Sydney knows he never will.

"But, the thing is, they tell you all that, all the statistics and where to try to find a job and how much money you need to live, and they don't even tell you what it's like to feel . . . to feel like a fucking old man and a teenager at the same time. Right? Like you've seen more shit than most people see in eighty years, seen people die on the ground, just drop and breathe their last breath right in front of you even though you're the last person on earth they'd ever choose to die in front of, and you were just playing poker with them six hours ago and talking about their girl they got back home. But then out you come out of the jungle dragging their—their bones behind you and you're still stuck the same way you were when you first stepped onto the fucking boat. No change at all. Nobody tells you what to do about that."

The defeat in Jimmy's voice is absolutely unbearable. Sydney has the completely unprecedented urge to wrap his arms around him and pull him down under his own body, shielding him from the air. Then he remembers that that would only choke him, fill his lungs with saltwater and sand.

He waits. Jimmy keeps talking as if the only person even listening to him is the restless sea.

"And then there's surfing," he says, his voice a bit clearer. "I've been doing it my whole life, I mean, minus some years in the middle, but it's so fucking stupid. Just hop on this plank of wood and float on the water, and the earth will just randomly decide for you whether you're gonna have a good time or not. Nobody else gets to decide that for you. It's just you and the earth. It's just that. It doesn't . . . mean anything for other people, do anything good for anyone. Not even a team sport. It's just . . . selfish. But I still do it. I swim out there, and I don't make any decisions, and I just float around on some wood for a couple hours every day instead of actually  doing something with my life. And you know what?" Jimmy clears his throat as his voice threatens to break, then powers through. "I don't feel any age at all when I'm surfing. Nothing. I just feel like I'm alive."

He shuts his mouth, takes a deep breath in through his nose, then rolls back his neck. The silence is electric. Jimmy runs a hand roughly over his face and sniffs softly.

Sydney can tell he's on the verge of crying, and furiously trying not to. He's shocked at the weight of these words. Breathless and guilty with the dawning realization that he's the first person to ever hear them. A long-forgotten memory, hazy around the edges, pops into his head, and his mouth starts speaking before he can even decide to share it or not.

"Lahela always used to tell me '*Ukuli'i ka pua, onaona i ka mau'u.*' The flower may be tiny, but it scents the grasses around it."

Jimmy's head pops up immediately at the sounds leaving Sydney's lips. "Wait—who?"

"Lahela. My mother."

Sydney suddenly freezes, piercingly aware that it's the first time he's ever referred to Lahela using that word.

Jimmy doesn't appear to notice, but scrunches his eyes as he stares at the side of Sydney's face. "You're really half-Hawaiian?" he asks incredulously, tears on his cheeks momentarily forgotten.

Sydney forces himself to shrug and continues to look out at the water. "Well, step-mom. Anyway, I always used to roll my eyes at that."

Jimmy snorts a quiet laugh next to him, a laugh that means "*gee, I can sure imagine that,*" and Sydney smiles.

"Real surprise there, I know. But it didn't make any sense—it still doesn't. I mean, the size of a flower has no impact over how much pollen it produces, or whether bees will pollinate that flower and help track the scent to other locations. And how can a flower's scent rub off on the grass around it? And why in hell should I care? But she would always say it to me whenever I was—"

Sydney stops immediately. He hadn't meant to get this far in the story, to reveal this much. He can't very well tell the man next to him, the *hero*, that his step-mom whispered that through the thin door to his bedroom on the days he came home with a black eye from school, or missing lunch money, or with another note from his teachers that he skipped class. It all sounds so stupid and childish, so many worlds away from two pro surfers running down a Los Angeles beach.

Still, Jimmy's waiting patiently, cheeks still glistening, and Sydney finds he can't stop even if he wanted to.

He tries again. "She would always say it to me when I was . . having a rough time, after my father moved us to Oahu. Looking back, I see she was trying to tell me that even the smallest thing can make a big difference. Even the stupidest thing is allowed to make you happy, if you let it. Or something like that. Never quite got the hang of the whole 'inspirational quote' hippie trend."

He practically feels Jimmy's slow smile next to him. The thick fog between them clears under the new warmth in Jimmy's eyes, and Sydney gasps in a breath so deep he feels his lungs stretch out in his chest. He lets it out in tiny sips, silently, so Jimmy won't hear.

The newly comfortable silence drags on while Jimmy draws nonsense in the sand with his finger. Sydney finds his internal organs in tune with every cell in Jimmy's body—every beat of his heart and flex of his muscle. Every thought. Every pulse in perfect symphony with the steady thrum of the waves.

Finally Jimmy sits up and rolls back his shoulders, casual and competent and put together once more.

"That's amazing," he says out of nowhere. "So you speak Hawaiian?"

Sydney scoffs. "God, no. Just that phrase. Well, that and '*he alamakahinu.*'"

"Which means?"

"A 'greased forehead.' Basically someone who kisses ass. She'd lob that one at my younger brother every other day when he discovered he could pit the parents against each other to try and get Rock 'em Sock 'em Robots for Christmas. She saw through his shit in less than an hour, but there goes my father trekking down to the city and buying him the last damn one left in the mall."

Sydney hears a rumble next to him and turns just in time to see Jimmy burst out laughing, shoulder brushing against Sydney's as he leans back in the sand to take a deep breath. He shoots Sydney a smile then, warm and private on the tip of his lips, and Sydney almost closes his eyes and looks away.

He's never had a smile like that directed at him. Ever. It almost hurts to look at, like staring straight up into the sun over Oahu without his sunglasses covering his eyes.

Jimmy clears his throat and pushes to stand, waiting for Sydney to follow suit as he leans down to brush the sand from the back of his thighs and the tops of his feet. Without a word, and with the ghost of that smile still tracing over his lips, Jimmy gestures with his head back down the beach the way they came. He waits for Sydney to take off running beside him this time, and Sydney tries to tamp down the blooming feeling in his chest.

There's a sense of doom hovering at his elbow, crouching just to the side of the current happy peace that's settling warm and soft in his limbs. But then Jimmy Campbell looks over at him as they jog, and the look on his face is just so damn *grateful* that Sydney would face an entire crowd naked and stripped and exposed if it meant Jimmy would look at him that way again.

By the time they get back to where they started along Hermosa beach and Jimmy grabs his sweatshirt from the lifeguard stand, the sun is already hot and heavy above them, sizzling across the sand. The rest of the run back had been pleasantly silent, their arms brushing against each other every few steps and neither one bothering to move any further steps apart. Something had been crackling at a low hum between them. Something tense and sweet and thick. And now Sydney finds himself for the first time in his life trying to think of a reason *not* to say goodbye to somebody.

Jimmy solves the problem for him by pointing towards the beach showers after running the hem of his tank top over his face.

"Need to get some of this sweat off my skin before I can walk up the road in public," he says, already heading towards the building.

Sydney swallows hard and follows, venturing further into new territory with every step. His eyes track slowly up the back of Jimmy's body, tank top wet and clinging to every muscle on his back with sweat, thighs tan and glistening, glittering with a dusting of sand, blonde strands plastered to his forehead the same way it had looked at the dockyard.

The air is suddenly too thin in Sydney's lungs. Too fragile.

No one else is inside the dim shower house—it's still too early for the typical beachgoers with their umbrellas and shovel-toting kids and supermarket paperbacks, and most of the exercise nuts prefer the stretch of beach up north near Venice. Their footsteps echo loudly on the wet concrete floor and walls, which are covered in a muddy layer of wet sand and fill their noses with damp salt. A long, thin window around the top of the room lets weak beams of sunlight into the open communal shower space, illuminating specks of sand and dust swirling in the air.

Sydney finds himself hovering near the doorway, uncertain and tense, as Jimmy walks calmly inside and strips off his shirt like it's nothing, heading for the far left of the three shower heads against the wall and flipping it on, testing the water with the tips of his fingers.

He steps under the spray, and Sydney holds his breath as the water sluices in sheets down Jimmy's body, clinging to his stomach and the crease between his thighs, causing his shorts to glide along every contour of his skin. Revealing the soft bulge between his legs.

"You just gonna stand there and watch?" Jimmy says, joking.

It knocks the wind out of Sydney. He jumps, then hastens inside and strips off his shirt, also leaving on his running shorts. It's ridiculous. He's been shirtless in front of hundreds of people—thousands. He's a champion of a sport where the entire point is to *be* shirtless. And yet here in this poorly lit, muddy, chlorine scented beach shower, in front of a man who's already even seen his tattoo up close and gasped at it in wonder, Sydney feels nerves roiling through his gut.

His fingers tremble as he goes for the far right shower head, and his stomach sinks down into his toes when he realizes it's broken.

"This one's broken," he says unnecessarily out loud. He wants to kick himself.

Jimmy just hums, now tipping his head back to let the water run through his hair, down across his face, dripping down the front of his neck and over his Adam's apple. Sydney swallows and forces himself to move to the middle one closer to Jimmy, hating with every fiber of his being this sensation of being completely out of his depth.

This isn't Danny Moore, showing up to a major international surf competition to a stunned and awestruck crowd, blowing surfers from all over the world out of the water. This isn't Danny Moore, silently scanning the surface of the ocean, figuring out the force and timing of an upcoming set of waves by sight alone while the hushed beach anxiously waits, hearts in their throats while their hands shield the sun from their eyes.

No—this is just him, plain old Sydney Moore from bumfuck-nowhere Iowa with the armful of books and the weird name, standing in a shower just one foot away from Jimmy Campbell. Just him trying to force his goddamn hands not to shake as he turns on the water and lets it slap sharp and icy against his skin, blasting away the salt and sand while it gradually warms.

Jimmy suddenly hums next to him as the now-hot water pounds against his back, massaging sore muscles. It winds its way along the concrete walls. And just like that, it's the most erotic thing Sydney's ever heard.

A horrifying warmth starts to pool in the pit of his gut, and he presses his forehead against the freezing concrete wall to try and blast some sense, any sense at all, back into his brain. He takes a slow breath under the spray and assumes the stance of Danny, shoulders back and chin high, chest puffed out. Jimmy's probably showered in front of tons of other men in the Navy. He's faced a bullet and won. Faced '*the* Danny Moore' on the starting line of a surf competition unexpectedly and didn't even blink an eyelash. So surely Sydney can handle a fucking post-run shower.

But then Jimmy turns so that his back is to Sydney, and takes a slow step back so his shoulders are just inches from Sydney's clenched chest, and any attempt to retain a hold on his usual, unflappable persona becomes instantly null and void.

They both realize at exactly the same moment just how close they're standing.

There's a mutually held breath hovering in the room like a secret. A bomb waiting to drop. The water hisses over both of their half-naked bodies and echoes softly across the floor, a steady trickle of wet slaps on concrete and sand.

Sydney pushes the wet hair back out of his eyes and takes a deep breath. His chest is just inches from Jimmy's shoulder blades. One small lean and there would be physical contact, his peaked nipples able to just barely trace the outline of Jimmy's spine. When he breathes out, shaky and slow, he sees goosebumps form all along Jimmy's back. An invisible imprint of Sydney's lungs. His skin shivers, muscles twitching. They're breathing in tandem, quick and shallow. Wet skin surrounded by hot, swirling steam.

Sydney takes one tiny step forward, his chest now just a finger-width away from the man in front of him, and Jimmy tilts his head back gently on his neck, letting the water drip down the front of his collarbone and chest.

Sydney can see the dip of Jimmy's collarbone from over his shoulder, can see the droplets of water cling to his skin and slowly roll down over his pectorals, catching on his nipples and trailing down onto his stomach.

Sydney wants. He wants like he didn't even know it was possible to want. Wants to lean that last inch forward and press himself against Jimmy Campbell like a ship pulling in its anchor. Wants to press his nose into the hollow of Jimmy's neck and shoulder. Wants to taste the water dripping off his skin, taste how the salt of his sweat differs from the salt of the sea. Wants to run his hands up his slick wet sides and hold on.

He feels attacked, barraged on all sides by thoughts he's never even known could exist. The air between them starts to thrum and crack, humming as it pulls their skin closer and closer with each moment they don't move apart, each breath that passes without a denial.

Sydney licks his lips and starts to lift up his hands, tracing ghostly touches up the sides of Jimmy's arms, their final destination still a mystery waiting to make itself known. His fingers hover over the tops of Jimmy's shoulders, left fingertips just a hair's width away from the raised, pink scar. A soft and broken sound escapes the back of Jimmy's throat. Sydney lowers his fingers towards his wet and warm skin. Breathes in the smell of his neck, dips his nose closer to his hair, lowers his fingertips and lowers, lowers, lowers—

A bang in the doorway startles them both, and they leap apart. Sydney's heart clangs in his throat. His hands hover awkwardly in the air, grasping at nothing. Jimmy quickly turns his back to the door as two more men walk in, talking loudly now and throwing down bags onto the wooden benches in the center, barely paying any attention to the two forms standing stock still in the corner of the showers.

Sydney tries desperately to get his breathing under control, to tame the unbearable shaking throughout his body. He hazards a glance to his left, just under his eyelashes, and sees Jimmy staring resolutely at the ground, letting the water splash directly onto his forehead. Sydney's eyes flicker downwards against his best intentions, and he holds in a gasp.

The front of Jimmy's running shorts are tented.

Sydney rips his gaze away to look down at himself and sees, mortified, that he's in a similar state. That he's trembling and aching and visible. Exposed in the corner of a muddy concrete beach shower.

In a barely controlled panic, he slams off the water and books it to his shirt, holding it awkwardly over his front and making for the door before the other two men, still talking loudly and stretching over in the other far corner, can see him.

The outdoor world hits him like a slap to his face. It's an assault on his senses. The sun and sand and salt and breeze and people all swarm around him in an electric daze. He stumbles on numb legs towards the shore and then stands frozen. He can still hear the sound of Jimmy's quiet moan mixing with the soft slap of water on skin in his mind. Jimmy's indrawn breath as Sydney's lips had quivered just above the top of his neck, the cascade of goosebumps down his dripping spine.

He tells himself that he has absolutely no idea what the fuck just happened.

An eternal minute later, he hears what must be Jimmy exiting the showers back behind him. Hears him stop and hesitate in the sand, probably debating whether to yell at Sydney for ever stepping closer to him in the shower, for causing his body's private natural response to the wetness and the heat to be exposed, or just to cut his losses and book it for good. Stay far away from Danny Moore just like everyone had warned him to.

Sydney waits and holds his breath, listening for Jimmy's footsteps to run the other direction, to head straight for Hermosa Avenue to his apartment and never look back.

He stares blankly at the sand in front of him, head tipped down. When he hears a person walk up next to him, he half expects to turn and see one of the other men from inside, waiting to greet his face with a punch after they belatedly realized what had been going on (*about to go on?*) in the dim corner of the showers. He thinks of all his belongings in a trash bag on the porch.

Instead he looks up, half-wincing, to see none other than Jimmy Campbell. He's holding out a cheap towel he'd grabbed off a rack back inside, physically placing it in Sydney's fingers when he doesn't immediately move to grab it.

Sydney holds the towel helplessly in front of him and stares down at his fingers. He licks his bone-dry lips and nearly coughs trying to swallow.

"I—I'm sorry if . . . that wasn't . . ."

"Nothing to be sorry for. Nothing happened," Jimmy says. His voice is calm, but Sydney can hear an odd sharpness concealed beneath it. Sydney nods dumbly and finally runs the towel over his face, chest, and stomach, the shock from earlier having thoroughly and mercifully killed his erection.

Jimmy clears his throat, continuing to over-do it in pretending all is business as usual.

"Look so, I don't have tomorrow off, but I don't start my shift 'til eleven. Figured we could start early and drive down a little bit south, check out a new stretch of beach to surf," he says, voice lighthearted. He doesn't quite meet Sydney's gaze.

Sydney blinks. There's no way he's hearing this correctly. Absolutely no way on earth that Jimmy wants to spend even thirty more seconds in his company.

In fact, Jimmy's already far outlasted anyone else Sydney's ever come into contact with besides his own damn family. Surely that's enough of a victory for him. Now Jimmy can cross 'try to befriend the enemy Danny Moore even though he tried to do something nasty' off his bucket list and go back to his normal friends and surf with people who aren't assholes eternally damned to Hell.

But Jimmy stands there, still looking up at Sydney with an absolutely unreadable expression, and he doesn't walk away. All Sydney can do is ultimately nod yes.

Jimmy nods once back, his neck a bit stiff and tense, then pulls his shirt back on over his still-wet skin.

"Right, then. Same time. I'll pick you up from here in my car," he says quickly, thrown over his shoulder as he turns to leave.

Sydney watches him walk two steps away, then belatedly calls after him, voice thin and rattled.

"James!" He visibly winces at his mistake. "Sorry, I mean—"

Jimmy holds up a hand to halt the apology as he looks back at Sydney. The expression in his eyes is one Sydney would swear he's never seen before in his life. It's thrilling and infuriating and beautiful all at once.

Jimmy's lips grow soft, and he gazes back at Sydney for a few silent beats. He rubs his palm once over his left shoulder, then drops his hand back to his side. His hair glows in the brilliant sun.

"You can call me James," he finally says.

And then he's gone, leaving Sydney open-mouthed and rattled in the sand. Wanting to break his own mask and chase after James. To grab his wrist and desperately whisper, "*Who the hell are you?*" and, "*Please, not yet. Please don't go.*"

# 9

Sydney fiddles with his motel room key as he waits at the edges of the dirt parking lot, staring down blankly at his shuffling flip flops.

He's early. Again. He wants to roll his eyes at himself. He never would have stood for this a week ago—standing in a parking lot alone waiting for a ride when he could very well already be surfing perfectly fine on his own. He certainly wouldn't have been standing there waiting for someone who now *knows*, without any shadow of a doubt, that the "fairy from Oahu" felt a physical attraction towards him, accidental or no.

His mind keeps telling himself to walk away. Let James pull up to an empty parking lot and realize that it all would've been a horrible mistake anyway. Let him shrug, and go meet up with his normal friend for the morning, and one day tell the story at a bar of the few days he humored Danny Moore when he was stranded in L.A.

It's the plan Sydney came up with the day before after they'd parted ways outside the shower house. He'd stood in the sand for who knows how long staring at his own toes and convincing himself that the ache between his legs was well and truly gone. And then he'd taken four different busses and almost three hours to travel all the way across the city to the Griffith Observatory, where he'd looked out over the hazy, smog covered city and tried to guess the occupation of everyone that walked by. Where he'd decided that he would definitely, without any second thoughts at all, *not* show up to be picked up by James Campbell the next morning.

But he's here, shuffling his feet at a crisp six-twenty-five. And he hears the sound of a station wagon pulling up alongside him in the dirt.

He scrunches his nose even as his heart skips a beat in his chest. As he watches the wheels come to a stop in a cloud of dust, that long dormant part of him that had held a torn and faded photograph of Hawaii in his hands is suddenly alive again, face young and open and turned towards the sky. The feeling of a warm palm cupping his hand. The way his momma's cross necklace would tickle his cheek.

He picks up his board and straps it down on top of James' on the roof of the station wagon without saying hello, taking more time than necessary to try and calm the shaking in his hands.

He hops into James' cool leather passenger seat, preparing himself for the atmosphere to be tense and awkward, and barely catches the banana lobbed at his chest.

"Figured you didn't get any breakfast in that motel of yours," James says nonchalantly instead of a greeting. He keeps his eyes on the road as he pushes the car into first and peels back out onto the winding coastal highway. His shoulders visibly relax right before Sydney's eyes as Sydney settles into his own seat, his left knee suddenly just inches from James' right.

A hot, tingling weight quickly evaporates off Sydney's chest—a weight that had been sitting there since James walked away from him in the sand the day before while the blood still pooled in his groin. And now, not twenty-four hours later, here's James still calmly driving him in his car like it's nothing at all. Body loose and relaxed even though he has to work later that day, as if Sydney's mere presence is some sort of buffer or balm. Sydney bites down too hard on the inside of his lip when he realizes he hasn't responded yet.

"Thank God," he says at the window. "How did I ever last living on my own the last seven years without you to remind me that fruit exists?" He peels the banana open anyway and takes a bite.

"Seven years?"

Sydney can practically hear James doing the math in his head. He sneaks a glance to see that James' brow is furrowed as he concentrates on the empty road, zooming along the palm tree-lined highway with the windows down, letting in swirls of fresh ocean air. Sydney just hums.

He takes a too-large bite of banana to fill the silence. He wants to slap himself in the face. Two minutes in to his last ever morning with James and he's already gone and said something unbearably stupid—

reminded them both of the fact that he's ten fucking years younger than the man smoothly navigating a stick shift down the Los Angeles highway. Revealed that he apparently did something so absolutely horrible that his own family didn't even want to see him through until he turned eighteen.

Stupid.

James breaks the silence after scratching the side of his jaw. "Did you teach yourself how to surf?"

Sydney swallows hard and stares out the window, letting the fresh wind blow his curls into his eyes. He starts to reach into his pocket for his sunglasses, then freezes, feeling that somehow, in some way, wearing them would ruin everything now.

He nods, then realizes James can't see him while concentrating on the winding road.

"I did, yeah."

Out of nowhere, James laughs. One golden, breathless chuckle. Sydney turns to stare at him.

"What's so funny?"

James wipes a hand over his grin and leans his elbow on the open window. "Nothing, just. Of course you taught yourself how to be the top surfer in Hawaii."

Sydney scoffs. "I'm not the top surfer in Hawaii."

"Oh what, are you getting humble on me now, Moore?"

"Of course not. Don't be an idiot. I'm not the top surfer in Hawaii—I'm *the* top surfer."

And James laughs *again*, free and open into the clean air. The sound of it fills Sydney with a tingling warmth. It settles deep in his gut, right in the center of his chest, up the muscles surrounding his spine.

He finds himself chuckling along too, cheeks fighting against his grin as he gazes out at the distant blue horizon through the trees whizzing by. He feels like an imposter of himself sitting just inches away from James Campbell's warm thigh as they zoom down the empty highway—as if Danny Moore has a secret twin brother who laughs, and surfs with other people, and who has someone coming to pick him up to intentionally spend time with him like it's nothing special at all. Like it isn't revolutionary.

Sydney settles back into his seat, watching out of the corner of his eye as the wind ruffles James' hair in the breeze.

"And you?" he asks back a beat too late. "Who taught you to surf?"

James grins, eyes soft with nostalgia. His thumb taps a rhythm on the steering wheel. "This guy who lived in the trailer next door to me and my mom. I thought he was so ancient growing up, but he must've been only fifty. He surfed in Florida in the 20s. Can't really remember how it started, but he must have taken a liking to me, or maybe my mom just asked him to look after me when she was off at work. Who knows. But anyway, he'd keep an eye on me when I was down by the water, and when I was six or so he put me on a board and spent a whole year teaching me how. I don't even remember his name, actually. Just called him Mr. Cool."

"And your mom—she knows he taught you? Does she come out to watch you compete?"

A thudding silence follows, and Sydney immediately realizes his mistake. He feels sick. He should have known, should have seen it and realized. Who on earth could have heard the tone of James' voice talking about his home and his mom and *not* realized it? And yet here he is so captivated by the smooth sound of that very same voice, and James Campbell's knee just inches from his own, that he goes and asks about a mom who he should have understood, from the first moment James mentioned her at all, was dead.

He stares straight ahead. He's too uncomfortable to see what James' face looks like.

James' voice when he speaks is soft and calm. Resigned. "She died," he says.

Sydney wants to ask a million things. He wants to ask how and when. Who took care of him, and where Mr. Cool is now, and if James still remembers the exact sound and cadence of her voice. He wants to tell him that she would be proud of him for even being alive—proud that he's a professional surfer. Wants to tell him that he's sorry for even bringing it up, and that the Bible apparently says that all shitty things happen for some unknown precious reason, and that he can still hear his own momma's voice in his dreams (*"Not Sydney. Please, not Sydney!"*) and that he wishes to God that he didn't.

Instead he asks, "What was her name?"

James turns to look at him. His eyes are shocked, raw and open. Like nobody had ever taken the time to ask him that question before.

James clears his throat and turns his eyes back to the road, fingers tightening on the gearshift.

"Helen," he says, a ghost of a smile just at the corner of his lips. His mouth forms the word carefully like he hasn't uttered it in years.

"Helen," Sydney whispers back. Without thinking about it, he slowly shifts his knee along the bench seat, letting it briefly press up against James' for just a breath before pulling it away again. The soft hairs at the top of James' shin brush like velvet along his skin.

He waits anxiously the moment to feel like the shower all over again—all hot and tense in his muscles, nervous sweat prickling sharply at the back of his neck, a blaring internal alarm screaming *wrong, don't, dirty, mistake!*

Instead the touch feels calm and warm. The bright, clear waters off Oahu lapping gently at his toes. James exhales a long, slow breath beside him.

"You know, her favorite thing in the whole world was a strawberry-flavored milkshake," he says with a smile in his voice. "She only ever got one once a year. We'd go on her birthday to this place down on the pier—some old shack that doesn't exist anymore. And she'd always tell me we would split it fifty-fifty, but then she'd give me way more than half. Plus all the whipped cream."

Sydney's lungs are straining against his chest. He wants to fly, spread his arms like wings and soar up bolstered on the gust of James' words—on his evident relief at finally saying these words out loud. They glide to an easy stop at a lone red light, and James looks over at him all easy and soft and grinning and *light*. He looks twenty years younger now than he did when Sydney first ran beside him into the waves following a blaring air horn.

"When's her birthday?" Sydney asks, not fully understanding why.

James takes a few moments too long to answer. He bites the inside of his cheek as he shifts the car back into first, revving the engine a bit too hard.

"The day after the Billabong finals, actually."

An odd pang thrums through Sydney's chest, one he can't quite pin down. He has the feeling that if he spread his wings now to fly, he would just thump straight to the ground. All he can do is hum, and James doesn't add anything more.

Despite that, the rest of the drive passes in a startlingly easy silence. Sydney watches the palm trees and stop signs zip by like the steady ticks of a clock. By the time James pulls off the road nearly an hour later, they're down somewhere near Laguna, and Sydney marvels that any time passed at all.

"Rob and I found this place last year," James is saying as he parks in the dirt strip alongside the road, one that looks out over the bluffs leading down to the shore. "Usually empty this time of day, but great surf."

Sydney hates his own body for tensing at the sound of the friend's name, flinching away from it like it's some sort of intrusion. It makes him feel like a child, clapping his hands over his ears to block out the sound of the word "prayers" or "chores."

He climbs out of the car, following James' lead, and gets down his board in silence. He's suddenly desperate to reach the water, as if this will all just disappear up in smoke if he doesn't get down to the waves fast enough—if he wavers at all.

James carries his board over his head, biceps bulging, then sets his board down in the sand beside Sydney and strips off his shirt without a moment's hesitation. He gracefully drops to his knees and starts waxing as if they do this every morning. Business as usual. All the time in the world.

And yet, for some idiotic reason, the liminal space of the sand— caught between the silent comfort of the car and the open freedom of the waves—licks sharp and threatening at the edges of the fragile, tender little flutter of *something* that Sydney always feels in the air between himself and James Campbell. That warm thrum of a spark that flickers and pulses, pulling on his bones like a magnet. And now it's on the verge of being put out forever—snuffed by the wind on the breezy shore.

Sydney waxes his board in half the time it usually takes, then leaps up and runs straight to the roaring water, haphazardly kicking up sand in a way he never, ever does. His breath catches in his chest when he glances over his shoulder and sees James following on his heels, full-out sprinting with his board under his arm. He hurls himself into the whitewater just after Sydney as if he can't reach the swells fast enough either.

"Fuck, Danny, give an old man some warning before you sprint off to start!" he calls, grinning as he paddles in his wake.

Sydney's left breathless as that spark flames into a crackling heat. "I thought you 'weren't that fucking old,'" he yells back.

"Alright, so that's how you want to do this, huh?" James pauses to sit up and catch his breath for a moment, then smirks before tilting his head back to slick down his hair. Sydney grips his board hard and tears his gaze away from James' long, dripping column of tan neck before that internal alarm starts blaring again.

James just shoots him a grin. "Try and keep up, kid," he says over his shoulder, voice dripping with a challenge.

Before Sydney can even think of a response, James is off, rocketing on powerful strokes across the surface towards the rushing wave. His chest is heaving, shoulders flexing under the sun, as he turns his board and readies for the drop in down the face. Sydney clutches the sides of his board with both hands and lets out a shaky breath of anticipation. The hair on the back of his neck stands up in a silent, shivering thrill as he stares breathlessly at James Campbell dropping in on the powerful wave.

He can't look away. Wouldn't look away if someone was holding out a million dollars just over his shoulder.

James zooms along the face, shooting off spray behind him as he pumps hard with his legs for speed. He reaches down to grip the side of his board, shoots out the other arm for balance, and then absolutely soars up into the sky. The sound of it settles with a thud in Sydney's gut, hovering right at the base of his throat. James lands his jump solidly on the lip of the wave and glides smoothly to the end of the shoulder, fitting in one fierce cutback before letting the whitewater swirl around his shins.

When James finally falls gracefully into the shallows on his back, sinking down into the earth, Sydney hears a quiet moan slip free from his own throat. He swallows it away.

James surfaces with a great gasp and reaches for his board bobbing on the waves. He runs his hand through his dripping hair and catches his breath before flopping down on his stomach to paddle back out towards the calm water. Sydney perches on his board, frozen, and pretends he isn't counting the number of strokes it takes James to reach him.

"You gonna sit on your lazy ass all day?" James huffs out as he glides up to his side. "Come on, Mr. Top Surfer. Show me what you can do."

Those words, said in that voice, send a zipping trail of heat straight down Sydney's spine. He rolls his eyes to gain a moment to recover before laying down flat on his stomach to start paddling.

"I just wanted you to have your precious minute of victory before I embarrassed you," he says in his usual smooth voice.

James barks a laugh and mutters "unbelievable" behind him as Sydney's arms start cutting through the icy water, propelling him forward. The sun beats warm and dry on his back, draping over his shoulder blades like a blanket of fresh heat. The horizon stretches out before him like a piercing slash across the heavens, and the salty air settles down around him in a silent cocoon.

And out of nowhere, he hears his momma's voice in his head.

"*And God said, 'Let there be a firmament'—that means cut 'em in half, Sydney—'in the midst of the waters, and let it divide the waters from the waters.' And that's how come the sea and the sky look the same.*"

And he remembers his small voice asking, "*Have you seen the sea? Is that how come you know it looks the same?*"

He hears her voice, faint around the edges, whisper back, "*No, honey, but your father has. He told me all about it.*"

Sydney halts his paddling and waits for a good enough swell to come in. He's achingly aware of James' eyes on his back, probably tracing the tendrils of his tattoo. He shuts off the voices in his head and looks out over the water, eyes scanning rapidly for signs of a good swell, following the drifts of the current and the tides, judging the depth and composition of the ocean floor beneath him.

He sees the familiar physics rise up in front of him like they're written plain as day in the air. Equations and predictions and models all hovering over the face of the waters.

"*And darkness was upon the face of the deep. And the Spirit of God hovered upon the face of the waters.*"

He gasps at the sudden clarity of her voice, relegated for so many years to his dreams and now crisp and sharp in his ears. It hurts. A dam he never even realized he had built suddenly cracks open and breaks, releasing a floodgate pouring out from his skin and into the sea lapping at his hips, causing the water to rise, and rise, and rise. He hears the clack of her cross necklace falling to the floorboards. Hears the imagined sound of Helen Campbell telling James he can have the whipped cream. Hears his own momma calling out his name, snot dripping from her nose, down across her smeared pink lips.

"Danny?"

James' voice shocks him from his thoughts. He turns around sharply, and sees that James has paddled out a bit to meet him. His brow is furrowed in confusion, tense like he's approaching a wounded animal about to strike.

"You alright?"

Hot embarrassment flares across Sydney's cheeks. Everything is quiet—silent save for the gentle lapping of the water against the undersides of their boards in tandem with both of their breaths.

"Yeah, I—sorry."

James twists his mouth like he wants to press him for more, but then settles on a faint smile. "Stop thinking so hard about it all, Einstein." He nods his head towards a far off swell, one that looks particularly large. "Here, drop in on that wave with me."

Sydney nods dumbly and follows, mind still reeling. He allows his eyes to zero in on the broad, quiet strength of James' back as he paddles out ahead of him, and all the while his own arms and legs move thickly like molasses. His heart pounds in anticipation as the wave starts to build and crest behind them, lifting up the tails of their boards where they wait about ten feet apart. He's never ridden a wave with anyone else before, aside from someone else snaking in on him to try and screw him over in a competition.

The misting wind rushes against his face and stomach as he drops in on the wave and lets his muscles take over. He follows in James' wake as James snaps off the top and then does a quick cross-step so he can hang five. Sydney knows James is showing off on purpose, trying to snap Sydney out of his own mind and goad him into a competition of friendly fire. But Sydney can't get his own limbs to move. He soars in a frozen stance across the face of the wave and closes his eyes. Feels the droplets of spray flying off James' board splash against his cheeks, his eyelids. Feels the solid, comforting weight of the heaving earth beneath his feet.

When he opens his eyes again a second later, he gasps out loud. He sees James Campbell before him, hanging five and smirking like the smug juicers back in high school, outlined by the stunning Laguna beach mountains and a clear, open sky. For the first time in his life since he ever picked up a magazine advertisement in his small hands, he sees something in the waves besides muscle and adrenaline and physics.

He opens his eyes wide, and he squints against the gushing wind on his face, and he sees a vast, incomprehensible beauty, laid bare for the two of them alone.

They surf for another hour, trading off dropping in double on waves and showing off with trick jumps and over-cocky flips.

It's the least amount of real, competition-approved technique Sydney's ever used during a surfing session, and simultaneously the most fun he can ever remember having. James Campbell moves and breathes like an entirely new person, utterly unrecognizable from the small, haunted man on the moonlit sand, or down at the dockyard, or panting after a three-hour-long training session, exasperated and sore. The blue of his eyes now indistinguishable from the blue of the sea.

James gestures to the shore for a break after a particularly punishing wipeout and Sydney follows, legs and arms pleasantly aching along his bones. He can't quite keep the stupid grin off his face. It feels out of place and entirely natural all at the same time. He rubs a hand over his salty lips to hide it.

James rummages in his bag for a towel once they reach the sand and quickly dries himself off before pulling on his tank top. He throws back his head to take long, slow gulps of water. Sydney stares for a moment at the saltwater trickling down over James' Adam's apple, mouth open and dry, then does a double take at the metal bottle in his hand.

"I'm pretty sure you were supposed to give that back," he says with a pointed look.

James glances down at the Navy-issue canteen and shrugs. "Turns out if you get metal blasted through your body you get to keep it as a souvenir. Or at least they never ask for it back." His eye twinkles with a near-wink.

Sydney wants to cup James' face in his hands and yell at him that it's the most remarkable thing that's ever happened on earth that James Campbell is suddenly laughing, making a *joke*, about his time in Vietnam. And that he's choosing to share it with Sydney of all the goddamn billions of people.

Sydney takes a step closer so that they're standing chest to chest and opens his mouth to reply when someone beats him to it.

"Jimmy fucking Campbell!"

They both jump apart and turn towards the sound of the voice, and Sydney's stomach drops like lead down to his toes. It's the cop.

He looks back to James hoping to see a similarly disappointed face—that their glorious time alone has been interrupted by an intruder—but James' face has broken out into a dazzling smile, giddy and sizzling with warmth. The perfect picture of pleasant surprise. Sydney wants to vomit.

Rob jogs towards James and throws an arm around his neck before rubbing his fist into his hair like a schoolkid. "Thought that was your car up there, old man," he says. "You've been ditching me for ages!"

James places a firm hand on Rob's shoulder, keeping it there for a beat longer than Sydney feels is necessary. Sydney can't see anything but the tips of James' fingers caressing the skin just above the neckline of Rob's t-shirt.

"Come on, be decent," he laughs. "I've been busy learning the ways of the professionals from this lunatic." He shoots a smirk and a quick glance towards Sydney.

Rob looks over at him, too and freezes, as if he hadn't even realized he was standing there before. He rocks back on his heels and lets out a long whistle.

"Well fuck, Jimmy, you weren't yanking my chain after all."

Rob stares slightly open mouthed at Sydney as he sticks out a hand. "I'm Rob. Rob Depaul. Jimmy's friend," he adds.

It's only been a day and already the name "Jimmy" sounds foreign to his ears. Sydney reluctantly takes Rob's hand and gives a single shake. "I know."

He doesn't offer anything more.

He's realizing with each unbearably awkward second that passes that he's grown far too accustomed to being alone in James Campbell's company over the last few days. Undeniable facts quickly slot into place in his head: that he's leaving tomorrow morning, that he just finished his last-ever surf with James, that now James' 'real life' has come calling to take him back, that James is shooting the same private smile at Rob now that Sydney thought was meant only for him just yesterday. Like a naive idiot.

He sets his mouth in a firm line and tries to simultaneously look intimidating and invisible. Rob takes his hand back, saying, "Ok, then," under his breath, and James is shooting him a look that Sydney refuses to meet head on. He can't bear to see what it is. What it means.

He tunes out the next part of the conversation, noting with a piercing ache that Rob and James are gradually taking small steps away from him in the sand, drawn into each other with quick words and even quicker laughs. He starts to plan his silent escape, flipping through options in his head of how to get back to his motel now that he knows he doesn't have a ride back with James, when even more voices come bounding down from up on the bluff.

"Well look who's still alive!"

"Jimmy, you narc, you made Rob cry like a fucking baby all week—left us to babysit him!"

Sydney swallows down the fresh wave of nausea in his gut as he turns to see a group of four more guys making their way towards them across the sand. They're roughhousing with each other and cracking more jokes as they jog, startling a group of nearby seagulls into flight.

He notices James' body language tense as they approach, and his stupid brain instantly supplies him with the reason why—now everyone knows, can see with their own eyes, that James just willingly spent time with Danny Moore. He's probably afraid they'll think he's just a pushover, or an ass kissing fanboy, or a guy who thinks he's too good for all of them now that he's made pro. Probably afraid they'll pity him for not having the guts to look at Danny Moore and say, "Thanks, but no."

105

But it doesn't matter what the reason is. The end result is the same: James looking quickly at Sydney with a flicker of fear in his eyes, masked by undeniable embarrassment in his cheeks.

Sydney's startled from his thoughts when someone claps a hand hard on his shoulder.

"So it's true, then. Our little Jimmy went and left us for *the* Danny Moore," the guy says, barely hiding his snicker.

"Aw right on—and we even get to see you without the shades!" chimes in another.

Sydney's heart sinks in his chest. He's heard this all before. And it would feel just mildly irritating and dull if only James wasn't still looking at him with that damn unreadable expression, eyes narrowed and wary while his body leans ever closer to Rob's beside him.

Sydney stands up straighter. He can feel James' eyes on him like a laser, prickling the hairs on the back of his neck and causing sweat to drip down his sides. He wishes desperately he had his sunglasses on his face instead of folded at his feet in the sand, or at least that he was wearing a shirt. As it is he feels completely laid bare, skin ripped back and showing his internal organs no matter how much more he tries to puff out his chest to hide his lungs.

"Yes, well, we've been training together. For the Billabong," he says, voice flat and steady.

The uncomfortable silence that follows his statement settles like a block of ice right in the middle of the beach. Apparently that explanation was too vanilla to make fun of. Everyone shuffles their feet for a beat before Rob clears his throat and steps in.

"Come on, Jimmy, you owe us some hang time," he says, wrapping an arm around James' shoulders. Sydney wants to cough. Loudly.

"Yeah, man, we were just on our way down here to get breakfast at Norm's when we saw your old station wagon along the side of the road," adds a third guy, one who'd been silent up until then.

"Come swimming with us, at least. These losers get cranky when they're too hot," Rob says with a jokingly icy glare at the group of other guys.

Sydney can sense the easy camaraderie among them all flying over his head and sailing past his sides, impossible for him to latch onto even if he wanted to try. He steps back and pulls on his shirt as the rest of the group starts to rip off shirts and strip down to boxers for their impromptu swim.

He doesn't miss the wary glare directed at him from two among the group, daring him with a look to do something queer. As if he'll jump on anything male that breathes if it has even an inch of bare skin showing. It would be humorously childish, something to make him roll his eyes over and scoff, if he didn't see James Campbell notice those looks directed at him too and frown.

He reaches back down and grabs his sunglasses and t-shirt to avoid their eyes, slowly continuing to back away as they all jog off down to the water. He's formed an alright plan over the last thirty seconds—just fake going for a walk down the beach and then come back to grab the rest of his stuff and leave when they're all busy swimming. Somehow it feels too pathetic to simply grab his board and leave now.

He's startled for the second time that day by a hand on his arm. This one is gentle and soft.

"You're not coming?" James asks. Sydney notices he's still wearing his own tank top.

Sydney huffs out a laugh, short and harsh, as he yanks on his shirt and flicks his aviators over his eyes. "Obviously not."

James opens his mouth like he's about to say something, then shuts it after a beat. Something passes quickly across his face, too fast for Sydney to fully catch. More embarrassment? Fresh irritation?

Hurt?

He fights with himself not to lean forward as James takes a step back. The air in front of him is too empty and cold in his absence.

"I'm gonna join them for a bit," James finally says in a flat voice. "Rob's right, I haven't really seen him all week."

Sydney nods as James starts walking away, wishing his board shorts had pockets for him to shove his hands into.

James pauses and speaks over his shoulder. "You know I'll still drive you back, yeah?"

It's even worse than if James had simply left him to fend for himself. This feels too kind, too overly accommodating, like Sydney's a kid whose parent forgot to pick him up from the middle school dance, and someone else's dad is offering him a pity ride back home.

He knows it wouldn't work to argue with James about that now, though, so he quickly nods his head and turns away before James can continue, striding off in the opposite direction as fast as possible without thinking too hard about it.

He knows, as he reaches up to wipe some stray sand off the lenses over his eyes, that he'll never see James Campbell like this again. That it's ended.

Sydney wanders aimlessly a quarter mile down the beach until the soft, sandy shore opens out onto a bed of rocky tidepools, washed over gently by the incoming waves and brimming with coral and starfish.

It's surprisingly empty for this time of day—no little kids with buckets and shovels running through to catch sand crabs, no frantic parents chasing after them, terrified they'll fall.

He perches himself on a flat stretch of rock and hunkers down to bide his time. He'll wait until the group he can just barely still see down the shore is distracted enough that he could sneak in and grab his board and bag without being seen. Without being accosted or pitied.

Exhaustion from the day settles like mud over his body. The conversation with James which already feels like years ago in the car, the unexpected memories of his own momma's voice, the revelatory comfort of dropping in with James on the waves—it's all left him feeling completely wrung out and dry. Hell, the last four days have done nothing but wring him out, over and over and over again until he's been wiped completely clean beneath James Campbell's steady blue gaze.

But that steady blue gaze won't be on him anymore, not after today. Not with Sydney's flight back home looming over his shoulder, and not with the way James let his fingertips touch the policeman's bare skin beneath the collar of his shirt. So Sydney wills his mind to go blissfully blank as he waits, staring out to sea and listening to the soft whirls and crackles of the foam as it hisses into the crevices of the tidepools and retreats.

It's a mistake. After what feels like only two minutes have passed, he hears footsteps clomping their way towards him in the sand. He reluctantly turns his head, expecting to see an eager, noisy kid with a mom trailing behind them, and instead sees James taking careful steps across the rocks. He moves cautiously, as if Sydney will up and run away if he approaches too fast.

Sydney nearly groans out loud at his stupidity. He should have just booked it out of there when he had the chance, not waited around like a sitting duck so that James could tell him to his face what Sydney already knows in every cell of his body—that he's appreciated the help, and it's all been good fun, but he really has to get back to his real life now. That's it's awfully awkward trying to hang with his friends with Danny Moore waiting around for a ride home from the beach.

He turns back to the sea and closes his eyes, already imagining the way James' lips will form the words.

"Thought you'd gone," James actually says.

Sydney flicks his hand in a gesture towards himself that says "*still here.*" "Also, do you really think I'd leave my board?"

He hears James sigh. "Yeah, guess not."

Heat blooms along his side as James approaches him, legs just inches from Sydney's shoulder. When James doesn't move to sit, Sydney sighs inwardly and stands, meeting him chest to chest. He has the sudden, blinding desire to see the true color of James' eyes one last time, and he slowly removes his sunglasses and folds them over his shirt, pretending he doesn't notice James' raised eyebrows as he does so.

James licks his lips against the sun. "Rob's been wanting to meet you."

"Yes, well, now he has."

Those same lips set in a firm line. "You know what I mean. He wanted to actually talk to you—to have a conversation."

Sydney rolls his eyes. "No he didn't. He just wanted to say he'd met me. A cool story to share at the next post-competition party at the bar. Get him laid."

James opens his mouth and takes a step back. "I'm sorry, I missed the memo when we decided you could go back to being a dick again."

"Did you? I believe that memo was sent out when you invited all of your *friends* to come gape at Danny Moore," he sneers. "A rare sighting outside of a competition, from what I hear."

"Oh lay off it. You heard what they said, it was a coincidence."

"You believe in those?"

"Well, I'm a living breathing human, so yes."

"I see. Was it also a coincidence that you lit up like a smitten schoolgirl when Rob walked towards you in the sand?"

He hadn't meant to say that. He really hadn't meant to. But now that it's out and open, Sydney's chest is practically roaring for a fight, gunning to let off some of the weight left behind by having to watch James' fingers graze the naked skin at the base of Rob's fucking perfect tan neck. By having to watch the rest of his friends take a wary step away from him while they changed in the sand.

James goes deadly still. "Excuse me?"

"You heard me correctly. It's written all over your face."

James clenches his fist at his side, eyes blazing. "What the fuck are you implying?"

Sydney tilts his head and narrows his eyes—a silent answer. He tells himself it's satisfying when James reels back, as if he's been punched.

"Swear to God, Moore, you watch yourself. Fucking watch yourself. You have no idea."

Sydney wants to scream. "Don't I? It isn't that hard to figure out watching you tuck his hair behind his ear and whisper sweet nothings into his ear."

James moves in abruptly like he's going to shove him, then yanks himself back at the last second, breathing out harshly through his nose. Sydney wildly wishes he hadn't backed away—that James' strong hands had collided with his chest.

"Jesus," James breathes, "that's really fucking bold coming from the man who got caught with his tongue down a rent boy's throat in a fucking bathroom."

Sydney's eyes blow wide with surprise, then he guffaws. "Seriously? *That's* the story they're telling these days?!"

A beat passes, and James' expression almost imperceptibly softens, confusion seeping into his enraged glare. "You're saying that's not true?"

Sydney laughs again, quick and harsh, then flails his hands out at his sides. He can't remember when exactly either of them started yelling.

"Of course it's not true!" he cries. "Do you think I have a fucking death wish?"

"Could've fooled me! Certainly seems like you do the way you walk around on your fucking high horse all the time, sneering down your nose at everyone else—better than all of us kooks."

"Oh great comeback. A real zinger, James. I can't believe I've never heard that one before."

"Fuck you! What the fuck do you know about me? About any of this?"

"I know you seemed pretty damn keen on spilling all your little secrets to your precious 'friend' the other night at the bar," Sydney bites back, gritting his teeth so he doesn't feel like a petulant high schooler.

James sucks in a breath and grabs a handful of his bangs. "Spilling all my—*Jesus*, Danny I was going to tell him about being shot at in fucking Vietnam. How much it meant to me that I won that day. That he had been there with me. You think *I* have a death wish?"

"So you don't deny it, then," Sydney immediately lobs back.

James goes still again, every inch of his skin almost steaming with heat. Sydney has the overwhelming sensation that James is towering over him, ready to punish him and push him down into the rocks and sand, and a terrifying thrill zips up his spine at the thought—one that almost drowns out the despair brewing in the pit of his gut. The air between them is sucked of oxygen as they stare each other down.

They're both remembering the shower.

Finally James takes a step forward and lowers his voice, pointing a finger straight at Sydney's chest.

"Look, all of this shit you think you know about me, all this shit you're trying to trick me into saying . . . Who the fuck did you talk to, huh? How the fuck have you known so much about my life since day fucking one."

"Who did I—who did I *talk* to?"

"Swear to God, was it Lori?"

Sydney looks up at the sky and feels his chest clench in frustration. "Lori? I don't even know who the hell 'Lori' is! I didn't *talk* to anybody. Didn't have to ask anyone."

"Then how?"

"I just *looked* at you and I figured it out, that's how!"

James shakes his head. "You don't know a thing about me, kid. Not a fucking thing."

Incredulity blasts across Sydney's face. "Not a thing? What the hell ever happened to 'I've never ever talked to anyone about the war, Sydney,' or 'Here, Sydney, let me tell you all about how I learned to surf'?"

James pulls at his hair with his hands and frowns, then sputters, "Who—what—who the hell is Sydney?"

Sydney freezes. He hadn't even noticed the name slip out. Panic starts to blare through his limbs, even more than it already is. The air crashes down onto him, burying him under too much breeze and oxygen and bright sun.

He desperately hopes he didn't pause too long, and his voice when it finally leaves his lips is churning with frustration. "Look, that's not the point. Just, what the hell are you so afraid of? You're so terrified of me seeing into your little head—knowing more than just the smallest fucking detail about you. And while you're at it, what the hell is stopping you from leaving your shitty-ass job you hate so much, or your shitty-ass apartment? From actually moving on?"

"Oh, you're one to talk! Why are you so afraid of someone actually having a real conversation with you? Answer me that, Mr. Sunglasses."

"That's a low blow, James, even for you," Sydney spits back. He can't breathe, chest heaving against clenched muscles.

"You know what a low blow is, Danny?" James asks. There's a dangerous fire blazing around the blue edges of his eyes. "Telling a fucking veteran who's had a bullet blasted through his fucking chest that he doesn't have anything to be afraid of—that he should just *move on.*"

Sydney's legs start carrying him away before he even decides to do it, striding off across the rocky tide pools and leaving James Campbell as far behind him as he can get. He calls back over his shoulder with a final roar.

"Sorry for taking up so much time of your precious second chance at life, then!"

"Oh, you want to run away?" James yells at his back. "Turn and face me like the fucking man you pretend to be all the time!"

112

At that, Sydney bolts around and plants his feet, squaring his shoulders. There's a furious and ashamed and absolutely panicked retort on the tip of his tongue when he sucks in a gasp and freezes—retort forgotten.

He barely has time to register the enormous wave rushing towards James' back, and the way his bare feet are clinging precariously to the edge of the slick rock. The way his back is to the sea while he screams at Sydney as he runs away like a coward.

He barely has time to scream, "James! Look out!" before the wall of forcing water crashes into James with a booming slap, throwing him to the ground and smashing his head straight against the craggy rocks.

Sydney's vision whites out to everything but the sight of James' limp body being dragged out to sea by the wave, tumbling and thrashing in the whitewater like a ragdoll. His legs are numb. His tongue feels too big for his mouth. He's running faster than he ever has in his life, sprinting into the foam and nearly slipping across the slick bed of rocks and coral.

He hears someone screaming, and he realizes distantly in his mind that it's him—screaming James' name. Screaming out into the void.

A second wave crashes over James' body, burying him in a cloud of sand and foam, leaving only the backs of his calves barely visible on the surface of the churning water.

Sydney reaches him right before a third wave slams down and grabs the first part of James' body he can reach. He yanks him as hard as he can, heaving his body against the rushing pull of the tide. With gritted teeth and a wild noise in his throat, he finally hauls the dead weight of him up out of the waves and onto the rocky stretch of shore.

He grabs him under the armpits and flips him onto his back. Wet sand covers James' still face, plastered through his hair. A stream of deep red blood pours down from the gash in his forehead, mixing with the saltwater. His eyes are closed, and his lips barely parted.

He isn't breathing.

Sydney curses out loud as a panicked hotness prickles at the back of his eyes. He can't lose it now. He absolutely cannot.

He sprints through his memories searching for something, *anything* to help, and a certain memory flies up and smacks him in the face—he's seventeen, spying on the lifeguard training course from the shady wall of trees, wishing they would just get on with it so he could have his stretch of beach back, watching them practice CPR.

His hands and fingers move without him, ripping open James' tank top to see his chest, plastered with more wet sand and flecks of broken seaweed. He doesn't even know if this will help—if this won't just hurt him even more. But James' chest stays frozen and flat, and his lips stay still, and Sydney can't fucking watch James Campbell die on the sand knowing the last thing he ever saw on earth was Danny Moore running away from him like a coward, accusing him of unspeakable things and telling him he's been anything but brave.

The memory of the lifeguard training flashes like a sputtering film through his mind as he positions his shaking hands on James' chest. He doesn't even pause to take a calming breath, but starts to push. Hard. Pumping down with all his might until James' ribs creak and sag under the weight of his trembling palms. He hears his momma's favorite hymn in his head, steady in time to his beat.

*"Be Thou my vision, O Lord of my heart . . . Naught be all else to me, save that Thou art . . ."*

He stops after fifteen (*Was it supposed to be fifteen? Thirty? Five?*) and grasps James' jaw, moving his lifeless head back to open up his neck, hating the heavy weight of it as it flops in his hand. He brushes the blood off his face, and shivers as it clings wet and sticky to his palm. He can't stop to think about it. With a deep breath he holds James' chin with his hand and leans down over him, pressing his dry lips to the grimy sand- and saltwater-covered skin.

James' lips are still warm. Sydney puffs up his lungs with air and forces the breath into James' throat, hearing the roaring rush of the air pump down into his lungs. His own cheeks are vibrating, stiff and sore as he leans up just enough to suck in another breath before covering James' mouth again with his own. The tide pushes and pulls at his shins, cradling James' body before trying to pull him back out to sea. Sydney holds on to James' upper arm so tightly he feels straight through to the bone.

After three breaths, he suddenly hears a soft gurgle in the back of James' throat, a quick catch in his chest. A tremor.

Sydney's heart pounds uncontrollably as he forces another breath into James' body, praying like he's never prayed in his entire life that this will do it—that this will be the one to keep James' lips from growing any cooler beneath his. He's so earnest in his thoughts, lost in the haze of blindingly focused panic, that he doesn't immediately notice the slight change in pressure beneath his mouth.

Out of the chaos, out of the swirling noise, he feels a subtle pushback on the air he's forcing into James' throat—a backflow of outgoing breath moving steadily out of James' lungs. Sydney moves to lift his mouth up, to see if he should place his hands back on James' chest to try pushing again, when suddenly James' lips move beneath his own, softly latching on to his bottom lip and giving a wet suck.

For exactly one second, Sydney freezes.

The soft jaw below his moves to further capture his mouth, and James exhales a beautiful, steady stream of breath from his nose straight onto Sydney's trembling upper lip.

Sydney's eyes fly open. He feels his own mouth start to move softly against James' wet lips, tasting the hints of crackling salt, and then he sucks in a startled breath. He yanks back from James' face just as James starts to cough and heave in great gasps. With numb fingers, Sydney turns him over onto his side and watches wide-eyed as James coughs up mouthfuls of seawater and gulps down air.

"Thank God," he hears himself whisper. He can still feel the warm, wet, ghostly pressure of lips gliding against his mouth.

Just as Sydney goes to lean over and glimpse James' face (*brush back his hair? touch his cheek?*), rough hands suddenly grab his shoulders, throwing him back from James.

"The fuck are you doing to him? Get the fuck off him!"

Sydney looks up wildly to see Rob and the rest of the guys sprinting towards them in the sand. The one who got there first hauls Sydney to his feet by his collar, practically spitting with rage.

"You fucking perv—making a fucking move on him when he just fucking drowned!"

Sydney doesn't register the punch in time to duck. The man's fist slams into his cheek, throwing him down into the rocky sand with a flash of white. He cradles his face with his hand on his knees and grunts out at the pain shooting through his skull. Sydney marvels that he had no idea it was possible to time-travel back to high school again.

He squints open his eyes, still flexing his aching jaw, and looks up from the wet sand just in time to see Rob brushing the wet hair back from James' face. To see him whispering to him, gently holding his hand. To see James' eyes open and blinking, chest rising and falling as he steadily breathes.

Sydney stumbles to his feet as one of the guys sprints past him to the road, presumably to find a call box for an ambulance. He stands back from the little group in the sand, gasping and helpless, still clutching his throbbing face as the rest of the men kneel around James amongst the tidepool foam.

He hears James' voice rise above the murmurs and wants to weep at the sound.

"I'm fine, I'm fine," he's saying in a thin voice. "Just got sucked under, that's all, I'm fine."

He says the words over and over; Sydney wonders if he actually believes them. If he realizes that he'd lain there in the wet sand beneath Sydney's shaking hands without breathing. If he, too, still feels the ghost of lips pressed hotly against his own.

All of a sudden, Sydney knows he can't take a single minute more. That the longer he stands there staring at James Campbell lying limp in the sand, the more he'll never, ever want to get on a plane and leave.

He tears his gaze away after reassuring himself one last time that James is, in fact, breathing, and then turns to walk as fast as he can back across the sand to his board. He wipes furiously at a tear that escapes down his cheek, James' dried blood cool and thick on his palm. His other hand still clutches at the blooming bruise beneath his eye.

He hears footsteps chasing after him in the sand, and he turns and tenses his body, ready for round two of the fight. Instead he sees it's the other friend running his way—the quiet one.

"Hey man, don't go!" he calls out, panting as he sprints. Sydney stands still and waits for him to catch up, even though he desperately wants to turn and flee far away in the other direction.

"Sorry about Kip, man, he was just scared," the friend says. Sydney huffs and experimentally flexes his jaw, then winces at the fresh shoot of pain.

"I know you were just doing CPR on him," he adds.

"Yeah, well, you could've shared that with your friend over there before he fucking decked me," Sydney snaps. He turns and starts striding away again, feet numb and heavy in the sand.

"He's asking for you!" the friend calls after him. "Jimmy's asking for you!"

Sydney's chest pangs, and a small moan escapes the back of his throat. He licks his lips against the ghost of James' mouth pressed against his own. Feels the memory of James' head rolling heavy and limp in his palm.

He doesn't respond.

He makes it back to his stuff and heaves his board under his still-shaking arm, steadfastly not looking at James' board lying next to it unassumingly in the warm sand. Then he books it up towards the road to hitchhike back to Hermosa.

He doesn't once allow himself to look back towards the shore.

# 10

The love affair never even began.

It was broken. Dead on arrival. The part of the "J" in James' name where the pen briefly ran out of ink while he stood leaning over a desk and signed his name on an enlistment form. The part of the "J" he never went back to try and fill in.

It was already dead when James stepped up out of the station wagon one foot at a time onto the already-hot asphalt of LAX at four o'clock in the morning, Auntie Cath's mostly-for-show sobs echoing out across the empty drop-off lane and Uncle Ron's hand slapping his back just once, hard enough to bruise.

Dead when he touched down onto a muddy training field next to the base camp outside steaming Saigon and *Run, seaman, I said get your ass into gear and fucking run or them Viet Cong'll cut your balls off!* And dead when the Lieutenant shoved him off the top of the diving platform into the freezing cold, chlorinated pool below, and he thought he was gonna die of fear before his back hit the water.

*You need to know how it feels to fall off the side of a ship without pissing yourself,* they said.

They also said *hold this gun like you've been holding it your whole life* and *don't fucking shoot at anything that's got the damn Stars and Stripes on it* and *if the ship goes down with a fucking torpedo and those sons of bitches capture you, you don't say a fucking word about our Intel no matter what they do to you, you fucking hear me, seaman?*

"Sir, yes, sir!" with no soul behind the words. "Sir, yes, sir!" before hunkering down in the back of a camouflage jeep alongside the hidden jungle Navy dock and whipping out packs of cards, and smuggled cigarettes, and little folded up photographs of naked pinup girls wearing fishnet tights and sailors' caps.

"Sir, yes, sir!" when James was dismissed from his midnight to five a.m. shift keeping watch up on the deck, and *you scrub the hell out of that grease stain on your uniform collar before the next time I see you, seaman, or you'll be scrubbing decks wishing you were a POW instead.* He went down into his tiny, swaying hammock bunk and pulled out a sheet of lined paper and pen to write to Auntie Cath and Uncle Ron for the first time since he stepped onto the boat. To tell them "All is fine," and "The food on the ship is alright, but not as good as your tuna casserole," and "Last week I saw a monkey climbing along the trees on the shore."

Instead he wrote a tear-stained letter to Helen Campbell. Told her that he wished he'd gone on and stayed in college instead of enlisting. That he'd just taken the chance with being drafted into the Army, destined never to return home.

(*You have a hell of a lot more chance in the Navy,* they'd said. *Boy your age oughta enlist out on the sea before they draft you and drop you in the middle of the jungle face to face with the barrel of a Viet Cong gun*).

Told her that this was the first year he couldn't go drink half a strawberry milkshake alone on her birthday since that night she never came home. The first year he couldn't eat all the whipped cream. Told her that he didn't want to die.

Written, but not signed. Dropped into the ocean before the whistle for first watch. Gobbled up quick by a fish.

Keith Hartman knew that James Campbell's mother's name was Helen.

He knew it in the dead of night, standing shoulder to shoulder on the starboard deck looking out over the lifeless, glassy sea, necks rubbing raw under starched uniform collars and eyes drooping shut to the steady lull of the ship rocking on the waves.

Keith Hartman's love affair began when he signed his name on that crisp white piece of paper, pen ink flowing smoothly throughout the whole entire "K."

He had green eyes like the grass on a baseball field, and hair that'd been cropped in a military cut since he was born, and a whole hallway back at his momma's home in Alabama covered in Navy medals going all the way back to 1805. Straight gleaming white teeth that could be their own lighthouse in the middle of the foggy, black nights out at sea.

He wrote letters home every Tuesday night to his girl Lila May, waiting and praying for him on an Alabama farm. He told the other sailors during mess hall that her tits were the prettiest little buds you ever did see. He told James in the black of night, shoulder to shoulder on the starboard deck, that really she was keeping her skirt pulled down and her blouse buttoned up until the day she had a wedding ring on her finger.

He had danger in his eyelashes and adventure between his toes. Lit up like a firework when he stood at attention with James at his side and found out the two of them were among those chosen for The Mission.

"Sir, yes, sir!" when James followed in Keith Hartman's trail like the tail on a comet as they strapped themselves with dark green and rusting supplies and not enough water and too many bullets. Surely there were far too many bullets.

It was supposed to be easy. Deliver the supplies. Pass off some Intel. Say hello to the Army buddies exhausted from trekking on foot through the jungle. In and out in five hours. Come back on board with the same amount of bullets they left with.

Instead it was far, far too quiet along the coast, where they hunkered down in the silent camo dinghy with guns drawn and pointed at the lifeless shore. Far, far too empty along the stretch of beach where the Army men were supposed to signal them down to meet them. Far, far too still.

They docked in absolute silence, crept up along the messy jungle shore with pounding hearts and unsteady hands. Whispered orders. Whispered curses. Camouflage uniforms disappearing one by one into the thick and airless jungle weeds. Wet, green leaves tugging softly at gun-toting arms. Swallowing up the boots on their feet and reminding them all that they were far, far away from the sea. Keith looked like he wanted to fly.

The first bullets felt like little puffs of wind. A respite from the heavy, wet sun hanging above them and dripping down onto their backs.

Then the world exploded.

There was chaos, and an explosion of sound, and orders screamed out into the void, half at the sailors, half into buzzing old radios. There was sweat dripping down into terrified young eyes, and James followed Keith Hartman in front of him and ran and ran and ran. And that's when it started to rain.

There wasn't time for "sir, yes, sir!" when the order came to *get the hell down* and *find some goddamn cover* and *hold your fucking ground* and *shoot the hell out of anything that moves, I said shoot, goddammit!*

James trembled on his back on the other side of a dirt mound and felt the earth shaking beneath him under the force of the bullets and the fire and the bombs. Hot and steaming water poured down onto his face, into his eyes. Dirt clods ricocheted off his metal helmet and hellfire rained down above him, pounding down into the earth and sending up towers of fire into the smoking sky. There wasn't enough time to ask for orders. Wasn't enough time to be scared.

James fired off bullets shoulder to shoulder with Keith, feeling Keith's gun's recoil shoot straight through to his own body. They fired searing metal into a wall of thick, choking smoke. The enemy emerging from the flames of hell.

No time for "sir, yes, sir!" when the order finally came to *move out, goddammit I said fucking move out!* And Keith Hartman pulled James by the collar to his feet, and they ran and ran and ran.

James didn't know whether they ran towards the sea or away from it. Bullets whizzed like fire past sweaty, trembling cheeks. Eyes stung shut against the blinding smoke. Jungle leaves and vines wrapped around legs and ankles and pulled sailors down into the heaving, hot palms of the earth. Reminding them they weren't on a ship that could glide away into the horizon.

(*You have a hell of a lot more chance in the Navy,* they'd said.)

James turned to see a wall of screaming fire explode on top of Roy and Lawrence. Their bodies disappeared, swallowed up in crackling red smoke. There wasn't enough time to stop and register the noise— hear the ripping booms of exploding bombs, or the screaming orders, or the thrash and crack of the palm trees riddled with bullets, or the rain pummeling down into the soft, steaming earth. To hear the last screams of Roy and Lawrence deep in the red mud.

Keith ran and ran and ran away from it all. And James followed.

They ran for hours, days, years. They ran for eleven minutes. And then Keith Hartman tripped and fell flat on his face, and James looked down and saw he'd tripped on Jack's muddy, smoking body, with three limbs left instead of four. And Keith hurled Jack up onto his shoulders and screamed at James to *run ahead and save yourself, Jimmy, for God's sake save yourself and run!*

So James did.

He ran for eight more minutes. Eight more years. The jungle was thinning out, and he could tell he was on the verge of reaching a safe, silent shore, and his lungs were burning in acid and legs on fire with trembling adrenaline.

That's when the enemy jumped out in front of him from the snarling green shadows, holding a black gun. And James wailed from the deepest part of his chest, and raised his gun arm without even thinking about it, and shot him before he could even check the uniform for a sign of the Stars and Stripes.

When he did crouch down and crawl on his hands and knees to check, he saw the face of a kid staring up into the sky, one eye covered in long black hair. Not even old enough for a driver's license.

No Stars or Stripes.

James hurled himself to his knees and ran towards the shore, vision blacking out except for the tiniest slip of ocean peeking out through the palm trees. His numb legs carried him through the last dense brushes of the jungle, hot and screaming at his back, and the crystal blue water in front of him lapped gently at the soft white sand.

The silence was a slap in the face.

He looked up towards the sky, with his mud and sweat and blood covered cheeks, and spotted a rescue helicopter swerving toward him way out in the distance, hovering over the calm sea. He ran out knee deep into the ocean, and waved his arms like a madman, watching the swinging ladder sway in the breeze, and the rain cleared up just like turning off a faucet.

He turned back one last time to the churning chaos of the jungle, praying he would see Keith Hartman burst out alive from the smoke and fire, and that's when his chest just under his left shoulder exploded.

James learned it all later, when he was laid up in a hospital bed near base camp under crisp white sheets, folded down at the corners.

How Keith Hartman finally did come running out of the jungle, vomiting with exhaustion from carrying Jack's corpse on his back. How he'd seen James' body floating face up in the shallows, sinking deeper into the red water, rising and falling in the blood-soaked foam.

Keith won a medal for it all, in the end. For saving Jack's body for his funeral and saving James Campbell's breath in his lungs. He visited James in the hospital, holding his thin hand in the uncomfortable silence, and James clamped his mouth shut so he wouldn't ask Keith why the hell he didn't just leave him to rest in peace on the beach.

It was hard to talk if they weren't standing shoulder to shoulder on the starboard deck. Keith slipped a bullet casing into his hand before he left, and neither one of them said goodbye.

They promoted Keith Hartman after that. Shipped him off to a war office with a comfy leather chair. And James never saw him again.

Later, when James tried to think about it—what happened after his chest just under his left shoulder exploded—he could only remember two things, but they were crystal clear.

That someone, somewhere on the pristine little beach was screaming out in tears for their momma, and that the last conscious thought he had was of whipped cream on a pier.

*Get down there to China Beach, Jimmy. It'll cheer you up in no time,* they said.

So James hauled himself from his crisp white sheets and clutched his creaking shoulder and hitched a ride on one of the supply jeeps traveling thirty minutes south from Da Nang.

The beach was a zoo. A rolling stretch of white sand covered in camo and GI's, with a hand-built driftwood lifeguard tower splattered with graffiti paint jobs and a line of shirtless soldiers all along the shore watching two men surf out in the waves.

*Watching two men surf.* Surfing in the middle of the chaos. Surfing on the other side of the world.

James sucked in a breath and stared speechless, hovering at the edges of the crowd. He felt like he'd just entered a time machine with a sick twist—doomed to stand frozen like a statue forever while he viewed a scene from his past life in Los Angeles. He stood there gaping until someone came up and handed him a lukewarm beer, and another laughed and said, *relax, dude, you're in paradise now,* and another one handed him a surfboard, dripping wet from the sea.

It was hand built from extra Army supplies—wood painstakingly sanded down and covered in cheap Army issue wax. A big white peace sign painted on its belly.

*How did you know I can surf?* James asked.

*Because everyone who watches the waves like that knows how to surf,* they said.

They told him to take a breath. Take it for a ride or two and enjoy himself. So James Campbell stripped down to his fatigue pants and an undershirt, and threw his old boots down into the hot sand, and waded out slowly into the crashing waves. One foot in front of the other, sinking into the soft, cool deep. His first time touching ocean water without bullets strapped to his back in lifetimes. Touching the same molecules of water, the same great, breathing sea, that he touched growing up outside his little Long Beach trailer.

It was painful to paddle out with his wounded shoulder, and his back spasmed as he tugged himself along one-handed. The water was too flat and his mouth too dry. He wanted to turn back. End it all before he embarrassed himself, or ripped open the stitches in his skin.

But a little swell came in, and he paddled out to meet it, and before he knew it James was standing on his board on shaking legs, feeling the wind and spray rush against his face in a long lost kiss.

He was surfing.

He was *surfing.*

He felt the smile take over his face in a great burst, and a tear on his cheek mixed in with the salty spray. He rode that wave until it was just a whisper of foam across the shallows, and the smile stayed on his lips even as he leaned back and let the wave finally swallow him up, enclosed in the sea. It threatened at the corners of his lips as he dragged the board behind him back up to the sandy shore, handing it off after that lone ride to the group of soldiers lounging around in the sand with a quiet *thank you.*

They looked into his eyes and nodded. They understood.

He blinked the saltwater out of his eyes and breathed as he walked slowly along the shore, feet sinking deep into the soft, wet sand, the sound of joking and laughter from the group echoing at his back. He looked up to the clear blue sky, free of smoke and fire, free of the sound of screaming.

James smiled, and he licked his lips, and they tasted like a crusty old shrimp.

On Day One of his new life, James woke up in the back of the station wagon which Uncle Ron had left him after he and Auntie Cath assured he was still alive and breathing. They'd visited him in the VA recovery hospital down in the Valley in between church and bingo on a Sunday (*Well, what can we say, Jimmy? You've been gone for so many years. We're glad you're alright.*) and then packed up and moved to Sacramento two weeks later, three days after James hung up the phone from giving them a call to tell them he was out and looking for an apartment. *Better house prices up there in Sacramento*, they'd said. *Take the car, you'll need it. Got less traffic up there in Sacramento, you know.*

James brushed his teeth over the gutter, buttoned up a shirt and walked into the work office for the Long Beach dockyard. *Can you be on time?* Yes. *Can you work manual labor?* Yes.

They never asked if he knew how to fall off the side of the ship. If he knew how to hold and shoot a gun at anything that moved.

He stayed alive for two months. Working and eating and sleeping. Breathe in, breathe out. Eyes open in the morning and closed at night. Keep an ice pack in the freezer to put on his shoulder the second he crawled in the door from work each day at six-forty-five.

And after two months of only being around other people when he was bent over at work, one day he made his way with a sagging spine and lowered neck down to the shoreline next to the pier. He'd never gone down there before, always packed up and left right after the end of day whistle.

He stood awkwardly in the sand. Fiddled with the bullet casing in his pocket. There was a group of surfers out there, laughing and playing in the ocean spray, faces turned up towards the sky. Just a few years younger than him.

James stood there and tried to remember how it felt to surf that little swell along China Beach and couldn't anymore. Just couldn't.

Instead he thought of wanting to tell Keith Hartman that he should have just left him there, should have left him to rest in the shallows with his last conscious thought about whipped cream on a pier.

And then a man appeared in front of him, all tan shoulders and wet hair pulled back and saltwater dripping from his calves. He put out a hand and waited for James to shake it, his grip wet and warm and firm.

And he said, "Hey, man, my name's Rob. You surf?"

# 11

The air tastes like flowers, soft and warm on his tongue.

James stops in his tracks on the curb outside the Honolulu Airport terminal and takes a deep breath in, letting it fill up his lungs, replacing the stale air from the plane in his system.

The healing cut on his forehead throbs as he looks up to the full, bright sun, and he winces as the dull ache makes its way behind his eyes. He hadn't even ended up needing stitches—head wounds always bleed ten buckets more than you'd think they would from the size of them. It's just a tiny line now, barely visible unless you knew it was there.

The ache remains, though, to remind him. Remind him that he had bullets shot at him halfway across the world, and yet the thing that almost did him in was a puny little tide pool on a sunny Laguna Beach shore, right in the familiar safety of broad daylight an hour away from home.

It's fucking embarrassing. James' feet are rooted to the pavement as he watches taxi after taxi pass him by. He can't bring himself to wave one down. If he does, then he'll have to open his mouth and give an address, and he'll have to let himself be driven clear across an unfamiliar island, and he'll have to follow through with this absolutely insane, ridiculous, moronic plan.

He'll have to see Danny Moore again.

It all started in a hospital room four days ago. He'd spent the previous six hours nearly begging and pleading to be released. He was fine, he felt totally normal, his chest was just a little bit sore, no his heart wasn't stuttering. But they'd ordered him to stay overnight for observations since his body had done the goddamn inconvenient thing of

127

trying to stop breathing, and Rob had stood in the doorway of the room with his arms crossed over his broad chest and practically dared James with just his eyes to try and get past him.

So he'd lain there under crisp white sheets, folded down at the corners, and tried desperately not to think of the last time he was left to stare up at a hospital ceiling. He instead focused all his attention on the sounds of Rob and Lori's voices, nervously chatting about anything and everything to keep the room from falling into silence.

He'd stared at the ceiling and remembered it all as if it had been caught on film. How Rob had pushed his hair back from his forehead there on the beach with the tide rushing in around his weak and sore body, trying to drag him back out to the depths. How Rob had held his hand and leaned over him and whispered, "*Christ, Jimmy you could have died. You could have died on me. Don't know what I would've done if Danny hadn't pulled you out and known how to get you breathing again.*"

And James had stared at the ceiling and realized that it hadn't all just been a dream. That he really had come back to consciousness to the feeling of warm, wet lips pressed against his own, and he really had thought for one fleeting, ridiculous second that he would open his eyes to find Rob's deep brown ones gazing back at him. And instead he'd seen two little droplets of ocean, blown wide with fear and covered with a mop of brown curls, a whispered, "*Thank God*" passed between full, trembling lips.

He'd realized, lying there in the drone of the fluorescent lights, that that zing up his spine, that overwhelming, soul consuming feeling of "*I have to fucking survive this,*" had come upon him at precisely the moment he'd looked up at those two terrified eyes. Had felt it *because* they were blue and not brown. Eyes that were frantic and young and powerful—desperate.

He'd known then that he didn't want to be left to rest in peace on the beach, floating in the blood-soaked foam. He'd known that he didn't want to die. Again.

And James had remembered how he'd coughed up another lungful of seawater and choked out, "*Where is he?*" And Rob had gone silent as Kip bit his lip and muttered, "*Sorry, man, I thought he was doing something nasty to you, so I . . .*"

James had gritted his teeth and turned his head. Had seen Danny walking, no, *running* away from them all in the sand, one hand clasped up to his face, the other one covered in blood. Running away as fast as he could from Dean's calls.

The memories had continued to flash through his mind the whole time he'd been in the hospital, an endless hellish loop. Until finally he'd gathered his courage and asked Lori if she could finagle one of the girls who'd worked the ISF check-in table with her for the pro circuit surfers if she could get her Danny's address in Hawaii.

Rob had looked at him like he was insane while he explained to them that he'd probably get a week off work in sick time after this, and he already had his plane ticket bought for the Billabong, and he obviously wasn't going to surf it now, but maybe he could still take a Hawaii vacation? And maybe he could watch the competition and pick up some tips for next year, if he ever even made pro again? And maybe, just maybe, he could thank Danny Moore for pulling his lifeless body from the surf?

Rob never even asked him why he didn't just want Danny's phone number to give him a call.

And then Kip, Dean, and Steven had come in, with hands held awkwardly behind their backs and their heads turned so they weren't looking directly at James in the hospital gown.

"That's a gnarly scar you got there, man," Dean had said. "Your shirt got ripped open when . . . you know. Never noticed it before."

And the air had turned thick and tense when James shrugged his shoulder and said, in a too-casual voice, "Yeah, I was shot."

Kip had missed the unspoken explanation and asked, "Where?"

And James had looked up at the ceiling and whispered, "Not here."

And now, after four long days of staring out his apartment window thinking more than he ever had in his whole damn life, even on the nights he'd kept watch on the ship without Keith by his side to talk to, James finds himself standing on the curb of the Honolulu airport, with a rucksack slung over his shoulder and an address written on a folded-up note in his pocket in Lori's script.

He tastes the flowers in the air, squares his shoulders, and flags down a taxi.

The drive across the island is gorgeous. It leaves James with his jaw hanging open and eyes scared to blink out of fear they'll miss another waterfall, or another tropical flower, or another craggy mountain. It reminds him of Vietnam—the beautiful coastlines they passed from the decks of the ship, the breathtaking, endless green they trudged and clamored through in guzzling camo jeeps.

It takes him by surprise, to sit there in the back of the taxi and think of Vietnam with even the smallest tinge of nostalgia, of appreciation. He somehow feels completely at ease with the memories as he gazes through the smudged taxi window, even despite his nerves at seeing Danny again.

He tells himself that it's impossible for him to feel this at peace *because* he's about to see Danny again. That would be ridiculous. Everything aside, he's only known the man for a little over a week.

*You felt like an entirely new human being after just one day of knowing Rob,* his brain supplies.

James frowns as he looks out the window, the foliage and rolling hills fading into a rainbow blur. No, the landscape is just beautiful. That's all. Even someone as fucked up as him can appreciate that. Even he can feel relaxed by it as the perfumed air surrounds his skin.

The taxi driver doesn't ask any questions the whole drive. He drops James off near Mokuleia forty-five minutes later, along the Northshore of the island. It's a small little town—dirt roads and somewhat ramshackle houses strewn about like they were tossed down in a handful from the sky.

"Keep walking down that trail you see there for half a mile and you'll see it," the driver says. "My taxi'll get stuck if I try it on that road."

James nods and shoulders his pack, starting off down a rutted dirt lane abutted on either side by rows of blooming trees. The salt of the ocean rushes into his nose, and the wind gently rustles as it drapes over the surface of the island.

His heart is pounding. He'd sat white-knuckled the entire plane ride and thought about what he would say—how he would somehow justify that he basically, at the heart of it, flew all the way across an ocean and hopped in a taxi for the sole purpose of saying, "Thanks for not being a dick and letting me drown."

It feels humiliatingly unnecessary. Who in their right mind would have stood there and watched him be carried limply out to sea without even trying to save him?

Then he remembers. *"Turn and face me like the fucking man you pretend to be all the time!"*

And that right there is why he didn't just ask Lori for Danny's phone number, he thinks as he trudges down the lane, purposefully taking slow steps. Because he wouldn't have faulted Danny one goddamn bit if he hadn't just left James to drown in his own defensive anger and self-pity in the sand. If he had told everyone at the funeral that he wished he'd noticed James fall under the wave before walking away.

The road turns a corner and opens up to a small clearing, a two-story farmhouse in whitewashed wood sitting primly in the center. James gapes. It's the absolute last thing he expected to see. He triple-checks the address in his hand with the painted numbers on the house and frowns. There's perfect blooming flowerbeds hanging off the porch in floral rows, and a peeling wood rocking chair, and wind chimes swaying from the eaves. The long, salty grasses covering the clearing fan out in waves from the house's walls, as if the house had been dropped in the middle of the sea itself, and the water drained.

James shoves the paper back in his pocket and stares straight at the brass doorknob. He doesn't allow himself to hesitate and strides clear up to the door, praying to God that whatever eventually comes out of his mouth will somehow be the right thing to say.

He knocks, and a few moments later the door creaks open on screaming hinges. James stops midway through the word "hi" when he sees it's an old man looking out at him, suspenders over a thin white tank top and old khaki pants. The man doesn't say anything, and they stare at each other. He keeps the door open just enough to poke out his face and the tip of his nose.

Finally James shuts his mouth, licks his lips, and tries again.

"I'm looking for Danny?"

The man doesn't say a word, just slowly points a shaky finger down a side lane that James hadn't noticed walking up, leading out from the clearing and down a winding dirt road in between the trees, cutting down a slope to the distant beach.

When James turns back to thank the man, the door's already shutting in his face. He stares blankly at the whitewashed wood in front of him as the slam echoes in his ears. When he finally wills his body to start moving towards the lane, he finds the wind gone from his sails. The false start robbed him of any courage he'd mustered up, and he shakes his head at himself, feeling pathetic and foolish as he starts to make his way through the sagging trees.

He can just make out the roar of the ocean building as he walks, beckoning out to him through the warm air. He hasn't even been in the water since the accident. He'd tried to, just yesterday. Put on his trunks and grabbed his board and left his apartment with confidence in his step and determination in the set of his shoulders. And he'd stood there on a crowded beach watching a pack of surfers already in the water, ripping across the pounding waves with security and ease.

And he'd gasped as he again felt the harsh slap of the water against his back, and the sharp pain of the rock slamming into his forehead, and the trembling, guttural moan of the sea as it dragged him half-conscious out into the cold, dark deep. He'd tried to blink the fear out of his eyes, looked side to side to make sure no one was staring, picked up his board and walked straight back up the road to his apartment. Called the World Surf League people the second he set down his board and said he had to drop from the Billabong—unexpected injury.

And now, as he puts one foot in front of the other down the shaded lane of cocooning green, James tells himself to stop in his tracks, turn right around, and go back. That Danny will be embarrassed for him if he says what he has to say—that he came all this way just to see a man who probably hates him. To thank him for doing something that anyone in their right mind would have done.

James fiddles with the bullet casing in his pocket, unbuttons and re-buttons the top of his quarter-neck grey shirt. Before he can force himself to turn back, he rounds a bend and freezes.

The thick brush opens up before him to a small white sand beach, perfectly cradled on either side by rocky outcroppings which frame an endless sea of clear blue. A wooden hut covered in faded teal paint emerges from the dark green shadows of the trees, jutting out over the sand with a thatched roof and huge windows, an overhang of eaves draped with hanging braids of shells blowing in the breeze. James barely has time to take any of it in before his ears register soft music, slowly plucked strings. His gaze zeroes in on the hammock besides the house strung up between two palm trees, swaying slowly back and forth and with one long, bony foot hanging off its side.

When James had first taken that folded up paper with an address on it from Lori's hand and shoved it in his pocket, he'd briefly pictured a tiny apartment by the sea, the mirror image of his own. Maybe a small, ramshackle house, or a room on the outskirts of the city if he really thought about it—he had no idea what you could afford on an island like this.

But this, this perfect bubble of paradise, floating on the calm sea as if the earth was cupping its palms to hold together Danny's private world, it makes James fiercely embarrassed for having intruded.

In a blinding panic he realizes this is all a mistake. He shouldn't be here, stomping into this secluded stretch of beach without an invitation, without the calm or the beauty within himself to fully appreciate it. With every breath he takes, he can practically see himself contaminating the glittering shore, polluting it with the haunted darkness seeping out through his skin—a grey cloud of smog exhaled with each breath from his lungs.

It's a lost cause. James grits his teeth and turns to leave, already debating whether to even stay on the island for the Billabong, when the music in the air suddenly stops.

He instantly knows he's been noticed. James waits with a sinking heart as the hammock creaks against the tree trunks, and one long leg reaches over the side to stand up on the soft sand. James doesn't even move as Danny turns his head back warily to look towards the road, and his eyes fly wide open when he sees James standing there in the clearing of the trees. Danny bolts up to standing, the uke left hanging from his fingertips.

"James," he says, breathless.

They stand there staring. Danny's mouth is wide open, his eyes blinking rapidly and fixed on James' face. James is absolutely pinned by the gaze, unable to form a sentence to say why or how or what—none of the words he'd been lamely practicing in his head since first sitting down in the plane. The calm breeze winds through the seashells hanging from the eaves of the house, softly clinking in the still, clear air.

Danny looks like he's broken. He's dressed in pajama bottoms and an old, thin t-shirt in the middle of the afternoon. His hair is frazzled and big, face fresh and young. He gapes at James with his mouth still open, chest rising and falling, eyes pouring over every inch of James' body in wide disbelief.

And James realizes in one glorious second that Danny isn't angry. That for some reason the sight of Danny Moore like this, unmasked and shocked, surprised in the warm cocoon of his private haven, is causing every muscle in James' tense body to relax like warm water. He knows now why he didn't turn back in the lane.

James keeps a light voice and casually shrugs his shoulders. "Guess you didn't predict this one, huh?"

Danny blinks once more slowly, then shakes his head back into focus and snaps his mouth shut. His brain seems to come back alive, and he stands up straight, shoving his hands in his flannel pockets and clearing his throat. James stops himself just in time from letting out a laugh.

"Yes, well, it's obvious you still had your plane ticket for the Billabong, and I'm sure you got a week of sick leave off work, so you thought you might as well at least give yourself a vacation and scope out the competition for next year," he rattles off smoothly.

James takes a careful step forward in the sand. His shoes sink too deep into the soft grains. "Sure, yeah. But that doesn't explain why I'm actually here."

Danny's eyes lose the sharp burst of confidence for a beat, and his body sags like air let out from a balloon. "No, it doesn't."

He looks wary, uncertain. James knows he needs to get this over with quickly before he loses his nerve. He's so tempted to keep on with the joking conversation, pretend nothing's happened between them since James sipped water from his Navy canteen and joked with Danny on the sand two minutes before Rob walked up.

He has to do this, though. He thinks of Danny on the pier, and he thinks of Keith Hartman handing him a bullet casing in the terrible silence of the hospital room, and he *has* to.

"Look, well, I'm sorry I dropped in like this. On this." James nods out at the house and the ocean. Danny's eyes don't leave his face.

"I just wanted to—needed to . . . ah shit." James looks down at the sand and takes a deep breath as he rubs a hand over his mouth, already hating every phrase that comes into his head. It all sounds so trite. So pathetic and lame. Like a poorly veiled excuse just to spy on Danny's private world. He puts his hand in his pocket and rubs the worn, smooth metal with his thumb. He tries again.

"This is the second time someone's saved my life, and the first time I never said thank you. So I couldn't . . . I can't move on from this without thanking you. You know, saying the words."

Danny shrugs his shoulders and glances down at his toes. "I hardly saved your life. Like you said, you just got sucked under. And whoever did it before wasn't expecting thanks anyway. It was their job. There's nothing you need to say."

"But I do. You did. I mean, we were . . . I'd just said . . . and you came back after me and pulled me out—"

"I just did what anyone would do."

"But this wasn't just . . . I wasn't just sucked under, and you saved me. You—"

"You were fine. Anyone would've helped you out, but—"

"—you got me to breathe again."

James stares at Danny's toes for the following beat of thick silence, then looks back up at his speechless face when Danny doesn't say anything more. He notices for the first time the faint bruise on his cheek, just under his eye. The sight of it makes James sick to his stomach, prickling hot sweat forming up along his spine, followed by a cold shiver.

He forces himself not to lick his lips, refuses to remember the wet, soft mouth against his. He's ashamed by it now, standing in front of Danny. Ashamed that this man dropped to his knees in the pounding spray and pushed air into his struggling lungs only for James to interpret it as a kiss in a feverish half-daze.

Danny's eyes are soft and sad. There's another cautious emotion hidden in the corners of his mouth, one James can't quite interpret, not from so many feet away. James takes another step forward in the sand and wills his face to look as earnest as possible.

"Look, I—I just need to say it," he says in a steady voice. "You saved my life. Thank you."

Danny doesn't retort this time, just hangs his head for a moment before looking cautiously back up at James. He runs a hand over the back of his neck, eyes roving like they're lost. "You're welcome," he finally says. His voice is so gentle James has to strain to hear it.

And just as Danny's voice reaches James' ears, he feels the moment start to tingle at the edges, threatening to pulse and thrum the way the air always does whenever he's anywhere near Danny Moore. He swallows, then shivers as a bead of sweat drips down into the hollow of his throat.

James wants to stand in it forever—this unspoken, unprecedented question of *what now?* Wants to feel the air warming in slow, electric tingles up his arms and straight into the center of his chest.

But then he sees in his mind's eye how out of place he must look standing on Danny's beach in his too-hot shirt with his shoes in the sand. The rolling warm air turns sharp and stale, and in a blink James is back to being an intrusion again. Unneeded and irrelevant now that he's finally got out what he needed to say.

He lets the easy silence, the flickering pulse still clinging to his skin, last for one more indulgent moment. Then he clears his throat loudly and takes a casual step back, breaking the air back into an average, stable calm.

"Right, well, I'll leave you be. If you come down to watch the competition, don't be a stranger."

He turns to leave before Danny can even respond, hating the fact that every fiber of his being wants to stay rooted to his spot in the sand. He's only half a dozen steps away when he hears a word called out sharply into the peaceful quiet.

"James!"

He flashes back to Danny calling out his name in desperation outside the showers—that second ever time Danny's mouth had formed the sounds. He turns slowly, looking just over his shoulder. He raises his eyebrows in a silent *"yeah?"*

Danny runs his fingers through his curls and opens his mouth twice before saying anything. His feet shuffle in the sand.

"Would you—do you want to see the island tomorrow? Just that the competition isn't for two days, and you'll just be here with nothing to do, and I thought that maybe . . . well there's this road we can drive down that people think is scenic, and I have a Jeep, or there's some choice spots to swim, or I could even tell you where you should go check out on your own, or—"

"Yes."

Danny pauses mid-word and blinks. "Yes . . . you'd like that?"

James fights to keep the smile from brimming over onto his face. His heart feels tight and warm in his chest, the same way it did whenever he woke up and saw the pale blue swimming shorts laid out on his tiny bed.

"Sure. I mean, famous local like you. I'd be an idiot to say no to that."

Danny smirks, glancing away toward the rest of the beach with a twist in his mouth. But James catches the hints of a smile there, a real, soulful smile lighting up the contours of Danny's face, turning the corners of his eyes into little pieces of glittering sky.

Rob had told him something once, in one of the quiet, raw moments between a set. Something about how Lori made him want to fly and bury himself below the earth at the same time. How the grounding brush of Lori's hair on his cheek when he held her always got all tangled up with the wing-like curves of her shoulders beneath his arms.

Ridiculously, James thinks he suddenly understands more of what Rob was saying than he ever had before, even on the nights when Rob's hair was against his own cheek in his foggy dreams.

"Well, guess I'll come back here in the morning, then," James adds, turning once again to go. It's easier to turn away this time, knowing he'll see this specific piece of horizon line again tomorrow.

Danny nods, standing stock still in the sand. "Any time."

James thinks he hears a whisper when he's already halfway down the lane, a voice carried faintly on the breeze, hidden deep in his mind. It's illusive and far away, shivering up his spine and trembling through the boughs on the swaying trees.

"*Thank God*," the whisper says, in a voice more desperate than when Keith had screamed, "*For God's sake, Jimmy, save yourself and run!*"

# 12

James lies awake, staring at the ceiling of his Honolulu motel room at four a.m., counting down the seconds until it's a reasonable hour to get up. He'd spent the rest of yesterday wandering in somewhat of a daze. He'd tried to do a bit of sightseeing along the sleepy North Shore after leaving Danny's beach behind him down the lane, but found he couldn't focus long enough to even look at what was right in front of him.

It had felt wrong, somehow, seeing those sights alone with Danny Moore back in his hammock just a few miles away. So he'd hopped on a bus he hoped was heading back towards the city and spent the rest of the evening hunting down a cheap motel, a cheap dinner, and a cheap paperback to pretend to read in his motel room until his stinging eyes finally closed in sleep.

At 5:45, he groans and allows himself to pop up from the shitty mattress. He figures if he takes extra long to get dressed, and walks as far as he absolutely can to find coffee and something to eat for breakfast, and then walks all the way back to his motel before hopping back on the bus he now knows will take him out near Danny's home, he'll be there just late enough in the morning that it will be reasonable. That it won't be absolutely pathetic what time he's there.

He's burning with questions that swirl maddeningly through his mind as he navigates the unfamiliar city streets. What Danny does for a living, who he surfs with along the shore over on the other side of the island, how he ended up with that house, how he ended up with his own fucking private *beach*, if he sways alone on that hammock all the hours he isn't doing . . . whatever the hell else he does.

James' mind is whirring so intently that he doesn't even check his watch until he's just stepping off the bus, five minutes away from the dirt road leading down to Danny's hut. James curses under his breath and groans. It's only quarter to eight.

He really is a chump. He's a nervous, sweating teenager on the doorstep of his prom date's house, realizing he's thirty minutes early and too afraid to knock on the door. He's a sore thumb in the middle of tropical paradise.

He certainly doesn't feel like a grown-ass man, a fucking professional surfing vet on a relaxing vacation in Hawaii. He doesn't feel like he's even lived a day of his own life.

He looks around him at the small, sleepy town, though, and quickly realizes he doesn't really have another option. It's either wander around Danny's little stretch of beach until he wakes up, looking absolutely stupid and trying not to feel too small or embarrassed, or it's wander around this town as the new town creep. With a resigned sigh, he moves down the now-familiar path towards the beach, quieting his steps through the brush as much as he can.

He eases his way around the last bend in the shaded lane, watching the early sunlight drift through the trees in swaths of swirling gold. He's expecting to find a quiet, sleepy hut with gently lapping waves, still enshrouded in the cocoon of stillness from the night before.

Instead he nearly jumps out of his skin when he hears, "James, you're here! Excellent. I see you ate breakfast. Coffee before we go?"

Danny Moore is standing on his patio, leaning out over the railing and gazing at the sea, fully dressed in khaki shorts and a black t-shirt with a mug of coffee in his hand, sunglasses hanging off the front of his collar.

James stops in his tracks and tries to mentally catch up. He feels like a kid caught out sneaking around after bedtime. "I, uh—I honestly didn't think you'd be awake."

"Yeah, yeah, sure. And you thought I'd wake up and see you on my beach and think you were a creep and then you'd be humiliated forever. Dull. This way we get a head start on the day, dig it?"

Without waiting for James to answer, Danny ducks back into the hut for a moment and emerges with a backpack and a thermos which James barely catches after it's tossed his way. Without even being on boards out in the waves, James is back in the whirlwind, back to being the breathless disciple chasing after the sunlit storm. Back to being completely out of his depth.

He ignores the small voice in the back of his head that feels patronized by Danny's impersonation of a goddamn tour guide leading the way in front of him. Instead he lets his excitement and curiosity cautiously grow, drawing him forward with each step as he follows Danny back down the lane and through the trees up to the whitewashed house.

He follows him in silence, looking at every branch and leaf he passes instead of the back of Danny's calves. Danny's walking the same way he did that day on the dockyard—the way James watched him walk up to the starting line in Hermosa a lifetime ago. Legs long and confident, back swift and straight.

"You're probably wondering whose door you knocked on yesterday," Danny says.

James rolls his eyes. "You know, I almost forgot after four days how much you love showing off."

To his surprise, Danny doesn't argue back, but just tilts his head to the side. "Bummer for you," he says, slightly out of breath from their brisk walk just as the red Jeep parked to the side of the house comes into view.

Before James can clarify he was just joking, Danny continues, "Anyways, his name's Chuck Hobbs. He's a writer. No idea what the hell he actually writes—never seen it. He never leaves his house, goddamn terrified of it. But he complains all the time that he can't write stories if he isn't around people, right? So I told him I'd meet with clients at his house and use it as an office, and he can watch and take notes in the corner like he's my ancient secretary, and then in return I get his old beach hut for dirt cheap."

James climbs into the Jeep besides Danny and says an automatic, "Yeah, right on," then halts as he tries to slot all the rapid-fire information into his head.

"Wait, your clients?"

Danny starts the Jeep with a roar and revs the engine as they pull out of the weeds. James barely fastens his seatbelt in time.

"I fix people's broken shit—not sure what you'd call that." Danny keeps his eyes square on the road, one arm hanging out the rolled-down

140

window as he rattles on. "Technology, mostly. Televisions, radios, phones, that sort of thing. Do it for a lot of businesses too down in the city. I'm half the price of any other shop."

James' mouth is hanging open. "But that's . . . how do you even know how to do that?"

Danny shrugs and steals the thermos in James' hands to take a long sip of coffee. "Dunno. Just tried it once when I was a teenager and realized I was good at it. Way to make a living—most of the time."

James gapes at him in silence, then bursts out into an uneasy laugh. "Shit, man, you're something else."

Danny smiles over at him quickly, the expression a little stiff on his face, then turns back to the winding road to focus. James can feel that something is off between them—too wired and tense and frantic. It dawns on him as Danny navigates them through the narrow dirt roads that he knows more about Danny Moore right now than he ever has by a landslide. That Danny's lobbing the answers to his unvoiced questions right back at him one after the other. And yet in the same moment, the air between them sits thickly with a cold, dull thud. The little pulse, the little flicker, is nowhere to be seen.

James looks down at his own hands held unnaturally formal in his lap, the way his back is straight and his knees pointed perfectly forward. It dawns on him with a surprisingly sickening roll of emotion: they're both trying too hard.

And the problem is, James doesn't know what he's even trying to do in the first place. To be buds? Rivals again? The life saver and the life savee? Two people who happen to surf together? Casual strangers?

The subtle wrongness of it all builds in his chest as they continue to drive, Danny pointing out facts about the island here and there in quick, unemotional words, and James left trying to absorb it all from the passenger seat. Danny's left knee bobs incessantly as he flies across the familiar roads, and James knows he hasn't sat up straight for so long since inspections back in Vietnam—not even for his interview to get the job at the docks.

After over an hour, Danny pulls off the winding road and parks, ending his explanation of a new flower that was recently discovered on the mountain towering behind them. The silence without the revving engine is deafening. Neither one of them moves to get out.

The air settles around them, thick and choking. Nothing like how it fizzled the last time they were in a car together back in Los Angeles, all warm and rested and clear. James wants Danny to move his leg over and press it against his like he did before. To hear him ask him quiet questions and watch his body melt into the car seat, muscles completely relaxed.

But instead, when he closes his eyes, all he can see is his mind's recreation of Kip's fist meeting with Danny's cheek. All he can hear is his own furious, threatening voice screaming at Danny until he chased him away on the shore, yesterday's *"thank you"* and *"you're welcome"* well and forgotten.

James knows the day can't go on like this, surreal as it is to be sitting in a Jeep on a gorgeous Hawaiian island beside the greatest surfer of her waves—beside *the* Danny Moore. James sits up a bit and clears his throat. His mind whirrs for the right thing to say to try and make things right. Wonders if he should apologize or make a joke or take his leave. If he should ask Danny if his bruise hurts, if what James told him about the war was all too much, if he felt James' lips move beneath his for that horrible second by the rushing tide.

He starts saying the first words that come to mind, just to end the silence. "Look, Danny, you've done me a solid today with . . . with showing me around like this. Would've been hell sitting around in the motel, but I'm—"

"I'm sorry, James."

James stops mid-word. "What?"

Danny takes a moment to think, scrunching his lips, then sighs through his nose as he gazes out over the floral blanketed cliffs in front of them, weighed down by the strong breeze.

"What I said to you that day. About the policem—about your friend. I'm sorry."

James takes a slow breath. Danny's voice is low and sincere, the apology carefully formed on his lips. The intimacy of it, sitting knee to knee in a silent car with nobody around for miles, discussing insults hurled at each other moments before Danny pulled James from the waves, it bears down on him with a heavy weight.

James runs his palm along his thigh. "Yeah, well, I shouldn't have said any of the shit I said either. You know, about the rumor or . . . or that shit about the man you're pretending to be."

Danny lets out a single laugh, low and brusque. "I think this entire island would line up to disagree with you there," he says, the sarcasm not quite hiding a darker tone.

Without thinking about it, James moves his leg so that it brushes against Danny's, and he holds it there, letting the warmth grow between their skin. He waits, heart pounding, as Danny's body tenses up next to his, the air in the car vibrating with tension. Long seconds pass.

And then, with a long exhaled breath, Danny pushes back warm and firm against James' touch. He settles back into his seat. James unclenches his fists.

The icy, frantic vastness of the air between them suddenly vanishes, and the cold weight is lifted off James' lungs with the change in the atmosphere. They sit together, gazing out over the gorgeous landscape, as the breeze rustles gently through the car's open top and sides. James knows he doesn't have to say anything more. His leg against Danny's is somehow enough.

After a minute, Danny steals the thermos again for another sip of lukewarm coffee and grimaces.

"God, how have you been drinking this shit on the whole drive?"

James laughs. "You haven't had coffee on a Navy ship. Makes that taste like something you'd drink in Paris."

"Oh, were you in the Navy? I didn't know," Danny shoots back with a smirk, and James pushes him in the shoulder and curses at him, not even bothering to fight the grin creeping onto his face. And for the first time in years, James Campbell feels eighteen years old again without the familiar accompanying wave of shame—that he should be moved on from a racing heart at another man's touch, from the sound of another's laugh wrapping itself around his own lungs.

Everything changes.

They spend the entire morning touring the island in the Jeep, stopping now and again to get out and look at the view. Danny makes fun of James for gasping every ten minutes, and James rolls his eyes when Danny gets twenty minutes too deep into a discussion of one beach's waves or a specific site's historical fact. It's the sort of vacation his mom used to talk about with faraway eyes, licking the spoon from her annual milkshake, and then she'd shake her head and tell James that they already lived in paradise, in the City of Angels, so what more could they need?

Danny knows the island like an intimate friend. Can read every rise and fall of the earth like a novel waiting to be cracked open and adored, the same way James watched him predict every swell of the waves. James listens to Danny's warm, smooth voice vibrate with energy and sits back as the words rush over him like warm, gentle water. He feels wide-eyed and light, desperate to take in every sight to see in this new and brimming landscape, and at the same time he can't help but feel absolutely assured, as if he's been to these same places hundreds of times before. Danny Moore at his side.

They stop for lunch at a little stand Danny knows about that seems to appear out of nowhere next to the one lane highway stretching alongside the beach. Danny orders for them both before James can get a word in and then leaves James with his mouth hanging open when a man inside the trailer home behind the food stand leaps out the door and bear hugs Danny after running to him across the grass.

The man is older, a native Islander. They whisper quietly together for a moment, both sets of eyes darting quickly once to James off to the side. Finally the man pats Danny once on the back with a smile and goes to speak to the boy in the little kitchen.

James shoots Danny a look that says *"what the hell was that about?"* and Danny merely shrugs.

"I rigged up his cash register for him a few years back, made some improvements."

It's the most anticlimactic explanation James has ever heard. He's also never seen someone bear hug another human being over a cash register. But Danny turns back to get their food, leaving James alone with his questions. Danny silently hands him a bowl made of banana leaves once James is sitting on a wooden bench overlooking the ocean by the road.

"Poke," Danny answers James' silent question. He sits down so their knees are touching. James thinks it's a mistake, but neither one of them shifts or moves.

Danny talks over a stuffed full mouth. "Lahela used to make it for us all the time. My father would make her grill him a separate steak or something and my little brother wouldn't touch it with a ten-foot pole, so I got triple helpings of it every time."

James takes a bite and almost moans. It's the most delicious thing he's put in his mouth in years. He thinks of his usual dinners of plain boiled pasta with canned sauce and feels a blush spread across the back of his neck. Danny practically devours his share next to him.

"You have a little brother?" James asks, suddenly needing their voices to cover up the small moans and sighs of Danny's chewing.

Danny pauses, food midway to his mouth, then finishes the bite and swallows, taking twice as long to chew.

"Had," he finally says.

"Shit, sorry, I didn't—"

"He's not dead."

James frowns, then watches Danny place another unenthusiastic bite of food in his mouth out of the corner of his eye.

He doesn't know what to say. He feels small and out of place sitting in this sacred landscape, holding up a bowl of food to his mouth that he's never even heard of, digging secrets from the man next to him whom the entire island would gladly pay to watch surf across their own waves, jackass reputation or no. That sensation of being an intruder starts to settle slowly upon his shoulders once more. That his haunted thoughts are contaminating—unworthy of what's so far been one of the most perfect, easy days of his life.

That Danny could be doing literally anything else that day, and instead he's choosing to waste his time ferrying around the *old washed out vet.*

Then Danny's knee presses gently against his, and it stays there as they sit at the edge of the earth for all the ocean to see. James blinks hard against the sudden sheen of water in his eyes. His lungs expand. All he can feel in the moment is calm.

"I'll be right back," Danny says with his mouth full, wiping a hand over his lips. "Need to make a quick call on his phone."

James finishes his food while Danny's back inside the little shack, still not quite believing his dumb luck that he, of all the goddamn people on the planet, is being given a private tour of a Hawaiian island by the champion of her waves—the man who made an entire Los Angeles beach hold their breath with fear and awe.

Him, James Campbell, who was just lying in a fucking hospital bed four days ago because he'd turned his back to the sea like an absolute moron, and gotten knocked down onto some rocks like a little kid. Who looks ten years older than he is and moves with a tired ache in his limbs. Who should've died on a beach all the way across the world, or spent this whole day sitting around blankly in a Honolulu motel room, or been back at a dockyard loading shipping containers. *He* is the one to feel Danny Moore's hand on his shoulder, warm and soft, asking if he's ready to go.

They step back into the Jeep and Danny pauses, fiddling with his keys. "I don't mind dropping you back near the airport," he says, voice slow.

James hopes he's not imagining the vague sense of "*please say no*" behind those words. He takes the leap. "Please don't make me sit in a fucking motel room the rest of the day."

Danny's face softens, a small grin on his lips. The sight of it makes James want to pump his fist. "You have a point. If you just moped around for the rest of the day, you'd be a real drag at the competition tomorrow. They'd never invite you back."

"Oh, sit on it. Just take me somewhere I can take a piss unless you want me to wreck your car."

"What are you, six?"

"Give or take a few decades, yes. Now step on it."

"Let's boogie, as the kids say?"

"You *are* 'the kids.'"

Danny tilts his head in the now-familiar gesture of assent, and James smiles when he sees Danny's driving them back in the direction of his house. The drive passes by in peaceful silence, only the wind roaring as it rushes through their hair.

They park in the patch of grass by the house and walk down the shadowed lane together with ambling steps, Danny kicking a small rock ahead and doing soccer tricks with it with his sandaled feet. James thinks about joining in, but holds himself back. He pictures what his coworkers back at the docks would think if he did—watching him act half his age playing around in the middle of a paradise postcard. Watching him steal a hidden glance at the flex of muscle across Danny's lower stomach when his shirt flies up.

James catches himself sighing in relief at the sight of the hut. He has absolutely no reason on earth to be thinking of this place as home. No reason to feel his body relax when it comes into view. And yet . . .

Danny does, too. James is watching him too closely to miss the quick release of breath, the small tension in his lean shoulders which had been there all morning which instantly leaves the moment their feet hit the sand. Danny kicks off his shoes and leaves them haphazard outside before running up the few steps to the still-open door.

He points to the bushes next to them and says, "There's your bathroom," even though James can see the pipework from plumbing running along the side of the hut. James gives him a sharp look and catches Danny's self-satisfied smirk as he disappears in front of him into the hut.

James takes the bait and relieves himself outside, trying to calm the sudden fluttering in his chest. When he's done he wipes his hands off on his shorts, puts one foot on the steps, and pauses. This action feels momentous, even though James can't come up with a clue as to why. The way the wooden stair creaks under the weight of his leg, as if it wasn't used to a body besides Danny's climbing into the house. The way Danny's hesitating just inside the door, out of sight but clearly waiting to hear James walk up to the door.

James tells himself that it's the burning curiosity to see the inside of Danny Moore's house which is making him take the stairs two-at-a-time, even while a small part of him whispers that he can't stand the thought of Danny waiting inside alone. After one last look at the ocean he steps through the front door, eyes blinking to adjust to the dimmer light.

The inside is small—a main room with a kitchen along one wall and a door he suspects must lead to a bed. Almost every wall is made of windows, looking out to the trees and the sea through a dusting of sand. And the books—textbooks, from what James can quickly see—are covering the table, parts of the floor, the little shelves built into the kitchen walls which were meant to store plates and bowls.

A basket of random wires and metal parts sits overflowing in front of the worn, hand-me-down couch. Standing in one corner is an old surfboard James didn't ever see Danny use back in LA, cracked and worn along the surface, with traces of paint stained into the waxed wood.

James does a quick sweep with his eyes and hides a small frown. He can't quite match the room before him with the man he's just spent all day with in the Jeep, let alone the man who towers above people on the beach, or wins Billabong Masters championships, or understands every inch of a breaking wave. The man who'd just played soccer with a rock in his sandals walking down the lane, hands shoved down in his pockets, curls in his face.

The room seems hollow, somehow. Empty like it's still waiting to be lived in and filled. As if it exists as merely a roof for Danny to sleep under after he's spent a day working his ass off out in the waves.

It looks like James picked up his own irrelevant apartment and plopped it right in the middle of an Oahu beach.

He takes a step further inside, acutely aware of the fact Danny's standing, frozen, watching him from the corner. His eyes roam over the few pieces of furniture in the room, made of thick and sturdy wood, and he says the first thought that pops into his head. Anything to interrupt the silence buzzing in the air.

"Not many people your age who have a house full of handmade furniture," he says. "Well, not many who have a house on a fucking beach, either, but . . . you know."

Danny stands awkwardly and grips one elbow, watches James look around, then shrugs. "Didn't really need to buy any of it. I built it."

James lets out a chuckle that sounds more like a sigh and grips the back of the nearest wooden chair with his hand. "Of course you did," he says under his breath. He wants to go home and throw his Goodwill couch and crooked table in the trash. Wants to ask Danny if sanding the wood leaves calluses on his hands. If the ocean softens them again.

His eyes catch sight of a single photograph sitting on top of a side table in a corner. Besides the surfboard, it's the only personalized thing in the room. He's drawn to it like a magnet, quickly stepping across the creaking floor.

A young curly-haired boy looks back at him, shit-eating grin over his whole freckled face. A woman crouches behind him and holds him around the middle, eyes bright behind huge cat-eye glasses with a smile that's just barely forming on her lips. There's a row of military jets behind them, lined up on hot white cement and steaming asphalt.

Before he realizes what he's doing, James picks up the framed photograph in his hands. There's writing just along the bottom in a long, feminine scrawl, and he squints hard to read it.

"*Me and Sydney. Ft. Knox, 1962*"

"That's my momma," Danny says quietly from the corner, with the hint of an accent James has never heard him use before.

James looks up startled, palms starting to sweat. He has the prickling sensation of being caught out. Then, with a great clunk, something suddenly slots into place in his brain. The day of the accident. Their argument by the shore.

"Sydney—that's your real name?" he asks.

Danny nods, looking down at his bare feet shuffling on the floor. "My first name," he says in a near-whisper, then he quickly straightens his spine. "But nobody ever calls me that. Only her. She named me after Sidney Howard, apparently, but my father said it sounded too much like 'sissy'—made it so I only ever went by my middle name."

"Daniel?"

Danny huffs under his breath. "Wouldn't know it, considering I've only ever been called Danny. I would've given an opinion, but, you know . . . couldn't talk yet and all that."

James hums under his breath and half grins, still staring at the woman's bright smile, then he pulls his gaze away from the photo and frowns up at Danny. "Sidney Howard?"

Danny rubs the back of his neck and shrugs a shoulder. "He wrote 'Gone With the Wind'—was her favorite film."

Pain flashes through James' chest. "Was?"

Danny quickly cuts him off with a tight smile: "Not dead, either."

James nods slowly, unable to tears his gaze away from the brimming little boy in the photo, small, thin hands holding on tight to his mom's freckled arms.

"So, your dad's military, then?" he tries.

Danny just hums.

James feels the air immediately start to turn tense. Watches Danny close off from him bit by bit the longer he holds the photograph in his hands. With one last glance, he sets it back down on the table, matching up the angle with how it was before.

He's overflowing with questions, exploding with curiosity in his mind. He knows there's only one thing he can ask, though. Only one way to show Danny that he understands living in a house with only one photograph decorating the entire place.

"What's her name?"

Danny lets a quick breath out his nose and shoots James a knowing smile. "Ruth, after the woman in the Bible. Hence the 'Daniel'."

James runs a hand over the back of his neck, trying to hide his shock at the word 'Bible' coming so casually out of Danny Moore's mouth. "Man, I wouldn't know who the hell either of those people were if you put a gun to my head," he finally says, and he feels warmth tingle through his body when Danny's face breaks into a laugh.

"Nobody came up and asked you that question in the middle of the jungle then?"

"Shockingly, no. We were all busy."

James walks toward him in the kitchen, enjoying the loss of tension in the room, when his eyes alight on a contraption taking up almost half the counter—wires and tubes and switches in what looks like a tangled heep.

"Aw shit, this whole hut is a bomb, isn't it?"

Danny rolls his eyes at the poor joke. "It's nothing. Just something I'm tinkering with."

"That's what people who make bombs in their garage tell the police—just ask Rob."

He nearly flinches at the name slipping out of his mouth, but relaxes when Danny doesn't appear to register it at all.

"I highly doubt the criminal classes are most concerned with coffee."

"Coffee?"

Danny turns towards the contraption and points at the parts, trying somewhat unsuccessfully to sound bored. "Coffee. It's a machine that connects with my alarm clock through a wire I ran in the wall. When it goes off, the electricity creates an imbalance of air pressure, which forces water through the tubes here across the induction burner, and meanwhile the battery operates this lever here which scoops up the grinds and places it in the filter, here, and so when the hot water reaches the end of the boiling process it drips through and starts making fresh coffee. Hands-free."

James stares. "You built an automatic coffee maker that's triggered by your alarm clock in an entirely different room?"

Danny suddenly seems unsure of himself. He doesn't quite meet James' eyes. "Yes . . ."

James shakes his head and lets out a breath, crossing his arms over his chest. "That's fucking brilliant."

When Danny genuinely smiles, chest puffing out a bit, James goes on. "Seriously, how you even . . . Whatever college I'm sure you went to when you were still in kindergarten must have snatched you up. I mean, this is unreal."

An odd look flashes across Danny's face, but it disappears before James even understands it's there. He clears his throat and leans against the counter. "Yeah. They must have."

Something feels off, and James tries to smooth it over with more mindless talking. "But I'll shut it. You must get tired of explaining it to all the idiots like me that trudge through here."

Danny's face grows even more serious, and his eyes narrow at James in thought. A silent moment passes before he speaks. James wonders why everything he's said in the last thirty seconds has felt like massively fucking up.

Danny gives a casual shrug, but his eyes turn a shade of dark grey. "Actually, nobody else has ever been here," he says.

James stands dangerously close to Danny in the tiny kitchen, watching his chest rise and fall in the buzzing air of the frozen room. He knows he should say something about that, can see the way Danny's eyes are trying to read his face for a response. He should change the subject or take a step back or ask him what for or *something*.

Instead he stands there, breathing in tandem with Danny's chest, feeling for the first time the close intimacy of their shared air in the quiet hut, the sound of the distant waves echoing through the windows.

James swallows over a dry throat, then looks up into Danny's face. Their eyes meet. James tries, but finds he doesn't give a shit what his coworkers would think watching him have to stare *up* into somebody's face.

What Rob Depaul would think.

"Okay," James hears himself say. His voice rasps across the word—a word which he's never noticed in his life could carry so much meaning.

Danny's own voice is a low whisper. "The sun will set soon. You want a good view?"

James nods, and still they don't move apart. He can't look away from Danny's eyes, the two little droplets of ocean that had made him want to suck in some oxygen and live. There's a loose eyelash draped across Danny's left cheek. James realizes he could brush it off with his nose if he rose up on his toes and tried.

Finally, Danny slowly moves his hand toward James, then hesitates, hovering over his skin. James holds his breath, lips dry, as Danny gently places his hand at the top of James' forearm, gripping his skin beneath his elbow in a warm touch. James' legs turn to water.

"Let's go," Danny whispers. His palm gives a brief squeeze.

They break apart, but the moment stays. It hovers over them as James follows Danny outside and down the private beach, sighing at the velvet-soft sand in between his toes. They climb up the rocky slope at one end of the inlet, using moss and grass for cover under their bare feet as they slowly ascend. James follows in Danny's footsteps up the rocks with total confidence, never more than one small step behind. He listens to their breaths, and realizes they're in time together more often than not.

When they finally reach the top of the rocky overlook, James gasps. Danny chuckles under his breath. The sun hangs low and sweet over the sea, dipping its orange and yellow ribbons into the blue depths and swirling through the clouds. James knows Danny's eyes are on him as he looks out over the view, breathless with the realization he's standing on the edge of the earth. His mind is free of fear. He thinks that if he squinted hard enough, if he peered through the orange haze, he could just make out the trees which had sheltered him from the hellfire on the beach. Just glimpse the fronds from which Keith had emerged with blood on his face.

He meets eyes with Danny, expecting to see the warm, soft gaze from earlier, and instead sees a glint of mischief.

"Oh no. . ." he starts to say, but then Danny is pulling off his shirt and stripping down to his boxers.

"Oh yes," he says back, staring hard at James until he groans and starts to reluctantly pull his own shirt over his head.

"I haven't even been in the water since I almost died, in case you forgot," he says through fabric stretched over his face.

"I haven't forgotten."

"My head isn't even fully healed, it still aches all the time."

"I noticed."

"I'm not even surfing tomorrow. I'm supposed to be out here resting and enjoying myself."

"You are resting, and you are enjoying yourself."

"How do I even know this fucking water's deep enough?"

Danny pauses at the edge of the cliff and gazes back at him over his shoulder. The air between them crackles, alighting into flame. Goosebumps rise in waves across James' bare skin. His hairs stand on end as he looks at the tattoo covering the muscles in Danny's back for the first time on the Oahu shore, dripping down the length of his spine towards sculpted hips.

And Danny's eyes are roaming over every inch of his own body as James simply stands there in his boxers, hands down at his sides. They trace across his ribs, land briefly on the scar. The earth itches with anticipation beneath the soles of his feet.

Danny smirks. "Because I've done this before," he says. And then he jumps.

James runs to the edge with his heart in his throat and peers over just as Danny flips once in the air, curls flying wild in the wind. He crashes into the crystal blue waters below in a heap of limbs, causing the ocean to heave and ripple in frothing waves.

James' chest stays clenched until Danny finally resurfaces, running his fingers back through his curls and spitting out a stream of water. He swims in place and looks back up at James, warm smile on his face.

"Come on then, Mr. Navy," he calls up. "Show me you can swim!"

James goes to laugh, cheeks just starting to grin, when suddenly the wave is booming against the back of his skull, and the rock is slamming into his forehead, and the tides are pulling him, gripping him out to the snarling sea. Icy fear crawls up the back of his neck and swells up his tongue. He's back on the top of the diving platform, waiting for the Lieutenant's hands to shove him from behind. He's back in the tidepools, limp and blue.

He's waking up to no waitress cap hanging from the door.

"James."

The voice breaks him from his trance, slapping him awake. James opens his eyes to see Danny looking up at him, worry in his eyes. James can barely look down over the ledge. He can't form a reply. Hot embarrassment creeps up the backs of his legs, rooting him firmly in place.

"It's alright, James," Danny says. His voice is calm and assured. He isn't lying.

James tries to nod, but it comes out as a strange jerk of his head. The water slaps against his back, the rock rushes up to meet his face.

His mom in the box.

"James. I'll be right here. I'm not going anywhere."

Like a rush of cool spray, James suddenly feels every muscle in his body release, his feet untethered from the ground. The words hover around his body, shielding him from even the harsh rays of the sun itself. It's the relief of seeing that rescue helicopter waiting just off shore. It's the sight of two terrified blue eyes staring down into his.

He takes a step back from the edge and nods down once at Danny without saying a word. Then James Campbell grits his teeth, takes one last deep breath, and runs.

He jumps.

His body soars weightlessly into thin air, floating in the void for an eternal moment before falling towards the earth. The wind roars and thrashes against his body, and the saltwater pounds into his lungs through his nose, and he lets out a whoop from the pit of his chest as the horizon line rushes past.

The ocean water that hits his skin parts beneath him like smooth velvet, enveloping him with a sudden, cool silence. His lungs burn as he makes his way back towards the air, the orange and red of the sunset lighting his way just above the rippling surface of the water.

He finds Danny's eyes and laughs, wide-eyed at himself. At his own daring. "God, you are something else," he pants.

"So are you," Danny responds, smiling. "Well done." His voice is deep and warm. They swim towards each other in the weightless sea, bobbing among the little swells left over from their jumps. James lowers his chin into the water and lets it lap against his lips as he glides. The sound of their combined breathing echoes across the surface, the little droplets falling from their hair like splashes in a vast, wet cavern.

James watches the water gently rise and fall over Danny's chest, tracing smooth, rippling lines over his collarbone, his nipples. The sunlight illuminates Danny's skin, painting it gold.

They stop swimming towards each other when they're nearly chest to chest, cocooned in the sounds of their breathing, the water gently slapping against their bodies, droplets falling from eyelashes as they blink.

Danny licks his lips. "It's shallow enough to stand just a little ways to your right. Sand bar juts out."

James gazes at him and gives a delayed, "okay." It dawns on him with a sickening lurch that he wants, more than anything, to close his eyes and focus on the sound of Danny's voice echoing on the surface of water, trapped between their bodies. The war rages inside him, churning in his stomach. He looks at Danny's kind eyes, his soft mouth, his young face. The droplet of seawater hanging on tight to the tip of his nose.

Danny starts swimming away, seemingly completely ignorant of the fact that the man sharing the water with him is the real one the other surfers at the competition should warn people about. James grimaces and swims behind Danny until they can stand up to their navels out of the water, expecting Danny to continue to walk towards the shore.

Instead Danny turns so that they're face to face, sharing the heat from their dripping chests.

James finds unexpected words hovering just behind his lips, pressing madly to get out. Apologies for staring at the hollow of Danny's neck, for not having an apartment filled with photographs and beautiful furniture, for having a gnarled scar blasted into his skin instead of inked art. For having killed a man.

But before James can say any of this, Danny blinks the water out of his eyes, takes a step forward, and opens his mouth.

"You were brave," he says.

James shuts his eyes hard and shakes his head. A rueful grimace forms in the corner of his trembling mouth. "That was stupid, back there. I . . . I shouldn't have been scared like that. . . I don't know why the hell I couldn't just—"

The breath is stolen from his lungs as Danny's hand suddenly rises from the water, palm placed firmly right down over the scar on James' chest. James freezes. Danny's hand doesn't flinch.

"James," he says, in a voice that cracks over the word. A voice that pounds within James' own chest. Danny's thumb strokes once across his skin. "You were brave," he says again.

James tries to breathe properly under the feeling of Danny's palm on his chest, covering the most intimate part of his skin, willingly touching the haunted darkness etched forever into his body. He trembles beneath the weight of it, afraid to look Danny in the eyes. He feels deep down that when he does, he will be stripped bare. No longer able to conceal any of his needs or thoughts, not even from himself.

"*Steady on, Jimmy,*" Keith had once said to him, grinning, right as they stepped off that dinghy onto the fatal shore.

James steels himself, and he finally raises his hand to cover Danny's own, sturdy, tan fingers covering long and thin. He meets Danny's gaze and nearly falls forward with a rush of sudden recognition.

The man from the pier.

"I missed you," Danny whispers. His eyes grow wide, as if he's shocked those words just left his mouth.

James nearly groans. He wants to draw the man before him into his body. No—he wants to *be* drawn into his. Kept and protected and held with steady arms.

Danny blinks hard. His hand twitches beneath James' fingers. "I . . . well, not—not really. Not like . . . I know it was just a few days, and you were hurt, and . . . and we barely—"

"Shh," James whispers. His hand travels up Danny's arm. He leans forward, licking his parted lips, at a complete loss for what to say. Danny Moore's wide eyes are indistinguishable from the Oahu sea. "Danny . . ."

James' words fade to a sigh as Danny suddenly reaches out and grasps him in his arms, pulling him close against his body and cupping the back of his neck with his huge, warm hand.

James closes his eyes as his cheek meets Danny's chest. "Fuck, I missed you too," he breathes into his skin.

Danny holds him as the gentle waves lap at their skin, right there in full view of the ocean and sky. James has never experienced anything like this in his entire life. Desperation rolls through his body—hands practically clutching at Danny's back, clinging to the tendrils of the jellyfish, the bones of his shoulder blades. He shivers when Danny's cheek rest against his forehead with a slow glide.

"Is this okay?" Danny whispers. James feels Danny's chest tense against him, anticipating his response.

James opens his mouth to say something back and can't. Finds the words blocked and choked in his throat. He turns his face into the hollow of Danny's neck as an answer. He holds on tighter, sighing as Danny's body relaxes under his once more.

He hears a wet breath in Danny's throat, a shaking sigh. A sudden thought pops into James' head just as they both start to shiver in the evening breeze, the heavy sun having just slipped below the waves. He clings to it like a lifeline.

*This is why Keith Hartman didn't leave you to die on that beach.*

James keeps waiting for the night to turn tense and awkward—for that panicked, internal alarm he'd felt flare through his system in the Hermosa Beach shower to start up again, loud and fierce now that they've held each other skin to skin in the shallows of the waves.

Only, it doesn't.

James is sitting on one of the chairs Danny moved out to his porch, practically devouring the spicy rice dish Danny seemed to whip up out of thin air once they made their way back to the hut from the shore. He's wearing a borrowed pair of Danny's sweats and an old, worn Grateful Dead t-shirt that he doesn't fully believe Danny just randomly bought at a Goodwill.

They sit and look out over the moonlit ocean, illuminated by the lights still on inside the hut, pouring golden pools through the windows onto the sand. James feels like he's lived in this place for a hundred years. The thought of leaving to go back to his bare hotel room churns in the pit of his gut like lead, yanking him down from the heavenly daydream he's been living in all day.

"Just stay here," Danny says, somehow reading his goddamn mind. "Can't catch a bus this late, and there aren't any taxis out here this side of the island. Couch isn't that bad—I've slept on it plenty of times."

James breathes out slowly. He's terrified of how much he wants to say yes.

"Besides, you've got an early-ish morning tomorrow," Danny goes on. "I think check-in is at seven-thirty or eight."

James' mind freezes, frantically running back over that sentence again and again. He starts to frown. "But I don't need to be there for check-in . . ."

He turns to look at Danny and sees a look on his face he's never seen before. He looks. . . sheepish? Somehow curling back into his seat.

The realization slams into James, knocking him breathless and forcing pounding blood in hot waves through his limbs.

"The fuck's going on?" he asks, voice dangerous.

Danny sits as a statue, gazing purposefully nonchalantly out to sea. He holds his chin high even while his spine sags. "You're surfing tomorrow," is all he says.

James clenches his fists. "No, I'm not," he says, keeping his voice as steady and flat as possible.

"You are. You can borrow a wetsuit I have I think will fit you. And my board."

James' skin turns to ice even as a bead of fiery sweat drips down the side of his face. "Since when am I fucking surfing tomorrow?"

Danny swallows hard and finally turns to look at James. He doesn't look quite so casual anymore. He looks ruffled, now. Squirming and unsure.

"Since I called when we were eating lunch and re-registered you."

"Since you called and—*Jesus* you just don't fucking stop, do you?" James leaps to his feet and paces across the deck, one fist clenched in his hair.

"Seriously," he goes on, "what even made you think that's a good idea? I was just in the fucking hospital, for God's sake. I haven't even surfed!"

"It's only been four days; you haven't lost any strength." Danny rises to his feet and faces him. "You proved to yourself just now that you aren't afraid to be back in the water."

"Oh, so that was just a test?"

Danny flails his hands. "Well, it worked, didn't it?"

James huffs, reeling at the memory of the heat of Danny's bare skin. "Look, what made you even . . . I haven't prepared for one fucking second. Don't know a single thing about who's surfing, or what's going on, or where the hell I'm even supposed to go. What on *earth* made you think this was a good idea? That I wanted this?"

"Of course you wanted this! This is your dream, why you came all the way out—"

"I'm not even supposed to fucking be in it! You know that's not why I came here!"

James glares at Danny for a long moment, then goes completely still. "I shouldn't even have the points to be here," he says. The ice in his voice startles even him.

His mind flashes back to Danny whipping off his sunglasses midride down a pitiful swell off the Los Angeles coast, staring James down just before flinging himself back into the waves on purpose.

Danny steps back and runs his hand through his curls. "Come on, man. Don't try that on me. You wouldn't have even been that far behind me in scores anyways. You don't understand, James. This is what you need to do."

"Need to do? I don't *need* to do anything. Especially not something you just decided for me not five fucking days after you had to fucking resuscitate me!"

"But you're already here! You have a board and they'll put you up against a Wild Card and you can surf," Danny pleads.

"God, I just—you know what? No. I'm not letting this ruin my fucking day. You're going to sleep, and I'm going to sleep, and we're waking up to go watch the fucking competition tomorrow, got it? Whether you're down with it or not."

Danny stands still staring him down, hands fidgeting at his sides. James dares him with his eyes to try and keep fighting—to put up another ridiculous, pointless, goddamn *unbelievable* selfish excuse why James should go out and embarrass himself on Danny's home turf tomorrow. Why James should have to be the one to take on the uncomfortable stares instead of Danny fucking Moore, for once.

But Danny ducks his head and eventually just nods, taking another step back.

"Shower's in the back," he says low into the awkward silence. "There's an extra towel."

"Right," James says as he strides inside. He doesn't wait to hear whether Danny follows him as he tears off his clothes and steps into the shower. He scrubs his skin furiously with his hands in the steaming water, rubbing until he feels pink and raw.

By the time James makes it back out to the main room, the door to the bedroom is closed, light pouring out from underneath . He flicks off the lamp by the couch with such force it nearly topples over, then flings himself onto the couch. He hates himself when he notices Danny left a folded-up blanket and a pillow for him, stacked perfectly neat. He huffs onto his side, forces his brain to shut off, and stares blankly into the dark.

James barely sleeps. He's awoken just before dawn to the sound of footsteps softly padding through the room, making their way carefully out onto the deck. He lies awake staring at the ceiling, waiting for Danny to come back inside, hating the fact that he feels so alone knowing that Danny's no longer also in the house.

When he doesn't return what feels like ten minutes later, James pushes himself from the couch and groans, cracking his neck. He blinks blearily at the soft, grey light starting to bathe the beach in silver as he looks out one of the windows. He instantly spots Danny down by the shore, standing still and gazing out to the sea, shoulders slumped.

James sighs as his feet carry him out to the sand, shivering once at the chilled dawn air. He makes his way slowly down to where Danny stands, giving himself hundreds of missed opportunities to give up and turn back.

Danny doesn't even look over at James when he joins him by his side. He doesn't seem surprised. His curls ripple back from his face with the light salty breeze.

"Couldn't sleep," James says to fill the silence. Even the sound of the waves feels muted.

Danny hums. They stand in silence for long minutes, looking out over the sea as it slowly lightens with the oncoming sunrise. The man next to him feels soft and gentle as the new day dawns, fading effortlessly into the peaceful landscape instead of standing out against the horizon, powerful and bold. A pathetic shame creeps across James' skin when he remembers how he yelled and stomped off the night before.

He takes a deep breath in through his nose and smells the salty air. His palms itch to get in the water. To get their grip on a freshly waxed board.

"You aren't messing with me," he says quietly. "You really think I can hold my own for a round without embarrassing myself?"

He turns to look at Danny, and frowns when the man shakes his head.

"No," Danny says. He meets his gaze, eyes focused and intense. "I think you can win."

James huffs and looks away, heart suddenly pounding in his chest. "Nobody's that optimistic."

"James."

James sighs and looks back, resigned to hear whatever new wild excuse or explanation Danny has at the ready—perfectly designed to goad and convince him into doing this stupid thing anyway. He raises his eyebrows at Danny to continue.

"James," he says again. Danny hesitates, then turns towards him, waiting for him to do the same.

James holds his breath as Danny's hands slowly reach up to settle on top of his shoulders, his grip warm and firm. Danny's pale eyes flicker in the morning light, and his curls blow softly across his forehead in tangled strands. James feels an unexpected moan on the tips of his lips.

"Think what you want about me," Danny says. "Whatever people say, whatever they've told you, I—I don't care. But I'm not cruel. I wouldn't embarrass you."

James is gutted at the expression on Danny's lost face. He gazes helplessly into the little droplets of ocean and takes a step closer, shivering hard when Danny's fingertips trail lightly at his collarbone.

James licks his lips. The roll of his tongue sounds unbearably loud. His body is pulsing, shaking, held together only by the hands on his shoulders. Danny's breath fans across his skin.

"No," he whispers, and the rightness of his words washes through him with a calming hum. "No, you wouldn't."

The air between them changes. Danny's eyes widen, and James finds himself slowly leaning forward into the heat of his chest. He barely registers what's happening as Danny tips his head down towards his, lips dry and parted. His own hands reach up to touch Danny's warm, firm waist, afraid to press too hard, afraid to make this all disappear.

James tries to relax his neck and closes his eyes. Feels Danny's breath dance across his lips, the warmth from his cheek illuminating James' skin. The taste of his mouth already swirling across James' tongue on the cool air.

Suddenly Danny sucks in a breath and pulls back. James flings opens his eyes to see Danny staring down at him in disbelief.

"You want this," Danny breathes, his voice uncharacteristically shaking.

James' answer falls effortlessly from his lips. "Yes."

Danny swallows hard and blinks. "With me?"

The question is so small, so tiny and fragile in the air. The unspoken *"and not Rob"* hands like a trembling secret between them. James closes his eyes and thinks of holding a picture of a curly-haired little boy in his hands.

"God, Sydney, yes. More than anything."

Sydney's chest hitches on his breath. He looks at James with pure, absolute, radiating wonder, and he breathes James' name on a sigh into the dazzling sunlit air.

He cups James' face in warm, trembling hands and kisses him with a soft smile still on his lips, leaving James melting and breathless in the sand as the oblivious sea laps at their bare feet.

# 13

James Campbell is kissing him.

*James Campbell is kissing him.*

Sydney tastes the groaning sigh that leaves James' mouth as James' hand comes up to hold the side of his face, fingers trailing through his curls and holding on. It brushes gently across Sydney's cheek, soothing that bruise that came from the end of a fist while James had struggled, gasping in the wet sand ten feet away.

James Campbell tastes like the cool layer of wet sand buried just beneath the top layer baked in the sun. Like the first burst of ocean water at the start of a new day across his bare skin. Like soft, warm heat.

A moan escapes from the back of his own throat as he tilts his head to capture more of James' sleep-soft lips under his, wet and pliant and gentle. Consumed.

Fire burns up his spine and crackles in the pit of his chest as he pulls James' body flush against his, and the rapid beating of James' heart pounds straight through to his own skin. James' peaked nipples brush against him. An electric shiver through his blood.

And James' body is somehow both solid and soft beneath his hands—hands which he can't believe are still steady despite the fact that *James Campbell is kissing him.* Steady, coursing, overwhelming desire burns in his chest, and he pulls back to speak before he loses his nerve.

"Say it again," he whispers, lips brushing against James'. The air between them is warm and wet, shaky exhales on the salty ocean breeze. Sydney keeps his eyes open despite the flush of hot embarrassment creeping across his face. He needs to remember exactly what James Campbell's eyelashes look like up close, count the number of faded freckles on the bridge of his nose, the lines at the corners of his eyes. Needs to burn this image into his memory in case they never . . . in case it doesn't . . .

To his relief James seems to know immediately what he means. James smiles a breathy laugh and looks into his eyes, brushing the curls from Sydney's forehead with gentle fingers.

"Sydney," he breathes.

The sound of his name in James' voice reverberates in his ears, then floats out over the sea and towards the distant horizon. Sydney wants to cup the sound of it in his palms and hide it away inside his skin forever. He wants to paint it across the sky.

"Sydney," James whispers into the side of his neck. Says it again nestled into his cheek, breathing warmth across his shivering skin.

Sydney turns his head to capture James' lips once more, and they both groan as their tongues brush, quiet trembling gasps mixed with the steady crash of the waves. Sydney lets his mind go blissfully still, utterly lost in the feeling of James' skin against his, the gentle caress of his lips, the careful, reverent traces of his warm fingertips. The visceral, exploding relief.

James Campbell is *kissing* him. *Him!*

Then he remembers why James stormed away the night before. The anger in his spine, the hurt trembling in his face.

Sydney needs to know—can't stand there on the beach with his palm across James' jaw for another second without knowing. He lets his fingers trace back through the strands of James' hair below his ear, imagining what it would feel like if he gave him one more soft kiss in the corner of his mouth. If he just pressed his lips to James' skin and breathed him in, quiet and still.

He pulls back, though, the air cooling the edges of his kiss-sensitive lips. For some reason, the fact that he almost *did* kiss James in such a way sends a shiver of fear down his arms. And James' eyes as they look back at him hold the depth of the sea. They bore into him the way a wave envelops his skin. Unrelenting and powerful, terrifying and known.

"Surf today, James," Sydney says in a weak voice. "Go out there and . . . just do it for you. Please."

James Campbell is a marvel. He's standing on a beach willingly holding Sydney's body in his arms, letting him touch and mark and feel

164

his skin with his hands, letting him ask him, beg him to hold his ground against his fear. James' eyes don't leave his, as if he's trying to read the results of the competition in Sydney's own pupils. The creamy, warm water continues to lick at their ankles, leaving their toes in cool and damp pockets of sand.

"You'll be there?" James eventually asks.

Sydney nods. He can't help himself. He brushes his fingers once more through James' hair and refuses to blink as he watches James lean into the touch. *His* touch. Refuses to wonder if James thinks it's childish how much his palm is shaking.

"I'll be there," he responds.

Then James smiles. It washes over his face in a bright wave, and Sydney can feel his own cheeks responding in kind. His chest swells, as if he's going to rise up into the air, bolstered by the power of the look on James' face and the wind blowing steadily off the surface of the ocean.

He wants to run down to the competition and laugh in everyone's faces that the bravest man on earth just said that he wanted him, right there for the entire sunrise-covered ocean to see.

Sydney dips his head and tentatively brushes his nose against James' to strengthen his answer, breathing in the scent of James' sleepy skin. James hums, then shakes his head and lets out a husky laugh, placing his hands on Sydney's chest and leaning slightly away.

"This is insane."

Sydney's smile freezes on his face and turns stale. The breath in his lungs sinks like lead.

He knows this. Doesn't James realize that he knows this? He's the most irritating, risky, un-liked man in all of surfing and James Campbell just willingly *kissed* him. Of course it's insane. Why else would he have had to wait to find the bravest man on earth for someone to finally say they wanted him? Yes—he knows all of this like he knows every part that makes up a television, a radio, a toaster oven, a car.

And yet, he'd thought it would last a bit longer before James went and pointed it all out. At least just long enough to kiss him one more time (lie on top of him, peel his clothes from his body, hold him down into the sand, hear him gasp, feel his back arch). At least until James wins the competition and walks away with a garland of flowers. At least until he has to leave and go back to Los Angeles . . .

Sydney's so lost in his head he realizes a few seconds too late that he's gone entirely stiff. James frowns, taking in the new tension in Sydney's body, then sucks in a quick breath with wide eyes.

"No no no," he says. "I didn't mean *this*."

James hesitates, eyes narrowed as if he's gauging Sydney's reaction, then he leans forward and kisses Sydney softly on the mouth, exactly in the spot where Sydney had longed to do the same to James just minutes ago. The soft pucker of his lips sounds louder than all their previous kisses combined.

Sharp relief immediately courses through Sydney's body in pounding waves. He moans on a soft sigh as he relaxes under James' brief touch, still shocked at the taste of James' lips—*James Campbell's lips*—against his own.

James pulls back and gives a small grin. "No, this is not what's insane," he says. He bites the inside of his lip in a way that he must have been doing since he was six-years-old, and something about the innocence of it makes Sydney want to somehow strip away the bullet scar and hurl it into the sea.

The moment turns heavy. James clears his throat and quietly goes on.

"Actually, this feels like the least insane thing I've ever done." He pauses, tongue jutting out quickly to lick his bottom lip. "You know I wasn't actually drafted? That I enlisted?"

The whispered words vibrate in the air between them. They drown out the sound of the breeze rustling through the seashells hanging off Sydney's porch, the murmur of the waves forever rushing over the sand onto the shore. Sydney dips his head, then takes James' hands from his chest and holds them in his own, running his thumbs along the length of James' sturdy, calloused fingers.

He suddenly feels incredibly young.

"I'd guessed as much. If you'd been drafted they would've just sent you straight to the Army, based on your age at the time. You probably figured you'd be safer in the Navy. It's why you haven't asked for any help from anyone since you got back back—you feel like you only have yourself to blame for being over there in the first place."

Sydney realizes he's nervous saying all this out loud. He doesn't know what's changed now—what should be different. If he shouldn't just say whatever the hell's running through his mind now that he's tasted James' lips. He wonders if James realizes the hours Sydney spent lying awake at night thinking them all through—the intoxicating puzzle pieces of James Campbell—knowing with absolute certainty that he'd never get to speak to James ever again to figure out if any of his guesses were right.

James looks up at him, scrunches his lips together, then laughs. Sydney's heart pounds in shock at the bright sound.

"You're a genius," James says. He pushes playfully against Sydney's arm. "Wacked as hell, but still. That head of yours is something else."

Sydney can't react in time to stop the humiliating blush that's spreading across his cheeks. James sees it and smirks, crossing his arms over his chest and planting his feet. "So, genius, is there anything you *can't* take one look at and know fucking everything about?"

Sydney knows he's joking, but the answer that falls immediately from his lips comes from the truest pit of his chest.

"You."

The air crackles. James looks at him with an unreadable expression, holding his gaze. Neither one of them breathes. Then James squeezes his hands one last time before letting go, turning back to face the sea and standing close enough for their arms to touch. James takes a deep, slow breath in, and Sydney's eyes track the rise and fall of James' chest below the thin fabric of his own t-shirt.

"What I meant to say, before," James finally says. "The thing that's insane. . . I mean, I'm standing here in Hawaii—in paradise—and apparently I'm about to surf the fucking Banzai Pipeline, and I've got *the* Danny Moore saying he doesn't think I'll make a complete ass of myself. Eighteen-year-old me is pinching the shit out of his arm right about now. It's unreal."

Sydney hums. "Eighteen-year-old you definitely wouldn't have been pinching himself about an eight-year-old know-it-all kid with greased, parted hair in a Midwest Sunday school," he says, smirking.

James laughs and leans against him. Sydney feels the touch shiver straight through to his bones.

James runs a hand through his hair and speaks while gazing out at the water. "But honestly, that's not even the insane thing. The insane thing is that I so badly just wanna say 'fuck the Billabong,' and fuck all those things that I wanted, because what I want more than anything right now is to stay here and kiss every inch of you." James turns and pins him with a wild blue gaze. "Of Sydney Moore."

Sydney almost moans. James' words rumble through his skin, settle deep in the pit of his gut, between his legs. He feels a ghostly press of James' warm lips at the dip in the small of his back. In the crease between his hip and thigh. His skin breaks out in rolling shivers.

It takes him three tries to fully clear his throat. He absolutely forbids himself to look sideways at James, now. If he does, he won't be able to stop himself from wrapping his arms around his strong waist, and pressing him down into the earth, and covering him with his body. He won't be able to stop himself from blurting out that even in his midnight fantasies, the other man didn't want to actually spend *time* with him before and after.

Finally he speaks, his voice low and gravely from savoring the taste of James' mouth left on his lips.

"You're not allowed to kiss me again until you're a Billabong finalist," he says, raising his chin.

James huffs. "Yeah right. You're fucking mad."

Sydney turns to him and smirks. There's a fire in James' eyes— the same look Jimmy Campbell had given him just before he chased after what he thought would be a closed-out wave off the hot and muggy coast of Hermosa.

"Oh, trust me," Sydney says, tilting his head. "I know."

"I spent all night going through the latest *Surfer's Journal* news and—"

"You what? I told you last night I wasn't doing this. How did you possibly know—"

"—I've come up with who I think they'll pit you against in the Wild Card round today based on recent rankings. Pay attention, James, those flowers will still be there in two days and you can come back and look at them then."

"Jesus Christ, don't you ever—"

"Shane Hamilton, Australian, won the East Coast championships at Virginia Beach in '66 but he had a nasty wipeout the next year that threw him out of the circuit for a few seasons. Back problems, apparently. He's even older than you, probably this is his last ditch attempt at getting through to a quarter or semifinal so he can go out on a high note, or at least—"

"—fuck! Sydney, watch where you're fucking driving!"

"That goat had at least a foot of room, chill out. Anyway. Hamilton. He's gun-shy now. He'll be cautious with his back. Drops in super late on swells only once he sees they're gonna be an open barrel that won't close in on him and trap him inside. Use this—look for one's he's hovering on and sneak in before him to take it before the barrel fully presents. You can handle a few wipeouts if they topple—it'll be worth it to rattle him. Following?"

Sydney turns his gaze from the winding, dirt road to look at James for the first time since they pulled away from the house. His own heart is racing, as if he's the one who's going to have to surf his ass off all day against the top surfers in the world, not James. In fact, ever since they both jogged back up to the house from the shoreline, stealing sheepish glances at each other as they stumbled in the loose sand, his brain has been an absolute whirlwind—no off button in sight.

He'd been running potential strategies for James through his mind, trying to predict the way the waves would be that day, making a list of everything they'd need to do and bring, when suddenly James had grabbed him by the shoulders and pressed him up against the back of the doorway and kissed him. Hard. Licked into his mouth and rolled him back into the rough wood and groaned, pulling on a quick fistful of his curls. And then James had pulled back before Sydney could even begin to respond and murmured, "Fuck, Moore, you got me," with his eyes pointed straight at the hollow of Sydney's throat.

Sydney had thought he would melt into a puddle and never walk again. Fuck the Billabong Masters. Fuck Waimea.

But they'd yanked themselves apart, eyes on the clock, pacing around the hut trying to throw things together for the competition, tossing items back and forth in a way Sydney passingly imagined an old married couple might pack for an overdue vacation.

Coffee was started, and while it was brewing, Sydney had taken a deep breath, squared his shoulders, and quietly taken a step towards James in the moment of waiting silence. When James didn't move away, he'd wrapped his arms around James' tense waist from behind and whispered into the back of James' neck, "You're gonna surf like hell today." And James had gently leaned back against him and placed his hand right on Sydney's forearm and squeezed, letting Sydney hold him in the quiet stillness of the room. And somehow that little squeeze had meant more to Sydney than anything they'd said standing on the shore that morning.

And now they're here—speeding along in the Jeep through clouds of dust while Sydney dumps out absolutely everything he's packed into his brain over the last twelve hours, hoping James is catching at least some of it even though he knows he couldn't slow down the stream of his thoughts if he wanted to.

He's nervous. He's nervous *for James.* And isn't that an absolutely remarkable thing?

An absolutely terrifying thing.

James looks over at him and gives a tight smile. He's nervous, too; Sydney can trace the lines of it through his tense shoulders.

"I'm listening, genius, keep going," James says. He reaches over and puts his hand on Sydney's thigh, keeping it there as they continue to drive. Sydney has to tear his eyes away from the sight of James' tan fingers resting on the line where his boardshorts meet his skin and force himself to look back at the road.

"Right—" His voice wavers, and he tries again. "Right. So. Other Wild Card they'll throw in there is Peter Fu. From Maui. Now he's the exact opposite of Hamilton. Attacks every wave whether it's a clear open barrel or not. He's decent at skirting on the foam, so he'll take a wave he knows is gonna collapse and he'll ride the barrel as long as he can before just hopping out and coasting along the foam in front. Then he'll do some fancy show-off leap at the end to finish the ride. He's nineteen. Paddles like hell the entire set. He'll take every wave he can get his hands on, which sort of takes care of Hamilton for you, but Fu will rack up enough medium level scores on waves that if you don't get your three good waves in he'll end up winning based on sheer quantity alone. Plus he's got a bit of home turf advantage, if you believe in that sort of shit. Got it?"

James clears his throat and nods, staring out the window with a look on his face like he's going to be sick.

Sydney can tell he doesn't want to be left alone to his thoughts, so he keeps talking, hardly even aware of the words coming out. He talks about the weather conditions, and the currents, the topography beneath the water along the Banzai Pipeline shore, and the way the social scene usually works at this competition (not like he's ever actually been part of it, but he has eyes).

He talks until he feels his voice growing hoarse, and he only shuts his mouth just when the outskirts of the Banzai sand come into view. The beach is spotted with boards stuck in the sand and stretching surfers, the sleepy town already alive and buzzing for competition day. James gives Sydney's thigh one final squeeze, then runs his hands over his face and gives a long sigh before leaning back to look out at the sky through the open ceiling of the Jeep.

Sydney doesn't want to leave the car. When he does, he'll have to be Danny Moore, just like usual. James will separate from him and pretend they didn't just arrive together. He'll go off and be surrounded by surfers from all over the world wishing him luck and catching up on the latest news and gossip, warming up together and strategizing from where they perch side by side in the hot sand.

And meanwhile Sydney will be off to the sidelines with his sunglasses on, dodging all the shocked looks he knows he'll get when word spreads he isn't surfing in the competition this year, trying to avoid fangirls and ass-kissers and rivals all at once by looking as unapproachable as possible. Just like it's always been.

Only, now, after just twenty-four hours of knowing that James Campbell flew to Hawaii for *him*, he doesn't want James to see him like that— to see him as Danny Moore on the Oahu shores. He doesn't want to stride like a freight train through the crowd, or snap back at anyone who even looks his way, or surf the entire day and leave without even having to say as much as a "hello."

He wants to sit with James. Talk to him about the weather. Ask him if his muscles feel ok.

And at the same time, the thought of the entire beach whispering *"what the hell got into Danny Moore this year?"* if they see him trying to casually sit and chat with poor, random, longshot Angelino surfer Jimmy Campbell is more terrifying than the tallest Waimea wave.

He wants to turn the ignition back on, turn the Jeep around, and drive like hell back home with James by his side. To feel the weight of him in his arms and memorize every detail of his skin so that he'll have the memory of it forever—for years beyond the day when James gets on a plane headed to LAX.

Sydney hears James trying to calm his breathing next to him, and he realizes that James will never move from the car unless Sydney forces them to start. As he shifts to open the door, something presses against his thigh, and he suddenly remembers that he has the most precious object on earth hidden in his pocket.

"James."

James hums and keeps staring out the window. He doesn't turn his head. When Sydney waits and doesn't answer, James slowly meets his gaze. His frowning eyes are churning storms.

"Yeah?"

"When I went back up to the rocks last night to get our clothes, there was—your . . . the bullet was still in your pocket. Was gonna give it back last night, but then . . . well, I have it now, if you want it." His swallow resonates through the Jeep, and he holds his hands awkwardly in his lap. "Just didn't want it to get lost," he quietly adds.

James stares at him, and Sydney couldn't decipher the lines on James' face if his life depended on it. The moment drags on, and Sydney starts to worry that he did something terribly wrong by taking it out of James' shorts and pocketing it in his own. That somehow that action was akin to picking up the gun and shooting James himself.

His palms sweat. He tries to wipe them silently on his boardshorts, but they noticeably rasp against the fabric. Finally James speaks, and his voice is thin and hoarse.

"I think I'd rather know that you have it," he says.

Sydney places his palm over the bulge in his pocket and swallows over the sudden lump in his throat. He can only nod in response.

They take a mutual breath and both reach for their respective door handles. Sydney feels his body change the instant he steps outside the car. Already his shoulders are back, chin higher, eyes itching to get behind their protective dark lenses. He leaves them off—just a few minutes longer. This continued desperation to hold on to his final seconds as Sydney Moore takes him by unwelcome surprise. He helps James unload his board and bag in silence, makes sure he has the water they packed and some food.

"Take extra time stretching your left calf muscle," Sydney says, breaking the thick silence as James shoulders his borrowed bag. "It looks tight."

James nods and picks up the board under his arm. He turns to leave. Sydney keeps talking.

"And watch out for that rip current if your heat ends up starting after 9:30, it'll make dropping in on any waves that are angled southwest impossible and you'll get sucked backward into the bottom of the pipeline."

Again, James only nods. Sydney swallows over his rising internal panic. The desperate need to say something, *anything*, that will snap James out of this somber silence he's fallen into—like a robot preparing for his doom of being taken apart by Sydney's very hands.

"Your strong suit is staying low and tight around the board. Your height, obviously. Plus your strength. You'll be gouging into the face of the wave while Hamilton and Fu will just try to zoom out of the pipeline as soon as possible. Judges here love when you go deep and spend extra seconds inside the barrel, so try and use that to your advantage—"

"Alright, mom, I get it. Thanks."

James' tone is icy, and Sydney stops mid-word, mouth hanging open. He feels like he's been slapped. A blush burns across his cheeks, and his fingertips tap against his sunglasses still hanging over the collar of his shirt, itching to pull them on.

Of course James doesn't need his help—doesn't need Sydney rambling on about things he already damn well knows when he's trying to calm himself and focus on the task ahead. For the first time in an achingly long time, Sydney remembers what it feels like to be a child scolded by the favorite parent. Except James Campbell has *kissed* him, man to man, and Sydney considers simply sticking his head down in the sand and never taking it out again. Not even when James wins.

Sydney takes a step back from James and reaches for his sunglasses, taking one last look at the true golden color of James' skin before slipping them on over his eyes and running a hand through his curls to smooth them. He sets his mouth in a firm line and steps aside wordlessly to let James go by, fists clenching at his sides.

He looks away from James, out towards the end of the street, when James' voice draws him back. He sounds tired and small. He hasn't taken a single step away.

"Sorry, I—Sydney, come on. Don't be like that."

Sydney tries to resist—after all, he's going to have to resist for the entire rest of the long day—but James Campbell just said his name twenty feet away from the Banzai shore, without a hint of hesitation or shame, so Sydney turns back to him. He leaves the sunglasses on.

James sighs and looks up towards the clear, open sky. "I just . . . I—" he sighs again. "Shit, I feel like such a fucking idiot. I have no clue what the hell I'm doing."

Sydney frowns and takes a step forward. "Why do you say that? You know exactly what the hell you're doing. You can read the waves. You're a good surfer. Just trust yourself."

"No, I know, it's not that. It's . . ." He grimaces, hums with a low growl in his throat, and Sydney starts to wonder whether he should be preparing to duck another punch when James says, "I just wish that I could stay with you today. On the beach, between heats. While you're off . . . being the reigning champion and I'm sitting alone shitting bricks. God, man, I wish that so fucking badly."

James' face looks like he's embarrassed to admit the words, and Sydney's chest clenches, completely overwhelmed. Without a second thought, he reaches up and yanks the shades off his eyes, blinking against the harsh sunlight. He takes a quick look side to side on the little dirt road, then steps chest to chest with James, walking them a handful of steps backwards to be shielded by the Jeep.

He slams his eyes shut, leans forward with a pounding heart, and brushes his lips against James' forehead. The breath shakes from the tips of James' open lips. Sydney smells the remnants of his own bar of soap along James' hairline, takes a precious moment to breathe it in, and the loudest thing on earth is James' swallow in the air between them.

"Surf like hell, James Campbell," he whispers into his skin, and then he does something absolutely insane, completely reckless, because they haven't even fucked, haven't rocked against each other just to get off and then yanked up pants while avoiding eyes. They haven't said or done anything at all, just *kissed,* in front of a sunrise that it would be impossible not to want to look at with someone's hand stroking your cheek. They haven't and they aren't and they don't. It's only been two hours.

But still, Sydney kisses James softly just beneath his hairline—a single press of his dry lips.

James sighs, long and slow, out through his nose. Sydney feels the tension seeping out from James' body in front of him, feels the hot lines of nerves running rigid through his muscles somehow soften and relax.

Without trying to give any sort of excuse for what he just did, Sydney forces himself to step back, trying to casually mask how stunned he is at his own daring. He shoulders his own bag, flicking back on his sunglasses and mentally preparing to enter the churning crowd. Beside him, James squares his shoulders, doing the same.

They share one last look before James turns to walk down towards the beach alone, leaving Sydney behind by the Jeep. They'd discussed this—how they should arrive on the sand separately, careful minutes apart. The last thing they need—the last thing *James* needs—is a rumor flying around about why the hell he showed up with the reigning champion he embarrassingly defeated two weeks ago in LA. Not when he's trying to focus. Not when he's trying to win.

When James is ten steps away, Sydney can't help himself. Suddenly the sight of James walking away from him towards the thronging beach feels too final—like a goodbye he hadn't even known was coming until it had already come and gone. A wild pulse shoots through his gut, the sudden need to open his mouth and call Jimmy Campbell "James" one last time that day.

"James!" His voice cracks, but he can't bring himself to care, and James jumps before looking back over his shoulder with a raised brow.

"I'll be there," Sydney says to him, voice steady and low. He wills his body to remain still, trying to pour assurance out of every inch of his own nervous, shaking limbs.

James' answering grin is more beautiful than the entire blooming mountain at his back. It's the same smile he'd given Sydney on the beach just after telling him about the war, only this time Sydney doesn't feel the need to look away.

Sydney shuffles his feet in his flip flops for another fifteen minutes by the car, perfectly imagining every step James must be going through down at the competition. He can see the beach clearly in his mind—the crowds lounging across the already blazing hot shore, the canopies of palm leaves, the sea of surfboards all stacked and standing in the sand, waiting to be waxed, the cliques of surfers from all over the world standing in huddles with their beards and their long hair and their girlfriends hanging at their sides.

Sydney closes his eyes and remembers back to his nineteen-year-old self, hiding alone in the dense trees near the beach and waiting for his opportune moment to run out and steal a board and prove to everyone that they were all absolute novices at surfing the Banzai. That he was the only man on that beach who wasn't just a sucker.

He huffs now, remembering how unbelievably irritated he'd been watching the world's so-called best pipeline surfers wipe out in wave after wave for getting stuck too deep in the barrel, or for failing to stick low and close to the face for fear they'd be pitched over—as if the entire point of surfing was *not* to get wet.

He remembers the beautiful, soaring recklessness of that moment—when he'd taken a breath, and run full speed from his hiding place, and told everyone in his path that they were morons and to fuck out of the way and let him through. When he'd sensed the perfect set just on its way in from the horizon, tingling in his fingertips, and he'd known that he couldn't miss it if he was gonna show everyone who was *really* the best at pipeline surfing.

And he had been the best, hadn't he? They'd mailed him the prize money (well, they'd mailed Chuck Hobbs the prize money, and Sydney had found it a week later taped to one of the trees near his house with a bill or two missing), and they'd given him an automatic spot on the pro circuit. They'd sent him the competition schedule for the rest of that summer and the next, and he'd placed in the top four at every major competition since.

The realization of how easy it had all been makes him ashamed in retrospect, thinking back to James' somber, determined face that morning. Thinking back to the look of sinking devastation on his face in Hermosa when Sydney had been just about to beat him in their round.

176

A fiery, foolish part of him wants to run down to the beach and scream, "*For God's sake, please let James win. He almost fucking died protecting all of you, and he won't tell any of you to fuck off, and he didn't get caught with any photos in high school, so you have to let him win this. You don't understand but you have to!*"

And then he remembers James' terrifying face in the moonlight when he'd accused Sydney of losing on purpose, and suddenly that desire is replaced by the need to go down there and find James Campbell and scoop him up and carry him away from it all and back to Sydney's home, back to the beach where no one will stare at the way his raised scar shows through his wet shirt.

Shit, he's never had so many ridiculous conflicting desires all at once in his whole life. He's felt nothing *but* reckless for the past forty-eight hours. He could have let James Campbell walk away from him down the road and gone back to his peaceful solitude and his hammock and his music, and instead he'd called after him and practically begged him to come back to him the next day, like the world's neediest travel agent. Like a total spaz. Like someone who had never experienced finding another person good looking before, forbidden or no.

And he still doesn't even know what came over him when he'd placed his hand on James' chest there in the shallows and blurted out loud what he'd been thinking as James leapt from the cliff—*you were brave*—and he sure as hell hadn't planned on reaching out and wrapping his arms around James' body, holding him close against his own bare skin like he'd wanted to do when he was watching him change in secret behind the lifeguard tower, what feels like lifetimes ago.

In fact, he has no idea who he even is anymore—this man who suddenly wishes he could be back at home with another human being instead of out surfing, clobbering the competition again and again. Doesn't know if that man is Danny or Sydney or 'the fag from Oahu' or some version of himself he hasn't even had a chance to meet yet. He's not even that old, for God's sake.

And speaking of God, *goddamn*, he can still feel the ghosts of James' hands on his skin from when they stood there in the evening waves. The way James clutched at his back and buried his face into his neck, letting the stubble on his cheek rasp against Sydney's collarbone, being willingly held in his arms for the entire ocean to see.

177

And then Sydney had looked at James in the soft, grey light that morning, and burned up with desperation at the need for James to know that *he could win,* and he'd heard James' perfect lips forming the sounds of his name—*his name*—and he'd leaned forward and kissed him.

And there, standing next to the Jeep alone and grinning like a total loony, Sydney realizes for the first time all day that he'd never actually leaned forward and kissed anyone before. That that part of his body had been left completely overlooked. Untouched.

He brings his fist in front of his mouth to secretly touch his lips, as if they'd somehow feel different now, molded by James' own. Then he coughs before pulling his shades back on and grabbing his bag.

It's time.

He slicks back his curls and takes a deep breath, reminding himself what it feels like to be Danny Moore again, and then he quickly makes his way down to the buzzing shore, already starting to receive shocked stares the closer he gets to the beach.

The first day of the Billabong Masters is never quite as insane as the Finals on Day Two. Sydney restrains himself from immediately searching for James in the smaller crowd once his feet finally reach the beach and he kicks his sandals off, leaving them in the middle of the sand. The Surf League guys are running cables to set up for the announcers' stand, and the judges are starting to arrive—old surfing dudes with greying hair who work with typewriters and journal articles now instead of ankle straps and wax.

Sydney wonders how far word's spread that he isn't going to be surfing. If it hasn't, there's going to be a stupid high-school gossip mill exploding in about two hours once everyone figures out he doesn't have a board with him. If it has, that same high-school gossip mill is currently tearing itself to shreds wondering whether he injured himself, or had a mental breakdown, or is playing some big trick on everyone, or finally got arrested for one of the ridiculous activities he supposedly does when he's not just being a stuck-up asshole. He tells himself 'supposedly,' as if the times he's surfed in San Francisco and Australia don't really count (or the *activities* he's done once the surfing was over . . .).

Oahu's a small island, and surfing's a small world. Sydney Moore's not gonna kid himself by pretending he isn't a topic of conversation, and a favorite one, at that. He has been for the last four years.

He finds a spot in some shade at the base of a tree and sits to wait it out, trying to look as simultaneously intimidating and invisible as possible. He breathes in the sea air and tries to calm himself over the next couple hours, watching the beach slowly come even more to life—as the surfers begin warm-ups out in the waves, and the announcers start going over the day's match-ups.

He watches James stretch his left calf muscle over and over again. Keeps constantly searching for a golden blond head moving throughout the sea of tanned bodies and native Hawaiians, bobbing among the other surfers warming up in the massive swells. James looks tense. He can see it from a mile away. It takes all of Sydney's willpower to stay where he is, to just let James be. The best thing he could possibly do for him at a surfing event in Oahu is stay as far away from him as possible. The raw truth of that hurts somewhere deep and unfamiliar in his chest.

The first heat of the day is completely forgettable. All three surfers struggle to hold their ground against the sheer velocity of the Banzai waves, clearly all new to the terrain, and none of them make higher than a six on any of their three scored waves. It would make Sydney feel smugly victorious, if he wasn't ready to throw up at the thought of James losing his nerve under the pressure.

Fifteen minutes before James' Wild Card heat is set to start, Sydney takes a deep breath, pushes off from his hiding spot, making his way down into the crowd with head held high.

The inevitable happens. The crowd parts before him like Moses entering the Red Sea.

Some are silent. One surfer Sydney's never cared enough to try and recognize calls out, "Danny! Yo, Moore!" to no avail as he strides by. Last year's rivals give him the reluctant but expected head nod. There's a snicker, a "Well, look who the fuck finally decided to grace us all and show up," and the fans who don't know enough yet to know they should hate him gasp and plead with him to hear if it's true he isn't surfing the Masters. If he hurt himself, if he got sick of winning, if he's embarrassed as hell about Hermosa. If an Undercover finally caught up with him in a stall. If he's single.

He stays silent.

He makes his way to the far side of the judges' area and finds a clear spot of sand to sit as close to the waves as possible. To be able to see James. He can feel the crowd hovering in a murmuring cloud at his back. He gives a silent, mental thank-you to the few locals who only know him as "the winner" who gave him soft applause and then went back to their lives.

All of it, in the end, makes him feel prickly and sick. He knows exactly what they're saying now that his back is turned—an exact copy of what they say to his face, and then some. And he can't blame them, if he's honest. Half of it probably pales in comparison to the way he's insulted his fellow surfers' abilities in years past in the sand. Those kooks deserved it, every word. But, still.

Before, he used to find it all mildly amusing—the various rumors people came up with, the stares, or the new complaints they had about his surfing or his personality or his tattoo or whatever the hell else people decided to take issue with as his reputation grew.

*"If only our champion wasn't a miserable asshole." "If only our champion didn't think he was God's gift to surfing and actually knew how to make friends." "If only our champion wasn't such a fag."*

He'd be caught dead before he admitted there wasn't a twisted, invigorating challenge to being infamous.

Now, though, knowing that James is somewhere on this beach, hearing the whispers and seeing the stares and feeling the odd energy following Sydney around, the reality of it all makes him want to hide his face under the sand. Embarrassingly hot tears suddenly prickle at the back of his eyes behind his aviators, and he hates himself for the way he wants to turn around and tell everyone to just leave him alone. Let him be.

He hates that he woke up when he was fifteen with a dream to be the best surfer in the world, and all he's managed to do since then is piss off an entire island and create a worldwide reputation for himself as "that dude we wish would just lose."

He shakes his head and blinks hard before settling his elbows around his knees to watch. He tells himself James needs him to pull it together, even though he doesn't believe that at all. Somewhere behind him, James is zipping up his wetsuit and walking towards the starting line over to his right, confident and at ease in this world, probably completely unaware Sydney has even purposefully perched himself so close to the waves to be able to see him.

With a huff, Sydney blocks out the sound of everything but the announcers and the sea. His own ridiculous thoughts can wait.

James has a heat to win.

*"And here for round two of Day One of our Billabong Pipeline Masters, folks, we've got our Wild Card heat. The Aussie Shane Hamilton coming fresh off an injury at Bells Beach back in his home surf, and what a wipeout that—"*

*"Yeah, man, that wipeout bugged out everyone standing on that beach. Stayed under for almost a minute, if I heard right. But, you know what, he's been looking strong with his paddling during warm ups earlier this morning. Back doesn't look like it's giving him too much trouble."*

*"He's here hoping to make a semi-final if you ask me. A little too weak yet to be aiming for anything higher, especially with the power of these waves we got here along the Pipeline. He's been dropping in late all season—you think he's gun-shy?"*

*"Hamilton's got some radical speed down the pipeline when he drops in early enough, but you're right, he's been looking a little cautious all summer. Didn't even make it out of his first heat back in Hermosa at the ISF, and that was a Wild Card heat, too."*

*"I'd sure like to see him make it today, just to give us old and greying hodads some hope. And then we have Peter Fu—what do you say, man, the new Hawaiian wunderkind?"*

*"Woah, dude, wouldn't say that quite yet. You can hear the home crowd sure agrees with you, though!"*

*"Right on."*

*"Tell you what, kid's been looking fierce all summer at the local competitions. Been taking wave after wave and barely slows down to catch his breath. Crazy stamina in him, that's for sure. But I'm wondering if he's got the patience to wait it out here at the Banzai, where taking a*

wrong wave can be a much bigger problem for you than just a little wipeout."

"That's true, man. He's gonna have to sit some out and wait for the clean barrels if he wants high enough technical points to push him up into tomorrow's Finals heats. And if he doesn't want to end up straining something in a wipeout—or worse."

"Ominous words, man. And now, what about Jimmy Campbell?"

"Bit of a surprise, there, I gotta say. I heard he dropped out with an injury, but it looks like he's back here today to surf!"

"Someone called in for him last minute and got him back on the list is what I heard. And I think we can all agree that the main reason he was let back in was his stunning upset two weeks ago in Hermosa against Danny Moore."

"He beat Danny Moore on a single wave! A single wave!"

"It was a gorgeous ride, man. Just beautiful. Hugged in close to the face and stayed deep in that barrel, which is exactly what judges love to see here at the Banzai. Not sure what the hell got into Danny Moore, though—that wipeout came out of nowhere. His first one in years?"

"Definitely the first one I've ever seen from him in competition."

"Damn, he sure can't argue with that record, can he?"

"Was it nerves, do you think? Normally you don't have to win a whole round on just one wave—

the surf that day was gnarly. Way too flat for surfers at this level to get in a good run."

"I'd agree with you, but Campbell's also been making a name for himself on the SoCal qualifying circuit the last few years—dude came out of absolute nowhere and started competing, from what I heard. Not sure what to make of his chances today. He may have beat Danny Moore, but I think it may be hitting it on the head to say that was a fluke."

"Yeah, man, hate to say it but I think Jimmy's just here today to show his face and get a little recognition. He only just made pro back at Hermosa the other week—these types of powerful waves we got here aren't at all what he's used to surfing."

"With Danny Moore apparently not competing, though, who knows what the hell will happen?"

"I hear that, man. I hear that. I don't know what to think about that news—didn't think he was injured? Word is he's here today to watch, and some of you folks in the crowd have probably seen him milling about. And I think you know what I mean when I say this, that I'm not really sure why he's here if he isn't surfing."

"You're preaching some truth there, dude. We'll have to ask him tomorrow what his 'famous' predictions are for the Finals. I'm sure he'll have a lot to say... But now, folks, we got the Wild Card heat lining up at the starting line, and some bomb fresh swells coming in off our beautiful Northshore coast..."

Sydney's never felt this nervous before a surfing competition in his life, and he isn't even the one goddamn surfing.

He finally lets himself look over at James waiting on the start line next to Fu and Hamilton and feels his heart leap up into his throat. James Campbell is the most beautiful thing he's ever seen. He's standing tall holding Sydney's board (the extra one no one's seen before—nobody will ever know), and wearing Sydney's old wetsuit (just barely too big for him—nobody will ever suspect), and looking for all the world like he's about to fight like hell.

The look on his face steals the breath from Sydney's lungs. Watching James stand there calmly in the sun, scanning the waves as if he isn't about to surf for the first time since nearly drowning, Sydney can't bear to stay sitting and just watch. He leaps to his feet and jogs a ways down the sand, just past the crowd. A grandmotherly type who has no idea who the hell he is asks if he's alright, and the surfer sitting three feet from her asks which bathroom he's heading to so he knows which one to avoid.

Sydney stalks right past them. He plants his feet apart in the empty patch of sand and crosses his arms over his chest, willing himself to look bored. As cool and icy and as 'Danny Moore' as humanly possible.

Inside, he wants to faint. He watches James slowly, casually turning his head left to right, scrunching his eyes, and Sydney realizes with a jolt of shock that James is searching for him. *Him!*

He curses himself for ever leaving his spot closer to the starting line and the water. Now James will think he left him, that he heard the idiotic nonsense the announcers were spewing out and decided that they were right, and that Jimmy Campbell really is just here as a consolation prize for knocking Danny Moore on his ass in front of everybody in Los Angeles, and he could never in a million years survive this round without mildly embarrassing himself—or much worse.

Then James turns his head in just the right direction, and his eyes lock on Sydney standing alone and aloof in his aviators, a statue at the edge of the chaos, and even from this far away Sydney can see every bit of tension leave his body. Impossibly, James' bad shoulder relaxes beneath within the tight wetsuit clinging to his skin.

Sydney's insides turn to lava. He nods his head once just enough for James to see, as casually as he can, and he sees James do the same. An emotion hits Sydney so strongly in the chest he nearly buckles over at the sheer force of it.

James Campbell is going to fucking win this round.

*"And Peter Fu takes a wicked hit on that last wave! Wild!"*

*"That barrel sure slammed down onto him. It was really a bad choice to go in on that one."*

*"He's been making easy points so far, trying to go for style holds and grabs on smaller foamy waves, but man, hits like that are really slowing him down."*

*"Shane Hamilton looks like he's considering this next swell, he's paddling forward to meet the crest, woop, looking back over his shoulder like he can't decide how tall this wave will be—"*

*"And oh! Jimmy Campbell drops in right before he can make his decision! Campbell's flying down this wave, look at him go. He's in deep now, crowd's holding their breath to see if he'll make it out of that barrel—"*

*"Just look at the spray coming out of that pipeline! Right on!"*

*"And Jimmy Campbell's out! He's out! Looks like he's stalling trying to stay tight in that tube ride as long as possible, just gouging into the wave with his hand, crouched nice and low, what a beaut—"*

"And a gorgeous nose grab at the end there as he flips forward into the whitewater to end his ride."

"That's gonna be the biggest point wave we've seen so far, and he knows it. He's pumping his fist as he surfaces and the crowd's loving it. Heat's only 7 minutes old but these surfers have been attacking everything that comes at them. I don't think a single wave's gone by without somebody trying it—these dudes are showing they deserve to be here for a reason!"

"Oh . . . Hamilton's not happy about missing that one. That was a bangin' wave, clear and open in the tube."

"Looks like Campbell definitely knows what his strengths are. If he'd tried to pump on that face he would've zoomed out too quick onto the shoulder and missed the slow barrel behind him."

"You might have been wrong about Campbell, man. He's already powering towards his next wave and didn't even stop for a break after his last ride. And I hope he forgives me saying he's on the older end of dudes here. Looks like he's out here to make more than just an appearance . . ."

Sydney's heart pounds like a siren in his chest. His weak legs tremble in the sand. Watching James conquer that wave was unlike anything he's ever experienced in his life. He feels breathless and awestruck. He wants to laugh and turn to the entire beach full of people sneaking stares and glances his direction and yell, *"He kissed me this morning! That man kissed me!"*

The ridiculousness of it all fills him, bursting in his lungs. There's a tingling at the base of his spine—one that started the moment James popped up on that last wave and dropped in, wet hair flying in the wind, calves bulging and clinging to his board. When his back was broad and strong as he crouched low and practically flew into that pipeline, and the crowd around Sydney back on the shore gasped and held their breath in anticipation.

And at the same time, can still feel the memory of the muscles on James' back beneath his own fingertips. The taste of those chapped, salty lips on his tongue. It's an absolute miracle he's managed to stay completely still, face betraying nothing. He should be nominated for some sort of award.

It suddenly occurs to him that this must be what his momma felt like on the inside when she would stand up in church and raise her hands up to the ceiling. When she would shout, swaying and clinging at her cross necklace like she'd fall apart without it, like her skin just couldn't contain the wild joy bubbling up inside of her. The need to swing her body and bellow with her lungs, no matter how much his father shushed her or begged her to sit back down.

Maybe James Campbell is his new Jesus Christ. The thought makes him wish his momma were here beside him with a sudden pulse of longing, watching his first and only friend in the world surf across the sea she's never seen.

He startles from his thoughts when the announcers start yelling. Shuts the lid back down and locks it tight.

James needs him now. Somehow.

*"—that monstrous snap off the top of that wave!"*

*"Shane Hamilton just proved that he's still in this heat—only a surfer with his experience could read that wave like that. That was beautiful."*

*"He knew exactly when to execute that turn at the end to create the most spray. He may have missed the tube ride on that one, but that was a powerful ride straight up the face of that wave at the end. One of the tallest waves we've seen so far in this set, and he owned every inch of it."*

*"Fu's shaking his head at himself. I think he realizes he's in trouble unless he starts choosing quality over quantity. Twenty-one minutes in and he's gotta be aching."*

*"I gotta go back on what I said this morning, man. Fu's got real potential for some great trick wave competitions, but . . . well, he's no Danny Moore."*

*"Nobody's a Danny Moore, man. Dude's in a class of his own, in more ways than one."*

"Ha! I dig it. Well now, Campbell out there is sure trying to remind us of why he deserved to be the one to knock Moore out of Hermosa. Just look at him paddling to meet this wave coming in . . ."

"His left arm's looking a little stiff—definitely paddling harder with the right. You think he strained it?"

"Hard to tell, man. He's got two solid waves up there already, a 7.2 and his first huge ride with an 8.0. I think Hamilton's last ride is gonna put him just ahead, though."

"Do we think Fu's out?"

"He may have the most rides in, folks, but they've all been under 7. Let's see if Fu can advance before our home crowd here. Just listen to the cheers!"

Sydney holds his breath as James goes in for another wave, tracking his sun-bleached hair bobbing among the distant swells.

It's a monster—rushing in under James' board and soaring him straight up into the air. Sydney can tell James' shoulder is hurting him. He wants to kick himself; of course it's hurting him. He hasn't surfed in four fucking days besides the warmup time this morning. Hasn't even been at work to keep up basic conditioning.

Sydney should have helped him stretch it, or given him a Tylenol, or brought him some ice, or scrapped this entire idea, or *something*. And instead that morning he'd just told him to win and kissed him on the forehead and basically said 'good fucking luck.'

Stupid. Naive. He wants to dive out into the water and hand James his own arm to use. *"Here, paddle with this! Don't mind the blood, I just ripped it off for you!"*

Sydney shakes his head at his own idiotic thoughts and watches breathlessly with clenched fists as James drops in on the wave, soaring down the face. Instantly Sydney can tell it was the wrong decision. The barrel is already breaking, too heavy to hold a proper pipe, and James isn't pumping fast enough to get out ahead of it. He doesn't have the speed . . .

Sydney watches in horror as the top of the tube crashes down onto James with a booming roar, causing the announcers to wince and the crowd to gasp as his board flies up rider-less into the foaming air. It's the worst wipeout yet of the entire set. Sydney's toes grip furiously at the sand as he counts the seconds in his head and waits for James to surface. He doesn't blink.

One, two, three, *Goddammit James,* four, five, *no, God no . . .*

*"Folks we're all keeping an eye out here for Jimmy Campbell to surface. Hamilton and Fu have turned back on their boards from out past the breaking line and seem to be looking for him, too. With only four minutes left in this neck-and-neck set, you gotta commend them for putting on a pause to make sure he's alright. I would, too if I was—"*

*"There he is! We see his head coming up now, ladies and gents. Right there at two o'clock. He's reaching for his board and climbing back up, it seems."*

*"And it looks like he's waving off the lifeguard—how is that possible?"*

*"What the—and folks what do you know, Jimmy Campbell after the worst wipeout we've seen yet today is paddling his ass off, back out to the breaking line."*

*"I can't believe it! He just nodded at Fu and Hamilton and then took off like a rocket. I haven't seen him paddle so fast yet this round."*

*"Well he's got to if he wants to try and make some insane comeback—clock's reading only two minutes left. How is he even breathing!"*

*"And Fu and Hamilton don't even know what just hit 'em. I think they were waiting for a rescue to happen—definitely not this!"*

*"This is bangin', man. Jimmy Campbell's turned his board around and he's paddling like hell to catch this last wave of the set, and boy is it a beauty."*

*"He drops in . . . and oh boy, look at that tube! He's deep inside. Deep. Look at the spray flying outta this thing. Will he make it o—"*

*"He's out! Jimmy Campbell is out, and look at that huge cutback to the cheers of the crowd, throwing up some spray and looking up to the sky. And oh! There's a shout as he sinks down into the whitewater to end his ride."*

*"What a powerful comeback on that last wave. If that's not at least a 9 I don't know what is."*

*"And it's a 9.4! The highest wave we've seen so far today goes to Angelino Jimmy Campbell, and he has officially moved on to Day Two of the Masters."*

*"Listen to the crowd! This feels like the biggest underdog story of the entire competition, and we've only seen two rounds of surfing so far—still have hours to go!"*

*"And let's also give some love to Peter Fu and Shane Hamilton—no weak rides today on that tough surf, that's for sure. They each surfed their asses off in this Wild Card round, but Jimmy Campbell came back from that wipeout to somehow surf the best barrel we've seen today. What a show, folks, and it's only the beginning!"*

The crowd is up and cheering on their feet for James Campbell, rushing past Sydney in a humming wave to meet him at the shore. James emerges from the shallows with a dazed smile on his face, board held high over his head and his chest still heaving from his last ride.

It's a moment that Sydney's been at the center of dozens of times, and yet he's never felt a wave of energy quite like this—such a churning force of genuine happiness directed at just one person the way the crowd on the beach is currently looking at James. He wants to burst through the crowd and run to him and wrap him in his arms. Badly. Desperately. He needs to prove to himself that everything that happened that morning wasn't just some dawn fever dream.

Instead he stays by the edges and watches, arms still crossed, sunglasses still pulled low. Danny Moore would never run to congratulate a competitor, let alone a surfer in a competition he isn't even surfing in. It would only throw suspicion on James.

He's not quite sure what to do. The elation coursing through his body is so intense he barely knows how to contain it. And yet, at the same time he has an overwhelming sense that he's intruding—that his presence is somehow dampening the celebration still happening on the shore of which he was once the untouchable champion. He tracks the golden glow of James' skin moving through the crowd, and sees that the announcers have hailed him over and pulled him near a mic to say congratulations. Sydney can't even hear James' quick, one-word replies over the sound of the cheers still rolling through the crowd.

Sydney realizes with a sinking feeling that they never talked about this part—about what they would do and how they would meet up again if and when James wins. Sydney knows how it goes, for the other surfers at least. You win an amazing round, and the other surfers want you to chill with them with a beer while you watch the rest of the day's surf, and then you go out that night to one of the local bars to celebrate and hype each other up for tomorrow, and then you don't get back to your house or hotel room until three a.m. with sore muscles and the promise of a hangover for the Finals.

At least, that's how some of the surfers do it—the ones that Rob seems to be friends with. The ones James is probably used to back in his normal life where he doesn't have to wake up on a boring beach and be stuck kissing Danny Moore.

But still, the thought of going back to his house and waiting alone for the rest of the day—hoping with a tinge of doubt to hear James' footsteps coming down the path in the middle of the night—feels worse than suffocating. Sydney knows he's fucked. Knew it, if he's honest with himself, from the moment he leapt up from his hammock and saw James Campbell standing there saying, "*Didn't predict this one, did you?*" with his hands casually stuck in his pockets. With his deep grey shirt open just slightly at the neck.

And Sydney's supposed to be standing on the brimming beach as Hawaii's most decorated surfer of '75 and '76, and instead he's waiting on the edges like a teenager with a crush on the high school football captain. Ridiculous.

An idea finally occurs to him, that he could at least walk back up to the Jeep and give it an hour. Wait and then come back down and peek if James is still hanging out with people. He can't spend one more second on this beach with James just fifty feet away from him and a complete inability to take one step any closer. With a resigned nod, Sydney tears his gaze away from James' back and makes his way up towards the top of the beach. He quickly winds down the familiar streets of the town, avoiding everyone's gaze like he knows how to do.

He's just turned the corner onto the side street they parked on that morning when he hears footsteps running up behind him. His gut clenches, an unexpected fear zipping down his spine, then he hears a voice.

"You fucking bastard, where the fuck are you going?"

He leaps around and comes face to face with a furious James Campbell. He opens his mouth to answer, but no sound comes out.

"Seriously, where are you going? Why didn't you come to me?"

Sydney realizes in a wave of hot shame that James looks incredibly hurt. Far more hurt than angry, the way his deep blue eyes have turned a shade of black,and his lips sag.

Frantic words rush to Sydney's head and pour out of his mouth before he can think them through. "Look, I—I'm sorry, James. But you won and everyone was there and looking and I didn't want them to see you with me because they love you, I mean, you saw it, and I thought you would hang out with the other surfers, and I could wait here for an hour and see if you still wanted to go home with me, but I totally understand if you don't w—"

James Campbell is kissing him.

*James Campbell is kissing him.*

On a tiny side street in the middle of broad fucking daylight after just annihilating his first round of the Billabong Masters, James has his hands tight on Sydney's neck and shoulders and Sydney is gasping against his lips, holding on for dear life. He swallows down his groans and breathes out against James' mouth "you fucking did it," and "thank God," and "I'm sorry," and "*James.*"

The kiss is rough but quick. James pulls back after just a few seconds, lips already red and swollen, then he quickly glances both ways down the empty street before holding the back of Sydney's head with his hand and bringing their foreheads together.

Sydney can barely breathe. He grips handfuls of the t-shirt James threw on after unzipping the top of his wetsuit. His skin beneath the shirt feels hot enough to burn Sydney's hands.

"I'm sorry I wasn't there. I didn't know you . . . that—I should have stayed. Please, I'm sorry."

James shakes his head against Sydney's skin and breathes quick through his nose. "You *were* there," he says roughly. "Hey now, you were there."

Suddenly Sydney knows—that James *did* hear the announcers teasing him, and did hear whatever everyone else whispered behind his back all morning, and did see the stares directed his way, some awe, some disgust, some resentment. That he saw it all, understood everything. That he knows from experience that Sydney wasn't just an innocent bystander wracking up an undeserved reputation all these years.

James knew, and he still came running after Sydney like hell when he noticed he was gone, and he's still here now holding his curls in his hand and risking it all just to taste his mouth, just to press his forehead gently to his.

James Campbell is a marvel.

James pulls back and looks up at Sydney, knocking the wind out of him for the tenth time that day.

"You're alright?" Sydney asks.

James blinks hard and nods. "I saw you on the shore, right when I came back up from that wipeout. Was far away, but, you looked like shit," he says.

Sydney tries to laugh, but can't. "I thought that . . . James, I thought you weren't gonna—"

James takes his hand gently. "Shh, I know. I wasn't sure either there, for a second. Made me realize I needed to get back out there. I didn't even know the round was still going on—thought it had timed out while I was under."

They stand in buzzing silence. They're both remembering that day. Sydney thinks of pulling James' limp body from the water, and forcing air into his lungs, and running his tongue over his own lips in stunned silence after James started breathing, trying to figure out if the taste of his skin was now forever changed. A sudden laugh comes bubbling up out of nowhere from his chest.

"Those other surfers didn't know what the fuck hit them when you started paddling again," he says. "Thought you were a corpse come back to life."

And James starts laughing too, leaning over to catch his breath and eyes lighting up with the thrill of his victory, with exhaustion from the morning's surf. Sydney wants to taste that smile on his lips, but holds back, awkwardly crossing his arms.

"Yeah, well, there's only so many times I can almost die before it gets old," James shoots back, which has them losing it all over again, staring openly at each other and trying to hide their chuckles over the fact that James Campbell almost drowned twice before Sydney's very eyes, and James Campbell just fucking won his first heat of the Billabong Pipeline Masters.

James insists they find an out-of-the-way place to watch at least another round or two, and Sydney leads them to the place in the trees where he'd watched and waited for his chance to jump in and surf all those years ago. They sit shoulder to shoulder in the shade while Sydney tells him blasé facts about the other competitors. It's the first time he's ever had a willing listener to talk to about anything related to surfing (about anything at all). It feels exquisite. Soft, velvet honey dripping from his tongue for only James to see.

By the time they make it back to Sydney's home in the Jeep, the sun is late and heavy in the sky. Sydney can tell James' shoulder is bothering him. The adrenaline of victory has finally worn off, leaving James sore and exhausted, and he's holding his upper body too carefully when he moves. Sydney can't quite understand the feeling that comes over him when he sees James' entire body visibly relax the second they come within sight of his little hut.

James sits out on the porch, rubbing at his shoulder, while Sydney tries to throw together some food that doesn't look like a ten-year-old made it, somewhat anxious at the easy domesticity of it all. They haven't even kissed once since they've been back from the beach, haven't even really touched, and Sydney wonders if he minds—if he doesn't feel like the warmth will slip away unless they tear at each other the same way they did by the Jeep. As if James can still back out any second since neither of them has taken off their clothes and actually seen each other naked, or stared at a full erection and reached out to *touch*—

Sydney bites his lip and shakes that thought from his head. He quietly reaches down and adjusts himself in the privacy of the kitchen, wondering when he grew up to be such an absolute idiot who couldn't even make *dinner* without thinking of James Campbell's cock. Of James Campbell wanting to reach out and touch *his* . . .

He sets a plate of pasta down in front of James out on the porch and pulls up the chair beside him, stretching out his legs to crack his toes. It feels completely reasonable, totally normal that someone be sitting at his side—a habit of eating seven years' worth of dinners alone broken in the span of five minutes. It's also the most bizarre occurrence he can ever remember happening on his little beach, cock-related thoughts aside.

"I'm surfing in the Finals day of the fucking Billabong tomorrow," James says after a long stretch of silence.

Sydney chuckles, grateful for the distraction. "Surprisingly, that fact hasn't changed since you last said it an hour ago."

James elbows him in the arm and digs into his pasta. "Oh right, I forgot that's old news to you," he says over a full mouth. "You're so humble about it all, it's easy to forget you've won before."

Sydney's hates himself for finding something endearing about a man like James Campbell talking with his mouth full, and he simply shrugs before they spend the rest of dinner in easy silence. The breeze rustles through the seashells hanging from the eaves, and Sydney realizes they've never sounded so beautiful to him before. He knows he would've cut them down long ago, just meaningless remnants of the previous tenant, except for the fact that the first shell on the first strand he held the scissors to looked just like the pearl from his momma's necklace, and he hadn't gone anywhere near them again.

"I'm not gonna be able to fall asleep any time soon," James says once they've finished. The sun is starting to set over the ocean horizon before them.

"I have an old Pendleton—use it sometimes to go down and watch the sunset by the water, if you want."

James looks over at him and smirks. "You watch sunsets on a beach on a blanket by yourself? What, do you live in a fucking romance movie?"

Sydney laughs and goes to get the blanket anyway. He knows James' interest when he sees it, and it shocks him deep in his core to realize that he could even know another person so thoroughly. It makes him wonder what James can read in his own face, even after such a short amount of time, and he wants to cringe at the thought of what he must be able to see. That, or the thought that maybe James actually doesn't see anything at all.

They lay the blanket out on the lower part of the shore and relax over the soft sand, just out of reach of the waves. James goes to lean back on his elbows and winces.

"Your shoulder's tight," Sydney says. "I could see you were having trouble paddling with it. Gonna feel like shit tomorrow."

He's almost surprised when James doesn't fight him on it, or call him out for being blunt. Instead he just nods and continues to knead at the sore muscle with his hand.

"You're right, there."

Sydney says his next words before he even realizes what he's saying, before he can stop to think of the implications of his question, or the myriad of reasons why James *wouldn't* want him to do this—place his hands on the most guarded part of his body, skin to skin. And then James' answer to his ridiculous question stuns him so thoroughly he's left to gaze helplessly out at the sunset-colored waves, gently lapping at the shore and bathing the world in shimmering gold.

"Do you want me to give you a massage?" Sydney had asked.

And James had sucked in a breath, and let out the tiniest little moan, and turned to look at Sydney with his beautiful deep blue eyes bathed in the golden haze of sunset.

And James had whispered, simply, "Yes."

# 14

An electric shiver ghosts down James' spine the moment Sydney's warm fingertips rest on his skin. He sits on the blanket in the sand with one leg bent, looking out over the rolling hush of the ocean, dripping in pearls of orange and red and painted with foaming gold. He holds his breath tight in his lungs, afraid to exhale and release the moan hiding in the back of his throat, emerging from the tense pit of his chest to shatter the thin silence.

Sydney had taken his time to slowly kneel behind him. He'd waited a careful foot away for James to strip off his shirt after James had awkwardly stared down at the sand for too many seconds, the image of Sydney's hands on his bare skin emblazoning itself onto his mind, halting his thoughts.

The echo of their last words still trembles quietly in the air, thrumming in the space between the open V of Sydney's thighs and the dip in the small of James' back. The simple, almost-too-easy dinner and their casual walk down to the shore have been replaced in an instant by a breathless anticipation, crawling slowly up through James' stomach and shivering in the shallow breaths leaving his lungs, mixing in with the restless thrush of the ocean as it hums.

James listens to Sydney's steady, even breathing behind him, and he envies him for the millionth time in two days how he can remain so goddamn stoic all the time. So effortlessly in control. He thinks of the way Sydney stalks across a beach, the way he can respond to absolutely anything thrown at him with just a single word, and meanwhile he remembers his own admission by the Jeep from earlier that day and burns with shame. As if Sydney Moore wanted to spend his day babysitting James on the sand. He walked away at the end of the day, after all, did he not? Excuse or no.

James wonders, as he wondered right after he emerged from the waves and saw Sydney wasn't clapping or coming his way, whether he's gone and fucked everything up by telling Sydney multiple times now to stay by his side—unnecessarily trying to voice it all out loud when all they've done is explode the building tension between them with a kiss. And he doesn't even know what this 'everything' is, if this 'everything' is even allowed, or if it exists.

They *kissed.* Goddammit.

He's achingly aware that he's not wearing a shirt. *Goddammit.*

It's embarrassing—to feel so unbelievably affected, right on the verge of a shiver or a moan from the second he feels Sydney's body heat radiating up his back from behind. Sydney's hands are still and smooth, not a hesitation in his fingers. He glides slowly up and down the slope of James' sore shoulders, fingertips just barely alighting on the sensitive skin of his neck, leaving shivers in their wake.

The silence sits around them, heavy and deep. It's a warm blanket in the cold dark of a storm—and the storm itself. Sydney's breaths gently rustle the hair at the top of James' head, leaving tingling warmth to drip like slow, salty water down the rest of James' scalp.

James waits in silence for the unspoken moment—the moment when he somehow knows that this will turn from shoulder massage into a caress of something more. He wants to lean back into it, and he wants to sprint away from it. When he's still making up his mind, finally, with the tiniest hesitation, Sydney's hands move to firmly grip the tense muscles of James' left shoulder, reaching around to place his palm flat over the scar and kneading into the tissue.

James moans, and Sydney's hands immediately still. The silence thrums.

"You're not hurting me," James whispers.

His words break every last wisp of tension that had still been hanging over them in a cloud. With a long, shaky sigh Sydney scoots forward so that James' body is suddenly cocooned within the V of his thighs, resting along the length of his lean body.

James frowns when he realizes he doesn't even remember Sydney taking his shirt off behind him. He can feel Sydney's heart racing straight against the muscles of his back, the slightly uneven rhythm to his shallow breathing, and James realizes in a moment of piercing clarity that Sydney doesn't feel stoic about this at all. That the touch of his fingertips on James' marred skin does not feel like some commonplace occurrence to end the day—does not effortlessly flow from his hands like some sort of post-workout stretch with a friend.

No—this is more. This is letting the entire ocean see that Sydney Moore is touching the physical imprint of the haunted darkness on James' skin. That Sydney Moore, the man who can read the sea herself like a lover, is sitting at the edge of the earth holding James upright from falling back into the sand. That he's placing James' weary body securely in the warm space between his thighs, in full view of the same particles of ocean that James' mom used to wade into with her stockings on to make James laugh.

James doesn't know enough vocabulary words to describe the sharp emotions rushing through him. Doesn't have enough space inside himself to contain them.

Sydney's thumbs dig deep into the muscles in James' shoulder, rubbing out the dull soreness from the day. James can feel every second of surfing he did aching through his body, from his neck all the way down to his ankles and toes. He's completely spent and limp, body still rising and falling beneath his skin in tune with the bob of the waves.

He feels Sydney's cheek rest against the side of his head, nuzzling gently into him as he slowly, patiently works out the tension in James' shoulder. James leans into the touch. There's a safety in the warmth coming from Sydney's skin. Safety, and also danger, whispering against his back as he stands right on the vast, unknown precipice of *something*. Toes itching to jump.

And Sydney lifts his cheek, and presses his lips firmly into James' hair while his palm strokes warm feeling into the raised scar on James' skin without hesitation, and that's when James feels himself start to cry.

He's silent. Stunned. His chest clenches on his breath, and he shudders through his core, and the tears slide gently down his cheeks, leaving cool trails in the evening breeze. They drip down onto his collarbone, pooling in the hollow of his throat. The churning emotions that had been slowly piling up inside him since first setting foot onto Hawaii—hell, since first opening his eyes in the shallows to see two terrified blue ones staring down at him—suddenly spill over inside of him, pouring shivering streaks down his face.

He sees Sydney from earlier that day in his memory—standing apart from the crowd on the beach, looking radiant and beautiful and *strong*. Sees the way Sydney's face was threatening to break and crumble just after James surfaced from the water, gasping for breath and desperately scanning the shore for a head of curls before he could even think to be thankful for being alive. He thinks of that moment—bobbing alone in the water and gulping down air and realizing that he absolutely had to paddle back out and catch the next possible wave. To prove to himself that he still could. To prove that he had the courage to jump off the cliff. Straight into Sydney's arms.

He remembers lifeless black eyes covered by long wet hair, lying frozen still on the floor of a red and steaming jungle, pumping out gurgling blood into the screaming void. Remembers the terrifying, sharp, nauseating fear that had coursed through his body two seconds after the world had exploded through his very chest. The feeling of his numb lips moaning out the word "mom" into the shattering gunfire, hoping that maybe, now that he was drifting between the worlds themselves, she could finally hear him again.

James realizes, sitting there with Sydney's hands on his skin, tear tracks on his face, that he's furious—furious at everything and himself. Angry that he doesn't have the strength in this moment to sit up on his own away from the support of Sydney's body behind him. To let himself be darkness and fear all on his own without contaminating the radiating sun of a man holding him up.

He's angry that his mom wasn't there to kiss him on the cheek when he first stepped onto the gleaming boat. That he was thinking of Billy Madden's hands when Lisa Kerny trailed her fingernails across his skin in the sunset tidepools. That the ocean that keeps him alive just by letting him ride her waves is the same one that pushes him back, back, back to the shore—back to existing and breathing and working, eyes open eyes shut, when he just wants to keep swimming out to the horizon and finally *rest*.

Angry that he's too young to be this tired.

And on top of all of this, he apparently can't be a normal person and sit and appreciate a fucking beautiful sunset, with a fucking beautiful man holding him, without falling apart and cracking into pieces like someone who belongs in an asylum for the vets who've lost it. Angry that he can even sit there and think of a man as beautiful in the first place.

He wants to tell the universe to just give up and lock him away since he doesn't have the decency to appreciate a good thing when he sees it. To banish him into the black since he can't laugh and pump his fist and overflow with joy that he's surfing in his dream competition tomorrow. That the best surfer on the whole damn island somehow believes that he won't embarrass himself. Somehow sees something in him to believe in.

And here he is crying instead like a child. In a *kid's* arms.

No, not a kid. A man. A man with a deep voice and stomach muscles and thick hair and—

Sydney's fingers are running through his hair. James has absolutely no idea how long they've been doing that. They card through the saltwater-stained strands slowly, gently, and then Sydney reaches around and wipes his thumb across the wetness on James' cheek, without saying a word.

His long, strong arms surround him, softly pressing him into his body in a way that makes James wonder if he'll ever physically be able to let go. For a startlingly fierce moment, James wants to escape, to break free from Sydney's hold and run out into the ocean and finish what he meant to do years ago. To let himself finally be one with the sea.

Then he hears Sydney's voice in his head, or maybe it's somewhere in his chest, or maybe it's out loud over the steady thrash of the sea.

"I'm here, James. I'm here."

For the first time since he wrote a letter to Helen Campbell on a Navy ship in the middle of the ocean, James allows himself to actually cry. Sydney pulls him closer into himself and holds him steady as James' chest heaves on choked breaths, and his hands come up to cover his eyes. He curls himself tight into a ball, willing his bones to disappear. Letting Sydney's bones take over.

James isn't sure how long they sit there. Sydney doesn't move a muscle behind him—doesn't shift or fidget or tense. He swallows down the sea breeze, opens his throat and mouth, and presses his spine back into a warm chest.

When James can finally take a full breath again without making a strained noise, he almost laughs. His lungs feel one hundred pounds lighter in his chest. It's the same sensation from when he'd hovered weightlessly in the air, right after leaping off the cliff into the gentle, steady blue, Sydney's eyes tracking him as he flew.

He knows somewhere deep in the pit of his soul that he doesn't need to tell Sydney a single reason behind what just happened. He tells himself he doesn't have to pretend that there aren't any tears still on his face, or that Sydney didn't just physically hold him as he broke apart, or that Sydney's hands weren't caressing the ugliest part of his skin like it was the petals of a beautiful, fragile bloom.

Sydney's arms are still wrapped around his waist, and James lets his head rest back onto his shoulder as they look out over the heavy sunset still slowly streaking its way across the sky. It feels impossible that he's only known this man behind him for two weeks, and that he's spent probably half of that time being a combination of intimidated by and infuriated with him.

James muses as he lies back against Sydney's chest, and their breathing starts to align, that he could probably spend the rest of his life naming emotions and still never name each one he's experienced since the moment he first locked eyes with Sydney Moore on a pier.

But James knows now. He knows Danny Moore, and he knows Sydney Moore, and he *knows.* The same way Sydney had looked at him on a moonlit beach and told him how he knew he'd been in the war. James can't imagine now how he's ever spent a sunset in his life apart from Sydney. Sydney who feels like the vitality of life itself effortlessly holding him up and out of blackest depths of the sea.

After a while, James pulls forward out of Sydney's reach and turns to look at him on the blanket. He tries to stop himself from feeling hotly embarrassed that his eyes must be puffy and red.

Sydney holds his gaze for a long moment, then smiles. *Smiles.* Like there's something in James' swollen, wet eyes that's pleasant for him to see. James sniffs and wipes his face one last time before breathing out the last bit of tension from his chest. He waits for the moment to feel uncomfortable, sitting silently alone together while James clears his stuffed-up nose.

It doesn't.

"Here, let me return the favor," he finally says, looking down at the blanket for Sydney to lie down.

Sydney smirks. "I don't really have anything I feel the need to cry about right now, but thank you."

James huffs as a strange warmth bubbles over in his chest. "Not that, you asshole. Lie down and I'll get your back."

Sydney looks steadily into his eyes. An odd look crosses over his face for one brief, fleeting second. A slight quiver of uncertainty. And then he gives a tiny, crooked grin—one that James notices doesn't quite reach his eyes—before turning onto his stomach on the blanket, settling down into the sand.

James has never seen the tattoo this up close before without moving, and he drinks it in, taking advantage of the last rays of the red sun still streaking the sky. The ink forming the body and tendrils of the jellyfish swirls in delicate, fluttering black lines across the smooth skin of his back, gliding over muscles and dripping down his spine. The detail is miniscule and sharp, unlike anything he's ever seen. James sucks in a deep breath and holds it, somehow reluctant to blow his exhale out across Sydney's bare skin, then leans in closer to get a better look.

Sydney instantly tenses up beneath him the moment James draws closer, and James realizes from the tense lines of his shoulders that he's nervous. James bites his lips as a wave of sadness washes over him. He honestly doesn't blame Sydney one bit for tensing up at the feeling of someone looming so closely over the lines on his back, seeing every intimate detail of the history inked onto his skin.

In a rush, he remembers the shit he heard all day at the competition about 'Danny Moore' from the other surfers as he tried to focus on the waves—the tattoo just one thing on a list of his sins. The faceless memories make James feel nauseous, hair prickling on the back of his neck as if the memories themselves have populated the empty beach behind them. He wants to shut his eyes tight and force out the memory of those words, get on with the simple back rub like he promised—return the favor.

Then he looks at Sydney's back, still lying deadly frozen beneath him. Even his ribs aren't moving, chest clenched waiting for James' reaction.

James keeps his eyes open, then licks his lips and warms his palms with his breath before placing them down squarely on Sydney's shoulder blades, anchoring him down into the earth.

"This is pretty beautiful, you know," he whispers.

To his relief, Sydney immediately relaxes beneath him, and James begins to run his palms up and down the length of Sydney's back. He presses deep into the skin, gliding smoothly from the tops of his shoulders down to the divots above the backs of his hips. The tattoo stares back at him, forcing him to remember that this is a man's back, Sydney's back, the man he's kissed's back. James gathers the new lightness in his chest, his eyes still stinging and red at the corners, and he stares right back, watching his own hands trace the tan skin.

Then Sydney just barely arches his spine, pressing his hips down into the earth and his back up against James' palms. Deep in his rough throat, Sydney sighs.

It's the most erotic thing James has ever heard.

Sydney's marked skin slowly undulates beneath his hands, rocking to the rhythm of his touch, seeking more pressure between James' shaking fingers and the sand. James doesn't even stop to think as he lifts a leg to straddle over Sydney's hips, sinking down onto the solid warmth of his body beneath him. Sydney shivers as James lightens the touch of his fingers and picks up the trail of one of the tentacles etched into his back, following it slowly down his trembling skin.

"Tell me about this," James says. "The story."

He continues tracing and following the lines of the tattoo, leaving shivers in the wake of his fingers, as Sydney takes a deep breath in and huffs out a gentle laugh.

"I don't think anyone's ever asked me before," he says back, voice low and muffled by the blanket. He pauses for a long moment, arching his spine up into the pressure of James' hands, then goes on.

"You're probably wondering by now how everyone knows I'm gay if that bathroom story isn't true."

James sucks in a breath and freezes. It sounds obscene to hear that sentence fall from his mouth so casually. So carelessly. A bomb dropped nonchalantly onto the cool, peaceful sand.

*I'm gay.*

Sydney turns his neck and peeks one eye up at James when he doesn't respond.

"You can't tell me you didn't realize that part was true," he says, brow furrowed. His eyes glance down to James' thigh across Sydney's lower back, and he raises his brows in a silent question.

James is suddenly acutely aware of the fact that he is indeed straddling the top of Sydney's ass between his thighs. That he'd grabbed Sydney by the neck and pulled his mouth to his in broad daylight by the Jeep not five hours ago. He stops himself just in time from flinging himself off Sydney's body into the sand.

"No, I—" He clears his throat. "I knew, I guess . . . Just never heard anyone say it out loud like that before."

Sydney hums. James thinks he's going to go on with the story of the tattoo. He waits with impatience, sweating under his arms, hot prickles on his cheeks.

Instead, Sydney says, simply, "You're gay, too."

The air slams into James' skin. His body prepares to flee, ready to tense up hot and defend and deny and refute. Ready to fight and run. Scream.

But then James hears himself say back, in the smallest whisper, "I know."

Sydney relaxes beneath him once more, and James' fingers resume their path along the lines of the tattoo. The air tingles, and James finds himself unable to draw in a full breath.

He feels like a completely new person in the wake of this admission, as if the shape of his mouth has been forever molded and changed by the words. He also feels exactly the same.

He drinks in the words when Sydney goes on, desperate for a distraction.

"When I was fourteen," Sydney says into the blanket, "I was in this little record store near the Pearl Harbor base where we were living. Trying to kill time before I had to go be home for dinner or something. Guy who ran it had this little counter in the back of the store with . . . magazines. You know what I'm saying. I saw this photo and I—I had to have it. He sold it to me for a penny. Now I think about it he must have been a queer, too. Maybe took pity on me or something, just wanted me to have it."

James can't help himself. "What was the photo?"

He watches with wide eyes as a blush forms along the top of Sydney's neck and back, blooming across his skin as James continues to run his fingertips over the inked lines.

Sydney swallows thickly. "It was of a sailor."

"Like a Navy ID? A portrait?"

"No, James. A *sailor.*"

James feels his own face flush bright red. He clears his throat and subtly shifts his position sitting across Sydney's hips, suddenly feeling a bit warm and heavy in his own gut.

"Right. Go on."

"Well, surprise surprise, I was fourteen and an idiot."

"That admission must pain you."

"You're hilarious. I kept it in my private notebook—this one I used for notes I took reading other textbooks after school. Didn't want my brother to find it because we shared a room. But then some of my stuff got taken—was only about two fucking weeks after I bought the damn thing. The wrong kid saw the photo and . . . Oahu's a small island."

James realizes his hands have grown still, resting firmly just under Sydney's neck and fanning across his shoulders. He picks up rubbing his back again, letting him know he's still listening. His ears tingle in the clear, salty air at the sound of Sydney's voice, vibrating up from his chest against James' palms.

His own heart pounds, anxiety churning as if he himself had been caught out in the high school halls—the worst nightmare he used to think about in the middle of the night when he woke up in a cold sweat with damp warmth between his thighs, the wrong face having been the one touching him in his dreams.

Sydney continues, seemingly unaware of James' trailing thoughts. "Word got to my father at work on the base pretty fast. You already know about all the church stuff, so you can imagine . . . Day I turned fifteen, I was coming home from being at the beach really early in the morning and all my stuff was in a bag on the front steps waiting for me."

"He kicked you out?"

Sydney hums. James' heart races in his chest, and a sickening feeling tightens his throat. He has a million questions. He chooses the least important one.

"Why were you on the beach so early? Surfing?"

To his surprise, Sydney smiles warm and soft, tinged with sadness and longing. James catches it on the corner of Sydney's lips not pressed into the blanket. "Actually, it was the first day I ever tried to surf."

"You didn't surf 'til you were fifteen?"

"I told you I taught myself, didn't I? Can't well do that if I'm still in diapers."

"I wouldn't put that past you, of all people."

"Your faith in me is heartwarming," Sydney says with a smirk, but when James opens his mouth to joke back, he finds he can't find the words.

Sydney's words hover over them on the beach, not fading away. They mix with the last golden rays of sunset still floating through the cooling air. The raw truth of them burns in James' chest, aching to be let free.

James licks his lips, then rubs his hands up over Sydney's back, across his neck, through his hair and down across the dip in the low of his back. His silence will have to be answer enough. Then he remembers why this conversation even started in the first place, and jumps at the chance to say something else.

"So what does all that have to do with the tattoo, then?"

Sydney chuckles. "Oh, right. Well that first night on my own I slept on the beach—didn't have anywhere else to go. Just had the clothes I was wearing and my bag of stuff and my board. Woke up in the morning and I was mad as hell. I'd never been so pissed off in my life. I went down to the water and the only thing I could think to do was yell 'fuck you' as loud as I could at my father. Well, not at him, but, you know, at the waves."

"I get what you mean."

"And then this jellyfish suddenly swam right up next to me where I was standing in the water. Thought it would sting me, but it just . . . hovered there by my leg and let me watch. And for whatever goddamn reason, looking at that thing, I—I don't know. I wasn't mad anymore. It was all completely gone. So I saved up money fixing shit and found out about an artist over on the Big Island that would tattoo a kid my age if I showed up alone. Flew down and got this the first chance I could. Never been mad about any of it again since. Stupid, but, that's the story."

"It's not stupid at all," James breathes.

It's the least stupid thing he's ever heard in his life. He wants to take his splayed open heart right out of his chest and press it against the tattoo covering Sydney's back—the tattoo he now won't ever be able to look at without seeing a young kid, lost and alone on a beach.

He wants to lean down and press his lips to the inked skin and taste it. So he does.

Sydney gasps when James' wet and parted lips touch his skin, kissing the top of his spine before slowly, carefully, dragging them down along one of the inked lines. He refuses to hesitate, in case even a second's pause makes him lose his nerve, and he follows the jellyfish across the muscles of Sydney's back and down towards his hips. James releases a shaky breath, stunned at his own daring, unsure if this is even happening in reality, or if he's just dragging his lips across his own palm, deep in a dream.

But the ocean rushes in, and the salty wind caresses his bare back, and James knows it's not a dream as he watches goosebumps form across Sydney's back, shivering under the touch of his lips. James keeps tracing the lines up and back, following the flowing tentacles across his skin. He kisses them with his lips, licks and tastes them with his tongue, runs his nose along the smooth lines of muscle and breathes in the scent of him, salty and floral and warm.

"James."

Sydney's voice is low and ragged. The sound of it shoots heat through James' veins and pools deep in his gut, throbbing once between his legs where he still sits pressed over the bottom of Sydney's hips. Sydney quivers and rolls beneath him as James tastes every inch of the skin of his back, the tattoo as a tender guide for his wet tongue.

Without thinking about it, James grinds his hips down slowly, suddenly feeling his hardening cock press deep into the warm crease of Sydney's ass through his shorts.

They moan simultaneously. James freezes, and the cool air crackles around them, rushing across James' skin and sensitizing the tips of his fingers.

"James." This time it's a whisper. The air around them releases.

The breeze coming off the ocean rushes in to weave through Sydney's curls, and James rolls his hips down once more onto Sydney's body, rubbing himself off slowly, glacially on the heat radiating out from the dip of Sydney's ass. He can't remember the last time he even got close to being this hard. Can't remember the last time he was lightheaded and breathless, muscles trembling and lungs shaking and lips wanting to taste, taste, taste. Hot and swollen between his legs, already tenting the fabric of his shorts.

A small part of his brain, the tiny alarm from the shower that now feels like a lifetime ago, starts to go off in earnest.

James is sitting out in the open air in front of the entire world with an erection between his legs and a man underneath him. A man who's arching up into James' touch, and reaching back with a shaking hand to grab tight onto James' hip and squeeze. A man who's panting on ghosts of little sighs, hovering on the tips of his full, wet lips. Who's grasping a fistful of sand.

Who calls him James.

James Campbell tells the alarm in his mind to shut the fuck up. He raises himself up off of Sydney's hips and leans down to press an open, wet kiss to the tattoo one last time.

"Turn over."

He barely recognizes his own voice. It's rough and hoarse, desperate—an entirely different kind of desperate than the way Keith Hartman had screamed over the chaos for him to run. Sydney turns slowly beneath him until he's splayed out on his back, chest heaving and eyes blown wide, looking up at James with barely parted lips. The dying sun illuminates a sheen of wetness from when he must have licked them.

James licks his own lips and stares. Sydney's skin is painted gold, bathed by the warm colors of the sun just barely hanging on in the sky. It molds across the muscles of his chest. Drapes over his stomach and down his lean, tan arms. James' eyes track down the whole length of Sydney's body, knowing Sydney is watching him look. He takes in his nipples, dark and peaked in the cooling air and the salty breeze. Takes in his hard, rippling stomach and the trail of hair leading from his navel down to the quivering waistband of his shorts. Down to the thick, bulging erection that's now just inches from James' own, throbbing and hovering in the air as a tented mound.

He meets Sydney's eyes again and swallows hard. He's on the cusp of a decision—one somehow more potentially dangerous then signing his name on an enlistment form. As if he could simply walk away right now if he chose to, even having kissed Sydney and willingly straddled his body. As if he could go back to Los Angeles, and return to his job, and have sex with women again and completely forget that the hardest he'd ever gotten in his life was when he was poised over the crease of another man's body, imagining a stubble-covered cheek rubbing against his.

He can see a separate stream of thoughts playing out across Sydney's pale and glittering eyes—nerves mixed with uncertainty and drowning in arousal. He watches Sydney blink a few times, as if he's trying to clear them, then James reaches forward, still hovering just above Sydney's body, and gently brushes the hair back from Sydney's forehead with his fingers. Sydney leans into the touch and sighs, body going limp into the blanketed sand.

It's a decision.

James gives a small nod, and at that, Sydney sucks in a breath and sits up quickly onto his elbows. He grips James firmly by the hips and, after a brief pause, pulls him down onto his lap. James settles his weight with a deep hum, and Sydney's throat rolls with a hard swallow.

They stare at each other. James feels as if he's never actually looked at this man before, never truly understood the physicality of the bone and muscle, the lines of his face. The young wrinkles starting to bloom from the corners of his eyes. He looks at those same eyes which spotted the jellyfish, which conquered the sea, which watched him take his first breath through blue lips on the rocky shore.

And while he's still looking, lost in an eternal pause of time, Sydney tilts up his head, wraps his palm around James' neck, and calmly captures James' mouth in a kiss.

The taste of Sydney's lips shiver down through his body and pool in thick warmth in the deepest part of his belly. He continues to straddle Sydney's hips, sinking his full weight into his body, and an odd shiver of pleasure runs of his spine when he realizes doesn't feel like he's in the lesser position at all. Rather, his own thick erection presses down against the heaving skin of Sydney's stomach through his shorts, pushing into his body with the force of his want.

James looks down at the bulge of his cock tracing the lines of Sydney's tense abdominals and moans. Sydney's hands are clutching at his back, running up his chest, cupping the side of his face and neck as his warm, wet lips once again caress his mouth. James tastes him. Their tongues meet, trembling in between them while they breathe gasps of hot, groaning air into each other's mouths.

James disappears. The edges of his body blend and smear into Sydney's warm skin. The spray of the pounding ocean waves showers his back, and droplets of cool air dripping from the earliest stars run down his neck. His knees are caressed by the gentle warmth of the sand through the blanket as he looks down at Sydney's face and kisses him deeply, not daring to pause for breath for fear that everything will suddenly halt. He thrills deep in his chest when Sydney's lips and tongue press back against his, eager and firm.

His skin is electric—every touch, every grip, every caress from Sydney's fingers pulsing through his body with a hot jolt, leaving permanent imprints of his fingertips on James' back and chest. James runs his hand through Sydney's hair and grips a handful of soft, velvet curls. His fingernails scratch warm scalp. Sydney gasps, his panting sighs melding with the hiss of the waves rushing over the shore.

James licks one last time into Sydney's mouth across his tongue, tasting the salt on his lips as Sydney gasps in surprise. James sighs out through his nose with their mouths wetly pressed together before pulling back for air, fingers still clutching at a handful of curls. He wants to say something elegant, something casually important. Something that could somehow convey even one tiny portion of how he feels in this moment, where he's a man who's kissing a shirtless Sydney Moore on a goddamn Hawaiian beach. But, for some reason, the thought of opening his mouth to try to say any of that makes him feel like parts of him would fly out from his lungs, tumbling away into the open sky, and he'd never get those parts back again. And Sydney would see.

Instead all he can do is shake his head and whisper, "Fuck . . ."

Sydney lets out a breathy laugh and runs his nose along James', trailing his fingers through the hair on James' chest with one hand while the other grips under his thigh. Sydney opens his eyes, blinking a few times in the thin light from the dying sun, and James finds that he can only stare into them for a few seconds before having to close his own. He wants to press his lips right onto Sydney's eyelids and feel his eyelashes brushing against his mouth. He wants to somehow taste the irises themselves on his loose tongue—the eyes that only he gets to see so bare and up close.

Sydney licks his kiss-swollen lips. "You are a marvel."

James laughs, then prickles under his arms, acutely aware again that he's basically sitting in Sydney's lap. "Feel like I should be in the 50s hearing you say that. Wearing a petticoat."

Sydney tries to smile back, but the steel glow of his eyes is intensely serious. "Well, it's true."

James' skin runs hot, and he half-heartedly scoffs.

*He's* the marvel? He's thirty-two living like he's twenty with no plans, no direction, a chain of dog tags in his sock drawer and a cheap surfboard taking up half the space in his tiny studio. And here's Sydney Moore, with his private beach house and his own business and a list of championship titles longer than a sheet of lined paper. Smarter than James by half, with the body of a fucking model, who steps one foot onto a beach and sucks everyone's breath clear out of their lungs.

An unwelcome mixture of indignation and embarrassment churn in his system. He starts to shift, lifting his weight back up onto his thighs and knees. The way Sydney's lap has been cradling him, bony knees holding him close, suddenly feels a lot like pity.

But then Sydney runs his thumb along James' cheek, still slightly damp from his tears. He doesn't stop James from shifting away, but leans in and leaves the softest ghost of a kiss just on the corner of James' mouth, tongue darting out to taste his skin.

James realizes that he's never been more wrong in his life. Realizes that the man he wants to compare himself to, the man he tries so hard to convince himself is too good to be true, too good to willingly cup James' cheek and kiss *him*—that man is not Sydney Moore. Not the Sydney Moore he thinks he knows.

Sydney's mouth brushes against his once more, and James re-gathers the courage he'd flown through from the cliff. He whispers against his lips, in a voice that sounds too thin and fragile to be his own.

"*Sydney.*"

Sydney hums and tilts James' head back gently with his hand before bringing his lips to his neck, leaving soft, wet kisses from his shoulder to his ear. James gazes up at the stars, tingling through his entire body, and tries to breathe. He feels himself growing hard again against Sydney's stomach, and he lets himself press forward just once against the hot friction of Sydney's body. He whispers Sydney's name up to the stars, so softly he can't even hear himself, just hot breath over his tongue, and he shuts his eyes tightly as the barest hint of stubble from Sydney's jaw rasps over his throat.

Sydney's wet, rolling tongue on his neck sends a zip of fire down his spine. The damp heat of his panting breath, saved for James' skin alone. James rocks his hips down once more on to Sydney's body, settling his weight, then, with a rush of boldness, looks down as he rubs the tip of his erection through his shorts against Sydney's stomach.

Sydney watches too, eyes glossy and wide, and whispers a curse through his full lips.

James needs more. Now. Sydney pants more wet, hot breaths onto his shivering skin, devouring his neck, and James' free moans echo out across the sea. Without warning, Sydney reaches around and grabs James' ass firmly in both hands, pulling him forward hard and crushing James' cock into his abs, and James' hips explode in a white hot flame of want.

He grips Sydney by the shoulders and pushes him down into the sand with a grunt, looming over him on his hands and knees. Sydney whimpers as James leans down and kisses him fiercely, groaning into his mouth and biting his full, wet lips between his teeth. Sydney melts beneath him; he runs his hands down James' back, grabs his hips hard and pulls, and James collapses down on top of Sydney's warm and writhing body. Their bare chests touch, pearled nipples brushing over sensitive skin. James shifts his weight up just an inch so that their erections align, and they both gasp out of the kiss and moan.

"God . . ." James hears himself groan, and he feels more than he hears Sydney's response rumble through his hair, "Yeah, come on . . ."

James aches between his legs. It's a consuming, throbbing heat he's never before felt while pressed against another person—one that makes him hyper aware of every place their skin touches, every groaning puff of breath from Sydney's close, open mouth. He closes his eyes and simply feels Sydney arching up into him, pressing his hard cock up against James' own as they rock into the heat of each other. James' hand flies out, gripping the sand above their heads for balance, and he shifts his hips so he can rub his balls slowly along the length of Sydney's erection through the fabric of their shorts. The thick, solid cock beneath him throbs and trembles at his touch.

Shocking words fly up into James' mouth and slam into the back of his teeth. He wants to close his lips around Sydney's ear and tell him he's *huge*, that the sweat pooling between their bare chests is hot and slick across his skin, that Sydney's giant hand trailing from the back of his neck to his thigh is driving him crazy, *desperate*. He wants to moan, for some insane reason and over and over again, the words, "*your cock . . . fuck, your cock . . .*"

Instead James yanks Sydney's head to the side and bites the thin skin in the crook of his neck. Sydney whimpers, whole body pulsing, as James holds him down so he can rub their cocks along each other, hot and slow and smooth. He's clenching tight through his thighs. Aching at the evidence of Sydney's thick want for him bulging the front of his shorts, dripping fat, wet drops of precum onto the fabric as they move as one.

And Sydney's huge, hot hands are everywhere at once, consuming every untouched inch of James' sides and back. Long fingers grasp hard at his ass, at his neck and shoulders, at every bone up his rolling spine, quivering and dripping with beads of sweat in the salty breeze. James lifts his cheek from Sydney's neck and realizes he's been cradling the back of Sydney's head in his palm for who knows how long. Something sharp flashes through his chest at the sight of the dark curls wrapped gently around his fingers, letting him protect them from the sand being flung onto the blanket. He hesitates for a moment, then keeps his hand there.

Just when James realizes neither of them has said anything for a long time, too long a time, that they've just been lying together in their shorts breathing shallow kisses and naively touching bare chests, not even naked, not even thrusting, not even touching *cocks . . .* Just then, Sydney's hand suddenly slides under James' waistband to grab the bare skin of his ass in his palm, gripping hard and rough.

The breath leaves James' lungs. He rests his head with a crash on Sydney's shoulder, running his hand up over the contour of Sydney's chest and nipple, and Sydney lets out a cry, high and breathless, as James sucks on the smooth skin just beneath his ear.

"James," he rumbles, voice nearly gone. The single sound seems to echo forever across the still, moonlit shore—so loud that James fears that all of Oahu just heard it, so deep that James feels it straight through to his own chest and bones.

And then Sydney's lips are on his again, gasping breath straight down James' throat, and his mouth pants wet, open, frantic kisses against James' swollen, sensitive lips. James ignores the wave of crippling unease that slaps across his back as he tries to build a thick rhythm, his aching erection grinding down onto the pulsing heat of Sydney's cock. He keeps time to the unprecedented moans and grunts escaping his throat, vibrating against Sydney's lips.

Sydney catches on. Of course he does, he's a fucking genius, isn't he? James refuses to let his mind keep wandering down that trail—imagining the more sculpted bodies, the more impressive surfers, the more confident, desirable, arousing men who've felt Sydney's hands on them before, no scars in sight. Instead he moans a reckless curse when Sydney's palm snakes without warning between their bodies and cups James' erection.

James freezes, terrified that if he moves, Sydney will snatch his hand back. He feels himself growing impossibly thicker and heavier in Sydney's palm. Before he can look down at the sight of Sydney's fingers caressing the thick bulge in his shorts, Sydney's lips are on his, in a touch so light and soft it brings an embarrassing tightness to James' throat. James holds his breath. Sydney kisses him there as his hand strokes, just once, along James' erection, sending vibrating sparks through his thighs, so powerful James nearly throws himself off and sideways into the clear sand.

But he doesn't, and Sydney traces the wet spot around the crown of James' cock with his fingertip, then he slips his hand to James' back, back beneath the waistband, and he grips hard at James' ass, pulling James close against every inch of his body. He wraps his leg around James' calf.

James pauses, just for a second, with his nose alongside Sydney's, trying to summon the same level of courage he had when he stepped off that dinghy into the silent jungle. He looks down into Sydney's face, expecting to see eyes dark with desire, heavy-lidded and sharp and piercing with need.

But Sydney's clear blue eyes are blown wide, glossy and wavering as they rove across James' face. He looks uncertain as they lie still, James' body covering his. He looks young.

To his surprise, Sydney's eyes suddenly banish James' unease away. James looks down at him, licks his lips, and gives an almost imperceptible nod. Something in Sydney's eyes grows impossibly warm, softening the edges of his pupils. He nods back.

Then James reaches down and takes hold of his own bare cock in his palm, groaning at the pressure from his fingers. He strokes himself, still heavy and hard from before, as Sydney's palm slowly kneads and grabs at his ass. James is ridiculously close as he quietly thrusts into his fist, closer when his pearled nipple brushes across Sydney's chest, closer as Sydney's long fingertips barely ghost into the crease of his ass, brushing unashamedly over James' hole.

James drips onto his fingers, clenches his stomach with a wild moan, stares down into little droplets of ocean. He flies his hand over his cock, twisting hard at the tip, and then he's coming, free and open under the moonlit sky.

James groans as he falls apart into an exploding bliss, burying his face in the mess of Sydney's curls. His orgasm pulses hot and thick through his limbs, pooling into his shorts. He distantly registers Sydney's arm brushing against his side, feels for a shocking second as Sydney pumps his own erection up against James' softening cock, then a breathless cry leaves Sydney's throat. The body beneath him jerks, then tenses. James pulls his own hand away and collapses on him just as hot cum seeps into the front of Sydney's shorts.

James goes to push himself off and roll to Sydney's side, hating the reluctance that sits like lead in his chest, then gasps in surprise when Sydney's hand grips his jaw. Sydney crashes their lips together, panting a wet and heavy kiss against his mouth. James kisses him back deeply, feeling limp and heavy in his skin, and Sydney's hands gently stroke up and down his sweat soaked back. He grazes his lips against Sydney's one last time, licking his own spit off the skin, before pulling away.

Sydney's head falls back limp onto the top of the blanket, spreading his curls out into the sand. His eyes are half-lidded and blazing, chest heaving, irises glittering silver in the light from the stars. Lips red and full.

It's painfully intimate, lying chest to chest, thigh to thigh, with a mess of wet and cooling fabric trapped between them. Sydney is lightly rubbing just the tip of his thumb across James' side, as if he's hesitant for James to even feel that he's touching him there.

James bites his lip as he realizes that this was simultaneously the most tame and the most erotic sex he's ever had in his life.

And he feels deep down that he should be bothered by that— that and a million other things that just happened. He should be above coming in his shorts having sex in his thirties on an open beach, rocking against each other like two teens trapped in a backseat. And at the same time he is so far, far below the man who just watched him masturbate in his arms—who just kissed and held him as he came. And he survived a *war*, took a *bullet*, and his heart is pounding harder now than it had after he crawled on his belly to check who he'd just killed on the jungle floor.

Something burns in him at those thoughts. Without thinking too much about it, James leans down and kisses Sydney's forehead, the same way Sydney had done to him just that morning by the Jeep. Something flashes through Sydney's eyes when James pulls away, something mournful and sad, but it's gone before James can even process it, replaced by an easy calm.

James hesitates, waiting for Sydney to speak, but when he doesn't, James scoots to the side and falls limp onto the blanket, still pressed against Sydney's side. Sydney reaches over and pulls across one edge of the blanket to cover their skin from the cool sea breeze. He pauses with his arm holding the blanket hovering over James' side, looking at him with a small frown, and James swallows over the rush of emotion as he nods okay for Sydney to drape across his shoulders with his arm. James scoots closer, places his ear right just against the thrum of Sydney's heartbeat.

It feels like they've done this a thousand times. There's a wobbling flutter in James' throat at how perfectly his cheek rests against the top of Sydney's chest. How his leg slots just so along Sydney's warm thighs. How the softness of Sydney's cock inside his shorts pressed against his own skin feels warm instead of iron hot, making him want to lean into it, not flinch away.

Sydney turns and presses his nose into James' hair as James places his hand on Sydney's forearm, and they lie in each other's arms, breathing in time to the hush of the waves. They listen to the breeze rustle the shells hanging off the eaves of the house, bathed in golden light from the lamps through the windows.

James eyes are actually drooping shut when Sydney reaches up to hold James' face once more, thumb resting at the corner of his mouth.

"You have another early day tomorrow," he casually says, his voice cocooned in the warm, close air between them. "Should get some sleep."

James hums. He wants to ask Sydney if he doesn't also think it's wildly unbelievable that they just had sex and haven't needed to say a single word about it. Then Sydney chuckles softly into his scalp, and reaches down to quickly grab James' ass with playful fingers, and James realizes Sydney's actually wondering the same exact thing.

It's fucking unreal. Like hovering in the air moments after leaping off a cliff, wondering if the soft, cool water will really catch him. Wondering if he really did just jump. Knowing Sydney Moore is there.

James finally shifts to stretch his legs and mumbles "ok" into Sydney's skin, and they sit up and pull off the blanket in easy silence. James stands on sore thighs and calves and marvels that the ache in his shoulder is actually gone, even after holding himself up over Sydney for so long in the sand.

He catches Sydney shooting him a small smirk as he folds up the blanket, shaking the sand from its edges.

"I didn't *just* suggest giving you a massage so I could have sex with you," Sydney says.

James huffs and rolls his eyes, even as the rawness of the words flash through him with a tight knot. "Yeah, right, Mr. 'I know fucking everything and I'm going to remind you about it every five minutes'."

Sydney laughs, and James almost gapes at how easily the sound of it falls from Sydney's mouth. James can't even begin to imagine what Danny Moore would look like laughing—standing tall on a beach with his sunglasses on and his arms crossed and his lips in a permanent straight line. And here is Sydney Moore, all loose-limbed and calm, looking over at James with a quiet warmth James can feel tingling across his skin.

James follows him as he starts to walk back up to the house, oddly aware of how many inches are between them. Their bare feet sink into the soft, cool sand, arms brushing as they walk. James is just starting to wonder who the hell is going to have to break the ice and ask whether he's still sleeping on the couch, when suddenly it grips him that he absolutely cannot leave that beach, cannot wake up and surf in the Billabong Finals tomorrow without doing something first which he'd never, ever thought he needed to do before.

He stops and turns to Sydney. His mouth is dry and numb. "Do you still have it?"

Sydney frowns in confusion, then follows James' line of sight down to his own pocket. He nods slowly in understanding, reaching inside to pull out the bullet casing he'd kept in there during the competition. He twirls it once in his fingers before holding it out to James on a steady palm. James stares at it a moment, then takes it with equally steady fingers. He walks calmly back to the shoreline, knowing Sydney will follow.

James stops just when his toes reach the calm, lapping froth, and he lifts his chin as the cool wind rustles through his hair. It whispers raised shivers across his bare chest and arms, pearling his nipples. He holds the bullet in his hand and looks down at it in the moonlight glow.

The earth freezes. He looks at it, and he tries to think of a pair of lifeless black eyes on the floor of the jungle, or the look on Keith Hartman's face when he'd screamed at him to run, or the way the beach had transformed itself in his final conscious moments to a Long Beach pier with a gigantic whipped-cream topped milkshake waiting at its end. Waiting for him as he collapsed down into the blood-soaked foam.

He stares at the metal in his palm and tries to think of the memories it always invokes. The ones that soothe his exploding heartbeat when he wakes up in a cold sweat in the middle of the night, and remind him that there must be some godforsaken reason he survived, and whisper in his ear that he should put off walking out into the sea for one more day. Just one more day. And one more. That first wet handshake from a grinning Rob Depaul.

But all James can see now reflected with the emerging stars in the gleaming metal is the brilliant smile that had swept across Sydney's face right at the moment James had emerged victorious from his Wild

Card heat. Sees the color of Sydney's half-lidded eyes as he'd let his head fall back gently into the sand just minutes ago.

James rubs his thumb once along the metal, saying goodbye.

Then he curls it into his fist, reaches back with his arm, and hurls it with all his might out over the vast moonlit sea. He watches it soar and glint in the air, reflecting the light of the stars, and he sucks in a breath as it plunks down into the water with barely a sound at all.

A single tear, still hovering at the back of his eye from earlier in the night, falls slowly down his cheek, and he lets it. He can feel Sydney's body heat radiating from where he stands a few feet behind him in the shallows.

James stands still and waits for his body to erupt with panic now that it's gone—that he'll never again feel the smooth metal he'd been tightly gripping the moment Rob had walked up to him in the sand and asked if he surfed.

Instead he feels utterly, incomprehensibly calm. He closes his eyes and sees the massive waves he's going to surf across tomorrow in his mind, and he hears Sydney's steady, even breathing at his back, and he lets out a breath he's been holding in for over two years.

Sydney walks forward to stand at his side, and they gaze out over the water, letting the foam pool around their shins.

"The hippies'll be all over your ass if they find out some fish choked on that," Sydney says, stone-faced.

James turns to look at Sydney—standing there, nonchalantly staring out to sea like absolutely nothing has happened since they first laid the blanket down onto the sand—then he bursts out laughing. A weightless, giddy, exhausted happiness flows smoothly through every vein in his body. Sydney looks at him out of the corner of his eye and quirks his lips in an answering chuckle.

James shakes his head and turns to walk back up to the house without responding. Sydney jogs to catch up, and James steals a glance at Sydney's moonlit profile just as Sydney quickly looks away.

James suddenly knows, without a hint of doubt, that they're currently walking back to the same room—the same bed and the same sheets. That he'll wake up tomorrow morning on the day he surfs in Day 2 of the Billabong Pipeline Masters with Sydney Moore by his side, sleepy and warm.

He takes a deep breath, stops himself just in time from looking side to side on the deserted beach, then steps closer to Sydney and wraps an arm around his waist. His chest tightens when Sydney immediately reaches out and pulls him close by the shoulders.

Just when they reach the sagging front steps, Sydney tightens his grip, not letting James step away. James is just about to turn to him to ask what's going on when he feels soft lips pressed into his hair. They hesitate for a moment, hovering above his scalp, then kiss him again.

And James swallows over an unexpected wave of hot gratefulness when Sydney whispers into his hair, "You surfed like hell, James Campbell."

# *15*

James flutters awake behind his eyelids, fighting against the bleary pull back to a heavy sleep. He stretches his tongue in his mouth and drowsily wonders how much longer he's got until his alarm will go off to wake up and go surfing with Rob before work. His ears fixate on the rolling sound of the distant ocean, waves cutting through fresh dawn air and pouring their pools of cool froth over the virgin sand. It sounds closer than it usually does—more steady and consuming and insistent. James takes a deep breath in and smells the hint of salt in the air, carried on a bed of blooming flowers.

His apartment never smells like flowers.

He sucks in a breath and flicks open his eyes, trying to focus their vision on the plain white ceiling above him while his heart kicks in. It pumps blood through his body, which feels sore and sated in a way he never usually feels after even the longest day of work.

The angle of the ceiling is wrong, and the diagonal slants through the air—just the barest hints of light—are pouring in from the wrong sides. He can't hear the early morning commuters making their way down Hermosa Avenue at twice the speed limit, or the dull, insistent way the gas pipe of his apartment building constantly hisses and squeaks. His confusion mixes thickly with the usual aching dread of another full day spent at work, and he lies almost petulantly on his back, waiting for the alarm, slowly stretching his sleepy lungs with air.

When the alarm doesn't come after a few minutes, James wakes up enough to turn his head to look over at his bedside clock. He freezes.

James doesn't see his bedside clock. Instead he sees a sleeping face just inches from his own, a vivid dusting of freckles in the pale, grey air, half-covered by a wild mop of frizzy curls.

The memory of the last few days crashes down on him with the slapping force of a crisp, thick wave. He stares dumbfounded at Sydney's sleeping form beside him, stretched out on his stomach with one arm curled up over his head and the other one lying gently in the small space between their bodies, tattoo rising and falling with the pulse of his breathing, sheet bunched in a tangle around his waist.

James stares at him, and he takes in a deep breath of salty flowers and sleep-soft skin, and a shocked, tentative smile curls at the corners of his mouth. Tingling relief courses through his body. He doesn't have to crawl out of the water and throw on a hard hat and go to work today. He doesn't have to spend the entire day waiting to go home to an empty apartment.

He's in Hawaii. He's going to surf in the Billabong. He isn't even *nervous.* The reigning champion is gently sleeping next to him, face relaxed and easy like he already knows James is there, even in his dreams. James feels like he just won the goddamn lottery and solved world peace and found eternal life all at once.

James scoots his face closer on their shared pillow, close enough to feel the soft puff of Sydney's breaths on the tip of his nose. He basks for a moment in the quiet unbelievability of it all. That little more than two weeks ago, Danny Moore was just a terrifying, barely real legend stepping up next to him in the sand. And here James is watching the rise and fall of his bare back as he sleeps. In his home, in his room, in his bed. Free and welcome to breathe his same air, and know the most intimate touch of his skin, and wait with bated breath for his unguarded eyes to finally flicker open and land on him.

His chest is awash with a thick wave of conflicting emotion— protectiveness over this trust that's been placed so willingly into his palms, leftover embarrassment from the beach the night before, and a raw, pleading whisper in the back of his mind to get up, get out, go back to his real life and the real world and leave hazy Oahu fantasies far behind. Leave the surfing and the trophies and the soft linen sheets to Sydney—to Danny.

And he will have to do just that in about thirty short hours from now, won't he?

But Sydney had held him as he wept, had wiped the tears from his cheeks with his thumb without pity, without asking for anything, and had offered his bare skin to him in full view of the sea and stars.

James rests in the moment for a minute longer, then quietly reaches out to touch Sydney's hand with the barest brush, just to feel his warmth and prove to himself he isn't asleep back in Los Angeles. He traces one of Sydney's knuckles with his thumb as he muses that this is the first time he's ever woken up next to someone and not had his first thoughts be *"where are my pants, what was her name, and how am I going to get home?"* He feels Sydney's living, breathing warmth on the pads of his fingers, and then he closes his heavy eyes as he relives the rest of the night before.

How they'd slid their arms off one another once they set foot in the quiet house, and Sydney had calmly handed him a towel and an extra pair of boxers and nodded at the shower. How James had only just covered his salt-dry hair in shampoo when the shower curtain had eked open, and Sydney had stepped inside, slowly and one careful foot at a time.

They'd stared at each other, neither one looking down past their eyes, James furiously blinking away stinging soap, and then Sydney had taken a breath, raised his chin, and wordlessly turned James around by the shoulders so that he could wash the soap from his hair, like it was something he did every evening without thought. James had held his breath, holding still as Sydney washed the salt and sand from every inch of his skin, and Sydney started to ramble in a smooth and steady voice that mixed with the splash of the shower spray all he knew about James' competition tomorrow—the competitors and their weaknesses and his predictions for the weather and the swells.

The thick knowledge of Sydney Moore's steaming, wet body behind him, his fingertips massaging across James' scalp, rubbing up his back with his deep voice right in his ear, both of them naked . . . James had looked down and seen himself growing noticeably hard and full.

Alarm pulsed through him as Sydney calmly detailed the preferences of one of the judges for tomorrow, and James had tried to listen, tried to forget that they were just inches apart in a shower, that

Sydney could see the bare skin of his back and thighs. He'd slowly moved his hand towards his groin, making to cover himself and try to will his erection away before Sydney noticed.

And then wet fingers had gently touched his wrist, Sydney's monolog grinding to a halt.

Their mutual breathing swirled around them in clouds of fresh steam. James tried not to visibly shake his head as he moved his wrist out of Sydney's grasp to drape his palm over his cock.

"Sorry," he'd whispered, at the exact same moment Sydney's lips brushed the top of his wet shoulder, and he breathed, "*James.*"

Something shifted, clunking into place with a deafening thud. James hardly knew what he was doing until he realized he was turned around and facing Sydney in the tiny shower, staring at his eyes through the mist, his hand now cupping the barest amount of pressure along his erection despite himself.

Sydney had traced his face through dripping eyelashes and sucked in a breath through his nose. And James had known, as if the words themselves were written through the steam, that he was remembering the beach shower.

A mutual blink happened—somehow, a silent *yes.* Then James had slid his hand away, and they'd each simultaneously looked down at the sight of their hard, dripping cocks almost brushing up against each other in the thrumming space between their bodies, flushed and bobbing in the force of the spray.

Sydney was flushed and long. Somebody whispered, not more than a wavering moan, "*yeah . . .*"

And James had watched with his breath in his throat as the water dripped down and soaked through the dark curls surrounding the base of Sydney's cock—the first one he'd even seen erect that wasn't his own. He'd let the water drip down from his eyelashes and off his nose, then bit the inside of his cheek as Sydney gripped his own erection in his shaking hand. He'd stepped forward, soaked curls hanging in his eyes, and shifted his hips to slowly trace the pulsing tip of his erection up the length of James' cock, panting into the hot steam of the shower and trembling with restraint.

That time, James had known that it was himself who'd whispered, "God."

James had raised quivering fingers and placed them right on Sydney's muscled chest, letting the pads of his fingertips stroke down slowly over Sydney's nipples until they hardened and shuddered beneath his touch. He'd rubbed and swirled and flicked the hardened beads of wet, soapy skin as Sydney arched into his hands, shutting his eyes tight when he gasped in breath. And Sydney had continued to drag just the tip of his leaking cock slowly up and down the length of James' aching erection, electrifying the warm skin covering James' rock-hard penis.

James had realized, with a sharp jolt that nearly sent him to his knees on the slick tile, that they were both standing there feeling each other without any intention at all to climax. That they were just touching. Looking. James had torn his gaze away from their cocks rubbing against each other in the buzzing air of the shower and looked up at Sydney's piercing pale eyes. And Sydney had given him a half-lidded look, wet lips parted, as if he couldn't believe that their bodies were doing that either.

Sydney had leaned forward, hovering for a moment to lick his already wet lips, then pressed the softest ghost of a kiss to the corner of James' mouth just as the water started to grow cold. James had breathed through it, not quite kissing back, but his palm cupped Sydney's elbow, somehow the safest part of him he could reach.

Without saying a word, they'd stepped out of the shower, both still erect, and dried off side by side like they weren't doing anything life altering in the least. Had pulled on two pairs of Sydney's boxers over half-hard cocks, and tiptoed across the creaking floor, and climbed into his bed without even discussing who would sleep where, a careful foot of cold sheets between them.

And James had taken a deep breath and reminded himself of the man he'd just been all evening—the man who hurled away the bullet into the sea, and kissed Sydney Moore in view of the stars, and caressed his soap-slick skin—and then he'd turned into Sydney's body and slotted his leg against a warm thigh. He'd put his arm across Sydney's slightly trembling stomach, his hand fanned across his side. And he'd shut his eyes just as Sydney reached up to hold his arm there with huge, strong hands. He'd let the sensation of his slowly softening penis pressed into Sydney's hip be relaxed and intimate and known without flinching away.

James opens his eyes out of the memory to see Sydney still fast asleep beside him, nose twitching gently in the throes of a dream, chest heaving deep and slow. James stares at him and waits for his insides to churn with nausea. Waits for the realization to dawn hot and sour in his gut that he'd finally given in to the desire he'd forbidden himself from since he was sixteen on a sunset beach and found himself wishing that Lisa Kerny's painted fingernails gliding over his skin could be replaced with Billy Madden's solid, callused fingers.

He waits for five minutes, watching the tips of Sydney's eyelashes flutter in warm, soft air, intimate and vulnerable in the breeze caused by James' breath. He waits as he reaches out a hesitant hand and places a ghostly light touch over the stubble on Sydney's cheek, running his fingertips across the side of his strong jaw before reaching into his hair to scratch his scalp.

He waits as Sydney's eyes suddenly flutter open all at once, completely awake in less than a second, surprised gaze focusing immediately on James. James looks directly into his eyes, tracking the fluttering droplets of sea in his irises, the way the corners crinkle when Sydney's lips curve into the hint of a grin pressed into the pillowcase.

"James," he whispers, voice raspy from sleep.

In an instant, James knows he doesn't have to wait anymore. The nausea simply isn't coming—not now, at least. Not for a little while. He returns Sydney's lazy smile, heart inexplicably pounding, and he brushes a curl off Sydney's forehead with his thumb, amazed at how frighteningly easy it is to gaze into his eyes without looking away.

Sydney reaches both arms above his head and stretches luxuriously across the sheets before shuffling closer to James, facing him with his hands folded in between them, appearing utterly relaxed. There's a question in his eyes, though. An almost-invisible frown hidden between his brows. The sight of it unexpectedly tugs at James' chest, and he shifts, painfully aware of the rasp of his bare skin on the sheets, then covers Sydney's hand with his, smelling the combined, sleepy warmth of their limbs.

Sydney does a slow blink; the easy contentment in the relaxed lines of his face almost hurts to look at. James has never had such a force of such . . . such guardlessness directed at him before, not even from Rob on all the mornings they sat side by side on the waves, completely at ease with each other.

Well, maybe not at ease. Not when Rob's palm had never stroked his scar, not when Rob had never held James' gaze instead of looking away, not when James had never told him that he had a bottle of untouched pills in his cupboard the day they met, just in case. That he'd killed a man before checking his uniform shirt.

But Sydney Moore doesn't know those terrible things, either—probably couldn't even comprehend them, not in the safe sheets of his private bed—and yet he's staring at James with a look of total *rest.* Rest in James, and with James, and because of James.

James Campbell, who didn't stop to carry anybody's lifeless body out of the red jungle for the waiting caskets. Who hugs Lori hello after getting off to thoughts of her naked boyfriend the night before.

James sighs, suddenly unbearably sad and unable to pin down why. The emotion in Sydney's eyes is young and clear, unclouded and stripped bare for James to drink in his fill. The back of James' throat tightens at the intimacy of it, somehow more meaningful, more dangerous and risky, than standing naked together in a shower with their erections pressed together.

Sydney clears his throat, and a light glimmers in the corners of his eyes. "You know what I'm gonna do tonight?"

James raises his eyebrows and hums.

"Gonna have sex with the Billabong Pipeline Masters champion."

James huffs out a laugh and as a flutter of shocked nerves soar up his throat, along with a heady, thick heat zipping down his spine at the rawness of the words.

"You're something else, Moore," he manages.

Sydney's grin widens, and he shuffles closer to James in the bed so that they're chest to chest, nose to nose. James imagines he can hear the sound of Sydney's heartbeat thrumming into his skin, in time with the steady beat of the waves onto the wet shoreline just outside the quiet hut. Golden rays of dawn light slowly seep in through the windows, illuminating Sydney's tan skin with glowing, sunlit warmth. James feels as if he's embracing the sun itself.

"You know what you're gonna do right now?" Sydney asks, fake serious and voice deep.

James' eyes pool black at the sound. The breath leaves his chest, and all he can do is shake his head like some naive, innocent kid. He is aware of every place where the warm sheets caress his bare skin, humid from sleep, and Sydney's nearly-too-small boxers feel tight around his thighs.

Sydney puts his warm hand on James' shoulder and pushes him onto his back, rolling to hold himself over James on his elbows, hips raised. A groan escapes James' throat at the heavy weight of Sydney's hand pushing his body, muscles still lax from sleep.

James holds his breath as Sydney dips his head towards him, licking his lips for a kiss. When they're nose to nose, Sydney pauses. James sees a flash of uncertainty suddenly blaze across his eyes—cutting through the playful teasing and easy confidence. Their lips hover inches apart, halted in time. Sydney's eyes search James', a hesitant, yearning look hidden in the folds around his mouth, and James remembers a flash of conversation from just two days ago.

*"Nobody else has ever been here."*

James wants to cup Sydney's face in his hands and whisper to him, *"Come on, man, tease me. Be cocky like that because I'm here. I'm not going anywhere, and you fucking got me."*

Then the reality of his plane ticket back to LA tomorrow slaps him in the face, leaving a stinging bruise. He tries to hide the realization in his eyes, but he knows Sydney catches it first. The moment turns dense and uncomfortable, tension radiating through Sydney's body as it hovers just above his skin, as if touching him will cause James to leap from the bed and run away for good—to escape the reality of a man touching his skin in the slow, relaxed, purposeful light of day.

James wonders if Sydney's right to be so cautious. If he really would . . .

But James finds himself raising a hand to Sydney's waist. He glances down at the clear sight of his tan fingers on the pale, smooth skin, kept hidden from the sand and sun. He watches the pre-dawn light illuminate a wave of shivers down Sydney's thigh as James slowly rubs his thumb, then he closes his eyes, relaxes his neck, and presses Sydney down onto himself.

They both groan. Heavy, thick heat floods down his front, and his thighs tense. James breathes deeply as Sydney settles his full weight, then rubs the sleep from his eyes before placing a hand in Sydney's lopsided curls.

"Well, what am I gonna do right now?" he whispers, playing along. But the words hang heavy in the room like too many questions at once, leaving Sydney's playfulness far, far behind.

Sydney leans forward so that their lips can graze together, open mouthed and shaky. James starts to grow hard at the heavy weight of Sydney's lean, muscular frame on top of him as Sydney's hot breath trembles against his own panting lips. James can tell that even now, Sydney's still holding himself back—still moving in slow motion, waiting for it all to disappear. That same tug from before gives a great, rushing pull through his chest, and James gently pulls Sydney's face down to capture his soft lips in a kiss, moaning at the taste of him bursting across his tongue.

Sydney barely moves, frozen and trembling above him, then he pulls back with a gasp and licks his lips, eyes wide and locked on James' face. James lets him look, lets him drink in every line of sincerity on his face, plane flight tomorrow be damned. A tiny flicker of sadness passes over Sydney's eyes, quickly replaced by the same easy desire from before.

"What you're gonna do right now," he finally whispers, shifting his weight along the warmth of James' body, "is you're gonna have sex with a Billabong Pipeline Masters champion."

And James barely has time to process those words before Sydney is scooting down James' frame, bringing his wet, parted lips to the center of James' chest. He kisses his way slowly down the center of his stomach as James gasps, abs clenched. Sydney pauses to lick at the dips of his pelvis, and James imagines he can feel the slick slide of Sydney's tongue straight through to his bones and muscle, raw and stripped bare.

James groans under his breath and grabs at the bedsheet with his hands to keep himself from bucking up into Sydney's touch. He gazes at the slowly lightening ceiling, eyes hazy with arousal and unable to look down as Sydney's fingers dip into the waistband of his boxers. After a second's hesitation, Sydney pulls them down off his legs, leaving James exposed to the morning air and the rushing hiss of the waves through the window.

He can't look. He can't see his erection bobbing near Sydney Moore's lips. He can't see it, he can't—

James takes a wild, deep breath, and he looks down just in time to see the grey light dappling across Sydney's long, bare back where he's bent over James' thighs, his curls trailing down his stomach, when suddenly hot, wet lips press to the base of his half-hard cock.

Air punches from James' lungs. He throws back his head, spine limp, as Sydney leaves a gentle trail of open-mouthed kisses from the base to the tip of his cock. His cock which is quickly thickening beneath the hot velvet of Sydney's lips.

"God," James whispers, unable to stop it. "Oh my God."

The touch feels unbearably obscene—Sydney's lips kissing his not even fully erect cock, just like he would his mouth, suckling and tasting the hot, steely skin. James ears' shiver at the raw, wet sounds echoing through the room. He grows even harder with each little gasp and lick.

Sydney's huge hands finally grip his hips. Hard. He reaches the tip of James' now throbbing erection and pauses, looking up at James with piercing eyes through a mop of curls. He licks his lips.

And James is just about to reach down desperately with his hands, to grip Sydney by the shoulders and pull him off and tell him, *"You don't have to. You don't have to do this. You don't—"*

Sydney's mouth closes around the tip of James' erection, sucking at the tip with his lips. The words die in James' mouth, everything except a high, breathy sound. Sydney's tongue rolls in slow circles across James' dripping slit as groans deep in his throat, then he closes his eyes, tilts his head, and inhales down James' aching shaft until a line of spit drips down his chin.

James can't look away. Can't move. His wide eyes are locked on the sight of Sydney's full, wet lips swallowing down the tip of his cock over the view of his own heaving chest. And God, fucking God, it's been *years* since even a woman did this to him—before he ever set foot on a Navy ship.

Long, quiet years. And he's certainly never looked down and seen the fucking hard, muscled lines of a man's broad shoulders in between his thighs, or felt the heady rasp of stubble scrape across the hair at the base of his cock, or heard a rumbling moan so deep he feels it rattle straight through to his bones.

"Fuck," he groans. Sydney moans again at the sound of his voice, and pulls slowly off the tip until just his tongue is laving at the swollen, dripping slit, licking down into his foreskin with wet sighs.

James tries to suck in enough oxygen to breathe. Sydney looks up at him again with those pale, half-lidded eyes and absolutely pins him with his gaze. His tongue curls under a fat drip of precome and sucks it into his mouth.

James' voice cracks and rumbles as his mouth spits out the least-arousing thing he could say. "Have you ever done this before?"

He wants to punch himself in the face.

Sydney presses a last kiss to his cock before letting it fall hard and throbbing onto James' tensed stomach. He leans up on an elbow, and the air turns focused and clear, cutting through the fog of arousal as Sydney clears his throat.

"Not with you," he says, eyes quiet and serious. A wash of something like embarrassment, like insecurity hides behind them, and James reaches down to place his thumb at the corner of Sydney's mouth.

He nods, madly hoping Sydney will be able to read everything James means in the only word he finds himself physically able to say.

"Okay," he whispers. Sydney bites his lips, then dips his chin.

James exhales a shaky breath as he watches Sydney's wet, full lips once again descend to the aching tip of his cock, still glistening with his saliva.

All at once, it dawns on him in full force that he's watching the two-time Billabong Pipeline Masters Champion suck him off. That *the* Danny Moore is giving him a blow job with spit on his lips and sweat down his back.

James lets out a breathy laugh, stunned. He rubs a hand over his eyes and pinches between his brows. "Who the hell are you?" he asks, embarrassed at the awe in his voice.

It's just a *blow job,* for fuck's sake.

But Sydney's lips quirk into a smile, and he flashes a half-wink at James, clearly reliving the memory, too. Then his hand is on the base of James' full cock, and he licks his smirking lips, and he takes James down his throat all the way to the base in one smooth glide, pressing his tongue hotly against the veins on the underside of James' erection and groaning vibrations through the sensitive skin.

James shatters.

A high, breathy moan erupts from the back of his throat as his head crashes back onto the pillow, hips fighting not to thrust up into the tight, wet heat of Sydney's mouth. Sydney strokes him with the flat of his tongue and sucks him root to tip in a rolling rhythm, and James lifts his neck and watches with his breath in his throat as his cock disappears again and again between Sydney's dripping lips, bobbing against the back of his throat and arching into the heat of his moans.

He's trembling, fighting to stay still on the damp sheets and aching down his thighs as Sydney pulls up to swirl his tongue around the head, sucking at the slit. He pumps James' cock with his hand, pulling a deep rub along the foreskin as he takes a wild breath before engulfing James in his wet mouth once more.

James can't help the curse that passes through his lips. He feels it like an electric shiver radiating down his spine. The air grows hazy, and his vision fades. Sydney suddenly snatches James' hand from where it's still gripping the sheets and pulls it down hard onto the back of his head, moaning deep in his chest when James' fingers reflexively clutch at a handful of curls.

It's all James needs to know. Like an unleashed floodgate, a stream of forbidden words fall free from his lips as he pushes Sydney's bobbing head down onto his cock, thrusting up into his throat, ears tingling at the wet slap of saliva on skin as Sydney moans and sucks him deep.

"Fuck yeah," James breaths. Sydney's shaking hands clutch hard enough at his hips to bruise, groaning as James fucks into his mouth.

"God, take it . . ." James feels another moan from Sydney's throat radiate through his body and pushes Sydney's head farther down onto his erection, pulsing and hard as steel.

He arches his back as the tip of his cock brushes the back of Sydney's throat, and his lungs ache. "Fucking *take it.*"

Sydney's lips are wide and stretched around him, pink and swollen as they suck him deeper into his mouth. James notices he can feel the bed rocking, and he glances down to see Sydney's own hips thrusting against the bed. One of Sydney's hands is gone from James' waist, and a fresh wave of heat courses through James' body at the knowledge Sydney is fucking into his own fist while James pumps into the heat of his mouth. His fingers clutch Sydney's curls so hard he's surprised he hasn't ripped out clumps of hair.

Sydney slows his rhythm, takes him down deep enough that James feels Sydney's lungs expand between his thighs, Sydney's nose breathing out hot air into the blond curls at the base of his cock.

For some reason, that's what causes everything to change.

The words fall from James' lips like a wave, somehow so much easier to say now in the morning light than they were last night on the beach. The aching pulse in James' groin is reaching a peak, coiling hotly as he fucks into the rumble of Sydney's moans against the throbbing wet skin of his cock.

"God, Moore, suck me," he growls.

Sydney keens high in his throat, and James pinches one of his own nipples, harder than he's ever done alone at home.

"Fucking look at you," he gasps. "Fuck, just look at you. Yeah, that's it. . ." He rocks deep into his throat. "That's it . . ."

And the bed thuds against the wall to the pounding rhythm of Sydney's fist pumping his own cock in his boxers, and James has the sudden, blinding, shattering vision of a white stream of his own cum shooting straight down Sydney's throat, dripping over those full, pink lips he'd first seen set in a hard, impenetrable line on the Hermosa Shore, and he's got Danny Moore between his legs, swallowing him down, Sydney . . .

"Suck me," James groans, his limbs starting to vibrate and peak. "Suck me down and take it . . . God *take me.*"

James throws his head back and comes with a cry, heat pulsing through his body from the center of his aching cock still sucked into the tight heat of Sydney's mouth. He spills down Sydney's throat and pulses as Sydney swallows around him, sucking him down with his tongue on a long, deep groan.

Then everything is quiet, pure and calm like his first glimpses of the shore through the jungle. And the helicopter in the distance isn't making any noise, no sound at all. Crystal blue waters shimmering in the heat, calling him home.

When James forces his eyes back open, he sees Sydney up on his knees, wiping the back of his mouth with his hand. His sweaty skin is glowing from the light pouring in through the window, reflected off the bright surface of the ocean. His lean chest heaves as he catches his breath.

James opens his mouth to say something. A *"fuck yes,"* or a *"thank you,"* or a *"that was the most powerful fucking orgasm I've ever had,"* and all of the options are *terrifying,* but then Sydney throws his body on top of him in a crashing heap. Sydney's lips slam into his. James moans a surprised grunt from the back of his throat as Sydney kisses him with an unprecedented fierceness, hands clutching at his face and neck, tongue licking into his mouth in long, hot pants, filling James' mouth with the taste of himself until he can barely breathe.

All of a sudden, the force of Sydney's mouth feels wrong—too frantic and uncontrolled, clouded over with a choking, desperate grey. James grabs Sydney's shoulders and gently pushes him back as he gulps down oxygen into his lungs, letting the air rush over his swollen, tingling lips.

Sydney looks torn apart. His curls are wild around his face, and his lips are kiss-swollen and pink. Chest flushed and glistening with eyes locked on to James like he's forcing himself to never look away. To never blink.

James glances down the small space between their bodies and sees that Sydney's erection is gone, lying soft now behind a wet stain on his boxers. The fact that Sydney probably just came with James' cock in his mouth should make him flood over with fresh arousal—want to crush this man to his body, and grasp the strength in his waist, and run his hands up the muscled, inked lines of his back.

And it would make James do all of those things, if not for the expression on Sydney's face as he stares at a place just above James' eyes, the sudden tightness of Sydney's lips making him look small and lost—unbearably naked. James feels an incredible sadness wash over him. Without having to be told, he knows Sydney's thinking of his flight.

James sighs—a kind of sigh he never thought he'd give after just having sex in bed with a man for the first time. He reaches up to cup Sydney's face in his palm, and Sydney turns his face softly into the touch, breath shuddering out his nose as a wet sheen glosses over his eyes. James' chest clenches—that inevitable, painful tug.

"You'll be there today?" he finally manages.

Sydney's voice is a whisper, much higher than normal. "I'll be there."

James tries to smile, but knows it doesn't quite reach his eyes. "And you won't fucking run off to the car if I win?"

Sydney relaxes above him and sighs through his nose before turning his face to press a soft kiss to the inside of James' wrist. The sweat on his cheek smears across James' palm.

"When you win," he says into James' skin, "I'll be there."

And James huffs and gives a hard glare at Sydney's absolutely ridiculous, misplaced, jinx-worthy confidence, even as his thumb can't help brushing gently across Sydney's chin. He answers Sydney's raised brow with a nod that says "*I'm ready,*" even though he feels absolutely anything but.

# 16

"—most likely pit you against Mark Florence and Dale Trent in the semifinal rounds. Try to create some ridiculous battle of the unexpected underdogs, so—"

"Coming from the man who keeps saying I'll win!"

"Well *I* know that, but that doesn't mean everybody else isn't still an idiot."

"Seriously, *everybody* else is an idiot?"

"Well, you didn't see any of them winning the Masters the last two years, huh?"

"That's because you—God, and you wonder why everyone else on the circuit thinks you're an asshole?" James says back, laughing.

Sydney shoots him a sly grin before turning back to the road, right palm resting warmly on top of James' thigh when it isn't using the gear shift.

"I don't wonder why," he says, squeezing James' leg. "And clearly not everyone thinks I'm an asshole."

James' cheeks hurt as he tries to contain his smile. He grabs Sydney's hand with his own and gives a brief, answering squeeze, slightly ashamed that doing so makes him feel so foolish and young.

"No, they don't," he says, just loud enough that Sydney can hear him over the engine.

He looks out the open window, letting the breeze rush against his face as the patchwork of white and pink flowers dotting the rolling green hillside fade into a nauseating blur.

"Keep going, then," he prompts. "The other idiots."

"Florence is new—first time surfing outside the UK. He's used to choppy surf, cold fast breaks with a lot of whitewater. Don't think he even has a fucking clue what he'll do on a huge open pipeline. My guess is he'll take the waves that have already closed and ride over the top of the pipe. That or he'll take the ones that are short enough to stay open faces. Day like today, though, with the wind the way it is, don't think he'll see many waves come in that aren't huge barrels."

James sucks in a breath and tries to let it out without shaking. "Right. K, Trent?"

"Trent's from your neck of the woods. Santa Cruz—"

"That's a fucking seven hour drive from Los Angeles!"

"Well that's shorter than an entire ocean!"

"Oh, sorry, Mr. Geography."

"You're the one who flew all the way to Vietnam and didn't realize that all of California is just a tiny, insignificant dot compared to other countries and oceans. What, did you have your eyes closed on the pla—"

"Oh my God, man, you are something el—"

"*Anyway,* the thing about Trent is he loves to show off. Completely unnecessary—"

"Seriously, are you hearing yourself right now?"

"I'm hearing me giving you excellent advice and you pointedly not listening—"

"Watch the fucking road! That's a fucking tree!"

"James, you're from *Los Angeles*—aren't all the streets there just a fight to the death anyways? Why you're concerned about a goddamn tree that had a good three inches is absolutely beyond me, and I'm trying to get us there on—"

"Shit, I think I'm gonna be sick."

James actually is going to be sick. His easy, lazy contentment from that morning—the blissfully calm acceptance of the fact that he was about to surf the fucking Banzai Pipeline—is completely gone, replaced in an instant by a churning, nauseating fear.

Sydney turns and sees the look on his face and immediately pulls over to the side of the deserted road, parking alongside a wall of bright green fronds and cutting the engine.

They sit in silence, the sounds of the Jeep still echoing across the oceanside mountains, mixing with the rising clouds of dust billowing out from the wheels. James wasn't even this nervous when he stepped out of the camo dinghy into shin-deep water with a gun in his hands and a too-silent shoreline in front of him. He realizes he's had a similar thought multiple times over the last few days, then wonders how the hell his life managed to get so much more terrifying since escaping LA and landing in paradise.

Sydney's hand is suddenly on the side of his face, gently turning his gaze.

"James, look at me."

James turns his head against the headrest of the old Jeep, pressing his cheek further into Sydney's steady palm. It's hard to believe they're not the only two people on the island. That five minutes down the road there's a massive swarm of people from all over Oahu—from all over the world—gathering to watch him try to prove he somehow deserves to surf those waves.

Sydney's eyes are wide and clear, boring into his with such focus it sends a self-conscious shiver up James' spine. He lets the silence linger for a few more moments, his mouth twisting like he's flipping through possibilities of what to say, then he licks his lips to speak.

"Look, when I was six, I came home from Sunday school all upset, crying and everything, because we learned about the seven days of creation and I was terrified of the water. How he separated the sea from the sky. And my mom sat me down and told me how it wasn't scary at all, and how it was where all the beauty that the earth couldn't hold overflowed to."

James sighs as Sydney's thumb strokes across the day-old stubble on his cheek, rasping incredibly loud through the calm silence in the Jeep.

"She'd never seen the ocean, probably still hasn't. When we left, she . . . she stayed behind in Arizona. That's why she isn't . . . well, anyway, I'm pretty sure she just read about the ocean in the Bible. So the first time I ever tried to surf—the morning I got thrown out, before everything else went to shit. . . I remembered the way the Hawaiians always say a sort of prayer before they walk out into the waves—Lahela would take me to watch for an hour on the days I had to go run errands

238

with her. So that morning I dipped my hands in the water and held a handful of it and told my mom out loud that I was seeing the ocean for her. I think . . . maybe you should do the same."

James forces himself to speak. "What, you mean say a prayer?"

"No." Sydney's eyes frown, like a silent apology. "I mean don't . . . don't just do it for yourself. Surf for Helen."

The entire earth falls silent after the name. James swallows hard and stares, grounded in the reality of sitting in the warm Jeep only by the slow swipe of Sydney's thumb across his cheekbone.

He wonders if it's humanly possible for Sydney Moore to somehow understand that James sometimes *hates* Keith Hartman for lifting him out of the foam. That it's *his* fault James couldn't run with open arms across the floor of the sea, straight towards Helen Campbell, and be reunited with her and laugh forever in the shade of the waves. That every time James' toes have touched the water since coming back, there's a momentary punch through his chest that Keith took it all away.

James tries to match the man sitting next to him with the man he'd first heard Dean and Kip and the rest of them talk about that day at Hermosa—the sick fucker strutting across a beach of losers against the gentle hand patiently resting on his cheek. It seems to James that the only things those two men have in common are a pair of piercing steel eyes, when they're not hidden from sight by dark lenses or curls, and the ability to surf their ass off across nearly any possible wave.

Well, those things, and the fact that apparently both of them have wanted to spend time in the presence of James Campbell, of all goddamn people.

James briefly presses his face into Sydney's palm, then pulls away out of his reach. He rubs a hand over his mouth before wiping it off on his shorts.

"Gotta say, it's weird having you know all this about me sometimes. Everything about . . . I mean, shit, you know, we haven't even known each other a month."

He instantly regrets his words. But, to his surprise, Sydney's lips quirk into a small smile, despite the fact that James has noticed a troubling sadness in his eyes since that morning.

"You think I'm used to the fact that you're the only person on earth who knows that I'm an Army brat who still knows the order of all the books of the Bible?"

James laughs, surprised. "I didn't realize your family was *that* religious."

Sydney shrugs, his eyes bright as he huffs a laugh through his nose. "Well, unfortunately, now you know." He shakes his head. "Could probably walk in right now without any studying and pass whatever the test is to become Ordained."

"Oh, so you're gonna brag about this, too, huh? Surfing's not enough anymore for you?"

Sydney's face is a warm, easy glow. He shrugs one shoulder. "Apparently."

The air feels clearer now, as if some thickness has been lifted straight out of the Jeep. James traces the toned lines of Sydney's tan bicep and shoulder with his eyes, watches his chest rise and fall beneath the thin fabric of his tank top, until their gazes meet.

James licks his lips. "You know we saw each other before our round at the ISF? Earlier in the day?"

Sydney's swallow sounds incredibly loud in the fragile stillness. His voice cracks. "Yes. On the pier."

"I didn't know who you were, then, actually. That you were . . . you."

Sydney rapidly blinks. "I realized that."

James refuses to feel ashamed when his voice doesn't quite come out steady. He whispers, "What were you looking at?"

Sydney stares at him, mouth half-open, then tries and fails to say something—aborted breaths and starts of words. There's a rising blush across his cheeks. A tightness squeezes down James' throat when he sees embarrassment on Sydney's face, mixed with something like apprehension, like fear . . .

James doesn't wait. He lets out the breath from his lungs in a rush and lunges forward across the gear shift to grab Sydney's shoulder, then pulls him into a barrelling kiss. Sydney gasps, surprised, then melts as his tongue rolls into James' open mouth.

It's the only way James can think of to tell Sydney Moore that, somehow, in some ludicrous way, maybe he didn't meet him for the first time on that pier. That maybe he met him in the moment he opened his eyes to blink groggily at a white hospital ceiling. When he realized he wasn't still dead in the blood-soaked foam, left to sink forever in the waters off Ha Long. That maybe waking up in Sydney's arms softened the terrifying sharpness of all that Keith took away. Made Keith actually *give* him something, instead.

James sighs into Sydney's mouth, and caresses his soft lips with his own, tasting Sydney's lost words on the tip of his tongue. The way Sydney's kissing him, the urgency in his mouth, it's almost like he thinks this is the last chance he'll get. It stings James somewhere deep in the pit of his gut. He wants to tell Sydney it'll all be okay. But the plane . . .

James places one last gentle kiss on Sydney's wet lips before pulling back and resting their noses together, drawing in the warm scent of his skin—the salt of the ocean embedded in the freckles on his cheeks.

He takes a final deep breath before pulling away, slapping his hands once on his knees and shaking out his shoulders.

"Alright," he says in a too loud voice. "Fuck. Let's go."

Sydney blinks for a second, frozen like he forgot how to speak, then cracks his neck as he shifts up in his seat. He smirks as he revs the engine and pulls back out onto the dirt highway. "Not gonna cry again on me, old man?"

James huffs, boldness burning through him. "Did I seem like an old man to you when my dick was down your throat?"

Sydney doesn't answer, but James looks over just in time to see the goosebumps rising on his skin.

They park in the same place as yesterday, and James has to remind himself as they step down out of the Jeep that it really was only just goddamn yesterday. They move as a synchronized team, unloading Sydney's extra board and their bags in quick, easy silence, nodding stiffly at anyone who passes on their way down to the shore.

James hikes up the board under one arm and slings the knapsack over his shoulder, then turns to face Sydney, thinking of what to possibly say. He grimaces as his eyes scan the brimming town and shore. There's far too many people here today for the Finals; kissing Sydney would be like a death sentence screamed across the beach.

Immediately James wants to hop back in the Jeep and drive somewhere private where he can kiss the living daylights out of this man.

This man who's already got his sunglasses in his hand like a shield, and whose very skin seems to prickle under the weight of the sets of eyes already staring at him from afar. James steps closer so their bodies are just barely obscured by the back of the Jeep, then reaches out to take Sydney's hand. He already looks so much stiffer, completely alone.

And it's the *Billabong Finals*.

"Don't fucking leave my sight," James says under his breath. His heart hammers so hard he fears it'll burst through his thin ribs.

Sydney gently threads the tips of their fingers together. James watches him also scan the crowds, and he thinks he sees disappointment sag his lips.

Sydney grimaces. "Pretty sure I'll have to take a piss at some point today. While I'm at it, might find a nice man to make out with, so it could be a while . . ."

James rolls his eyes and gives Sydney's fingers a final squeeze before walking away, emblazing the image of Sydney's soft, warm smirk into his memory.

"You're a fucking looney," he calls back over his shoulder.

He almost doesn't hear Sydney's response over the noise of the crowd—old friends greeting each other, car horns honking to try and find parking, the rushing crash of the waves, an old Eagles song blaring somewhere from a cheap, crackling stereo.

But James does hear it. And he feels the ghostly press of Sydney's lips against his forehead as a shiver sends its way down his spine, tattooing the words onto the veins beneath his skin.

"Surf like hell, James Campbell," Sydney calls.

James finds a small patch of free sand within the crowd and kneels to fish out the wax from his bag. The other surfers are more tense today—less talkative as they each sit and stand in their own private bubbles, gazing out at the waves and memorizing their every curve and swell until the clock ticks down enough for their own turn to soar across the water.

James prefers it this way—anything to escape the half-hearted attempts at small talk he'd had to make all of yesterday while casting secret glances at Sydney from across the beach, standing tall and apart and godlike on the sand, attracting the gaze of everyone within fifty feet and not even twitching in acknowledgement.

He shifts to bury his knees deeper in the already-hot sand and blocks out the sound of everything but the rough swish of wax over the surface of his board and the crush of the waves onto the shore. The barrels are huge today—Sydney's prediction was right. The familiar spark of fear James always gets when faced with monster waves flicks to life in the back of his mind, clearing his head of the chaos around him and focusing his mind on one thing only: surf. And survive.

He waxes his board in slow, steady circles and goes back over everything Sydney's told him about his competitors in his first round, about the swells and the strategy, weaknesses and strengths. For ten minutes, he successfully remembers Sydney's words and advice. *"Let Florence chicken out on his own, watching you take on one of the first bomb swells. The barrels today will be tighter—don't spend as long in the pipe. Take your hand off the face and let the water propel you out before it closes in on you. Let Trent have smaller, frothy waves so he'll try to pull off a trick. He's not used to the velocity of the Banzai and he'll wipe out."*

Then, out of nowhere, ghosts of Sydney's hands are on his wet, naked shoulders, rubbing soap into his skin as a voice rumbles deep in his ear. The whispering steam of the tiny shower cocooning their heat. The hair between Sydney's thighs, around his full cock, growing thick and heavy with streaming water . . .

James grits his teeth and blushes down to his chest as his skin replays the physical memory of Sydney's wet, open kisses down the center of his stomach, and the soft sheets against his back, Sydney's shoulders spreading open his thighs, his wet lips sucking down his—

Tension in the air, tightening like a drum. James he looks up just in time, tongue numb and sweat on his brow, to see every other surfer's gaze zoom to James' right. James follows their stares, nearly moaning out loud in relief that they weren't looking at him, then he gasps through his nose.

Danny Moore is jogging through the thick crowd towards the shoreline, holding a board up over his head that James knows immediately has been stolen ("*borrowed*" Sydney's voice supplies in his mind).

But Sydney Moore is gone—completely subsumed by Danny's puffed chest and high chin and slicked back curls. James stands there in shock; he tries and utterly fails to picture this man's hands on his own skin, falling asleep with his nose tucked into the crook of James' neck, holding him by the shore as he wept, cupping his palm to James' cheek just an hour ago in a Jeep pulled over to the side of the road.

He can't. It's equal parts fascinating and sad. James stares at the dichotomy as the rest of the beach swarms to murmuring life, feeling sick to his stomach watching everyone look at the charade he too had once gazed upon with intimidated, shivering awe. The spectators part before Danny as he effortlessly glides across the sand with leaping strides, aviator-covered eyes staring straight ahead at the booming waves.

"Well fuck me, Danny Moore is surfing in this now?"

The other surfers around James are starting to whisper and fidget, gathering into a standing clump to watch as Danny plunks the tail of his board into the sand, rips off his shirt, and then throws the board under his arm once more as he runs out into the waves.

The murmur of whispers around James grows into a chorus, crushing him with the weight of their sound.

"Did he add more to that tattoo? Looks even fucking bigger than last—"

"Couldn't let somebody else have a chance for a year? Feel like I just time-traveled to three years ago . . ."

"You know what that fairy said to me last year? Told me I was gonna lose before we even got in the fucking water, some shit about my left ankle—"

"You heard what he did in the bathroom in Laguna, yeah? Fucking si—"

"Think he really has the guts to go after the Big Wave record next week?"

"He's just having fun," James says over the chorus of the crowd. He sets his feet apart in the sand and holds his ground as the surfers around him turn to stare. Sweat prickles under his arms, and he scratches at the beard of two-day stubble over his jaw.

A man James recognizes from a competition last year in San Diego speaks up next to him. "What's that, Campbell?"

James clears his throat. "He isn't surfing in the competition. He's just having fun before it starts. Look."

James gestures with his head out towards the waves, and the guys around him follow his line of sight. Danny's paddling out in front of a powerful rushing wave, oblivious to the crowd holding their breath on the shore as he lets the rising swell raise him up towards the sky. In one swift movement he pops up and soars down the face of the open barrel, cutting a massive wall of spray. The crest of the wave curls around him and crashes into a smooth, glittering pipeline, and the crowd of spectators release an open gasp across the sand as more spray shoots out from the opening of the barrel like a rocket.

"Shit, man, that's the biggest fucking bomb we've seen all morning," one of the other surfers says under his breath.

They all nod. The wave is easily twenty feet tall, towering above the rest of the horizon line and blocking out enough of the sun to cast a shadow along the shore. James' ears pick up the sound of the announcers cutting through the thick, tense silence on the beach.

"—not surfing this year, but our own reigning champion Danny Moore is deep in this barrel, folks, and boy is it a beauty."

"I'm getting a little worried we haven't seen him pop out, yet . . ."

"It's always tense to wait, any second now—and Danny Moore emerges from the barrel! And look at him fly! Cuts back along the crest for some massive spray and grabs the nose of his board for a tap across the lip."

"This ride is to the max! Fits in a third cutback . . . oh, and Moore isn't done yet! Look at him squeeze every second he can out of this monster wave!"

"And a soaring, one-eighty turn to end his ride right at the end of the shoulder."

"Folks, you're all giving this ride standing applause and we have to agree—Danny Moore may not be surfing in this Billabong, but I think he's just reminded us all that he is still the champion of these Oahu shores. What a treat, my ladies and gents. What a thrill!"

James' heart is in his throat, sweat on his palms, when he realizes the surfers around him are cheering.

*Cheering.*

"Fucking hell, Moore, that was a beauty!"

"Son of a bitch can ride, can't he?"

"Powerful, man. That was insane."

James can't believe it. This group of surfers around him who were practically lining up to give Danny Moore shit are now standing here respectfully clapping one of the biggest waves of the year, not an "asshole" or "fairy" or "fag" to be heard.

James can't even bring himself to join in the applause. He watches breathlessly as Danny emerges from the waves, saltwater dripping in sheaths down his bare, muscled chest, his soaked board shorts clinging to every contour of his thighs. Danny straightens the aviators still magically over his eyes and runs his hands back through his dripping curls, then jumps, and raises a hand once to the crowd in acknowledgement as if he just noticed other people were there. He calmly glides back through the chaos, hands the board back to a bewildered local spectator, and disappears off into the trees lining the beach without uttering a word.

It takes every ounce of James' self-control not to drop his things in the sand and chase after him. A rushing mix of adrenaline and shame flood his system—adrenaline that he himself kissed that powerful surfer only that morning, and shame that James' kiss has made half the terrible rumors about Danny Moore true.

And God, Sydney looked like he didn't even break a sweat, wasn't even panting when he came back to shore. James wants to taste the fresh saltwater on his lips, and shove him against a wall, and fucking *own* the Billabong Pipeline Masters champion. Hold down the incredible power in his limbs and press into him, press into his heat—

Ah, back to the nausea. James forcefully swallows down his train of thought just as Sydney's words from that morning float to him on the warm, floral breeze:

*"Tonight I'm gonna have sex with a Billabong Pipeline Masters Champion."*

James' stomach thuds, tied in knots. Nervous sweat prickles over the back of his neck as the heat times start to be announced across the buzzing beach. He's up in thirty minutes.

He wants to panic. Wants to swim out into the sea and dive beneath the waves until he finds the bullet casing. Wants to clutch it in his palms and think of how easy it all was just two weeks ago when he was sitting in the sand with Rob and looking out over the familiar Hermosa swells, his only care in the world wondering if anyone down below on that beach knew about the scar on his chest. If he would win enough money and points to surf in only the next competition.

Now he has a professional status to prove, and a fucking semifinals heat to not embarrass himself in, and a man—a gorgeous, soft, warm man—to somehow convince to still be around him after he inevitably loses. He has a plane ticket sitting in a long-abandoned hotel room back by the Honolulu airport that he needs to force himself to forget all about for the next twenty-four hours.

Sydney's absence from the beach tugs fiercely at the back of his mind. It nags him incessantly as he finishes waxing his board and starts stretching off to the side to prepare for his heat. There's a pull at the center of his chest—a knot around the warmth inside his skin that's connected to a long string which Sydney Moore wears effortlessly on the tips of his fingers, pulling him helplessly along in his wake.

There's a low boil of anger churning in the pit of his stomach. Anger that he apparently can't even focus for five fucking minutes without Sydney nearby, the previous three decades of his life be damned, and even more anger that not two hours ago Sydney had held his hand and looked him in the eyes and *promised* not to leave James' sight.

And now he's gone and disappeared entirely from the hot sand after hurling himself into the waves and stunning the crowd like James didn't even exist. And now he's alone.

And it's his first pro *semifinals.*

Panic prickles at the back of his throat. He can't do this. He absolutely cannot fucking get on a board and paddle out into the Banzai in front of hundreds of people and somehow surf well enough to win, or well enough to even get a sponsor. He should just quietly leave Sydney's borrowed board leaning against a tree for him to find, pocket his wax, and leave. Nobody would even notice he was gone. Jimmy Campbell?

Who the hell is he? That guy from LA that Danny Moore lost to on purpose? Out of pity?

He misses Rob, those quiet, early mornings, and his carefree laugh . . .

A harsh whistle startles James from his black thoughts, and he whips around to find its source. Sydney flicks his hand out from where he stands concealed in the shade of the nearby trees, already back in a dry t-shirt, bag slung over his shoulder.

Embarrassing relief floods through James' system so quickly he thinks he might pass out. With a quick glance back at the crowd of surfers to make sure nobody's watching, James jogs across the sand to where Sydney waits in the shadows, hidden in the cool, thick air of a plumeria tree ripe with blooms.

"Thought you'd gone," James pants out as he joins him.

He shoves his hands in his pockets and hunches beneath the branches, and the rest of the beach disappears the moment he's chest to chest with Sydney Moore. Gone are the sounds of the crowd, the buzz of the announcers, the swish of the umbrellas and palm fronds and the chorus of laughter and music. All James can hear is the sound of Sydney's breathing.

Sydney frowns as he takes off his aviators, folding them over the neckline of his t-shirt with practised ease. "I literally just told you I'd be here. Why would I leave you?"

James is instantly ashamed for his earlier, childish anger. It must show on his face, because Sydney sucks in a breath, eyes wide with realization.

"*Oh*, you thought I just did that to show off and then booked it out of here to escape everyone," he says. He tilts his head. "Makes sense. You were standing right in the middle of a huddle of my particularly greatest fans."

James can't believe this is the same man who just utterly annihilated that wave, all dripping muscle and terrifying focus ripping across the surface of the ocean, stealing the breath of everyone on the shore in a mighty rip.

"How can you stand it?" James blurts. "Knowing what they say about you?"

"James, you've met me. Don't make me into an angel."

"Yeah alright, but—"

"Listen, that's irrelevant," Sydney cuts him off. He places his hands on James' shoulders, then quickly glances back at the beach to ensure no one has noticed them. His voice when he speaks is smooth and alive, rushing over James' entire body like a steady, soothing breeze.

"I just went out there to test the current," Sydney says. "Rumor going around of a riptide flowing southeast right after the breaking point, but that's total bullshit. Florence and Trent have heard about it, though, and they'll stay clear to avoid it. Use this. Hang back farther out than you normally would and wait for the largest swells that break first. You'll be able to catch them while they'll just have to dolphin dive under. You'll have to surf your ass off on them, and don't wipeout on one of those unless you want the lifeguards pulling you out, but if you can hold it down you've got this round in the bag. Move on to the finals."

A tight emotion stretches from the soles of James' feet to his scalp. He fights back a smile as he looks up into Sydney's eyes, blazing and alight with excitement.

"Who the hell are you?" James whispers.

There's a sudden laugh trying to break free from his chest. It is so unbelievably ridiculous that he was so afraid two minutes ago back on the shore. He's alive, and he's in Hawaii, and Sydney sucked him off that morning.

After all, it's only *surfing*, for God's sake.

Sydney grins knowingly and squeezes James' shoulders with his hands, his chest puffed up with pride. He leans forward towards James' face, then hesitates. James watches, fascinated as the thoughts play out across Sydney's eyes. Desire, then hesitation, then realization, then relief on the heels of something like joy. Sydney sighs and leans the rest of the way in and plants a quick, dry kiss on James' lips. James sways in his arms, and Sydney holds him steady.

"Go on, then," Sydney says, turning James by the shoulders back to the beach. "They're about to call your heat to prepare."

James walks forward in a daze, guided by Sydney's gentle shove against his back. He sets his shoulders, cracks his fingers, rivets his eyes to the incoming waves as if nothing else on earth exists.

He thinks of the time Rob and Lori ran out fully clothed into the water to hug him after he won his very first competition, entry paid for with Rob's extra cash. He thinks of the look on Sydney's face when he'd shot up from his hammock to find James standing there in the trees.

Sydney calls his name when he's ten steps away, and James throws a glance over his shoulder, eyebrows raised.

Sydney's eyes are sparkling, his entire body framed by a sea of white and yellow blooms. James wants to dive into the sight of it. Take a picture and ink it onto the skin of his own body.

"For Helen, yeah?" Sydney's earnest eyes look incredibly full and young.

James' own words catch in the back of his throat. Sydney nods his head at him to continue walking away, and all James can do is look at him for one beat more before turning back towards the competition, fresh determination in his step and a heavy warmth settling in the core of his chest.

The airhorn startles him, just like it always does.

James holds back his flinch and runs forward into the waves, throwing down his board into the shallows once he's waist-deep, then leaping on top of the solid, familiar wood. His heart races in his chest, pumping the blood through his body so harshly he can feel it pulsing through the tips of each of his fingers.

He's flanked by Hamilton and Trent, both breathing hard as the three of them pull themselves out to sea, diving under the whitewater waves that come their way before they make it out safely past the breaking point. James relishes in the comfortable familiarity of paddling out at the start of any competition—slowly leaving behind the sounds of the crowd and the announcers with each stroke of his arms. The pleasant burn wakes up the muscles in his back and shoulders while the bright sun beats down onto this skin. He memorizes the rhythm of the waves as they rock against his body, and he controls his deep breaths through his nose.

He does exactly what Sydney had said to do—paddles out even after he senses Hamilton and Trent have both stopped until he's out just far enough that only the largest waves will break before they reach him.

He's nearly alone in the middle of the sea, and yet that knot around his chest is still there—that woven, unbreakable string that grounds him back to Sydney on the shore with each paddle he takes. James blinks hard as he realizes that, for the first time in his entire adult life, James truly *wants* the sea to push him back to shore. Wants her to thwart his efforts to keep swimming out towards the horizon and forbid him from disappearing into the deep.

He doesn't have time now to think of how that might change everything, or nothing at all. And he definitely doesn't have time to think about how much of that was Sydney's doing, or his own.

Far off in the distance, James finally spots the deep roll of a huge wave rushing steadily in to the breaking point. In his gut, he already knows this one is his, as if his name was written across it in coral and foam.

Behind him, he can hear the sounds of Trent and Hamilton battling it out over the tighter barrels closer to shore, dropping one after another into the whitewater as the pipelines shoot them out too fast or close in over their heads.

Almost six minutes have gone by in the round. James knows that everyone on the shore thinks he must have lost it. That he's chickened out or lost his nerve or caved under the pressure of going up against two surfers known for doing trick rides on smaller waves. Going up against two surfers actually known for something in the first place.

"*Idiots,*" the Sydney in his mind suddenly says.

James smiles despite himself as the wave continues to build, heaving up the water from the deep and forcing it towards the sky. He has to start paddling now or it'll pass by right under him.

James grits his teeth, turns his board, and tenses his muscles, readying for the race of his life. He goes to place his first paddle, then he remembers.

"Mom," he whispers into the surface of his board, feeling foolish and alive. He doesn't even think he's called out to her since he screamed for her to help him on the painful beach. A strange peace settles over his body in the following silence, covering him in a layer between the surface of his skin and the force of the baking sun.

He closes his eyes and savors the taste of the word on his tongue, and he licks the salt from his lips.

Then the hurling force of the wave is there with a roar, pushing him up towards the sky by the tail of his board. The crest of the wave starts to form just under his center of gravity.

And with a smile on his face, beautiful danger flying back through his hair, James Campbell pops up onto his shaking feet and soars down the face of the barrel.

Everything is forgotten. Everything but his legs and the water and the board. James surfs like a machine, barrel after barrel, ride after ride, chase after chase. He's the only person out there in the water. The only person on the entire beach. The only person beneath the sun.

The towering waves push and shove against the bottom of his board, straining at the muscles in his legs and ripping at his core. They blast salty spray into his face and crush him in their whitewater—propel him faster than he's ever moved on a board in his life and shove him back towards the shore again, and again, and again.

He doesn't stop. The only sounds in the world are the hurling crash of the great walls of water around him and the echo of his breathing in the long tubes of the barrels. He gouges into the faces, rips cutbacks across the crests, soars up into the air, and crouches down low against his board.

When the airhorn finally echoes out to him across the water, it feels like he's been surfing for either five minutes or five days.

James has absolutely no idea what just happened. Every muscle in his body aches, and his throat screams out for clear water, and his eyes burn and crackle under a thick sheen of salt. He paddles in on aching arms and body surfs on the whitewater of the shallower waves, having no idea how Hamilton and Trent just fared in the round. He doesn't even know how many waves he himself caught, or if they really were as towering as they felt, or whether his two brief wipeouts left him looking embarrassing and clueless and small.

The crowd is roaring as he approaches. They're on their feet and waving their arms and yelling. Cheering.

James paddles in to where he can stand and looks back over his shoulders for Hamilton and Trent, wanting to know what or whom the entire beach is erupting for. He scans the horizon, but the ocean behind him is empty. He turns quickly back to the shore and sees the two of them standing off to the side, panting with towels around their necks, applauding for him.

*Applauding for him.*

James gasps and drops his board into the shallows. He sees the entire beach before him like he did that day at Hermosa, exploding before his very eyes, every gaze locked on him. He catches the sound of his name coming from the announcers' crackling loud speaker, and he gazes dumbstruck as a pack of smiling surfers jog down to meet him in the water.

Desperately, his eyes scan the crowd along the shore. He nearly moans when he finally spots a familiar head of dark curls standing in the center of the chaos, arms crossed over his chest and chin held high. He can clearly see the outlines of his own reflection in the familiar black shades.

He watches Sydney Moore pull the aviators down off his eyes, send James a wink, and smile softly at the corner of his mouth.

And that's when James Campbell drops to his knees in the wet sand of the foaming shallows, tears at the back of his eyes. When he witnesses the overwhelming scene before him for the second time in less than a goddamn month. Because he didn't just embarrass himself, and hundreds of people are currently applauding him completely unaware of the scar hiding just beneath his wetsuit, and he's moving on to the fucking finals of the Billabong Pipeline Masters.

And Sydney Moore is smiling freely at him, uncrossing his arms to clap.

# *17*

Sydney wants to sprint towards James Campbell at full speed and tackle him down into the soft seafoam and kiss the disbelieving smile on his lips. Wants to clutch his shaking muscles and the clinging wetsuit with his palms and crush the rushing heartbeat in James' chest against his own.

He physically grips the sand with his toes to force himself to stay put as James rises from his knees to stand and is quickly engulfed in a crowd of surfers gone running to congratulate him. They slap his back and tap his board and welcome him into their midst with open arms—the unexpected underdog no longer. He has proven his worth without leaving an inch of room for doubt, and they've gone running towards him like moths to a flame, leaving Sydney to stand in an empty patch of sand.

Nobody came running towards Danny Moore after he'd first ripped his way across the Banzai Pipeline.

Sydney shakes his head against the unwelcome thought and awkwardly grips his hands behind his back to stop them from clapping some more. James can't see him now, anyways, not when he's so surrounded. He steps back into the rest of the crowd behind him and wills himself to fade back into the masses, slipping down his aviators and silently thrilling that, for once, nobody is looking at him.

He tries to catch a glimpse of golden hair through the huddle by the water—a muscled, tan forearm, or a flash of stormy blue eyes. But all he can see is a thronging sea of bare backs and boardshorts and beards. Not the forehead he'd fallen asleep with his lips pressed against, or the hands that had gripped his curls and the bedsheets with strong fingers as

Sydney settled between his thighs and kissed the most intimate part of his skin.

God, but James' eyes had been beautiful when they'd locked onto Sydney's just moments ago. Sydney had watched, rooted to the sand, as the thoughts passed so freely across James' face. Exhaustion, followed by confusion and wariness, finally blotted out by sheer disbelief. By joy. And he'd sought out Sydney in the crowd as he stood there dripping wet, chest heaving on the shore, and he'd stared at him with a look that said *you gave this to me.*

Except that's beyond ridiculous.

Sydney hasn't give him anything at all. James did this for himself. For Helen. And with only the incredible strength and power of his own body and will. And his look at Sydney had simply been a reflection of his inner sense of well-earned accomplishment. It didn't have anything at all to do with the fact that Sydney himself was standing on that shore amongst the crowd.

Did it?

Sydney huffs and grips his hands even tighter behind his back. It's infuriating—experiencing such a wave of indecision on the beach where he's always felt more confident than anywhere else in the world. He's spent every day since he was fifteen cataloguing the world around him into a system that makes sense, a system that acknowledges Sydney Moore's existence but does not particularly care too much that he's there. And that's been good. It's been fine and perfect and left him peacefully alone and carried him through each hour until he can set foot back on his private stretch of sand at the end of the day and release the cold breath in his lungs.

And now, after just two days of being allowed to touch James Campbell's skin, he's walking around thinking that someone is *thanking* him. That someone is actually searching for his eyes in a crowd because they want to see that he's there.

Stupid.

Is it?

The airhorn starting the next semi-final heat blares across the hot sand, and Sydney blinks out of his thoughts to see that the entire crowd around him has resumed their seats, leaving him standing alone among the sea of sunbathing skin and beach towels.

In an unfamiliar flash of panic, his eyes scan the beach for James, wishing for the first time in his life that someone, well, some*one*, was saving him a seat on one of those beach towels to watch the next set of surfing.

He finds James easily, as if his body subconsciously knew his exact location. He's leaning back in the sand with a t-shirt pulled on and his wetsuit top hanging down by his hips, running a hand through his soaking wet golden hair and laughing like it's the only way he knows how to breathe. Laughing surrounded by a group of other surfers, all loose and at ease.

The rush of jealousy Sydney experiences looking at James' body so effortlessly surrounded by them is staggering. It's as if the sunlight has been blocked forever in the spot directly above his head, as if his skin is doomed to remain dry and hot and prickly for all time despite the cool ocean spray blowing steadily at his back. A sense of betrayal niggles, unwelcome, in the back of his mind.

*"You'll be there?"* James had asked.

And Sydney had answered yes, of course, always. Had crept along in the shade of the trees and called James over to him and assured him *yes, I am here, can't you see that it would physically hurt me to leave you? That the trails of kisses you left on my back would split open and bleed if I turned away? That I can't ever go back?*

God. He's a fucking insecure teenager all over again. And James is *James Campbell*, who just advanced to the *finals* after nearly drowning a week before. Who survived the *war*.

And meanwhile, in his tiny, insignificant little slice of the world, Sydney wants to strut over to James Campbell and step on the hands and toes of all the other surfers and demand why, when they still have one precious day left together, James is already imposing their separation. Why, not even an hour after Sydney had kissed him in the shady cocoon of flowers and opened himself up to the entire beach's scrutiny out on the waves just to make sure that James could win, James is now lounging back on his arm and acting like he doesn't even know that Danny Moore is standing on the same shore. Why James is laughing with them and acting like those same smiling lips didn't whisper the word "Sydney" over and over again in full view of the stars the night before.

And that's when Sydney realizes he is the world's biggest idiot.

Because his eyes suddenly focus, and the hazy fog of indignant hurt clears from his mind in the salty breeze, and he sees that James Campbell is not, in fact, lounging back on his hand and laughing like it's the only way he knows how to breathe. Instead James' entire body is tense, the smile on his lips is stale and fixed, and the hand pressing back into the warm sand is slowly, ever so slowly, pushing him up to stand.

Sydney watches with his heart in his throat as James nods along and slowly gets to his feet, waving a hand at presumed offers to stick around and watch with the group and instead looking straight at Sydney like he knew exactly where he was standing without even a second's hesitation. James gives a slight nod of his head before walking swiftly and calmly up the sand towards the road, smiling and acknowledging the well-wishes thrown his way as he makes his way through the crowd.

On numb legs, Sydney follows at a careful distance, pointedly looking everywhere but at the broad line of shoulders carving muscled arcs into James' shirt, or the smooth skin at the back of James' still-dripping neck, or the way James' thighs steadily carry him as if he didn't just surf his ass off on an infamous pipeline. He watches his bare feet sink into the sand as they gradually leave the sounds of the competition farther behind them.

He continues to follow James through the maze of palm trees and cars, basking in the warm breeze on his skin as uncertain anticipation starts to spark in his chest.

James walks like a God—the men blessed by the sea Lahela used to tell him about when they stopped to watch the surfers between boring errands. The wetsuit clings to his calves and thighs, drips over the firm curve of his ass. A tiny sliver of pale skin peeks out between the bottom of Sydney's old t-shirt James is wearing and the top of the folded-down wetsuit.

Sydney has the sudden, humiliating urge to run forward, drop to his knees, and press his tongue to that warm strip of skin, his arms around James' firm waist. To taste the salt, and brush the fragile hairs on James' body across his lips, and listen to the whispered shiver that would cascade down James' spine.

James turns down a side street off the main road and glances casually to his right before turning again behind the back of an old surf shop, surrounded on three sides by the beginnings of a stretch of lush, rolling green hills. With a bewildered frown, Sydney turns the same corner, only to immediately be grabbed by his shoulders and slammed back into the wall.

Sydney barely has time to grunt in surprise before a hand comes up to rip the sunglasses from his face and throw them to the ground, and then James Campbell is kissing him fiercely, pressing him back into the wall with the whole force of his body and gripping at Sydney's hair and shoulders as if Sydney will fall apart without the firm grasp of his hands.

James is already thick and hard against his hip.

The low heat that had been pooling in Sydney's gut from the moment James popped up on his first wave of the day explodes into a fire of want, pulsing down his legs and grinding against the heat from James' body. Sydney melts, surrendering, as James pants and groans into his mouth, forgets to breathe as James kisses every inch of his lips and steals the moans hovering at the tip of Sydney's tongue. Sydney brings his hands up to clutch at James' waist, helpless to do anything else but curl up against him and hold on.

And Sydney wants to laugh into James' mouth, or turn his face up to the sky and laugh in the face of the sun. He wants to cry out that the man who just stunned an entire beach to their feet left it all behind so he could kiss Sydney up against the back wall of a surf shop. It's more magnificent than every competition he's ever won combined.

James *looked* for him. He really did.

Sydney gasps for breath as James sucks his upper lip between his. There's a certain physical heat in James' mouth—one Sydney's never tasted before. It loosens his tongue and lips, makes him think of James gasping for grunted breaths as he pumps along a towering wave.

James grabs his face, pressing hard, and they moan one last time in unison before James pulls back to lick his kiss-swollen lips, eyes wild and dilated and absolutely locked onto Sydney's face. Sydney's hands still clutch at the fabric around James' waist, holding himself up from collapsing onto the grass.

He stares. James looks like a ray of sun plopped down in the middle of the velvet green blanket of the earth. The bright sunlight glints off the tips of his blonde bangs, and the saltwater dances on his eyelashes, and the colors of the jungle of flowers behind him reflect off his tan, rippling skin like a handful of sea-polished pearls.

James leans in towards him again and runs his nose along Sydney's cheek, sending a shiver down Sydney's spine until his bare toes clutch reflexively at the soft, warm grass.

"Couldn't get away from them fast enough," James whispers, eyes still closed. "Thought they'd never let me leave."

Sydney feels a bewildered smile curling at the corners of his lips, but he settles his mouth into a cool line just as James opens his eyes, pinning him back to the wall with the pure, earnest truth in the lines of his face. Sydney licks his lips and tries to speak, tries to pick out words that he could possibly say that would somehow do justice to the fact that James just willingly left a crowd of people who were fawning all over him just so that he could press Sydney's back into a wall and kiss him.

Sydney realizes he's been standing there with his mouth half-open, and James' brow furrows as he takes in the look on Sydney's face.

"Shit, man, sorry, you're shaking. I didn't mean to—"

Sydney cuts off James' ridiculous apology by gripping his shoulders and turning to slam James' back into the wall instead. He needs to taste the salt on James' lips. Badly. Needs to feel every inch of his strength and muscle surging up into his hands, touch the force of the man who conquered the Banzai's largest waves of the day. He needs to taste and subsist on the oxygen and carbon dioxide coming from his warm, wet mouth. To show the rolling mountains at their backs that James Campbell is letting him kiss him when he's just one surfing round away from becoming a champion.

James gasps in surprise the moment Sydney shoves him back, body going stiff for a moment. Fear flashes through Sydney's chest that he's pushed too far, gone completely over the edge, when James reaches out, grabs him, and finishes pulling Sydney into himself until James is trapped against the wall. Sydney moans on a sigh and presses his lips once more to James', licking into his mouth and tasting the proof of James' words—the proof that he really was seeking Sydney out on the sand.

James groans deep in his chest as Sydney caresses his lips, tracing them with his tongue. He cups James' face in his hands, growing shockingly warm and heavy between his thighs at the rasp of James' stubble across his fingers, when suddenly James' own hands are up and under his shirt, running roughly up Sydney's bare sides and clutching at his skin. He trails the tips of his thumbs over Sydney's nipples and grasps the whole span of his ribs.

The hot trace of James' hands on his bare skin, just five minutes away from a beach full of people, sends a fiery thrill through Sydney's core. He thinks of the way James' thighs had bulged through the wetsuit as he clung to his board and soared across the face of the wave, of the way the saltwater slipped down the inky black neoprene over his calves, and, in a rush of pure desire, Sydney reaches down for the underside of those thighs and lifts James up against the wall with a thick grunt. A pulse ripples through him when James immediately wraps his legs around Sydney's waist, trapping him with his thighs and pulling Sydney as close to his body as they can get.

Sydney is flying, held down to earth solely by the gripping muscles in James' legs. He carries the weight of James' powerful body in his hands, the quivering muscles that had carried him across the punishing roar of the ocean, the kiss of warm sunlight still lingering on his skin. Sydney pants into James' mouth and tastes the warm, wet heat of him, kneading his fingers into the firm curves of his ass through the wetsuit as he holds him up off the ground.

"Like that," James whispers with Sydney's tongue in his mouth. His thickening cock is pressing straight into Sydney's abs, bulging the clinging black fabric of the suit. Sydney grazes his teeth across James' stubble as James' head thuds back against the wall. James yanks on his curls. "Fuck, like that . . ."

Out of nowhere, the memory of the photograph Sydney bought when he was fourteen floats into his mind—the shirtless sailor with oiled abs and dog tags gleaming on his bare chest, a hand reaching down into the open fly of his tented uniform pants. And for the first time since leaning down to kiss James Campbell on the beach at sunrise just yesterday morning, Sydney's brain realizes that he *has* that sailor. Here. Now. Groaning with his ass in Sydney's palms and grinding his cock into Sydney's body. Desperate for friction just ten minutes after absolutely annihilating his semifinal heat, punishing the waves of the sea with the sheer strength of his body.

Biting his bottom lip.

It's the most erotic thought Sydney's ever had in his life. He hikes James higher up on the wall and gasps against his wet lips. He speaks before he loses his nerve, dipping his head to lick a stripe up the salty side of James' tensing neck.

"I want you," he groans. "Have wanted you. Hermosa, when you were changing—God, you . . ."

James' head hits the wall with a thud.

"Fuck, Sydney."

"Watching you out there. Fuck, you have no idea what I—"

A loud bang clatters from the other side of the surf shop wall, and Sydney whips his hands back from James' ass so quickly James barely catches himself from falling to the ground. Sydney leaps away from him, tripping in the grass, and tries to breathe over the wild pounding in his chest. Cold sweat prickles across his skin, smothering every last inch of heat.

He has no idea what just came over him, pinning James Campbell to a wall and hiking his legs up around his waist in broad fucking daylight, when James should be resting and preparing for his finals heat in just a few hours, when he should be off surrounding himself with his new community and watching the other surfers and studying the rises and falls of the waves.

James' hand is suddenly on his cheek, dry and warm. James doesn't look like a man who should be off preparing for a finals heat, or who was just slammed into another wall by another man in broad fucking daylight, or who wishes he was back watching the other guys surf.

Instead James pats his cheek once before letting his hand slowly fall away. Sydney thinks he sees a sudden gloss over James' deep blue eyes, but it's quickly blinked away.

"Stop thinking so hard, genius," he says in a surprisingly casual voice, still trying to catch his breath. "You'll pull a muscle and then my plans for tonight'll go to shit."

Sydney laughs despite himself. He stoops to pick up his sunglasses, then shoves his hands in his pockets to try to look less useless while the panic slowly fades from his body in rolling waves. His erection is long gone, and a quick, sheepish glance down at James sees him quietly adjusting himself in the wetsuit with his palm.

Sydney immediately looks away. He clears his throat and ducks his head, hating the fact that he suddenly feels ten years old.

"Sorry, I just—I didn't mean to do that . . . now. I shouldn't have just—"

"I started it, didn't I?" James says, an undercurrent of embarrassment behind his rough voice. He rubs a hand over his mouth and tries to fix his hair. He shoots Sydney the barest hint of a grin—one Sydney convinces himself isn't forced. "You can be a real idiot sometimes, you know that?"

Sydney chuckles again through his nose, and his eyes trace the lock of soft, gold hair that's fallen into James' face. A small rush of warmth finally breaks through the cold, dead weight draped across his skin. "I'm starting to realize that," he says.

James' body heat still thrums along Sydney's limbs, pulling him close even though they stand two feet apart. James looks like he's going to say something else, then shuts his mouth. Sydney wonders if he's imagining the way James' eyes quickly rove up and down his body. Then James drops his hands to his sides, shakes out his shoulders, and starts to walk back towards the road, tilting his head for Sydney to follow.

James walks back out into the world as if nothing at all unusual just happened. It takes Sydney's breath away—watching James hold his head high and walk down the street like this isn't one of the most nerve-wracking days of his life. Like he doesn't have to surf his ass off and try to win his first pro competition in a few short hours. Like he didn't just press his erection into another man's thigh and cling to his body in the hidden shade.

But then again, this is probably *last* on the list of nerve-wracking days in James' life. Sydney looks at the beach in the distance and once again feels a wash of shame over the complete irrelevance of his tiny life. That James Campbell wakes up every day having survived a war, continuing to *live*, and all Sydney has is a dozen useless medals from playing a game in the water.

"*This isn't just a game for me,*" James had told him once, standing in a sweat-soaked shirt with grey circles under his eyes, and Sydney remembers, not for the first time, that a Banzai win for James Campbell would mean a thousand things more than when Sydney had conquered the same waves.

He bites his lips, arguing with himself against his desperate, selfish need to have James to himself for just a little bit longer, growing stronger with each step they take closer to the crowds and waves. The answer finally comes to him when he notices the tightness in the way James is carrying his left shoulder—the careful stillness in his walk.

"Your shoulder's gonna give out on you unless you stretch it out," he says, catching up a few steps to be by James' side. "Got some food in an ice chest in the Jeep. If you eat now and stretch some you'll have enough time to get back down and watch the water for a while before you're up."

James stops in his tracks, then immediately turns to head in the opposite direction of the competition, back to where they parked the Jeep.

"I knew you were a genius," he smirks.

Sydney tries not to let his chest puff up too obviously with pride. Who feels proud of themselves after simply suggesting somebody else eat lunch? He passes a hand over his mouth, hating that what he's about to say will wipe the easy smile from James' face.

"Give me a chance too to fill you in on who you'll end up against this afternoon," he says cautiously.

James runs a hand through his hair. "Shit, hadn't even tried to find out before leaving with you. Who is it?"

James turns to look at him, and he must see the look on Sydney's face, because his immediately blanches like a sheet, dread in the lines of his eyes.

Sydney clears his throat and forces himself to hold James' gaze. "Duke O'Brien," he answers, as casually and apologetically as he possibly can.

"Oh fuck."

"Look, we've been over this. He's not as unbeatable as everyone says he is. Hell, I've beaten him—"

"That's because you're you!"

"*You've* beaten me, and I've beaten him, so I'm not sure why you're being so damn stubborn about this, after all—"

"I beat you because you fell off your fucking board! On purpose!"

263

"And as I've told you before, it still would've been close if I hadn't!"

"You haven't told me that before."

"My deepest apologies. I'm telling you now."

"You've gotta be—close is not the same as beating. Especially not in the fucking Billabong finals. Jesus . . ."

"You've made it this far, haven't you? And nobody's fallen off their board on purpose yet."

James opens his mouth to retort then abruptly closes it again. He slumps back into the seat and tears haphazardly at the crust on the sandwich in his hand.

Sydney smirks at James' silence, too wrapped up in their time alone together to be worried at how much it delights him to watch James Campbell act like a sulking child. The dichotomy of it warms him from a very specific and hidden place deep in his chest. He reaches across the gear shift of the Jeep to place a hand on James' knee.

"Come on, gotta eat something. Your body'll thank you."

James sighs again through his nose and stares out the front window at the distant beach like a man staring at his own gallows. Sydney moves his hand up to James' shoulder, loose and open now after Sydney helped him stretch it, standing in the shade of a nearby canopy of trees. This time, James hadn't flinched at all when Sydney's fingers touched the scar, which had caused a completely unneeded and sharp emotion to tighten Sydney's throat.

He's just about to fill the silence with something stupid, like asking him how the shoulder feels, when James' brow suddenly furrows.

"Hold on, when did you even pack this food? I was with you the whole morning."

Sydney takes his hand back to reach into the bag in his lap and lift out a handful of sunflower seeds. "Did it last night."

"In the middle of the night?"

Sydney hums and throws back the seeds into his mouth, overly enthusiastic and almost knocking the sunglasses off the top of his head. He quickly recovers, but knows that James without a doubt saw.

"Well, why the hell weren't you asleep?" James adds.

Sydney takes his time to chew and spit the shells out the side of the window, smirking when James makes a disgusted noise. He wipes his mouth with the back of his hand and decides whether to make up a reason or tell the truth.

The truth wins. He ignores the sweat forming at his brow and instead remembers the force of James' hands slamming his shoulders back into the wall.

"I knew I had . . . plans for the morning. Didn't want us to be late if we didn't already have your stuff packed for the day."

He shrugs, waiting for another disgusted noise, but James throws back his head and barks out a laugh. "You made peanut butter and jelly sandwiches at three o'clock in the morning just so you could have enough time to have sex with me?"

"No, that would be stupid. I did that so that I could give you a good-luck blow job. There's a critical difference."

"'Critical difference' my ass, you fucking loony."

"Well it worked, didn't it? You're here, in the finals."

James turns to look at him, and the sudden smile on his face takes Sydney's breath away. The tension seems to melt from James' body before his very eyes, slowly fading away on the warm, floral-scented air. James nods once and exhales a deep breath before sitting up straight in the hot leather seat, taking a full bite of sandwich and shaking out the remaining tension in his shoulders.

"Right," he says over a full mouth. He wipes away the crumb of crust caught in his stubble. "So, O'Brien. Tell me whatever the hell I need to know."

Sydney doesn't want to talk about Duke O'Brien. He wants to start the Jeep's engine and drive over to the other side of the island where no one else will be around and stand under the clear, open sky holding James Campbell's hand tight in his. For an insane moment, he almost opens his mouth to suggest it. To say that it's just some silly competition, and James has already proved he's a world class surfer, and can't they just go and be on their own now for every minute until he has to leave?

Then the image of James hurling the bullet away into the sea pops into his mind, just like it's done again, and again, and again over the last twelve hours, and Sydney bites his tongue against the reminder that James has a life extending far beyond the tiny bounds of the Oahu shores. Far beyond Sydney's reach.

Sydney squares his shoulders and spits out another mouthful of shells, forcing his mind to focus on the task at hand. A tiny part of his heart is yelling that James Campbell needs him right now, and the rest of his heart desperately wants to believe that's somehow true.

"Duke O'Brien," he begins. "Last year's Virginia Beach champion, as you know. Second in the Sunset Beach invitational, fifth in the Surfabout in Sydney, and came third in the U.S. Open over in your neck of the woods in '74—"

"See now, since Long Beach is in Los Angeles, this actually *is* the correct usage of 'your neck of the woods'—"

"Which, as I was *saying*, got him qualified for Virginia. But then there's his regional wins, which—"

"Oh this is really helpful, thank you. Tell me more about the competitions he's already won which I haven't, please."

"Well it's important to know what waters he's surfed on before! You can't just walk out there totally ignorant!"

James laughs and places a hand on Sydney's knee. "I know, I know, genius. Keep going."

A flushed, embarrassed grin spread across Sydney's cheeks when he realizes James was just goading him on purpose. He flexes his thigh beneath James' palm and watches the shimmer of the waves far out in the distance.

"Right, so, in the last year alone, he's surfed on every major coastline for big wave surfing. Word is he's using the Billabong here to pave his way for the World's in Australia in two months. It's a huge advantage if he wins this; they'll let him skip straight to Day Two. So he's gonna go hard and fast, isn't afraid to be a dick and drop in on a wave you're paddling for if he thinks it's a good one, so you can't hesitate at all with him. Don't pause up at the crest after paddling, just drop in early so you can get on the face, even if you miss part of the barrel. Yes?"

James groans. "Copy."

"He loves doing cutbacks at the foot of the wave. He'll zoom straight down the face just to get to the bottom and then stay there to surf at the base of the wall. Virginia judges liked it because the waves there aren't huge to begin with and it let him do some nice trick moves in the whitewater, but judges here want to see you take advantage of the pipeline. That's your specialty, just as long as you can drop in before he snakes in on you. And he *will*—"

"Oh, wonderful. Thanks."

"—*try*. He will try."

James closes his eyes and runs both hands through his hair before looping his fingers at the back of his neck, breathing deep and slow. Sydney watches, transfixed, as James' chest rises and falls beneath his own t-shirt covering his warm skin.

He wants to slip his head under the shirt and rub his face against the hair on James' chest and breathe in the smell at the base of his neck, under his arms, in the crooks of his elbows. The desire is so intense it startles him—this sudden need to possess, to *be* possessed, and he only just kissed him for the first time yesterday goddamn morning.

"What are you thinking about?" James suddenly asks.

Sydney hadn't realized he'd been quiet for so long, his monologue long forgotten. "Shouldn't I be the one asking you that question?"

James rolls his neck once on his shoulders to crack it. "I'm thinking about being scared shitless to go up against O'Brien on the Pipeline in an hour. And also that I want to crush his ass. Your turn."

Sydney's chest clenches tightly against the words that want to come spilling out his mouth. That he doesn't know how he'll breathe when James gets on a plane tomorrow and leaves. That he had it all planned out to take James over to the east side of the island tomorrow to a little place where he knew he could buy James a strawberry milkshake, but then he found out James' flight leaves first thing in the morning, and they won't have time. That finding James Campbell on that pier was more life altering than the first time he ever popped up on a board and rode a wave into the shore.

That James is about to win and go on with his life, and Sydney will just have to quietly go back to only ever being called Danny Moore.

He gathers his aviators and his keys so that they can leave the car and head back down to the beach, ignoring the dull, dreading ache in his chest.

"I'm thinking that you're about to surf like hell," he finally says, forcing out a calm confidence he sure as hell doesn't feel, and James nods once with a small, grateful smile on the corner of his lips before opening the door of the Jeep to the rushing noise of the real world.

*"—with a final three-wave score of a whopping 27.1, Terry Russell just proved that he is definitely the one to beat in this Billabong Finals. Is that a Billabong record?"*

*"Moore finished last year with twenty-seven even, so yes!"*

*"Right on, Russell! Gonna make Moore have to break a sweat next year!"*

*"What a performance, folks. Eight full rides, beautiful clear barrels, epic speed and a hang ten right at the end there to rack up the extra points . . . Georgie Davis surfed the set of his life, but looks like even that wasn't enough to come out ahead of Russell today."*

*"Gotta feel bad for Davis, man. 25.8 is the best he's put up in his career, but of course it had to be in the same Finals round where Russell seemed to pull together every ounce of strength he had and absolutely demolished that set—such an ace performance."*

*"Davis didn't even really have a chance from that first swell, you know."*

*"Right on there, man."*

*"Now Russell's in the hot seat—you think he's praying this second Finals heat goes badly?"*

*"Who wouldn't? He's sitting on the Billabong title right now and hoping one of these next two competitors readying themselves on the start line doesn't snatch it from him."*

*"And those two surfers are Angelino Jimmy Campbell and Duke O'Brien all the way from the faraway lands of the UK."*

*"What a matchup! Who woulda thought?!"*

*"Campbell had a solid run yesterday in his Wild Card heat, but man did he surprise us all this morning!"*

*"He had a radical set this morning, pure magic. No other way to put it. Not sure how the hell he knew that rip tide wasn't as strong as we all thought, but man did he take advantage of it."*

"He's gotta be feeling those monster waves in his legs now, though. Gotta be tired. O'Brien lucked out with his semi-final, as we all saw."

"That's right—small waves, perfect for his trick moves, and two fine surfers who caved to some harsh injuries. It's just about the perfect recipe for a surfer like Duke O'Brien to get a Finals seat without breaking a sweat."

"I dig it. Gotta admit, though, I'm bummed we aren't gonna get to witness O'Brien versus Moore."

"Now that would be the match of the century! The true battle of the giants. I think I'd have to split my life savings in half and bet on both."

"Let's pray to those gods out there that O'Brien decides to take on Waimea next week, then."

"Nope—look at O'Brien out there. He's shaking his head. Even Danny Moore isn't crazy enough to surf the Pipeline and Waimea right in a row."

"Damn. Such a let down . . ."

"You can cry about it later, brother. Now, though, we've got about five minutes until this last Finals heat of your 1976 Billabong Pipeline Masters—let's talk strengths. Jimmy Campbell."

"Campbell's been having a hell of a month—just made it out of qualifiers about three weeks ago at the ISF and already he's showing us all he deserves to be here with the pros."

"That's right, dude. Went from placing top ten and top five in some local SoCal competitions, did a few as far as San Diego from what I hear, but beyond that, he hasn't surfed outside that circuit. And we all know it's a whole different ballgame surfing international waters."

"Makes it hard to talk about what we'll see from him here. He's definitely on the older side for the surfers we see here on the Pipeline—it's a punishing stretch of beach we got here for the old bones. He's shown he can use some killer strategy against his opponents, and he sure as hell can hold his own against the big wave surf we've got here along the Banzai, but beyond that I have no idea what to expect from him up against a competitor like O'Brien, and, like you said, he's gotta be feeling the ache from that first round . . ."

"Sheer tenacity from O'Brien—that's what we're gonna see."

*"He's had a wild last two seasons leading up to that Virginia Beach victory—"*

*"So this is it,"* Sydney thinks to himself. *"This is how I'm going to die."*

There can't possibly be a way for him to survive the nerves roiling through his body—that his heart was somehow made to withstand the beats currently thudding explosions through his chest.

He tunes out the droning, pointless babble coming from the announcers and tries to eliminate everything but the sound of the waves, desperate for the steady rhythm of the breaks to try and slow his racing heart. The incoming swells are some of the largest they've seen all weekend, booming across the shore and roaring with whitewater and spray. Once, the sight would have thrilled him, burning with adrenaline through his core. But now it only serves to make his skin feel too tight for his bones, his throat aching and dry. Those waves aren't meant for him.

His eyes find James where he stands next to O'Brien near the starting line. To any one of the hundreds of spectators flocking to the beach to see this Finals heat, James Campbell probably appears utterly calm. He stands ready in his full wetsuit with his waxed board by his side and a wet towel around his neck, leaning forward to hang in a stretch between his open legs and calmly bobbing up and down like he has all the time in the world.

To Sydney, he looks anything but calm.

From the moment they'd stepped out of the Jeep and started walking towards the sand, James a careful fifty feet in front of him, Sydney had watched helplessly as each step closer to the beach brought a little more tension back into James' frame. The body that had been so strong and open as they'd held each other and kissed in the shade. Those same arms that had held him close in loose, sleepy warmth just that morning in the quiet comfort of his bed.

There's an undeniable thrill in the back of his mind at the realization that he alone in this sea of people knows the clues to reading the secrets hidden in the lines of James' body. That he alone has felt the raw power of those arms against his own skin, and that he alone knows that this man standing calmly on the shoreline, like he's simply waiting in line to buy groceries, holds a dangerous, conquering strength in every inch of his limbs.

That he alone knows the texture of the scar hiding beneath his wetsuit. That he alone can call him simply "James."

In a flash of panic, he realizes that James can't easily see him from where he's standing. He quickly scans the beach, knowing he only has a matter of minutes to find the perfect spot so that James can easily find him from the waves, when he hears his name cackle across the sand over the mic.

"—get Danny Moore up here to tell us his predictions for the Final!"

"Wouldn't be a Billabong without our reigning Champion!"

Dread settles in Sydney's gut with a sickening lurch as he looks over his shoulder and sees that half the beach is expectantly staring at him, stuck in an awkward standstill between wanting him to do something and wanting the heat to finally begin.

Sydney's just about to raise up a hand and simply shake his head no when he realizes that this is his last chance to speak to James in the two minutes before he'll run out into the waves. That this may be the last time he'll ever see James Campbell surf while knowing that James would actually want to hear Sydney's voice.

With a sharp nod, he walks back towards the announcers, zigzagging through the sea of lounging crowds and beach towels. He stands stiffly beside the two guys he recognizes from last year and shoves his hands in his pockets.

"So Danny, care to settle the rumors?"

"Yeah, man, fill us in. Why aren't you surfing here this year?"

Sydney takes a deep breath and clears his throat, fighting with himself not to stare across the crowds at the back of James' head where he waits for the airhorn to start his heat.

"Timing just wasn't right. I need to focus on Waimea."

"You heard it here, folks, looks like Danny Moore really is going for that world record!"

"Well, obviously. Everybody surfing Waimea is going for the record."

"Right, of course, but—"

"That's the whole point of doing it."

The second announcer awkwardly clears his throat, and Sydney wants to kick himself for not being able to act cool and casual for just once in his life.

The announcer tries again. "Maybe later we can go over how funky those Waimea waves are gonna be. You can convince O'Brien over there to join you. But, for now . . . thoughts for this Final? You know these waves better than anyone."

Sydney appreciates being thrown a bone, but can also still hear the faint insincerity hiding behind their cheerful words—the wavering undertone of disappointment that they aren't currently chatting with literally any other top surfer on the beach. Sydney flashes a desperate glance towards the starting line and sees that James is entirely in his own head, gazing out at the waves with seemingly no idea that Sydney's voice is even echoing across the sand.

He clears his throat again and bends over to make his voice louder in the mic, sending up a silent prayer to who-knows-what that this plan will somehow work. To his momma's God.

"You've asked me to predict the surf and the round, but I'll skip all that and tell you the winner of the whole thing."

The announcer's brows raise. "Oh, right on, man. Ok, give it to us!"

"Jimmy Campbell. Obviously," Sydney says in his clearest voice.

He watches James' head perk up at the sound of his name.

"Alright, dude, you can't leave us hanging. Gotta explain that one!"

"Yeah, man, I don't think any of us is doing him a disservice to still call Campbell the underdog here. I mean, he's gotta beat both O'Brien *and* Russell's massive score."

"This just because he beat you back in Hermosa?"

Sydney fights with himself not to audibly scoff. "Of course not. Russell put up an alright score, but he got all his points just by throwing in tricks at the very end of his rides. O'Brien's gonna chase after everything that comes at him, whether it's a smooth barrel or not. Campbell's the only surfer here today with enough experience to know when to wait."

"Enough experience you say—but he hasn't even been pro a whole season."

"Yeah man, he only came on the scene two years ago, so—"

"That doesn't mean he hadn't touched a surfboard before then," Sydney cuts in. "Doesn't take a genius to figure that out."

He can read in every inch of James' body that he's listening. Intently. The clock ticks down to thirty more seconds before the airhorn, and desperation floods Sydney's mind. He hasn't said enough. Hasn't done enough. Hasn't told James Campbell what he fiercely needs him to know.

Didn't kiss him one last time back in the Jeep before it was too late.

"Look at that, thirty seconds! We're just about ready to start here, folks. Moore, last thoughts on your underdog choice today?"

Sydney clears his throat and allows himself to look directly at James, remembering the feel of his warm, firm skin against the pads of his fingertips. The blue of his eyes juxtaposed with the white sheets of Sydney's bed.

"My prediction isn't wrong," Sydney says, hoping no one else can hear the shaking in his voice. "I'm more confident of this than any competition I've even surfed in."

"Wild claims, Moore. Keepin' it real, that's for s—"

"Far out! What makes you say that?"

Sydney takes a precious few seconds and closes his eyes. He sees the man he saw that day on the pier, so small and lost compared to the man standing now on the starting line, exuding a steady, fierce strength. He opens his eyes just as the back of his throat starts to close up, and he wants . . . God, he wants to reach out across the sand towards James Campbell with his fingers, hoping to grasp just a ghostly wisp of his same air.

"Jimmy Campbell will be the next Billabong champion," he answers, voice steady. "It's simple. O'Brien's going out there today to get his spot at World's, and we all saw Russell lay down his usual tricks, but Ja—Jimmy Campbell is . . . Campbell is treating this like a whole lot more than a game."

"Man, well there you have it folks. Danny Moore keeping it real, predicting underdog Jimmy Campbell for the win. I don't think I'm the only one shocked! We'll just have to see if he's—"

And the announcers go on blabbering about how Danny's gone and said another one of his ridiculous, cryptic one-liners, and the crowd has turned breathlessly to the starting line where the two surfers are lined up ready to race with their boards held under their arms, and Danny Moore is well and forgotten, lost in the hum of energy across the beach.

And in the last five seconds before the airhorn blares that will inevitably rip James away from him for good, James turns back and finds Sydney immediately with his eyes, and Sydney gasps at the realization that crashes through his body.

Sydney knows, more strongly than anything he's ever known in his life, that he is in love with James Campbell.

The horn sounds, blasting across the waves, and James doesn't even flinch this time as he sprints out into the ocean to a roaring cheer from the crowd. Sydney stands alone in the middle of the chaos, salty wind rushing at his back, and the spray on his face, and he feels a piece of his chest be dragged out to sea towards the largest swells on the face of the earth, kept safe and secure in the warm patch of skin over James Campbell's steady, pulsing heart.

*"Two wild first-wave scores from both of these surfers!"*

*"They're not playing around out there today, man. The championship is on the line, and they've both just shown that they more than deserve to be here with those first rides of the heat."*

*"Duke O'Brien's chasing after this next wave. Campbell's letting him have it."*

*"It's a beauty—he's letting himself be pushed up to the crest . . . and what a drop in! Look at the speed! O'Brien cuts down the face and he's pumping like crazy along the foot of this wave."*

*"He's searching for an open part of the face to fit in some turns . . . And look at this rad spray!"*

"He's smart not hanging back for that barrel—pipeline on this one is far too small. You'd get caved in on, for sure."

"And after two cutbacks, looks like he's ending his ride with a tap on the lip and one last shower of spray. He's gotta be pleased with that one as he dives back into the water."

"What a ride!"

"Tell it, man. Ace!"

"Look here folks, Campbell's getting ready to answer. I'm not sure if he can get in front of this wave in time. It's a monster . . ."

"Paddling like hell but it might be too late. He's pushing after it, straining to catch the crest. Oh! And this swell gets away from him. What a bummer!"

"He's disappointed. He could've caught that one if he started sooner, and he knows it."

"It's wicked hard to watch O'Brien take a wave like that and then answer to it—you think he's feeling the pressure?"

"With O'Brien looking like he's gonna catch this next one, three scores to Campbell's one is not gonna put Campbell in a great place to do well in this heat."

"And Russell's score?"

"Don't pin me down, man. Too early to tell!"

"One thing I do know . . . Danny Moore just might be wrong—for the first time in his life!"

Sydney clenches his fists where he stands off to the side, chest heaving as if he's the one out there battling against the force of the ocean.

James chickened out on that wave—there's no other explanation for what could have happened. That or his shoulder is already starting to give out on him.

He watches O'Brien cleanly finish his third major ride of the set, putting up a third score over 7.5 to a wild cheer from the crowd. O'Brien turns to give a wave back to the beach, huge grin on his face. James doesn't even turn his head to see if he landed the wave.

Sydney's going to be sick.

James paddles a little farther out from the main breaking point, dolphin diving under a few swells before letting himself be pushed up and over the next set. He looks small and fragile in the water—a little golden pearl pushed and rolled about by the towering waves. He looks like a ghost of the man who'd attacked the water with everything in him only just that morning. His limbs wilt off the sides of the board as he floats along in the swells, all the momentum from his first perfect ride already lost out to the sea.

Sydney stands there helplessly, watching as James chases and misses two more waves in a row, knowing that he is the only person on earth to blame for throwing James out there, making him struggle and fail in front of everyone like he is now.

He wants to grab his past self—the man who'd fallen off his board in LA, and told James he could win the Billabong, and sent him off with just a sandwich after stealing his precious recovery time to kiss him and selfishly hang out in the Jeep—and smack that past self upside the head. He wants to run out into the waves and cradle James' body in his arms and carry him back to shore, away from the punishing water, away from everyone's stares.

James starts to paddle after a third wave, smaller than the previous two, and Sydney's heart leaps up into his throat.

*"—but looks like Jimmy Campbell's going after this smaller wave, right after missing two in a row."*

*"Probably trying to win back some confidence. Easy points. He's gotta be exhausted from paddling so much in one stretch without a real break."*

*"I gotcha. Look here, Campbell's out well ahead of this wave, digging deep into the water . . . he's letting the wave catch the tail of his board—and he catches this one! Crowd's giving him some encouragement as he pumps along this swell."*

*"Look at the spray coming off his turns! He isn't wasting this ride!"*

"And a perfect nose grab before a tap off the top and a quick re-entry. He's milking every second he can get out of this wave, not letting the shoulder taper off without a fight."

"It won't be a huge score, but at least it'll be something!"

"Nineteen minutes left in this heat and you know he's gotta be feeling the pressure. He may not know the scores but he's seen O'Brien's waves."

"O'Brien's at a current three-wave score of 24.9, and with Campbell's latest coming in at 5.9, yikes. He's got a lot of catching up to do."

"He's still in the game, though, folks! Anything can happen here at the Banzai."

"See there! Campbell looking to catch another wave now, paddling hard after leaping back on his board from that last ride. Man didn't even catch his breath. And boy, this bomb's a big one—"

Sydney curses out loud. The woman next to him, who'd been carefully pretending not to notice his presence, shoots him an odd frown, and Sydney quickly looks down at his fingers and shakes his hand as if he just tore off a particularly deep hangnail.

His lips are pressed so tightly together he's sure they're turning white. James is paddling like hell after this next wave, one of the biggest ones of the set, but O'Brien is right on his tail, chasing him with strokes twice James' speed. Sydney actually does tear off a particularly deep hangnail and hisses through his teeth; he already knows exactly what's going to happen in the water.

The crowd holds their breath and starts to hesitantly cheer as James places his hands firmly on each side of his board to pop up, when suddenly O'Brien leaps to his feet and flies past him down the face of the wave, leaving James to awkwardly tuck and roll over the crest with his board flying up behind him in the spray.

"Shit," Sydney breathes. This time the woman beside him hums in sympathy.

The crowd groans for the appropriate beat, then switches to wild cheering for O'Brien as he whips down the towering pipeline, riding the first full barrel of the set. Sydney knows James is well aware of the time quickly ticking down. He's probably got a rough estimate of points in his head, same as Sydney and everyone else does when they're out past the reach of the voices back on the beach.

He knows James knows he only has one wave worth looking at so far—hardly enough to hold a candle to O'Brien and not even worth the embarrassing comparison to Russell, who sits off to the side near the other competitors with a towel half-covering his head and an anxious frown etched into his face.

James paddles back out past the breaking point as O'Brien finishes his ride, dropping in the backdoor of the barrel and riding the entire tube to a booming cheer from the crowd when he emerges through the spray.

He paddles until he's just a speck on the vast glass sea, dwarfed by the endless blue horizon and the infinite crystal sky. Sydney squints his eyes to see as James sits up on his board, nearly unheard of in the middle of a competition round, and he calmly gazes out towards the horizon, keeping his back to O'Brien, and the rest of the waves, and the crowd, and the entire Hawaiian shoreline.

He sits there for almost a full minute, utterly still and staring out to sea while O'Brien catches another smaller wave as a safety for his points, shooting through a small tube before cutting back across the whitewater. It's as if the crowd has forgotten James is even in this round as O'Brien flings himself back on his board to their applause and heaves himself back out to catch the next set—smooth and unstoppable.

Sydney watches, shamelessly shielding the sun with his hand after moving his aviators down his nose. He can just make out what's happening as James reaches down and cups a handful of water in his palms, bringing the water close to his bent-over chest.

Like that same rushing wave to the face that told Sydney why in hell he wiped out in Hermosa, Sydney realizes all at once what James is doing.

He's surfing in the Finals of the Billabong, and he has hundreds of people watching him do it, and he's a good four rides away from even coming close to catching O'Brien.

And James Campbell is stopping in the middle of it all to sit quietly in the waves and talk to Helen.

Sydney quickly shoves his shades back up his nose to cover his wet eyes. The last thing he needs—the last thing James needs—is for the Banzai crowd to notice that, for some ungodly reason, Jimmy Campbell's embarrassing grappling in the Billabong Finals is making Danny Moore *cry*.

Then, just as suddenly as he'd stopped, James springs into action again, flinging himself down on his board and paddling like hell towards the shoreline as a gigantic wave surges up behind him, blacking out the sky.

The crowd holds their breath as James chases it, buzzing with anticipation, and O'Brien looks on from the side with a grimacing scowl, and Sydney thinks he's going to jump right out of his skin and ignite.

James reaches the crest of the enormous, roaring wave, plants his hands firmly on both sides of his board, and pops up.

*"Just look at the monster Campbell's dropping in on now! Perfect nose grab as he gouges into the face, using that hand to slow him and keep him inside the barrel. Judges, are you seeing this?"*

*"Perfect pipeline, I could carve my own initials into that thing. Beautiful entry. Look at the spray on that tube!"*

*"Just waiting for him to emerge—"*

*"And he does! Jimmy Campbell zooms out of this pipeline standing tall, and looks like he's ending his ride with a powerful leap off the lip and into the whitewater."*

*"Whatever the hell Campbell was doing sitting on his ass out there, it worked—listen to this crowd!"*

*"I'm right there with them, man. That was a thing of beauty. Powerful wave, perfect fast drop in, ample time in the body of the tube. Judges gotta award that one at least an 8."*

*"And it's an 8.6! One of the highest waves we've seen today, and Jimmy Campbell just showed us all he is sure as hell still in this final. Two more waves like that and O'Brien could be in real trouble."*

*"Campbell's already paddling out for the next one, and O'Brien's on the chase—"*

Every muscle in James' body looks rippling and alive. Sydney can feel his energy all the way from where he stands tensely on the beach, carried to him on the force of the crisp salt spray.

Everything has changed. The atmosphere on the shore is electric, crackling with anticipation, the announcers are yelling and cursing at will, the other competitors watch with half-open mouths, and Terry Russell holds up his towel to hide half of his face from the view, afraid even to watch.

Sydney feels a smug grin threatening at the corner of his mouth. He wants to turn to the random surfers lounging near him, hold his chin high, and say, *"You know why Campbell's doing so well? It's because I gave him a good-luck blow this morning."*

The thought alone makes him have to force down a chuckle in his chest. He's lighter than air, fizzling along his skin, as if his body will simply float away on the wind rushing across the shore from over the tops of the thick green mountains at their backs.

He knows now that James himself knows he can win this. So yes, of course everything has changed.

But has *everything* changed?

*"O'Brien's certainly not going down without a fight, and that wave sure proved it."*

*"Huge air on that drop in—I don't think his board even touched the water until he was three-quarters of the way down the face!"*

*"And that's earning him another whopping score with an 8.1"*

*"It's pushed his three-wave score up to 25.3. Well within the possibility of trying to catch Russell's Billabong record of 27.1 set in the first Final round here this afternoon, but it would require some monster effort on his part."*

"Word, man. That mean you're saying Campbell's still too far back?"

"Never say never, especially after his last ride, but with only eleven minutes left in this heat Campbell would need two waves well over a 9, and I don't think he's even put up more than a handful of 9's so far in his entire career, especially not on the professional stage."

"You're right there, man. Judges definitely score harsher once you're up in the championship tour. Every up and coming pro surfer will tell you their first year pro is like a slap in the face."

"Not many surfers go pro by knocking Danny Moore on his ass, though, my friend!"

"True!"

"And look here, folks, we've got a hardcore battle out on the waves for this next drop in."

"Campbell definitely started paddling first, he has the right of way closer to the peak, but O'Brien's trying to snake in there like he does—and Campbell's not giving up! He won't let O'Brien have it!"

"O'Brien looks left, probably telling Campbell to get the hell off."

"Campbell keeps paddling! He's not backing down!"

"These two surfers are both at the crest. Someone's gonna have to give up or the wave will be a waste for both of them."

"And man, it's a bomb we've got coming in here."

"O'Brien moves to pop up—"

"Campbell drops in! Campbell pops up barely even using his hands and he's soaring down the face of this wave!"

"O'Brien can't believe it! He's had to wipe out to the side to keep from crashing down into Campbell's barrel."

"Campbell's bending deep. He's crouching as he pumps along this wave. Will it curve over into a pipeline?"

"It does! Campbell knew this wave was going to be a beauty, and boy is he thanking himself he didn't back down in that fight. This tube is a wonder—perfectly formed, crystal clear waters, rocketing spray . . ."

"Is that—? Ladies and gentleman, Jimmy Campbell's just exited the tube goofy foot!"

"How did he manage that inside that barrel? How?"

"We're all going wild as Campbell rips up the face of the shoulder. He's doing a floater across the whitewater along the breaking part of this wave—dude, what a way to end that ride."

"I can't even guess what score that'll get—how many techniques were in that ride? Four? Five?"

"Five hundred? Man, Moore wasn't kidding when he said Campbell would know to wait for the perfect wave. What a beauty!"

"9.3! 9.3!"

"Campbell can't hear us but he's pumping his fist as he makes his way out past the breaking point. He knows that was a winner."

"O'Brien's only got time for one more—maybe two if he hustles."

"Nah, man, these waves may be gnarly but there's no way he can paddle hard enough to fit in two."

"What's he need to pull one over on Russell?"

"At this point—looks like that would be a 9.4. Clearly not impossible, as we've just seen from Campbell."

"Two waves that much over 9 in a row, though?"

"Well, it is the finals!"

"And where does Campbell stand?"

"Campbell's surfing his ass off, but even with that 9.4, he'll need an insane 9.5 to push himself up past Russell."

"That's right, man. Campbell and O'Brien may be battling it out against each other out on these waves, but the real battle is between each of them and that massive 27.1 score put up by Russell. I bet it's taunting them."

"And Russell looks like he's about to pass out over in the competitors' area. He definitely didn't expect to be feeling this amount of pressure going into this heat. Think his seat is hot, or what?"

"Look here, O'Brien's going for his final wave of the round—"

Sydney wants to scream at everyone on the beach to just shut up already and let James think.

Which is ridiculous, because he knows from experience that James can't hear a single thing aside from his own breathing out there where he is on the water. But still, Sydney's hands are clenched into tight fists, and his eyebrows are furrowed behind his aviators, and he's never wanted to open up his lungs and yell so badly in his life. He wants everyone to close their eyes and turn away from the shore—to let James have his final moments out in the Banzai waves in peace.

Instead, in almost perfect unison, the entire beach rises to their feet as O'Brien gets ready to drop in on his final wave of the round, a collective gasp of anticipation hovering over the sand. Sydney rubs his palm over his mouth to hide his grimace in what he knows is a hail Mary attempt to look bored and aloof instead of scared half out of his wits.

O'Brien drops in on the massive wave, crouching low to his board right from the start, and Sydney sees exactly what will happen two seconds before it does:

He crouched too early, center of gravity pitched too far forward over the breaking crest of the wave, and the entire beach gasps as O'Brien tumbles forward off the lip of the fifteen-foot wave, board flying up behind him and limbs scrambling for purchase in the air before he crashes headfirst into the belly of the barrel.

The shore is pin-drop silent as they wait for O'Brien to surface, hoping that another wave doesn't break and force him into a double hold-down. Sydney tracks the flow of the current within the wave, watching the force of the water until his eyes pinpoint exactly where he'll come up for air. He starts to count, flashing back painfully to just that morning when he'd had to do the same horrible countdown for James.

Hundreds of people wait with shaking limbs for Duke O'Brien to let them all know he's still alive. Not even the announcers are breaking the silence, and only the ocean continues to roar. The lifeguards hover in the shallows, rescue boards held over their heads in preparation to leap into action if O'Brien doesn't show his face soon. The woman beside him shoots Sydney a pained, hopeful glance, as if he himself could somehow politely ask the waves to bring Duke to the surface.

After ten full seconds, he appears. The crowd lets out a chorus of sighs, groans, cheers, whistles, as O'Brien climbs unsteadily back onto his board, chest heaving as he gives a quick wave to the shore with stooping shoulders.

He knows his chance is over. All eyes turn to James.

Sydney closes his eyes for a beat, then pushes his sunglasses up to perch in his hair. He needs to see James Campbell fully. Needs to see the true color of his skin contrasted with the waves, and track the black speck of his wetsuit bobbing through the swells, and see the flash of golden light woven through his soaked hair.

He crosses his arms over his chest and squeezes as he watches James explode into action the second O'Brien starts paddling in to shore. James' arms paddle like mad through the swells and the spray, pulling him towards a thirty-foot wave rushing in from the horizon, and Sydney has to use every ounce of focus he has left just to force himself to breathe.

James turns to catch the wave, dwarfing him into a speck as it surges to hurl him up towards the heavens on its crest. The crowd holds their breath, every person on the beach deadly still, and Sydney lets out a soft moan as James prepares to drop in on the towering monster covering the sky.

He hears himself whisper a single word as James looks over his shoulder at the breaking crest one last time.

"*James.*"

"*Campbell's final wave now.*"

"*He needs a massive 9.5 to edge ahead of Russell for the title, let's see if he—*"

"*Getting ready for the drop-in. This wave has gotta be at least thirty-feet!*"

"*Wouldn't catch me dead on a wave like that, man . . .*"

"*No shit.*"

"*He drops in and crouches low—look at that speed! He's flying! Barely keeping on his board!*"

"*He's riding this barrel high up on the face, using his hand to gouge into the wave and let him stay in that tube just a little bit longer. I can't imagine the skill!*"

"*Shoulder's opening up, it's gonna spit him out early unless he— booyah!*"

"Oh my God! Oh my God! Jimmy Campbell just dropped down the face and he's caught the second break in this wave!"

"Riding low along the foot of this wave, and he's lower than we've seen him ride all competition."

"He's practically sitting on his board! Look at that dynamite force of spray!"

"And this barrel has him totally enclosed, can he even see?"

"Naw, man. No way—this tube's so tight I bet you he's the only surfer here short enough to have caught it."

"Killer on the knees! Just waiting for him to break free—"

"There he is! Jimmy Campbell emerges from the longest tube ride we've seen today—two tube rides in one wave!"

"That was unbelievable! Off the hook!"

"I can't believe what I just saw."

"Campbell here knows he just gave it everything he has. He's pumping his fist in the air as he rides straight out of this wave—I can hear his shout from here."

"And a perfect fall back into the whitewater to end this ride."

"If that wasn't the best ride we've seen all day I don't know what is. That was a once-in-a-season ride right there! Once in a lifetime!"

"This crowd is going wild. Even Davis is clapping on his feet! You gotta feel for poor Russell right now—he's sitting on pins and needles after that showstopper."

"This is madness—Jimmy Campbell comes from absolute nowhere to give a ride that . . . you know what? I'm just gonna say it. He gave a ride that was just as powerful as any you would see on this Pipeline coming from reigning champion Danny Moore."

"You're right, man. That ride had Moore all over it. The technicality, the expertise, the grace right up until the end."

"And Campbell is what—ten years older than him?"

"Twenty?"

"Nah, man, you're crazy! Campbell may be an old soul but he ain't forty if he's surfing a wave like that."

"Alright, alright. I dig it. But still, imagine the sheer strength!"

"That's right. Jimmy Campbell just showed us all he has a hidden talent to be reckoned with. No more tiny Los Angeles regionals for this dude."

"We're all holding our breath here as Jimmy paddles in—waiting on the score from the judges."

"Folks, I think you could hear a pin drop."

"Look at that—even Danny Moore looks nervous!"

"Campbell's walking up out of the shallows. He's tense. Judges are having their final consultation. I wouldn't want to have to assign that wave a score!"

"Any moment now, folks. Any moment now . . . God."

"Hang in there, Russell . . ."

"I might have to go over there and throttle the score outta one of 'em . . ."

"Campbell's waiting in the water like a statue, board floating in the foam—"

"9.8! Jesus Christ, a 9.8!"

"Campbell can't believe it! Would you look at his face, he can't believe it! I can't even believe it!"

"Listen to the roar from this crowd! We're cheering on the new champion of these Oahu shores."

"Ladies and Gentlemen, what a show. What a goddamn show."

"I'm shaking, man."

"Jimmy Campbell is your 1976 Billabong Pipeline Masters Champion, and boy does he deserve it!"

"What a performance!"

"Put this in your record books, folks. This is the first time in the six years of running the Billabong that a surfer in their first year pro—"

"—in their first month pro!"

"—clawed their way to the top to win the title. What a treat."

"We won't be underestimating Campbell anytime soon! What a guy to watch!"

"And look at O'Brien walking over to shake his hand. Excellent surfing we saw from him today, as well, and the crowd's letting him know it."

Sydney wonders why his cheeks feel wet, then realizes it's from the tears spilling over in his eyes. He runs his forearm quickly across his face, grateful everyone's too focused on James to be looking at him, then slams his aviators back down. He watches from a distance as every surfer on the beach sprints towards James where he stands, half-kneeling in the shallows, board still floating and bumping into his ankles with the tide.

Sydney catches a shocked, breathless smile flash across James' face before he's surrounded for the second time that day by a swarm of other surfers, cheering for him along with the rest of the crowd, reaching out to place their hands on his skin.

He *won*. He woke up that morning in Sydney's bed and he jumped on a board and he *won*.

Sydney's limbs are shaking. The minutes tick by, and the swell of energy exploding across the shore doesn't die down, and still Sydney holds his ground and waits, feet rooted in the sand. Even if James spends the entire rest of the day celebrating his victory with everyone else, Sydney needs this moment—just one moment to somehow catch James' gaze in the crowd and let him know that he's never seen anything more beautiful in his life than the sight of James Campbell soaring across that last wave.

He racks his brains trying to think of something Danny Moore would conceivably do for the man who just won the championship he's been known for for years. It frightens him that he can't automatically think of the answer—that Danny is so far away he has to stand there and think hard in order to conjure him up. That he has to be conjured up in the first place.

He's still standing there stiffly in the sand, not even able to bring his shaking hands together to clap, when a small gap forms in the swarming crowd before him. Sydney takes a step back, suddenly terrified that someone is about to point a finger at him and announce to the whole beach they saw him crying, when, like a burst of sunlight cutting through the fog, James Campbell breaks free from the surfers surrounding him.

He takes one look across the shore, swiping the wet hair back from his face, then immediately locks eyes with Sydney.

Sydney doesn't give a shit what Danny Moore would do. His breath catches in his throat as he starts walking forward on numb legs, closing the distance between them as James jogs out to his spot at the edge of the crowd. All eyes are on them, boring into James' back.

James slows to a stop when they're face to face, chest still expanding under the wetsuit with his deep breaths and tracks of saltwater clinging to his tan neck. He stops, and he looks at Sydney with so much emotion it would take Sydney one hundred years to catalog it all—to parse out each enigma of James Campbell's bared soul and memorize the look on his face, the sheen over his lips, the color of his eyes . . .

Sydney folds his sunglasses over his collar, and James swallows hard at the movement. Sydney feels James' eyes on the hollow of his throat. Then Sydney reaches out a shaking hand, pricklingly aware of every set of eyes across the shore, and James takes it with equally trembling fingers, palms squeezing hard, fingers locked firmly in a grasp.

Suddenly the entire beach around them vanishes. The only things on earth are the sunlight above them, and the sound of the waves still crashing into the shore, and the solid feeling of James Campbell's hand in his. James shakes his hand once, then simply holds on. Sydney feels another tear threatening to fall loose, and he lets it, knowing they're just far away enough from the crowd that no one else will see.

James sees, though, and he whispers Sydney's name into the wind, his thick voice breaking on the word. Sydney sniffs hard and reminds himself he can't hold on to James' hand forever. That he has to let go.

With one last firm shake, Sydney pulls his fingers out of James' grasp, mind flashing back to that first time they ever held hands at the dockyard. His skin still crackles with electricity, radiating out from his palm.

"Go on," Sydney says in a rough voice. His thumb briefly traces James' wrist. "I'll be here. I'll wait for you." He nods back towards the crowd behind James, meaning the winners' ceremony and the sure to be endless loop of congratulations.

James' eyes flash a painful sadness before he nods firmly and tears his eyes away from Sydney's gaze, taking a deep breath before fully turning and meeting head on with the crowd. Sydney immediately bites his tongue so he doesn't open his big mouth to beg him to come back.

He watches James walks away from him down the swarming stretch of shore. Stands frozen and alone in the sand as the lei of flowers is gently placed around James' neck, and photos are taken with him and Russell and O'Brien with their boards. He watches as James laughs and smiles and embraces every post-competition moment Sydney usually despises and avoids. Watches as James floats with happiness at all the things Sydney normally tries to escape from as soon as humanly possible without forfeiting the championship title.

He sees them through James' eyes now, and an unprecedented warmth settles over his skin as he waits, staring down occasionally at the palm of the hand James had grasped in his wet, salty grip.

And maybe James Campbell won't want to go back to Sydney's cheap little bed now that he's the year's biggest name in surfing along the Hawaiian shores. Maybe he'll tell Rob and everyone else back in Los Angeles that he had a little help from Moore, and the tips were worth it to put up with him for more than five seconds. Maybe that handshake meant, *"thanks for the help, kid. See you when I crush your ass at the next competition."*

Or maybe Sydney's being stupid again for the unprecedented seventh time that day.

But Sydney knows now that he'll wait for hours to find out. He'll wait for days, months, years. He'll wait forever.

# 18

Sydney finds a cold lemonade and relaxes under the shade of a tree for almost two hours, tracking James' movement back and forth across the sand, willing his mind to think of nothing but the way James had looked at him as he shook his hand in front of every single person on the beach.

He wishes he could use this time to get his own turn out on the waves. His body feels restless and agitated after being confined to the dry land for so long—cooped up for two days of watching everybody else surf along his favorite pipeline, aside from testing the current the day before. He finds he's already missing his morning surfs in Los Angeles with James after half a decade of managing just fine being out on the water alone.

The clock of their remaining time together ticks away like bombs in his head. He wants to run down there and yell at everyone to just go away—to let him have his last few hours of knowing that James Campbell's eyes will always seek him out on a crowded beach before he has to watch James fly back to his real life on a plane, leaving Sydney to go back to a silent house where his sheets smell like someone else's skin.

But James just looks so *happy*. He's giving an interview to the *Surfer's Journal* crew for next month's edition, and taking photos for the local Oahu paper—making everyone around him perfectly at ease and thrilled where Sydney had always just left behind stale air.

Just when he's starting to think he might run down there and physically snatch him away, James catches his gaze across the beach and gives a tiny nod towards the direction of the Jeep. He's ready.

With a flood of relief, followed quickly by an even larger flood of uncertain nerves, Sydney springs into action, making off towards the car, knowing James will follow a little ways behind. The sun is starting to set heavy and full above the ocean, casting orange and purple lights across the rustling mountains framing the shoreline. Sydney shivers when the cool evening air settles on his skin as he makes his way through the winding side streets towards the Jeep, now parked alone on a long dirt stretch once filled to the brim with other cars.

He throws their bags into the back and fixes his hair in the side mirror, as if that could somehow convince James Campbell not to ask him to take him straight back to the motel. Then he turns just in time to see James making his way towards him, dressed back in boardshorts and a hoodie with his board under his arm and a slow, aching weariness in his step. Sydney eyes the bulging bag thrown over James' shoulder where James has clearly shoved the lei and trophy inside, right on top of the sand-covered wetsuit, probably growing musty and damp.

The enthusiasm that had been emanating from James' body all afternoon is gone, and Sydney opens his mouth to ask what's wrong when James suddenly drops his board into the dirt, looks quickly side to side, and steps forward to throw himself into Sydney's arms with a sigh. Sydney quickly catches him as James leans like a dead weight into his body, letting Sydney cup the back of his head to hold him up.

James Campbell is a genius.

Sydney hadn't realized how badly he needed to feel James back in his arms until he has him there, deeply breathing with his cheek burrowed into the crook of Sydney's neck, arms wrapped tightly around the low of his back. The island seems to settle and sigh beneath their feet, quietly fading into the hushed tones of dusk, as the sunset colors gently pull the palm fronds down towards the earth to rest.

After a minute, James gives one last squeeze before pulling back slowly from Sydney's arms. He looks down at his feet. "Sorry, I just—"

"You won," Sydney whispers.

An odd look crosses over James' face before he finally meets Sydney's eyes. He shrugs, and a faint light washes over his skin with the fading sun. "Yeah, I did."

Sydney leans down and quickly places a dry kiss on his mouth before he can convince himself not to. James sighs through his nose, then brushes his cheek across Sydney's before pulling away.

All afternoon, Sydney had stared at James moving through the congratulatory crowd and fretted about what he could possibly say to James Campbell—the man who just conquered his fears, and stunned surfers from all over the world, and became a champion there for the entire earth beyond the horizon to see.

The man whom Sydney now realizes he loves more desperately than the feeling of his own wet board beneath the soles of his feet.

But he doesn't say anything at all as James turns to climb into the car. He rubs his palm over James' bicep through the soft fabric of the hoodie, giving a brief squeeze, then throws the surfboard into the back before climbing in and starting the engine. His heart constricts in his chest when James' hand immediately goes to his knee.

They're silent the whole drive back. James calmly stares out the window like he didn't just live one of the most insane days of his life, and Sydney pretends it's taking absolutely all of his concentration to drive on the roads he's known for years.

Finally, just when they reach the beginnings of the road leading down to Sydney's beach, James speaks.

"It's weird," he says under his breath, his chin in his hand. "I feel exactly the same."

Sydney wonders whether he missed an earlier part of the conversation, too lost stealing glances at the reflection of the island sunset off the tips of James' soft eyelashes.

"Hmm?"

James' other hand doesn't leave Sydney's thigh. "I just mean— I've wanted this, to win something like this, since that first day Rob told me about the surf scene after I came back from 'Nam. Going to work every day and surfing with him, every smaller competition back home, all the . . . all the fucking money I had to save, and the time—this is all I would think about."

Sydney stays quiet, impatiently gripping the wheel, as James gathers his thoughts. He pulls into his usual parking spot in the shade of the trees and cuts the engine, prickling a bit at the sudden silence in its wake. He watches James stare at the hints of purple ocean in the distance through the window, framed by golden palm fronds and liquid pools of glittering sand. A cool breeze winds through the Jeep, rustling James' hair, and Sydney wants more than anything to feel those locks of salt-dried hair against his cheek.

After another minute, James continues. Sydney wonders if he even realizes that they've parked.

"I thought I'd finally feel like I was doing what I'm supposed to now, I guess. Like I could move on and start actually *doing* something, you know? Live like everyone else in their thirties. Get a sponsor and solve all my money problems and surf as my job. Get a . . . get a magic house and a wife and kids to just appear in my life, nice car to drive. Better clothes."

James sighs and grips Sydney's thigh even harder with his palm as he continues to stare out through the sea of trees. Sydney wonders with a cold shiver whether James had felt him flinch at the word 'wife.' He wonders if he'd been imagining the way James had flinched, too.

James shakes his head, and his voice grows rough. "God, that all sounds like hell now," he says. "I mean I just . . . I just went out there and won the fucking Billabong and I don't feel a goddamn change at all. Just, exactly the way I was two days ago. A week ago."

Sydney grips the steering wheel tight with his hands. He wonders desperately where he himself stands in the continuum of 'what's changed about James Campbell and what hasn't'.

His inhale, when he remembers to breathe, sounds incredibly loud. "And is that a good thing?"

James shrugs. He rubs one palm over his mouth as the other slides down to Sydney's knee. "I don't know—I think so," he finally whispers.

Sydney doesn't know what to say. James is acting the complete opposite from what he'd expected. All day—since the moment James had caught that first major wave against O'Brien and proved that he wasn't backing down without a fight—Sydney had been waiting for a laughing, cheerful drive home (if James even decided to come back home with him in the first place). For breathless smiles and kissing in every corner of his house and letting James throw him down onto the mattress and take him.

But now, as he quietly follows James through the lane leading down to his house, dipping his head to duck under the lower tree branches and watching James grow visibly more at ease with each step they take closer to Sydney's beach . . . Now he realizes that they would never have had that breathless, laughing, celebratory evening in each other's arms, consuming each other and devouring strips of bare skin and calling each other the Billabong Pipeline Masters Champion.

Because James has a plane flight tomorrow. And James feels as if nothing has changed.

And suddenly Sydney realizes he still doesn't even know if James is staying with him tonight, or if he's expecting him to drive him back to his hotel by the airport once he grabs the rest of his things.

He follows James on shaking legs as James passes by the house and instead walks straight across the sand towards the water, gazing out at the sun spilling its evening warmth across the rippling glass sea.

"You'd think I'd be sick of it by now. Watching the waves," James says out to the water.

Sydney comes up behind him and hesitantly places his hands on James' shoulders. Immediately, James falls back into the touch, letting Sydney pull him close into his body and wrap his arms tightly around his chest, cheek resting in the salt-dried locks of hair.

"I never do," he replies. He's surprised his voice comes out as normal as it does with all the knots in his stomach.

James hums, and Sydney holds his tired muscles in his arms, willing his racing heartbeat against James' back not to give his emotions away.

He feels his lips moving before he even makes a conscious decision to speak.

"Stay with me, James. Stay for tonight. Please."

Sydney shuts his eyes tight as he feels James' breath shudder through his body. James makes a wet sound just at the back of his throat as his hand comes up to grip Sydney's forearm, and his head finally nods against Sydney's chest.

His voice is choked and rough. "Okay. Yes."

# 19

James wakes up all at once. The room beyond his cocoon of warm blankets is stormy and grey, fogged in by an overcast pre-dawn sky and the thick mist rolling off the humming surface of the ocean.

He squints through the half light at the ceiling and tries to piece together the night before, like flitting through photographs in an album from an old shelf. He remembers Sydney holding him on the beach for a long time—long enough that James had almost fallen asleep standing up—and he remembers leaning back into those warm arms while the sun dropped slowly over the waves.

He remembers Sydney silently taking his hand, and leading him up to the porch, and plopping him in a chair, putting a bowl of some sort of food in his hands. He remembers feeling wholly, achingly tired, every muscle in his body stiff and sore and begging to be allowed to just melt.

And that's when James remembers *why* his muscles had been so tired and stiff and sore. Because he won the fucking Billabong.

He won the 1976 Billabong Pipeline Masters yesterday.

He'd stood on the beach with the lei of flowers around his neck, and reporters in his face, and an entire shoreline of people applauding the way he'd surfed. They'd announced him as the champion, 'Jimmy Campbell' echoing across the sand. They'd taken his picture, shaken his hand.

And yet apparently the first thing that pops into his mind the moment he becomes conscious in a soft bed is standing on the cool shore with the warmth of Sydney Moore behind him, running his fingers up and down James' arms before asking him, begging him to stay.

James remembers those words a thousand times better than the words the judges said to him when they presented him with the championship lei.

And then James realizes with a sinking thud of dread that the last thing he even remembers from last night is him gradually drifting off to sleep on that chair out on the porch. And the last thing he'd seen had been Sydney leaning back in his chair with his bare feet propped up on the banisters, softly plucking at the ukulele in his hands. Sydney letting James drift off to sleep next to him as if they did this every evening—as if James hadn't just won one of the world's largest surfing competitions and claimed Sydney's reigning title just hours before. Like they didn't only have one last night together before James has to leave, and like Sydney hadn't begged him to spend that night with him in his home, in his bed.

James stretches out his legs and remembers he's naked under the sheets, skin dry and scratchy since he never took a shower the night before. He can see what must have happened in his mind like a film— how Sydney must have somehow gotten him from the porch into his room, and must have laid James down on the mattress and carefully taken off his sand-covered clothes, and pulled the sheets up over him so he could rest. How he must have lain there next to James wishing he was awake—wishing they were still out chatting on the porch, or holding each other close, or laughing on top of each other in bed calling each other the Billabong Champion in between breathless kisses. In between desperate, hungry kisses.

He finally turns his head to look at Sydney's sleeping form and instead sees two pale blue eyes staring back at him, clear and open and fixed on James' face.

"I didn't mind," Sydney whispers with a raspy voice.

An ache twists in James' chest; Sydney's eyes hurt to look at. "How did you know what I was thinking?" he whispers.

"You show your thoughts on your face." Sydney shrugs one shoulder. "Sometimes, at least."

James turns onto his side, his entire world shrinking down to the three inches of space between Sydney's eyes and his in the semi-darkness.

"And you can read my face that well, can you?"

Sydney hums. "You tell me."

James tries for a smile, but his eyes sag at the effort. He hears the seconds ticking by in the air like bombs dropping, each one pushing him further and further away from Sydney's air. Sydney is looking at him as if he could memorize every inch of James' face if he only stared hard enough, eyes roaming slowly from his forehead to his chin and back again, eyebrows furrowed in concentration behind a curtain of morning-soft curls.

James knows, with a terrible sense of foreboding through his core, that if he reaches out and touches Sydney now it will only feel like an electric shock, a heated pulse of aching need that would surge through his body from his fingertips, crippling his lungs. He keeps his arms tight against his own body, cramped in the tiny space between their warm, naked skin.

He licks his dry, chapped lips. "About last night . . . Look, I'm— I'm sorry that I fell asleep . . . that we couldn't—"

His throat closes up, and the words catch on his tongue. He's not even sure what he would even be apologizing for. For falling asleep last night before they could do anything together, or for keeping his plane ticket, or for stealing Sydney's title from him, or for even trying to talk to him in the first place that day out on the waves off Hermosa. Or for all of it at once and then some.

But Sydney's face crumples at James' cut-off words, shattering into tiny broken pieces. He barely gets out a hoarse whisper of James' name before James is reaching out towards him through the grey light and pulling him towards his body, tucking Sydney's head under his chin. Heated pulse of aching need be damned.

James grips him so fiercely he can feel Sydney's bones creak in his arms. Sydney lets out a choked noise and shivers against his chest, clinging to every inch of James' bare skin under the sheets, digging his nails hard enough into James' back and shoulders to leave a mark.

And James wishes Sydney's fingernails actually would pierce his skin and leave their mark. That they would draw blood and scar. His own version of the tattoo that rests warm and soft on Sydney's back beneath his palms, infinitely more beautiful than the mark blasted into James' own rough skin.

And Sydney is so small all of a sudden in his arms. His skin fragile and smooth. His muscles quiet and lean. And James wants to cover him forever with his own body, protecting him from the storm swirling outside their fogged-up windows, from every other set of eyes on earth, from the force of the waves . . .

"Goddammit," James chokes out. He buries his face face in Sydney's curls as Sydney gives a moan in muffled response.

The air grows damp and thick. James grounds himself in the warm, heavy weight of their limbs wrapped around each other, skin to skin. Feels Sydney's soft penis pressed into his thigh, bared and unashamed. The soft hair on his calves and thighs trailing along James' legs.

For one piercingly clear second, he wonders what the rest of the surfers—what Rob and his friends, what Russell and O'Brien—would think if they suddenly walked in on them now. Two grown men, two of their own kind, clinging to each other naked and trying not to cry in the dark. It's hard to believe that those other people even exist—that this embrace between them is something that's occurring in the same universe as everyone else's life. That it's something that could even be discovered or known.

Then Sydney looks up at James with wet cheeks, and touches the side of James' face so gently James barely feels his palm at all, and he leans up to place the softest ghost of a kiss on James' mouth. His lips tremble, and Sydney's thumb swipes once across his closed eyelid. They both hold their breath.

The other surfers in James' mind immediately disappear. He gives in to the kiss, the caress of Sydney's lips across his mouth, desperate in its timid, gentle touch. James quivers and responds to Sydney's body, pulling him close by the small of his back, knowing that if he gives in and does what he really wants—presses Sydney back into the mattress and tastes every inch of his skin—that no force on earth would ever be able to pry him off.

Sydney is still planting chaste kisses on his mouth, small and soft and wet, never-ending, when suddenly his alarm clock goes off, exploding in the velvet grey air and cutting through their sleepy fog. Sydney lets it ring and lifts his head to kiss James' cheek where it meets his nose, holding his lips against his skin for the span of three shallow breaths. Then he pulls back and turns over to shut off the alarm, the smell of coffee already drifting to them on the ocean breeze flooding through the house.

James' heart pounds. He's frozen—lips locked into the last position they'd been in when Sydney had pressed his tender mouth to his.

That kiss had felt an awful lot like a goodbye.

Sydney stretches his limbs before abruptly sitting up, swinging his legs over the side of the bed to stand. "Let's go then, soldier," he says, as if he hadn't just clung to James in the darkness and left a sheen of tears across the scar on his chest.

James wants to grip his arm and yank him back into bed. Fear runs through his body like thick ice as Sydney stands without looking back at him, spine straight and rigid. It's too soon for all of this, for everything. It's far too soon.

James turns his nose into the sheets and frantically gulps down one more deep breath, memorizing the combined scent of their skin, the hints of Sydney's shampoo, then he heaves himself from the mattress while Sydney already paces about the room, gathering James' things.

"Should take a shower. Don't want to smell like seaweed on the plane," Sydney says steadily, tossing James a towel he barely catches in time.

James shakes his head to try and fully wake up, pushing down the panic in his chest as he watches Sydney slowly transform into the man he'd been the morning James had met him to go out and see the island. Three days and three lifetimes ago.

"Right," he mutters. He catches the clothes Sydney tosses him, the ones that are actually his. The reason behind why he's had to borrow Sydney's clothes for days suddenly slaps him in the face, and he groans up at the ceiling. "Shit, I wonder if the hotel even kept my stuff. It's been three days . . . I didn't even think about it."

"No need. It's taken care of—they're holding your stuff for you."

James stops mid-crouch to pick up a sock. Both of them are still naked. "What?"

Sydney walks out into the living room, talking louder so that James can hear, voice crisp and businesslike in complete odds with the lazy ocean and palm trees right outside. "I made two calls that day when we were eating lunch. First one was to the WSL about your entry, and the second was to your hotel."

"What the—" James stumbles out into the main room of the house, awkwardly holding his bundle of clothes in front of his crotch as if anyone could see him through the wide-open windows.

Sydney stands tall and proud in the kitchen, pouring out a cup of steaming coffee with his back towards James. The silhouette of his bare, inked skin against the foaming grey sea through the window makes James want to gasp out loud at the piercing beauty.

Instead, he grips the bundle of clothes tighter and plants his feet on the hardwood. "How did you even know what hotel I was staying at?"

Sydney turns towards him as he takes a sip of coffee, frowning down at James' attempt to cover himself. "James, don't be ridiculous. You know there's nobody around here to see."

James does know. He had sex right right there out under the stars on that beach, and still he holds his clothes firmly in front of him with both hands. A fiery hot madness starts to churn deep down in his gut. The blinding need to grab something made of glass and break it.

"That's not—seriously, how did you know the hotel? And that I would stay here? We hadn't even done . . . you know. We hadn't even said I was staying here," he says.

Sydney fixes him with a look. "Well I wasn't wrong, was I? Why does that matter?"

"Why does that—of course it matters, Sydney!" James huffs as fights for his shoulders not to tense and hunch. "You can't just—how did you know?"

Sydney sighs like James is the most exasperating person he's ever met in his life. Maybe he is.

"James, it says the name of your hotel on your room key, which was in your shorts pocket that day with the tag hanging out most of the time. Even an idiot could have put two and two together."

James refuses to feel embarrassed, and in its place, indignation quickly bubbles up from his chest. He feels like an actor in a film, where everyone knows the script but him, and he simply woke up and found himself in the middle of a film set, harsh lights and painted backgrounds and all. He can practically hear the shower calling to him at his back, begging him to get in and get clean so he can pack up his stuff and just leave already.

He stares Sydney down. "Ok fine, I guess I'm an idiot. But that doesn't explain how—" James flutters his hand uselessly out towards the sand. "How you knew—"

"I *didn't* know. I saw that you were enjoying yourself, and you clearly didn't want to go back to your hotel, and I have a couch. You hadn't even thought of your hotel room that whole day. I figured I'd help you out."

"By calling and cancelling my own damn hotel room for me? Without even asking me?"

"I didn't cancel it, for God's sake. I paid them to hold onto it and keep your stuff together until today."

"Oh, so now you're paying for stuff for me, huh?" James hisses. "What, did you pay them to let me back in the competition too?"

Sydney rolls his eyes. "Aw, come on. Don't say shit like that you don't even believe. It's such a waste of time."

"Right, yeah," James says, and the words taste bitter as they leave his tongue. "Wouldn't want to waste anymore of your valuable time."

"That's not what I—"

Sydney cuts himself short, then wipes the surprise off his face and fixes James with one last icy glare. He shakes his head as he starts to turn back to the window, shutting James out as if his back is an unbreachable wall.

James stands there stranded in the middle of the floor, panicked and hot as he fights against the urge to sprint towards Sydney—to cling to his back so he won't be alone in the room.

Instead he practically growls, then grips his toes into the hardwood. "Oh no you don't. No you fucking don't."

Sydney whips back around, eyes blazing. "Don't what? Don't look out the window of my own house? Don't help you out? Don't breathe?"

"No, you dick, don't turn away and go all 'Danny Moore' on me when I'm trying to talk to you—"

"You're not trying to talk to me. You're trying to tie up all your loose ends before you have a flight to catch—"

"Don't turn your back to me and pour your fucking coffee like you didn't just lie there crying in my arms!"

Sydney freezes, coffee mug half raised to his mouth. He looks dangerous, and James swallows down a wave of bile in his throat.

"You say I'm 'going all Danny Moore' on you?" Sydney says, in a voice that would sound fragile and small if not for the terrifyingly sharp lines of his shoulders. "I didn't 'go all Danny Moore' on you, James. I *am* Danny Moore. You've been living with him for three whole days, or did you forget?"

"The hell you're Danny Moore!" James gulps down air as his legs shake, cold and exposed in the thin breeze. "Don't fucking lie to me like that."

Sydney glares at him, eyes glinting. He says nothing, then takes a slow sip from the mug in his hands, eyes boring into James and daring him to say something more.

James almost laughs. The silver light reflecting off the ocean covers Sydney's skin in gold like a glittering stone. The sight of him, statuesque and beautiful in the dim light of his kitchen, completely unashamed of his naked skin, fills James with sudden nausea—that, and wild anger.

"So what," he says, as if they weren't just yelling. "You're just gonna stand there drinking coffee and waiting for me to take my shower and leave like we haven't been fucking all weekend?"

Sydney scoffs. "Really? 'Fucking all weekend'—that's what you'd call this?"

"Well I'd like to know what else the *great* Danny Moore would call this, seeing as how you're such a fucking genius and all. You clearly moved heaven and earth just to get me to stay here in the first place, what with paying off my own damn hotel room and begging the league to let me surf."

Sydney slams down the mug on the counter and huffs. "I don't know, James! Maybe I wanted you to stay here so badly because I, the *great* Danny Moore, actually just hoped that I would maybe get to kiss you. You know, like a fucking normal person would hope for after meeting somebody like you. But clearly getting James Campbell to stick around is too much of a fucking challenge, even for a *genius* like me!"

"That's not fair. You know that's not fair." James doesn't realize until it's too late that he's already dropped the bundle of clothes to the ground. He stands naked at the opposite end of the house, wanting to crumple and scream.

"Well life isn't fair, as I'm sure you of all people would know," Sydney spits back.

James huffs out a bitter laugh, hands floating wildly up into the air. "I can't just stay here, Sydney! I have a job, my apartment, I have a whole fucking life back in Los Angeles. I can't just leave it all and move here to la-la paradise land with you!"

"That la-la paradise land is my actual life—and, in case you forgot, it really isn't such a paradise at all, even with the fucking palm trees."

"Oh, well keep going, now you're *really* convincing me to stay."

"Well what the hell else do I need to say to convince you then? What else do I need to do for you?"

"*Do* for me? I don't need you to do jack shit for me!" James yells.

"Apparently not, since your life was going totally according to plan before. And all of this definitely would have happened even without any of my help. You've made your point loud and clear."

"Made my—well if I'm such an annoying burden why do you want to keep me around?"

Sydney scoffs, eyes blown wide. "Why do I—you seriously have to ask that?"

"Yes, I seriously have to ask that," James glares, arms folded fiercely across his chest. He ignores the fact that Sydney's spine is slowly curving, making him look vulnerable and young, as if James' words were physically penetrating his bare skin.

Sydney swallows, and a small moan gurgles in his throat. "Why the hell wouldn't I want you around?" he gasps. "You . . . you make me—" Sydney looks lost, eyes desperately searching around the empty room. "You just won the championship!"

James blinks away the stinging water in his eyes, hating the fact that he knows he would hand the championship right back if it meant Sydney would finish saying what he originally started.

He sniffs, hiding it by clearing his throat. "Okay, so that's all this is? I'll just come to you each time I want to win something and you'll graciously bend over backwards to help me? As long as I give you something back in return?"

Sydney's body shakes. "How dare you? How fucking dare you?"

James wants to punch himself in the face. He holds his ground, feeling wild and desperate, unleashed—the same primal force that had yanked his finger over the trigger. "Well what the fuck else am I supposed to believe when you ask what you can do for me to somehow goad me into staying? And what . . . just—just fuck the rest of my life? Throw that all away?"

"You just told me thirty seconds ago that you don't need jack shit from me, so I doubt I've already forgotten that that's exactly what you *don't* want me to do."

"Oh, so *now* we're trying to do what *I* want, huh? First you wake up and all but shove me into the shower to leave and now you're begging me to stay?"

"I didn't want you to be late for your fucking flight!"

"Right, because you always know what's best for me. I'm going to lose, but you decide I should get a pity win. I get a hotel room, but you decide I don't need it. I come here to watch the Billabong, and you fucking decide I actually need to surf in it instead."

"But you fucking won!" Sydney groans and grabs his hair with both hands. "God, James, why the hell can't you just let yourself be happy?"

"I'll start letting myself be happy when you stop pushing me away!"

"Pushing you away? You're the one who's fucking leaving!"

Sydney's words echo through the house, falling like lead through the dense air.

James stares at him, wanting to drop to his knees. Hot, prickling water stings behind his eyes. He covers his face with his hands, feeling utterly fragile and exposed. "Fuck . . ." he sighs, and shame burns through him when his voice breaks. "Just what the hell are we even fighting about? How did this even happen?"

He pulls his hands away from his face and gasps when he sees Sydney. He looks devastated. Wrecked and small and trembling in the middle of the kitchen floor. Lost. The polar opposite of Danny Moore strutting across the sand in his aviators, head held high.

Sydney's lips shake as he whispers. "I don't—James, please . . . I don't know what to do if you leave. I can't just . . ."

James feels as if he's just been slapped in the face. "Fuck, Sydney," he breathes.

Sydney releases a loud, wet breath as James takes a hesitant step forward, forcefully scratching his fingers through his thick stubble. "Listen, I'd—I'd rather get shipped back to the fucking war than get on that plane. But I have to." He chokes on a rising sob and shrugs. "I just have to."

"I know," Sydney whispers, and then he starts to sink to the floor. For the first time since stepping out of the bedroom with his clothes held between his legs, James rushes naked across the vast space of the house towards Sydney. He grips Sydney's shoulders and presses his face into his own bare chest as Sydney's hands cling to his arms.

"It's my life, Sydney," James chokes out again. "There isn't a way to . . . this isn't my life. We aren't . . ."

James can't even finish the thought. Sydney nods while he gulps down shaking breaths, trembling and hot beneath James' hands. James grips Sydney's cheek in his palm and lifts his face towards him, and they share a brief, wild look before James pulls him into a fierce and desperate kiss. Sydney moans under the force of his lips, hands immediately going for James' chest as he straightens his shaking legs to stand.

With a heaving sigh, James walks him back him against the counter and licks into his mouth, swallowing Sydney's grunt. He pants harshly through his nose, pressing himself along the entire front of Sydney's warm skin while Sydney's huge hands grip and consume his shoulders and back.

James holds Sydney's face in both of his hands and whispers lost words into his sighing, wet mouth. "I'm sorry. God, I'm so sorry. I didn't mean any of that . . ."

Sydney shakes his head and turns his face to kiss along James' wet cheek. "*I'm* sorry. You know I don't . . . I shouldn't have s—"

James silences his words with another kiss, groaning as their tongues brush, and he clutches hard enough at Sydney's soft skin to bruise. His chest is torn in two—half hating himself that he couldn't let

Sydney finish what he was going to say, and half absolutely terrified to let him say a single thing more.

Sydney's hands on his skin are desperate—starved and crazed. James thinks of opening the creaking door to his own empty apartment later that day, the plain cold lines of his twin-size bed, and heaves out a stifled moan into Sydney's mouth, crushed by the weight of the reality that he's about to walk away down that tree-lined path.

His lips ache, swollen and sore as Sydney utterly consumes his mouth, limbs shaking as he grips trembling skin covered in rough shivers. Neither of their cocks are hard.

"This . . . this isn't it," James breathes into Sydney's mouth. "It can't—it won't be—"

Sydney grips him tighter and devours his lips on a desperate moan, like a drowning man finally finding air, sucking it straight from James' own lungs. He catches the bead of sweat starting to drip down the nape of James' neck.

James caresses the disheveled curls falling across Sydney's ear, caught between wanting to yank them and suck them gently into his mouth. Sydney's body hangs limply in his arms as if the man isn't made of pure, lean muscle. As if the second James steps away, he'll collapse and fall to the hard floor.

"Sydney, look at me," he whispers. For the first time, he notices that Sydney's palm has been warmly covering his scar, protecting the raised skin.

But when Sydney's pale eyes rimmed in red finally meet his, James realizes he has absolutely no idea what he could say. He struggles to get in enough breath, left speechless as he stares into the two little circles of clouded grey. "Look at me," he says again, an apology written in his face.

Sydney does look at him, looking somehow devastated and furious all at once, then he softly shakes his head no and reaches again for James' mouth, falling against his chest.

James kisses words onto his lips, mouth open and panting. "Sydney, you are—"

"James," he whispers.

"This isn't—"

"James." Sydney shuts his eyes tight, holding James' jaw. "It isn't just . . . fuck, I . . . I lo—"

"I know," James moans, the truth of it suddenly ripping through his chest. He nearly doubles over. "Fuck, Sydney, I . . . I know, it's—"

Sydney kisses him, somehow the saddest motion James has ever felt. "James."

And James doesn't even know what the hell he's promising when he whispers back, "I promise you."

# 20

"Beverage for you, sir?"

James presses his forehead against the cool glass of the window and looks down at the endless sea below. It feels like they're barely moving, just stuck forever, hovering in the same patch of blank sky. He keeps reaching for the bullet in his pocket with panicked fingers, never remembering in time that his pocket will be empty.

"Sir?"

The stewardess winks at him for the third time on this flight. James runs a quick hand over his jaw, wincing at the rough spot he must have missed when shaving in the plane bathroom with the cheap razor he'd gotten midway through sprinting across the terminal. He drums up his best courteous smile and shakes his head no, already turning back towards the window when she leans in and speaks again.

"Were you on vacation, then?"

James has the sudden, intense sensation of what it must be like to step on stage for a play, head popping out from behind the backstage curtains.

"Sort of, yeah."

The stewardess leans her elbow against the empty seat in front of him and relaxes the slope of her shoulders.

"I never get to go to the beaches," she sighs. "Never have enough time on layovers—just time to sleep and do it all over again. You see any good ones?"

James chuckles, hoping it doesn't sound too ironic. A very specific stretch of sunset-covered ocean drifts through his mind.

"A couple chill beaches. Palm trees, water, sand, the whole package."

She laughs, high and tinkling, and James notices a man across the row start to pay very close attention while pretending to read his newspaper.

"Oh, did you see any of that big surf competition they had? Was all anyone talked about for weeks leading up to it. Billabang something?"

James opens his mouth to just retort—say *"no, I've never even heard of surfing in my life, sorry to disappoint, just sat on my ass on a lounge chair all weekend with a beer in my hand, talking normal sports."*

Then he sees Sydney's face from the day before in his mind, eyes bright and a single tear on his cheek when he'd shaken James' hand in the sand.

James takes a deep breath and schools his features to look as casual as possible.

"Yeah, the Billabong Pipeline Masters—"

"Ah, that's it!"

"Right. I, uh, well, I won that, actually."

The stewardess laughs again, louder this time. James knows he shouldn't be surprised at all to see that she thinks he's joking.

He puts on a smile and tries again, hand awkwardly rubbing at the back of his neck. "No, seriously, I just surfed there this weekend— why I was on the island. I won the competition."

The stewardess leans in, giving James a full whiff of her crisp perfume. "Well you can show me the shiny trophy when I finally get my beach vacation time," she says low. She winks one last time, and sets a can of Pepsi on the seatback tray.

James stares numbly at it as she turns and makes her way down the aisle, acutely aware that every man's gaze but his is following her ass down the plane. He looks under the Pepsi can and confirms what he already knows—a folded slip of paper with a phone number in bubbling scrawl.

James sits back in his chair and closes his eyes, crumpling up the paper in his palm with a wash of guilt. He realizes he's never felt like more of a queer then he does in this moment, even when he'd had his own cock down Sydney Moore's throat. He's got the number of a beautiful woman in his hand, the invitation practically painted across the sky, and all his mind can see is Sydney's face when they'd finally pulled apart for breath that morning, naked and trembling in the grey light of his kitchen, brushing the sweat damp hair from each other's foreheads, cocks still awkwardly soft.

Sydney had kissed his forehead once after a second's hesitation, imprinting the feel of his mouth onto James' skin, and then they'd each stepped back with forced, harsh movements. James hadn't had time to shower, and they hadn't had the air for any more words. James had dressed and gathered up his things like a ghost roaming through the rooms, already feeling as if the house was abandoned and empty even with him and Sydney still standing right in the middle of it.

He hadn't allowed himself one final look out towards the sea when he jogged down the steps. If he'd looked, it would have been admitting he might never get the chance to see it again.

Then Sydney had driven him across the island to Honolulu, lips in a tight line, breathing uneven. He hadn't come close to hitting anything on the road, just drove straight and smooth and easily under the speed limit—perfectly in line. And James had gripped Sydney's thigh so tightly on the drive he was surprised Sydney even had feeling still left in his leg, trying to somehow force assurance through his skin and straight into his bloodstream, up the veins in his body into his heart and lungs.

Assurance of what, he's pretty sure neither of them fucking knew.

And he'd wished like hell that the island wasn't the most beautiful thing he'd ever seen. He'd pressed his fist tightly against his mouth as he looked out the window and watched the rolling green zoom past, dotted with pearls of flowers. He'd wished that it hadn't looked like Vietnam anymore—that it was just some meaningless mixture of pink and blue and green. The warm breeze had blown stiff and suffocating against his face through the open Jeep.

He'd stepped up out of the Jeep at the airport drop off after they'd quickly swung by the hotel, and only then had he realized in a jolt of panic that he hadn't hugged Sydney one last time back at the beach. Hadn't kissed him or held him or let himself be held. Hadn't known if Sydney would even accept that embrace.

And now they couldn't—not standing there at the airport terminal, one Jeep in a long line of taxis, surrounded on both sides by parting and reuniting embraces and tearful hugs.

Sydney had stepped out smoothly and handed him his bag, hands hanging limply at his sides after James carefully took it so their fingers didn't touch. Sydney had licked his lips, staring down unblinkingly at the blinding concrete, shattering the illusion of the man held carefully together he'd been through the whole drive.

Then he'd looked up, and shown James everything with his eyes.

"You surfed like hell, James Campbell," he'd said, just as the announcement to start boarding James' flight blasted through the crackling speakers. And James had only had the strength to barely whisper Sydney's name before he'd torn his gaze away from those pale eyes and practically run into the terminal, leaving Sydney alone and untouched on the sidewalk, looking like he'd just said goodbye.

The announcement to prepare for the descent sounds in the stale air of the plane, and James presses his forehead to the cold glass once more. The stewardess passes by one last time to pick up trash, and James feels like the scum of the earth for not even looking her direction. He doesn't know whether she tried another wink.

Instead he waits for her to pass, then opens the can of soda and takes a long gulp, telling himself that the brown liquid running down his throat is actually creamy and cold and pink. Topped with whipped cream.

He closes his eyes and shivers along his arms, remembering the gentle scratch of his mom's long, coral-painted fingernails across his scalp.

Remembering the press of Sydney's trembling wet lips on his cheek.

And he stares down at the ocean, at the hazy Los Angeles sprawl slowly sharpening into view. He imagines the salty slap of the waves against his skin, the velvet crush of the warm sand. Then he shuts his eyes tightly against the bright, sharp world, and he rolls the crumbled piece of paper in his hands until it resembles the shape of a bullet.

The LAX terminal looks exactly the same. James feels surprised as he navigates the hallways, dodging other harried travelers with their trails of luggage, until he remembers that of course it looks exactly the same—it's only been five days since he was last there, running like hell to catch his flight after being stuck in a taxi in traffic and praying to God that he wasn't about to do something extremely stupid showing up unannounced at Danny Moore's doorstep.

He'd had a different piece of paper in his pocket that time, in Lori's bubbling script.

With each step he takes towards the doors leading out to the sprawling maze of Los Angeles, James feels as if he's stepping father and farther away from home. Which is ridiculous, because up until five days ago the only place besides Los Angeles he'd ever even been to had been goddamn Vietnam, like the world's worst global traveler.

His palms itch to feel the warm saltwater underneath them, toes straining to sink into warm, soft sand. Nothing like the icy, seaweed-choked water and rocky grains that make up the SoCal shores.

Nobody's looking at him as he steadily makes his way towards the doors; nobody even smiles or registers he's there. He used to love that—the ability to walk through a public place and know with certainty that nobody could spot the scar beneath his shirt, or the way he flinched at loud noises, or the way his shoulder sometimes moved stiff in the joint. It made him feel alive, part of the thrilling, healthy vibrance of the city, leaving the haunted darkness behind at home where no one could see.

Now, though, he feels a small, foolish pang in his chest as he longs for the beach full of applause directed his way. For his name falling easily from everyone's lips, and for a piercing blue gaze constantly searching him out in a crowd, desperately wanting to find him, to know he was there.

"Jimmy!"

He keeps walking. There's millions of guys named Jimmy.

"Jimmy Campbell, you old fucker! Jimmy!"

James turns around, startled, as a familiar body accompanies the booming voice, bear hugging him without warning in the middle of the baggage claim.

James stumbles and drops his bag. "Rob? What the—?"

Rob pulls back and jokingly whacks him on the side of the head. "You turkey, you told us you weren't going there to surf, just going to watch—and then you fucking *won* it?!"

Rob goes to hug him again when he's pushed aside by Lori, who grabs the bewildered James and wraps her arms tightly around his neck, not saying anything.

James buries his face in her hair and inhales, an indescribable emotion flowing over within him. He can feel her heart beating just as fast as his against his chest. Finally, Lori releases him, quickly wiping the back of her hand once across her eyes, and Rob's arm immediately falls around her shoulders.

James knows his mouth is hanging open like a broken hinge. "How did . . . what—?"

"Never underestimate the power of a best friend with a police badge," Rob says with a smirk. "Had to whip it out three times just to figure out what goddamn flight you were on, and that was after I had to call and ask every fucking surfer on earth whether they heard correctly that *Jimmy Campbell* had just won the Billabong."

Rob tries to look stern, but the warmth shines through in his eyes, forcing a smile at the corners of his lips.

James has no idea what to say. He stands there stunned, bag still lying at his feet. "Shit, man, word travels fast," he finally grunts out.

"You're fucking right it does. Especially when a fucking rookie who just turned pro three weeks ago wins the fucking Billabong Masters from the Wild Card spot!"

Rob grabs his arm again and squeezes. Lori tucks her hair behind her ear, holding on tightly to Rob's back. "We're so proud of you, Jimmy," she says, eyes wet.

James clears his throat and bends to pick up his bag, stalling for time until he can speak. He runs his hand through his hair, knowing Rob and Lori know him well enough to see that he's touched.

"I don't know what to say," he finally gets out.

Rob pushes him forward towards the doors by the back of his shoulder, leading Lori along beside him as they walk. "I know what you should say. You should thank the only two people who'll put up with your miserable ass and still pick you up from LAX at rush hour even though you never called to tell them you won the fucking Billabong Mas—"

"It only happened yesterday!"

"—and then you say 'thanks Rob and Lori for inviting me over for dinner,' because that's what we're doing now."

"We got stuff to make that chicken dish you like, with the tomatoes," Lori chimes in.

"Plus," Rob says as they step out into the harsh sunlight, "you look like shit. Like some lost puppy in a cardboard box nobody wanted to adopt from the animal shelter."

And James laughs, truly laughs, for what feels like the first time since returning to Sydney's Jeep after he won—or maybe even since kneeling in the foaming shallows off the coast of Oahu, searching out Sydney Moore's smile in the crowd.

"Thank you," he says quietly when they reach Rob's truck, feeling completely inadequate, and like he should have to sit in some sort of child's seat for the drive back. Lori grabs his shoulder and uses it to hoist herself up, then scoots to the middle of the bench and pats the seat for James to follow.

"Of course, Jimmy" she says, and James wonders if he's imagining the way her voice sounds wet.

James sits back in the rickety metal chair in Rob and Lori's backyard, pleasantly full and sleepily watching Josie run circles in the dry grass. He breathes in the familiar air of Los Angeles, tense and thrumming and alive with the heat of the city—the claustrophobic energy bouncing between the highrises and freeways and hidden backroads, all swept over by the faint breeze of the freezing, kelp-choked Pacific.

Rob and Lori have been nursing beers and half-heartedly arguing for almost thirty minutes over whether it gets too hot for Rob to try and start a vegetable garden near their fence next spring. James watches them with sleepy, heavy-lidded eyes, simultaneously wishing he was alone in his own apartment while also realizing he's dreading the hour he'll have to leave the murmuring comfort of their little backyard.

Rob laughs, and leans in close to kiss Lori lightly on the cheek before sitting up straight to tie back his hair. James watches the familiar process out of the corner of his eye—the way Rob's fingers rake through the tumbling, tangled strands, and the way he arches his back.

Then James blinks hard, and he sits up so quickly that Lori asks him if he's alright, to which he awkwardly mumbles something about thinking he was stung by a bee. And all the while, James realizes that he hasn't, not for one moment, even thought about wanting to be with Rob since he surprise bearhugged him at the airport.

The revelation leaves him breathless—that, and a bit unmoored. He stares into the warm night air, mouth half-open, and marvels that he hasn't spent one second achingly captivated by the way Rob's hair curls around his ear, or the tan skin of his forearms, or the way his t-shirt hugs his muscled sides.

He hasn't felt nervous, or guarded, or giddy—sharply aware of where his own body ends and Rob's begins. He hasn't gone to say or do something and then pulled back with a terrified internal halt.

James leans back in the chair as Rob and Lori continue their garden debate, and he takes advantage of their distraction to look at Rob—really look at him. He sees the young man who walked up to him in the sand and asked him if he surfed, not knowing that when he reached out to shake James' hand it was the first time James had touched anybody since hugging his aunt and uncle goodbye his first day out of the hospital. He sees the man who met up with him nearly every morning for two full years without ever knowing where or who James had been in all the years before. Who'd brushed the soaked hair back from his wet face in the shallows, and sat by his hospital bed telling him too many details about the latest episodes of MASH. Who cried out in the hospital hallway in Lori's arms when they thought James was asleep, an hour before James asked Lori to track down the address in Oahu of one Danny Moore.

The experience is so wildly different from the way James looks at Sydney he can't believe he didn't have this revelation earlier in the day. A manic, bubbling laughter swells in his lungs. Gone is the heavy weight of careful dread, the fear of discovery and simultaneous intense desire to be known that he had always felt in Rob's presence, even when they were just laughing out on the waves. He can't decide whether he's lost a part of himself or gained something more.

He watches as Lori leans her head against Rob's shoulder, both of them content to leave James to his quiet thoughts, and all James feels looking at the two of them together is a deep, aching pulse of longing that Sydney Moore wouldn't be behind him to catch him right now if he were to close his eyes and lean back his head.

"Bed time for you, old man," Rob says.

James flicks open his eyes, not remembering when they'd closed. He shuffles to his tired feet, wincing at the instant fiery soreness in his thighs. "Think I could catch a taxi if I walk out to that main street—"

"And have you fall asleep in the backseat and get mugged like some loser?" Rob stands and puts a firm hand on James' shoulder. "Come on. Guest bedroom exists for a reason."

James starts to shake his head. "Aw, man, I couldn't—"

"You can and you will. Lori didn't spend seventeen hours trying to pick out a duvet cover just for nobody to end up sleeping under it."

"Oh, says the man who returned and bought a different toaster what—four times now?" Lori cuts back.

James follows behind them back into the house, feeling a bit like a child being put to bed by his parents as Rob smacks Lori's ass in front of him when she bends down in the linen closet to pull out a towel.

"Here, Jimmy. The blankets should be fine. It's hot as hell anyways."

For the third time in as many days, James is handed a towel and pointed to a shower that isn't his own. James is instantly grateful when they leave him to his own devices for the rest of the evening, not sure he could stand it if they'd wished him goodnight or tried to show him around the spare room.

He putters around in there for what feels like an unbearably long time, flipping through an old magazine until he finally hears Rob and Lori make their way off to bed. Then he creeps down the darkened hallway into the bathroom, ashamed that even the thought of taking a shower when other people are awake nearby makes his stomach churn.

He stands under the spray with his eyes tightly closed, frozen still as he showers off the remnants of the Oahu sand and salt from his skin— the last remaining wisps of Sydney's warm scent from the crevices of his body. Then he stares at the ceiling beneath Lori's pristine soft sheets for hours, pretending that the cars zooming past outside along the freeway are really the roll and hum of crystal blue waves.

"Come on, sleeping beauty. Up."

James groans out of a dead sleep and blinks blearily into the darkness.

"What the . . . ?"

"Hustle, man. My shift's at nine so we don't have much time."

James' eyes finally focus on Rob's ghostly outline in the dim light, and he sees he's already dressed in boardshorts and his pullover, hair piled on top of his head in a haphazard ball.

James groans again and turns his face into the pillow, for some reason intensely grateful that he'd decided to sleep in both boxers and a t-shirt. "You're dreaming," he mutters against the sheets. "No way. I'm tired."

"All you did yesterday was sit on your ass on a plane," Rob laughs. "Then sit on your ass in my backyard. I was there."

"Yeah, but the day before that I surfed my ass off winning the goddamn Billabong, you asshole," James moans.

Rob throws a pair of boardshorts at his head, not lightly. "Oh what, so now you're retired? Don't think I know you still have another day off before you start work again. Now get your ass up and surf with me before I disown you, miserable old fucker."

Rob quietly leaves and creeps down the hallway, trying not to wake Lori as James heaves himself from the bed and pulls on clothes in a daze. Rob's throwing his extra surfboard into the bed of his truck by the time James joins him out on the driveway, blinking into the thick, grey air.

"I feel like you're my dad taking me on a surprise trip to Disneyland that mom doesn't know about," James quips as he climbs into the passenger seat.

"That's true," Rob says, starting the ignition like a bomb on the sleepy, silent street. "Except mine and Lori's kid would be a million times cuter than you in the morning. You look like a wet paper bag."

James huffs a laugh out the window. "Real funny."

They drive to the beach in silence, passing through the sleeping city covered in a veil of slowly lifting darkness, fading from black into glittering silver. For one startling moment, James almost reaches out his hand and puts it on Rob's leg as he looks out the window, watching the lazy palm trees crawl by in the thin fog.

He lifts his hand to do it, fingers itching to land on warm, soft skin. Then he remembers it wouldn't be the leg he's hoping to find. He covers up the movement with a too-loud cough.

Rob doesn't say anything as they park along their favorite stretch of Hermosa shore and pull out their boards. They strip down to their bathing suits in silence in the sand, James pulling off his sweatshirt and shivering with his bare chest in the cold. It's the same as it's always been—the usual routine. Except this time James' eyes don't linger on the muscles of Rob's stomach as he re-ties his hair up into a bun, hair tie hanging out the side of his mouth.

James bites his lip as he finds himself missing the way the sight would fill him with a secret warmth while they stood shivering on the dawn shore. Finds himself wishing he was watching long, thin fingers comb through dark curls.

They jog side by side out into the crisp, icy waves, groaning and shuddering at the shock of icy cold. The cool grey air settles across the surface of the restless ocean, tinged with pink as the sun slowly rises above the glittering city at their backs. They paddle out just past the main breaking point, dolphin diving under waves to get used to the freezing slaps of water.

James follows, frowning, as Rob paddles out even further beyond the point where they'd normally stop to perch and wait for good swells, venturing out into the flat, glassy deep. James pulls up a few feet away from him and rolls his neck to stretch out his stiff shoulder, already feeling a sore ache in his joint.

"That feel alright?" Rob asks, breaking their silence for the first time since getting in the truck.

James nods, wondering whether he can remember Rob ever asking him about his shoulder before. "Just getting it warmed up, yeah."

Rob hums, and James looks over when he feels eyes on him, surprised to see Rob openly staring at the scar for the first time he's ever noticed. Rob meets his gaze, something odd passing across his face, then he looks away.

They wait, staring out at the flat horizon while the waves crest and break unridden behind them. They wait for long enough that James is just about to open his mouth and ask if Rob forgot how to surf without him the last three days, or if Rob's too nervous now to surf in front of a Billabong champion, when Rob takes a deep breath and releases it with a small hum.

"So, out with it, then," Rob says, speaking out to the horizon.

James frowns. "I haven't said anything."

"Exactly—you just won a pro competition, something you've been wanting to do for years, working your ass off . . . and it was the fucking *Billabong*, and you haven't said a single word about it. I don't even know your scores, who you beat, how it went, how you got back in. Nothing."

James opens his mouth to try and respond, completely caught off guard, when Rob goes on as if he's forgotten James is even there.

"And you know what? When they said . . . when word was spreading two days ago at the beach about who won, that it was fucking Jimmy Campbell, you know all I heard at first was just your name. Everybody talking about your name, over and over. And I thought that you . . . that you'd gone and drowned. That everyone was talking about you because you went off to Hawaii without me and did something fucking stupid and died."

"Aw, Rob," James hears himself say. He wants to curl in on himself at the sharp ache in his chest. Rob actually is hunched over, staring down at his hands, and James fights down a wave of shame that he would have once been distracted by the way it made Rob's abs appear chiseled into his sun-browned skin.

"Rob," he whispers again, at a loss for words.

Rob shrugs, sending James a brief, too-casual glance. A sudden cascade of shivers raises the hairs across his chest. "I just . . ." he tries, then swallows hard. "God, man, it—it fucking scared the shit out of me what happened before you left. I can't stop seeing it. Thinking about it. Think Lori thinks I'm going mad."

"You're not going mad," James immediately says. Thousands of possibilities of what he could say jumble in chaos on his groggy tongue. "I . . . you know it—the accident, for me, too, it was—it all happened so fast I wasn't sure I was gonna make—"

Rob nods and waves him off, giving an embarrassed half-smile. "I know, I know. You're still fucking half-asleep and I'm here going off, being a drag. Just needed to say that, get it out."

"I never thanked you," James says, nearly whispering, and Rob laughs.

"You mean, thank fuck I was there to fill out all the paperwork for your ass at the hospital?" He sighs, then straightens his spine. "Well, forget all that. Now *you* can say why the fuck you haven't even said the word 'Banzai' since you've been back."

James prickles, looking quickly over his shoulder back at the city—the jumbled, churning chaos of metal and glass rising up from the earth, totally opposite from the vast, empty sea and sky at their front. He turns back to look at Rob, feeling inexplicably far away and small.

"You know me," he responds lamely. "Just—I haven't processed it all, I guess."

Rob chuckles through his nose, a small, sad smile on his lips. "I do know you, Jimmy. So that's why I want you to tell me why you just had what should be the best two weeks of your life, minus the almost drowning part, and you look even sadder than you did that first day I met you."

James flinches and rubs the back of his neck. He speaks down softly at his board as embarrassment heats his face. "That obvious, huh?"

Rob shrugs apologetically. "Obvious enough to us, at least."

James sighs. "Man, I don't want to drag Lori into anything . . ."

"Too late—she's already dragged in. We both fucking care about you."

James swallows down a sudden tightness in his throat. "I know."

"We just want to help you ou—"

"I'm not a child," James hisses. He immediately runs a hand over his face and groans. "Sorry, I'm sorry. I didn't mean that."

Rob silently nods his head in understanding. He sits and waits for James to speak, and James fights against the urge to just swim out towards the distant, flat horizon, leaving every word of this conversation far, far behind him.

He doesn't even know what he could possibly say—how he could open his mouth and tell Rob Depaul that he has quietly, unknowingly kept James from walking out into the ocean for two whole years, and that James threw the bullet Rob never knew about far away into the Oahu sea, and that now James wants to keep surfing with Rob for an entirely different reason than simply grappling with both hands to stay alive—simply forcing himself to look away when Rob fixes his hair.

He doesn't know how he could possibly tell Rob Depaul that he missed him fiercely in the moment he knelt in the Banzai sand before the exploding crowd, and that he now sits next to him alone out on the water and feels the ghosts of Sydney Moore's smooth hands across his skin, in his hair, between his legs. And it's as if the entire Pacific Ocean suddenly sits between between him and Rob now, vast and lonely and uncrossable—a bottomless deep.

He's been silent for far too long. "You know I'm not good at this stuff," he finally whispers, scratching at his poorly-shaved jaw.

Rob hums. "Yeah, I know you're shit at it. But so am I." He turns to look at James, bobbing on his board with the rippling surface. He opens and closes his mouth a few times, then fills his chest with a deep breath. "I missed you, Jimmy," he says.

James' face grows hot. He looks back down at his board. "Aw, it was only a few days, man," he says, trying to keep his voice light, half-hoping Rob is leading up to one of his jokes.

"No, I mean . . . the past two weeks," Rob says. "Since the ISF. I've missed you."

The gentle slap of the water across the bottoms of their boards is deafening. James swallows over his dry mouth and wishes desperately he had some water nearby to gulp down.

He missed Rob, too. Missed him in a way he never knew he could, even when he was being held close in Sydney's arms. And James knows he could repeat Rob's words right back to him, and laugh it off and say, "*Sorry, man, about all that—you know I am. But I'm here now, right? We can start surfing together every morning again like old times.*

*Just because I'm a champion doesn't mean I won't still surf with the sorry likes of you."*

But just the thought of those words feels like acid in his mouth. He lets himself say the first part with shaking lips—the part that would have seemed absurdly impossible to admit out loud just two weeks ago.

"I missed you too, man." And then, to fill the silence. "I'm sorry."

Rob shakes his head. "Nothing in hell to be sorry for." He takes a deep breath, and James feels the moment suddenly shifting like the ocean itself rising to swallow them whole, forcing up from the deep until the whole earth tilts.

"You looked happy," Rob says quietly. "With him."

Everything changes. The air around them crackles and fizzles with sharp heat. James stares down at his board and thinks he's going to vomit. His limbs shake, and his gut clenches, and he closes his eyes as his vision starts to fade to grey around the edges.

*"Facing off against that fucking fairy . . ."*

*"You don't want him checking out your ass as you paddle out, sick fucker . . ."*

*"He's lucky we all still even let him surf . . ."*

James takes a shaking breath and finally forces himself to meet Rob's gaze, wincing as his blue eyes stare straight into brown.

Then James freezes; Rob's face is soft and patient. James realizes he isn't angry or jealous that James found a different surf buddy from him, or even accusing that out of all the people it had to be Chief Circuit Asshole Danny Moore.

He isn't implying . . . is he?

No—Rob's just stating a fact, *you looked happy with him*, and waiting to see if James will pick up the lifeline and answer.

James picks it up with sweating palms.

"He—he's been a good friend to me," James whispers.

Sydney holding him in the shallows, palm pressed up against his scar. *"You were brave."*

"Probably find that hard to believe," he adds.

Rob shakes his head. "Nah, man, if you say he's different, I'll believe it."

James has the overwhelming sensation that the entire ocean is listening, frozen and waiting on the tense cusp of his words. He grips the

322

sides of his board hard in his palms, reminding himself where he is, then closes his eyes and thinks of a beach far, far away.

"After I was shot," he says in a steady, flat voice, "back in Vietnam . . . I wished I hadn't woken up. In the hospital. I was . . . I was alone."

Rob freezes beside him. They've never talked about this. Never. Not even the day James took off his sweatshirt and bared his skin before Rob. Never even said the word "Vietnam" to each other out loud.

James licks his lips, speaking to the unbroken horizon. "These other soldiers there recovering told me to check out this beach a little way's south. Said there was a platoon stationed near there that had fixed it up, added a little lifeguard tower and made some surfboards out of the extra supplies . . ." James clears his throat, achingly aware that Rob is barely breathing over the sound of his words. "So I went, you know. Borrowed one of those boards, caught one wave. Nurses were pissed as hell later that I got the stitches wet," he laughs under his breath. "But I . . . when I came back . . . that was the one day I had where I knew that if I surfed, I wouldn't—wouldn't just wake up one day and swim out as far as I could and not come back."

He looks over at Rob and sees that his eyes are wet. Rob nods solemnly, fingers gripping tightly at his board. And something about the look on his face, the lines around his mouth . . .

Quite suddenly, James understands a critical piece he'd been missing before.

"I'm realizing as I say this out loud . . . you probably knew all of this, didn't you? Or, most of it. That's why you made me meet you every morning before work?"

Rob smiles, his eyes drooping and dark. "More or less, man, yeah. I mean, I didn't know . . . you know. But—was wondering how long it would take you to figure it out."

They look at each other, and James blinks hard as the air around them softens, lifting some of the fog. He thinks of the bullet lying somewhere at the bottom of the lost sea, and he knows that it's now or never, the raw truth of it yanking hard within his chest.

"Rob," he says, holding his gaze. Rob tenses. "There's something . . . I'm not . . . everything with Sy—with Danny . . ."

James suddenly can't look at him, tearing his eyes back out at the water. His voice when it comes is just trembling air, and James has no idea what it sounds like, or when he says it, or whether his mouth even works.

He shuts his eyes. "Rob. I'm gay."

James thinks he's going to slip off his board and sink down into the murky, cold deep, lost forever until the currents slam his rotting bones into a rusting bullet. The seconds tick by like hours, hammering across the sea.

Then, out of the thrumming, manic fog in his mind, he hears Rob saying his name. Realizes he's been saying it for a while.

"Jimmy. Jim, come on, look at me."

James does, trying to suck air into his lungs which have shriveled, his body crumpled and small.

Rob holds his gaze and keeps every line in his body completely still. "I know," he says softly.

James can't believe what he's hearing. "What—you guessed?" he whispers.

Rob shakes his head. "No, I *know*."

Realization crashes down on James like a slap of icy water. He shudders and runs a hot hand over his face. "Shit, I didn't think you remembered that."

Rob laughs once under his breath. "Hard to forget."

And Rob's voice is gentle, but James cringes all the same, face prickling with beads of cold sweat on his brow.

"*Hard to forget.*"

Hard to forget how James had stopped in his tracks when he was halfway down the street after leaving Rob and Lori's housewarming party early, hearing wild footsteps chasing after him. How he'd turned and seen Rob sprinting crookedly towards him, face loose and happy from drinking, begging James with half-slurred words not to leave, not yet. Not to leave *him* yet.

And James had been so overcome with adoration for Rob Depaul in that moment—chasing after him and begging him to stay in the middle of the warm, lamplit street—that James had taken two steps forward and grabbed the side of Rob's face and kissed him square on the mouth.

And for two breathtaking, beautiful seconds, Rob had kissed him back.

Then Rob had put his hands on James' shoulders and gently pushed him away, whispering, "*Wait, man, wait,*" and James had realized what the fuck he'd just done and jumped back from Rob's touch like it was a scorching flame, too horrified to even apologize, wanting to fall into the pavement and be swallowed up by the road.

Rob had tried to step forward and take his arm murmuring, "*It's okay, it's okay, it's okay,*" like he was trying to wrangle a terrified animal, and James had finally gasped out, "*Fuck, sorry,*" before taking off running down the street, madly wondering why he felt sixteen and one-hundred years old all at once. He'd run the four miles back to his apartment, not even bothering to stop for a cab. The sound of Rob calling out his name echoing down the street had rung in his ears the whole way back.

And the next morning he'd sat on his bed and stared at the wall after not sleeping a wink, wondering what his life would be like without ever seeing Rob Depaul again, wondering whether it was worth it, whether he should just . . .

When at six o'clock on the dot, he'd jumped out of his skin when he heard Rob banging on his door saying, "*Come on, lazy asshole, I've been waiting for you down on the beach for twenty minutes!*"

And James had opened the door with a shaking hand, and seen Rob looking at him like it was just any other morning, and thought that maybe, just *maybe*, Rob had been just drunk enough not to remember any of it at all.

Turns out he couldn't have been more wrong.

"Fuck, I'm so sorry," James says into his hand. "God, you know I never meant—"

"It's okay, Jimmy. I meant it when I told you. It's okay."

"But Lori—"

"It's *okay.*"

James' chest clenches painfully, erratically squeezing on his lungs. "So you knew this whole time, then?"

Rob nods, eyes serious. "I knew."

James feels an incredulous laugh bubbling up inside of him, mixed with the dramatic crash of the last two years of his life slotting into place. "And you still—how did you—you still stayed? You never said anything? You still . . . you still wanted to surf, and—"

Rob grimaces, shaking his head. "Don't turn me into a saint, Jimmy. I never fucking said anything to stop Kip and Dean and the rest of them when they got going about Danny, did I? You were right there, you could hear fucking everything, and I just . . . I let them—"

"I'd never expect you to do that."

"That's exactly why I should have."

James doesn't know what to say. He sighs through his nose and massages his shoulder with his hand.

The earth has permanently tilted on to its side beneath him, forever altering the way he walks on the ground, swims through the waves. The silence stretches on, frazzled and tense—pulsing.

Rob finally breaks it in a hesitant voice. "So, Danny. He really is gay then."

"Yes."

"And you and him . . ."

James clears his throat in the silence, then swallows down a rush of throbbing panic. "Yes."

"For how long?"

James huffs out a laugh. "Two weeks—not even that, two fucking days. I stayed with him in Oahu. That wasn't the plan, but it just sort of . . . happened." James looks at Rob, somehow feeling that this is critical to make clear. "We hadn't . . . we *hadn't*, before then."

Rob nods, slowly. James can't believe he's saying any of this out loud. The words falling from his mouth explode like bullets piercing the peaceful morning air, tainting the sleepy calm hovering over the ocean.

And yet Rob sits next to him, relaxed and easy, limbs loose and soft despite the fact he's barely moved in the last twenty minutes. James realizes he's never wanted to hug him more than in this moment—all those long nights, and the days with the beautiful sunshine on his tan skin, and that night in the streetlamps—never more than now.

Rob clears his throat and runs a hand over the back of his neck. "Well, in the spirit of admitting things . . . fuck, man, I feel like this is the shittiest thing to say to you. I don't . . . maybe I shouldn't . . ."

James gently splashes some water with his hands by his thighs, chest still aching. "Go on, can't be worse than any of the shit I just said."

Rob grimaces. "That's just it, I . . . well, listen." Rob quickly glances at him, and James bites the inside of his cheek when he sees Rob's eyes are wet. Rob grunts once under his breath as he looks away.

"Thing is," he goes on, "if we had met some other way—you and me. If it was earlier, some other time, if I hadn't already been with Lori . . . you know I love her, man. I love Lori. But if it was some other— I think that . . . I would've wanted to try, Jimmy. With you. I think—I *know*—I would have wanted you."

James' mouth is dry. "Like that?"

Rob's chest shakes. "Yeah, man. Like that."

"I didn't know you—that you had . . ."

"I fucking kissed you back, didn't I?"

"Well, that doesn't mean—"

"And, before that, too. I . . . around you. I knew."

James is shocked at the terror he can hear in Rob's defeated voice—the fear that what he's just said makes him the biggest asshole on earth.

"Does Lori know?" James whispers, because he needs to know the answer to that before he can feel any sort of emotion about it at all.

Rob rubs a hand over his face and sighs. "Yes. Fucking miraculously, she does. Thought I'd shit myself telling her and she just . . . she just—"

"She's Lori," James says in a gentle voice, hoping Rob will somehow understand.

A beautiful light washes over Rob's face, softening the lines in his brow. He shrugs as he smiles at the distant horizon. "Yeah, she's Lori."

And James realizes he's never heard anything more wonderful in his life. Because he's sitting out there, bobbing gently on the ocean, and he just heard the man he dreamt about for two long years say that he might have felt that way about him too, that he *did*. That he would have done *that*.

And all James feels in this moment is a bone deep affection for his friend—a clean wave of relief that he wasn't losing his mind on those mornings when their shins would brush together in the water, when they would sit side by side in the baking sand, and Rob would lean close enough that his hair fell down over James' shoulder. That he hadn't come back from the war completely lost and mad, unable to tell the difference between friendship and romance, car horns and bombs, swimming away from the shore and a silent death.

He wants to get back on a plane and jump into Sydney Moore's arms and let him finish everything he ever tried to say.

Maybe.

Rob's still waiting for him to respond, staring despondently down at the water.

"That's not a shitty thing to say. Not at all," James says.

Rob huffs and flings up a hand. "How are you not fucking pissed at me right now? I mean, I *knew* . . . I knew that you—even before that night, and I strung you along for two years, just—"

"You didn't string me along, man. You saved me. That day I met you? It wasn't . . ." James sucks in a wet breath. "You know, it wasn't okay. I wasn't okay. And you're my best—my only—you're my brother."

Rob sighs, sagging his spine. "James," he says, for the very first time. "I'm just so sorry I couldn't . . . well, I couldn't be that for you. When you needed it. When you wanted it. I'm fucking sorry."

James nods, letting Rob see the sheen over his own eyes. "I know. You don't need to be sorry."

The silence stretches on again, softened by the blanket of the waves. James briefly tries to imagine now what it would actually be like to kiss Rob Depaul—to sigh into his mouth, and comb through his hair—and can't. Every time he closes his eyes he sees Sydney Moore's lips. Sydney's face, and Sydney's freckles, and Sydney's curls.

"Listen, I'm glad you already had Lori," James goes on. "I wouldn't . . . I'd never wish this on you. Being like this."

"Fuck, Jimmy, I don't wish it on you either."

James looks over at him, shivering at the wave of warmth rushing over his skin.

"I know, man. I—I hear you." He shrugs, shaking out his shoulders. "Just . . is what it is."

Rob sighs, eyes still sad like he's just told James that the world is ending. James thinks that maybe it is, maybe these are his last few seconds on earth. He can't decide whether he's upset about it or relieved. A sudden weariness he's never known settles thickly in his bones, snuffing out the brief burst of warmth from before. He left

Sydney Moore's lips back in the middle of the Pacific Ocean—his face and his freckles and his curls. He left them behind.

James startles from his thoughts when Rob clears his throat. "But Danny. Is he . . . you know. Is he *that* for you?"

James remembers Sydney's face as he'd walked away from him that final time, leaving him alone on the airport sidewalk in a line of taxis.

"I think he tried to tell me that he loves me, right before I left," James says. "We were in his house, fucking fighting over nothing. I didn't . . . I couldn't let him finish saying it."

Rob whips his head to look at him, eyes blown wide. "Fuck, Jimmy, seriously? And you—is that how you feel?"

James shrugs his shoulders hard, arms falling helplessly at his sides. "How can I? You can't love someone after two weeks. Two days. That's not how it—it's impossible."

"Oh, fuck that. Who said there was a rulebook?"

James laughs. "Probably the same person who said two men can't fuck each other."

Rob chuckles in response, and James feels the air finally settle and relax, clearing away some of the thick, tense fog. "Anyway," James goes on. "You made the right choice. Lori's way prettier than me."

"Fucking right she is. Sometimes I get confused out here wondering whether something's you or a clump of old seaweed."

"You son of a bitch," James laughs, and Rob hits the water to splash him right in the face, grinning.

Rob hums a bit dramatically in his throat. "Fuck. So Danny Moore loves you," he says, and James finds himself nodding slowly, stunned to hear the words said out loud.

"I . . . maybe. Yeah."

Rob smiles wide. "When are you going back?"

"To Oahu?"

"Well, yeah!" Rob looks at him again, sees something in the look on James' face, then groans. "Shit, Jimmy, don't tell me you're not planning on going back."

James feels the anger from yesterday morning settle once more over his chest. "Well what the hell else am I supposed to do? I can't just . . . drop everything and move there."

"Why the hell not?"

"It was *two days*."

"And I've known you for two *years* and never seen you look as happy as you do when you're talking about him."

"When the hell was that?"

"Literally just now."

James shoots him a look. "Seriously? Jesus, you sound just like him."

"He asked you to stay there with him? On Oahu? Jimmy, why in the living fuck are you back here?!"

"I have a job!"

"That you hate and that you're way too fucking good for."

"—that *pays*. And honestly, I . . . I mean, I barely even know him."

"All this time I've heard about Danny Moore on the circuit and I can guarantee you, Jimmy, he's never even had a *single* conversation with another surfer. And you stayed at his *house*. You . . . well, you two—"

"I get it, yeah." James grits his teeth as his face flushes. "Look, man it's not just my job. You know that. I have . . . I have my place, the wagon, and you, and—"

"Exactly. You've got jack shit here in LA besides my sorry ass and you know it."

"It's not that simple."

"Of course it's not simple. But you've got a man who says he fucking loves you—yes, he at least thinks he does, you can't argue that— and you've got a bank account full of prize money because you're a fucking professional ass surfer who just won the Billabong, and you've got a best friend who thinks you're an absolute moron for not getting the hell out of here. You like being with him—don't lie to me. Tell me one goddamn reason why you aren't back on a plane right now."

James says the words before he can even think. "I'm scared."

The silence falls, heavy and buzzing. Rob waits, and James forces himself to speak, pushing out choked words.

"Look, if I go there—there's no turning back, right? Everyone will know, no matter how hard we try . . . People aren't idiots. They're gonna notice that Jimmy Campbell and Danny Moore show up to every surf competition together in the same fucking car. They're gonna . . . and

I can't just say nevermind in a year and go back to this. To how it is now. Nobody *knows*, Rob. It's you. My whole life, you're fucking it."

"And him."

James blinks hard. "Yeah. And him."

Rob's voice is soft and gentle. "But does he make you happy?"

James wants to keep fighting. "Well, you make me happy. You and Lori make me happy. Los Angeles makes me happy. The surf here. No reason why I need to change anything."

"Damn right we make you happy, but I'm sure as hell not gonna put stars in your eyes like he did that day on the beach in Laguna."

James sighs, not answering. He tries to think of something, anything to change the subject. Now that he's gone and revealed himself he feels a desperate, racing need for it all to be over. He doesn't want to sit there on the water and think of Sydney's face looking desperate and lost in his kitchen. Doesn't want to think about how neither of them said anything important in those last precious moments, caught in the heat of a frenzied kiss.

The subject refuses to change, though, and Rob still perches staring him down, waiting for another comeback to refute.

James gives in to the conversation with a resigned sigh. "We didn't say anything when I left. We . . . I kissed him. Goodbye. And he dropped me off. And I don't even know . . . I don't have his phone number. Didn't make any plans. I think he thinks we just won't see each other again—awkwardly wave at the next competition and that'll be it. I feel like a complete asshole."

"You're not an asshole. You said it—you're just scared."

James laughs, frantic and desperate. "Why is this more terrifying than stepping off a fucking boat with a gun in my hands? It doesn't make any fucking sense—"

"Hate to sound like a greeting card, Jimmy, but this stuff doesn't make any fucking sense. First day I woke up and knew I wanted to marry Lori she was dead asleep and had a horrible perm and was drooling all over *my* pillow. And I thought 'I need to fucking marry this girl.'"

James' brain halts. "Wait, you never told me you're getting married?"

Rob's face lights up with a brilliant, shy smile. "I, uh, haven't told anyone yet. I just bought the ring a week ago."

Every ounce of frustration leaves James' chest in a rush. He answers Rob's smile, reaching out to take his hand and hold it over the water. His throat chokes up on his words, and a million sentences float through his mind before he finally settles, lamely, on, "I'm so happy for you, for both of you."

Rob squeezes his hand and smiles, eyes understanding. "Me too, man."

The light moment quickly turns strained, the emotions from the past thirty minutes churning into a thick, heavy weight in the air—one that can't be cleared, only left behind. James lets go of Rob's hand and dramatically shakes out his shoulders, trying to breathe away the tension still in his limbs. "Right, well, tomorrow morning I'll bring a check and pay you for the therapy," he jokes.

"I've kept your sorry ass alive for two fucking years," Rob smirks. "You owe me at least a hundred grand at this point. Better get real good at surfing."

James rolls his eyes and, after a mutual nod, starts to paddle back towards the breaking point of the waves, knowing they've said everything that needed to be said. Rob joins him, paddling just behind him and panting as they reawaken stiff muscles from the cold.

"Look, Jimmy," Rob calls up to him as they paddle, "all I'm saying is, and this is the last thing I'll say about it, you decide to go back there, just say the word and I'll help you. We'll help you. I'll miss you like hell, man, you know that. But you just say the word."

James looks over his shoulder, more water glossing over his eyes. Rob smiles at him and raises his brows, confirming James heard, then nods over his shoulder at a fresh swell coming their way.

"You take this one," Rob says. "Show me how a Billabong champion rides our sorry little waves."

James flips him off and starts to get into position to chase the wave, but stops just before starting his first stroke. "Will you tell Lori, for me? Tell her . . . you know. I want her to know."

Rob nods. "Of course, old man."

Then James paddles like hell towards the Los Angeles skyline, a warm tingle zipping down his spine as he catches his first wave of the morning and soars into the spray. Rob's echoing whoop follows him all the way in to the shore.

James lifts his hand in a wave as Rob pulls away from the curb in his truck an hour later, wheels revving so he can make it home in time to change and shower before his shift starts at the station. The dust along the side of the highway swirls around James' shins in a sandy cloud, and the hot morning sun beats down onto his back, high and bright in the sky and quickly drying his damp shirt.

James shoulders his bag as Rob's truck disappears from view, turns away from the road, and is immediately slammed with the sensation of being a tourist in his own city. He shoves his hand in his pocket to make sure his apartment keys are still there, but the thought of going back to that stale, empty room feels like some sort of accepted defeat.

But he *should* go home. He should throw out the stale trash and open up the windows, run down to the bodega for some groceries to replenish the measly fridge and call in to make sure he'll still be allowed to show up for work tomorrow. He's got laundry to unpack, unused boardshorts to put away, a dead and crumpled lei of flowers to awkwardly throw in the trash and a trophy to decide whether to put on a sad shelf or hide in a closet.

Instead he walks down the beach towards the pier, already thronging with morning joggers and tourists. He hefts his bag higher on his shoulder and makes his way as gracefully as he can through the crowd. It feels surreal that only two weeks ago he'd stood on the sand just below this very boardwalk and emerged from the water having just beat Danny Moore.

He passes the exact place he'd been standing on the rough wood when he'd locked eyes with an unassuming stranger in the crowd, and James can't even believe that it's the same pier—the same physical place. Surely the spot where he first glimpsed Sydney Moore is too private for regular people to be unconsciously trodding over in flip-flops and trainers. Everything now looks like a flat façade—a cheap, thrown-together copy of the water and sand surrounding Sydney's home back on Oahu. Even the palm tree fronds don't look quite as green.

James makes it to the very end of the pier and leans his elbows against the splintered wood, shielding his eyes from the oppressive sun. He looks out along the southern stretch of shimmering beach, snaking around the coastline down towards Long Beach and the marinas. He imagines he can see the cranes from the dockyard piercing up into the hazy sky, heavy and rusted with the slow, eternal drag of labor. Covered in grime and sweat. He wonders if they even have a dockyard on Oahu. Maybe down by the harbor near Honolulu, a black, oily splotch in the middle of paradise.

The thought makes him cringe. Sydney Moore wouldn't want to wake up every morning next to an exhausted, sweat- and grease-covered dockyard worker. Not in his little haven of paradise.

Would he?

James stands there for almost an hour, letting the skin on the back of his neck burn under the sun and forcing his mind to stay completely blank. He doesn't think about how his hands have grown soft from a week away from work, or the fact that Rob Depaul admitted out loud that morning that he had kissed him *back*, or about how James can no longer remember the exact lines and shading of Sydney's tattoo. He doesn't think about the fact that Sydney Moore is currently preparing to hurl himself from the tallest waves on earth in just a few days at Waimea.

He just stands there, bag over his shoulder like a tourist kicked out of their hotel, and he watches the bustling beach slowly come to hectic life.

When the thirst in his throat makes him feel lightheaded, James finally turns to walk back down the pier with a resigned sigh, making his way towards his apartment with thudding, dreaded steps. The small incline up Hermosa Avenue has never felt so unbearably steep, and the screeches of the traffic make him constantly jump, as if he'd just stepped off the fucking boat that morning with his shoulder still in a sling.

The door to his apartment opens with a great shove, squealing on its hinges as it swings open into the airless, dark room. It looks like it's been ransacked; James' clothes are still scattered on the floor from the day he shoved them into his bag to try and rush to the airport on time. A dropped cup of instant coffee stains the old carpet. The hospital bracelet from his stay lies torn in half on the little wooden table, the still-to-be-dealt-with insurance paperwork folded up in a heap next to it.

James steps inside and shuts the door behind him with a thud, then takes one slow look around every corner of the room. He can barely hear the ocean over the hum of the cars rushing by just outside his tiny window. His left-behind surfboard is the brightest color in the place, standing limply in the corner as if it can't decide whether to be happy James is home.

There isn't a coffee maker taking up half the counter space. There are no photographs of his mom.

His bed, shoved away in the corner, is only big enough for one.

James gasps in a breath and closes his eyes. His knees buckle as the shocking wave of realization floods like fire through his chest and up his throat. He suddenly knows, more than he's ever known anything in his life, that he is somehow in love with Sydney Moore.

The realization leaves him trembling and shocked, frozen in the center of his room. He wishes Sydney himself were beside him to confirm that any of this is real—that James really is standing in his Los Angeles apartment with the utmost certainty that he is about to move across an entire ocean to go live with a man.

And not with just any man. But with . . . with—

James sprints to the phone on the wall and snatches it off the cradle, groaning in frustration when he doesn't hear the dial tone. He must have forgotten to pay the goddamn phone bill—what with all the drowning and championship winning and last minute flights.

In a mad panic, he grabs a handful of change from the dish on the counter and rushes out the door, running like hell down the block towards the payphone near the bodega on the corner, not giving a shit who happens to see. He shoves the quarters into the slot with shaking fingers and holds his palm over the smile blazing across his face, unable to wipe it off.

He flips madly through the crumpled-up papers and cards in his wallet until he finds the one from Rob's station, dog-eared at the corners with the number to reach him there written in Rob's own shaky scrawl.

The voice at the other end is crisp and professional—completely unaware that the man on the other end of the line is seeing Los Angeles in vivid technicolor for the first time in years.

"Los Angeles Police Department, Torrance Station, how may I help you?"

James clears his throat. "Uh, yeah, is Officer Depaul there? Rob Depaul?"

He hears papers shuffling on the other end of the line, muffled voices and beeping in the background. "I'm sorry, sir, he's out on patrol. Can I leave a message?"

"That'd be rad. Yes, just tell—tell him Jimmy Campbell called." James runs a hand through his hair, lifting his chin to feel the fresh breeze against his face.

"Tell him it's about what he told me earlier. I decided yes."

# *21*

Sydney stands on the shore off Waimea just before dawn, silently watching the waves surge and crash in the watery moonlight. The wind whips his untamed curls freely into his face, blowing across his cheeks and tangling with his eyelashes, hovering over the bridge of his nose.

He's been standing there since sunset.

His bare feet are cold and stiff in the sand, buried almost up to the ankle. The wind slices through his sweatpants and grabs ahold of his legs, crawling icy hands up his bare bones. He hunches his shoulders and tips his head down so that his nose is buried in the front of the soft sweatshirt covering his frame. He pauses as the fabric casts a calm, guarded warmth over the skin of his lips and chin, then he shuts his eyes tight, shakes his head at himself, and inhales.

He hates being so irrationally *stupid.*

The sweatshirt is the only piece of clothing James touched that Sydney hasn't been able to bring himself to wash. His sheets, his towels, his pillowcases, every article of clothing—all of it went straight to the laundromat in town the second he'd gotten home from dropping James off at the airport.

There had been no sense in delaying it—might as well jump straight back into his old life. His comfortable, usual, familiar little life. Where all his clothes just smelled like himself, and his meals lasted him for days on the leftovers, and his bed only had the imprint of one body in the morning. Pillowcases only strewn with long, brown curls of hair.

This goddamn sweatshirt, though. He'd gotten back from the laundromat dragging the huge sack of clean clothes behind him and seen it lying forgotten half-hidden under the bed, like some unwanted monument erected smack in the center of his home. And he'd left the damn thing there for three whole days until he finally picked it up with shaking hands in the middle of the night and held it to his face in a daze.

And now he feels moronic and utterly hopeless, standing on the beach like some swooning heroine in the secret books he knew his momma used to hide and read, trying to somehow breathe in a reminder of James Campbell's lost scent against the salty air and warm musk of the sand. Not even surfing, just uselessly watching as the thick black wind slowly lightens into the clean slate of dawn.

It's been one hundred and thirty-seven hours since he last held James Campbell. One hundred and thirty-six since he last saw him. The knowledge that that number will only ever grow towards infinity leaves a thudding, irritating ache in his chest, drowned out only by the heaving drone of the wind as it whips across the ocean's churning surface.

He needs to keep count, though. To track the number as it grows higher and higher and higher. Because watching the number grow to one thousand, or ten thousand, or one hundred thousand means that it had to have started at one, then two, then three. It means that James Campbell winning the Billabong and then coming back to sleep in Sydney's bed must have really happened at some time, in some place. That it can't all have just been a dream.

One hundred and thirty-eight hours now, as he braces himself against the wind and spray and tracks the current of the waves by the light of the graying stars, memorizing their rises and falls, completing the tables and formulas in his head that will help him pick the largest wave tomorrow at the competition.

He knows that to whoever the hell is watching over them all from above, this is what he was born to do. Or at least, meant to do ever since he picked up that sharpened red crayon and opened the stiff pages of an outdated, water-damaged textbook. He looks out at the ocean and sees her secrets hovering over the waters. Sees her currents and forces, the whispers of her underbelly and the pull of the tides.

It used to thrill him—that mental spark of muscle and adrenaline and physics coalescing into one bursting firework of action when he threw his board down into the towering waves. The possibility of winning in a challenge of man versus nature.

And then James fucking Campbell had gone and poured his emotions over the surface of the ocean, drowning Sydney's perfect calculations into the chaos of the whitewater and leaving him instead with the loneliness that comes from standing at the edge of the world just before dawn. Leaving him with an echo of his momma's voice singing prayers in his head that hasn't stopped since the moment he'd looked out at the sea with James Campbell no longer beside him. Five days and five centuries ago.

He feels as if he's really floating above in the darkened clouds, watching himself down below on the shore. And what a horrifying sight he is . . .

Sydney grits his teeth, growling at the empty air, stunned and indignant and repulsed that he's been stripped down to such a sorry state—that the man he's known himself to be since he was fifteen was really all just a façade, easily blown away by the breath from James' mouth when he'd first parted his lips and said, "*We actually haven't met, yet. My name's Jimmy.*"

It's all just a little bit ironic, he thinks, in a way that seen in any other person's life would have made Sydney roll his eyes and scoff, throw up his hands and mutter, "*Of course! What the hell did you expect?*"

Because here he is staring at the surface of the water, stripping bare her secrets and forces hidden beneath. All the while scoffing at the other surfers who only ever bothered to notice the height of the waves, maybe their basic shape or speed. And apparently he'd forgotten all this damn time to apply the same logic to himself.

And James Campbell had taken one look at him barreling across the sand with his head held high, aviators over his eyes, and seen straight down to the seafloor of Sydney's soul. James had taken shelter there, and kissed it gently with his soft, salty lips, and then calmly stepped onto a plane with a bullet-free pocket and a championship title to his name. Trophy tucked away in his bag.

Sydney wants desperately to stand there in the darkness and lie to himself like this—tell himself that James is living perfectly fine without him over there in Los Angeles. Probably tired of having a stuck-up kid hanging around him all the time, especially a kid that everyone agrees with no contest is a complete pain in the ass. He wants to pity himself standing alone and morose on the beach, trying to smell James Campbell's skin in the sweatshirt he'd worn for only a day.

The day he'd *won* and walked back to the Jeep and thrown himself into Sydney's arms, kissed his mouth, leaned his weight against his skin . . .

No. James Campbell is doing exactly what he's meant to be doing in Los Angeles. He's moving on and up. Thanks, Sydney, for the hints at the Billabong. You've been a real help. Don't be a stranger at the next competition on the pro circuit.

But then he sees James' face in his mind like a haunting ghost— the broken, shattered, desperate way he'd stood there naked and trembling in Sydney's home, right before rushing to his side to hold him together with his bare hands. The way the lines around James' mouth had deepened when he whispered his name before walking away into the airport.

And Sydney knows he can't lie to himself and say that he's the only one affected—that he's the only one who wanted James to stay.

Somehow that makes James getting on that plane feel even worse.

Sydney waits for one last swell to come in, noting the composition of the wave and adding it to the mental catalog he's been building during similar vigils and practice runs all week. Now more than ever he knows he needs to surrender himself to the giant pillars of water crashing down into the unsuspecting shallows. He needs to pick up his board in his steady hands tomorrow, and sprint out towards the uncertain horizon without looking back, and let the earth hold his life in her palms—man versus sea.

He needs to prove to himself that there is something higher at play than waiting on a moonlit beach for James Campbell's arms to come up behind him and kiss the back of his neck in a ghostly embrace.

He watches the rushing spray and foam settle back into the earth after the crash of the wave, the water fizzling down into the wet sand like tiny fireworks exploding across the sky. Then he holds the hair back from his eyes against the wind, tucks his nose down into the neck of the sweatshirt, and makes his way back to his Jeep, legs stiff and sore from a long night of standing watch.

He'll conquer the tallest waves on earth tomorrow. Gut strong and hands steady and neck held high, flinging himself down into the spray from the heavens, fighting against the great heaving force of the water and foam.

He'll do it whether James Campbell's deep blue eyes are seeking him out on the sand or not.

And he knows that they won't be. They definitely, unequivocally won't.

On the drive back home along the winding beachside road, Sydney blinks out of his aimless, boring thoughts to the sudden, intense desire to just grip the wheel and swerve his car off the dirt road towards the trees, wanting to hear James curse and panic next to him. Wanting to hear him laugh (well, mostly curse).

His fingers grip the wheel hard and he starts to do it—drive like a maniac in an action film who's gotta save the girl before the bomb goes off. His toes zing as they press the accelerator over the roaring engine. His fingertips buzz.

Then he realizes the car would stay totally silent if he did, only the wind as a witness to a random Jeep swerving across the road. The wind doesn't laugh like James Campbell, not free and deep and open like waves rolling over smooth rocks on the shore. The wind doesn't know how to curse, either. So Sydney drives the rest of the way home straight and narrow, five miles under the speed limit with careful turns.

When he gets back to his house, he throws his keys haphazardly across the room, missing the table, then turns to make a cup of coffee when he stops dead in his tracks.

The photograph.

As if the side table had been nothing but empty for the past five days, there is a *photograph*. *The* photograph. One he has carefully *not* looked at for nearly one hundred and fifty long hours.

In a daze his numb legs carry him four steps across the creaking hardwood floor to the little table, and he picks up the frame in careful, trembling hands. His momma's skin is golden and shining like the sun, eclipsing the tired metal and grey of the airfield surrounding them and covering Sydney's small frame in warmth.

He strokes across the surface of the photograph with his thumb, gently tracing over the locks of her hair as if he could feel the individual strands. He realizes he's never picked it up and held it in his hands before—not since he first set it down on the table on the day he'd moved in, when it took him ten hours to sand down the hardwood floors and just ten minutes to unpack all his belongings.

James Campbell had held it in his hands, though. He'd squinted hard at Ruth Moore's elegant scrawl, and studied her brilliant, crooked smile, and looked up and formed the word "Sydney" with his lips, fragile and perfect in the private, salty air.

It had been the first time Sydney had heard his real first name since he was ten-years-old on an Arizona porch. And now he misses the sound of it so badly he's tempted to whisper it just to himself in the stale and empty air of his house, feeling younger and more alone than he ever has in his life—even that night sleeping out on the beach. Feeling naked.

*"Sydney, baby, what's it say in Exodus chapter twenty?"* his momma had asked him that day in the car as she drove him, swerving down the road towards Ft. Knox, three miles away from their house. She'd looked back at him in the rearview mirror with half-glazed eyes and a nervous smile perched on her lips.

*"Exodus chapter twenty verse twelve: honor thy father and thy mother, that thy days may be long upon the land which the Lord thy God giveth thee,"* Sydney had recited proudly, not caring in the least what the verse actually meant.

*"That's right. So what's that mean we're gonna do when we see your father at work today?"*

*"It means just do whatever he says,"* Sydney had mumbled.

*"Sydney . . ."* she'd warned.

*"Aw, come on, Momma. You know he's just—"*

*"Sydney Daniel Moore."*

Sydney had sighed, loud enough that he knew she could hear. *"It means say 'yes sir' and be respectful,"* he tried again.

And he remembers, vivid as the photograph in his hands, how his momma had smiled back at him in the rearview mirror and wrapped a curl of her hair around her index finger.

*"You know Momma loves you,"* she'd said.

And he'd beamed in his chest and whispered *"I know, Momma,"* too young to realize that her words were heavy and slurred.

And James Campbell had held this photograph in his hands. He'd *held* it—held it with the same rough fingers that had run through Sydney's curls when his face had been down between James' legs, James' body in his mouth, and the same fingers that had touched Sydney's cheek first thing in the morning, pulling him from soft sleep to the quivering air of sunrise.

A wave of self-disgust suddenly washes over him, sharp and stifling and hot. He slams the picture frame face down on the table, takes two steps away, then reaches back and guiltily flips it right side up again. He clenches his fists and sets his shoulders, walking confidently towards the taken-apart record player in the corner that he was supposed to have finished over a week ago.

For the first time since James Campbell waltzed into his life across the sand, Sydney's fingers itch to get themselves back inside the intricate workings of a machine—the wires and knobs, switches and electrical currents. The knowable logic of a perfectly made system. Sydney takes his project out to the porch and sets up his usual workspace on the rough wood boards, out under the open sky and overlooking the sea.

He tells himself one last thing before he loses his mind to the steady zen and predictable logic of the broken parts waiting expectantly beneath his hands:

He has his work, and he has his waves, and he has his little place in the world. And James Campbell has reduced him to a lost and trembling shell of the man he created that morning after he turned fifteen for the very last goddamn time.

He ignores the tiny part of his brain that whispers to him that he still has the memory of James' lips against his own. One hundred and forty-one hours ago.

One hundred and forty-two hours ago.

343

# 22

The sun is bright and heavy in the sky when Sydney finally blinks hard and looks up from his work.

He's been switching back and forth between the record player and recording his notes on the waves from the night before in his notebook, working until the passing hours disappear like seconds as his mind buzzes steadily ahead, refusing to do anything but think. His stomach growls roughly, and his eyes start to droop closed against the harsh blare of the sunlight reflecting off the white sand. He suddenly realizes he hasn't eaten or slept in well over twenty-four hours, and shakes his head angrily at himself.

So much for taking back control of his life—he can't even keep his new resolve for four hours without letting himself sink to a state that will only come back to bite him in the ass tomorrow morning at the competition when he's tired and weak.

Idiot.

The warm breeze weaves through the old seashells hanging from the eaves, gently clinking in the wind with the soft hush of the restless ocean. He twiddles the screwdriver in his hand and tries to think. He could eat now, or he could take a nap, or he could get another few practice waves in down at Waimea. He could go for a swim to condition, or he could start on the project for his next client sitting untouched up at Chuck Hobbs' place, or he could sit here and close his eyes and remember the precise color of James Campbell's eyes in the moonlight just moments after he'd orgasmed, clinging tightly to Sydney's shoulders and covering him with the heavy, trusting weight of his body.

Nope. Not that.

Sydney groans and runs his hands over his face, gripping tightly enough at his hair to sting his scalp. He feels like a mess. He can't even decide what to do with his goddamn day without thinking of James fucking Campbell, and he's been deciding what to do with his days just fine for over seven fucking years. Even earlier than that, if he's really honest with himself, despite everything Lahela and his father tried to do.

He sucks in a frustrated breath and gets quickly to his feet, still gripping the screwdriver tight in his fist and hoping that his feet will somehow lead him on to the next activity for the day—the next meaningless thing to fill the time. Nothing but a series of steps and movements and thoughts that will carry him successfully through hour one hundred and forty-five so he doesn't go and do something pathetic again like stand lonely on a windswept and rocky shore with his curls blowing into his face.

He turns to head up the lane to Hobbs' place, thinking he might as well go and lose himself again in his work. Maybe Hobbs'll even have something semi-edible sitting out on a counter for him to shove in his mouth.

He walks down into the sand on stiff legs, and he takes two steps towards the lane while staring down at his feet, and he looks up quickly, already wincing, at the spot where James had once surprised him by appearing like magic out of the shaded, tree-lined path. And he freezes.

James Campbell is standing there.

*James Campbell is standing there.*

James Campbell is standing there with three bags slung over his shoulders and no shoes on his feet. Sunglasses perched in his hair and a tank top clinging to his abs and a brilliant light overtaking his face. A hesitant smile.

"Sydney," James Campbell says, voice breaking.

Sydney's heart explodes. It stops beating and soars up straight into the heavens all at once. He drops the screwdriver down into the sand. His muscles ache with adrenaline pumping through them like fire—adrenaline and shock and disbelief and fear that *James Campbell is standing there.*

*James Campbell is—*

His mouth is too dry to speak, and his tongue lays limp in the bottom of his mouth. Stunned.

James Campbell has tears in his eyes. "I missed you" he whispers.

James Campbell looks brilliant in the sunlight. It glints off his hair in brilliant golden streaks like the tails burning radiantly behind shooting stars soaring over the ocean. His skin is the warm sand, and his hands are the shade cast beneath the plumeria blossoms, and his eyes are the vastness of the ocean right at dusk. The depth and the secrets and the power of the waves.

And his voice is the calm, rolling moan of the lighthouse cutting through the storm. The hope of dry land in the wet darkness that comes from being trapped without oxygen under a booming wave. Sydney wants to stand frozen on the beach, not moving a muscle, and spend the rest of his life describing James Campbell, until the number of hours reaches all the way up to one million. One million and one.

Instead James takes a step closer to him, gesturing with his chin to the bags hefted around his strong, broad shoulders.

"This okay?" he asks. His voice is see-through and soft.

Sydney feels himself start to laugh deep down in his chest, and it comes out sounding like the choked back exhale of a sob.

"I don't understand," Sydney breathes.

He thinks that maybe he'll never be able to move again. His eyes are frantic, drinking in every inch of James standing calmly in front of him before James inevitably disappears up into the mist, turning back into a shadow to walk behind Sydney in the blackest hours of the night, guided by restless dreams and the ghostly echo of James' voice saying his name ringing in his ears.

James doesn't disappear. He stands firmly in the hot sand and waits, staring through the thick, crackling air between them and looking at Sydney in a way Sydney knows he's never been looked at in his life. Like Sydney is somehow a sunset covered ocean, and a velvet field of flowers, and the first warm hints of dawn lapping gently at the cool, silvery shore. Like Sydney is one of the beaches back in Vietnam, haunting and terrifying and unreal, catching the soldiers as they fall.

Like he is somehow something more than a stunned man standing frozen in the sand, curls frizzed wildly about his face and mouth half-open and eyes blown wide with disbelief.

James starts to look worried. Sydney stands there, helpless to move or speak, as James' thin façade quickly starts to fade, revealing the uncertainty beneath.

"Sydney . . . ?"

The spell hovering over Sydney's limbs breaks away in an instant, cracking in two, then shattering across the shore. He licks his trembling lips, wanting to yell and sink to his knees and fly and run all at once.

"You're here," he says on a whisper.

James nods, and Sydney can hear his swallow even from twenty feet away. "Yeah. I'm here."

"Here . . . on Oahu." Sydney doesn't realize it until the words are out of his mouth that he's asking a question, one that rises in his voice.

Because it suddenly dawns on him, sharp and hot, that James Campbell may be here on Oahu, but that doesn't mean he's really *here*. Here in Sydney's arms, in Sydney's home, in his bed. And Sydney doesn't think he will fucking survive it if James Campbell smiles at him and calmly suggests that they go for a surf together, or go and meet up with some of the other surfers James met along the pipeline, or have a casual chat.

But James is holding bags . . .

James must have heard the question, because his mouth twists. Sydney can tell by the way he's holding himself that the bags are hurting his shoulder, and Sydney momentarily wonders what color red his blood stained into the sand.

He shakes his head from the nauseating thought as James takes a deep breath. "I . . . I missed you," he says again, all the emotion in his voice landing hard on the 'you'.

"You . . ." Sydney starts, then he wipes a hand over his dry mouth. The breeze blows a lock of James' long bangs out of his eyes, and Sydney's fingertips go numb with the desire to feel it. "You look so beautiful," he whispers.

His own brows shoot up, stunned. But before Sydney can stuff his fist in his mouth, or bury his head in the sand, or try to backtrack and cover over what the hell he just said, James Campbell melts.

He drops his bags into the sand with a thud and runs the twenty feet towards Sydney, kicking up clouds of sand. Sydney throws open his arms and takes one desperate step forward and grabs James hard in his arms, not giving a shit when James knocks his sunglasses off his head. He pulls James close to his body in one fierce embrace as he lets out the last two minutes' worth of tense breath in his lungs.

James' back is shaking hard, warmed by the sun. A damp trail leads down his spine from dripping sweat, and Sydney shivers when the hair on James' chest seems to brush against his own skin through James' thin shirt.

"Fuck, Sydney," James chokes out. "Fuck."

"James."

"Ah, God . . ."

"*James.*"

Apparently, it's the only word left he knows.

James fits his head beneath Sydney's chin in a way that makes Sydney want to shield him from every gun left on earth, from the most dangerous waves, from the sky itself, and James hugs him hard enough to bruise, fingers gripping hard into his back, imprinting themselves on Sydney's bones.

"Say I can stay," James breathes. "I know we didn't say, before . . . not really . . . but you're—you—"

"James."

"I'm here now. Please . . ."

James whispers the words into his chest, and Sydney can feel the heat of them straight through his shirt, straight through his skin and ribs down to the muscles in his chest. Something inside of him releases. Something held hot and tight, bundled up and tied together, since the moment the doors had closed behind James walking away from him at the airport terminal. One hundred and forty-five hours ago.

Sydney melts around James' body. Places his cheek down in his hair and rubs his face against the soft strands, brushes his lips again and again across James' scalp, clean and warmed by the sun. He breathes in the scent of his skin, letting it spread through his veins like a salve. James smells like the seats in the plane, and floral Hawaiian mud, and sweat and salt and musky men's shampoo.

He smells like the worn, thin sweatshirt thrown back inside on the hardwood floor.

Sydney tilts his face up to the clear open sky and thanks whoever the hell is up there that his momma always used to talk to. Thanks them for flying James Campbell clear across the Pacific Ocean and placing him solid and warm in his arms, gripping so tightly that Sydney can barely breathe. Thanks them more than he did the moment James ended his final Billabong ride, and Sydney knew before the judges even opened their mouths that he had just won.

He cups the back of James' head in his hand, swallowing down a thick emotion at the warm, living weight of it in his palm. He coaxes James' face away from his chest, stares for a moment at the way the sunlight weaves through his blonde eyelashes, then leans down and kisses him with a rushing sigh. James exhales into his mouth, hands immediately flying up to hold Sydney's jaw in his hands.

"Thank God," James moans against his lips.

The relief is nearly debilitating. Sydney thinks he should climb back up on the cliff and announce to the entire world that it is actually *he* who is the biggest idiot of them all, because he thought he would be absolutely fine going about his days as if he'd never felt James Campbell moan against his mouth, or caught rasps of James Campbell's stubble on his own chin. As if he could just blink once and magically pretend they'd never kissed—never touched each other so closely, nose to nose, that neither one of them could close their eyes and pretend something else was happening, couldn't look away. As if he could simply wave at James at the next competition across the beach and conveniently forget the fact that James was the first person since his momma to call him Sydney, the photograph held carefully in his steady hands.

*God,* he's been a fool.

Sydney kisses him deeply, humming just to feel the vibrations rumble across their tongues.

"*God,*" James murmurs, out of breath.

Sydney chuckles against his mouth. "I was just thinking the same thing."

The smile threatening to burst across his face hurts his cheeks. The salty breeze tingles across his sensitive lips, carrying the taste of James' mouth across the sand on a gentle, soothing wind.

James' eyes are the ocean. He brushes the curls back from Sydney's forehead, looking like he has words waiting right at the tip of his tongue. Then he shakes his head in something like disbelief, even though *he* was the one who just strolled up unannounced in the oblivious sand, bags over his shoulders, and he pulls Sydney hard down against him by the back of his neck. He licks into his mouth, rolling across Sydney's tongue, and he groans against his chest, sending a flame of heat shooting straight down Sydney's spine.

Sydney kisses back, distantly aware in the back of his mind that the sky has never really seen them kiss—not like this. That the daylight is illuminating the places where their bare lips brush, desperate and wet. And the entire ocean is watching James' lips part under his, the way they consume the soft sighs from Sydney's mouth. And James' mouth tastes like the first gulp of seawater Sydney ever accidentally swallowed down.

That, and a hot, slick, rolling, *gasping—*

Sydney sips on the breaths spilling over from James' mouth. He touches the lips that once turned cold and blue beneath his, caresses the mouth that almost died in the foaming shallows of the ocean and still gulped in oxygen and *breathed.* The beautiful mouth that had looked death in the face twice and yelled, *"Fuck you, you bastard, I'm not ready to fucking go yet!"*

A laugh bubbles up in Sydney's chest at the thought, and he pulls back to chuckle breathlessly down at their feet. James cups his cheek in his calloused hand and frowns, a grin spreading across his wet and swollen lips.

"You laughing at how I kiss, asshole?" he whispers.

And oh, his voice is impossibly deep, and rough . . .

Sydney swallows his laughter, legs shaking. "No." He brushes his thumb gently across James' lower lip, watching the soft skin stretch with the pressure of his finger. "I was thinking that you have the most beautiful mouth, but you say the dirtiest things."

James gets a dark glint in his eyes, and a sudden shiver cascades down the back of Sydney's neck. He can hear James panting, barely standing still, as James' tongue slowly slides out to lick the tip of Sydney's thumb. They stare at each other, and Sydney holds his breath, then James' lips gently pull Sydney's thumb into his mouth.

Sydney watches his finger disappear into the warm, wet heat of James' mouth, a stunned shock burning its way up his bare arm. James sucks at his thumb gently, holding his gaze with a look Sydney imagines James had on his face when he crept into that jungle with a gun in his hands. His courageous, steady hands—hands which had held him, and brushed through his hair.

"*You're so brave,*" he wants to whisper to him, because James is standing under the open sun with Danny Moore's thumb sucked into his mouth, but he's already told James that once. No, *twice.* And James Campbell can't think he just flew all the way across an ocean to see a kid who blushes bright red at something as innocent as a *thumb* and can't even think of anything new or original to say.

James finally releases his thumb to brush against his lips, hot breath on his glistening skin sending goosebumps up Sydney's arm. "Good," James says, voice rough and low. "Because it looks like you're fucking stuck with this mouth, Moore."

But then James immediately closes his eyes, and his mouth twists in something like a frustrated question, like regret.

It only takes Sydney half a second to understand the question on James' face, and yet that's still half a second too long. He's standing here making out with James Campbell when he thought he was about to spend three hours fixing a radio on the porch, and James has asked to stay with him, James brought his *bags,* and Sydney "Idiot" Moore hasn't even said *yes.*

He clings like hell to the muscles on James' back—the trembling strength of his shoulder blades in the sun.

"Stay here with me" he breathes, even though James already asked. He needs to say the words—taste the way they burst off his tongue. His eyes grow embarrassingly wet, blurring out James' face into a brilliant spot of tan warmth, and he knows James sees before he blinks it away. "James, live here. Stay with me. We'll . . . we'll figure it out, whatever you need . . . and it's—I . . . I *missed* you."

James gasps through his nose and blinks hard, leaving a sheen of water across his own eyes.

"Okay," he whispers, nodding.

"Okay."

Sydney's breath chokes in the back of his throat. He leans in to kiss James again, and instead the million questions in his head start to pour out of his mouth. "I don't understand, though. You . . . you were going to—and your job? Your apartment, your friends? I didn't ever think . . . *ever* think you were planning to . . . how?"

James clears his throat roughly. "I'll tell you everything. I promise, I'll tell you, but—" He pauses and gentles his grip on Sydney's cheek, tilting his head down so that he can rub his nose once along Sydney's, breathing in long and deep. He whispers so softly Sydney can barely hear him over the roar of the waves.

"Can we?" he asks, in a voice that sounds so sad, and pained, and hopeful all at once that Sydney can't believe James Campbell is brilliant enough to fit so much emotion into two words. But, then again, he really shouldn't be surprised, should he?

Sydney nods desperately, nose bumping into James', then he crashes their still-wet lips together, the lump in his throat forgotten. He rubs his thumb along James' cheek, catching the drop of salty water falling from his eye. James groans deep in his chest, clutching at the back of Sydney's shirt and roughly pulling him a stumbling step forward in the sand, straight into James' sturdy body.

Sydney knows he's grown hard—can feel the low current of heat start to pulse between his thighs. He goes to move his hand to the back of James' waist to press them closer together, desperate for friction, his tongue between James' lips and teeth, when suddenly James pulls back, gasping from the kiss, and grabs his arm hard around the wrist.

"Fuck, I need to feel you. Now," he growls.

James pulls him quickly up the steps and into the cool darkness of the house, and a whimper escapes Sydney's mouth as he tries to keep up. The moment he's inside the doorway, James grabs his shoulders and pushes him back into the wall with a thud that rattles through the wood foundation. James runs his hands up Sydney's sides under his shirt and kisses him hard, pressing him back into the wall with the force of his body.

Sydney's chest is heaving. He slips down farther on the wall, bringing himself face to face with James, and pulls James into himself by the small of his back, perfectly aligning their hips and groaning when James' half-hard penis presses hesitantly into the dip of his own thigh.

It's exquisite. James' body is warm and solid in his arms, letting Sydney feel the full weight of him pressed up against his frame, and James' tongue slides against his as if they have all the time in the world, maddeningly hot and steady and slow.

It's the fantasy Sydney never even knew enough about to want—the one where it's calm, and in the middle of the afternoon, and in his own home. The one where he fears the windows of his house will burst because they can't contain the sounds of their combined sighs and moans.

The one where James Campbell came back with his *bags* sitting just outside in the warm sand.

James pulls back panting and looks straight into Sydney's eyes, gently arching his lower back more firmly against Sydney's palm. His warm hands slide up over Sydney's chest beneath his thin shirt, finally coming to rest just above his nipples, and he rubs warm, soft circles into Sydney's shaking skin. The swish of James' palms over his chest echoes throughout the quiet room, then James leans in towards his neck, hesitates for barely a second, and gently presses his warm, wet lips just under Sydney's jaw.

Sydney's skin explodes in shivers. "James," he gasps. He reaches up to caress the back of James' head with his hand, holding him closer as James slowly presses soft, steady kisses down the line of Sydney's neck, fingers still gliding over the thin hairs on his chest.

And Sydney suddenly remembers the toned lines James' own chest, how the thick blonde hairs felt when they brushed across his cheek, how they rasped against his skin, and how he kissed through them right before he licked his way down James' stomach, mouth watering to suck down his thick, dripping—

Sydney's head thuds back against the wall. He drowns in the sweet, wet drag of James' mouth along his sensitive skin—the puffs of warm air from James' mouth spreading throughout his entire shaking body.

Slowly, ever so slowly, Sydney reaches his other hand down to the low of James' back and presses, guiding James to roll his hips against him, rocking his hardening penis into the dip just above Sydney's thigh. James moans softly into his neck, voice high and broken, as Sydney's hand moves lower to the firm muscle of his ass and holds him there, rocking James' hips into himself in a slow, heated rhythm.

Sydney lets loose an unintelligible, embarrassing moan, right in the moment James licks his pulse and whispers, *"yeah, like that . . ."*

Filled with rushing boldness—which is stupid, because they've already seen each other *naked* for God's sake—Sydney presses his thigh between James' legs, his tense muscle rolling straight against the hot bulge of James' cock.

James' breath falters. He presses one last shaking kiss to Sydney's neck before lifting his head to rub his cheek along Sydney's jaw. Sydney shivers at the rasp of James' day-old stubble against his thin skin. James brings up one of his hands to cup Sydney's cheek, whispering low into the crook of his shoulder.

"I . . . I need you to understand, Sydney. I don't have a plane ticket back. I moved out of my apartment. Do you . . . is that . . . do you get me?"

Instantly, Sydney wraps his arms around James' back, holding him in a hug which one-month-ago-him would have called completely unnecessary and sentimental. James hands find his waist, and they share a long breath in perfect sync.

Sydney closes his eyes, his cheek in James' hair, and tries to convince himself for good that this is even happening. Just thirty minutes ago, he was sitting alone on his porch, trying to pep talk himself into eating something for the first time in over a day, counting the hours up to infinity to prove to himself that James Campbell had once desired his company—his conversation and his bed and his mouth.

And now James is here, in his house, with his bags, asking and promising to stay. Letting Sydney hold him and press their bodies together. Letting Sydney feel his cock against him with the understanding this is no longer just some unavoidable, convenient fluke.

He realizes he hasn't answered, leaving James hanging for the second unforgivable time that day. He pulls James even closer in the embrace. "I understand," he whispers. Then, in a rougher voice, "You came back."

James looks up at him with deep blue eyes and clears his throat, voice soft and intimate in the silence of the room. He doesn't take a step back, or pull his arms away.

"Honestly, I knew I had to come back the second I opened my apartment door," he says. "Just took me a few days to sort everything out—my stuff and my place and all that." Then he breathes out a sigh, suddenly shaking in Sydney's arms. "God, Sydney, I'm so fucking sorry I left. I didn't . . . I just didn't realize what we—"

Sydney hushes him with a kiss, just at the corner of his mouth. He understands now, as if it were written down for him in the size and force of a wave. Looking into James Campbell's eyes, holding his body against him, he sees that this is not the same James Campbell who walked away from him into the airport. Not even the same James who emerged victorious from the waves, or who hurled away the bullet into the sea, or who kissed him along the shore.

"I think you *had* to go back," he says gently.

James nods, understanding. He takes in a deep breath, as if he's going to say a lot more, then responds, simply, "I think I did."

They look at each other for a few seconds longer, James' hand idly tracing Sydney's spine, until Sydney thinks that maybe the moment has passed—that they'll get James' bags from back outside and talk through what the hell to do next. He wonders if James realizes that Waimea is tomorrow. Wonders what competition James plans to surf in next, and whether he'll need to get a bigger bed to fit them both, and how James will earn money, and if James is hungry or tired or thirsty or wants to go and surf or wants to go and be alone or—

James' mouth is pressed against his, and Sydney's brain stops short. He freezes as James softly draws one of his lips between his teeth.

"Stop thinking for five seconds and come fuck me," James murmurs into his mouth.

Sydney audibly gasps.

James steps back from him, smirking, but with his brows raised as if he's making sure Sydney's still alright, that he hasn't just asked for something too unbelievably obscene. Sydney wants James Campbell to think of having sex with him as the *farthest* possible thing from obscene, so he bolts upright again, then goes pliant as James takes him by the hand and leads Sydney back into his own bedroom—into *their* bedroom. Sydney's brain shivers at the thought.

"But it's the middle of the day," Sydney hears himself say.

James laughs, turning to lead him forward towards him by the bed. Sydney's wondering if he's imagining how James' laugh sounded more nervous than not.

"Yeah, no shit it's the middle of the day. I thought you were supposed to be a genius."

Sydney huffs, embarrassed. "Well how should I know. You're the only one who ever calls me that."

He means it as a joke, but James gets a sad look in his eyes and pulls Sydney close to him, placing his palms back on Sydney's chest above his shirt.

Sydney feels the air of the moment changing into something heavy and warm. James' breath ghosts across his skin like velvet when he speaks. He swallows, licks his lips, then swallows again.

"I . . . I've never actually been with a man before," he whispers.

Sydney frowns. He knows this. Of course, he knows this. Anyone who saw James Campbell's face when he'd looked down that night in the shower and saw Sydney's hard cock brushing up against his own would realize that he'd never gotten to be with a man before. Anyone who saw James Campbell's face after they first kissed.

Anyone who saw James Campbell look at his friend, Rob . . .

Sydney opens his mouth to say that he knows—he pays attention, so he knows—and then immediately shuts it again. He realizes James looks unbearably nervous, as if he's scared that this will somehow make Sydney step back from him and say, "*You know what, actually, I've changed my mind since you clearly don't know what the hell to do if another man's penis is involved.*"

James keeps talking before Sydney can think of a response, voice thin and uneven. "I've never . . . Sydney, I've *never* wanted anyone like I want you. Right now. But I don't. . . I might not know how—"

Sydney kisses him again, pressing back through James' lips with his tongue. He pulls off his own shirt, mind racing over his thudding heart. And it's so unforgivably inane, but Sydney suddenly feels that right here, right now, is the first time that he has ever truly taken his shirt off in front of James—two weeks of shirtless surfing and two nights of shirtless sleeping be damned.

There aren't enough words in the English language to convince James Campbell that Sydney has never wanted anyone, any*thing*, the way he wants James Campbell right now. That he has never even experienced such a breadth and depth of emotion in one moment. That he couldn't give a shit about who James touched before this because James is here. Now. On Oahu. In his room.

Because James *survived*, and he's choosing to spend his unpromised days in Sydney's arms.

James' hands immediately run up Sydney's bare stomach and settle over his chest. Sydney watches breathlessly as James' eyes follow the trails of his fingers over ribs and muscle. Then Sydney kisses him, letting James feel the full warmth of his bare skin, and James moans as he parts his lips to let Sydney in.

Sydney speaks against his lips. "James Campbell, you have no idea—" He kisses him over and over, hands planted on either side of James' face and living off the air coming from his mouth. "You have no idea," he says again.

With a rush of air, James reaches down and strips off his own shirt, then falls into Sydney's arms, skin to skin. "Come here," he breathes.

And *oh,* how could this feel so different from the times they've touched naked before? Sydney can't even believe that someone's skin could change in texture so drastically. His hands run up the hard, muscled plane of James' stomach, dipping across the curves of his abs and trailing through the hair leading down from his navel. James shudders beneath his palms, breathing hard through his nose and arching into his touch, and Sydney moves his fingers up over James' chest, pausing to rub softly over his nipples until they peak.

James looks down at Sydney's hands on his body and groans, closing his eyes. "God, your fucking hands." He lifts his own hand to cover Sydney's long fingers where they trace his nipple. "Fuck . . ."

Sydney chases the word on his lips with a searing kiss. James' voice reverberates through his body, sinking deep into his veins. They are alone on this beach, on this island—alone in the universe. The only sound that exists is James' deep, gasping breaths. The brush of skin on skin. Soft moans escaping from the back of desperate throats.

And Sydney realizes he really *is* desperate. He's looking down at James' chest and shoulders like he's never even seen another man before, and he's vibrating out of his skin with the desire to hold, to touch, to taste—to be *taken.*

Sydney grips James' sides and traces his ribs until he's pressing his chest into his touch, then he leans down and licks a slow stripe up James' neck, pausing to bite him gently just under his ear.

James cries out and grips the back of Sydney's head, holding him there in the crook of his neck. "Touch me," he groans, tightening his fingers around Sydney's curls. "Fucking touch me. Please . . ."

Sydney's hands move before he even fully processes James' words, working frantically at James' belt and the zip of his jeans. He pauses with his hands on the waistband, looking at James for a nod, then pushes his pants straight down to the floor, wincing a bit when the buckle clacks on the hardwood. He looks down, lips half open, and stares at the plain white pair of boxers clinging to James' hips and curving over the bulge of his erection.

A thrilling rush burns across Sydney's cheeks. He wants to drop to his knees and press his face into James Campbell's warm, erect cock. Wants to breathe in the scent of him and feel the wet tip of his cock through the cotton of his underwear. Wants to trace the lines of it with his lips, mouth it as it swells from just the damp heat of Sydney's breath.

Then he feels absolutely ridiculous. Because he's already seen James naked; he's seen James naked in the full light of day standing tall right out in his living room. He's kissed down James' naked body and settled down between his legs and taken James' cock into his mouth, letting his heavy thighs squeeze and tremble on either side of his shoulders.

And yet, everything is different now. Sydney can't even believe those actions happened between him and the man in front of him. James is different, and he is different. And this is the first time—the first of innumerable times, unless James realizes in the next hour, or day, or week that dropping everything to join Sydney in Oahu was the biggest mistake of his life. And still, Sydney trusts the promise of James' packed bags more than he trusts that the tide will push the waves in to shore day after day after day.

He shucks off his own jeans with shaking fingers, then drops to his knees like he wanted to with a grunt. He grabs the back of James' thighs with his hands and rubs his cheek slowly along James' erection, shivering when James curses under his breath above him. James' hands settle firmly on his shoulders, holding him down to earth, and time stops as Sydney kneads his hands firmly into James' ass, then turns his face and breathes hot air against the covered tip of James' cock.

He breathes until the fabric turns wet and warm under his lips, until James' thighs are clenching and trembling in his hands, straining to push forward against Sydney's mouth and back into his firm grip.

Sydney looks up at him through his eyelashes, lips resting right on the tenting bulge of James' cock. James' eyes pool black.

"Do you want this?" Sydney whispers. His voice is husky and hoarse. It's unbelievable how badly he wants to put his mouth on James' cock, how desperately he needs to feel the thick weight of him on his tongue, heavy and hard as steel and hot. He needs to taste the evidence of James' desire for him leaking thickly from the tip, staining his fresh, clean boxers.

Sydney knows his face is embarrassingly flushed. He rests his cheek against the top of James' thigh and waits.

James blinks hard and groans before finally shaking his head. "No," he says, tracing Sydney's ear with his thumb. He coughs a laugh. "Well, yes. Hell yes. Fuck. But . . . Jesus I need to feel you. Let me feel you."

James Campbell is a genius. Sydney can't believe he even briefly forgot.

Sydney reaches up from where he sits back on his heels and pulls James' boxers down off his hips, dragging them slowly over the blanket of soft hairs covering his thighs. He gets quickly to his feet, so quickly he gets dizzy, then pulls off his own underwear as James kicks his off his ankles.

They take a mutual deep breath and stand before each other naked. Sydney wonders why the sight of James standing tall, breath swelling his chest, is filling him with such a sharp rush of gratitude, enough to cloud his vision. Then he remembers that, of *course*, they've never stood in front of each other naked before—not like this. Not when Sydney can let his eyes slowly wander over every inch of James' bared body with the knowledge that his time left to look isn't slipping through his fingers like sand.

James catches his eye, a serious look on his face, and Sydney would bet anything—every medal he's ever won—that James is thinking the same.

"Sydney," James whispers, sounding like so much more than a name. And Sydney reaches for him, absolutely helpless to stay still, and pulls him close into his body, meeting his lips in a warm, deep kiss. He lets his unsteady hands roam up and down James' broad, muscled back, and James' gentle, rough fingers are on his waist, his ribs, his biceps, the dip in the middle of his chest, fingers curling softly through his fine, thin hair.

It's everything and it's not nearly enough. Sydney kisses the corner of James' mouth, lips open and panting, then pulls him back with stumbling steps towards the bed, somehow anxious not to let his hands leave James' skin. He thinks James is going to push him down and climb on top of him—hold him down. He wants to feel the solid weight of James' body on top of his, rolling and heavy until the sweat slicks the hot places kept hidden between them.

Instead, James walks straight past him and lies down first on his back with a small sigh. He stares at the ceiling, then closes his eyes in a long blink, then looks over at Sydney like he's waiting for Sydney to decide whether he actually wants to come and join him—like he's waiting for himself to suddenly leap up from the bed and run. James' chest is heaving as he tries to control his breaths. His stomach is clenched, and his thighs are shaking, and his cock stands proudly up from his stomach, red and swollen and full.

Sydney licks his lips, meets and holds James' thick gaze, then swings his leg to settle over James' hips. The bed creaks and groans. Sydney holds himself up on his thighs, hovering in the air, giving James—giving each of them—one last chance to change his mind. James looks down at the thrumming space between their bodies and bites his lip, then throws his head back onto the pillow with a moan, lifting his hips up into the air towards Sydney's body.

"Please," James whispers in a high voice Sydney's never before heard him use. "God, please . . ."

With a rushing sigh, Sydney settles his full weight down on top of James' thighs, and they both gasp, two unleashed moans, when their flushed erections settle heavily against each other. Sydney can barely breathe at the spark of heat radiating up his spine, greying his vision and constricting his lungs.

"*Oh*," he whispers, right as James grips Sydney's hips hard and grunts, "God, like that . . ."

The soft afternoon light pours in through the open window looking out over the shore, bathing James' bare chest and stomach in smoke-like ribbons of gold. The light settles across the muscles of his shoulders, drapes over his firm, tanned arms, illuminates the freckles on his sun-kissed skin. It makes the scar look like a beautiful whirl of sand in a rippling tidepool.

Sydney leans down and licks a stripe up James' chest, tasting the sunlight on his skin, his hairs on his tongue, and James' hand flies up to grasp the back of Sydney's head to hold him close. James tastes like the ocean, as if he just stepped out of the Banzai waves only moments before.

Sydney slowly kisses and licks across his collarbone, down over his pectorals, the sides of his shaking shoulders, all the while slowly rocking his hips deeper into James' body, his erection rutting heavy and full against James' pulsing cock beneath him, the heavy weight of his balls pushing James down into the mattress.

And James' hands frantically clutch at his hair, the back of his neck, the length of his spine and the very lowest dip of his back as Sydney leaves a trail of wet, open kisses across his bare skin. He stops to lick at a nipple, moaning around the taste of the hardening bud under his lips, and a shiver of heat erupts down his sides as James cries out breathlessly and pushes his chest deeper into the heat of Sydney's mouth. Sydney bites his nipple softly between his teeth before moving his lips down, tracing them reverently over the muscles in James' stomach, moaning kisses over the strong lines of his body, breathing softly over the spot where his dog tags would have lain.

He pauses when he gets to the scar. Sydney looks up through his eyelashes to see James staring down at him as if he's looking straight up at the sun, overwhelmed and desperate, shocked at being seen. Sydney stops his rolling hips over James' arching body and instead holds himself still against James' warm, naked skin. The soft, curling hairs about James' cock caress the most sensitive spot in the dip of his thigh.

For the very first time, Sydney suddenly imagines—really closes his eyes and imagines—James Campbell lying in hospital sheets. He imagines the blood-stained gauze, and the Army-issue cot, and the way his eyes would squint as he stared up at the ceiling in pain. And James Campbell has never really told him any of this, not the details or the who or the how or the where, but something hot and sharp in Sydney's chest knows that nobody was sitting beside that hospital bed—nobody but the hourly nurse.

He opens his eyes to see a small frown on James' face.

"I don't . . ." Sydney swallows hard. "I don't know what I would've done."

James' frown turns to a sad smile. He runs a steady hand through Sydney's curls. "You wouldn't've done anything," he says in a heavy voice. "You wouldn't have even met me."

Sydney's whole body tenses. "Exactly. James . . . James, I—"

He can't finish. Instead, he helplessly opens and closes his lips, willing James to somehow read his unspoken words in the sheen over his eyes, then he takes a breath and bends his head to kiss the center of the scar etched into James' skin, reaching up as he does to cup James' cheek.

Time stops once again as he kisses the gnarled skin. He traces its outlines with his lips, tastes its different warmth with his tongue, holds James' body firmly against himself as he anchors him into the earth with his mouth. He wants to feel the bullet's weight on his own tongue, swallow it into his body, rub his skin with the bloody sand and mud from wherever James fell, and he doesn't know why the hell he can't have *normal* thoughts about James Campbell being shot in the chest, why he can't just say he's selfishly glad James survived and then move on, but he can't just . . . he can't—

James' lips press softly into the center of Sydney's palm. Sydney stills, holding his lips on a ridge of the scar, as James whispers words into his skin, bringing his hand up to hold Sydney's palm against his lips.

"It was on a beach" he breathes. Sydney immediately holds his breath so he can hear every syllable, and James clears his throat. "We were ambushed in the jungle, and—Sydney, it was chaos. There were bombs, and the rain, and I saw people just drop . . . and I couldn't . . . Keith. Keith was the man who saved me—my deck watch mate." James swallows. "Keith Hartman. He told me to run. It—it came at me from behind when I finally reached the shore. The bullet. Keith found me there in the water. Carried me with him when they pulled him up into the helicopter." He sighs. "You can't imagine the noise. The screams. And then . . . whoosh. Silence."

Sydney presses another kiss to James' chest as James' hand comes to rest gently in his hair—unbearably soft, as if those same fingers had never felt the screaming metal of a gun. Sydney closes his eyes, losing himself entirely to the soothing sound of James' living voice.

"I surfed there, too" James whispers, a small smile in his voice. "Just once. After." He sighs, and his fingertips send shivers across Sydney's scalp. "China Beach, they all called it. I promise I'll tell you about it another day."

Sydney nods. He wraps his arms around James ribs and presses his cheek into James' chest, curling himself into a small ball, half on top of James' body. James holds him with a grounding, easy pressure, and Sydney thinks that maybe they'll just stay like this forever, who even cares about the surfing and the sex, who even cares about standing upright, but then he hears James' heartbeat skip.

"I shot someone," James says, so softly Sydney can barely hear him over his own pounding heart. He feels a cold sweat suddenly break out across James' skin. James' hand leaves Sydney's back. "When I was . . . I was just trying to escape. And he came out of the trees. . . I just—just shot him without thinking. Without looking."

Sydney looks up sharply at the desperate, horrible sound of James' voice. The grey fear choking out the blue of James' eyes makes him want to weep.

Sydney presses his palm right over James' racing heart. He tries to steady his voice. "He died?"

James' eyes gloss over. "He was . . . he was just a kid. He died."

Sydney Moore decides, right then and there, that he will do everything in his power—he would give up *surfing*—if it means James Campbell never again has an expression on his face like he does right now.

James' entire body is tense, held in a flinch as if he's readying for Sydney to hurl himself back from his skin, or yell in his face, and instead all Sydney's frantic brain can piece together to do is to breathe out, "*James*," right before taking James' head in his hands and rushing his lips to his mouth.

And *oh*, they'd never really kissed before either, had they?

James melts. Sydney groans when James' hands fly back up to grip Sydney's spine and shoulders, and the sigh James' breathes into his mouth could be Sydney's one source of air for the rest of his life. Sydney frantically tries to blink away the water in his eyes as he tells James a million things with the caresses of his wet lips that he could never hope to put into words—not even if he had an endless number of days.

What feels like hours later, Sydney presses one last kiss to James' mouth before pulling away, running his thumb along the soft, wet skin beneath James' eye. They breathe in time together, long breaths filling the quiet air of the house.

To his surprise, James grins, shaking his head as light creeps back into the lines of his face. He casually rubs Sydney's upper arm. "Who the hell are you?" he whispers.

Sydney smiles as James' courage overflows to his own limbs. He tilts his head. "I'm the best surfer in Hawaii."

James laughs under his breath, the warm puffs of air flowing across Sydney's face. He wraps one of his calves around Sydney's leg. "Hang on, though. I thought you were *the* top surfer?"

Sydney grins at the new lightness in James' voice before leaning down to plant a kiss to James' forehead. "Yes, well, I've grown a bit humble. Mellowed out a bit," he quips.

James raises his eyebrows. "Oh?"

"Yes. In fact, I've met someone—someone very old and mature."

James rolls his eyes and brings his other hand to Sydney's hip, gripping him firmly and briefly pressing his cock up into the inside of Sydney's thigh.

James plays along, eyes glittering. "Well, who is she then?"

Sydney scoffs, then dramatically frowns. "James, you haven't heard? I'm also the gayest surfer in Hawaii."

"Oh, right," James laughs, reaching up to run his palm up Sydney's lean chest. He pauses to run his thumb slowly over his nipple. "I might have heard something about that. Some wild rumors. So who is *he?*"

Sydney smirks and rolls his hips languidly, rubbing his heavy balls slowly up and down James' erection, causing him to shut his eyes and moan.

"He's a professional surfer," Sydney says, starting to pant.

James smirks with his eyes closed, hands gripping hard at Sydney's waist. "Yeah? He must be good, then."

Sydney leans down to barely brush his lips across James' mouth. "*Very* good."

Suddenly Sydney remembers holding James up against the wall behind the surf shop, picturing the way his uniform would drape across the muscles in his arms and thighs, the gleaming dog tags on his chest . . .

The thought leaves him dizzy.

"He's also a sailor," Sydney gasps.

James flicks open his eyes and smirks, a flush spreading quickly across chest. "Oh, so we're allowed to talk about how you have a thing for men in uniform, then?"

Sydney scoffs, freezing like there's a beam of light on him through pitch dark. "I do not!"

James' eyes are sparkling. He gently smacks Sydney's thigh on top of him. "You fucking liar! Admit it. You've got a thing for it."

"That's fucking insane. My *father* was a man in uniform."

"Oh yeah? So was your teenage wank photo. And so is the naked man you got underneath you right now. Well, so *was*."

James reaches around to grab Sydney's ass hard, causing them both to groan at the friction. Sydney looks back down at James and feels a thousand words get caught in the back of his throat. He runs a hand slowly up James' hard stomach, settling over his chest.

"Let's stick with '*is*,'" he says, trying to catch his breath. Then he rolls his eyes at himself. "Fine. You might have a point."

"Damn right I have a point. I'm not fucking blind."

"Well you don't have to rub it in. You've got your own weird shit, too."

"Me?" James rubs idly across Sydney's ribs. "No way, man. I'm normal."

"You mean you're a square."

"Fine, I'm a square."

"But you're *gay.*"

James laughs as he pinches one of Sydney's nipples. "Fine, I'm a gay square."

Sydney can't help himself. He leans down to kiss James, the smile still on his lips, and they both relax into each other as the moment settles. Sydney gets lost in James' warm eyes, becoming aware once more of every place their naked skin is joined.

"God, you're beautiful," he says again, voice low.

James breathes sharply out through his nose and blinks hard before reaching up and pulling Sydney down onto him by the shoulders. "Come here," he whispers.

Sydney falls forward and drapes himself across James' body from chest to ankle, letting the full weight of him sink down onto James' warm skin. James grips at his back and reaches up to meet Sydney in a deep kiss, open and wet.

"Fuck, you feel good," James pants into his mouth.

"God, James."

"So fucking good on top of me."

Sydney groans into his mouth, licking and sucking at his lips. James' muscles are warm and solid beneath his body, rolling up into Sydney's touch, legs entwined at the thigh. Sydney wants to press himself so solidly into James Campbell that they become inseparable.

But then James tenses beneath him.

Sydney pulls back with fear in his throat, struggling to think of how to ask what's wrong, when James' hands are suddenly gripping hard at his shoulders, and he effortlessly flips Sydney over onto his back with a burst of muscle. It knocks the air from Sydney's lungs. His head smacks the pillow.

And *fuck,* James is on top of him, slotting his leg between Sydney's naked thighs and pressing his cock down hard into his hip, stomach to stomach and chest to chest. Nipples brushing over nipples. Sydney tries to breathe as James devours his mouth, hands roving up his sides and gripping at his skin, reaching around under the small of his back and pulling Sydney closer against himself.

The heavy, angular weight of James' body on top of him is maddening. Sydney thinks he might disappear—float up out of his body and be carried out across the waves on the warm breeze, leaving poor James Campbell to hump an empty bed.

But he doesn't disappear. Instead, Sydney grows slick with pulsing sweat as James' hands hold him down into the mattress. James presses one last kiss to Sydney's lips before moving down on his elbows towards Sydney's chest. James kisses him, every last inch of his bare skin.

Sydney can feel him carefully tasting his skin with his tongue, covering his shaking, sensitized body with warm, wet traces of his lips.

Sydney looks down at the golden sunlight glinting across the top of James' bent head and curses under his breath.

And Sydney thinks he can feel the smile on James lips as continues kissing down Sydney's stomach, up his sides, and down below his navel, as Sydney clings to James' back hard enough for his nails to etch deep into the tan skin. James looks up at Sydney, gasping a breath through swollen, wet lips, then he places his cheek in Sydney's pubic hair and rubs.

Sydney moans, staring down stunned at James pressing his face into his groin, slowly, deeply breathing in the scent of his skin. James' stubble catches the hairs on Sydney's upper thighs and pulls, and Sydney unconsciously spreads his legs for James to settle down between them. He places his shaking fingers in James' hair before he can talk himself out of it.

If there was a medal for being the hardest you've ever been in your life, Sydney knows without doubt he would currently win it.

James lifts up his hand, hesitates for a moment in the air, then places his palm gently around the length of Sydney's erection.

"God . . ." Sydney breathes, then he realizes with a jolt James has never actually touched it before, and his cock swells impossibly harder in James' hand, aching to be stroked.

James twitches his fingers, testing the weight of Sydney's cock against his palm. Then he looks up at Sydney for a blinding moment before turning his cheek into Sydney's groin and closing his eyes. Without looking, James takes a deep breath, tightens his grip, and *strokes.*

Sydney nearly shouts, and James flings opens his eyes, looks at his own tan fingers wrapped around Sydney's red and gleaming erection, and groans out loud, long and deep.

"Fuck yeah," Sydney moans. "God, touch it. Touch me . . ."

He's honestly not sure if he'll survive. James looks up at him again with deep blue eyes the color of the ocean in a storm, and Sydney's amazed that his own lungs continue functioning to take in air. He watches, chest heaving, as James slowly brings Sydney's pulsing cock towards his lips, licks them, then places a soft kiss midway along Sydney's shaft. He places another kiss closer to the tip, and another, covering Sydney's erection with the open, wet heat of his mouth.

James sighs, and if Sydney wasn't half out of his mind right now he would think that the way James' breath just quivered through his lungs meant that he was . . . that he was almost—

James kisses his throbbing erection again, tongue tip tracing a vein. Sydney's mind goes blank.

He holds his breath tightly in his chest as he stares at James looking down at his cock, then James licks his lips again, groans, and opens his mouth to rest the tip of Sydney's cock against the flat of his tongue, holding the weight of him carefully in his mouth.

Sydney cries out in a rush and fights the desperate, surging urge to thrust. It's been *years* since anyone did this to him. Since he was barely nineteen and in the back of a seedy gay bar in San Francisco— fresh off his first win at the Billabong a few months before and right after placing second earlier that day in a local competition in Santa Cruz. And that man hadn't kissed him, or traced the lines of his chest and stomach with his tongue, or kissed his *erection*.

And now James Campbell is sinking the tip of Sydney's cock deeper into his sucking mouth, running it between his wet velvet lips, tasting the heat of his skin and moaning out loud at the weight of it on his tongue.

Sydney's neck gives out. His head drops back down to the bed with a thump, and he grips what he can of James' hair with his fingers as he gently rolls his hips, letting the tip of his cock start to thrust between James' open lips. He gets lost in it—the puffs of air ghosting down his erection coming from James' nose, James' firm, smooth hand slowly fisting along his length, the deafening sound of their panting breaths in the buzzing air of the room, the tiny, trembling moans echoing from the tips of Sydney's lips.

Then it's gone.

His cock is suddenly wet and cold in the air, lying flat against his stomach. James is completely silent. Sydney flings open his eyes and pushes up on his elbow to look down.

He sees James sitting up on his knees, one hand gripping Sydney's thigh and the other one covering his eyes, head tipped down towards the mattress between Sydney's legs.

Sydney's heart hammers in his chest, and he swallows down a punch of fear in his throat. James is regretting it; it was too much. Sydney pressured him, told him to touch it, made James take off his clothes and lie down with him in bed and put his mouth around another penis like a queer. And James was trying to tell him how he was forced to kill a man, telling him about the war, and he didn't *want*—

Sydney forces himself to speak, hating the weak whimper of his voice.

"James?"

James sniffs wetly through his nose and runs his hand over his eyes. "Fuck, I'm sorry," he chokes out.

Sydney's heart shatters in his chest. He tries to sound calm, forcibly ignoring the fact that they're both still naked in his bed, cocks now only half-erect.

"It's alright. We don't have to," he rushes out, perfectly even. "James, I . . . I never meant to make you—we can just . . . you don't have to stay in our . . . in the bed with me. You don't have to—"

"No, you idiot." James takes his hand away from his eyes, and Sydney realizes with a gasp that he doesn't look angry. He sits up all the way, cowering back in confusion, when James reaches out to grip his hand hard.

James' voice is breaking and choked. "Just, do you have any idea how long . . . how long I've wanted to do that?" He pauses again to catch his breath, eyes shining when he blinks at the ceiling. "I can't—seventeen fucking years, Sydney. I've wanted to do this. Be with a . . . with a man like this. And it feels—" He swallows down a cry, shaking his head self-deprecatingly before running his forearm over his face. "It just feels so fucking good."

"*Oh*, James."

Sydney rushes forward and cups James' face in his hands, immediately kissing him softly on the mouth. He can't stop. When James doesn't pull away, Sydney kisses him again and again, tiny sips of kisses against his trembling lips, reminding them both that this is real.

"You are a marvel," Sydney whispers against his mouth, wiping at James' wet cheeks with his thumbs.

James huffs out a laugh and sniffs hard again. "God, could I cry any more fucking times today, do you think? Make it an even ten or something?"

Sydney kisses his closed eyelid, brushing away the saltwater with his lips. "I don't mind," he says, honestly.

James pulls back and looks at him skeptically. "Come on. I'm not exactly helping the mood. Came here with big ideas to . . . throw you up against a wall or something."

Sydney tightens his grip on James' hand as James shakes his head and shrugs.

"Trust me," Sydney says, "I'll be the last one to stop you from doing that." He kisses his mouth. "Right now, though." Kisses him again. "God, you have no idea, James." And again. "You have no idea."

James deepens the kiss with a groan, the caress turning heated. "I think I do," he whispers.

A thought pops into Sydney's head so suddenly, so forcefully, he's amazed he hadn't planned it out in perfect detail before. It's dark and twisted, sending shivers across his skin. It's beautiful.

"Would you—" He pauses, licking his lips. He summons the courage he'll need to surf Waimea tomorrow and tries again. "Do you want to try doing that at the same time?"

James pulls back and frowns, thumb running over Sydney's bottom lip. "What, su—" He stutters, then pushes through. "Suck you off?"

Sydney tries to breathe. "Suck *us* off."

James' eyes pool black, blown open wide, lips trembling. "How can you even . . ."

Sydney leaves one last sloppy kiss on James' lips, then grips the back of his head and pushes him down hard onto the bed, overcome with hot desire thrumming through his veins.

"Fuck yeah," James breathes. "Sydney, *fuck . . .*"

Sydney twists away from him, lying down the other way so his head is near James' cock, now half-hard and swelling again, bobbing maddeningly into the air. Sydney licks his lips, shifting to awkwardly try and better position them both, mouth-watering.

His brain frantically flies through the potential steps—how they should move, where they should be. He thinks maybe he's taking too long, that maybe this was too twisted—too fucking much. Then James' hand is on the back of his head, gripping his curls, and he abruptly pushes Sydney's lips down hard around his cock as he groans.

"God, suck me." James' fingers tighten. "Take it."

Sydney takes it.

He grips the base of James' cock in his hand, wraps the other around James' warm thigh by his cheek, then takes James down as far back in his throat as he can, feeling him swell to hardness on his tongue.

He licks along the skin, sucking as he swallows, reminding himself of the beautiful weight and rhythm, and he knows that James is watching, his head resting on Sydney's hip. Sydney can feel the stubble from James' cheek on his bare skin like electric shocks of pleasure. James rubs at his side, wraps the other arm around Sydney's thigh, and rolls his hips slowly, pressing himself deeper into Sydney's open mouth as Sydney grabs desperately at the back of his ass, pulling him close against his face.

He groans around James' cock, half a curse and half James' name.

Without warning, the stubble is gone from his hip, and before Sydney can even process that he's dripping precome down his own erection, his aching cock is suddenly enveloped in tight, wet heat— *swallowed.*

James groans against his penis, sending vibrations through his throbbing skin, and Sydney cries out with his tongue wrapped around James' cock. James' erection is swollen and heavy on his tongue, leaking and hot, and James' cheek is rasping against his inner thigh, and James' lips are sucking down the length of his erection and groaning like he can't get enough of the taste. Sydney clings to James' thrusting body, face buried in his groin, James' full cock hot and throbbing in his mouth, and thinks that he could do *this* forever—forget lying innocently in each other's arms.

They roll into each other—press and push and thrust. The room is filled with the wet sounds of thick cocks slipping across lapping tongues. Sydney breathes out his nose, grips James' ass harder in his hand, and grinds him deep against his face, taking him all the day down until his pubic hair rubs a rash against his chin.

James pulls off and reaches down to grip at Sydney's hair. "Fucking hell, Moore," he pants. Sydney opens his eyes to glimpse spit on James' chin, and James licks his lips. "God, fucking look at you."

Then those lips are back around Sydney's cock in a deep moan, licking up the precome from his slit and moaning at the taste before sucking him down again deep.

Sweat trickles down Sydney's back as he bobs his head and rocks his hips, overcome by the sensation vibrating through both ends of his body. James' thighs are sweating under his palms, trembling as they rock into his mouth, every moan thrumming straight into his own cock.

He's not going to last. With a gasp, he pulls off, rubbing James' cock against his cheek. "Fuck, James, I can't—shit I'm gonna come." He squeezes his eyes shut and moans, wildly thrusting his hips, shoving himself across James' sweet tongue, straight down his throat. "I'm gonna come."

James sucks him hard and fast, cheeks hallowed around his cock while his hand slaps Sydney's ass hard and grips. Sydney buries his face in James' groin at the base of his throbbing cock and looks down to watch his own erection disappear again and again into James' mouth, wet and glistening, precome and spit dripping down his chin in a thick sheen. Spreading his lips.

"James," he moans. "James, I—*fuck*!"

James nods around his cock and grips his hip hard, and Sydney's climax explodes across his skin, pulsing out of his cock straight down James' throat as James moans deep and slow at the taste.

Sydney lets out a silent cry, gasping for enough air. James waits until the last pulses burst across his tongue, then pulls off Sydney's cock with a grunt deep in his chest. He places a wet kiss at the base, burying his nose in Sydney's hair.

Sydney's lungs heave. His limbs are loose and wild. He grabs for James' arm, yanking him hard back up towards him.

"Sit on my face," he hears himself beg.

James curses and hurls himself down to lick into Sydney's mouth, forcing Sydney to taste himself in a hot and frantic kiss, then he scoots forward on his knees until his hips are over Sydney's neck. He holds himself up over Sydney on shaking thighs and grips his erection with his hand, guiding it gently towards Sydney's lips.

Sydney looks up at him and wants to cry. He looks beautiful. The light off the ocean reflects and ripples across his sweating skin, and his hair is rough and wild, his skin glistening and flushed. Muscled chest heaving. Lips pink and swollen and wet. Sydney reaches around to grab James' ass firmly in both hands and pulls him towards himself, letting James guide his bobbing cock to the tips of Sydney's lips. Sydney laps out with his tongue at the wet slit, licking up the precome and swallowing it with a consuming moan, then he opens his mouth wide and pulls James forward until his cock sinks all the way in.

Sydney looks up at James, lips almost painfully stretched around his throbbing erection, and winks.

James laughs, eyes blown wide. "God, you're something else," he whispers. He plants one hand on the wall in front of him and grips Sydney's hair with the other. They share a brief, breathless look—raised eyebrows from James, and Sydney gives a small nod. Then James slowly rocks his hips forward on his sturdy thighs, driving his cock between Sydney's wet and open lips. Straight down his throat.

James bites his own lips and groans. "Fuck, just look at you. Look at your fucking mouth."

Sydney sucks hard at the tip as James pulls out again and immediately thrusts back in, hitting the back of Sydney's throat with a grunt. "Your *mouth . . .*"

Sydney stares up, eyes blown wide, as James traces the outline of Sydney's stretched lips with his thumb, feeling where they grip around his thick cock. James looks wrecked—thoroughly fucked. The most desirable thing Sydney has ever seen in his life.

Sydney grips him hard as James rolls his hips, clenching the muscles in his abs and brushing his tight and heavy balls against Sydney's wet chin.

James' hand on the wall turns to a fist. The deep thrusts of his cock pick up speed. "Shit, Moore," he growls, eyes black and mouth open. "Swallow me. God . . . Gonna come down your fucking throat." James gasps once up at the ceiling, baring his glistening neck and chest, before he stares back down at Sydney and grips Sydney's curls with both hands.

He wails. "*God*, Moore. Fuck, your mouth. Gonna come . . . come down—"

He lets out a breathless cry and grips Sydney's hair hard enough to sting, frantically fucking into his mouth as Sydney's tongue is blasted with a wave of hot and salty cum. He gulps it down, eyes blown wide, staring up at James Campbell's face as he comes with Sydney's name a moan on his lips.

He remembers he is in love with James Campbell, although he never really forgot.

Sydney pants for breath when James slowly guides his cock back out of his mouth, lips and chin and mouth absolutely dripping with James' cum, the hot taste of him still rolling down his throat. James looks down at him, shakes his head slowly, then flings himself down on top of Sydney's body, covering him with his weight and wordlessly pulling him into a kiss, deep and slow.

They moan as their tongues brush, trading the tastes of each other. Sydney clings to James' slick back and shoulders, nails digging into his skin, desperate for the weight of him on his chest. Then, finally, James sighs into his mouth before falling off Sydney's body with a grunt, rolling heavily onto his back.

He pants up at the ceiling, one arm thrown over his eyes. "You," he whispers. He laughs once. "God, you."

Sydney turns onto his side and pulls James gently into his arms, and a warm ache tugs in his chest when James easily rolls into the embrace, letting Sydney pull him close and hold him. They come down slowly together, panting breaths gradually evening out, sweating skin starting to cool in the breeze as heartbeats fade to normal.

Sydney buries his nose in James' soft hair and inhales over and over, memorizing the combined scent of them. James' penis is warm and soft now, pressed against his legs, the space between James' thighs still damp from his release mixed with Sydney's own spit.

Finally, Sydney cups James' jaw in his hand and pulls him back up for a last kiss, gentle and long. Sydney groans softly into his mouth, holding him close, reveling in every inch of their warm skin still pressed together. He shifts heavy and sated limbs, trying to grow impossibly close.

James smiles at him, eyes glowing and soft in the late afternoon sun, and the three words Sydney had tried to say in the middle of a desperate kiss five days ago come flying up once again into his mouth, perched and buzzing on the tips of his lips.

But he swallows them down. It isn't time—not yet. Then he brushes James' hair back from his face, resting with their legs entwined.

He licks his lips and whispers, knowing his voice will be hoarse. "You know that Waimea is tomorrow," he says.

James nods. "S'why I made sure I got back here by today."

Sydney's heart flutters hotly, and he leans forward to brush another kiss across James' mouth. The breeze off the ocean dances across their skin with rippling shivers, and Sydney reaches down to pull a blanket up over them, holding James closer in his arms.

James looks at him with serious eyes once they're settled. "It scares the shit out of me knowing you're surfing those waves tomorrow."

Sydney nods once. "I know."

He's well aware of what he's up against. Men die off Waimea. Brilliant surfers get flung from their boards, and crack their heads against the reefs and rocks below, and drown in the whitewater, bodies sometimes never to be found.

James' eyes are glistening. "I . . . Sydney, I don't know what I would do if you don't—I don't know."

Sydney tilts his head up to press his lips between James' eyes, trying to breathe a confidence he doesn't quite feel into his skin.

"Won't be that bad," he says, tone light. "I had to watch you surf the Pipeline, you know. You even wiped out and stayed under for a bit to give me a nice flashback. Test my nerves."

James laughs. "Those weren't fucking fifty foot tall waves, you dick."

"Well, compared to your short ass, they practically were," Sydney shoots back, desperate to see the fear fade away from James' eyes.

And it does. James barks out another laugh and rolls his eyes before smacking him hard in the arm. Sydney fights back, smirking, straining against James' grip, and then they're wrestling for leverage, the blanket pushed off onto the floor. James throws a strong thigh over Sydney's hip and rolls on top of him, pinning him down and settling his weight on Sydney's body. Sydney's hands rub gently at the small of James' back, the fine hairs tickling his fingertips.

James runs his hand through Sydney's curls, and Sydney lets himself arch into the touch, eyes falling closed. James' thumb runs along the thin skin under his eye.

"You look exhausted," James says. "I wanted to tell you earlier."

Sydney hums, warm tingles dripping down his neck and back as James' fingers run through his hair. He feels hotly embarrassed now about his sleepless nights standing alone by the waves, not knowing that James Campbell was at that very moment finding his way back to him for good.

He feels James' lips suddenly brush against his face, kissing the sleep-deprived bags under his eyes.

"Right," James says firmly, clearing his throat. "Here's what we're gonna do. I'm gonna get all my shit that's sitting outside melting in the sun, and you're gonna clear out a drawer for me so I don't feel like I'm in a fucking hotel. Then you'll sit down and eat something because you look like you've lost ten pounds since I last saw you. And I'll tell you about all the shit and fucking red tape I had to go through this last week so I could move my life out here, so you can be grateful I didn't give up and just say fuck it all."

Sydney opens his eyes, and James is looking down at him with such quiet fondness that Sydney wants to say fuck it all to James' plans and hold him against his body in bed all day instead.

James chuckles under his breath and continues to brush through Sydney's hair. Sydney feels like this should make him feel hopelessly young and naive, but it doesn't.

"I know," James says, reading his thoughts. "Tonight we'll . . . we'll be back here. But right now you gotta eat something so you don't drown on me tomorrow. You can tell me all about your strategy and whatever other weird science shit you've got going on up in there."

James leans down to kiss him softly, and Sydney melts under his touch. Then James pats his cheek and rolls up from the bed with a groan, standing to stretch out his arms above his head and giving Sydney an absolutely fantastic view of his ass.

"Thought my legs were gonna fall off in that plane," he groans.

Sydney heaves himself from the sheets and follows James out into the main room of the house on shaking legs, embarrassingly desperate not to let him out of his sight. "How the fuck do you think I feel in a plane—my legs are three feet longer than yours," he tries to joke back.

He feels drunk as James mutters something under his breath back at him. Half-asleep and half-dead and half up floating in heaven. James walks naked through the house with steady, confident limbs, not hesitating in his steps as he walks over to the kitchen cabinets and looks through them for something to make for them to eat.

Sydney watches him, openly staring. Amazed that James Campbell is naked in his kitchen, not clutching a bundle of clothes over himself, looking like he's been standing there just like this every afternoon for decades. The broad lines of his back and shoulders are silhouetted by the vast, rolling horizon of the sea through the window, painting wisps of deep golden light across his skin.

James talks casually over his shoulder. "Should take a shower while I do this. You smell like sex and it's fucking distracting."

Sydney turns like a sheep to follow James' instructions, then immediately whips back around.

He needs James to know—needs him to somehow understand that just that morning Sydney had stood in this very same spot and contemplated whispering his own name into the silence just to be able to hear it. To pretend that James' voice was echoing through his house, carried effortlessly on the salty breeze where it would never be carried ever again.

And now James is here. *Cooking.* Telling him he smells like sex because they just *had* sex and not looking uncertain in the least. And he told Sydney about the worst moment in his entire life, and his shoulders aren't even *tense.*

Sydney stands in the place where James had stood five days ago with a bundle of clothes in front of his groin, and he hesitantly calls out his name in a weak voice.

"James."

James pauses and turns around, feet firmly planted on the hardwood, brows raised.

Sydney opens his mouth to try to speak again, but can't. James Campbell is beautiful in his home. In *their* home. A powerful beam of the sun. Crackling and warm deep down in the pit of Sydney's chest.

James' mouth softly twists, and his eyes glitter for a moment. "I know, Sydney," he whispers. He gives a little shrug, as if that could somehow encompass everything they've just done. "I know."

His eyes roam quickly over Sydney's body, taking in his still-damp thighs, and his soft penis, and the curls stuck to the sides of his neck with sweat. Sydney holds his chin high, not letting himself shrink away. Then James nods his head at the shower behind him and turns back around to keep cooking, hands working open a bag of pasta from the back of a cupboard.

In a daze, Sydney tears his eyes away and wanders into the shower, leaving the light off as he does. He stands under the warm spray and looks down at his own body in the steaming darkness, tracing the faint marks he can feel from James' fingers and teeth and stubble all over his skin.

He'll conquer the tallest waves on earth tomorrow. Gut strong and hands steady and neck held high, flinging himself down into the spray from the heavens, fighting against the great heaving force of the water and foam.

He'll do it because James Campbell's deep blue eyes will be seeking him out from the sand.

And Sydney now knows that they will be. They definitely, unequivocally will.

Sydney covers his face with his hands, then slicks back his wet hair. He lets the steaming water pound against his face and chest, then finally whispers into the spray the words that had been hovering on the tip of his tongue for one hundred and forty-seven hours.

"I love you." Lost immediately to the rushing hiss of the water.

"God, I love you."

# 23

James stands in the middle of the darkened bedroom and looks down at Sydney sleeping on his stomach like the dead, sheets tangled around his waist and curls plastered to one side of his head.

It's just before six in the morning, and James has been wide awake since four. They'd fallen asleep early the night before; Sydney was so exhausted his eyes had been drooping shut over dinner, head slinking back in the chair out on the porch overlooking the ocean while James rambled on about finding a new renter for his apartment, and quitting his job, and finally getting that call from Val's, and deciding whether to ship his board out to Oahu or just say screw it and use some sponsorship money to buy a new one.

He hadn't told Sydney about Rob, though. The words had been certainly hovering there in the air the whole evening, desperate and yearning to come out. It would have been so easy to wait until Sydney's eyes were closed, his head sleepily rolled back, and whisper that he actually told someone he was gay, in those exact words and out loud. That the world didn't end. And that all he could think about in that moment was how the hell he was gonna get back to Sydney's arms.

But the second James opened his mouth to do just that, he knew he needed Sydney to be fully awake to hear it all, not drifting off in a doze with half a smile on his lips, one hand reaching out to gently cling to the hem of James' shorts, not even letting go when he drifted off to a deep sleep.

And James had done exactly what Sydney did for him a week ago. Had woken him up gently and lead him half-asleep by the hand into the bedroom. Slowly stripped him of his clothes and climbed into bed beside him after taking one final piss and washing his face. And Sydney had nestled against his chest and clung to him tightly as he started slipping back effortlessly into his dreams, breath hot and damp where it blew on James' skin. James had listened to him sleep while tracing the lines of his tattoo with his fingertips, watching the moonlight ripple across his back through the window.

At first James hadn't dreamed at all. Then he'd dreamed of Los Angeles—palm trees with giant green surfboards for fronds, and Lori begging him to find Josie, who was lost, and Sydney finding her miles out in the ocean treading water, then hauling her back through the sea in his arms only for all of them to realize he'd accidentally captured a dolphin instead.

James had fallen out of the dream with a jolting thud and blinked open his eyes to discover that Sydney was pinning him down to the bed—one thigh draped across both of his legs, one arm flung across his chest and his nose buried right in James' armpit.

And James had chuckled and kissed Sydney's curls. Smiled like hell into the darkness that this was his life. He'd taken advantage of the private dark to be awed by the sensation of hard lines of muscle weighing him down with tender sleep. And he'd blinked hard up at the ceiling knowing that this was now his home—that he *lived* here. With him.

Then he'd closed his eyes again and dreamed of Waimea. Of surging waves one thousand feet tall, black as tar, rushing towards the shore with the sound of screams echoing through a hot jungle. And Sydney had been dangling like a ragdoll from the crest, reaching down for his falling aviators, and James ran and ran and ran to catch him, but his shoulder exploded before he could get there in time to break his fall.

James had gasped awake and stared at the ceiling with greying vision, heart pounding and limbs covered in a thick sweat. Once he finally convinced himself that Sydney was safe and alive next to him, he'd realized that the ache in his shoulder was real. Pain radiated out from where Sydney's head was pressing down onto him, heavy with sleep. He tried to slip his arm away, but Sydney clung tighter to him in his sleep.

So James had tried and failed for almost an hour to look down at Sydney's soft and vulnerable face and not picture it pale and draped with seaweed, floating endlessly in the depths of the sea like a ghost. Swallowed up whole by the deep.

And when sleep failed him, and his shoulder felt on fire, James had pressed one last kiss into Sydney's curls then quickly slipped out from under him with a grimace, fighting against Sydney's pull. He told himself that if he lay there any longer, it would be like admitting that they might never get to do it again.

He'd stood in the kitchen and looked out the window at the moonlit waves. He'd paced. Taken a shower and fought back whimpers as he tried to stretch out his screaming shoulder under the hot and steaming spray. And then he'd come back into the room, *their* room, and just sat on the edge of the bed—feeling like the biggest creep in the world for sitting there in the dark just watching Sydney sleep. He'd reached up and gently held Sydney's hand, draped up over his head on the pillow like some wild kid who'd finally fallen asleep where he collapsed.

James had sat in the dark, and counted the steady thrumming pulse under the thin skin of Sydney's wrist.

And now James stands over the bed, counting down the seconds until he has to wake Sydney up to get ready, hating the part of himself that wants to climb back into bed and force himself to fall back asleep so they'll both sleep in too late to make it to Waimea on time, since he knows neither of them set the alarm clock the night before.

Sydney looks so young and open, strong and alive even in a dead sleep. The sculpted lines of his back rise and fall with his breath, glinting with the faint moonlight spilling into the room from the reflection off the sand outside.

James wants to ask him why they left his mom back in Arizona, and when he realized he was gay, and how many Sundays he's spent sitting in church—if he believes in God, and if he hates his stepmom as much as his dad. He wants to ask him where he's travelled, all the beaches he's surfed, all his different schools. He wants to ask him why he's never heard him say anything about going to college.

James feels as though he could trace every inch and corner of Sydney's body and somehow feel the answers in the lines of his skin. As if there had been an invisible barrier between them all this time, the thinnest film, which was only removed the moment Sydney Moore bent his beautiful head and kissed James' scar.

But James doesn't ask him any of these things, and he doesn't trace the lines of Sydney's soft skin. Sydney dreams on, lightly snoring as he breathes.

With a resigned sigh and a forced nod, James sits back down on the edge of the bed and kisses the center of Sydney's back, then rubs his hand along the warm skin in slow, firm circles.

Sydney starts to stir, and James leans down to kiss him again.

"Hey you," he whispers. "Should get up. Have something to eat."

Sydney groans and shoves his face farther into the pillow. James chuckles under his breath at the sight, filled with a rushing, nameless emotion, and Sydney immediately bolts upright at the noise, staring blearily in James' direction with fast blinking eyes. Then he collapses back into the pillows with a squinting frown.

"James?"

James can't help it. Sydney looks so confused and rumpled and *Sydney* in the soft grey light that he wants to take a photo and paint it onto his own skin, right next to his heart. He wonders just when over the last twenty-four hours he became a useless, emotional sap.

He leans down and places a soft kiss on Sydney's lips, and that's when Sydney completely freezes below him.

James frowns and pulls back. Sydney stares up at him, eyes blinking, mouth frozen open in the position it had been in under James' lips.

Then all of a sudden the light flicks on behind his eyes, and James' chest clenches as he watches a wave of pure, disbelieving relief wash over Sydney's face. Sydney surges onto his elbows, reaches up with both hands to cup James' face, then pulls him down into a deep kiss with a moan.

The kiss is perfect. Warm. Overflowing with honeyed joy and soft velvet comfort and home. James finally relaxes as the last remaining tendrils of fear from his nightmare gently wisp away from his body. The lines of his shoulders soften, and a bit of the churning anxiety deep in his gut slows to a temporary calm.

Sydney pulls back after one final press of his lips to James' mouth and heaves a great sigh, thumping back onto the pillow with his curls fanned out around his head and staring up at James with a bleary-eyed smile.

James laughs. "What, did you think it was all a dream?"

Sydney looks caught out for a moment, eyes wide and young, and then he snorts and shoots James a look that says he's an idiot. "Of course not. Obviously you're here. Your clothes from yesterday are right there on the floor, my mattress has a dip towards the side you were sleeping on, and the air smells like you. Plus I have a rash from your fucking stubble on the inside of my thigh."

Their rough, low voices sound crisp in the intimate darkness—etched permanently into the air of the house, and set apart from the rest of the world churning just beyond the windows.

James smirks, running his thumb across Sydney's chin. "Good. That way you'll remember me when the saltwater gets in it and stings so you don't do anything too stupid today."

They share a quiet look, and something tingles up the back of James' neck—something heavy and permanent. He clears his throat before the moment can turn too serious, needing to lose himself in a boring morning routine so he can pretend that Sydney's not about to go fling himself off the tops of the tallest waves on earth.

James leans down to kiss Sydney's cheek and gives his other cheek a soft pat. "I'll start coffee. You get ready and then we'll go. I know you'll wanna watch the waves for a while before it starts."

Sydney turns his face to press a kiss into James' palm and whispers, "okay," and with an internal sigh, James drags himself away and starts to pull on boardshorts and a t-shirt from the drawer Sydney had cleared out for him in his dresser the night before.

He makes his way out into the dark kitchen, listening to Sydney start to get up and rummage around for things back in the room. It sounds so right—hearing another person walking about, creaking on the floorboards, opening doors and moving clothes. James can't quite believe he survived for so many years in a silent apartment, only ever hearing the sounds of his neighbors through the thin walls.

He can't figure out Sydney's goddamn coffee contraption to save his life. After ten minutes of cursing under his breath, he gives up and puts on some boiling water. He finds a loose teabag deep in the back of the silverware drawer and bobs it up and down haphazardly in the steaming water, pretending that his stupid hands aren't shaking.

By the time he has a mug full of over-steeped and stale tea, the gripping fear is already back in full force, pulsing through his body in black, heated bursts. He looks out the kitchen window and holds the un-drunk tea in his hands, watching the calm tide lap gently at Sydney's shore and picturing towering walls of water in his mind, ripping across the surface of the ocean and roaring as they break over into a fury of whitewater and foam, crushing Sydney's limp body beneath them, burying him deep under thick, wet sand.

He startles when Sydney's arms wrap around him from behind.

"Why the hell are you drinking tea?" he mumbles.

James leans back into his body, heart still pounding, and tries to huff out a laugh. "Couldn't figure out your damn coffee machine."

Sydney reaches around and takes the mug carefully from his hands, places it on the counter, then wraps James fully in his embrace, pulling him back into his body until James finally lets his neck rest back against Sydney's chest. He can feel that Sydney is dressed and ready behind him, smelling like soap and toothpaste with just the tiniest hint of sunscreen.

James can't even remember hearing him get ready after those first few minutes. He'd only heard the screaming crashes of the waves, and the slap of choking clumps of seaweed, and the booming roar of the thick water bashing against the rocks.

Sydney hugs him tighter and presses his face into the side of James' neck.

"You know you can ask me not to do this," he whispers low. "One word from you and I'll listen. I won't go out there." Sydney presses his lips into a soft kiss on James' skin. "I really mean that."

James wants to moan. He reaches up to grip Sydney's forearm hard, fighting with himself to keep from shaking even more than he already is. They stand there for a long time. Sydney waits patiently, face pressed close into James' neck and breathing slow and steady at his back, holding them both upright on the cool wood floor.

James wants to turn around in Sydney's arms and press their lips together and whisper into his mouth, "*Yes, please, I'm begging you not to go out there and do this. I'm fucking begging you.*"

He wants to take Sydney's hand and lead him to literally any other beach along the North Shore, or any other beach in Hawaii, or in the entire world. Say, "*Here, come surf with me. We can surf together each morning and go home each night to our bed. Just not Waimea. Anywhere but Waimea. Please.*"

Then he sees a tattoo-less Sydney in his mind, standing ankle deep in the shallows on an empty beach and screaming out "*fuck you!*" across the still water, a trash bag of belongings waiting behind him in the sand. He sees Danny Moore standing alone and aloof on the shore with an empty circle cast around him like a curse, all alone in the middle of a crowd.

James closes his eyes and grits his teeth against the sinking pain in his chest. He's ashamed that it took him this long to figure it out—to see the truth deep inside the man whom he's been unable to take his eyes off for weeks.

That this isn't just a game for Sydney Moore, either.

Finally, James shakes his head no and sighs, sinking back into Sydney's arms. He clears his throat and tries to speak, but his voice is barely a whisper. "You let me get on that plane," he says. "I couldn't . . . I can't ask you not to do this. I want to, more than anything, fucking believe me. But, I can't. I won't."

Sydney nods, brushing his face against James' neck, and he moves his palm up to cover the scar under James' thin shirt. The warmth from Sydney's hand is hot like an iron—a kiss and a burn and a warm fire on the blackest winter night all at once. The tingling of his mom's coral fingernails scratching lightly at his scalp.

"Thank you," Sydney whispers. He moves his hand up to grip harder at James' shoulder, tightening their embrace, when suddenly pain radiates out in a burst of fire from his socket.

James winces with a hiss before he can hide his reaction, and Sydney freezes, then whips his hands off James' body. He stumbles back.

"You're hurt! You didn't tell me you were hurt."

James rolls his arm, fighting an angry blush, and turns to face Sydney, looking worried and something like afraid.

James shakes his head softly. "It's nothing, don't worry about—"

"God, I fell asleep on you. My head was on your shoulder. I pinned it down in the same position all night and then you woke up this morning in pain."

"Really, Sydney, it's fine. It's not your fault, just—"

"But I should have known. I should have realized before I fell asleep that I was hurting you."

Sydney's eyes are wide and anxious, chest wildly heaving, and James reaches out to grip his arm hard, trying to bring him back down to earth.

"Listen to me," he says in his steadiest voice. "Listen to me."

Sydney rapidly blinks and slowly focuses on James, his whole body trembling like he's coming out of a panicked daze. James tries not to wince again as he raises his left arm to grip at Sydney's other shoulder, holding him hard and firm.

"Neither one of us is talking about my goddamn shoulder right now," he says. "Yeah. I got shot. Sometimes it fucking hurts. But I also had nightmares half the fucking night of you drowning from a thousand foot tall wave, and you're scared right now that if you go out and do this I won't still be on the beach waiting for you by the time you come back. So listen to me."

He takes a deep breath, and relaxes his grip on Sydney's arm, stroking his skin. "I'm not leaving," he whispers. "You're going to do this. And we're going to have fucking mind blowing sex tonight because you'll still be alive, and I'll still be here, and I don't give a shit if my shoulder hurts for one day, okay?"

James shakes Sydney once gently, trying with every ounce of energy he can muster to mask the fear still churning behind his eyes—to look calm and assured and easy. Trying not to show how shocked he is at himself for talking so freely about the fact that they're going to have even more sex.

Sydney studies his face, pale eyes roaming over his features until they finally blink hard and settle. He gives a tiny nod, then smiles at the corner of his mouth. "Aye aye, Captain," he says.

James immediately huffs and shoves Sydney away from him, drawing in a deep breath of oxygen now that the air isn't thick and charged.

"You're fucking disgusting," James groans. "Now make us some coffee with your fucking spaceship here so I don't fall asleep today, and then you're gonna drive us *like a normal person* to Waimea because I swear to God I'll have a heart attack on you if you try and swerve us into a fucking goat again, alright?"

James turns to head back into the bedroom and gather his stuff when suddenly Sydney's hand is gripping his face, pulling him back quickly towards him and planting a deep, warm kiss on James' mouth. James reaches out and grabs a handful of Sydney's shirt in his shaking palms, sighing into the kiss. He can taste the relief on the tips of Sydney's lips—the warm, soft pulse of understanding, of gratefulness, that James didn't ask him not to surf.

James pulls back reluctantly, still clinging to Sydney's shirt. "Come on. You'll be late," he says roughly. He rubs his hands over Sydney's chest one last time before stepping aside to let him walk by, not missing the chance to slap his ass.

James lets himself stare at Sydney's back for just a moment as he starts to make the coffee. His eyes trace the firm lines of his back and shoulders, the strength in his arms, the dip of his hips and muscles in his thighs. Bony ankles perfectly balanced on hardwood.

He lets himself stare, and he tells himself that he'll be able to see this sight every morning until somebody walks in and physically drags him away.

And he tells himself that Sydney Moore will surf Waimea's tallest waves today. And that he will live.

# 24

"Oh, so you *can* drive like a normal person on the way to a competition. I wasn't sure if it was physically possible."

"Seriously? I drove just fine that first day I took you around the island. And on our way to the—on your last day here."

"Yeah, I realize that, genius. I said *on the way to a competition.* It's physically possible. For you. To drive without killing us before we get there."

"Well I'm not fucking nervous this time, that's why, Captain Smartass."

"No, no, no, this whole 'captain' thing has gotta go. Right now. Gone."

"Yes, Cap'n," Sydney smirks.

"Jesus Christ. Nevermind. You just—wait, hold on a second. *How* the hell are you not nervous this time? You didn't even surf before!"

"Exactly! You were the one surfing, and it was goddamn nerve wracking to watch."

"Oh, coming from the man who told me every five seconds I was *going* to win."

"Well that wasn't a for sure thing! I can't fucking predict the future!"

James laughs under his breath and shakes his head, covering his smile with his palm while he stares out the Jeep window at the fragrant rolling green.

"Seriously, you're about to surf down the most fucking dangerous waves on earth and you were more nervous sitting on your ass and watching me flail about? You're something else."

Sydney leans over and places his palm on James' knee, gripping tight. "James," he says. The sudden change in tone of his voice causes James to pause and turn his head. Sydney glances at him once, looking like he's about to tell him it's their last day on earth.

"James," he says again, when James' eyes are locked on to the side of his face. "I've never wanted anything more in my life than I wanted you to win that title. It was the most invested I have *ever* been in a competition. Do you get me?"

James swallows hard. He finds he can't bare to blink. Sydney's eyes when they look at him again are the clear open sky, pouring out emotion like they've never spoken a more raw truth in his life. James clears his throat and nods, covering Sydney's hand with his.

They gaze at each other, the moment quickly turning heavy, tumbling towards unspeakable words which James shockingly realizes he has already prepped on the tip of his tongue. Just as James starts opening his mouth to speak, half overcome and half terrified at what might pour out, he glimpses the barest hint of color out of the corner of his eye.

"Fucking God, Sydney, the cliff! Watch the fucking road, you fucking lunatic!"

Sydney cranks the wheel hard back onto the road, away from the precarious edge of screaming blue sky.

James' heart explodes in his chest, shooting right up into his throat. "Do you have any idea—we could have died! Goddammit, you can't fucking drive for shit!"

And then James realizes that the odd sound filling the car isn't him yelling, or even the sound of the engine.

It's Sydney laughing. *Laughing*. Leaning forward over his knees and thumping his palm on the wheel as he gasps for breath.

James sucks in a slow, furious whistle and tries to calm his voice. "You fucker, you did that on purpose, didn't you?" he says.

Sydney wipes a tear from the corner of his eye. "James, I could drive this road with my eyes closed, there's no way I could ever—"

"—fucking *don't*!"

"—*possibly* drive us off a cliff." Sydney pauses again to calm himself, trying to talk over the laugh warping his lips. "God, you . . . you're adorable," he says.

James stills. The word settles over his body like a warm shiver, starting at the base of his spine and ending in a tight burst across his scalp.

He's never been called that before in his life. Never imagined that he would ever want to hear that word directed at him from the lips of someone whom he had just fucked in the last twelve hours. And now the desire to get out and walk over to the driver's side door and kiss Sydney Moore is so strong that he nearly chokes trying to get the words out.

"Pull over."

The smile freezes on Sydney's face, and his eyes narrow. "What?"

James can barely think clearly. The thought that this might be his last ever chance to kiss Sydney hovers dangerously at the back of his mind, and his voice shakes when he repeats himself. "Pull the car over. Stop the car."

Sydney looks over his shoulder, then pulls over to the side of the empty highway, lips pursed with worry and something like confused exasperation. "James I didn't mean . . . look, that's not a *bad* thing, you know, I just meant—"

"Not a bad thing at all, just wait a damn second."

James practically flings himself from the passenger seat and jogs around the back of the Jeep. Sydney is already cautiously opening his door by the time James walks up beside him, setting one long leg down into the soft dirt. James feels the sudden urge to drop to his knees and wrap himself around the warm skin of Sydney's calf and thigh, feel the soft hair under his fingers, the curves of the muscles around his shins, and the bones of his ankle.

Instead, he opens the door the rest of the way, steps into the V of Sydney's thighs, and kisses him before Sydney can ask the question hovering on his lips.

James' heart clenches when Sydney immediately wraps his arms around him and draws him in. The tension melts—vanishing into the clear, floral air, carried away on the soft breeze ghosting over them from across the surface of the ocean far below.

Sydney tastes like the breath of life, the fountain of youth, the pulsing power of raw strength. He tastes like the way Keith Hartman's eyes had lit up when they were chosen for The Mission, and the way Rob

Depaul screamed James' name to the heavens the first time he won a heat, and the way Danny Moore whips the air out of everyone's lungs when he sets foot on a beach.

He tastes like Oahu—like home.

James presses a final kiss to Sydney's mouth before pulling back, bringing their foreheads together. "I'm sorry," he whispers. "I don't why . . . I just—I had to." He swallows hard, feeling unbelievably foolish for what he's about to say. "Just in case."

Sydney breathes out a sigh through his nose and holds James closer by his grip around his back. "I know," he says. James feels Sydney's body tremble once, and his hands clench around fistfuls of James' shirt. "Thank you."

James has a feeling that that *"thank you"* was for a hell of a lot more than just walking around the Jeep to give him a good luck kiss. He kisses Sydney one last time, gently breathing in the scent of sunlight from his skin, and then he pulls back, running his hands through Sydney's curls to smooth them from the wind of the drive.

"No more driving off a cliff jokes, you fucker," he says.

Sydney smiles, gradually lighting up the sadness that had settled in the corner of his eyes. He winks. "Noted, Captain."

James drags his eyes away from the road and glances again at Sydney once they pull up along the sand of Waimea beach. The waves are already crashing towering walls of water onto the shore, building up to the largest swells of the morning in a few short hours. The sea air blows through the open sides of the Jeep, rustling Sydney's hair, and the swish of palm fronds settles over the silence in the car like a blanket.

They look at each other after Sydney cuts the engine, and James takes in the slightly nervous clench of Sydney's fingers around the wheel, the small, eager excitement pulsing in the vein along his neck.

James wonders what the hell he's supposed to say in a moment like this—how to tell the man he lives with as of fifteen hours ago that it's far too fucking soon to say any of the words rumbling around in his mind but he might not get the chance, this might be the last time before Sydney goes and . . .

But Sydney gives a curt nod, his lips already set into a line, and James just tries to give a reassuring smile in response. They both exhale and reach for their door handles, stepping out into the bright air of the real world for the very first time that morning.

There's already a small crowd on the shores of Waimea Bay by the time they get there, gathering to watch the sun rise steadily into the sky, standing on top of station wagons and leaning against the sides of Camaros to point out at the incoming swells and judge the best routes to take. James follows Sydney through the thick green brush running along the edges of the sand, making their way through the rocky green over to the rest of the surfers.

There aren't any fans sitting back in the sand with cold drinks in their hands. No judges setting up their table, or announcers booming across the beach, or umbrellas dotting the shoreline in the breeze.

No, this beach is quiet, almost somber—light-years away from the young people with boomboxes sprawled across the Hermosa Beach shore, waving their beers. It's in a completely different universe from the packed shoreline of hopeful surfers and cheering Hawaiian locals stretched out along the Banzai Pipeline just a week before.

It's like the only living, breathing thing in all of Waimea Bay is the sea herself.

Every step James takes closer to the sand rattles in his bones like a dirge, the sharp wind against his face like a hissing warning. He can't even bring himself to look out at the waves rising up twenty, thirty, forty, fifty feet high. A voice in the back of his mind starts praying like hell for the waves to never reach past twenty—for the informal competition to be called off due to the puny swells, or for the weather to be too rough, or for a wrong current to make its way in and dash the hopes of clean, open-faced waves against the rocks lining the shallows like barbed wire.

Sydney's head is held effortlessly high in front of him. He pulls down his aviators over his eyes as he approaches the group of surfers already lined up along the sand by their cars, arms crossed and eyes intent as they gaze out over the waves. The group turns to look at Sydney approaching, and James can't quite stop his surprised frown when he sees their faces light up with warm smiles.

"What it is, what it is, Moore. Was wondering when you'd show up, you lazy ass."

"Here he is. Little bird told me you had your sights on Waimea this year."

"Banzai waves too small for you now, huh?"

"Come on, dude, look out and tell us what we're all missing."

James' mouth is half open. He doesn't recognize any of these men from the Billabong, not even the passing memory of a blurry face. These men look slightly older—more worn and weathered in the way their loose limbs casually lean. He stands dumbly in the sand as Sydney accepts their handshakes and pats a few of them on the back, effortlessly moving into their circle.

The last man in line, the first one to greet him from before, steps forward and gives Sydney an actual hug, slapping him hard on the back before they do a practiced handshake between them.

"My man," he says, looking Sydney once up and down. "Look even skinnier than the last time I saw you. These waves gonna pummel your little white ass if you ain't careful."

To James' surprise, Sydney laughs as another surfer rolls his eyes. "Hank here acting like he wouldn't be the first one out in the water to save you."

James watches, mouth half-open, as Sydney pushes his aviators up into his hair. He shoves his hands in his pockets, and James feels a rush of emotion at the way Sydney ducks his head like an embarrassed, starstruck kid. "Hank," he says to the man he just hugged, acting overly casual. "It's been a long time."

Hank tilts his head, talking only to Sydney as the rest of the surfers go on talking about the surf. "Got some family shit—why I wasn't out there in LA the other week."

Sydney hums in sympathy. "New York?"

"Just got back yesterday. Dickie here's letting me bum his camper 'til I figure out a place."

Their voices fade into a blur as James takes a step back and watches Sydney Moore freely converse with a group of people for the very first time, the sight of it causing an embarrassing lump in his throat.

James had heard that Big Wave surfing was different—little whispers he'd caught here and there back in LA from surfers who'd actually traveled out to surf along the North Shore. They'd all shaken their heads at this tiny, set-apart world full of the craziest surfers with the biggest thirsts for danger. At how they were all mad, too ruined now by the thrill of monster swells to get any enjoyment out of riding the surf off other coastlines. Thrill seekers who hurled themselves from the crests without second thought, riding on the shoulders of the group of boys who first threw down their boards into the infamous surf in '57 and swam out into the waves without looking back. Men who chased after the next record, and the next record, and the one after that simply because they could, and they had their boards in their hands, and because the waves were there. How *somebody* had to try to ride them and live to swim back to shore and tell the sane pro-circuit surfers all about it.

But now, standing here face to face with this world, James sees that it's actually an entirely separate *universe*. One where the rest of surfing—its competitions, and qualifying and pro circuits, and points, and heats, and judges—doesn't even exist. Where Sydney Moore can walk onto a beach and be welcomed with open arms and handshakes, and where the only spectators who dare to show up and watch are the ones who know they may end up seeing a corpse float back to frothy shore.

He realizes Sydney is staring back at him, beckoning him closer.

"You all heard of Jimmy," Sydney says to the group with a clear voice, drawing all eyes to him. "He just stole my title at the Billabong."

The other surfers seem to really notice James for the first time. A few of them frown in confusion, glancing quickly at Sydney and wondering how in hell Danny Moore just showed up to surf with a friend—with his winning competitor—but then they're beaming towards him, holding out arms to slap his back and shake his hand.

"So *you're* the wild card!"

"Fuck, man, heard about your 9.8. Fucking primo ride you had there. Out of this world."

"And you beat this miserable fucker back in Los Angeles, too!"

James smiles, embarrassed, and tries not to shrink into the sand under the praise. He can't even believe what he's seeing on this empty stretch of foggy shore. It's like he's stepped into that Twilight Zone show Lori's always begging Rob to watch—where the surfers here on this beach say all the same shit James heard the surfers say back at the

Banzai, the same exact words, except in this world they say it with warm grins, stepping back easily to welcome James and Sydney into their fold.

James prickles across the back of his neck at the feeling of being an imposter. These men are about to surf the highest waves on earth, following in the footsteps of the untouchable surfing giants before them like it's nothing revolutionary at all. And they still somehow profess to give a shit that little Jimmy Campbell from a Los Angeles trailer park came over to their shores a week ago and won a silly competition on a fluke.

Sydney's hand is briefly on his elbow, and James blinks out of his thoughts to look at him. The look on Sydney's face says everything, as if James had been narrating his thoughts out loud. The look says, "*It wasn't just a silly competition, it was the goddamn Billabong Masters,*" and it also says, with a tiny shrug, "*I know. I can't believe these guys don't hate me, either.*"

Sydney shoots him a soft smile, and the other surfers surrounding them vanish as James grins and flutters a quick wink back. Then Sydney clears his throat and crosses his arms over his chest, filling the beach with his presence.

"So, looks like the swells will be high enough today after all," he says, nodding at the latest incoming monster of a wave.

"Wicked early in the season for it, but Harry was right. These beauties'll definitely get over thirty today."

Sydney hums. "We got actual judging?"

A surfer next to him laughs. "Shit, Danny, did you just show up and hope there'd be a competition on?"

Another one steps forward. "Nah, he fucking knew. We woulda had a nice calm empty beach today, but *somebody* had to go and open his big mouth about this thing we're doing over a damn microphone last week at the Billabong. This place'll be thronging."

Sydney's cheeks turn pink as he looks down at his scuffling feet. He hunches his shoulders. "Well, the people requested an interview. You know how it is."

"Oh, and all of a sudden you want a little piece of spotlight?" another surfer laughs, warmly. "Tired of winning shit and then disappearing off into the trees—?"

"Ah, sit on it, Willis," Hank cuts in. He slugs the other surfer in the arm. "Just fuckin' jealous you ain't got competition wins to be all hot in the press for."

Sydney shrugs again, pointedly not looking up at James as he talks softly under the resounding conversation of friendly jeers. "Just seemed important," he says to his feet.

James tears his eyes away from Sydney and looks out over the empty stretch of beach, endless pools of soft white sand surrounded by rolling hills of craggy green and fluttering flowers. He frowns, hating the fact he feels nervous to make his voice heard. "Place looks empty enough to me," he says.

"Ah, my man, this ain't Los Angeles, but you'll see."

"They'll be here, just you wait."

"Curious sons of bitches can't pass up the opportunity to watch someone get reamed," another says, casually smirking.

"Anyways," cuts in the man who seems to be the unofficial leader of the group. "To answer His Highness Mr. Moore's question here, we got one of the WSL guys to come down and be the judge, make it official and shit. Not like we need him, but if one of us goes for the record . . ."

The rest of the group nods, suddenly solemn. They all turn to look back out at the waves, snarling against the shore and slamming into the barrier of reef and rocks, hurling up streaming spray into the sky.

James feels sick to his stomach, vision going hazy as he stares without blinking at the roaring walls of water.

"You joining us, then, Campbell?"

He blinks and turns to see that it was Hank who asked him. James takes a good look at him for the first time—just a twenty-something kid, barely older than Sydney, with a drooping black mustache and a faded orange baseball cap from Zion National Park. Realization dawns on James as he looks at him. He sees the haunted darkness hovering just beneath his skin, the careful set of his shoulders, the way he keeps looking over his shoulder and scanning the surrounding shore in a predictable cycle.

They share a small nod, alone in the group of surfers, and both of them flinch when someone slaps their hand hard on the metal roof of a nearby car. James wonders, fleetingly and with a sad tug in his chest, whether it takes running through a Vietnam jungle for somebody to see the hidden beauty in Danny Moore.

Then James clears his throat, a bit too late. "Nah, just here to watch the show. Make sure no one does anything too stupid," he tries to laugh.

Hank gets a sad grin at the corner of his mouth, then turns to the group. "Y'all know Chris got one of those new jet-ski's they're selling at Jack's shop over in Honolulu, rich son of a bitch."

Another frowns. "Heard he can't make it up here today." He clicks his tongue and sighs. "Woulda been good to have another set of surfing eyes on the beach."

James looks to Sydney, confused, and Sydney leans over to quietly speak. "You've seen them in LA, those motorized personal bike things you can ride out on the water."

Another surfer jumps in, short and stocky with a giant patriotic bald eagle tattoo buried under a forest of deep black chest hair. "Chris got one and started using it for us along the North Shore. Attach a board to the back of it and you've got your own little water ambulance. Figures that the first day in three years the waves off Waimea are ideal enough to surf some record breakers, he's got a fucking funeral to go to."

Another guy rolls his eyes. "Oh yeah, Dickie, blame Chris for having the fucking *nerve* to go to a funeral instead of saving our sorry asses. Relax, man."

"Well, it's true! Fucker knows what happens around here."

"Well don't go fucking jinxing it! Jesus, you have any concept of superstition?"

The group goes on half-jokingly arguing, laughing and teasing each other like they're just sitting around a bonfire with beers in their hands. It almost makes it easy to forget that one of them could drown that day.

James shivers. He can't forget. He seeks out Sydney in the group standing next to Hank and sees that his eyes are far away out over the ocean, focused intently on the rises of the swells barreling in towards the shore, growing higher and higher with every set until the entire bay turns into a churning, bubbling caldron of white foam and salt.

James can sense when his invitation becomes a bit strained— more based on the fact that he's sweating over having absolutely nothing to say than the way the other surfers are treating him. He seeks out Sydney's eyes, tilting his head away down the shore, then with one last smile he walks off and leaves the group to their strategy, making his way along the sand to sit down in the shade of one of the palm trees.

He watches the waves and meditates to the steady thrum of the water, incessantly rubbing the sweat on his palms off on his shorts. He watches people slowly arriving in waves at the beach around him, locals curious to see the first time Waimea's shown record-breaking surf in years, and fellow surfers come to watch and learn how to master the terrifying swells.

James isn't surprised at the voice in the back of his mind that tells him over and over again to grab a board and join them out in the water. That he should be one of the ones racing down the towering faces of the waves. It feels like that hot spark deep in his gut when he'd followed in Keith Hartman's footsteps into the thick and airless jungle, gun clutched hard in sweaty palms, trigger finger steady.

It's the part of him that had silently thrilled, in a twisted black way, when he'd first laid eyes on Danny Moore standing tall next to him in the sand. The part of him that had felt shivers up his spine, and screaming adrenaline in his bones, when he'd looked down to his right from under his eyelashes and seen Danny Moore's shorts tented in a steaming public shower.

It's also the part of him that he had willingly hurled out into the sea, knowing that Sydney Moore's arm would be there to steady him if he fell.

James listens to the voice telling him to run out there into the waves like a man listening idly to the radio, feeling the ghostly muscle memory of the tide yanking on his bones. And then he shuts off the station, and thinks of the look on Sydney's face when they'd placed the lei of flowers around his own neck, and suddenly the need to go out there and prove himself, to feel the rush of danger burn fire through his veins, fades away to a soft, clear mist.

He takes in a deep breath of biting wind and buries his toes deeper into the sand. His lack of sleep the night before is pulling at his eyelids, making them swollen and heavy. He looks back over towards the surfers one last time and immediately locks eyes with Sydney through the swarming crowd.

James nods, gesturing out towards the sea with a look he hopes means, "*Go ahead, I'll be here.*" And the smile Sydney Moore reveals for only him makes James feel like he's just won the Billabong Pipeline Masters all over again.

James is roused from his doze by a cheer rippling across the warm beach. He flings open his eyes and desperately, before his brain can even realize why, searches out Sydney in the crowd. His heart hammers in his chest, pumping hot sludge through his limbs. He frantically scans the beach, the shoreline, the water and sand. Checks the two little specks of surfers already paddling out into the menacing waves to see whether either of them has a head of dark curls.

He thinks one of them might.

With his heart in his throat, James starts to stand, thighs shaking and palms gripping handfuls of sand as he struggles to his feet, still blinking off sleep to realize that Sydney Moore just fucking surfed out into the Waimea waves without even saying goodbye, that absolute motherfucker, and James never even told him, never got the chance to hold him and say—

"James! James, I'm right here. I'm not out there."

Sydney jogs towards him across the sand, brow scrunched with worry. James flops back down into the sand and releases a shaky sigh, running his hands over his face and trying to hide his embarrassment that something as simple as Sydney being in the *water* just made him lose control of himself more than he's ever experienced in his life. More than the moment Auntie Cath told him to pack up all his things, that the trailer wouldn't be home anymore. More than the first bomb in the mud.

Sydney reaches his side and leans down, placing a hand on his shoulder. "Sorry—didn't mean to scare you. I was just running over here to see if you wanted to watch with me. We picked straws and I'm up last with Hank."

James still can't talk. His mouth is dry and his limbs sag frozen into the sand, heavy and limp. He hadn't realized just *how* scared shitless he was of watching Sydney paddle out into those waves until he'd thought it had been happening right before his very eyes, and now the realization that he'll actually have to watch that in a matter of hours barrels down on him like black mud, choking him off from the gorgeous beach air, the breeze and spray coming off the water, the swish of palm fronds at his back covering the green mountain.

Sydney's hand is still on his shoulder, waiting. Finally, James clears his throat and opens his eyes, forcing himself to look up at Sydney and hoping his terror isn't showing on his face.

Apparently it is. Sydney frowns and drops into a crouch. "James," he whispers. He pushes his sunglasses back up into his hair. "James, I would never go out there without knowing you were here watching my back, you know that? I . . . I couldn't do it without."

James swallows hard and nods, still loathing that he was so affected by a mere two fucking seconds of not knowing where Sydney was. He feels young and helpless, as if Hank and all the other surfers should be babysitting him in the sand.

"I know that," he says, wishing he believed it. "I know. Sorry, I just thought—"

He can't even finish the words, and Sydney twists his mouth, moving his hand up briefly to cup James' cheek in the shade of the fronds. "I know," he says low, with eyes that suddenly look twenty years older. "And I'm telling you that would never happen. Never."

Sydney squeezes his jaw before trailing his hand away, and some of the youth starts to burn back in his face. He smirks. "You're stuck watching my sorry white ass now whether you like it or not."

James forces a smile and looks back down the beach. "So how do you know Hank?"

Sydney wraps his hands around his knees. "School, surprisingly."

"That long?"

Sydney shakes his head. "His dad was military, stationed at the Harbor like mine. I don't think we ever actually spoke in school, not until we recognized each other later on the circuit—comp in NorCal, actually. His family had moved back to New York. Same year I . . . stopped going. To school, I mean."

James flashes him a stunned look before he can stop himself, and Sydney gives a thin smile, then briefly lifts his hands. "Never really graduated. Must've slipped my mind."

James schools his features and places that startling fact in the back of his mind to look at later, when Sydney isn't about to hurl himself down a deadly wave. Then he waits, sensing that more is coming, disbelieving that simply attending the same high school a few years apart would have caused Sydney to go out of his way to make a friend. Sydney looks at him and grins as if he can read James' thoughts.

"He started it," he says. "Our school was swarming with Army brats, but . . . he stuck out, for obvious reasons, and I . . ." Sydney grins, but it doesn't quite reach his eyes. "Well, you've seen how I get along with people. Guess we were the two outsiders. I didn't even know at the time he surfed, but he'd read about me."

"Your fame does precede you," James says, mock seriously.

Sydney shoves him with his knee. Off in the distance, the two specks of surfers have now made their way to the breaking point after agonizing minutes spent swimming over and duck diving under the roaring waves.

"We're not really friends, I guess," Sydney finally whispers, almost to himself.

It sounds like he's apologizing for actually having a connection with another human being, and James is about to say just that when Sydney shakes his shoulders and sighs, like a period to the conversation. "Well, but you know . . ." he says with his typical shrug.

James swallows down his million questions and hums, then takes Sydney's offered hand to rise to his still-shaking legs.

"Come on," Sydney says, turning back towards the punishing waves. "Watch with me. And then you can pretend to be in charge and force me to eat or stretch or some shit. Feel useful."

James rolls his eyes at the same time a wave of gratefulness washes over inside him. Gratefulness that Sydney somehow knows him well enough to know that he just heard screams and bullets as he sat panicking in the sand, and that he desperately needs to pretend that what just happened hadn't happened at all.

"Oh gee, thanks for giving me purpose in life," he smirks.

Sydney casually sticks his hands in his boardshort pockets as they walk back towards the crowd gathered along the beach. The floral breeze of the rising mountains gently pushes at their backs, mixing with the salty spray of the waves beyond.

"Well, jobs for vets are shit these days," Sydney says. "So I'm just doing my part. You could be my manager. Like those guys that holds the clubs for the golfers, fetch them their towels and water and keep track of their shit."

James slaps his arm and tries not to laugh. "You don't ever fucking stop, do you? You'd think by now, after . . . everything, you'd stop being an asshole with me at least."

"Oh no, James, now I have to be the *biggest* asshole to you. Can't have you thinking too highly of yourself that you snagged Danny Moore."

James sucks in a breath and glances around them quickly, hoping nobody heard. He sees Sydney blink once, like he was surprised by the words out of his own mouth. They look at each other, heat crackling in the air for an eternal beat, when James realizes that nobody could give a shit about what Sydney's muttering to him under his breath. Not when two surfers are paddling their way out towards the tallest waves Waimea Bay's seen in years.

He relaxes his shoulders, wanting desperately to reach out and wrap his arms around Sydney's warm, firm waist. "You're something else," he whispers, and Sydney looks over his shoulder to shoot him a wink before pulling his sunglasses back down over his eyes.

The crowd is nearly silent after the initial cheer that followed the first two surfers paddling out past the breaking point. Everyone is holding their breath, eyes never straying from the two little black dots bobbing and weaving through the towering swells. The surfers both paddle out to the side, just off where the waves are fully breaking, and pull up next to each other on their boards, probably talking through which sets to go for, what routes to take.

James follows Sydney around the edges of the crowd, cringing at himself for being afraid to even look down for fear he lets Sydney out of his sight, no matter what Sydney just promised him not five minutes ago. The three inches between their shoulders buzzes and thrums. It's all James can think about. How if he just leaned slightly to the right, if he just shifted his weight in the sand, he could feel Sydney Moore's warmth on his skin, a reminder that he's here and alive and breathing. Not floating pale and limp in the black deep with seaweed covering his face.

Sydney calmly watches the surfers while the wind off the waves picks up speed, clinging to his shirt and wrapping it around the contours of his chest and stomach. James forces himself to do the same, ignoring the electric space between them and instead watching the sets, trying and failing to come up with what his own route through the chaos would be.

Some of the waves are tall enough to partially block out the sunlight, casting the water in shadow like a sudden night. They crest and break over on top of each other without pause, waves as tall as three-story buildings smashing down into the foam, breaking over hidden rocks and surging against the palm trees tucked into the sides of the craggy rocks on either side of the bay. The sound is deafening, and the air is thin. James watches, and tries to breathe, and waits.

Hank eventually walks up next to him and stares out to sea without saying hello. "Betcha Don's gonna take that swell forming out on the horizon line. If he waits any longer, he knows he'll lose his nerve."

Sydney hums from the other side of James, still looking out at the waves. "It won't be a record-breaker, but it'll hold a clean face for him. Won't break too soon."

Hank chuckles under his breath. "Won't even ask how the fuck you can tell all that this early, but I been there, done that with doubting your little head."

Sydney just smirks.

James holds his breath as Don starts to paddle like hell out in front of the incoming wave, far sooner than James normally would for any of the smaller waves he's caught along Los Angeles. The ocean seems to rise towards the sky behind him, heaving up in one great surge to fling him up into the clouds.

The beach is silent. Every person frozen. Don paddles as the wave pushes him higher and higher up towards the building crest.

"Shit, man, I wish we had Chris out there with his raft," Hank whispers.

"He'll be fine. The current will take him straight down the face and he'll be well out before the crest breaks," Sydney says back, voice calm. "Got enough speed."

Don perches at the top of a thirty-foot wave, grabs both sides of his board, looks down over the edge of the towering crest, and pops up to his feet.

The beach gasps, and James leans to his right to press his shoulder up against Sydney's as Don rockets down the face of the wave, spray flying up behind the tail of his board—just a black speck against a wall of moving water being hurled back down to the earth.

James can see his legs shaking with the force of the wave from here—the way his board pumps and bobs against the face as it tries to carve in a steady path. The wave starts to break ten feet behind him as he zooms straight down, threatening to crash on top of him and bury him in thirty feet of solid, rushing water and foam. Hank curses under his breath, one hand covering his mouth, and James almost does the same. Sydney alone out of everyone on the beach stands calm and unaffected, lips not even pursed.

For one blinding moment, Don is swallowed up by the mist and spray, disappearing into churning ten-foot-high walls of rushing foam. Someone on the shore yells Don's name, cheering him on. The two lifeguards—James hopes they're lifeguards—stand calf-deep in the shallows, ready to run.

And then, like a ray of sunlight breaking through the clouds, Don reappears, backed by walls of whitewater and flying out towards the shoreline, still standing tall on his board. The crowd lets out a wild cheer as Don pumps his fist into the air and then dives off his board into the calmer water, staying under for the bulk of the wave to roll past before surfacing again to crawl onto his board and get some air.

James lets out a breath he hadn't realized he'd been holding, and Sydney presses back briefly into his arm.

"Well shit, my man, you were right," Hank says, shaking out the tension from his arms.

Sydney finally breaks his gaze away from the water. "Are you surprised?"

Hank grins. "Nah, I learned that lesson your second Billabong." James notices Hank quickly look between the two of them, as if James' very presence at Sydney's side is still a question niggling in his mind, then he stretches his arms behind his back and whistles. "I need to stretch, gonna go say my last rites and shit. Moore, see you out there."

Sydney holds up a hand, and James gives Hank a nod as Hank heads off towards his board stuck in the sand, still shaking the muscles in his arms and shoulders loose. James hates that he feels a wash of relief at watching him go—that the way Hank's eye had flickered between him and Sydney had been like a punch to his gut, sweat under his arms.

James stands next to Sydney, barely speaking, for the next three rounds. Two surfers a round, just one successful wave each, if they even manage that. Nobody has the endurance to try to catch more than one of these waves in the span of thirty short minutes. The beach feels oddly quiet without the blaring airhorn, or the crackling announcers, or the sounds of hundreds or thousands yelling, laughter spilling across the warm sand.

No—everything is calm. Understated. Surfers start and end their heats with a cheer, and a blanket of silent focus hovers over the shore the rest of the time. Sydney tries to call each ride under his breath as it's happening—which wave they'll take, how tall it'll be, what will happen. Three surfers wipeout, but all of them happen early enough in the wave to simply dive through the face and surface on the other side of the crest, missing the deadly crash of the breaking point.

James almost forgets that Sydney will eventually take up his board and join them—that he won't just spend the whole day standing by his side predicting the future before taking James' arm and leading them back home to their porch, and their gentle, safe waves, and their bed.

Then Sydney clears his throat and uncrosses his arms. "I need to get ready," he says.

James freezes, mouth dry.

"James?"

With an effort, he forces himself to turn and look at Sydney, standing beside him, looking infuriatingly beautiful with the sunlight reflecting off his aviators and the salty wind blowing in his curls. The warmth of the sand glittering across his tan skin.

James can't say anything. He licks his lips and nods. Sydney reaches out to tightly grip the top of his arm through his sleeve.

"I'll find you before Hank and I head out, okay?" Then he's off into the crowd, striding towards his board so he can wax up and stretch as if he isn't about to do something absolutely, deathly insane.

James fights back a moan as he watches Sydney walk away from him down the stretch of shoreline, framed by mountains of rushing water on his right and mountains of green velvet on his left. He looks back out at the surfers paddling up and over the gigantic swells across the horizon and tells himself that everything will be totally fine. They haven't had any major accidents today. Nobody's drowned. Nobody's died. These guys know how to surf this beach, have been training for it for years.

And that's when Dickie drops in on his chosen wave. And the towering force of water behind him caves in on top of his tumbling body, crushing him under the foam while his board soars clear up into the air, ankle strap broken.

The crowd on the beach lets out a collective gasp, waiting with bated breath for a tiny speck of a human to surface from the crashing, churning whitewater. The lone board slaps back into the water, and the roar of the wave is loud enough to tremble through the sand, pulsing against the soles of James' bare feet.

And then a second wave hits, even taller than the last. And that's when the other surfers start to run.

Sydney sprints ahead of them towards the shoreline, board held up high over his head before he throws it down into the shallows and paddles out with quick, powerful strokes, dolphin diving under the incoming swells. James takes two trembling steps forward in the sand, wanting to cup his hands around his mouth and scream for Sydney to come back, to let one of the other surfers go after Dickie caught in the walls of gushing water, to get his ass back on the sand and come and let James crush him into his arms so he can't fucking throw it all away before they've even begun.

But Sydney paddles out, Don hot on his heels. James tracks Sydney's soaked white t-shirt through the rises and falls of the battling swells; Sydney hadn't even changed into his wetsuit yet. James wheezes breath in and out through his mouth and tries not to sink to his knees in the sand. The crowd has moved closer to the shoreline, and the two lifeguards—God, why couldn't the fucking lifeguards be the ones paddling out on their boards—are up to their waists in the water, treading through the breaking waves as they stand ready with a thrown-together first-aid kit.

Nobody makes a sound. The edges of James' vision start to spark and blur.

The entire universe shrinks down to the speck of Sydney's t-shirt in the deep blue water. James can't tell if he himself is standing or kneeling, silent or screaming, sleeping or awake. He sees Sydney turn over his shoulder to call back towards Don before paddling up and over a twenty-foot wave just about to break, barely reaching the crest before it topples over into a barrel.

Someone from the beach suddenly yells. "I see him! I see him out there to the right!"

Sydney's already paddling straight towards Dickie, as if he knew exactly where he would surface. James covers his mouth with his hand as Sydney reaches out for Dickie between two massive swells and pulls his limp body onto the front of his board. They're just to the right of the main breaking point, dangerously close to the crashing falls of the waves as the ocean continues to barrel towards the shore, completely unaware of the three men trying not to drown in her foam.

Don arrives at Sydney's side, clearly exhausted from the sprint, and helps hoist Dickie's body onto Sydney's back, wrapping his arms under Sydney's stomach so he can try and limply hold on. Then they're racing back to shore, barely avoiding being flung and slapped about by the breaks.

James can see the straining of Sydney's muscles from here, pulling with all his strength against the thick current and fighting to get enough air as his board sinks beneath the weight of two people. Sydney catches a few smaller waves in towards the shore, body-boarding in on the whitewater, and Don reaches the shore just a minute before him, panting and sprinting towards the surfers all standing in the shallows.

"He's alive, but we can't tell if he's breathing," he pants out. The two lifeguards swim out to meet Sydney where he's paddling in. Sydney slides off his board once his feet can reach the bottom and catches Dickie under his arms. He limply passes Dickie's body over to the two men who drag him backwards up to the sand and out of the last clutches of the hissing waves.

James is running before he even notices what he's doing. He's running right past the group crowded around Dickie being looked over lying in the sand and sprints straight towards Sydney instead, white shirt plastered to his skin and dripping with saltwater, trails of wet sand wrapped threateningly around his thighs and calves.

Sydney's chest is heaving as he pushes his wet hair back from his face, stepping back from the surfers kneeling in the wet sand to make sure Dickie's okay. Sydney's eyes are blown wide open where they stare down at Dickie's limp body, mouth twisted and taut, and as James reaches his side, he suddenly realizes what Sydney must be thinking of as he watches the lifeguards open Dickie's airway and try and force air into his still lungs. How he must be seeing James himself lying there lifeless in the wet sand, sand-covered lips slowly turning cold and blue.

James reaches out for his arm, and Sydney flinches at the touch, hands still clutching at his hair.

"Sydney, I'm here," he says, not giving a shit about calling him Danny. "Look, I'm here. It's me."

Sydney blinks hard and sucks in a breath, then whips his head towards James.

"I'm *here*," James says again.

Sydney releases all the air in his lungs, stepping back further from the men kneeling in the sand and taking a stumbling step towards James. He lets his arms fall to his sides and leans his weight against James' shoulder, sagging like air let out of a balloon.

James takes him by the wrist and starts to lead him away. "Here, let's get you some air, get some air," he says, over and over. "There's nothing more you can do."

The beach is eerily silent as he pulls Sydney away, his limbs moving thickly through the sand in a daze.

"Moore, you alright?" Hank calls out behind them.

Sydney blinks hard, then turns around, leaving his wrist in James' hand. "I'm all good," he says in a weak voice. "Just need some air."

Hank looks relieved as he puts up an understanding hand. "Looks like he's alright," he calls out, nodding down at Dickie. "He's breathing now, just a little stunned. He's fine." Hank shakes his head and passes a hand over his mouth. "You fucking did it, man."

Sydney nods that he heard but doesn't respond, letting James lead him quickly up towards the shaded canopy of the trees right at the edge of the line of parked cars. His legs feel numb, whole body going into an automatic mode he never even knew he had, completely unaware that any other breathing person exists on the beach besides Sydney, his warm, wet wrist still clutched in James' hand.

James gently pushes Sydney down into the sand against a palm trunk and rifles through their nearby bags for the canteen of water he brought along. He kneels in front of Sydney and puts a hand on his shin, trying to exude nothing but a strong, calm peace.

Sydney gulps down the water and takes a deep, shaking breath, pushing the curls back from his forehead again.

"I'm alright," he says, still panting.

James huffs, and his voice cracks. "Like hell you are."

"I'm fine. I'm good. Just needed to catch my breath."

James shakes his head in disbelief as Sydney shuts his eyes and leans his head back against the trunk, taking careful breaths. The saltwater glitters across his skin, and the muscles of his chest rise and fall under the clinging wet contours of his white tee. There are small lines of exhaustion painted around his eyelids, and a little smear of mud clings to the pulsing vein in his neck.

James looks at him for a long moment, his hand innocently clutching his shin, and he wants to lean forward and grab Sydney's face in his hands and kiss him and growl, *"You promised me you wouldn't go out there without saying goodbye. You fucking promised me."*

But James also knows he would never really say that, not in a million years. Because Sydney Moore knew that he was the fastest swimmer on the shore, and he knew that he would know exactly where Dickie would eventually surface. And James knows that Sydney just saved that man's life without even a second's hesitation—a man who's maybe given him shit in the past, or called him a fairy, or whispered behind his back, big wave camaraderie aside.

And Sydney called *James* brave.

James lets himself reach forward for a brief moment to hold Sydney's hand, shielded from the rest of the beach by his own body. Sydney opens his eyes and gives a tired smile, and James feels his heart sink deep in his chest. He'd suspected, but now he definitely knows.

"You're still gonna go out there, aren't you," he says.

Sydney gazes into his eyes and nods, body tense and waiting for James' reaction.

James takes a deep breath and releases it with a nod, and Sydney's eyes widen in surprise. James squeezes his wet hand before letting go.

"I said you should do it. I won't take my word back now," he says. He stares into the eyes of the man he'd slept next to that morning, the man who knows every secret, horrible, intimate inch of James' skin. Who knows it, and who still wants James Campbell to be by his side, in his home, in his life. Who admitted that he, the top winning surfer in all Hawaii, would only feel confident enough to swim out into Waimea if he knows James is there.

Sydney closes his eyes and leans back against the tree, whispering James' name once softly into the warm breeze, and James doesn't say anything more as he sits by his side, watching the wind slowly dry the salt from Sydney's skin.

They wait in the shade for another half hour as Dickie recovers on the sand, and the crowd tries to recover from the scene.

But all too soon, Hank's waving over in their direction.

"You still joining me, Moore? Or did you get your fill already?"

Sydney immediately opens his eyes from what James thought was a nap and smirks, then starts to rise to his feet. "Gotta show you incompetent idiots how it's done," he calls back, and Hank flips him off and laughs. "Five minutes!"

Suddenly, James needs to say everything, so strongly that the beach around him reels and tilts on its side. He grabs Sydney's hand before he can start walking away to change into his wetsuit and prepare and yanks him back into the palm trees, slamming him up against a trunk with a surprised grunt from them both.

They're still in full view of the crowds by the water, and James finds himself wishing more than anything he's ever wished for in his life that he could just lean forward and press their lips together one last time. That he could strip off their shirts and press their chests together so he could remember the warmth of Sydney's skin, the rhythm of his breathing lungs.

Instead, he holds Sydney at arm's length and grips his shoulders hard. Sydney watches him, lips parted and eyes wide behind a curtain of half-wet curls.

James' voice is choked. In his mind, he sees Sydney young and asleep earlier that morning in their bed, with the moonlight illuminating his face and his curls softly falling across his pillow.

He blinks again, and he sees the open, shocked face of the man on the pier.

"Don't you dare not come back to me," he whispers. His voice is hoarse.

Sydney's focused eyes are the vastness of the sea. They stare straight through James' skin into the red, swelling muscles of his lungs, and his large hands come up to grab hold of James' forearms. James looks down, throat embarrassingly tight, at the sight of Sydney's long fingers over the blanket of golden hair covering his own skin.

Sydney takes a deep breath, and the earth disappears.

"James," he breathes in a fragile voice. His eyes grow wet. "I love you."

James shuts his eyes quickly as a moan escapes the back of his throat. He shakes his head and huffs out a wet breath, trying to force his voice to work, but Sydney goes on.

"I know . . . I know it's soon. That we . . . we aren't really—but I need you to know. Before I go out there, I need you to—"

"Sydney."

James is shocked he was even able to form a coherent word. He grips Sydney's shoulders so tightly he can feel the contours of the bones, and he lets Sydney see the tear that rolls down his cheek without wiping it away. "God, you . . . come back to me and I'll tell you the same thing, you—" A thousand curse words zoom through James' mind, and his mouth opens and shuts, his head shaking. "You . . ."

Sydney's mouth crumples, and he smiles with wet eyes and nods. "I will," he whispers. "I promise you, I will."

And James knows that that's the *last* thing Sydney can promise. That he's just about to let the man who kissed his scar without pity walk away from him in the sand without getting to hear that he's loved back.

And Sydney does walk away from him, then, after one more heart-stopping look. He holds his head high, and pulls his wet shirt off his back, and makes his way towards his board to join Hank out in the surf. Leaving James grasping at cold, thin air in the dark shade.

James stands dumbly at the edges of the beach as he watches Sydney rejoin the surfers as if nothing's happened, waving off what looks like Hank's reminder to don his wetsuit and instead attaching his ankle strap wearing just his boardshorts. He slips off his aviators and drops them into the sand.

James watches Sydney act as if he didn't just risk his life saving one of their own, or as if he didn't just look into the eyes of James Campbell and say, in full view of the clear open sky and the vast blue sea, that he *loves* him.

That he loves *him.*

James wants to turn his face up towards the covering of thick, soft clouds and laugh at the top of his lungs—a gigantic "*take that!*" to the universe that's tried to drag him down over and over again. That whispered to him for nearly three long years that he should just walk back out into the sea and never swim back. Leave Rob Depaul to show up to surf together the next morning only to find an empty shore.

But then he watches Sydney walk confidently with his board towards the waves, the crowd gathering closer to watch and cheer them on. Sydney turns back just when his toes reach the water and looks over his shoulder, giving James a wave where he still stands by the trees, and then he's running out into the thrashing sea, not once looking back.

James stares as the crisp black lines of Sydney's tattoo gradually disappear into the spray. He tries to breathe in the choking, salty air, grateful that it smells like the sea and not like blood, and mud, and jungle. He refuses to be embarrassed at how his throat is burning and tight, and how he's blinking back the hot tears threatening to spill over in his eyes.

That man out there—the one dwarfed by skyscraper waves—he *loves* him.

James goes to stumble closer to the water so he can see, when he catches a small movement out of the corner of his eye. A woman appears from the line of thick trees, long black braid streaked with grey curling over her shoulder. Her long skirt blows gently across the surface of the sand, and her blouse ripples and clings in the strong wind pouring across the shore from the waves. She walks towards the water with small, hesitant steps, then stops in her tracks and raises a hand to her mouth, eyes completely fixed on the two surfers paddling out into the fierce walls of deadly, roaring water.

In a flash of clarity, James realizes exactly who she is.

"*Lahela always used to tell me 'Ukuli'i ka pua, onaona i ka mau'u.' The flower may be tiny, but it scents the grasses around it.*"

He quickly scans the waves, making sure Sydney is still paddling within the safety of the shallows, and then he slowly walks towards the lone woman where she stands completely frozen in the sand.

He gently clears his throat by her side so he won't startle her. "Are you here to watch Danny?"

She still jumps at his voice, and turns to face him like she'd forgotten she wasn't alone on the beach. Her deep brown eyes are wide with fear.

"Yes," she whispers. She doesn't ask him how he knew. James looks down at her face, not bothering to mask the fear in his own eyes, and she clutches at a little golden cross hanging down around her neck.

In a silent decision, they walk side by side closer to the shoreline, off to the side of the rest of the rapt crowd. Lahela's skirt blows against James' ankles in the sand, grounding him on the earth as his heart flies out across the waters to the place where Sydney paddles through the waves, fighting against the water to let him ride her swells.

James watches the man who just said "*I love you*" swim steadily towards the most dangerous waves on earth, leaving James completely powerless to save him on the dry shore. And beside him he hears whispered words escape from Lahela's trembling lips, carried away on the salty breeze and nearly covered by the roar of the sea.

"*Ka mana o ke Akua e ho' opakele mai ia kakou,*" she whispers, gripping the cross with her fingers. "*Ka mana o ke Akua e malama mai ia kakou.*"

Sydney paddles out just to the left of the breaking point, perched on his board above the heaving swells of the deep. He looks back once towards the shore, straight at James, a silent signal that he's about to take the next wave barreling in towards the shore.

And James whispers his own prayer softly into the wind, just as Sydney's powerful arms cut through the storming water.

"Please . . ." he murmurs across the sand. "Come back to me."

# 25

The wind scours across the surface of the waves and whips the cool saltwater into his face, hurling droplets into the rolling void of the deep surrounding his board. Sydney grips his thighs tighter around his board to steady himself against the rocking water beneath him, trying to breathe slow enough to keep his heart rate steady after the harsh paddle out to the breaking point.

Hank is still battling behind him—stuck in the shallows and trying to get past the barrier of cresting waves, pushed back again and again by the whitewater no matter how fast he tries to paddle over the tops. And Sydney is alone out on the water, gasping for breath with a burn in his arms and limbs, shaking with exhaustion since he already battled through these waves once not even an hour ago to help Dickie.

He tears his eyes away from Hank pushing through the breaking waves and instead looks out towards the horizon. The vastness of the sea suddenly looms before him with a moan. He can hear the empty groaning of the void across the surface of the ocean, stretching out to infinity with no break in sight. No people, or whispered words, or family, or jobs, or money, or competitions on crowded beaches.

No James Campbell.

The empty horizon line had always been peace for him—a welcome reminder that he always had an out. He could simply swim out towards her unreached depths and never look back if he wanted. He could take a deep breath and swim forever in the blessed, lonely silence. He could wake up one day in his house, step out into the sea, and let his feet leave the steadiness of the ground for the very last time, abandoning the whispers behind him on the dry land.

But now James Campbell is at his back, strong and brave and beautiful standing on the shore, letting Sydney be out here in the raging swells just so he can prove to himself that he's capable of reading the secrets of the ocean. That it's possible for him, Sydney Moore, to have one place on earth where he actually belongs. To dare the sea to welcome him with thrashing, outstretched arms.

Time stretches out before him like eternity, dripping with smears of danger and promise. Sydney knows he's only been in the water for about five minutes, and that he only stopped paddling and stopped to perch on his board thirty seconds ago. But now Sydney also knows, deep in the pit of his soul, that James Campbell is waiting for him back on the sand, waiting to tell him, in his sweet, smooth voice, "*I love you.*"

And Sydney knows, for the first time in his entire life with certainty, that the ocean will carry him back to shore. That it will not leave him to roam over the lonely horizon forever.

Sydney tracks the next two waves rolling in to shore and spots his opening—an incoming swell that'll be at least thirty feet. Forty if he's lucky. But probably more like thirty-two.

It isn't the record; it wouldn't even be close. It would be a small blip on the radar of Big Wave surfing history—nothing for anyone to remember or note down. And even as Sydney registers this fact in his mind, suddenly, as if it blew right into his face with the fresh breeze, the record isn't important to him anymore. It has been blown away without fanfare, lost to the distant foggy tides.

The record doesn't matter when he still has the scent of a sleeping James Campbell hidden in the crevices of his skin. Not when he's just opened his mouth back on the shore and said the most terrifying three words he ever has in his life without fear. Not when James brought his bags.

It's time.

He takes a deep breath to slow down his racing heart, steadfastly ignoring the fresh bursts of fear and adrenaline pumping through his veins. Without meaning to, he looks quickly back to the shore, and immediately his eyes find James, standing frozen in the sand with the wind blowing his golden hair back from his face. Looking like sunrise light pooling across a soft, cashmere beach. Looking like the crystal clear waters, rippling with glittering light, in which Sydney had looked into through angry tears and first seen the jellyfish bobbing gently by his feet.

Looking like the feeling of opening the door to his little house and seeing someone else's shoes already sitting just inside. *James'* shoes.

He sees only James Campbell, who looks back at Sydney with such steadfast focus that Sydney wants to say "fuck it" and race back into shore as fast as he can. Abandon his board in the shallows, and sprint madly towards James, and tell him that saying "*I love you*" was the easiest thing Sydney has ever done in his life. The most poignant moment of clarity—more deeply felt in his bones than the moment he'd first stood up on a surfboard on trembling, fifteen-year-old legs.

James nods from the shore. Sydney can see his lips just barely moving, whispering something to himself in the breeze. He hears James' voice clear as day in his head, crisp and warm over the sound of the roaring waves.

"*Don't you dare not come back to me.*"

Now it's time.

Sydney swallows hard against the lurch of fear in his chest and turns back to that perfect wave barreling towards him from the smooth horizon. He looks quickly down at the water pooling over his board and around his legs, cups a palmful of it in his hands and thinks of his momma. Thinks of her God. Thinks of survival.

Then he's paddling like hell out in front of the heaving mass of water, vision blocking out everything but the sight of his hands sinking again and again into the blue, pulling himself steadily along. His breathing echoes off his board, amplified across the vibrating surface of the water.

The salt tangs on his lips and tongue. The spray coats his face in foam, pulling strands of his hair down into his eyes. It feels strange to see the brilliant blue of the waves without the cover of his sunglasses—the way the sand glows like a blinking pool of pure light beaming from the edges of the waves. The way the sunlight ripples through the whitewater, surrounding his body in shimmering blue as he tugs himself towards the shore. Towards James.

The wave starts lifting him up towards the sky by the tail of his board. The ocean surges beneath him, rumbling and churning as it gains rushing speed. Sydney blinks, and he sees the speed and the height hovering over the waters like he always does. Sees the angles and drop in, the perfect path to take and the precise moment to stand up on his board and drop in.

He is alone in the ocean. Alone in the world.

Except, he *isn't*, because James Campbell is in the water, the sky, the sea. And the molecules of his blood poured into the Vietnam foam are here, now, wrapping snuggly around Sydney's shaking skin and guiding his way.

He grips the sides of his board with unsteady fingers right at the crest, and he peers over the massive drop towering down from the cliff of pure water. His heart screams and beats like a war drum in his chest, echoing until it is the only sound against the rest of the silent, muffled earth.

Sydney sucks in a wet, salty breath through his lips, thinks of the color of James Campbell's eyes in the earliest morning light, and then leaps up to standing, ready to fly straight over the edge.

He soars down the face of the wave in near free-fall, zooming straight down the three-story drop with nothing but the screaming wind at his front and the ripping force of the ocean beneath his legs. His knees tremble with energy, his thighs ache and grasp at his board, desperate to stay standing so the sea doesn't fling and pitch him away.

He feels one-thousand feet high in the air. As if he could angle his board just so and soar off, carried on the wind into the sky. Like he could spread out his arms and fly across the island through the clouds. And he could land back in his home, slipping straight between the sheets, James Campbell already waiting for him with a warm smile on his lips and no fear left in his eyes.

Sydney grunts against the force of the wave pummeling him from all sides. He hunkers down against his board, arms flying out to catch his balance, fighting against the wild, thrashing current beneath him. He's almost to the foot of the wave, just barely ahead of the breaking crest. He needs to pick up a little more speed to make it out from under the crushing force of the barrel. If he doesn't, he'll be pummeled down into the deep, cast off like the smallest piece of seaweed thrown limply across the spray.

He bends his knees deeper and sucks in a breath, fighting like hell to reach the bottom without flying off into the spray, or being bucked from his board. He hears the wave crash in a screaming roar behind him, feels the slapping rush of spray and foam slam at his back with the force of a moving train. It shoots him forward like a rocket across the surface of the water, blinding him in a cloud of whitewater that slaps at his bare skin and burns in his eyes. He can't tell if he's up on his board or hurtling through the water. If he's breathing in oxygen or salt. If he's traveling towards the shore or being sucked back down into the claws of the deep.

Sydney's heart pangs in his chest. He needs to reach the shore. Needs to reach James. Needs to *live* . . .

Suddenly, like the brilliant sun piercing through the clouds, Sydney's lungs suck in a gulp of pure, dry air. His eyes catch a glimpse of dark green mountain backed by an open blue sky.

The deafening roar in his ears subsides. He can hear himself breathe again, and the droplets of water from his curls drip into his eyes in little splashes. He can tell that he's standing upright, still clinging to his board with numb and shaking legs. His stomach is on fire, abs clenched so tightly he thinks he'll never draw in a full breath again.

And he's alive.

Suddenly, he laughs. A smile and a sigh and a sob all at once as the pent-up fear in his body escapes from his muscles in a rush. He looks up once towards the bursting blue sky, noting one solitary egret flying across the sea of soft, white clouds, and then he looks back towards the shore, running his fingers through his curls to see.

James Campbell stands tall and sturdy in the crowd, illuminated on the beach by a ray of sunlight that seems to shine directly onto his body, and his alone. The rest of the people on the beach are waving their arms and cheering, calling out and clapping and rushing in closer to the water to celebrate his ride. But James stands silent and unmoving among them all, arms clasped tightly behind his neck, with hints of a brilliant smile illuminating the corners of his face.

Sydney smiles back, breathless and panting. He thanks his momma's God who separated the sky from the sea, thanks the ocean for carrying him safely to shore, and then leaps off his board into the swirling shallows, the cool water like a kiss across his aching skin.

He waits underwater for the bulk of the wave to pass over him, then surfaces into the calm between the swells. The bubbles of foam sizzle and pop in his ears, and his hair falls limply into his eyes with stinging salt. Like a madman, he paddles farther into the shore, catching the smaller breaks to propel him forward, then he rips off his ankle strap and leaves his board to coast up to the sand.

He runs in the soft shallows, shins slapping against the receding waves. The other surfers are running towards him in a group—Don and Dickie and Willis and the rest, Hank with a wet towel still around his neck, never having made it past the punishing break during the round. They're calling his name and cupping their palms around their mouths, looking at him like he's the goddamn sun.

Sydney makes his way on numb legs into the warmth and noise and bright light of the real world, where the earth doesn't heave and roll beneath his feet, and he isn't left floating on the hazy, intangible tips of the open sky. He walks towards the small crowd like he's hearing the entire earth for the very first time.

"Fucking primo ride, Danny!"

"Largest wave of the day, dude!"

"Shit, Moore, you just showed us how it's done! That's how it's fucking done, man!"

The ocean continues to pound at his back, rushing in over and over again onto the sand, covering his feet with tingling foam. He lets them pat his back and reach out to touch his board bobbing in the shallows like a trophy. He hears their words and cheers as one giant sound, crackling in his ears and blowing heat against his face.

Sydney isn't even sure what he says back, or how he looks. If he smiles or waves or says, "*I know, man, didn't think I was gonna make it out of that one without needing one of your sorry asses to come out and do the rescuing this time.*"

Then the crowd parts, and the sound fades away, and all he can see is James.

James, who has his hands clasped behind his straight back as if he's standing watch on the deck of a ship. James, whose eyes are sparkling like the sunlight dappling the surface of the sea.

James, who is walking towards him slowly, eyes locked on to his.

Sydney runs to him like he's never known what it is to truly run until this moment. The saltwater stings his eyes, and the sunlight blares, and his curls fall down into his face over and over, and still he runs towards James Campbell like a clear beacon of guiding light, clearing his path across the shore.

His toes trip in the sand, his calves and thighs burn, and James' calm face breaks just before Sydney reaches him and crushes him into his arms, feeling James' hands grip hard enough at his bare, wet back to leave a mark—a brand new tattoo of the memory of James' touch on his skin.

James' back is shaking, and his face is buried deep into Sydney's neck. Sydney holds him tight against himself, breathing in the sunlight from his hair, cupping the back of his neck in his palm.

They are the only two souls in Waimea Bay.

And then James huffs out a breath and moans. "Who the hell are you?" he whispers into Sydney's quivering skin. He grips him even tighter. "God, Sydney . . . I love you."

Sydney wants to take a deep breath and dive under and drown in James' words. Wants to breathe them in and keep them down in the pit of his lungs so they can never escape from him out in the wind across the ocean.

The water from his skin is seeping into James' clothes, making them cling to his body. Sydney wants to pick James up and fucking carry him back across the island to their home. Let James throw him down onto the bed and take him. Have him. Let James cover him with his lips and fingers and tongue and let Sydney know that he belongs to him until the day a force of nature kicks down the door and physically drags them apart.

He wants to hold James' face in his hands in front of everyone and kiss him on the shore, letting James taste the fresh saltwater on his lips. Wants to pick him up and feel James' legs wrap around his waist like the girlfriends of the other surfers do when they're kissing in the sand after they've won, kissing to the sounds of cheers and whistles echoing down the beach.

Their embrace lasts less than five seconds—just short enough to be two surfing buddies, champions of the Billabong congratulating each other in the sand.

James sucks in a deep breath when he pulls back, like he's really breathing for the first time all day. His eyes are shining and clear, and Sydney nearly gasps. The darkness always lurking in the corners of

James' eyes is suddenly gone—eradicated completely and replaced by a warm, glowing pride. By relief. A strange sense of security washes over Sydney as he looks down into James' open face, more thoroughly than the waves that just crashed over every inch of his skin when he was alone out in the bay.

And the bravest man on earth just said that he loved him. His body and his voice and his home and his mind and his surfing. *Him.* And Sydney just happened to look up from his feet and find him on a crowded pier.

James holds his gaze for another second before he pats his arm once and takes a step away, putting empty space between them again. "You are something else," he whispers, then, with a tilt of his head, "Later." Sydney glances up at the crowded shore and reluctantly understands.

Then James grins one last time at him, his beautiful lips curving up just at the corners in a smile meant for him and him alone, and then he steps just barely to the side, and Sydney absolutely freezes.

It cannot be her. It absolutely cannot.

But it is.

Sydney blinks hard then gapes at James, making sure that what he's seeing isn't just some dehydrated hallucination in the middle of the hot beach. He can feel his mouth hanging half-open, his face slack. James looks at him with eyes as deep as the sea and nods gently, his face carefully blank.

Sydney can sense the surfers behind him retreating back to their own groups—going over the best waves of the day, making plans to go grab a drink, passing along the latest news and gossip from the circuit beyond Oahu. The wind from the waves rushes in streams across Sydney's back, pushing him closer to where Lahela stands motionless in the sand, her silk skirt billowing in a ripple across the grains while the breeze whips through the loose strands of her braid.

She looks back at Sydney with watering eyes, and her hands hang helplessly at her sides. Sydney takes one hesitant step forward, toes sinking blindly into the sand.

She whispers in a thin voice into the breeze. "Oh, Danny."

Sydney takes another step closer and shakes his head. "I don't understand," he whispers back. His voice is nearly lost in the wind.

She smiles, and her mouth trembles at the corners. She holds out her hands, fingers shaking. "Can I see you?" she asks.

Sydney feels that if he does take three steps forward and hold her hands in his, she'll disappear into mist. He hasn't touched those hands since he was newly fifteen, walking down a hot sidewalk with a trash bag slung over his shoulder and his father's yells still echoing in his ears.

He's afraid they'll be thinner than he remembers. More frail. He's afraid they'll feel like his momma's hands did gripping at his shirt on their Arizona porch with a half-empty liquor bottle spilling over onto the splintered wood. And he's afraid that if he touches her, and feels the bones of her hands, then maybe it will be James who vanishes into thin air. One good thing gained, another taken.

He's suddenly more afraid than he was twenty minutes ago at the crest of the wave.

James clears his throat and speaks gently at his side. "Sydney," he says. It travels through the tense muscles in Sydney's shaking body like a salve, loosening the icy stiffness in each joint.

With a rush of air, Sydney moves forward in the sand and reaches out his hands to take her outstretched fingers. She immediately grips him with a surprising, frantic strength.

"My boy," she says, voice shaking.

Her voice sounds just like he always remembered it—deep and fragile, gently lilting over the vowels like flower petals bending under the weight of a warm, soft breeze.

Sydney doesn't even know what comes over him. He blinks hard, letting the sight of her sink crisply into his vision, not fading away into a ghost after all. Then he steps forward and lets her wrap him in her arms, feeling her thin bones under his hands as she stretches up on her toes to reach her arms around his bent neck and shoulders. Her long braid rests against his cheek—the same way she'd always worn it for the five years that she had made his lunches and sent him off to school and held ice to his cheek all the evenings he came home with bloody noses or black eyes.

Her hair smells like flowers. It's the smell of mornings when Sydney would wake up at three o'clock and make his way on silent bare feet down the hallway to the kitchen, only to see her standing there in her nightgown drinking tea. The smell of the fragile chamomile on those special silent nights they sat across from each other at the kitchen table, doing nothing at all. The smell of her perfume that had wafted over to Sydney across the tense air when she had chased him down on the sidewalk, grabbed his wrist hard, and begged him not to turn his back on the Lord.

Her hair smells like burned wax candles and sand. The citrus of his father's sharp aftershave, and the slightest hint of fried fish from dinner the night before—a dinner which Sydney hadn't been at to help eat the leftovers.

And her hair somehow smells like the time his momma took him out of school in the middle of the day, and drove him to town to see *West Side Story*, and bought him his own box of Good and Plenty to eat. And she had left him there at the theater, accidentally, and his father came by with red in his eyes to pick him up four hours later, but that hadn't mattered at all. Not to Sydney.

Lahela pulls back from him with wet eyes, smoothing out the front of her now damp blouse. Sydney opens his mouth to apologize, but instead hears himself ask, "How did you know where to find me?"

Lahela smiles with sad eyes. Sydney finds he can't tear his gaze away from her, not even to blink. If he does, she'll disappear into the sand, vanishing forever and never to return. He can still feel James' presence standing calmly at his side, grounding and safe.

He gazes into the face of the past he'd screamed "*fuck you*" to out across the surface of the waves early that one morning, and he tries desperately to convince himself that the past two hours—the past two weeks, the past seven years—have been real.

"I heard about you after you won that first time," she says. "Everyone was talking about it, boy. It was in the papers." Her voice sounds wistful like she's describing the plot of an old and favorite book. One with a very sad ending.

Sydney barely remembers to nod.

"And I saw you the next year there, competing. When you won again."

Sydney's eyes widen in shock. "You were there?"

She nods. Sydney wants to question everything he's ever experienced in his life. The thought that he was standing along the Banzai holding his board while his own step-mom was secretly among the

423

crowd without him knowing makes him feel like everything he's ever seen has maybe been just a mirage.

Like maybe James Campbell never appeared out of nowhere in the tree-lined lane—neither time.

"You stopped writing to me, boy," she goes on. "Did you get my letters?"

Sydney looks at his bare feet encrusted with sand and feels a flush of shame spreading up his neck. "I did."

He's not sure what else he could possibly say. "*I did, but I didn't want you to be associated with the new black sheep of the family, the queer?*" or maybe, "*I did, but you think I'm going to hell anyways so I didn't really think it would be worth the time to respond?*" or really he could just tell her the truth and say, "*Because every time I picked up the pen I remembered that I hated my lonely fucking life a little bit more. And because you let him make me leave.*"

Lahela doesn't wait for him to elaborate. Instead she takes a calm breath and looks out at the sea, gesturing so the bracelets around her wrist tingle together. "So is this what you do then? To make your living?"

Sydney follows her hand to see the waves still pounding at their backs, and he realizes he'd completely forgotten the entire Pacific Ocean was even there.

He clears his throat, suddenly feeling ten-years-old again, that first day she ever shook his hand and asked him what was his favorite food. "Um, no. I—I work. I just . . . I do this. Too."

He winces at himself—the pathetic jumble of words leaving his lips that is somehow supposed to stand in for the story of his life.

But Lahela's expression doesn't change at his vague answer, and she turns her gaze away from the sea until her eyes see straight through his skin. "You surf like were born out there in the water," she says. Her eyes are focused and grave. "A true master of *he'e nalu.*"

Sydney feels his eyes watering. He hears what she's saying—what she really means—even though it feels inordinately difficult to hold his chin high and believe it. That somehow a kid from bumfuck nowhere Iowa worked his ass off enough to call what he does on a board an art. A religion.

He thinks of James, fists clenched and eyes furious in a way Sydney hasn't seen him look like in what feels like a long, long time.

"*This isn't just a game for me,*" he'd said, as if it physically hurt him to spit out the words. Sydney suddenly understands those words in an entirely new way, deep in his bones. He wonders if Lahela can somehow understand any of the rapid thoughts flashing across his face.

He can still feel James' quiet presence at his side, hovering in the background as if he's expecting to simply be ignored, or be introduced as a surfing buddy Sydney's seen a few times on the shores. And James looks perfectly fine with this arrangement, not bothered in the least that Sydney's gone nearly a whole ten minutes without introducing the only two people he's talking to on this entire beach.

In an instant, the thought of speaking a single word more to the lost memory of the woman in front of him without her realizing who James is feels worse than drowning.

But, God . . . he wants desperately just to stand there and look at her forgotten smile. To talk about surfing, and ask how she is, and if they still live in the old house, and pretend that his past is behind him—that his father hasn't gone seven years without speaking his name. He wants to pretend that the reason he ever had to leave in the first place is now long dead and gone—just some teenage mistake mixed with coming-of-age confusion. He wishes he could look the woman who just called his surfing *he'e nalu* in the eyes and say he was no longer the man with a photograph of a sailor in his pocket—that he's changed.

But James Campbell loves him, and the betrayal of not latching on to that with both hands shakes him to his core.

Sydney steps back from Lahela and looks over at James with a pointed gaze, and James immediately takes a breath and steps closer to his side. Sydney drinks in his last calm look at Lahela, while she's still looking at him with warmth and pride in her eyes, and then he opens his mouth to speak over the sound of the waves.

"This is Jimmy Campbell," he says. "James. He's the new Billabong champion." He waves his hand between them. "James, my stepmother, Lahela Moore."

Lahela's eyes widen, and she reaches out her hand to shake James'. "The new champion?" she gasps with sparkling eyes. "You're as good as my boy, then."

*My boy.*

425

Sydney tucks those words away in his mind so he can revisit them after this interaction inevitably goes to shit—after Lahela runs away from him, embarrassed and disappointed. He feels James stiffen beside him, and Sydney guesses James realizes roughly what he's about to say. And James Campbell does absolutely nothing to stop him, just stands tall, his steady chin high.

"James is . . ." Sydney swallows hard over a bone dry mouth. He shuffles his feet so that their shoulders are nearly touching. "James is with me. We—he lives with me."

Sydney stares steadily at Lahela, willing her to somehow understand. Eternal seconds tick by, as if the crash of the waves themselves is keeping time.

Just as a fresh wind blows her braid across her chest, she sucks in a breath, her eyes wide.

But Lahela doesn't run away from them in the sand. Instead, she stands frozen. She whips her head back and forth a couple times between them both, then settles on James standing at Sydney's side, looking strong and tensed and ready for a fight.

Sydney watches, helpless, with his heart in his throat as Lahela seems to study James with focused, narrowed eyes, her lips thin. The beach is silent and deafening all at once. Sydney hears his own breathing echo harshly in his ears, as if the water behind him has turned into sand paper thrashing and cutting against the rocks along the shore, filling the beach with snarling white noise.

Finally, Lahela reaches up to clutch her fingers around the cross at her neck. She looks at James as if she's about to pop up on one of Waimea's waves.

"You don't look like a . . . you don't look like it. One of them," she says.

To Sydney's surprise, James' eyes soften. The corner of his mouth curves in a gentle smile. "No, I suppose I don't," he answers. "But I am." He looks quickly at Sydney, eyes full and blue. "With him."

Sydney has never wanted to scoop up and kiss James more than in that moment. He wants to run his fingers through James' perfect hair, warmed by the sun, then look back at Lahela and ask her if she can even fucking believe it that he got this man to somehow love him—pack up his life and leave behind everything he's ever known to move to Oahu with Danny Moore. To be *with* him.

Lahela is still standing frozen, watching them both. Sydney bites his tongue so he doesn't beg her to speak—to just fucking say something, anything at all, instead of leaving them in suspense. Yell at him, curse him, tell him he's going to hell, just anything instead of this silence.

She clears her throat and eventually reaches out her hand again, fingers slightly trembling. James frowns, surprised, then takes it.

"It's nice to meet you, James," she says, in a very even voice. "My boy was not happy. Before."

James looks down at their clasped hands with a slight frown and shakes hers once before letting go. Sydney stares at the empty space where their joined hands used to be, scared to breathe unless everything around him dissolves into a dream.

"Danny," she says softly.

He looks up at her, his eyes wide and unblinking. She takes him in, letting the wind blow the loose strands of her braid across her face as she blinks into the sun hanging heavy and full over the blinding ocean.

"You need to trim your hair," she says. "Too many tangles at the ends." Then, before Sydney can even react, she reaches forward and touches his arm. "When will you surf next?"

Sydney feels like his brain is thirty seconds behind, frantically trying to play catch-up, still waiting for her to shake her head at him in disgust. "Sunset Beach is in three weeks," he hears himself answer back.

She nods and releases her grip. She doesn't smile, but there's a clarity on her face Sydney hasn't ever seen since the first day she showed up in their living room with his father's hand on her shoulder and a new engagement ring on her finger.

"I will try to be there, then," she says.

And then, after one last steady look, she's turning to leave, skirt blowing out across the sand as she makes her way back to wait for a bus to take her clear across the island, on her way home to cook dinner and do his father's laundry and sit with her Bible in her special chair to pray for his soul. And probably to pray for James' soul now, too.

A flash of panic suddenly shoots through Sydney's stomach. Dread claws at his mind—that despite what Lahela just said, despite everything he just learned, that if she walks away now Sydney will never see her again. That he'll lose everything he thought he might have just hesitantly gained back.

He takes two running steps forward in the sand. "Wait!"

She turns, holding the blowing strands back from her face.

"Mikey," Sydney says, the name completely foreign in his mouth. "Is Mikey okay?"

Lahela smiles, but her eyes are sad. "Yes, your brother is well," she says. She pauses and licks her lips, then goes on, still turning back awkwardly at the edges of the beach. "He's going to UC Berkeley in the fall. For engineering."

Sydney finds he can't ask a single follow-up question, and Lahela doesn't offer up information about anyone else. Instead, she glances one last time at James, then turns to keep walking toward the palm tree-lined road.

Sydney stands stunned in the sand as Lahela's skirt disappears into a cloud of dust and leafy green—her thin form, both familiar to him and alien, swallowed up by the island from which she came. His brain feels like it's churning through thick, wet mud, dragging him back and slowing him down.

His brother is going to Berkeley. His brother, who always begged Sydney to finish his homework for him under the covers with a flashlight each night, is going to Berkeley to study engineering, probably making his father beam with pride when he tells the other Lieutenants on the base. And meanwhile Sydney stands on a beach without even a high school diploma, with a tiny ad in the phone book naming himself as a pseudo-mechanic for cheap, and saltwater and grease stains permanently etched into his fingertips.

It's a shock, even though it really shouldn't be—the fact that the world kept turning even after he turned his back on it and swam out into the sea. The fact that his brother isn't still eleven years old, and that Lahela's hair is streaked with grey. Fuck, maybe his father isn't even Lieutenant Moore anymore.

His pride from before at conquering Waimea suddenly leaves his body in a rush. He feels pathetic and young in the sand. Left behind.

But Lahela had been proud of him, hadn't she? She'd stood tall and looked at him with pride and called his surfing *he'e nalu*.

And James doesn't care that there isn't some fancy framed diploma on his wall.

Right?

"Sydney?"

Sydney realizes he forgot that James was even standing there, or that the rest of the beach was filled with surfers probably wondering who the hell Danny was just talking to, or that he'd just surfed one of the biggest waves Waimea's seen in years and lived to tell about it.

He'd forgotten that James had held him close and whispered into his ear, "*I love you.*" How could he *forget* that?

He turns to look at James, still speechless, and James smiles in that way of his, lighting up every grain of sand on the beach into a brilliant burst of sunlight with just the lines creasing the corners of his eyes.

"Come on, then," James says. "I just had a birthday standing here waiting for you to move. You need to say bye to any of these guys or can we get the hell out of here and be alone?"

James Campbell is a genius. Of course they should leave. Of course they should go back to their home together now that the fear is over. Of course they should go and kiss each other and fall asleep in each other's arms. Because James Campbell *loves* him.

Sydney nods, and James lets out a breath like he's relieved as they start to make their way over to Sydney's board and bag. Sydney looks one last time out at the raging waves, frowning at the eerie sensation that he'd surfed across them thirty days ago instead of just thirty minutes, and then they turn to go, shoulder to shoulder, leaving the group still mingling behind them in the sand.

"Moore, come on, man! You ducking out on me?"

Hank jogs after them across the beach, waving a hand for them to wait. Sydney realizes that if any other surfer on that beach had just flagged them down, he would have felt an unprecedented surge of annoyance.

Hank lifts up his hat to wipe the sweat off his brow with his forearm before jamming it back down. "We're all gonna head down for a beer if you guys wanna join. You know, celebrate not dying and all," Hank says with a wink.

James chuckles sarcastically, and Sydney fights the urge to reach out and take James' hand. "You know me, man," he says back. "Not much for sticking around. We're just gonna head back home."

He realizes his mistake too late. Sydney bites his tongue in his mouth, waiting for the inevitable awkward clarification on what the hell he just implied with his words. By his side, James spreads his feet to plant himself in the sand.

Hank barely hesitates, just blinks and looks quickly at James with just his eyes. Then he smiles in the corner of his mouth and scratches at his jaw. "It's casual, Moore. You out-surfed all of our sorry asses today. Guess you weren't too skinny after all—deserve to be rid of all of us for a nice break."

Sydney lets out a breath he hadn't realized he'd been holding. Or maybe he had realized it, the way it had burned like fire and ice in his concrete lungs. Hank nods over at James, hands in his pockets. "You'll be at Sunset in a few weeks? To surf?"

James nods yes, and Sydney suddenly catches the gaze of understanding between them. He feels like a moron for not having spotted it before. Too focused on himself, on the waves, on his ride. James looks at Hank like he's seeing a friend from his past, still covered head to toe in camo with the jungle at his back.

And Sydney wonders, fleetingly, if it takes having run through a Vietnam jungle with a gun in your hands to be a person who wants to have a conversation with him beyond hello. He wonders if that's something that would bother him, or fill him with an oddly undeserving pride.

James rubs the back of his neck. "Guess I am, now that I've tricked everyone into thinking I know what the fuck I'm doing. You?"

Hank laughs. "Nah, man. Not much one for competitions this year. Just been sneaking out here when I don't have to worry about points and heats and shit. Leave all them fancy trophies to Moore, here."

Hank leans forward to hold Sydney firmly on the arm before Sydney or James can answer him. "Go on, then, you fucking hermit. You both earned it."

The look in Hank's eyes as he quickly glances between them instantly confirms just how much Hank understands. Sydney fights to hold his head high as he lifts up a hand, barely muttering, "Catch you later" in time for Hank to hear it as he walks back to the group of other surfers still lounging on their boards in the sand. Casually, as if he hadn't just knowingly shaken the hand of the gayest surfer in Hawaii and told him to go home and be with his man.

"So, he knows," James says under his breath, not a question.

Sydney's eyes don't leave Hank's hat in the crowd. "Yeah. He knows."

He's just about to try and concoct some sort of apology when James taps his arm before turning to head to the Jeep. Sydney follows silently, watching his feet carve footprints into the sand. By unspoken agreement, Sydney hands James the keys when they get near, and after throwing his board in the back, he gets into the passenger seat, placing his hand firmly on James' knee when James lets out the clutch to start driving them home.

The drive is silent. James whistles a Stones tune through his teeth as he drives, slowly meandering the winding seaside road back down along the North Shore towards home. Sydney stares out the window, letting the wind rush against his face, and he breathes in the salt sea air in deep gasps—the hints of warm flowers and earthy mud. Salted fish and grassy straw and sweet, milky coconuts wafting on the breeze. James' deodorant, and the musk of sweat mixed with saltwater and hot sand, and the worn, cracked leather of the seats in the Jeep.

Sydney closes his eyes to the sea and trees rolling by, and with a rush of emotion he realizes for the first time in his life that this is home— the first time since he stepped off the plane in Honolulu holding his father's hand with a Jetsons rolling suitcase behind him. That his little hut with its peeling paint and empty beach and creaking wood floors is the absolute best place in the universe. That he's one lucky son of a bitch.

He looks over at James, driving with one hand hanging out the window and the wind rustling his golden hair, and he grins so wide it hurts his sunburned cheeks.

"Remind me," Sydney says over the sound of the engine. "I've already forgotten." He leans back further in his seat, letting his curls blow across his eyes.

James' eyes light up even as he shakes his head in exasperation at the winding road. He covers Sydney's hand on his knee with his own. "I love you," he says. He wipes across his mouth with the hand that had been hanging out the window, and the corners of his eyes crinkle as he continues to shake his head. "You are something else, Moore. But fuck, I really do."

# 26

Sydney gratefully steps back when James gets his board out of the back for him after parking out in front of Chuck Hobbs' place in the usual spot. To Sydney's tired, drooping eyes, the world feels like he's living inside a film. One where he has James to drive him back home after a morning spent surfing Waimea, and James to carry his board for him and casually walk down to the house—*their* house—and James to look back over his shoulder and say, "Come on, you lazy ass, your legs are like five inches longer than mine and I'm carrying your goddamn board and I'm *still* beating you."

Sydney jogs to catch up with him, wondering if he just ran a little bit faster if he'd sprout wings and fly up into the clear blue sky at the lightness in his chest.

James sticks the board down in the sand and leans it up against the house, then shucks off his shoes. "You must be starving."

On cue, Sydney's stomach growls. James smirks and walks into the cool darkness of the house, heading straight for the small fridge and looking at the contents inside with a frown on his face, muttering to himself under his breath.

Sydney stands frozen in the doorway, watching James casually look through the fridge in his bare feet as if he hadn't just picked up his whole damn life and moved it here just yesterday. As if he hadn't just watched Sydney surf the most dangerous waves on earth, or whispered "*I love you*" into his ear on the crowded beach.

A low sense of dread—the complete disbelieving anxiety that all of this can't possibly be real—finally surges up and spills over in Sydney's chest, and he takes a step forward into the room, heart pounding.

"James."

The tone of his voice makes James pop up his head over the refrigerator door. "Something wrong?"

Sydney gestures limply with his hand around the silent, empty house, not even sure what to say. "You—you gave up so much for this. For me."

It's not at all what he'd meant to say. He'd meant to say something inane to break the silence like, "*I think there's some chicken thighs in the freezer,*" or, "*Did you bring anything you wanna put up to decorate the room?*"

He sure as hell hadn't meant to stand there looking young and stupid in his doorway, reminding James of everything he gave up to be here. That he doesn't have a job yet, and that he left all his friends behind. That people like Lahela and Hank will look at him closely now standing next to Sydney, and some of them will *know*. That he'll be the fag from Los Angeles who fell for the fag from Oahu.

He wants to sink to his knees and apologize and tell him to pack his bags and run—go back to his normal reality before it's all too late. But before he can do anything, James shuts the fridge door and leans back against the counter, arms spread casually out behind him.

James nods slowly at Sydney's words. "Yeah, in a way I did."

Sydney swallows hard. His voice sounds too small in the echoing house. "I'm sorry."

James frowns, taking a step forward. "Why the hell are you apologizing?"

Sydney shrugs. His mouth is dry. "Because, you . . . you aren't—I don't want you to go through what I do. You don't deserve that."

"Well you don't deserve it either, love."

Sydney shuts his eyes at the name, caught off guard by the pulse of longing through his chest.

James goes on, as if he hasn't even realized what word he just used, or its effect. "Sydney, look at me." He waits until Sydney looks back up from the floor. "I wouldn't have gotten back on that plane in LA if I wasn't sure about this. If I wasn't as fucking close to one-hundred percent as I could be."

Sydney reels as the room about him spins, causing everything to blur except the clear lines of James' limbs. "I'm sure, too," he whispers.

James nods and clears his throat. The house seems vast and silent, warping around them in its own private universe where nobody else even exists. "You know," James starts, rubbing the back of his neck. "I . . . when I was in LA, I stayed with Rob and Lori that first night back. I told Rob that . . . that I'm gay. When we surfed in the morning."

Sydney gapes. "You told him?"

"Yeah, I did." James shrugs his shoulders. "He helped me get everything together so I could get back out here, actually. Told me I was an idiot for not coming back to you sooner."

"A week is still pretty damn soon. Less than a week."

James grins, then it falls from his face as he stares out one of the windows over Sydney's shoulder. "I think you know this. That—that with Rob . . . I've always—"

"You loved him."

James frowns. "Actually, no. Well, I mean, yes. In a way. But it's not the same as . . . as this. Not at all." His palm rubs once over his chest and shoulder. "I was in a bad place when I met him," he whispers. "Really bad."

Sydney's throat closes up. It's almost physically impossible for him to calmly think about James sitting alone in an empty apartment with his scar still angry and red and knowing that nobody will call on him that day, or the next, or the next.

"I'm glad that you met him," Sydney says. "Extremely glad."

James' eyes are dark. "Me, too." He sighs, and his eyes squint like he's in pain. "But it's not just . . . Rob told me, last week. Admitted, I guess. If he hadn't already been with Lori when we met . . ."

James looks at him like he's waiting for an explosion, and Sydney suddenly remembers the way Rob's fingers had brushed James' wet hair back from his face in the tide pools. The way Rob's entire body shook.

Surprisingly, the realization comes with a wave of relief. It means James was never going to sit in an empty apartment knowing that nobody was going to call on him for the rest of time.

"I understand," he says.

James stares at him for a long moment, then grins in the corner of his mouth as he slowly shakes his head. "Yeah, I guess you do."

"He's the only person you ever told," Sydney says, not a question.

James huffs a laugh. "Yeah. That and you—well, you told *me*. But . . . God, the world didn't end, you know? It's—" James runs his hand through his hair, looking over Sydney's shoulder. "Shit, Sydney, I wanted to kiss you on the beach after you came out of the waves today. I wanted to so fucking badly. I wanna tell people that I'm with you. That I just moved in with you, because that's the kind of shit people get to be excited about."

Sydney's eyes grow wet. "Me, too."

James sighs, then walks forward and takes Sydney's cold fingers in his. He looks down at their joined hands. "But, this—what we have to do . . . it isn't right. I mean, *this* feels right, for me. Being with you. It's the first time I've ever felt like the war wasn't just *it*. That I have the whole rest of my life. And you . . . you helped give that to me. But I can't tell a fucking single person about it because we just can't. Not everyone's Rob, or even Hank."

Sydney grips James' hand hard in his. "I know. But James, I didn't give anything to you. I'm just . . . I'm only just—"

"Listen to me. I don't think either of us knows what the hell this is yet. What . . . what it will mean. How hard it'll be. But that sure as hell doesn't mean I'm leaving you, or that I don't want to live here with you."

"But you shouldn't—"

"No, no buts." James' head rises bravely. "I haven't wanted to fucking kill myself since the second I met you, and I'm pretty sure I'm not totally off base when I say I think you've felt the same. So unless you tell me to leave—"

"I'd never tell you to leave."

"Right, so unless you tell me to leave, I'm in this. I'm with you. I wouldn't have come back if I didn't feel that it was worth it to try, okay?"

Sydney can barely breathe. He gasps in a deep breath, then reaches forward to pull James into his arms. He rests his cheek against his hair and runs his hand up the muscles in James' back.

He wonders if James can feel the hammering thuds of his heart through his chest. "I never kissed anyone before you," he admits, hating that his voice cracks like he's actually still fifteen.

He feels James' smile against his neck. "I know. It's never . . . it's never felt like that for me, either. It's just been wom—"

"No, I mean *literally*. You . . . you were it."

James pulls back and looks up into his face, and Sydney uses every ounce of energy left in his body to keep his eyes open. He knows his face is beet red.

James frowns. "But, I thought you . . . you'd been with—"

"It was all just . . ." Sydney glances down between them at the lower half of his body. His face burns even hotter. "You know."

The following silence is so thick Sydney wonders if all the air in his house has been sucked away. Then, to his complete surprise, James laughs. He runs his hands up Sydney's chest and grabs two handfuls of his shirt.

"So, the infamous Danny Moore's first kiss, huh?" He runs his thumbs once over Sydney's nipples, then winks as he looks into his eyes. "Lucky me."

Sydney melts. He collapses forward against James' chest, holding him tightly as he he smiles into James' hair. The house doesn't seem quite so large or silent anymore. "I'm not sure what the hell I did to deserve you."

James huffs as he runs his hands up Sydney's spine. "I'm not sure either, because you can be a fucking asshole sometimes."

He pulls back and grabs Sydney's cheek, bringing him down for a kiss. "Now stop doubting me. I'm a fucking decade older than you, I know what I'm choosing here."

Sydney laughs despite himself as James steps back. "Seriously, you're gonna play the age card? Now?"

"I'm gonna play the age card if you keep doubting that I have more feelings for you than I even know how to deal with," James says. He walks back towards the kitchen. "Now go and shower, you smell like hot beach. And when you come back, we're gonna eat whatever I can whip up out of this sorry ass fridge and drink beers and you're gonna help me come up with what the hell I can do out here for a real job."

Sydney stares at James' back as he effortlessly navigates the small kitchen. The world straightens itself out again around him for the first time since he'd set foot in the doorway.

James looks back at him over his shoulder when Sydney doesn't immediately move. "Go on. I'll be here."

Then he turns back to the fridge and leaves Sydney standing in the middle of the house. The house that's filled with the sounds of James

Campbell whistling while he rummages through the fridge. And the warmth of James' skin reaches out across the hardwood floor and spreads through every inch of their home, caressing the tired soles of Sydney's water-wrinkled feet.

"So your step-mom knew, then. About you."

Sydney takes another sip of his beer out on the porch, bringing his knees up to his chest.

He hums. "Wasn't exactly a secret. I'm pretty sure the whole street heard what my father was yelling that day."

James winces. "The usual names?"

"The usual, and then some. He got fairly creative."

James stretches his legs out, resting his feet on the banister of the porch, and cradles his icy bottle in his lap.

"I sorta thought she was gonna react more when you told her about me today."

"So did I." Sydney takes another drink, then lets his beer hang between his fingers by the neck, swaying softly in the breeze coming steadily off the ocean. "I don't think she's ever actually met any gay people before, who were known at least. Think you threw her for a loop with all your manly muscles and shit. No lipstick or feather boas or lisp or anything."

James huffs out a laugh and runs a hand through his hair. "Never understood it—those guys you hear about up in San Francisco or New York or whatever who dress like that. Never understood how they could be that brave, letting everyone know like that. I'd be scared shitless to even go to one of those bars, scared of a raid. And they just . . . go out there and do it. Probably have bigger balls than any of the men I even served with—I'd bet money on that."

Sydney chuckles. "You know, I went to a gay bar in the Castro once, couple of years ago after a competition in Santa Cruz."

"No shit?"

"Was like a whole different world up there. Whole blocks where everyone outside on the streets was a man holding another man's hand. Leather, high heels, the whole thing. I felt like I was on a movie set."

James smiles wistfully. "Did you take advantage of it?"

Sydney smirks. "Best blow job of my whole damn life, until you came along."

James rolls his eyes, then finishes off his beer and cracks open another on the porch railing. "You're impossible," he says. Then he sighs and settles back into his chair. "So, you're gonna see your step-mom at Sunset?"

"Looks like it."

"Will you write to her again?"

Sydney shrugs, looking out over the calm flat horizon as the sun begins to slowly drip down towards the waves.

He wants to say yes, that he could effortlessly get out a blank sheet of paper and pick back up right where he left off in his final letter. But the past seven years hang over him like a lead weight, crushing him slowly with a choking weight from the sky. He isn't eating his post-competition dinner alone in his empty kitchen, and that's enough for now.

"Don't think so," he finally says. "It still feels too soon. Might always be too soon."

He looks over at James, hoping he gets what he's saying, and James nods understandingly as he gazes out over the ocean. Then quiet peace on his face turns into a small frown, and James licks his lips like he's nervous. Sydney watches him hold his body carefully still.

"Your actual mom. . ." James trails off.

Sydney knows that it's a question. It's *the* question. And for the first time ever, the thought of answering it doesn't fill him with dread at all.

"She drank," he says simply, holding up the beer bottle in his hand with a shrug before taking another sip. "I was too young to know. Only in looking back that I've figured it out."

James nods, waiting patiently, and Sydney continues. "We moved from Ft. Knox to Arizona when I was nine. I don't even remember what city, to be honest. Near some base down there in the desert. One day there was a church picnic after service on Sunday. It was like a hundred

439

and three fucking degrees outside. I remember whining because they ran out of lemonade and I ended up pouting under a tree waiting to go home."

James laughs like he can perfectly imagine little Sydney Moore, whining and hot and sweaty at a church picnic. Sydney takes a deep breath. It's been years since he's even thought about this day, and he's certainly never said any of it out loud.

James waits, quiet and gentle on the porch, and Sydney looks at the sunlight glinting off his eyelashes before he goes on. "So my momma shows up late to this thing. Totally out of her mind already. I heard all this yelling and went over to see what the hell was going on, and there she was, standing by the food table calling the pastor's wife a bitch because she copied her potato salad recipe. Then she picked up the bowl and threw it on the ground in the dirt. And for some reason, the only thing I remember being shocked at was that her bra strap was hanging loose down her arm. She was always dressed up so perfectly. I'd never seen her bra strap before."

James hums, listening, and Sydney feels a smile grace across his mouth. "You know, actually I remember laughing. Because momma pointed her finger at the pastor's wife and said that she was jealous of all the people on earth who hadn't had to meet her. Then she turned to the pastor and told him that she could spill a can of alphabet soup on the floor and it would still be more eloquent than his sermons."

James laughs beside him. "So that's where you get it from."

Sydney hums. "Momma was the queen of calling out other people on their shit. I just didn't realize at the time she only ever did it when she was hammered."

James lets the smile gently fade from his face. "So what happened then?"

"I remember she fell. My father was screaming at me and Mikey to get her back home and he stormed off. But Mikey followed him, and everyone else just stood there staring. So I had to try and help her up by myself. And as I was trying to help her up, she just kept telling me she was okay and that I should go and play with my friends. Except I didn't have a single goddamn friend there. Everybody could hear."

Sydney suddenly feels bad for telling such a horrible story, ruining their first real evening together out on the porch of their home—

440

an evening without the knowledge that one of them is about to leave or do something completely crazy the next day.

"Sorry, man—" Sydney winces, that word now tasting sour in his mouth after everything that's happened between him and James in the last day. He presses on, hoping James didn't notice. "I know it's not really a nice story to hear."

James shakes his head. "I'm gonna start making you put a dollar in a fucking jar every time you apologize, and then you can buy me a brand new surfboard. What happened next?"

Sydney shoots him a grateful smile. He realizes he couldn't stop telling this story even if James had asked him to can it and let them sit out there in peace. It feels so good to let it fall from his lips, like releasing the image of his momma kneeling in the dirt to fade away over the sea— like setting her free, after all this time.

"I finally got her back home down the street. One of the other women came and helped me—can't remember for the life of me who she was. When we got home, my father was on the phone, sounded like he was talking to some higher officer than him. I don't really remember much of what happened after that. But a few weeks later, he woke me and Mikey up really early and said to pack everything we had and be at the car in fifteen minutes. And when we went out, my mom was already out on the porch, like she'd been there all night."

Sydney's throat tightens, and he takes a moment to let his words settle. James waits beside him, steady and calm.

"She grabbed my arm, and my father grabbed my other arm, and she was crying, yelling at him not to take me. Then I remember her cross necklace fell on the ground—just that specific detail—and then suddenly I was in the car. That's when we moved out here, to Pearl Harbor. My father never spoke of her again and I've haven't seen her since. Lahela moved in about six months later."

James lets out a slow, deep breath. "Shit."

Sydney chuckles softly. "Shit is right."

"You ever think about trying to find her?" James asks.

"Think about that every day. I don't even know where I'd start. I don't know what her maiden name was—can't remember if she ever had a job before my father, where her family was from, if she went to school, nothing."

441

A familiar shame creeps up the back of his neck, the ever-present muddy weight of inadequacy that drags him down whenever he stops to think about the fact that he should be able to just hop on a plane and find her.

He should be able to take a few hours and find out her maiden name and her family and her job. And then he wonders if he would still get on that plane even if he had the ticket in his hand and was standing on the tarmac at the bottom of the stairs.

James reaches over and touches his arm, breaking him away from his thoughts. "You're a genius, yeah? You ever get too creaky and old for surfing, you got a career as some sorta private investigator all set— already got your first case."

Sydney smiles then, and briefly covers James' hand, inordinately grateful for James dropping the subject with a joke. He takes another sip of beer and feels it settle in his stomach, releasing the ache in his muscles from the full day of battling the waves. James watches the waves beside him, lost in his head. Sydney wants to let him sit there all calm and relaxed for hours, but he also doesn't know when he'd ever get another chance, or work up to the same courage, and so he opens his mouth and tries to look as casual as possible.

"And you? You never said how your mom died."

He half expects James to be offended, or to say that it's none of his damn business. Instead James hums like he was expecting the question, then leans back further in his seat to relax.

"I was ten. She went to work one night—was the third shift waitress at this diner—and just . . . never came back home. Woke up to an empty trailer. Then the neighbor—you know, the surfer guy, Mr. Cool—he came over and got me, finally, a couple hours later. And he didn't tell me what happened, just drove me out to my Auntie Cath's place in the Valley. And then my Uncle Ron finally told me like ten fucking hours later that she'd been hit by a car, and I was staying with them."

Sydney winces. "Did she . . . was it—?"

"They told me it was instant, yeah. That's the story I'm going with."

Sydney breathes in the ocean, melting back into the chair. "Your aunt and uncle?"

James shrugs. "They did alright by me, I guess. Not like they really wanted a third kid, or could afford it. I was never really . . . never really a *part* of the family, but I don't hold it against them. Least they took me in."

"They didn't take you back in when you were sent home," Sydney says, not really hiding the ice in his voice.

James rubs his shoulder. "Was partly their idea I enlisted in the first place. I spent a few years out of high school working odd jobs and wanted to go to college—something my mom always told me was non-negotiable, even when I was just a kid. But then . . . you know, it was the early days of the war at that point. We didn't quite realize how bad . . . well, and they were offering incentives to enlist. Uncle Ron told me to take a few years of vacation on a ship in the tropics and then come back with money for school." He laughs and rolls his eyes. "A real win-win."

Sydney swallows down the rage still bubbling in his throat. "But after?"

James hears the tone in his voice and softly smiles over at him, even though his eyes are sad. "You can't hold that against them, love. They were . . . they made sure I was alright, yeah. Helped me get into the rehab facility in LA where I was at for a few weeks, before I moved out and found my job. But then they were already moving to Sacramento. And I was alive, just recovering." He tilts his beer. "Plus, they left me the station wagon."

"Where is that now?"

"Sold it." James' mouth twists. "Only got a hundred bucks for it, though."

Sydney wants to argue more, wants to scream up at the sky that it should be *illegal* for someone to have taken a look at James Campbell, who'd just been *shot* in his country's fucking uniform, and just leave him a barely-functioning car and tell him good fucking luck.

But James' thumb is calmly tracing the hairs on Sydney's forearm, and he looks so handsome in the glowing evening light, and Sydney blinks to realize his anger has completely fizzled away.

"Well, it does make sense then," he says.

James turns and looks at him. "What makes sense?"

"Well, you know, 'lack of a true father figure'—it's what's supposed to turn you into a queer, isn't it? It's a Bible truth."

443

James barks out a laugh, face turned up to the sky. "You're something else, Moore," he says, grinning. "Man, who the fuck knows who my father was—some sailor that was in Long Beach on leave, probably. My mom never said anything, I was too young."

"Well there you go," Sydney says. "Absent father, single mother imprinting all of her feminine ways on you—"

"Don't make me kill you only two days in to living together, you fucking loony."

Sydney ducks as James throws his balled-up napkin at his head, then rises on aching legs to his feet, stretching out his body with a groan. He feels shockingly lighter than air, as if he didn't just sit there and have a conversation about his family for the first-ever time in his life. He thinks for the thousandth time that James Campbell is a marvel.

"Must be exhausted," James says behind him.

Sydney hums, even as his eyes fall closed. "Getting there."

James' arms suddenly wrap around his waist from behind, holding him close.

"My man," James whispers into the nape of his neck. "My sleepy man. Come on to bed."

And Sydney realizes it would take the force of the entire ocean, or every one of Waimea's waves combined, to stop him from following James between the cool sheets.

It's six in the morning.

Sydney's eyes blink awake to the sight of the fading yellow numbers of his alarm clock, and he thinks that maybe time travel really *is* possible, because there's no way on earth that he closed his eyes what feels like thirty seconds ago out on the porch, standing in James' arms and breathing in the salt of the sea, and now he's naked, in his bed, and it's *six in the morning*.

The sheets are warm and soft against his bare skin, radiating a cloud of heat, and he winces as he shifts and his sore abdominal muscles scream in protest. Something tightens around his waist, something heavy and constricting, something warm and smooth and firm with a blanket of soft hairs . . .

"Did I wake you?" Murmured in a rough, intimate voice into the back of Sydney's neck.

Sydney immediately feels around with his hand until he touches James' arm wrapped around his stomach, pulling James' palm up to press it to his lips. James settles his hand over Sydney's chest when he lets go.

Sydney's throat feels like sandpaper. "How long did I just sleep?"

James chuckles, a puff of hot, damp air on Sydney's skin. The day's worth of stubble on James' jaw sends prickles down Sydney's spine. He slowly becomes aware of the lines of James' naked body against him, his broad chest against his back, his stomach and the tops of his thighs cradling his ass, their intertwined calves.

"About ten hours," James whispers. He presses Sydney closer into his body. "We were both pretty exhausted, I think."

Sydney hums, his body melting like warm water with the pull of James' strong arms. James taps his side gently. "How do you feel?"

Sydney considers. "Like I'm dead and just woke up in the heavenly gates."

James kisses him right where his neck meets his shoulder, sending a hot cascade of shivers across Sydney's skin. He shifts back into James, suddenly piercingly aware of the warm, soft bulge of James' cock pressed against his buttocks.

They lie there in silence for what feels like days, or even years. Sydney wonders if it's possible for his mattress to have gotten one thousand times more comfortable overnight. For the air to have gotten sweeter, and the oxygen more pure, and the breeze to have transformed the simple cotton of his sheets to fine linen.

Then, so slowly he wonders how many minutes have passed without him noticing, he feels James' body start to wake up and tense behind him. His mouth opens and closes, and Sydney hears the roll of his tongue as he licks his lips.

It sounds as if James is working himself up to say something, something important which can maybe only be said when his face is pressed against the back of Sydney's shoulder, and he waits, leaning back into James' body for what feels like the thousandth time over the last few weeks.

It feels exquisite—like waking up from a nap in the warm sand, then standing up on his board on a wave that he knows will travel on in a perfect barrel towards infinity. He realizes he isn't afraid of what James will possibly say.

James sighs into Sydney's back, and his warm breath softens across his skin. "You're still awake?" he asks, even though Sydney would bet anything he already knew the answer.

Sydney hums, and James nods against his shoulder and clears his throat. "I couldn't really sleep," he says. "Couldn't stop thinking about what . . . what the hell I'm gonna do. For a job."

Sydney closes his eyes and rubs his hand along James' arm. "You forget you're a professional surfer now. You'll have money coming in. Competitions are every few weeks, plus you got Val's backing you. And there'll be more."

James sighs through his nose. "I know, but . . . I can't live off hoping I'll somehow finish in the top three all the time. I'm not like you. I'm not—I don't have assured wins. And I can't," James swallows. "I can't go back to a job at the docks. I don't think I could do it. Not anymore. Not here—"

"Who the hell told you that you need to go back to the docks?"

James shrugs. "Well, besides standing up and balancing on a slippery board there's jack shit else I'm good at. It's not like I went to college—finished it, I mean."

"You're speaking to a high school dropout."

"Yeah, but you're *you.* And I . . . it's all I have."

In his mind, Sydney sees the man he'd seen that day on the docks, angry and embarrassed, reaching out to snatch back the bullet and shove it into his pocket, looking like a corpse walking around in broad daylight.

Sydney can feel James' weariness bleeding through his back and straight into his chest, and Sydney wants to turn around, and kiss James' frowning lips, and tell him that he can live in a jobless paradise forever now that he's here. That everything is perfect now that they have each other, and that he doesn't have to worry or sweat through his work shirt or be sore.

But Sydney isn't an idiot. And he begrudgingly knows as well as he knows the timing of the tides that James is one-hundred percent correct—that a man like James Campbell wouldn't ever feel right about living his life trusting unpredictable surfing wins and sponsorships to pay for plane tickets to competitions and food in the fridge.

And he also knows that a man like James Campbell would rather die than accept some sort of hand out from Sydney trying to find a job for him. Unless . . .

Sydney traps that thought and hides it away in his mind to look at later. He traces the veins on James' hand with his finger where it rests against his chest. The soft heat of the bed is quickly growing stifling against his limbs, and his sore muscles itch to get up and stretch instead of lie motionless with a gnawing ache.

"We'll figure out something," he finally says, lamely. James squeezes him with his arm, and sweat prickles along Sydney's back when he considers what he's about to say.

"That isn't all you have," he whispers, for some reason embarrassed at the shaking in his voice. "You're not . . . James, you're not *nothing.*"

James' entire face is pressed into his back, and Sydney feels the trace of his lips when James finally says, in a defeated voice, "I know."

Sydney wants to say it again, again and again and again until James says "*I know*" like he really means it, but instead he taps on James' forearm. "You know what you don't have, though?"

James hums in question, but it sounds like a moan or a sigh.

"You don't have long enough bones. How can you even breathe back there all smashed into my shoulder blade?"

James huffs and shoves him forward, and Sydney closes his eyes in relief, a silent sense of pride, when James laughs.

"You're impossible," James groans. "Swear to God I'm gonna get an eye deformity from rolling them at you every five minutes." He leans up on his elbow and pats Sydney's hip. "Come on, you want breakfast?"

Sydney stretches out the length of his body, then catches James' arm, stilling him before he can stand up from the bed. "Later. Come swim with me."

James shoots him a look. "Seriously. You want to go swimming. Right now."

Sydney fights down the grin at the corner of his mouth as he shoots up from the bed and starts to head, fully naked, towards the door. He notices James' eyes quickly trace down his back.

"Come on, old man. Don't tell me you're afraid of a little cool water."

James shakes his head up at the ceiling even as he starts to follow him out into the kitchen. "You're not tired? Sore? Hungry?"

Sydney just shrugs.

James dramatically sighs. "What the fuck did I ever do in life to get saddled with the most irritating dick on the planet?"

Sydney holds up a middle finger without looking back, filling a glass of water in the sink. "You sure as hell didn't think my dick was irritating a couple days ago. Now stand there and argue all you want, but you know you want to."

He slams down the empty glass and heads out the door without waiting, grabbing his board from the side of the house as he goes.

James halts in the doorway. "What the—Sydney put some shorts on, you can't just—!"

Sydney hefts his board higher in his grip and looks back. "Name one random stranger you've seen come on to this beach since you've been here."

James sighs, averting his eyes from Sydney's naked body and instead looking out across the waves, still peeking out from the doorway. "We're still in fucking public . . ."

"Grab the extra board laying by the hammock, will you?"

Sydney grins to himself as he hears James finally stomp out the door and down the stairs.

"There's no way in hell you can surf here," James calls from behind him. "The water's totally flat."

"I'm aware."

Sydney runs his hands through his hair to loosen out the curls, then bends over to drop his board in the sand and quickly stretch. He shivers down his spine when he looks between his legs to see James following with the extra board, naked under the rising sun, his beautiful cock swaying down between his thighs, and his golden hair, and his eyes tracking the length of Sydney's bare legs, pupils black.

He straightens upright and turns to the sea, letting the salt spray fan out across his skin, covering him in goosebumps and settling deep in his groin with a thud. He takes two steps out into the foam with his board, wanting to run forward and laugh up towards the sky that he is at home, with James, and that he will wake up tomorrow morning all over again, with James.

He wants to glide out into the waves with James beside him and tell him everything, spilling words out across the surface of the calm, quivering ocean. He wants to pull James' bare body into his arms in the waves they call home and tell him that he hopes James realizes that Sydney's pretty sure he's in this for good. For life. He wants to hold James' hand in front of the endless sea and make a declaration in front of heaven and earth that he is finally the man he was always meant to be with James Campbell—with and because of and alongside *him*. He wants to celebrate and kiss him and not feel naive or afraid, the same way all the other couples get to do in fancy chapels with a three-tiered cake and expensive photographer. And James had mentioned it that one day, right after winning, about the wife and the kids and the house and the nice car, and maybe he'll wake up one day in a year and realize he actually still wants that, the wedding and the rings . . .

No, Sydney shakes that thought out of his head with an affronted grunt. The morning is too beautiful for thoughts like that. The ocean too calm.

He thinks of something else, anything else . . . Ah, right. He wants to lick the saltwater as it drips down from the hairs covering James' chest. That's what he wants.

He hears James hiss from the cool, early morning bite of the water as he wades in behind him. Sydney looks back over his shoulder as he holds his board up high above his head, the tiny swells slapping softly against his stomach and thighs, cradling his skin in foam.

James stands naked and beautiful and grounded in the shallows. Sydney licks his lips, throat bone dry, as his eyes roam over James' body in the rising sunlight. James halts where he is, the water just up to his knees. A breeze blows Sydney's curls over his eyes, and by the time he brushes them back with his palm, he's shocked to see that James' eyes are glistening and wet.

Sydney summons his best grin and tilts his head. "You coming, Captain?"

The last thing Sydney sees is James rolling his deep blue eyes, right before Sydney dives with his board straight into the waves, letting the salt wash away the last remnants of tension from the day before. He takes a few lazy strokes through the clear and calm waters, relishing in the soft caress of the waves against his bare skin, so different from the snarling waves off Waimea hurling stinging foam.

Then he hears James finally splash into the water behind him, and Sydney's skin covers in goosebumps as James' smile seems to spread its warm tendrils straight down to the depths of the ocean, filling the cold, dark deep with the fresh sunlight of a new day.

# 27

The sun is soft and pink in the sky as it slowly rises above the grip of the gentle waves, lapping at James' ankles like melted cream. James shivers as the cool breeze brushes across his bare skin, watching transfixed from the shallows as Sydney holds his board over his head and wades out into the waves, the water pooling around his thighs and rippling just under the firm curves of his ass.

James' mouth waters. The image of Sydney Moore wading naked out into the golden sunrise sea is so beautiful he feels tears building up in the back of his eyes. The soft sunlight drips down over Sydney's golden skin like honey, clinging to his spine and draping across the muscles in his shoulders. The tattoo shimmers across his back as he twists and works to hold his board aloft in the sky.

James stares at Sydney's hips as they sway deeper into the water, gently rocking in the small, splashing waves. Crystal clear saltwater rises and falls over the firm curves of Sydney's ass, frothing in the space between his thighs. Fat drops of seawater drip down the length of his spine and into the dark line of his buttocks, leaving glistening trails.

James suddenly halts his steps, toes clenching in the wet sand, and tries to breathe. Tries to move.

Sydney looks at him over his shoulder and calmly brushes the curls out of his face, as if he isn't doing anything extraordinary at all. He looks beautiful and trusting, like the only thing he wants in the world is for James to follow him out into the sea and go for a swim. Like somehow, despite everything, James' mere presence makes him happy.

"You coming, Captain?" Sydney smirks, just as James finds himself blinking back the water in his eyes. Then Sydney flings his board down and dives into the water, sending up a small plume of crackling spray into the air.

James rolls his eyes, or at least he thinks he does, and then he takes two steps forward on numb legs, and throws down the board he'd been holding limply under his arm, and follows Sydney into their own little strip of ocean, diving through the water with a crash.

The saltwater weaves through his smiling teeth as he kicks down under the rolling, incoming swell, and then he surfaces to a burst of sparkling sunlight and the crisp, clear air of the island. He licks the dripping cascade of seawater off his lips,and it tastes like flowers instead of smog and asphalt. Tastes like warm skin and thick salt and a hint of shrimp.

Sydney paddles steadily in front of him, breathing calm and easy to the rhythm of his long and lazy strokes. James follows in his wake, not able to look away from the water rippling and splashing over the backs of Sydney's bare thighs. He watches it pool in the dip between his shoulder blades and catch individual ringlets of hair in the sunlight.

James breathes in deeply and revels in being back in the water for the first time in over a week. There hadn't been any time back in LA, not after he'd picked up that payphone and called Rob to tell him he'd already made up his goddamn mind.

He'd seen Rob and Lori nearly every hour when he wasn't finishing out his last days at work—bowing to their staunch insistence that he let them be selfish and hoard all his time while they still had the chance. And he'd been busy packing boxes, selling his car, deciding what to ship and what to keep and what to leave on the side of the road in a cardboard box.

And sure, there'd been moments when he'd looked up from his boxes and stared out the window the way he always used to before. He'd watched the icy waves rush into shore and splash over the early morning surfers, and the afternoon families, and the evening lovers who all waded out into the water off Hermosa. But the thought of grabbing his board and running out to join them when he knew that Sydney was thinking he was all alone again forever on Oahu had felt like wanting to take a sip of sweet strawberry milkshake and instead getting a mouthful of sand.

So he'd waited. He'd stayed inside and inland and salt-free and dry. And he'd joined Rob and Lori for beers in their backyard far away from the water, where they asked him all about the beaches on Oahu and sent him wet smiles when they thought he couldn't see. Where they carefully avoided any mention of Danny Moore or his surfing or his house, just in case James showed back up on their doorstep a week later with his tail between his legs.

Now, though, as he follows smoothly in the wake behind Sydney's board, watching the curves of his back glisten in the sunlight, and the tattoo writhe across his paddling shoulders, James feels that the water is a kiss over every inch of his skin. It wakes up stiff joints as he paddles through the calm ripples as if he'd been swimming since before he learned to walk. It caresses his dry skin, softening it like a dried-up sponge dropped into fresh, cool liquid—finally pliable instead of unyielding stone.

It feels strange to be lying down on his board naked, the thought humming in the back of his mind that something feels out of place even though he's paddled out to sea hundreds of times before. The waxed surface scratches at his chest and clings to his stomach like it always does whenever he feels safe and warm enough to swim without a wetsuit on.

But it also tickles the insides of his bare thighs, and digs in gently to the bones of his hips. His board rustles the thatch of wet pubic hair waving in the water as it rushes past his groin, and the waxed surface presses up against his soft penis in a way that feels grounding and vulnerable all at once.

It's just him, and his board, and the water, and the sky. No crowd at his back, or wetsuit covering his skin. No time limits or post-surf work shift or tiny airless apartment waiting for him alongside the long stretch of traffic and smog and skyline.

It's just him and Sydney Moore.

Sydney paddles out ahead of him towards the smooth, glassy horizon, then stops fifty yards out from the shore and turns back to James with a warm and easy smile on his face. He sits tall and unashamed on his board. The saltwater pours down from his wet curls plastered onto his neck, and runs across his chest towards his abs and cock, which James notices is half hard where it's bared between his legs. Sydney catches him looking and smirks, then takes a full breath, swelling his glistening chest, and scans up and down the shore.

"Feels like a year ago that we jumped off that cliff, doesn't it?" Sydney says, squinting off towards the far end of the beach where the cliff stands silhouetted against the pale blue and purple candy sky.

James blinks, surprised. "Shit, it does."

Sydney smiles wistfully as James pulls up next to him and perches on his board to rest.

"You know, the days always used to run together here before. Like one giant, never-ending day with a few work contracts thrown in or a competition to catch. And then this last month has felt two fucking years long."

James hums. He feels alone on the earth with Sydney out in the middle of the ocean, their voices echoing loudly across the velvet surface of the waves which lap at their boards. He feels as if the shoreline could suddenly disappear, and they could be surrounded by nothing but the sea, and it really wouldn't bother him in the least.

He expects that thought to gnaw with fresh anxiety in his chest, dragging him down towards the little piece of shiny metal that he knows is still resting at the bottom of the sea, worn and smooth from years spent warm and dry in the palm of his hand. But instead all he feels is a far-away calm, slowly approaching his bare skin before reaching out to cover him with soft and easy warmth, sheltering him from the bite of the breeze.

James suddenly remembers his first real glimpse of Danny Moore in his mind—standing next to him with his aviators glinting in the sun and stripping off his grey hoodie that day back at the ISF. The power and strength that had radiated from every inch of his tanned, confident skin. The picture is vivid in his memory—etched into his brain in perfect, brilliant detail.

"I feel the opposite, actually," James eventually says. "It seems like I first looked at you next to me at the start line five minutes ago, looking all too-cool-for-school with your aviators and shit."

Sydney chuckles. "Well it's good to know I make such a lasting impression that you've forgotten everything that happened in between."

James splashes a handful of water his way, shaking his head at Sydney's smirk. "Ass."

Sydney sends him a quick wink that sets James' heart racing before James closes his eyes and tilts his head back to the billowing clouds. He takes a deep breath and exhales slowly, letting it settle every muscle in his body, and Sydney lies down on his back on his board and sighs lazily up at the sky. He holds out a hand towards James, wiggling his fingers to come, and James' heart clenches all over again as he paddles himself forward on the water, aligning their boards. James grabs the other side of Sydney's board to steady them beside each other, and Sydney places his head up on James' thigh with a contented sigh.

James takes him in, eyes crinkling just at the corners. "There's no fucking way that's comfortable for your neck."

Sydney shrugs. "Works for now."

Sydney closes his eyes and lets out a deep breath, and James lets himself gaze straight down at his upside-down face. He runs his fingers through Sydney's curls swirling in the water, pooling around his head as they bob on the surface of the calm and sleepy sea, and Sydney hums as he stretches his legs down and cracks his toes.

James blinks when he realizes he'd completely forgotten they were naked.

Finally, Sydney licks his lips and cracks open one eye, staring up at James through the pale wafts of sunlight.

"What you said earlier . . . about your job."

James shrugs one shoulder to hide an odd wave of shame. "Ah, don't worry about that. Just . . . half-asleep rambling. I'll figure it out. Maybe the Navy employs professional surfers now—I can re-enlist."

James half-chuckles under his breath, but Sydney's expression doesn't lighten at the poor joke. Instead, he lifts one hand over to rest on James' board, keeping them close together on the waves. He closes his eyes.

"You know . . . something that came to me, this morning. An idea—"

"What, in the last ten minutes?"

"Ten minutes is more than enough time for an idea."

"A fleshed-out one?"

"I think quickly."

James scratches once at Sydney's scalp as Sydney cracks open one eye to shoot him a smirk, then Sydney's face sombers, and James' fingers freeze.

"I have some savings," Sydney says. "A good amount. Money I've saved up over the years from work and winnings. Built up pretty fast since I barely have to pay Hobbs any rent. And I was thinking . . ."

Sydney pauses, turning his cheek into James' palm as James once again strokes through his hair and down along his neck. James shocks himself by leaning down to kiss Sydney's forehead—easily, without any second thoughts at all. "Go on. You were thinking?"

Sydney takes a breath, steeling himself. "Look, maybe you'll just rag on me for saying this, and maybe I deserve it. But . . . you and me, with what we know, what we want to do—we should open up a surf shop. Our own place."

James huffs out a surprised laugh, rocking them both unsteadily on their boards. "Oh right, and cars can fucking fly," he says. James pats Sydney's head gently and ruffles his hair. "Stop shitting me. What's the real idea?"

Sydney sits up suddenly, then angles himself so that he's facing James with their boards side by side. He grabs onto James' knee hard as James stares back at him in disbelief. The look on Sydney's face—his earnestness, the flash of hurt deep in the pale blue of his eyes . . .

James realizes with a thud in his gut that Sydney is completely, one-hundred-percent serious. He tries to keep his face blank as he runs a disbelieving hand through his own wet hair.

"Shit, you're serious."

Sydney nods, then goes on, glancing down nervously at the water and chewing his lip as he spits out the words as fast as he possibly can, as if he's afraid James will try to cut him off if he doesn't.

"Look, it's . . . it's all just coming together now in my mind, but listen. I have the money. I know of a few places along the North Shore that could be for sale. I know how to use all the tools—how to make and fix boards. I could . . . I could *design* some. And you could own the place flat out and run the front. Give . . . I don't know, give kids surfing lessons or some shit if you wanna feel humanitarian about it since you've almost died a million times—feel like you're giving back. And then we'd—we could find a third partner to run it for us when we're off at competitions, and you wouldn't have to run all over trying to find a job somewhere that you'll hate like hell anyway. Our entire lives could be right here with the water. Not wasting time trying to do or be anywhere else."

James freezes, stunned. He almost doesn't want to allow himself to hear what Sydney's saying. It sounds like a goddamn dream he never even realized he's had. His own shop. His own place. Sydney at his side and at his back and at his front. Locking up the door of the shop and coming home every night to their own bed with the smell of wood and salt and seaweed on their skin. Tasting like the sun.

Then the dream shatters in his mind, cracking into a million pieces like the center of a punctured mirror. There's a reason things sound too good to be true.

James sighs and grabs the back of his neck, trying to work up the words and hating that the light behind Sydney's eyes is about to fizzle out.

"I don't know the first fucking thing about running a shop, Sydney," he groans. "I mean, shit, I could run it into the ground. And I don't have a dime to put into it up front. I can't just rely on you to pay for everything for the rest of time."

James wonders just when he started thinking of his relationship with Sydney as 'for the rest of time,' and then wonders why the words 'relationship with Sydney' make him feel hot in his throat, and all the while expects Sydney to roll his eyes and shoot back some witty retort. Call him an idiot and a spoil sport and afraid. Or say that James is right . . .

Instead, Sydney calmly nods to himself, then he looks over at James with an expression on his face that causes the entire world to freeze.

"You make me happy," he says quietly.

Self-disgust suddenly rises within James in a choking rush. "God, I'm sorry . . . I shouldn't have—I didn't mean to shoot you down like that. Everything is just—it's a lot."

James reaches forward to place a wet hand on Sydney's bare chest, and Sydney immediately places his fingertips on James' cheek. They're close enough to breathe straight into each other's mouths, and James wonders if he blinks if the entire rest of the world will have disappeared.

"It is a lot," Sydney agrees.

Sydney swipes his thumb gently across James' cheek, and James' throat grows tight against the words that want to come spilling out of his mouth. Sydney looks radiant in the sunlight. Golden and strong in the buttery pink wisps of light slowly streaming across the pale sky from the sun.

"But, look," he goes on, his voice barely a whisper. James leans in close enough that one of Sydney's curls touches his own face. "We can try. I don't see any reason why we can't try. And I—I just want to be happy. With you. It's something I never expected to have and I hardly know what the fuck to do with it but—"

James barely chokes out a watery "fuck" before he launches himself forward into Sydney's arms, cutting him off with a grunt of surprise. He hugs him awkwardly across the distance between their straddled boards.

Sydney huffs out a wet laugh into the side of his neck, clutching him close by his nape. "You are a marvel," he whispers.

James pulls back and cups Sydney's face in his hands, trying and failing to think of anything he could say. He kisses him gently, tasting the ghosts of the words on Sydney's lips with a soft hum. Still amazed in the corners of his mind that he's kissing a man beneath the wide open sun.

He looks over his shoulder back towards the shore. He sees their home, the peeling teal paint framed by lazy palm fronds and golden sand. He sees a ghost of himself from not even three weeks ago—standing nervously at the end of the lane in the shade of the trees, looking at Sydney—at Danny—Moore's foot draped over the side of a hammock and wondering how in hell he was ever going to thank him for saving his life without looking like a pitiful fool.

Sydney's staring at him now with eyes the color of crystal glass sea. He looks young and fresh and open. He looks like the man who conquered the waves at Waimea without falling to his death into the black deep, and he looks like the man James woke up next to the morning after he first let himself lay his hands on another man's skin.

"You already growing nostalgic on me?"

James shakes his head at Sydney before looking back at the shore. "Not rising to your bait," he says.

Sydney dramatically shrugs and looks out over the water. "Not my fault you wear every emotion on your face. I mean, shit, didn't they teach you how to be stone-faced in the Navy?"

"Aw, fuck you," James groans, trying not to laugh. "Can't handle your shit right now. It's too early." He splashes Sydney with a handful of water, and Sydney dodges it, then gets a mischievous glimmer in his eyes right before grabbing James' shoulders and shoving him clear off his board.

The ocean swallows James up in a cool gulp, cutting him off from the sound and the sunlight and the air. James chokes on a lungful of saltwater and kicks to the surface, shivering once in the cooler water hidden just beneath the surface layer warmed by the rising sun. He spits out a mouthful of water right at Sydney's eye when he surfaces, shooting him the best glare he can.

Sydney yelps when the water hits his face. "You're disgusting!"

"Not like you haven't tasted my spit and ocean water before," James smirks.

Sydney cocks an eyebrow. "You don't have a problem with tasting ocean water then, Captain?"

Before James can groan, Sydney's leaping on top of him from his board, shoving him down under the water again and fighting with him to keep him under the waves. James grips at slick, wet skin with his palms, feeling Sydney's muscles ripple and flex in his hands as he struggles to fight back towards the surface and get a breath.

He finally gets a grip on Sydney's curls and yanks before bursting up through the surface and gasping down a lungful of air. "You fucking dick!"

Sydney surfaces and immediately shoves James away, panting. He clutches his head with his hands and frowns. "Jesus, that hurt!"

He's also laughing—face wet and glistening with soaked ringlets dripping across his forehead and neck.

Before James can decide whether it's a smart idea or not, he reaches through the water and pulls Sydney's bare body against his, then licks the salt off Sydney's lips with his own gasping mouth.

Sydney immediately clings to his body, nearly sinking them both as they try to tread water. Wet skin meets wet skin, sliding slick and smooth.

"Come on," James breathes, grasping Sydney's sides. "Come here . . ."

They kiss and wrestle in the small swells, James' legs kicking and fighting to stay afloat while Sydney's huge hands roam and grip and stroke. James' cock begins to thrum in low, steady pulses as his erection grows in the warming water. He grabs Sydney's slick, wet thighs and wraps them around his own waist, then moans as Sydney presses his thickening cock into James' clenched stomach.

"Shit," he breathes.

Sydney's thighs squeeze him harder. "James . . ."

James grabs Sydney's ass as his legs wildly kick to keep afloat, pressing Sydney's bobbing cock closer against the hard, muscled plane of his own stomach, and they both choke down wet moans in their throats. Sydney kisses him deeply, his rough hands grasping James' face, before pulling back to gulp down air, lips full and pink.

His voice is low and gravelly—foaming waves rushing over a rocky shore. "Get on your board."

James runs a hand up Sydney's dripping wet chest, running his fingers through the soft hair and catching Sydney's nipples under his thumbs. He can barely think straight. He wants to drag Sydney from the water and throw him down into the sand and fuck slow and deep against Sydney's wet skin. His erection bobs in the water, resting just under the crease of Sydney's ass. He wants to press it against Sydney's body, slide between his warm buttocks, the slick pressure of his saltwater-soft skin . . .

Sydney had just said something to him, hadn't he?

"Wait—what?"

Sydney kisses him again, gasping into his mouth, before falling away from James' body and pulling James' board back towards them through the water. "I said, get on your board."

James heaves himself up onto the waxy surface without asking why, shivering up his spine as his aching cock brushes across the board. He straddles it, erection standing proudly between his legs, then clenches his abs and thighs as the board suddenly rocks deeply to the side.

"You're gonna sink it!" James cries out.

But Sydney still slides on behind him, gripping James' shoulders as they both fight to steady themselves and keep balance. "Be cool," he whispers into James' ear, right as the board sinks down into the cool, clear water, bringing it up past their waists.

James looks down to watch Sydney's arms wrapping around his waist, sliding slowly up his stomach and chest. His fingers look even more pale against James' tan skin and soaked hair. He can feel Sydney's chest pressed up smoothly against his back. Can feel his hard cock pressed into the low of his spine, warm and thick between his hips just under the water's surface.

Sydney's voice is lower than James has ever heard it. "It won't sink. I didn't study physics for nothing."

James barely huffs out a weak laugh as Sydney's hands start to rub firmly across his skin, trailing up and down over his nipples until they peak. James' thighs start to shake with restraint, the effort of keeping them steady on the rocking board, and Sydney's breath echoes loudly in his ear, mixing with the splash of the water lapping at their bare skin and sides.

James lets himself lean back into Sydney's body, trusting the the stability of his warm, lean chest. Sydney's arms caress and hold him close—holding him up out of the sea.

And James thinks that maybe he would've been content to stay just like that for a long time, calm and relaxed and watching the sun smear gold across the grey sky. He would have, if not for the pulsing want settling deep in his thighs.

*God*, he's hard.

His flushed cock bobs obscenely under the surface of the water. It rocks with the movements of the board beneath them—the waxed board which keeps rubbing gently across James' ass, teasing at the hole Sydney had stroked with his fingertip the first time James had ever come in his arms, right under the stars.

With a groan, James rocks his hips down against the board, pushing himself deeper into the V of Sydney's thighs, and Sydney licks a stripe up his neck, humming at the taste.

"God, this is . . ." but James loses his train of thought on another deep sigh.

"*James.*"

Sydney's hands move down to James' bare thighs, running slow and firm up the length of the muscle, rustling against the hair on James' legs through the water. Sydney leans forward to rub his cheek against James' stubble, humming deep and low in his chest. "*Fuck*, James."

James thinks he must be floating in a hovering bubble of sea and sky, effortlessly held up by the touch of Sydney's hands on his skin, roaming across his sides and chest, dipping down under the water to caress his waist. To stroke up the inside of his sensitive, quivering thighs.

James leans his head back on Sydney's shoulder, baring his chest and neck, and he dips his hands under the water to grip the outside of Sydney's legs, clenched tight around James' hips.

Deep down in his brain, James knows that he should probably feel too vulnerable—too naked and open before the edge of the earth with Sydney's full cock pressed thickly against his back. With Sydney's hands roaming possessively over his wet and trembling skin for the entire open ocean to witness.

But James also recognizes that he's never really felt safer in his life. It washes over him like a burst of fresh oxygen blasting across every inch of his skin. It brings a watery smile to his lips as he closes his eyes and continues to relax, focusing on the strength of Sydney's lean muscles keeping them upright and afloat. He basks in the pure, breathtaking fact that he hasn't once yet felt shame that he is the one being held, not doing the holding.

Then his eyes fly back open, and he gasps as Sydney's large hand suddenly grips the base of his erection, holding his cock in callused fingers as James' pubic hair ripples in the water.

"Jesus," he breathes. His neck falls back onto Sydney's shoulder. He pushes his hips forward unwittingly, needing to press himself deeper into the tight grip of Sydney's palm. Sydney's other hand comes up to rest across his chest, fingertips just barely caressing the edges of his scar.

James stops himself from thrusting for just a moment, using the entire force of his will. "You don't have to," he barely grunts out, not even knowing why. "You must be tired. You—you surfed yesterday. We can go ba—"

Sydney's hand pumps slowly along the length of his erection, immediately knocking the breath from James' lungs. He shivers down his spine as Sydney's voice rumbles against his ear, breath tickling the hairs at the back of his neck.

"I want to," he whispers. His fingertips trace the tip of James' cock peeking through his foreskin, swirling the water around his wrist. "Let me . . ."

James groans as Sydney's mouth leaves a wet trail of warm, prickling air along his neck. Sydney's hand keeps caressing his cock beneath the water, splashing gently into the buzzing air as his fist pumps along James' aching erection, following it up towards the surface of the water before plunging back down to the base. His touch is gentle, as if he's feeling James' skin for the first time. James watches Sydney's fingers on the most intimate part of his body, slow and callused and warm. Wet.

The splashing water echoes loudly in James' ears as he starts to thrust his hips harder into Sydney's fist, hot pulses starting to thrum and build from between his thighs. He watches the tip of his own throbbing cock disappear again and again within the tight grip of Sydney's long fingers, blurred and hazy beneath the water in the thick golden light.

"Look at you on me," James hears himself groan. He stares down between his legs, barely wanting to blink, and he barely recognizes the wild, rough sounds coming from his own throat. "God, your hands . . ."

Sydney's voice rumbles in his ear as his other hand on James' chest holds him close. "Can you imagine," he breathes, "if you were sliding your cock into my ass?"

James almost screams. The thought slams into his mind with the force of one of Waimea's waves, knocking the breath from his lungs and clenching every muscle in his stomach.

Sydney gasps raggedly in his ear as he lets James continue to slowly fuck the tight circle of his hot, wet fist. He keeps talking, voice like gravel, and James' can feel the panting shakes of Sydney's chest along his back.

"If I was on my hands and knees in front of you," Sydney moans. "My cock hanging down between my thighs. If I was dripping . . . begging you . . . if you were watching my balls sway, full and heavy."

James' face burns. "Jesus fuck, Sydney. The fuck are you doing—"

"If you looked at my tight little hole and saw it pulsing and wet." Sydney gasps and trembles behind him, his voice coming out in ragged pants. "Begging to be filled . . ."

"What are you . . . God, I don't—"

463

Sydney's lips brush his bare neck. "If you shoved your fingers into my mouth . . . got them dripping wet. Ran those fingers around my ass . . . feeling how hot it is . . ."

James grips the back of Sydney's neck with his hand, barely processing the words pouring out of his mouth. "Shit . . ."

Sydney grunts deep in his throat as his fist pumps James' throbbing erection. "How tight. . ."

"Fuck. . ."

"*Fuck* me."

Sydney's wet lips burn hot and filthy in James' ear, pouring streams of shivers down his sides and across his spine as Sydney grips him from behind so tightly James can barely draw in air. His long fingers trace the length of James' erection—holding and caressing the rock-hard skin, skimming gently along the veins, brushing with an aching touch just across the slit.

James looks down through the ripples caused by Sydney's hand and sees precome leaking from the tip of his cock, slowly dissipating into the ocean water in a long, opaque stream, swirling in the little waves caused by Sydney's restless hand on his body.

James swallows over his dry mouth and runs his shaking hands slowly up Sydney's thighs, bracketing his hips. It's dangerous and it's thrilling and it's reckless and it's *a lot.*

He arches his back slightly away from Sydney's own erection pressed into his spine, needing to try and force conscious, clear thoughts through his melting brain. He tries to speak. "I . . . Sydney, I didn't know—"

He stops, swallowing hard. He's not even sure what the fuck he wants to say.

He wants to turn around and double check that it really is still Sydney Moore behind him—the man who tried to apologize for loving him just twelve hours ago. That it's the Sydney Moore James has known and held and kissed who's currently whispering about being fucked in his ass in James' ear.

He wants to say that he didn't know Sydney *thought* of these things, or that he even wanted them. He wants to tell Sydney that even in his deepest, darkest fantasies about Rob, it was never, ever *this.*

And he wants to tell Sydney that he didn't think he would ever have this in his life—another man wanting him, plain and fucked up James Campbell, to be *inside* them.

James closes his eyes against the vast horizon and centers himself in the feeling of Sydney's arms around his skin. His brain meanders and swerves, idly trying to come up with a way to say all of the above and then some, when suddenly James realizes that Sydney's hand has stilled on his cock.

"Syd—"

Sydney's hands immediately fly off James' body, flinging space between them on the board. His voice comes out in a frantic rush. "I'm sorry. God, I'm sorry. I didn't . . . I don't know where that came fr—"

"Shh, Sydney—"

"I didn't mean any of that. I don't even know what I was saying. You don't—"

"Love, listen to me."

James marvels at how effortlessly that word now falls from his lips, then turns around as much as he can on the board without tipping them over, twisting his spine so he can look back over his shoulder.

Sydney looks like he's just run twenty miles and seen a ghost. For some reason the sight of him now, looking wrecked and shocked and nervous just seconds after groaning the word cock into James' ear, fills James with an easy confidence—a fierce protectiveness he never knew he had. He reaches back to put a hand on Sydney's drying shoulder.

"I'm sorry," Sydney whispers again, looking down at the board between them.

James shakes him. "You owe a couple dollars for that jar now, remember?" He moves his hand to Sydney's face. "Don't say sorry."

"I didn't mean to upset you."

"I wasn't upset. I'm not."

Sydney swallows hard. "I . . . I didn't mean that. Any of that."

James traces his thumb along the corner of Sydney's mouth, waiting for Sydney to finally look up and meet his gaze. His cheeks are flushed, and his eyes squinting like he's in pain, and his curls are wild from the grasp of James' hand minutes ago. James isn't sure if he's ever seen anything so beautiful.

He dips just the tip of his thumb between Sydney's lips, and watches as goosebumps cascade down Sydney's chest.

"Didn't you?" James whispers in a low voice. "Mean it?"

Sydney's eyes grow wide.

James has the sudden sensation that he's gone back in time, back to those eternal seconds before he'd placed his hand on Sydney's bare erection for the very first time, mouth watering at the thought of finally getting to taste a cock—*his* cock. The electricity in the air, the crackling against his skin, the sensation that he's tilting, tilting, tilting off the edge of a cliff and he can't go back. He's going to fall.

Good thing Sydney's right behind him.

"I just wasn't expecting it before," he says, still tracing Sydney's lip. He laughs under his breath. "Didn't know you had it in you."

Sydney immediately blushes from his throat to his hairline, and James can't help it. He twists his aching back even further around so he can brush a quick kiss across Sydney's half-open lips. When he pulls back, Sydney rapidly blinks, then sucks in a breath.

"So, you would want that?" Sydney whispers.

The answer forces itself so strongly into James' mind he nearly laughs. "Yes," he breathes. Then, because it feels important to be unmistakably clear in this moment, "With you."

Sydney bites his lip, then tentatively puts a hand back on James' thigh. His eyes look very far away. "And . . . that's okay?"

James' mouth twists. He can hear the hidden question behind Sydney's words—the fear that it would be painfully, utterly wrong for either of them to want to touch each other that way. And despite it, maybe even because of it, James feels a sudden courage fill his chest, even though he sure as hell doesn't know the proper answer to Sydney's question. It's a question he's asked himself unsuccessfully ten thousand times.

"I don't give a shit about what's okay," he says, fully aware that Sydney might hear the part-lie. He looks at Sydney's Adam's apple bob, the beautiful curve of his throat. "It's okay for me."

Then he frowns. "But you? Is that actually what you—?"

Sydney's sigh explodes from his mouth. "Shit, James, more than anything."

"Fuck, come here . . ."

The board dramatically rocks to the side as James immediately turns back around, rolling his spine back into Sydney's chest and bringing Sydney's hands up from his thighs to once again wrap around his sides.

Sydney doesn't hesitate; he sighs and plants a wet, open kiss at the base of James' neck as he rolls his body back against him, sending shockwaves of ripples out across the quiet water. His hands rove slowly up James' stomach and chest, trailing fresh saltwater across his shivering skin and covering his muscles with his huge, warm palms. James presses forward into his hands, head leaning back and lungs full of air as he lays himself open to Sydney's touch before the horizon line.

He loses himself in the touch of Sydney's palms ghosting up his sides, fingertips trailing over the muscles in his stomach and thumbs stroking in small circles just around his nipples. James looks down and sees his own body as he's never seen it before—as capable and muscled, as something desired to be *touched*, not just a left behind mishmash of useless aches that got shipped back halfway across the world.

For the first time since stepping up next to him in the sand in LA, James doesn't feel too old and worn out for Sydney Moore.

Sydney's hands make one final pass, starting at James' thighs and slowly, firmly trailing up his body all the way to his neck, caressing James' skin with his palms and covering him with frothy ocean foam. Then James groans in the back of his throat as Sydney's hand dips back beneath the waves and strokes once again up the full length of James' cock. He brings him back to full hardness in just a few rolling pumps, sending shivers down James' bare thighs, his hair swaying gently in the waves.

James tightens his grip on Sydney's neck as Sydney bites the lobe of his ear. He steels himself to feel that horrifying, familiar uncertainty coil thickly once more in his gut, cutting him off from the sparks of pleasure caused by Sydney's hand on his cock. But when the feeling doesn't come, James releases the air in his lungs and moans, wondering if it's possible to feel light enough to just float up into the open sky.

He gasps as Sydney's thumb traces a slow circle around the tip of his penis, painting it in a cool, thin layer of saltwater fizzling against the heat of his skin—seeping between his foreskin and his full, bobbing cock. James reaches down into the water and touches the meeting place of

Sydney's fingertips against his unmistakable, screaming erection, stroking long and slow and firm.

He groans, sounding shockingly loud in the still silence of the flat sea. The drips of saltwater from Sydney's pumping forearm crackle in his ears. Echo across the rolling swells.

James turns his face into Sydney's chest. "What happens next?"

He can feel Sydney's small smirk against his ear, and James presses his hips back against the inside of Sydney's thighs, biting his lip at the rasp of the board against the skin of his bare buttocks.

Sydney kisses along his jaw from behind, barely controlling the shaking in his breathing. "Next you'd push just the tip of your finger inside me," he breathes. "I'd clench around you. Hot and tight and pulling you in—"

"God . . . yeah . . ."

"Pulling you deeper. You'd watch your finger disappear inside me."

James nearly chokes on the air in his lungs. The thrumming desire building between his tense thighs suddenly shoots up his spine with a crackling heat, spreading down to his toes dangling limp and free in the water.

Sydney thumbs at the dripping slit of James' cock beneath the rippling ocean, causing the water to cloud with the small drips of precome leaking from the tip. Sydney breathes in deeply against James' back, pressing into his spine, then James feels him look down over James' shoulder at his own hand on James' cock. Sydney curses under his breath, and James grabs frantically at Sydney's thighs.

"Take me in," James whispers up at the sky. "Take me in you. Syd—"

"You'd grab my hips so hard it hurt, and you'd push another finger in. You'd feel me stretching around you, sucking you inside so slowly."

James' aching balls swell heavy and hot in his groin at the rumble of Sydney's words. "Shit, Moore . . ."

"You'd feel how tight I am." Sydney's unsteady voice pants in James' ear. "How wet and hot. God," he whines, "it's been so fucking *long*."

Ah, that's what does it.

James' hand flies down to grip Sydney's wrist, stilling it on his cock just seconds before his orgasm explodes in a shockwave of shivering heat through his limbs. He laughs under his breath as he tries to get in enough air, and Sydney rests his curls against James' shoulder, seemingly content to wait. The water flowing against his cock makes it bob obscenely in the current, begging to be stroked.

"That was a close one," James mumbles, unable to keep the smile from his lips.

Sydney hums and licks his shoulder. "Hmm, problem?"

James winds his fingers through a handful of curls, and he registers, distantly, in a half-dreaming and inappropriate-for-the-moment sort of way, that they feel just like the old, worn cotton of his childhood bedsheets. He realizes that he's grinning in a way he never has during sex, the centuries ago that he last had it.

His thumb twitches on Sydney's smooth wrist. "Can't finish yet. Need to get to the end of the story."

He feels Sydney's cheek move into a smirk where it's pressed against the side of his face. Sydney hesitates for a moment, turning his wrist within James' palm, then reaches forward to trace just his fingertips around the base of James' cock. He whispers, slowly, as if he's going to be whispering in James' ear until the end of time, and as if the ocean herself could hear. "Then I'd beg you for it. Beg you to hold me down and fuck me."

James' entire body prickles, and his erection shoots up into Sydney's hand. "Yeah . . ."

"Beg you to *take* me." Sydney pumps James' erection until the water churns.

"Shit . . ."

"Pushing into me."

"God."

"Slapping into me."

"*God . . .*"

James' entire consciousness is focused on the tight grip of Sydney's hand on his cock, which is hot and pulsing and thrusting once more into his fist. The roll of James' hips rocks their board and shoots tiny waves through the calm water, rippling out from the center point of James' body resting in the V of Sydney's thighs. The saltwater rushes in smooth ribbons across his erection in Sydney's hand, slicking the slow, deep slide of his palm on James' skin and causing his pubic hairs to push and pull at his groin, leaving trails of shivers.

Sydney cradles him in his huge palm, then twists hard at the tip. "Beg you to let me have it while you fuck my ass with your fingers."

James sighs, his stomach held so tense his muscles have become solid rock. He listens to the dangerously loud splashing of the water filling the whole expanse of the sea. And he thinks how he's never felt sensation like this before in his life, pumping through his body in thrumming hot pulses the same way the fear had blasted through his bones in the jungle rain. How he's never even had the guts to think about the words currently pouring from Sydney's mouth. And he drinks them in with an open mouth and a moaning tongue; drinks them in like a man dying of thirst on dry land, gasping against Sydney's chest as he lets himself be lost at sea to the sound of Sydney's voice in his ear—the sweet pressure of Sydney's hand, the hand which conquered *Waimea*, caressing James' erection.

"Come on," he breathes, just as Sydney raggedly pants, "Can you see me? Can you see me on my hands and knees with your fingers fucking into my ass?"

"Look at you . . ."

"Can you hear how wet it is sliding into me? Hear me panting underneath you?"

And God, his voice. It's dangerous and throttling and electric and *male*. James moans as Sydney bites the lobe of his ear. He can feel Sydney's own steel erection pressed into the low of his back, slowly thrusting against him for friction, adding to the splashing in the water. James nods, lost, and Sydney groans on a breath behind him.

"You'd hold your own cock in your hand, wouldn't you?" Sydney swallows hard and shudders, grasping to James' body as if he's going to collapse and sink. "Look down at how thick it is. Think about how you're gonna shove it inside of me, wouldn't you? How it'll stretch me open—"

"*Fuck*." James does look down at Sydney's huge fingers wrapped around his cock—pale, ghostly fingers through the clear water against flushed red. Looks at Sydney's thin wrist plunging over and over again into the water as he strokes James slow and deep. James swallows hard over a wild sound in his throat, and Sydney Moore is so effortless, so brimming, so alive, and he wants to be fucked by *him*—

"You'd grab your cock and brush it across my hole," Sydney moans.

His hand suddenly reaches down below James' cock to grab roughly at his balls, rolling them in the water between his fingers while the tip of one finger strokes lightly over James' perineum, sending a burst of tight, crackling heat up through the tip of James' aching cock.

James' cries out, an embarrassingly high sound, and Sydney gasps in his ear.

"Watch it flutter around you. Watch the tip of your cock drip around the rim of my ass. You'd watch that, wouldn't you?"

"God, yeah, Moore . . . look at you . . ."

Sydney grips him harder, hand flying faster over James' hard cock, turning the water into a churning rush of foam and spray between James' legs.

"You'd push your thick cock inside of me, wouldn't you?"

James groans as Sydney's other hand pinches his nipple, and he pushes his chest into the touch of his hand, desperately arching his back.

Sydney licks a stripe up the side of James' neck, messy and uncontrolled. "You'd sink into me and feel how fucking tight it is. Watch your cock disappear into me. Listen to me pant for it."

"Fuck yes, Moore, God I'd fuck you . . . I've *wanted*—"

"You'd fuck me, pump your thick cock into me, push inside of me and stretch me open around you—"

"Shit—"

"You'd be so *heavy*—"

"Sydney fucking Moore."

"Can you feel it? Can you feel yourself fucking into my ass? Can you feel me hot and wet around you?"

"God, you're touching yourself . . ."

"Feel your balls slap against me, full and heavy and hanging—"

"God, take it. Fuck, I'm in you. I'm inside you. *Take* it—"

"Fuck me," Sydney suddenly cries. "Shit, that's it. That's it . . ."

James thrusts into Sydney's fist, eyes shut tight and watching his own cock sink deeper into Sydney's body again and again in his mind, disappearing between the curves of his ass to the wet, frantic slap of skin on skin. He grips at a handful of Sydney's hair with the hand reaching behind to his neck, feels Sydney's ragged breaths shaking against his cheek. The aching hot steel of Sydney's cock rutting against his back, thrusting through the waves.

James burns through his fingertips and summons his deepest voice. He thinks of the way Sydney's curls had elegantly fanned out into the sand after that first night on the shore. His open, bright face . . .

He steels himself and licks his dry lips.

"You'd feel my tags hanging down onto your back, huh?" James growls.

Sydney yelps. James could sit there for a million years and not be able to come up with a better word than 'yelps'. The sound of it pours a fat, curling drip of precome from James' cock into the sea, and Sydney isn't even sitting up straight anymore, but leaning onto him, leaning against him, as if he's relying only on the strength of James' body to keep him afloat in the sea—*the* Danny Moore.

His Danny Moore.

James tries again. "Think about my hands gripping you like a gun. Fucking gripping you like I'm crawling down in the mud. Pounding you like firing off a bullet—"

"Oh my *God*—"

"Or would you want me in uniform? All pressed and clean. No sweat. Just my cock hanging out of my zipper, fucking you down . . ."

Sydney grunts a frantic curse and works James faster, twisting his wrist at the top of his cock before plunging back down again and again to the base. "God, you'd feel so good," he moans, like he's drifting and gone, like he's being held down with his face pressed into a table, like he's shaking the whole ground.

James' hand joins Sydney's on his cock, guiding his hand to squeeze harder along his already hard as steel erection, freely leaking into the water and coiled tight. "Fuck, you . . ."

Sydney collapses against his back, rolling his hips hard against James' spine. "So fucking good in me. *James.* Taking me . . ."

"So tight—"

"Fucking me until I can't breathe," Sydney cries. "Filling me with you. Holding me down and—"

"Shit, I'm gonna come. I'm gonna . . . Syd . . . *Fuck*—"

James gasps hard, gulping down a lungful of air as Sydney's hand grips his cock harder than ever before and *pulls.*

Cool saltwater rushes over his cock in the wake of Sydney's palm, exploding across his hot and pulsing skin in bursts of cold foam as James groans deep in his chest and finally comes.

Sydney's other arm grips him by the chest, pulling James back and close into his body as he plasters himself along James' skin. His shaking fingertips reach up to trail along James' neck as James throws his head back towards the sky, groaning out the last waves of his orgasm shattering through his bones. It gushes across the surface of the sea, hurtling out towards the horizon from the point of Sydney's palm still caressing his loosening balls in the churning water.

Sydney whispers into his ear like he's just run a marathon and swum across the entire Pacific Ocean in a row. "I . . . I didn't know you had it in you."

James laughs up at the fully risen sun, his voice raspy and nearly gone. "Well . . ." he clears his throat. "Turns out we both have our . . things."

Sydney's answering hum and chuckle vibrate down his back like warm water. James looks down as the last humming pulses of his orgasm roll through his body in hot waves. He watches Sydney's hand barely touch his cock in the water, thumb ghosting slowly up his length. The once-crystal water is clouded with his semen, swirling gently in the waves caused from the thrusting rocks of their board.

James breathes out a deep sigh and collapses back against Sydney, one hand still reaching back to grip a handful of his curls.

"Shit," he whispers. It sounds like the tingling wave of muffled silence that had descended on the pristine Vietnam beach right after he fell.

Sydney's cock is still pressed thick and hot into his back, but somehow, it only makes James feel even more relaxed and calm. James closes his eyes and hums limply as Sydney's hands cup palmfuls of the saltwater clouded with James' release and brings them up to pour it down James' chest. It cascades in a cool stream over his sensitive nipples and pools in the muscles of his stomach before trailing back into the rippling sea.

Sydney tucks his arms around James' waist still submerged beneath the water and rests his cheek on James' shoulder, utterly still. James tries to slow his breathing, focusing on the rise and fall of Sydney's chest against his back, and the fizzling waves of release still silently pulsing out from between his thighs and through his muscles. The sun-warmed kiss of the water against his skin.

Sydney kisses James' shoulder for a long time, holding his lips just there in the dip of James' collarbone. Then he whispers into his skin in the newly formed silence. "I really do love you, you know."

James smiles with his eyes closed against the piercing sun, his throat tight. "I know," he whispers.

James is just about to try and turn around to get his hands on Sydney's body—to kiss him and sigh into him and feel Sydney utterly fall apart in his safe, stroking hands. But Sydney suddenly slips off the board behind him, back into the water, causing James to jolt up to the surface and scramble on the board for balance.

He watches, utterly confused, as Sydney's naked body glides effortlessly through the water over to his board, which had floated a ways away, cutting through the sparkling surface with his cupped palms and causing light, tinkling splashes to echo in James' ears. Sydney climbs up onto his board with a grunt and paddles back towards James until they're side by side. Then he straddles his board and perches beside James looking straight out at the horizon, his erection still rising proudly between his legs.

James watches this silently, tongue caught in his mouth.

He's not sure what the hell just happened. A slow fear starts to build at the base of his spine—that he said something wrong, or didn't say or do enough, or said or did too much. That what had come out of his mouth when Sydney's hand was on him had taken the fantasy way too far, too fast.

Sydney sits beside him, somehow godlike and untouchable, pink light dripping down across his bare and glistening skin as his chest rises and falls with his even breathing. James clenches his fist not to reach out and touch him, wanting to bridge the sudden distance that had expanded between them in the seconds between James' orgasm and Sydney sliding off his board.

Then Sydney takes a deep breath, licks his lips, and speaks calm and firm, eyes still roaming out over the horizon.

"You told me, before, that you wanted to get married."

It's the absolute last thing James expected Sydney to open his mouth and say. He reels for a moment, desperately trying to sort the last few days of his life into place like a puzzle blown to pieces by the wind. Like he's still got a lieutenant over his shoulder screaming bullets at him to put the fucking thing back together, missing pieces or no, *I said now, soldier!*

And then he's gripped with an unbearably sharp sadness. Because Sydney can't still think . . . not after everything, after what they've said, that James is still thinking of getting back on a plane, of saying, *"peace, man, later"* and then finding a pretty girl, getting down on one knee . . .

And he's also angry, because after everything he's done, everything he's said, Sydney *can't possibly still think . . .*

And James Campbell knows that he was supposed to end up going absolutely mad, or begging for spare cash on the streets, or drinking a gallon of liquor a day, but he *surfed*, and therefore he didn't end up doing any of those things, and if Sydney Moore recognizes all that and *still* thinks James is somehow incapable of commitment, of sticking true to his word, to himself, then . . .

And James may not have been fully himself for the last three decades but he sure as hell is now, and even the stars saw it, and he came back fully expecting to be turned away on the shore with all his belongings in his hands, knew that Sydney had absolutely every right to say, *"Thanks but no thanks, remember you left?"*

But James still came, and he told Sydney he'd never been with a man before, and he said *"I love you."*

James wonders if Sydney didn't just find some sort of switch for his emotions that first time they met. If he didn't shoot magic spells at him from across the pier and flip on the invisible switch that had been switched off since James woke up to an empty trailer. Since he saw whipped cream in his own blood.

And shit, Sydney's still sitting there, quiet as stone. Waiting.

James finally kicks into gear a few seconds too late and barely stops himself from stammering in complete incoherence. "Sydney, you can't be—yeah, I know I said that. I did say that. But that was before. I don't still . . . I mean, I just told you last night, I'm in this, so you can't still thi—"

"I actually *do* listen to you *sometimes*, you know."

Sydney's tone is oddly light, and James looks over to expect to see him laughing. But instead Sydney's gaze is still focused on the horizon, as if he'll sink down into the sea if he even looks away from it or blinks.

James frowns. He glances down to Sydney's now-flaccid penis, tucked between his legs and resting against his board. For some reason, the sight of it looks incredibly vulnerable, and James wants to reach over and cover it, protect it with his hand.

He releases some of the tension in his chest with a long breath, unable to believe that just minutes ago they were gasping hot filth in each other's ears, wild and reckless, naked and grasping and erect, and now he's tongue-tied and trying not to hunch down over his board.

"Okay . . ." he tries in a steady voice. "Right, so what—"

"I mean, *now*. Marriage. Being . . . being bonded like that. Is that something you still want?"

"Now . . . what—with *you?*"

Sydney doesn't even blink. He stares straight ahead, and his chin rises the tiniest inch. "Yes, with me."

James' brain stops, then a surprised laugh explodes out of his chest. He thinks he must have sunk down beneath the waves and died without realizing it, and now he's living in a dream world where Sydney Moore sits next to him out on the ocean and says absolutely unthinkable things like, *"marriage . . . with me . . ."* after James has just orgasmed with a screaming, filthy groan into his hand.

James forces his lips to move, words exploding into the buzzing silence. "What the . . . I thought you meant with, you know a . . . a wom—Sydney, we can't even *get* married," he finally chokes out.

Sydney doesn't move, pale eyes still fixed on the thin silver line between sky and sea. He swallows, and if James wasn't so completely out of his depth already, he would think Sydney looks *scared.*

"Maybe not technically," Sydney says, tilting his head in that way he does, but it's a bit more exaggerated, a bit too choreographed. "But we could get as close to it as we can."

476

James gapes, mouth open, watching Sydney calmly sit on his board like he hasn't just said the most earth-shattering and ridiculous words James has ever heard in his life—more unbelievable than when the nurse asked him if he was finally awake, and told him yes, he was still in 'Nam, and yes, he was alive.

James coughs to clear his throat and tries to speak again, voice shaking just below his forced calm. "Look, Sydney, I'm not sure where this is coming from right now, but it's . . . I mean, you're right, I guess. Technically. I'm sure people have done it. People like us. But it's . . ." he stops, not even sure what he wants to say. Then he hears himself blurt out, of all the goddamn things, "But you're so young."

Sydney laughs, the sound bursting out of nowhere to vibrate over the water. James watches his eyes crinkle at the corners.

After what has felt like ten years without seeing his eyes, Sydney looks over at James, blue eyes reflecting the sunlight rippling across the waves like a perfect mirror. "That hasn't bothered you before," he says, shrugging.

"I didn't say it bothered me. I mean, hell, you practically don't even have an age. You're something else. But, still . . ." James allows himself to trace Sydney's body with his eyes, the smooth and marbled lines of lean muscle, the unscarred skin, the sturdy spine.

He pictures the same man before him as just a kid, waking up alone on that beach. Remembers him dropping in on the massive wave the day before, raising the hair on James' arms. "Still, Sydney, this is *new* . . ."

"You know I didn't know what the ocean looked like when I was little?" Sydney suddenly says. His voice sounds far away, like he's telling this story to the farthest island on the other side of the world. "I mean, really little. I didn't know at all. Just knew what my mom told me from the creation story—you know, the seven days and the guy's rib and shit."

James laughs, shattering the tension like a pick through ice. "Yes, I believe even a heathen like me has heard of the 'seven days and the guy's rib and shit.'"

Sydney grins at him, and his voice grows crisper, more present. "Well, I saw it for the first time in a magazine. Playboy, actually—"

"Ha, you were probably vastly disappointed at the male options in there . . ."

"James, I was *six*." He huffs, and it's the most beautiful sound James has heard since arriving back on Oahu. More beautiful than "*stay here with me*." Sydney rubs a hand over his mouth. "It was . . . it was just a painted ad, actually. One of the airlines, if I remember right. But that picture . . . all I wanted in life after that was to see the ocean. Just, get the hell out of the landlocked hell hole Army bases we lived on and *see* it."

James blinks hard at the way Sydney's eyes have lighted up, shining brighter than the reflection of the sun on the water. "I can imagine," he says quietly.

"Well, obviously you can. I'm doing a damn fine job telling it to you. But, James, the thing is . . . you have to understand . . ." His voice grows thin. "When I was staring into space in my hammock and I stood up and you were just there? That was like finding that picture. And I've kept that picture for fifteen years—still have it folded up somewhere—and my entire life is in the ocean and I've never looked back. From that first moment, I knew. And I haven't once regretted it or doubted myself or gone back. And you are . . ." He shakes his head and helplessly shrugs. "You *are*. Do you see?"

James *does* see. It's the most beautiful, terrifying, unworthy thing he's ever seen in his life. More beautiful than those two men surfing off China Beach, more terrifying than the lifeless black eyes on the jungle floor, more unworthy than a man like Rob Depaul asking him to surf with him the next morning.

James grins sadly at the corner of his mouth despite himself. He feels a part of his chest sinking without fully understanding why. It all seems too good to be true, like a ghost of his potential future passing right before his eyes that will disappear into the clouds if he doesn't reach out and grab it fast enough. Like trying to grab at a handful of water and hold every bit of it in his palm without leaking.

And this is unbelievable—that he could say the words "I love you" to another person for the first time and then realize, just thirty-six hours later, that he had the definitions of those words all wrong. That they mean so much *more*. Bafflingly more.

"We just met," he says, nearly laughing, and then instantly realizes his mistake.

Sydney bristles. "I thought we were beyond 'we just met'? What about the 'nearly one hundred percent sure' and the coming back and the moving here and the 'I love'—?"

"No no no," James quickly paddles to be closer to Sydney's side, then reaches out to place his palm right over a rapidly beating heart. Sydney freezes, as if James will fling his hand away again if he moves.

James takes a breath, remembers what it feels like to wake up next to a man like Sydney Moore, and leans forward to kiss his shoulder. "Sorry, shouldn't have said it like that. Just . . . you were a fucking stranger to me a month ago. A terrifying stranger. And now you're . . . you're my entire life. You've picked everything up inside me and flipped it all around. It's hard to believe."

James holds his breath as Sydney looks straight at him, curls frizzed and drying in the sparkling sun and eyelashes wet at the tips from the saltwater. James forces himself to meet Sydney's gaze head on, not turning away, and he watches, amazed, as a thick emotion passes through Sydney's clear eyes.

Sydney smirks, but his lips shake. "I'm your entire life, huh?"

James laughs through his nose. "Don't get a fucking big head about it. It's already too big to fit through doors—it's why you gotta do a sport that takes place completely outside." He tucks a curl behind Sydney's hear. "But, yes. It seems you are." Then he bites his lip. "But why this, now? Bringing up what I said before. Why marriage?"

Sydney blushes again, and James can't stop himself from quickly glancing down at Sydney's soft cock before adding, "We were kinda in the middle of something."

This time, Sydney laughs, but it quickly fades from his face, replaced by something that looks like he's in pain. "What I said last night, about you giving up so much . . . and I heard you, what you said. That you made this choice and you're a brave, strong, independent adult and can make your own life decisions and won't be pushed around and all that—"

"Wow, way to make me sound like an ass—"

"*But*, that doesn't mean that I . . . I don't *want* you to give up anything for this. To have me in your life. And I want to . . . to celebrate that you've actually deemed me tolerable enough to *live* with and *sleep* with, and I don't want you to wake up one day and realize that you've given up something gigantic just to be with *me*."

"I don't feel that way. I wouldn't feel that way. I feel the *opposite* of that wa—"

"I'm not saying it needs to be now. Just, I want you to know. Maybe you don't have to give that up. Because I know you want it. And it . . . it could really *be* something."

"I just wanted to stop being lonely forever, Sydney, not specifically marr—"

"You had Rob."

"For one hour a day when he wasn't at work or with Lori, yeah."

"Look just keep it in mind, would you? I'm telling you I would do that for you. I would want that for you. That's all I'm trying to say."

Something finally clicks in James' mind as he watches Sydney cross his arms in irritation—the missing puzzle piece to all this that had still been drifting wildly in the wind for the past five minutes. "This isn't just about me," James says quietly, as if it's a question. "You bringing this up, it isn't just about what I want . . . ?"

Sydney stares down at his board, uncharacteristically twiddling his fingers. "You're *it*," he finally whispers. He tilts his head. "I dunno." Then he sighs and flings one hand out towards the horizon, scrunching his mouth. "And fine. I guess you're right. I do . . . this isn't only about what you might want. Maybe I . . . well, I want things, too."

James takes one last look at him, beautiful and glowing and earnest in the sun, then he closes his eyes for a long blink, chest panging. The cool surface of his board suddenly feels invasive against the bare skin of his buttocks and thighs. He wants desperately to cover himself. To shield his skin from the open horizon and block the water from rushing across his naked legs and groin.

He swallows hard. "It wouldn't be a real wedding, Sydney," he says gently, voice breaking. "It wouldn't . . . it wouldn't mean anything. Just words. We don't need to have that to make any of this real, yeah? And who the fuck would even be there? Who would do it?"

Sydney sighs softly beside him, chest deflating as his skin glows a gentle gold in the early light. "It would mean something to us," he says back quietly, still staring down at the water. He shrugs. "I just think . . ." He whips his head up to look straight at James. "Why can't we celebrate?

Why can't we have that part of it? I . . . I *found* you and I can't do fuck all about it!"

James blinks back sudden tears, breath stolen from his lungs. He has the vivid, undeniable sensation that he's staring at a vision of himself from the day he first set foot onto that ship, his brand new uniform freshly starched, and the dangerous, unknowable excitement in his limbs, and the wild fear behind his eyes that everything could catch fire, could go up in red smoke. When he'd wished his mom was there at the bottom of the gangplank to kiss his cheek, and wondered if he should have looked Billy Madden up in the phone book to give him an awkward, haven't-seen-you-in-years goodbye.

And at the same time, James feels like he's looking at a version of himself he hasn't even met yet—one who is incredibly brave, and *feels* things, and won't settle for absolutely anything less in his life except the very pinnacle, beyond anything anyone thinks he deserves. Beyond what's humanly possible.

He's looking at Sydney Daniel Moore.

And it makes James want to wrap him in his arms and kiss him— gulp down a deep breath and hold him close and scream, *"I lived, I lived, thank God"* up to the heavens.

"Love, listen to me," he finally says, his voice choked. He takes Sydney's wet hand in his and holds on tight. "The only thing that I will ever suddenly realize when I 'wake up one day' is that you and I haven't killed each other, and we aren't destitute and out of jobs, and I'm not stepping back on a plane to LA, and you'll be asking me to swim with you at six in the morning, and then the only thing I'll realize in that moment is that I remember every word of this conversation. And we can do whatever the fuck we want with that. Whatever this . . . marriage could look like. I don't care if a piece of important paper isn't involved. Yeah? You . . . you've just told me everything I ever need to know. And I won't forget it. And I hear you."

Sydney sniffs hard as he stares down at their joined hands, which catches James so completely off guard he almost asks if he's just gone and upset him, or somehow broken his heart. But then Sydney looks up at him with eyes the color of the sea across the tidepools, and he kisses James once before pulling back with a small smirk. "It's a shame," he says.

James finds himself smiling for no reason at all. "What's a shame?"

"That you didn't stick around in the Navy long enough to get to the level where you get a nice dress uniform. You wouldn't look as handsome in anything else, if we ever did do it."

James barks a laugh up at the clouds and kisses Sydney again, open and uncontrolled with his relieved lips. "You're something else, you know that?" he whispers against Sydney's mouth.

Sydney licks his grin. "How could I forget with you telling me every five fucking minutes?"

They hold each other, stretched almost uncomfortably across their boards, and yet James finds himself utterly relaxed as the water bobs under his board, breathing in the scent of Sydney's sun- and salt-covered skin. A cool breeze rushes along the surface of the water, washing away the remaining sleep from his skin and covering him in shivers. He suddenly wants to be back in their bed with Sydney resting on his chest more than anything, buried deep and safe under the sheets and breathing in the scent of his curls for the rest of the morning.

"You're shivering, and I'm still tired and hungry," Sydney says. "Should head back. Swimming at this time is a stupid idea."

James rolls his eyes, then swallows hard as Sydney reaches forward and presses one last soft kiss to his forehead before lying down on his board and paddling in towards the shore.

James follows behind after one last glance out at the water, watching the last tendrils of the dawn fog wind their way across the surface of the black and blue deep.

Sydney calls back over his shoulder, effortlessly even as he paddles. "I've had more emotional fucking conversations in one week than I have in twenty years combined. So you owe me a fucking mind blowing orgasm when we get back to the house. Or money for my resulting therapy."

James laughs into the surface of his board, grinning as the water rushes past his skin in a cool kiss. It sucks away the tense ghosts of fear still clinging to his bones from the day before, washing him clean like he never even used to keep a bullet casing in his pocket. "The orgasm I can owe you, at least," he calls back. "Can't pay for your mind doctor until you get our shop up and running."

James waits to ask him until they're in the sand walking up to the house, after Sydney has risen out of the water like a god, golden bare skin glittering in the full sunlight and shoulder blades clenching as he lifts his board up under his arm. James waits until he walks just behind Sydney, following his footprints in the sand, transfixed by the movement of the backs of Sydney's thighs, the curves of his buttocks, the sway of his hips as he walks naked across the soft shore, calves and ankles sinking deep into the cool, velvet grains.

James waits, until he realizes he has to say it now, before they reach the house. One last question niggling at the back of his mind that won't let him easily climb back into their bed and wrap his arms around Sydney's body, holding him impossibly close.

"What made you do it?" he asks quietly, stopping to stand still in the sand.

Sydney freezes ahead of him and turns, a frown forming between his brows. "Do what?"

James shrugs, frustrated at himself that he didn't just get straight to the point. "To . . . in Hermosa. Your wipeout. And I know it's stupid I'm still stuck on that, but, I need to know. It's the only mystery in all this I still have left, and you're already a pretty fucking mysterious person to begin with. So . . ."

Sydney looks back at him straight through his skin, the same way his eyes had peered into his chest that first moment back on the pier. James holds his breath as Sydney walks towards him naked in the sand, the fresh clouds casting rippling shadows across his smooth skin as he seems to glide above the earth.

Sydney stops just inches in front of him, and James lets himself drown in Sydney's eyes. They're glittering. They look like the little glimpses of crystal ocean water that had peeked out at him through the thick and steaming jungle when he'd run for his life with fresh blood wet on his palms—the promise of safety and silence and life.

The whipped cream-topped promise of shelter.

Sydney bites his lip like he's thinking of just what to say.

"You don't think it was out of pity anymore," he says, not really a question.

James shakes his head. "No."

"And you don't think it was just me being nice to a serviceman, or me fucking with you just to see what would happen?"

James bites down a grin. "No, and no. Hence the remaining mystery."

Sydney squints at him, like he's trying to read James' sincerity in the lines of his face, then his eyes suddenly clear, open and wide and staring down at James like he's the only thing worth looking at in the world.

"You seemed to be the only person on earth who could stand my miserable ass."

"That first conversation? We just argued and I paddled away."

"But you tried to talk to me."

"That just means I'm not a worthless pile of shit of a human being."

"You introduced yourself."

"Again, same response. Plus we had fuck all to surf on that day."

Sydney touches his chest, his fingertips tracing the edge of James' scar. He swallows. The moment turns incredibly thick. "I wanted to see you again," he whispers, and James draws in a breath at the raw sound of Sydney's words. Sydney traces the scar. "I thought you were beautiful, and I wanted to see you, and I wondered what it would be like to hold you, and if I didn't see you again for certain at the Billabong I would have been chasing you for months trying to track you down at the next lower circuit competition, trying to secretly ask around who and where you were, and when you were surfing, and then I would have had to somehow finagle my way all over again to be in your same heat, and that would have been an unbearable waste of time when I was trying to focus on Waimea, so I wiped out so I could pinpoint your location specifically to the Banzai in two weeks, and then the universe smiled down on me when you yelled at me so fiercely you dropped your bullet into the sand. Everything else just . . . happened."

James bursts. He's leaning forward to kiss the shit out of Sydney Moore when Sydney stops him with a finger in the middle of his chest.

"Now my last remaining mystery," he says, slightly breathless.

James quirks an eyebrow. "Hm?"

Sydney blinks a few times. "Why, actually? Why introduce yourself to me when you'd already been told that I was . . . when you already knew what I was like?"

James doesn't need to think for longer than a millisecond to know his answer. He shoots Sydney's customary smirk right back at him, kisses his confused, waiting lips in a quick peck, then turns to start walking up to the house, warm sand on his feet. He turns back at the hammock, awestruck at the silhouette of Sydney's naked body against the golden light billowing out across the sand of their home. Against the glass sea.

"Honestly?" he says, loud enough so Sydney can hear him where he stands frozen in the sand. "Because you were hot as fuck."

And as James turns to mount the steps into their home, something deep down in his chest tells him he already knows exactly what he's going to do when he 'wakes up one day' in the future, and he realizes with a relieved smile that he's not able to find one single goddamn reason to fight it.

# *Epilogue*

## *Late summer, 1977*

The soothing sea rushes through his ears in a frothing whisper, gently pulling James from his dreams until his eyelids blink slowly into the thin, grey light. He listens to Sydney's deep and even breathing beside him, blowing against the mop of curls covering his face. He's sleeping like the dead on his stomach with his arms thrown up over his head, just like he looks every morning—painted in rested gold twinkling off the tips of the hairs on his bare arms and back.

James sighs, waking up his lungs, and turns on his side to stretch back his tight shoulder. He stares at the small photograph pinned to the wall by his side of the bed. He'd taken it on their trip down to surf Bells Beach in Australia back in February. James smiles now to himself looking at it for the thousandth time—remembering how Sydney had rolled his eyes so hard they'd nearly popped out of his head when James had pulled a brand new camera out of his bag when they got to the hotel.

"Lord spare me," he'd said. "Please tell me you're fucking joking."

James had smirked, holding it up and immediately snapping a picture of Sydney glaring at him across the room with his hands perched on his hips. "Definitely not joking."

He'd pulled the film from the camera and waved it in the air to develop, smirking at Sydney's shocked expression as his hands flew up to grab in his hair.

"That film is expensive, James! Don't tell me you just wasted a photo on *that*!"

"I wouldn't say I wasted it," James had said, glancing down at the slowly forming picture like a ghost emerging from the black, watching as the fog cleared to reveal Sydney's judgmental eyes with a perfect ringlet draped across his forehead.

Sydney had waved his hand, giving up, and turned back to continue unpacking his bag in his room, creating the ruse they'd done many times before of making it look like both hotel room beds had been used and slept in. "You'll regret whatever money you spent on that within the week, I guarantee you," he'd muttered, elbow-deep in his suitcase. "Those cameras are a bitch to maintain. Break constantly."

James had come up behind him and wrapped his arms around Sydney's chest, stroking gently over the soft fabric of the shirt James had given him for Christmas. "Good thing I know a good mechanic, then," he'd whispered, right before biting the lobe of Sydney's ear and letting his hands rove below the waistband of his shorts.

And then, four days later, after James had surprised literally everyone on the beach by coming in fourth at Bells while Sydney remained stuck in fifth place, and after Sydney had grabbed James' arm at the end of competition day and dragged him back to their hotel and threw him down hard onto the bed, fucking him through the mattress and covering James' groans and cries with his hand, and after they'd woken up early to spend their last day in Victoria watching the sun rise steadily over the empty beach, James had let Sydney walk along ahead of him, bare chested in the glittering morning light.

He'd pulled the camera from the bag slung over his shoulder, and waited until the jellyfish on Sydney's back shone just so in the reflection from the sunshine and the waves, and he'd snapped a picture of him looking just barely over his shoulder, waiting for James to catch up and follow.

And Sydney hadn't made fun of him at all when James had pinned it up quietly next to his side of the bed, a handwritten "*Sydney and me. Victoria. February 1977*" written across the white part along the bottom.

"You're not even in the photo," Sydney had whispered, lying behind James their first night back at home and hugging him close in his arms.

James had wrapped a hand around Sydney's forearm and stroked, fingertips brushing over the shivers on his skin. "Yes, I am," he'd whispered. And Sydney had hummed understanding and kissed the back of his neck in the dark.

Sydney stirs, shifting in his sleep behind James and burrowing his face deeper into the pillow, rousing James from his sleepy thoughts. James tears his gaze away from the fading photograph and turns onto his other side to face him, grinning silently as Sydney huffs a lazy breath to blow the long curls off his forehead, nose twitching, then immediately falls back into a deep and heavy sleep. James lifts his arm over Sydney's bare back, gently running his fingers up Sydney's spine and watching, transfixed, as his breath falters in his sleep at the touch of James' palm.

Sydney's skin smells like salt and sand and sun. The sandalwood shavings from working on his boards in the back of the shop, and the lacquer that coats his hands no matter how many times he washes them, and the dark, musky hint of sweat and semen from the sex they'd had the night before. James presses his cheek to Sydney's upper arm where it's thrown up lazily over his head, letting the new layer of scruffy beard on his face rasp against Sydney's skin, deafening in the silence of the room. He breathes in the scent of him. Kisses wet and slow up Sydney's arm towards his shoulder. Kisses over the fresh and crisp lines of the new tattoo draped across the contours of his body, still bright and bold over the shaved skin of his arm and practically glowing in the morning light.

James traces the lines with his lips. The barest hint of tongue. He hums softly into Sydney's skin, remembering back to the day only three weeks ago when he'd come home from a long day spent up at the shop and opened their front door to an empty house and a barely legible note taped to the fridge.

*"Gone to the city. Be back late. That beef you were hoping to use in your lasagna tonight has gone bad. You can use the mushrooms from Hobbs instead in each layer and it'll taste just fine."*

James had run a hand over his face and rolled his eyes, knowing full well he'd never mentioned to Sydney at all that day or the day before that he'd been planning on making lasagna for dinner. Then his eyes had caught the words added to the bottom of the note, flooding his chest with a still unfamiliar warmth, even after a year.

*"Don't worry—not doing anything stupid."*

So James had used the mushrooms in the lasagna instead, and it had tasted fine when he ate it by himself at the kitchen table, and the next morning he'd woken up to an empty but slept-in bed and walked out into the kitchen to grab a cup of coffee from the machine it'd taken him a whole goddamn month of silent struggling to figure out. He'd turned around at the soft pad of Sydney's footsteps behind him, embarrassingly eager to see him again, and then nearly dropped his full mug at the sight of Sydney bare chested in worn sweatpants with a fresh new tattoo covering his left upper arm and shoulder, protected by a thin layer of plastic.

And before James had been able to say anything besides, "How—?" Sydney had walked forward and kissed him right on the forehead, saying, "Took me three goddamn hours to find a place that actually made strawberry milkshakes because the first place I went to was fucking closed, and they half melted on my way back home on the bus, but they're in the freezer for later today and you can thank me by finishing the sanding on that new board and then fucking me tonight."

Because of course Sydney had known what day it was—that it was Helen Campbell's birthday—even though James hadn't said a single goddamn thing about it. And while James felt hot tears building up in the back of his eyes, Sydney had taken the shaking mug of coffee from his hand and wrapped him in his arms, whispering into his ear, "The tattoo wasn't planned, obviously. Just walked by a place that looked relatively clean and got an idea. 'S why I wasn't home until the ass crack of dawn."

He'd held James in the silent kitchen for a long time, letting James breathe roughly against his chest. James had stood stunned, arms hanging limply at his sides, feeling numb and small and completely overwhelmed. Then he'd felt Sydney's lips press gently into his hair, just like he'd now done countless times before, suddenly filling James' bones with such a sense of *right* that James had nearly laughed.

Instead, he'd pulled back slowly, staring at the floor while he passed a hand over his wet eyes to try and pull himself together. He'd been utterly calm—those first breathtaking moments when he'd popped up on the makeshift board off the Vietnam coast. He'd felt braver than the cliff.

"What you told me, a year ago. Just after Waimea," James had said, voice choked. "You know. What we talked about? What you asked me if I wanted?"

Sydney had frowned, then quickly nodded, his eyes quiet and focused, waiting patiently for James to speak.

Finally James had shaken his head and held Sydney's cheek in his hand, trying to talk over his own trembling lips. He raised his chin—Sydney's careful breaths like the wind on his face from his winning Billabong wave, from the first wave he ever learned to ride.

"I think I may have just 'woke up one day,'" he'd said wetly. "We should celebrate."

And Sydney's face had crumpled as he pulled James into a deep and groaning kiss, thumbs brushing softly over the tears falling silently from the corners of James' eyes, moaning, "Oh my God" into his mouth. Breathing sighs of James' name.

Now, just three blink-of-an-eye weeks later, James continues to run his lips over the tattoo, waiting for Sydney to slowly wake up beside him. He can practically feel the ink beneath his lips, as if the lines are raised into more than just a flat picture. Feels the ship's anchor etched forever into Sydney's arm, surrounded by the winding rope and lying against a bed of white plumeria blossoms, which fan out over his shoulder and drip down his arm and back until they just reach the tip of the jellyfish.

James keeps his eyes closed and kisses the exact place where he knows his initials are just barely inked into the bottom of the anchor, hidden in the details of the design for only James to see. It had taken him ten full days to notice them, much to Sydney's private delight.

"Your beard tickles," Sydney grumbles into his pillow, halfheartedly shrugging his shoulder under James' mouth.

James grins, climbing further onto Sydney's back and running his lips across his shoulder blades and neck.

"Should I press harder, then?" he asks.

Sydney's breathing changes beneath him, growing faster. "Then you'd just cover me in marks."

James hums, licking a slow stripe up Sydney's spine before rubbing his gruff cheek at the nape of Sydney's neck, breathing shivers into his skin.

"You like having marks from your man all over you," he murmurs, rolling his hips slowly where he lies now completely on top of Sydney, letting his warm, thickening cock press just barely into the curve of Sydney's ass.

Suddenly, Sydney tenses and flips onto his back beneath him, then he runs his hands up the small of James' bare back and pulls him down to lie across his body. James settles his full weight down, groaning deep in his chest as his cock presses warmly against Sydney's own lazily growing erection. Sydney's hands run up the length of his spine, up into his hair and tangling into the loose, blonde strands.

Sydney's voice is low like gravel from sleep. He rolls his hips under James languidly as he speaks, eyes still swollen half-shut. "My man, huh?" he says.

The words tumble down James' back like sparks of heat, and he leans down to capture the words on Sydney's mouth with a wet and sloppy kiss, panting across his lips and tasting the morning slowness on his tongue. James hums contentedly into Sydney's sleep-warm skin beneath him, slowly tangling his fingers in Sydney's curls and moving like they have all the time in the world—deep and heavy and slow.

After a few minutes of James slowly licking into his mouth, Sydney pulls back panting, lips pink and wet and pupils blown wide. He grins at the corner of his mouth, holding firmly onto James' waist and tracing up his sides with his fingertips. "Aren't we not supposed to see each other beforehand?"

James groans and reaches down between them to cup his palm over Sydney's balls, rolling them gently in his hand and letting his wrist trace just barely against the base of Sydney's swelling cock. "You're ridiculous," he breathes.

Sydney sucks in a breath and fights a moan as James slowly strokes up his hardening length with the barest tips of his fingers, caressing the hot skin like satin. Sydney closes his eyes and tilts his head back, arching his back and hips up into James' touch. "It's bad luck, though," he grunts out.

James grins and leans down to press a soft kiss to the corner of Sydney's mouth. "True," he whispers. He props himself up fully on his elbow and reaches up with his other hand to press his fingers into Sydney's mouth, gliding between his full and parted lips and caressing his wet tongue. Sydney's eyes fly open wide as he moans around James' fingers, vibrating against James' skin and coating them with his spit. James shoves in a third finger, watching Sydney's lips stretch around him, and he rolls his hips hard and slow against Sydney's groin, rubbing his balls slowly along the length of Sydney's full cock.

"You want me to stop?" James rumbles. He slowly drags his fingers out from between Sydney's lips, skin glistening and wet, then reaches down to grasp again at Sydney's erection, running his slick fist along the length of his cock from base to tip before swirling his thumb gently over the leaking slit.

Sydney groans and huffs out a breath which James knows is supposed to sound annoyed, but completely misses the mark when he's writhing and panting beneath him, hips thrusting to roll himself up into James' palm. "Fuck you," Sydney moans.

James kisses wetly beneath Sydney's jaw, tongue dipping out to taste his skin. "You already did that last night," he says low.

Sydney grabs at the back of James' neck and chuckles breathlessly. "God, how could I forget?"

For a moment, James revels in Sydney lying heavy and soft beneath him, letting James work him, pulling soft moans from the back of his throat and running his lips over every inch of Sydney's face and neck. Sydney's fingertips cling firmly to the sensitive skin of James' nape, anchoring him in his arms, and James moans at the rasp of the hair on Sydney's thighs against his own as they twist and tangle beneath the sheets, limbs moving heavy and slow.

Sydney's hand comes up to cup James' cheek, thumb running across the scruff on his face. James' chest clenches at the look on Sydney's face—a look he'd seen often since that moment three weeks ago standing in their kitchen.

James stills his hand on Sydney's erection, for some reason wanting to slow everything down, to savor the seconds, and instead drapes himself across Sydney's thigh and chest, his palm cupping his balls.

Everything grows muffled and still. "I wish you'd keep this," Sydney whispers, fingers tracing along James' jaw.

James frowns, surprised. "I thought you weren't a fan. Just humoring me while I tried it out."

Sydney hums, reaching his neck up to kiss once in the center of James' cheek. "The opposite."

"Even though it leaves burns all over you?" James traces his thumb just under Sydney's lower lip, where already a soft pink rash is forming from the rasp of James' beard against Sydney's smooth skin.

Sydney grins wickedly, and James barely has time to react before Sydney's muscles tense beneath him and he's flipping him over in one smooth motion onto his back, pinning James down into the mattress with a grunt. "Especially because it leaves burns on me," he growls.

The words sear in James' brain, shooting down his spine and pooling in between his hips even as he laughs at being thrown onto his ass. Sydney grips James' waist after pressing a wet kiss to his lips and motions for him to turn onto his stomach, which James does with a moan at the back of his throat, anticipation thrumming hotly through his quickly waking muscles.

Sydney's already trailing his lips and tongue down James' back by the time James can force any words out of his breathless lungs. He sure as hell isn't laughing anymore. "*Jesus . . .*"

Sydney bites at the skin over James' shoulder blade hard, sending a piercing thrill through James' chest, before laving at the mark with his tongue, hands roving firmly up James' sides. "Should I be concerned that you're calling out another dude's name during sex?" Sydney quips into his back.

James reaches back to grab at a handful of Sydney's curls and pulls, other hand gripping tightly at the pillow as Sydney's wet, open lips travel lower . . . lower . . . straight down to the dip in the small of his back. "Fuck you," James groans.

Sydney hums, lips perched just at the top of the crease of James' ass. "Let me do this first," he says, right before grabbing James' buttocks hard in both hands and dipping his tongue into the crease, slowly traveling down in a cooling, wet slide.

"God, yeah . . ."

Sparkling pleasure radiates out from the center point of Sydney's soft tongue gliding between James' cheeks, leaving an icy trail in its path as his hands grip hard and squeeze. James frantically reaches up with one hand to press against the wall, pushing himself back against Sydney's tongue as Sydney's groans vibrate through skin. James can feel the bed gently rocking from where he knows Sydney is getting himself off against the mattress, using the friction of the warm sheets against his cock as he breathes in deeply across James' skin.

James' chest is trembling, hips pushing desperately back against Sydney's mouth while also trying to grind his throbbing cock deeper against the mattress, shooting coiling heat through his groin. Sydney's lips and tongue slowly, gently kiss down the crease of his buttocks, nearing his hole with their warm, wet trail. James flutters in dark, wicked anticipation, gut tensing and breath held tightly in his lungs.

Suddenly Sydney's mouth is gone, cool air rushing against the spit trailed down along his ass. "You didn't get up in the middle of the night to take a shit, did you?"

The air in James' lungs releases all at once in a surprised laugh. "You know I didn't, you dick. Only an idiot could get that close and not be able to tell."

James can feel Sydney's answering grin in the air, brushing softly against the skin on his quivering lower back. "Never hurts to ask," he says lightly.

James is just about to shoot back a Sydney-inspired retort when the words die on his tongue in a rushing gasp, pushed out with an uncontrollable moan as Sydney spits loudly against his hole and then presses his mouth fully against him in one slow, open-mouthed kiss.

James cries out from deep in his chest, hand on the wall shaking. Sydney's lips suck and kiss over his fluttering hole, leaving him wet and open and aching. James' buttocks ache where Sydney's thumbs hold him open, pressing around his rim to make room for his lightly stubbled cheeks, rubbing roughly against his sensitive skin as he licks. James fights the urge to reach back and grab the back of Sydney's head and shove him deeper into his ass, needing to feel every inch of Sydney's mouth against his body.

"Come on . . ." someone is whispering, maybe it's James, it's probably James, James isn't the one with his tongue up someone's ass—

"Fuck, baby, come on . . ."

Sydney's warm, wet tongue slides roughly inside, shooting straight past the rim and igniting the heat in James' groin, and Sydney groans loudly against his skin. He pulls back, words whispered like ice against the wetness surrounding James' hole.

"Fucking shit, James, you're still open from last night."

The memory slams into James' mind with a heat-filled crash, causing him to reach back and grip a handful of Sydney's curls and push his mouth back against his ass. Sydney groans into him, grabbing at his hips hard enough to bruise and pressing his tongue so deep inside James feels like his entire self is being stretched open for Sydney's wet mouth.

James closes his eyes and lets himself remember, reliving it like a fantasy as Sydney's lips continue licking deeper into his hole, rolling and sucking wet echoes through the room.

He remembers . . . how they'd been sitting out on their chairs on the porch, after-dinner beers in hand and watching the sunset like they did almost every night. How Sydney had been plucking idly at his uke, thinking out loud through a new board design he was going to try out soon at the shop once he got the right materials shipped in. And James had sat there feeling lighter than air, letting Sydney's words wash over him like a soft blanket pulling him deeper into a heavy, relaxed daze.

Then Sydney had stopped talking, and played his uke for a few more minutes into the silence. And then he'd casually said, "So Chris is gonna meet us here tomorrow at ten, if that's okay?"

The reality of everything had hit James, then. That he was essentially sitting out on the porch with his fiancé, talking about what time they were going to get fucking married. And even though that small part of his heart had still tried to pang and pull back thinking that it wasn't even a real wedding at all, the rest of him wanted so desperately to hold Sydney Moore close to him in that moment it had nearly gutted him, ripped him in two.

So James had risen to his feet on unsteady knees, reached down to pull Sydney up to his feet, then kissed him without warning, grasping Sydney's face in his hands. "I need you. Now," he'd said against his lips, and Sydney had followed behind him gripping his hand tightly on the way to their bedroom, eyes wide and soft and hungry all at once.

"Are you thinking about it?"

James flings his eyes open in the present where Sydney's words tickle against his skin, and his large hands glide smoothly up the muscles of James' back. Sydney leans down and suddenly bites the skin on James' buttock hard between his teeth, causing James to cry out and grind his cock deeper against the mattress, needing the friction and heat.

"You know I fucking am," he breathes.

Sydney hums deep in his throat, wetly kissing his bite mark before moving his lips back between the crease of James' ass, kissing their way back to his open and dripping hole. James shivers up his spine as Sydney licks a slow stripe across his opening, starting at the thin and sensitive skin of his perineum and ending up in the small of his back.

"Tell me about it," he growls. "Tell me why you're so open and wet."

James moans breathless as Sydney shoves his cheeks back against the skin of James' ass and sucks his lips around his hole, running his thumbs hard up the backs of James' thighs. He feels dizzy with want. Sydney's mouth sucks and hums and licks open his hole while closes his eyes and remembers the ghosts of Sydney's body from last night on his skin. James swallows hard and presses his hand harder against the wall, speaking low and trying not to let out a wild cry.

"You pushed your fingers inside me," he groans, face burning.

He gasps as Sydney grips his ass harder than he ever has and makes a noise that sounds like falling apart, pressing his tongue even deeper inside of him with a moan. James can barely breathe.

It's rare he finds himself saying anything coherent at all during sex. Anything besides an "oh God" or a "fuck" or Sydney's name. He leaves the beautiful, dripping, piercing sentences of scorching words to Sydney, on the nights when either of them has the breath left to speak. He loses himself in Sydney's voice, his fantasies, his wants, his brash desire, and he indulges the secret part of himself that wants to lie there and be utterly taken, completely overwhelmed.

Now, though, he shivers as he feels the mattress rocking even more as Sydney thrusts against the sheets. James flushes red up his neck where he gasps at the ceiling and shudders at what he's about to say, his throat tight.

"You stretched me open," he pants out. "Fucked into me. Filled me."

Sydney pulls back from James' hole and cries out breathlessly. "*Shit*, James."

James feels the desperate heat of Sydney's words travel straight through his body to the aching, leaking tip of his full cock, pressed hot and thick into the sheets. It rolls through him like a wave, thrashing him helplessly onto the wet shore.

He thinks back frantically to the night before, how in the middle of kissing, tangled naked in the sheets, Sydney had started to reach down and prepare himself like they did things most of the time, when James had stopped him with a hand on his wrist and shaken his head and whispered, "No, I *need* you."

How Sydney's eyes had blown to huge black disks when he looked down and watched his fingers sink into James' ass the way they'd done only a handful of times before, moaning out loud at the wet slide of his fingers into James' shaking body.

James takes a deep breath, feeling bold and reckless. Sydney's curls tickle against his ass where he still licks into him, stopping every few kisses to spit into his hole before diving in to press him open further with his lips. In his mind, James sees Sydney from the night before, gorgeous and kneeling before him with his muscled chest heaving in the moonlight, holding his cock in his hand at James' entrance with a hot sweat dripping down from his curls.

James presses back harder against Sydney's lips and curses under his breath. "You held your huge cock in your fucking hand . . ."

"Fuck, tell m—"

"Pressed it up against me. Pushed it inside me."

"Oh my God . . ."

James reaches down frantically under his lifted hips and grabs his own cock in his hand, gripping hard and moaning at the release of sweet friction. Sweat beads along his spine and in the small of his back as Sydney still bites and licks along the crease of his ass, alternately fucking him deep and wet with his tongue. Suddenly, Sydney gives one cheek of James' buttocks a light slap, shooting heat straight down through James' toes curling against the mattress.

He starts to keen as he pulls hard on his own cock, words pouring out of him that he'd only ever heard Sydney say in the heat of the moment on their filthiest nights.

"You were so fucking huge," he groans. "Swelling in me . . ."

Sydney whimpers high in his throat, and James feels Sydney take one hand off his ass to reach down to start working his own erection.

James goes on, prickling up the back of his neck. "Fucking into me. Pumping your cock in my ass. God you were so big. Didn't think I could take it—"

"*James.*"

James closes his eyes again and sees Sydney from the night before. How he'd covered him with his body and thrusted his cock into him again and again while James lay panting and arched on his back, fingernails leaving red trails along the skin of Sydney's shoulders. How Sydney had held James' face in his hands and kissed his bearded cheeks, his eyelids, across his forehead, just the barest hints of panted kisses brushed against his mouth. He thinks of how Sydney had pulled out all the way then knelt up to watch himself disappear into James' body in one long, slow, glide, both of them moaning at the wet slap of skin against skin, sparking through the room.

How Sydney had laid his whole weight on top of him, just barely rolling his hips so that he hit the spot inside James that made his toes curl and the breath knock clear from his tight lungs. And how he'd whispered softly against his mouth, voice nearly gone, "dearest love" as he'd reached between them and gripped James' cock in his hand and pumped him until he came.

James flings open his eyes and knows he's getting close. He pulls and twists on his cock, fire shooting through his veins, and swallows over his dry throat to keep talking, knowing Sydney's hanging on his every word as his tongue traces a slow, hot circle around the rim of James' ass, barely dipping inside for a sloppy lick.

"I'm still open now," he pants out, nearly biting his tongue. "That's how much you stretched me."

Sydney whimpers behind him where he still lies on his belly between James' legs, tongue flicking frantically against his dripping hole. James arches his back to push against him. "Fucked me so fucking good. So hard. I can still feel your huge cock in me." James grunts as the heat of his orgasm starts to coil at the base of his erection, hot and dripping in his hand, hard as steel.

He gulps down air. "Can still feel your cum dripping out of me, dripping down my thighs . . ."

"Jesus Christ—"

"God, I was tight, wasn't I? Open just for you to take me. Only you inside me." James whines as his cock throbs. "Getting fucked . . ."

"Fucking *fuck*."

And with that, Sydney presses his face hard against James' ass, fucks his tongue deeper into James than he ever has, flicks the tip against the sensitive skin inside him, and *groans.*

James comes in his hand with a breathless cry, spilling onto the sheets and dripping over his fingers still frantically flying up and down the aching steel of his erection. Distantly he hears Sydney's voice murmuring, and feels his hands running up and down the cheeks of his ass.

"Fuck, yeah that's it. Come for me . . ."

James collapses onto his stomach, not giving a shit that the sheets beneath him are wet. He takes a breath that expands every inch of his lungs, feeling dizzy and tingling and heavy like lead. Then he heaves himself onto his back as Sydney pushes himself up to kneel over James' hips, hand desperately pumping his own cock.

James runs his fingernails up Sydney's thighs, then reaches under to grab his balls in his hand, feeling them hot and tight up against his groin. Sydney's cock is swollen and leaking from the tip, shaking from the force of Sydney's huge hand flying over it where it juts out proudly just above James' stomach. James reaches his other hand forward and brushes a finger just across the slit, collecting the drip of precome leaking there, then brings his finger to his mouth and sucks, licking it clean.

Sydney curses, eyes desperate and wild. James looks up at him and blinks hard. Sydney looks undone. Curls wild, spit still dripping from his chin, lips bright pink and swollen with beads of sweat dripping slowly down his chest and over his nipples, illuminated by the sunlight pouring through the windows off the surface of the ocean.

"You're beautiful," James breathes, his throat surprisingly tight, because he knows exactly how to make Sydney Moore fall apart.

Sydney does. He pulls himself once more, long and slow, starting from the thatch of dark hair at the base of his cock and squeezing hard out towards the leaking tip.

"Gorgeous man," James whispers to him, his hands on Sydney's heaving sides. "My man . . ."

Sydney whips his head back and keens as he comes, semen spraying across James' chest as they both groan—two pairs of eyes blown open and fixed on the sight of Sydney's cum painting the muscles on James' stomach and chest.

Finally, Sydney releases himself and collapses forward onto his elbows, bracketing James' head and leaning down for a kiss. He hesitates just above James' face, realizing where his mouth just was with a slight frown. James grabs the nape of his neck as he whispers, "Come here, you," then pulls him down the rest of the way to crash their mouths together, still panting and open, lips sensitive and wet.

He kisses him for a long time in the early morning air, relishing in the heavy weight of Sydney's muscled limbs lying limp on top of him, trusting him to hold him up and not let him fall.

When Sydney eventually pulls back to breathe, James nearly gasps. He forgets, sometimes. Forgets how wrecked and open and *young* Sydney can look—how alive. They hold each other's gaze in the new silence, breathing hard into the vulnerable air, then James pats the side of Sydney's cheek and grins.

"Still all in a fit about seeing each other the day of the wedding?" he asks.

Sydney blinks once, registering his words, and then the look on his face is slowly replaced by his usual gaze—piercing and cocky with just a tiny hint of smirk. James drinks it in as Sydney sits up and wipes his mouth with the back of his hand.

"You don't realize this," he says, "because you have an absolutely shit internal clock. But it's nine-fifty right now, and Chris is coming at ten—"

"Shit!"

James leaps up from the bed as Sydney laughs, eyes bright. He paces across the room, frantically searching for his robe among the heap of clothes thrown onto the floor from the night before, then looks back at Sydney still casually kneeling on the bed, one hand working out the tangles from his curls while the other one strokes languidly at his soft, wet penis nestled between his muscled thighs.

James wants to drop the robe in his hand back onto the floor. Leap back into the sheets and pull Sydney down and kiss him senseless until his cock is thick and hot again, pressing into his skin. Wants to taste the laughter on his tongue and kiss the dimples on his cheeks.

God, he's really lost it over the past year, hasn't he? He's fallen hard and gone.

It feels spectacular.

James stands with his hands on his hips, trying to look stern as Sydney chuckles. "You couldn't have fucking said anything about the time twenty minutes ago?"

Sydney raises his eyebrows, eyes darting quickly to James' ass. "I was busy!"

James curses and flings on his robe before heading for the door to the bathroom. He catches Sydney's pleading look out of the corner of his eyes as he heads for the door and stops. "Oh no no, you don't get to use the shower. You'll end up taking a fucking half hour, and *I'm* the one who has fucking cum sprayed all over me, thanks to someone."

Sydney rolls his eyes and huffs at the ceiling. "Well fine, I'll just have to look like I literally just had sex in all your memories of today then."

James mutters under his breath as he walks into the bathroom and shuts the door. "You better be fucking clean and dressed by the time I come out of here. Seriously, Sydney."

He hears Sydney's laugh continuing behind him, spreading warmth through every inch of his chest.

"Quit whining, you old grump, we'll be ready on time. Didn't they train you to take fifteen second showers in the Navy?" Sydney calls through the door.

James can't fight the grin on his face as he frantically flips the shower on and fusses at his hair in the mirror. "They also taught me how to effectively drown someone in the Navy, so watch it with the sass, you dickhead," he calls back.

James hears a muffled, "Aye, aye, Captain" through the door before he steps under the warm spray, letting it wash the smell of sex from his skin. He takes a deep breath of the humid air to fill his lungs, trying to steady his racing heart.

It feels real, now. Standing in the shower trying to look presentable in eight minutes so he doesn't look like he just fucked another man when a stranger will knock on their door for the very first time.

He thinks to himself for the hundredth time over the past few weeks that if someone had walked up to him a year and a half ago when he'd just finished a morning surf with Rob, or just ended his shift at the dockyard, and told him that today he was going to somehow bind himself forever to another man in front of a living, breathing witness, he probably would have passed out or vomited or punched whoever told him, or all three.

Fear coils thick and sudden in his chest, a little voice in his ear begging him to hide behind the door like a child when Chris comes. Apologize to Sydney later when he finally crawls out of his cave and say, *"Come on, man, we've already said we love each other, so there's no real reason to actually have some sort of ceremony for it, is there? Is there?"*

Then, through the sound of the pounding spray and the ragged breathing from his chest, James hears Sydney whistling as he gets ready in the next room—some tune James has heard on the radio but can't quite place. He hears Sydney's brave, brilliant voice again in his mind, crystal clear and sharp as if Sydney were standing right behind him in the shower.

*"Yes. With me."*

The fear dissolves, rushing from his body like the foam fades back from the shore with the rise and fall of the passing tide. He blinks back the water forming in his eyes and ducks his head to be battered by the spray, flinching when it hits him as if he's flayed open and raw.

In a sudden rush, James shuts off the water with a shaking hand and wraps a towel around his waist, then immediately peeks his head out of the bathroom door, steam billowing out around him into the living room while he drips wet puddles onto the floor.

Sydney's standing by the window already in his clothes with his hair tamed and styled, calmly looking out at the shore with his arms crossed over his chest. He turns to look over his shoulder when he realizes James isn't moving from the doorway and frowns slightly, confused.

James' heart races.

"I love you, you know," James says, his lips numb.

Sydney smiles, free and open, and traces his eyes gently up James' dripping wet skin. The moment pulses between them, and James has a sudden flashback to those mornings they'd spent on the beaches in Los Angeles together before everything had been laid open and made known. Mornings when the air would spark with electricity and buzz in the space between their bodies, tantalizing and hinting at more—fierce and dangerous and vulnerable like an open flame.

A harsh knock sounds at the door, breaking the thick, warm silence. Before he turns to answer it, Sydney shoots James one last look that banishes the last icy fingers of anxiety still clutching tightly at his heart.

"I know," he whispers softly, eyes crinkling. And then he gestures his head for James to go on and finish getting ready while he goes to answer the door, hand perfectly steady on the doorknob.

"Shit, do you think we should have worn ties?"

James runs a hand over the back of his neck, feeling odd and itchy in his skin. Sydney snorts under his breath and shoots him a sidelong look, and James can tell that he's irritatingly trying to suppress a fond grin.

"For what?" Sydney whispers back, gesturing with his head to the empty beach. "To impress the adoring congregation?"

James huffs and shoves his arm against Sydney's shoulder. "You know what I fucking mean."

Sydney gasps quietly, eyebrows comically raised up his forehead. "James Campbell, cursing in a church? Wash out your mouth."

"Oh for God's sake—"

"And using the Lord's name in vain!"

"*Jesus* spare me."

"I'm sure he's got better shit to do then come and look after your sorry ass."

"Sure doesn't seem that way when he swoops down and saves me every couple years."

"I'm sure he makes mistakes."

"Do you ever fucking stop?"

"Do I need to make you put a dollar in a jar for every time you curse on our wedding day?"

"God, you, sir, are fucking something el—"

"You two all set?"

James startles and looks up at Chris watching the two of them with an amused smirk, then coughs to clear his throat while something like embarrassment fizzles in his skin. He can practically hear the laughter he knows Sydney is hiding back in his chest standing next to him.

"Yeah, sorry," he forces out.

Chris holds up a patient hand, then gestures with a nod towards the rocky cliff far behind him, silhouetted by the slowly purpling sky. "Let's go then," he says.

James takes a deep breath and starts walking beside Sydney, both of them trailing behind Chris as they walk along their stretch of beach just like they've done hundreds of times. Only this time, James feels each grain of sand against his bare feet as he takes step after step, tickling against his toes and gently pushing him forward across the shore towards the place where he'll take Sydney's hand in his and be expected to say words that will actually somehow *mean* something. Words that could somehow convey even half of what he feels as he listens to Sydney's steps gently swish beside him in the sand, echoing back and forth with his own. Because that's all they have, isn't it? Just words?

No. More than words. So much more . . . and yet . . .

James thinks as they walk in mutual silence that Chris is absolutely nothing like the man he'd been picturing when Sydney first said he'd sniffed around and learned who he was. His name, and the fact that he was willing to perform a ceremony like this, meant James had been picturing some young New Age dude from San Francisco or New York, freshly arrived in Hawaii with a string of fake puka shells around his neck, chanting something about Krishna like the parades of people he'd seen the last couple years in orange robes along the downtown LA streets.

He definitely hadn't been expecting the elderly Hawaiian man walking carefully in front of them now across the sand, with a simple garland of leaves about his neck and a plain canvas bag slung lazily over his shoulder, grey hair glinting in the thick sunlight.

James had done an embarrassing double take that morning when he'd walked into the living room dressed and ready where Sydney was already talking casually with Chris. It was a shock to see someone else in their home for the very first time, and even more of a shock when that person was the complete opposite from what James had been expecting.

He'd paused, irrationally waiting for Chris to look him up and down, look back at Sydney, and then give a face of shock or disgust—a mirror image of Lahela's face that day she told James he didn't look at all like 'the others'. Because now Chris *knew*.

But when Chris didn't look at him oddly, or say any of these things, James had been the one to stare as he stood like an idiot in the corner of the house with his mouth half open. Until Chris had said, laughing, "Ah, so you're one of the ones who was expecting me to be some young guru from the mainland. A common mistake, I assure you." And Sydney had snorted down into his mug of coffee before gazing at James with twinkling eyes and gesturing silently for him to come sit by his side, as if they had coffee every morning with a stranger who knew that they kissed in the safety of the dark. And James had just noticed how tightly Sydney's hands were holding his own mug, as if he needed James to be by his side for them to finally relax.

So James had joined them, neck beet red with embarrassment, and then grown even more surprised when Chris hadn't immediately taken them outside, joined hands, said the magic words, and been done with it all and gone by ten-thirty. Instead he'd leaned back comfortably in their rickety wooden kitchen chair and drank his coffee so slowly James had to get up to use the bathroom twice before Chris was done getting through his first cup.

He'd asked James about his life—where he grew up and what he did and where he'd surfed. And when James had glossed over a few years of his life with a low, "I was away," Chris had taken one long look at him in the silence, then stuck out his hand and shook James', hard and firm over the rough kitchen table, giving him a nod that James knew in his tight chest somehow meant, "*Thank you.*"

Then Chris had turned to Sydney, still sitting loose and comfortable at the table without even a tapping finger or fidgeting leg in sight, despite Chris' endless list of questions, and despite the fact that James had noticed Sydney was seeming to turn and scan out the window every ten minutes. Chris had smirked a bit and said, "So, the infamous Danny Moore. I hear you're designing a new style of board in that shop of yours?"

And James had watched, chest fluttering and warm, as Sydney had come absolutely alive—eyes bright and hands flying and lips talking through physics and waves and materials faster than even James could fully keep up with, and he'd heard it all a hundred times before. Chris had sat there and nodded and asked questions like he actually knew what the hell Sydney was talking about, all while Sydney's knee pressed warm and steady against James' own under the table.

Finally, Chris had leaned back in his seat, set down his empty mug, and taken a deep sigh, smiling at them both. "If you don't mind, I'm going to take a few minutes for myself," he'd said. "I'll come back when I'm ready for you two and we can go?"

James' heart had started racing, and Sydney had nodded when neither of them said a thing.

"Do you have a specific place in mind?" Chris had asked, pushing up from the table.

Sydney had shot James a quick glance, placing his hand hesitantly on James' knee. James covered it with his own, even as his mouth went dry.

They hadn't discussed this before. The question hadn't even crossed his mind. But then Sydney had squeezed his leg gently and looked up at Chris standing in the doorway, head steady and high. "There's a small cliff just at the end of the beach," he'd said. "I think we'll do it there."

And just as Chris was about to disappear outside, James had blurted out the question he knew he had to ask before he could stand up on that cliff and let this man somehow bind him to Sydney forever.

"Why do you do this?" he'd asked suddenly.

Chris had paused, looking thoughtful. Then he'd looked across the shore towards the waves for a minute, patient in the buzzing silence. "I practice the old religion," he'd finally said, words slow and carefully formed on his thin, chapped lips. "The old beliefs of my people."

James had felt Sydney go rapt with attention beside him, eyes clear and focused and fixed on Chris' silhouette in the doorway. Chris had taken a breath and gone on, his voice somber. "Then one day we were no longer free, and those beliefs became outlawed for hundreds of years." His voice had grown haunted, shaking slightly as his body grew still. "People were thrown in prison. Or killed. It is a very long story. I am giving you the book jacket version."

Sydney and James had both quietly hummed.

Then Chris had slowly turned back towards James sitting frozen next to Sydney, meeting his gaze with unbearably soft eyes. "So it seems we have a small something in common, no?" And with a final nod, he'd disappeared through the doorway, ambling down towards the shore. Leaving James and Sydney to sit in a house that now felt oppressively silent without Chris' voice to fill it.

Now, twenty minutes later, James follows along in Chris' footsteps in the sand, Sydney's presence next to him flowing out to cover every inch of his skin. James smells him in the air, feels the ghosts of his warm touch still hovering on his face and hands, tastes the words from his lips on the thin ocean breeze, mixed with a frothing layer of salt.

James is walking to a wedding, *his* wedding, which would be the most absolutely absurd phrase he'd ever heard in his life if it wasn't undeniably true. It's unbelievable, and it's nerve-wracking, and it's beautiful, and it's *final.* And it's also sad, as James looks around them at the empty beach, the oblivious rush of the waves across the sand, and the distant birds in the sky.

And James can't turn back now, couldn't turn back even if he knocked his head and wanted to, but he also wants to wake up next to Sydney just one more time before everything changes. Except, nothing is changing. Except, *everything* is changing. And Chris is walking so fast, flying across the sand, even as his footsteps amble so slowly he doesn't even kick up any warm grains.

Sydney still keeps glancing over his shoulder back to the house, eyes keenly darting across the trees, and James is finally about to ask him if he's afraid someone is going to walk by and see them when Sydney halts, puts a hand on James' arm, and abruptly stops them in the sand, an odd look on his face. James looks down at Sydney's hand on his arm and frowns as Sydney calls quickly up to Chris ahead of them. "You mind if we take a quick moment?"

Chris nods and turns to keep walking away, leaving James and Sydney alone on the beach that James suddenly feels has never looked so open or so vast. Sydney takes both of James' hands earnestly in his own—the new rough spots and scars across his fingers from his time in the back of the shop. The scars James has cleaned, and patched up, and kissed.

Sydney's voice is surprisingly soft and low, blending in seamlessly with the steady thrush of the waves at their backs. "Are you alright?"

James' heart unexpectedly melts, churning in his chest, and without thinking, he leans forward with a sigh and falls into Sydney's arms, burying his face against Sydney's neck and feeling Sydney's hands come up to hold him steady around his back.

They stand there in silence, heartbeats synchronizing to the same even beat of the waves. James feels Sydney press his lips into his hair, styled for once, and warmed by the sun. Listens to Sydney breathe in the scent of him as Sydney's arms run slowly up and down his back, holding him close.

"Thank you," James whispers into his skin.

Sydney kisses his hair again and hums. "For what?"

James pulls back and takes in the breathless sight of Sydney Moore glowing in the light of the glittering afternoon sun. The crisp white of his button-down shirt is nearly blinding, and James can just barely make out the faint colors of the tattoo spilling across his shoulder, which peek through the fabric made transparent by the radiant sun. The shirt hugs the lean lines of his chest and stomach, tucked into khakis that cling to his hips and drape across his thighs.

James takes him in, eyes roving slowly from his bare feet in the sand up to his eyes like the sea, and he swallows as emotion chokes the back of his throat for the innumerable time that day. James smooths down the front of Sydney's shirt with his hands, fixing up his open collar before gliding his hands down his chest, stopping to rest just over Sydney's heart. He prides himself that he didn't just look over his shoulder to check if Chris could see, and Sydney smiles down at him, his eyes sparkling and wet.

James takes a deep breath through his nose, willing the irritating nerves still crackling through his body to disappear with his exhale, pushed out and away across the sea. "For doing this," he finally answers. "Just, slowing things down for a second."

Sydney nods silently, understanding. James has a strong feeling Sydney didn't just stop for him. He stares at the dip in the hollow of Sydney's throat, fanned by the crisp white lines of the new shirt James had given him for his birthday—because James had come to realize over the past year that Sydney owned approximately two shirts that weren't tattered almost to bits, one of which James had seen him in that day Sydney appeared out of nowhere on the docks, and so James had made it his mission to supplement Sydney's wardrobe over every possible holiday in the future, bit by bit.

"You look handsome," James says, the word gliding across his tongue.

Sydney blushes across his cheeks, then blinks hard and smirks. "Aren't I supposed to look beautiful? I'm the bride in white, after all."

James huffs a laugh and groans, slapping Sydney on the arm. "You're so full of shit," he whispers so Chris can't hear, chuckling.

Sydney grins and runs his hands slowly up James' chest in return, smoothing down the dark navy shirt Sydney had thrust at him the night before saying, "If you don't wear this, I'll pose an objection at the altar." Sydney's thumbs run gently over his collarbones, then he traces the fingertips of one hand around the scar hiding under James' shirt, finally covering it with his palm in a gesture James has come to realize stands for a thousand unspeakable words.

"You sure you're alright?" Sydney asks, even as he himself glances back at the trees over James' shoulder. "You seem . . . there's something on your mind."

James almost laughs. Only someone like Sydney could pull off asking if James is alright when meanwhile *he's* the one who keeps making sure they can't be seen down the lane, or across the beach. But then, James would also be an idiot if he thought Sydney couldn't tell that he isn't exactly prancing carefree up to the cliff, either.

James looks once more towards the sea from where he's sheltered from the salt breeze by Sydney's chest, watching the sunlight dance and dapple across the surface of the water, then he covers Sydney's hand on his chest with his own. He waits until Sydney's pulse seems to flow straight through the veins under his own skin. "It's just sort of sad, isn't it?" he finally says. "I mean, this is the celebration you wanted—*we* wanted. But we're doing this alone."

Sydney's lips tremble, just barely, then he shrugs one shoulder. "We have Chris as a witness," he offers, right before he scans the trees once more.

"I know," James says. He can't find words to express how unbearably heartbreaking it is that Sydney seems to want to *keep* it that way—shoo everyone away from the beach, lock the doors. And James also can't find the words to express how shattering it is that he finds himself agreeing with him. That even the thought of Chris knowing, when he already full-on knew, made James stand dumbly in the corner just a few hours ago.

Sydney cups James' cheek in his hand, his fingers steady. "But that's not really what you mean," he says, with a sad smile.

James mimics the sagging slope of Sydney's mouth. "No, it isn't."

"We'll see Rob and Lori in September when we're there for the U.S. Open though, yeah?"

"You realize we're also there for their wedding, too? Not just for surfing?"

Sydney fake huffs and rolls his eyes. "Fine, and we'll be there for the wedding too," he groans.

James grins and fixes the crease of Sydney's collar one last time. "You're impossible," he says.

"Clearly I'm not *im*possible if you're promising to stick around."

"Fine, what are you, then?"

Sydney acts like he's thinking hard. "I'm *nearly* impossible."

James shakes his head and curses under his breath with a soft laugh, then moves to start walking again towards the cliff.

He does feel a little more grounded, the sadness pushed back from the forefront of his mind. He thinks he just might even feel ready now for the first time in three weeks—ready to stand up in front of the sea and the sky and let the edge of the earth see that he's in love with Sydney Moore. Say the words and kiss him, and at least Chris will be there to witness it all.

Then Sydney sucks in a quick breath behind him, and his hand shoots out to stop James by his wrist. "What if," he starts, "James, what if we didn't have to do this alone?"

James frowns, turning back to face him. His mind races for what Sydney could possibly mean. "What, you mean Hank? I thought he was watching the shop for us."

Sydney bites his lip, glances at the trees, then looks down quickly at the sand, and suddenly a spark of something lights up in the back of James' mind, burning hesitant and bright. "Hold on, wait a second. Why the fuck do you look so suspicious right now?"

Sydney looks up at him, eyes open and warm, then stares over James' shoulder back towards the path in the trees without immediately looking away. James' heart races without him fully knowing why, then he looks over his shoulder to follow Sydney's steady gaze.

His eyes focus, squinting against the glare of the sunlight reflecting off the sand, and then he freezes, sucking in a gasp.

Rob stands at the edge of the beach with Lori beside him, holding up a hand over his eyes to shield them from the blinding sun. Lori waves back at James from where she stands close next to him, grin threatening to leap off her face and her other hand tucking her hair behind her ear out of the breeze.

James whips his head back towards Sydney and gapes at him with wet and burning eyes. He can barely speak. "What did you do?" he whispers. "How did . . . ?"

Sydney looks at him for a long moment, like he's trying to seriously study James' shocked face, then he smiles at him like somehow James just hung the sun. He hesitates for a moment, then leans forward and softly kisses James' cheek, and James is too shocked to realize that it's the first time anyone's seen them kiss.

He doesn't even flinch. Doesn't move.

"Go on, then," Sydney says, pushing James gently forward by the back.

James is terrified that if he turns back around they'll be gone, faded away like a mirage into the hot sand. "You're something else," he chokes out, and Sydney laughs and says, "I know," as he turns James around by the shoulder and pushes him forward again towards where Rob and Lori still wait impatiently in the trees.

James stumbles forward on numb and shaking legs, then looks up from his feet. They haven't disappeared. They're still standing there—

standing at the entrance of his home like Los Angeles just plucked them up and dropped them clear in the middle of Oahu.

James wants to run towards them but can't trust his shocked legs to move. Instead he walks, barely feeling the sand beneath his feet, and Rob finally emerges from the shade to jog out to meet him instead, Lori on his heels.

"Who the fuck gets married without inviting their only goddamn friends?" Rob calls out to him.

James laughs wetly and shakes his head, still blinking in disbelief. "Me, apparently," he manages to say back. Then Rob reaches out and pulls him into his arms in a thick hug, clutching him to his chest.

They've never hugged before—not like this. James holds his breath as his body melts against Rob's bones, breathing in the scent at the crook of his neck that James suddenly realizes smells just like the sand outside a little red and white seaside mobile home.

"Shit, Jimmy," Rob whispers. "Missed you, man."

James can't bring himself to say anything back. He finally pulls away and holds Rob firmly by the shoulders, staring and staring and staring into the brown eyes he hasn't seen in over half a year since he and Sydney competed in San Diego. They'd been so busy with setting up the shop, and surfing around Hawaii, and saving every last dollar they had, and James wants to kick himself now for ever letting it get like this, after he'd sat in Rob and Lori's warm backyard with Josie's head in his lap and promised them he wasn't disappearing forever, that they would still have—

"How the hell did you get here?" he hears himself ask.

Rob chuckles. "Well you see they've got these newfangled things called planes now. Big tubes of metal that fly you high up in the air over the ocean—"

"Oh, close the shades, you dic—"

"And then there's these machines called *cars* that are like mini planes on land with wheels that—"

"You fucking ass, why don't you ever—"

"Jimmy!"

Lori flings herself into his arms, legs wrapping around his waist, and James holds her up out of the sand with a surprised laugh. Lori kisses

512

his cheek before jumping back down to her feet, reaching forward to smooth out the wrinkles from James' shirt.

"Sorry, but if I didn't interrupt that you two would have just had the 'insult Olympics' for an hour while me and Danny stood here waiting," she says. "To answer your question," and she gives a pointed glare at Rob, "Danny called us a couple weeks ago and somehow pulled plane tickets out of the air, and Rob had some vacation days left and I skipped some class and here we are."

James looks back over to Sydney near the shore where he waits staring out at the sea with his hands in his pockets, carefully not looking their way. James' chest expands almost painfully, overflowing with an emotion he can't even name. "I didn't even know he . . ." he trails off.

When he turns back at Rob and Lori, Rob wraps his arm around her waist, his eyes turning serious as they lean against each other.

"Really, though, Jimmy, you know you could have told us," he says, sounding a bit hurt. "You know we woulda dropped everything to come."

Hot shame creeps up the back of James' neck, and he fights the urge to run a sweating palm over his tingling face. "I'm sorry," he says. "I just didn't . . . this all happened so fast, yeah? And it's not like . . . well it doesn't really mean anything official, you know?"

Rob slaps him gently on the arm. "That's bullshit and you know it."

Lori nudges him with a frown, chiding, "Rob . . ."

"You know what I mean," Rob adds. He reaches forward to take James' arm once more, his grip warm and firm in a way that instantly takes James back to that Los Angeles beach right after his backbreaking shift, when Rob had been panting and radiant and dripping wet.

"This does mean something, Jimmy," Rob says.

James blinks hard and swallows over a dry throat, feeling like a wrung-out sponge. He ducks his head and nods, rubbing his palm over his neck. "I know," he whispers.

The moment turns thick and heavy, settling between the three of them with a thud. Lori looks over James' shoulder towards Sydney and forces a smile, speaking lightly into the grey fog of sudden emotion.

"Well come on, then," she says. "He's waiting."

Rob starts walking with his arm still around Lori's waist, the other one clasped firmly to James' shoulder. James sucks in a full breath for the first time since turning around and glimpsing Rob Depaul standing on an Oahu beach, and his legs move thickly through the sand like rubber. He walks towards Sydney like a lighthouse in the fog, as if each step he takes is really on a pier in the middle of Hermosa instead of over the soft, private sand of their home. He belatedly realizes Rob is talking and turns his head to hear.

"Yeah, Jimmy," Rob's saying, grinning. "Make him wait any longer and he'll start writing pining love letters to you—send them tied to little bird wings flying across the beach."

A laugh bursts from James' chest, and he shoves Rob away from him. "Jesus, between you and him, the only person on this beach who I actually fucking like is Lori," he groans.

"Well that's because Lori's too nice to make fun of you for growing a fucking beard like some hermit living in a cave. I mean, shit, do you eat grasshoppers now and only bathe once a year?"

Lori huffs. "Rob, I swear to God, I'm gonna purposefully lose this engagement ring in the ocean if you can't just can it for two hours on the most important day of Jimmy's life."

"Well if it's the most important day of his life, he shouldn't look like he just crawled off a deserted island where he didn't have a razor for six months," Rob shoots back.

Just then, they reach Sydney, who's slowly turned to greet them, hands stuck in his pockets and shoulders slightly slumped, like he's trying to make himself look smaller in the air. Rob grows oddly quiet as they stop in the sand, and James feels a hot wave of sudden nerves churn in his gut.

He needs to say something—somehow bridge the vast, gaping hole between the two halves of his life suddenly clashing together in the sand. He opens his mouth to try to speak, hands clammy and awkwardly clearing his throat. But Sydney reaches out a hand before James can manage to say anything, and Rob takes it in a firm and silent handshake, sharing a quiet look that somehow makes James' chest physically ache to witness.

Sydney turns to take Lori's hand then, and leans down to kiss her cheek. James gapes, mouth wide open. He's barely seen Sydney shake another person's hand before, let alone this. He burns the image into his memory, hiding it deep in his mind.

"Thank you for coming," Sydney says formally.

Rob and Lori immediately echo, "Thank you."

James has the sudden sensation that Rob and Lori are his parents, and Sydney's his school principal inviting them down for a formal meeting. The thought makes him want to laugh at the sheer, unbelievable impossibility of it all, then he again notices the look that Rob and Sydney keep sharing with each other, and feels that he's missing something desperately important instead.

Rob breaks the silence and clears his throat, putting on his usual grin. "Well, someone had to come out here and make sure you weren't just marrying this old man for his life insurance. You sure as hell aren't marrying him for his looks."

*Marrying him.*

James' heart stops at the effortless words—a screaming bomb piercing the peaceful sky over the ocean with exploding flames. But nobody even flinches.

Instead, Lori huffs and rolls her eyes as Sydney laughs. It lights up his entire face, and James finds himself staring at him breathlessly for what feels like the hundredth time that day. Without thinking, he reaches out and places his hand on Sydney's cheek, touching the smile still on his face, and then he stills, realizing what he's just done right in front of the two other people he loves most in the world.

Some prickling, black part of him waits for Sydney to turn his cheek away with an embarrassed laugh, or to crack a joke and turn to quickly walk up to the cliff, ending the awkward silence and leaving James behind in the sand.

He waits for Rob and Lori to gasp, for them to quickly look away. For them to say they didn't fly across an entire ocean for *this*. This isn't *our* Jimmy.

But everything is quiet, and the ocean sings, and Sydney brings his hand up to hold James' fingers against his cheek. He turns his face to kiss the center of James' palm, plain as day.

The earth stops, and James' breath catches in his throat.

"Shall we?" Sydney says quietly, speaking only to James.

James has never known the answer to anything more fiercely in his life. He strokes his thumb across Sydney's cheek, swallowing hard, then whispers, "Thank you."

The wind at the top of the rocky cliff wraps around his skin like soft velvet, shivering across the hair on his forearms below his rolled-up sleeves.

James clutches at Sydney's hands in his, unable to keep his eyes off Sydney's warm and glowing skin, swathed in the white fabric of his shirt and bathed in the reflection of light off the waves down below. The wind blows his curls across his forehead, down into his eyes. James wants to rise up on his toes and bury his face in Sydney's hair, inhaling the warmth of him straight down into his lungs over the floral salt scent of the sea.

Instead he holds on, and looks only at him, and tries to focus on what Chris is saying next to them as Rob and Lori watch on from just off to the side, arm in arm.

"The sky and the sea were once one," Chris is saying. "A vast expanse of the same unbreakable blue, stretching unbounded for eternity. Hovering over the surface of the earth."

Chris is speaking very softly beside them, his voice just barely carrying over the sound of the swirling wind and crashing waves below. Sydney shoots James a quick look, eyes nervous with the barest hint of a smile at the corner of his mouth, and James squeezes his hand in return, trying to breathe. Trying to stay rooted in the ground instead of flying clear up into the clouds.

Chris goes on, his voice evolving to a steady, calming hum. "One day, the earth realized that the sky and sea could no longer remain one entity. That they had individual gifts, and individual paths to take. And so she softly divided them evenly down the middle, separating wet from dry, water from air, the waves from the clouds."

Chris gestures behind him towards the vast horizon line, brilliant and shimmering in the hazy afternoon sun. "But you see," he says, "they are not separate at all. They are the full sky. And they are the full sea.

And yet they are also joined together seamlessly into one by the horizon line you see. And the sea sends its waves up towards the heavens to greet the sky, and the sky sends its wind down to kiss the surface of the water. And in that way, the sky and the sea are still one."

He looks back and forth between James and Sydney a few times with a somber expression on his face, the breeze picking up strands of his long hair. James feels a slight prickling in the back of his mind that maybe Lori and Rob are finding this all ridiculous—that they're wondering where the hell Sydney even found this guy, or embarrassed that they're the only two guests at not-real wedding, like some unsuccessful play put on by a jobless actor friend. James steals a glance towards them out of the corner of his eye, then suddenly grips Sydney's hard so hard he feels the bones creak.

He's never seen Rob cry before, but now he is, one tear sliding down his cheek while his arm grips Lori hard around the shoulders. His hand shakes.

The prickling in the back of James' mind vanishes, blasted away over the cliff and across the waves, and he looks back at Sydney, glowing and beautiful in the sun. Sydney winks at him, softly under the cover of his eyelashes, and James fights the urge to press him down into the earth and kiss him until the sun finally sleeps.

"Sydney," Chris says, and James wonders how he even knew the name, "you are the sea. And James, you are the sky. At your horizon line, you meet. It is never broken, and never bent. It is eternal, holding your two souls together at the seam, and you may reach across it to share your gifts with each other, from now until the day you part."

Chris reaches into the bag at his feet and pulls out a small box. James had nearly forgotten—that morning already seems like years ago. When Chris had passed them each the rough, wooden box and told them to place their rings and the chains to wear them on inside it, and James had nervously slipped his decidedly-not-a-ring for Sydney under the lid, then desperately fought against his curiosity not to peek at Sydney's ring for him when he passed him the box.

Now Chris opens the small box, shielding the contents from them with the lid. He cradles the box in his hands, and continues in a voice that floats effortlessly on the wind.

"In my hands are the symbols of your love that have each decided to wear over your hearts, chosen by each other as the deepest symbol of your entity as sky or sea." He reaches in and draws out the dog tags James had placed in there that morning, freshly engraved with Sydney's full name across the back. July 9, 1976—the date of the International Surf Festival in Hermosa—right beneath it.

Chris hands the chain to Sydney, who reaches up with a shaking hand to cradle the tags, before gasping up at James with a crumbling look on his face.

"Really?" he whispers.

James' sleepless nerves over Sydney being upset that it wasn't a real wedding ring vanish when he takes in the shine across Sydney's pale eyes. He nods. He can't speak. Sydney huffs out a wet laugh and carefully settles the chain around his neck, then tucks the tags underneath his shirt, dropping them over his chest.

James startles when Chris holds up an object right in front of him, and it takes a moment for his eyes to adjust before he reaches up to grab it with numb fingers.

It isn't a ring.

It's a small medallion on a chain, made of sanded, gleaming wood. James holds it in his palm and runs his thumb along the smooth, flat surface. Something about the coloring of it looks familiar to him. Then he notices the barest trace of spray paint at the edge. Realization slaps against his face, and he gasps.

"Your first board?" he breathes.

Sydney nods, eyes hesitant. James can tell he's waiting to see if James will understand why. Why Sydney felt the need to cut apart the first board he ever caught a wave on, and carved out a piece at the center, and sanded and sanded and sanded it until it became something beautiful that shone. Why Sydney felt the need to include the barest hint of old spray paint that never fully scrubbed off, which James knows once formed a word sprayed across Sydney's board that still shoots icy fear into his own chest.

*Oh*, Sydney . . .

James places the chain around his neck, adjusting his shirt so the smooth wood hangs just over his heart. He looks up at Sydney with wet eyes, biting his lip, and Sydney's entire body relaxes like releasing a lungful of air.

James nods, just barely, and he knows that Sydney sees—that he understands. It's more than any of the words they could say.

James nearly forgets that the two of them aren't alone on the entire earth, and he flinches when Chris suddenly picks up where he left off, his voice warming the cool frothy spray carried by the wind flowing across the rocky cliff.

"Aloha is the welcome and the goodbye," Chris says like a hum. "It is the welcoming of this new union—this horizon of sky and sea. And it is the goodbye of the fully separated self—the goodbye to a life lived solely on one's own path, with one's own gifts."

He turns to James. "James, before you say goodbye to your old life as one man, and welcome your new life as sky, is there anything you wish to say to Sydney?"

James blanks. He hadn't known Chris would ask them this. They hadn't known anything about what he would even say—no vows or lines or any of it at all. Which is unbearably stupid now that he thinks about it. Who walks into their own wedding without knowing what they're about to promise and say? But he's stuck here, and Chris is waiting for him to make a life changing declaration, and he suddenly can't think of a single word beyond Sydney's name.

He glances up at Sydney with wide eyes, feeling like the entire ocean is frozen waiting on the cusp of what he's about to say. Then he sees Sydney's patient eyes, the little palmfuls of clear ocean water on the safe shore, and the words come rushing out of his mouth before he can even plan them, flowing calm and effortless from his lips.

"You saved me," he says, throat tight. "And I love you."

A thick moment of insecurity beats in James' ears, and he grits his teeth as he thinks that maybe Chris had expected some longer, more eloquent vow after all the gorgeous things he's been saying to them all afternoon. That maybe he'll scowl, and tell the Champion of the Waves Danny Moore that he should at least find a man who doesn't sound like an uneducated, unprepared rock, if he's going to be with a man at all.

But Chris simply nods, a soft smile on his lips, and he turns towards Sydney, who's looking at James like he's stunned. Chris repeats the same thing to him. "Sydney, before you say goodbye to your old life as one man, and welcome your new life as sea, is there anything you wish to say to James?"

James stares transfixed as Sydney swallows hard once, then twice. He reaches again for Sydney's hands, and Sydney's fingers immediately lock onto his in a strong, tight grip. James waits patiently, wondering what grand speech Sydney's about to deliver, as Sydney looks down at their joined hands and blinks.

The moment drags on. James' breathing starts to pick up. He feels unprecedentedly helpless watching Sydney struggle for what to say for seemingly the first time since James introduced himself out on the waves.

Then Sydney looks into his eyes and gruffly whispers, "James."

Sydney opens his mouth to say more, but nothing comes out. He looks back down at their hands wide-eyed, then releases a shaky breath and looks back at James with one tear slowly sliding down his cheek. His lips tremble as he barely gets out the word again.

*"James."*

Then James watches in awe as Sydney starts to cry, tears streaming freely down his face as his lungs clench over a wet sob. James completely forgets about the ceremony. Forgets Chris and Rob and Lori and the fact they're even standing up on the cliff saying their vows.

Sydney's crumpling face is the only thing that exists in the world, and James immediately steps forward and holds Sydney's wet cheek in his hand, thumb wiping away the water dripping down from Sydney's eye. His own eyes grow wet as Sydney's chest vibrates against his, and James waits patiently until Sydney looks up from between their bodies and briefly meets his gaze. He would wait here forever.

"Hey now," he whispers, pulling Sydney's face down closer to him. Out of nowhere, an odd sense of calm drapes over his skin, banishing the panic of watching Sydney Moore break down and replacing it with warmth spreading through his veins—the soft heat of the sand against the soles of his feet when he shook Sydney's hand on the Billabong shore.

He grips Sydney's wet cheek harder in his hand as Sydney tries to hold back the choked sounds in his throat. "I'm right here," he whispers. "Look at me."

Sydney's wet eyes fly back open and lock onto James' face, wrecked and lost with a hint of embarrassment burning in the vivid blue of his irises. James rubs his cheek and smiles, letting Sydney see his own lips shake. "Here I thought I was gonna be the one to lose it," he says.

Sydney laughs wetly, coming to life and wiping the back of his hand over his cheeks and nose. "So did I," he says roughly, eyes crinkling. "But then again, you had all that Navy training."

James shakes his head and sniffs. "Ridiculous man," he whispers.

With a final pat and one last swipe of his thumb across Sydney's cheek, James pulls away his hand, pausing briefly to straighten the collar of Sydney's shirt. Sydney rolls back his shoulders, running his forearm over his eyes once more and sniffing hard.

When he's ready, he gives James a small, grinning nod, and they both look at Chris and gesture to go on. The vows are done; they both know that Sydney just said everything he ever could with one word. He doesn't need to say anything more.

Chris appraises them both, his face gentle and solemn, then he bends down to pull a gleaming conch shell out of the bag, cradling it softly in his large, rough hands.

He clears his throat. "With this sound, we will ask for the attention of the sky and sea as witness, to see that you, James Campbell, and you, Sydney Moore, have chosen now to join together as one, binding yourselves to each other with your hearts as the unbroken horizon line. May no man, no law, and no force of nature cause that horizon to bend or break. When I sound this horn, the sky and the sea become one."

With one final serious glance at each of them, Chris turns his back to face out over the ocean, raising the conch shell to his lips. The wind whispers in the silent pause. Then Chris takes a deep breath and blows a deep and mournful note through the shell, echoing out across the waves and billowing over the sea.

James' chest vibrates with the groaning hum. He looks up at Sydney, whose eyes are burning brilliant blue framed by long, wet eyelashes. Sydney smiles and runs his hands across James' shoulders, and James closes his eyes and hums as Sydney presses a long, soft kiss to his forehead, his thumbs coming up to rub along his jaw.

James reaches up to hold onto Sydney's wrists as the conch shell continues to blow out over the sea. And the brilliant wind in his hair, the foaming salt in his nose and the back of his throat, and James breathes in the scent from the hollow of Sydney's neck as his toes grip at the foundation of the sun warmed earth.

Sydney pulls back and looks at him just as Chris finishes the final call on the shell. James moves to step back from Sydney, unsure what Chris will do next, when suddenly an unexpected voice breaks the bubble of silence.

"Aw come on, give him a real kiss!" Lori cries.

Sydney laughs as James shoots Lori and Rob a breathless smile, and then before he can even lick his lips, or raise his brows at Sydney to silently ask what he wants to do, Sydney's wet lips are on his mouth.

He caresses James' surprised lips, moving slowly against his skin while a moan builds deep in his throat. James feels the kiss right down to the soles of his feet, wrapping around every muscle and bone. He smiles against Sydney's mouth, grips the back of his neck, and pulls him closer against his lips to deepen the kiss with a soft moan, not giving a shit that three other people are watching him place his mouth on another man's skin. Watching him taste the sound of his name still trembling on Sydney's tongue, or weave his fingers through a head of dark curls, or swipe his thumb along a sharp, angular jaw.

It feels an awful lot like flying. Like soaring down the face of a wave with nothing but the ocean spray blasting against his grinning face.

Sydney presses one last kiss to the corner of James' mouth, moving his lips gently across the edge of James' beard, then he steps back, dropping his hand after one final squeeze.

James belatedly realizes that Chris is placing the shell back in his bag and slinging it over his shoulder, quietly starting to step away behind them. James quickly steps in front of Chris before he can leave and tries to think of what the hell he should even say, feeling somber and giddy in his chest all at once.

He catches the deep brown eyes framed by unruly, grey brows and forces himself to speak. "Thank you," he says. "I don't . . . I don't know what we would've done."

Sydney stands beside him and nods once, his eyes full of meaning. Chris steps back and looks between the two of them thoughtfully for a moment before giving a small smile and bowing his head.

"It was a privilege," he says. Then he nods towards Rob and Lori waiting behind them. "Go and celebrate, then. And one of you better win for Oahu next month in Huntington Beach." Then he looks once more at the sea, shoulders his bag, and calmly walks back towards the path leading down to the beach, stepping smoothly along the way with his head held effortlessly high, not looking once behind him.

James watches Chris leave with the strange urge to reach out and beg him to stay, oddly sad and empty with each further step the man takes down the cliff path. James waits until Chris' silver head disappears behind the rocks and into the trees, then startles when someone gently touches his shoulder. He turns to see Sydney guiding back around towards Rob and Lori where they stand near the peak of the cliff.

"I think Rob's gonna pass out if you don't go over there," Sydney whispers in his ear, and James only has the chance to take two steps forward when Rob covers the distance in three leaping strides and crushes James in his arms, gripping hard at his back.

They don't say anything. Rob's chest presses the smooth, unfamiliar weight of Sydney's medallion against James' skin, the wood already warmed by the heat of his body. James breathes into his shoulder, and Rob's hair tumbles loose from his bun across the side of James' face.

Then Rob thumps his back hard once before stepping aside so Lori can jump in, and she squeezes her arms around James' neck as he buries his face in the top of her hair. Sydney steps up behind him, running his palm up the small of James' back, and James has the sudden sensation, forming a lump in his throat, that he has never been alive until this moment. That his heart has been beating half-speed from the morning he woke up alone as a kid until now. That he has never, truly never, felt the real kiss of the sun against his skin until these specific rays. This specific sky and sea.

But then Lori steps away from him, slipping out of his arms. A buzzing silence falls, and everyone stands frozen still, and James fears that everything in his entire world is about to turn strained and uncomfortable for the rest of time—that all four of them will stand at the top of this cliff without any idea what to say until the earth dies, the memory of Sydney's lips on his forever burned into everyone's minds.

Then Rob clears his throat and turns to Sydney. "So, who the fuck is *Sydney*?" he asks.

Sydney laughs, the sound of it washing over James like smooth, warm water. The earth unfreezes, and time starts ticking away again in a rhythm with the waves. They all shuffle their feet, unconsciously moving a few steps away from where the ceremony just took place.

Rob turns to James and sports a wicked grin. "And what the hell is this about him calling you 'James? Who the fuck are you, now—some middle-aged pastor from Kansas? I taught you better than that, man. Be cool."

James rolls his eyes as the last wisps of tension break, giving way to clear, fresh air as James starts walking down the path besides Lori, Rob and Sydney walking a few steps ahead of them. But Rob and Sydney slowly pull away as they all eventually make their way back along the stretch of beach, and James prides himself that he doesn't immediately break into a sprint to keep up like a desperate kid.

Lori walks beside him in easy silence, one hand playing with the tips of her hair draped over her shoulder. When Rob and Sydney are too far ahead to hear, James sticks his hands in his pockets and breathes in the familiar spray of the sea.

"Rob's not giving him the 'break his heart' talk, is he?" he asks.

Lori snickers under her breath. "No, he gave him that over the phone when he called a week ago. I was terrified just sitting in the next room over," she laughs.

James chuckles, peering into the distance as Sydney and Rob pause by the shore in front of the house, their toes dipping into the wet and foaming sand. He watches Rob lean forward to put his hand on Sydney's arm, holding him there. They learn towards each other, both speaking low and occasionally nodding. Something tells James he already knows the gist of what they must be talking about—something about the fact that James damn well knows that these are the only two men on earth he's ever looked in the eyes and told that he used to want to swim out forever into the water and never look back.

That he still does. Some days. After the long nights filled with red mud and lifeless black eyes. When he thinks maybe the warm arm around him is really a deadly jungle vine, pulling him down into the smoke.

James blinks. He hadn't even realized he'd stopped walking, and Lori's shoulder brushes against his as they both stare at Sydney and Rob standing in the shallows. The sight of the two people James loves most in the world currently holding each other by the sea burns fresh, sharp warmth through his chest, making him have to blink away.

"How long are you guys staying?" he hears himself ask Lori.

Lori takes the bait and goes along with the change in subject, taking a breath and flipping her hair back off her shoulder as they resume their walk. "Only until day after tomorrow," she says like it's an apology. "You know it's hard for Rob to get time off like this. And me, too."

James rubs the back of his neck. "Shit, of course. I didn't realize—we could take you out somewhere tonight? Try and find somewhere in the city? Or I'm not sure if we have anything to cook –"

"Oh please, I've already made Rob get us reservations to the most expensive restaurant in Honolulu tonight by our hotel, and you're gonna stay here and enjoy yourself. Don't worry about us."

"But you came all this way, you took time off—"

"Jimmy, we'll see you tomorrow, I promise. I'll probably wake up tomorrow morning to find Rob's already snuck out at the crack of dawn and hitched a ride back to you because he'll be too impatient to wait for poor old me."

James snorts under his breath and grins down at his bare feet, watching them sink into the sand just as they finally reach Rob and Sydney standing quietly on the shore. Sydney immediately reaches for him and pulls him close to his side by the waist, kissing the side of his head without hesitation. The plain, blatant fact of it makes James' heart tug in his chest.

He wants to call up to the heavens for somebody up there to take a picture of them all—of James standing on the beach of his home in front of his two closest friends with Sydney Moore effortlessly pressing his lips into his hair. Of him breathing easy and open with the warm weight of Sydney's wedding gift hanging around his neck and over his chest, protected by the thin navy fabric of his shirt and with the cool chain brushing the edge of his scar.

Rob puts his hand on Lori's shoulder with an air of finality. "So, we'll see you guys tomorrow?"

Sydney tilts his head. "I guess we can spare you some time."

Lori squints at him. "I don't think I can ever call you Danny ever again. Just doesn't fit."

"Oh, you'll get used to it again, trust me," Sydney says, right at the same time Rob loudly whispers, "He'll kill you and bury you at sea if you don't!"

A silence falls on the group after Sydney laughs through his nose, and James has the choking urge to say something—anything. That he should thank them again, or talk about what just happened, or somehow put all the chaos in his head into words. That he needs to keep them forever in their huddle on the beach before anything has the chance to break away or fall apart.

"Alright, Jimmy?"

Rob's looking at him with the same questioning expression he was wearing the very moment they first met.

James shakes his head, reminding himself that he's in Oahu, and that he owns a surf shop, and that he's *married,* and that he'll never again be all alone. He smiles apologetically. "Yeah, yeah, sorry. Just lost in my head."

Rob and Sydney look at each other and explain, at the exact same time, and in the same superior voice, "He does that."

Lori huffs. "Oh, God; the world can barely handle one man obsessed with Jimmy Campbell. We don't need *two.*" She grabs Rob's arm and raises a hand at Sydney's open mouth to gently cut him off. "We'll catch the bus," she says to his silent question. And then, to an affronted Rob, "You have to pass on your crown now that you're not married to him. Leave them be. It's their *wedding night.*"

And after Lori looks back at them over her shoulder and rolls her eyes, and Rob looks back over his shoulder and gives a puppy-dog frown and a wink, they walk together back down the tree-lined lane, Lori turning to give one final wave before she wraps her arm around Rob's waist and leans her head on his shoulder.

James is left alone on an empty stretch of beach with Sydney at his side, still blushing hot across his cheeks from Lori's words, and all he can think to do is laugh.

"Well, what do we do now?" he asks into the silence.

Sydney grins down at him, eyes glittering and creasing at the corners, and then he looks out over the sea and takes a dramatically deep breath, settling his shoulders as the sun pours across his face.

"Now we surf," he says, and he walks off without another word towards where their boards are kept leaned up against the side of the house.

And James knows that Sydney knows that he'll follow him. Would paddle behind him to the edges of the earth.

"Why did he choose you as the sky and me as the sea?"

James hums in response as he paddles out into the waves behind Sydney. They're skirting just to the side of the main break of the waves along the deserted beach they'd driven to at the very edges of the Banzai, swimming out smoothly towards the slowly setting sun.

James calls up to him as he paddles through the soft, clear water, voice echoing across the frothy surface. "Probably because you're like a deep, black pit of terrifying mystery, and people are afraid of the ocean."

Sydney huffs. "What, and you're just sunshine and puffy clouds and rainbows all the time?"

"Obviously Chris thought so."

"Well shit, I didn't want to think he was an idiot, but now I have to," Sydney mumbles.

"Hello? You need any help up there?" James calls back. "I'm pretty sure you're sinking under the weight of your gigantic fucking head."

Sydney chuckles ahead of him and stops paddling in a clear spot of water, sitting up to perch on his board. He pulls his arms behind him to stretch his shoulders, chest heaving. James' mouth waters at the sight. The flowers spilling across his shoulder ripple and shine in the thick purple light, which billows out over the waves from the low and heavy sun and reflects back onto his smooth, tan skin.

James pulls up next to him and sits up, too, cracking his neck. Already his chest feels naked without the warm, smooth wood hanging down across it; they'd left their necklaces back at home out of fear of losing them in the waves. Now James finds himself rubbing idly the spot at the middle of his chest with his fingertips for a moment, breathing deeply into his lungs and catching the soft scent of flowers floating across the ocean's surface.

"I miss mine, too," Sydney says quietly beside him.

James holds out his hand across the water and Sydney immediately takes it, dipping their joined hands just below the surface of the waves and holding on.

James sighs. He wants the world at his back to just disappear for a week. Wants to take Sydney's hand in his wherever they go and let Sydney lead him to the edges of the earth so he can follow him there. Wants to lead Sydney to the depths of the seas. He wants to see only his face, smell only his skin, hear only his voice.

"I wish we could escape," James says. "Just for a week."

"Aw, come on, James, why would you ever want to escape paradise?"

James rolls his eyes as Sydney squeezes his fingers. "You know what I mean, you dick."

Sydney hums softly, and suddenly the yearning in James' chest grows so strong he thinks he'll moan out loud at the clutch of it. "I know Hank's already watching the shop for a few days, but . . . you think we can ask him to add a few more?"

Sydney shrugs one shoulder, looking out calmly at the horizon. "Seeing as how he owns a third of the place, I don't see why we can't ask."

"We could go somewhere," James sighs. "Just the two of us, and no competitions or anything. Just, get out of this bubble for a week." He turns to Sydney and says the words hiding in the back of his throat. "Somewhere we can . . ." He briefly lifts their joined hands out of the water and nods down at them. "You know, somewhere we can do this. Out in the open. Would be nice."

Sydney nods understanding, rubbing his thumb along James' hand. "I know of a place on Maui we could stay that might be nice. It's really private from what I hear. And there's hiking there. Volcanoes and shit you can climb to feel all adventurous to match your beard."

"God, that sounds like a fucking dream."

Sydney hums and squeezes James' hand once more before letting go. He cups a handful of seawater in his palms and leans his head back to pour it down over his hair, plastering his curls to his head. James watches the beads of water drip slowly down his chest and stomach, wanting to lean down and lick them off one by one with his tongue.

Sydney smiles with his eyes closed, face still turned up towards the sky. "Good thing we already have that place booked for the rest of the week, then," he says.

James blinks hard, mind reeling. "What? What about—"

"And good thing Hank already said he'd watch the shop for the whole week."

The water tickles against James' thighs as he sits there dumbly with his mouth hanging open. He doesn't know whether to laugh or cry or take Sydney by the shoulders and kiss every inch of his face, bit by bit. "You're fucking serious?" he pants out.

Sydney looks back at him with glittering eyes, barely holding back the smile from his lips. "Of course I'm serious. Our flight's around the same time as Rob and Lori's the day after tomorrow. We can ride with them to the airport. Be a surprise for them, too."

James huffs a disbelieving laugh and stares blankly out towards the endless horizon, trying to calm his racing heart and the quiet shaking in his hands gripping his board. He licks his lips and tries to talk without laughing. "Is this what being married to you is like, then? You surprising me once every three goddamn hours?"

Sydney suddenly stills next to him, and James feels an ache in his gut when he thinks he understands the reason why. "God, baby, I feel bad. You've done all of this for me, found Chris and planned it all, and then I had my friends there today." He groans quietly and rubs the back of his neck, feeling hot under his skin. "I haven't done jack shit for you back. Not anything."

"That's not true," Sydney says immediately.

James gestures limply out towards the waves with his hand, not knowing what to say. He wants to cup the entire ocean in his palms and hand it to Sydney on a platter. That or reach up as high as he can to write Sydney's name in the goddamn stars. Something to feel like less of an absolute dud.

Sydney reaches out and grabs his hand again, grip steady. "James, that's not true at all," he says again.

James looks over at him and bites his lip. "What have I done, then?" he asks. The question trembles across the gently rolling waters, hovering and waiting for an answer.

Suddenly Sydney's face breaks into a breathless smile, sending grateful shivers down James' spine. "You married me, you idiot," Sydney says, and then he leans across the space between their boards, grabs the side of James' face, and kisses him, wet and slow, sitting at the edge of the earth.

James moans against his mouth, letting himself feel and taste every good part of Sydney's lips. He pulls back just far enough to speak, the air from his lips brushing across the tip of Sydney's tongue.

"When was the last time I told you that you were something else?" he whispers.

Sydney chuckles and presses another kiss just below James' mouth, his lips in a grin. "It's been at least an hour. Better remind me."

James kisses him again, deep and open-mouthed and groaning when Sydney's fingertips come up to run over his scar. "You're something else," he whispers against his lips.

Sydney pulls back and gives James a look so trusting, so open, so *content* that it explodes through his chest, tilting the world onto its side. Like the perfect pipeline barreling towards the shore in the middle of a set, James knows what he can do—what he can say to somehow feel like he's given Sydney something precious back.

James steels his shoulders and clears his throat, looking straight out across the horizon. Sydney had told him once, like he was teaching a class on James Campbell, that he's a man who leaps head first into risks when he isn't busy being boring with things like jobs and money and plans.

And this sure as hell is one of those risks.

"I found your notes, you know," James says gently.

Sydney's eyes widen quickly in shock, and James laughs. "Well come on, I'm not an idiot," he chuckles. "You hid them in the pocket of my own goddamn pants."

"Well you never wear that pair!" Sydney cries. "Not even once! They're practically the only fucking thing in our house you've never touched besides the new coffeemaker prototype—!"

"*That's* what that is?"

Sydney's jaw drops. "What the fuck did you think it was all this time? Don't say a bo—"

"I dunno. A bomb?"

"A year later and you still think I'm building a secret bomb, how could you even—"

"Well, it's not like you don't have all the pieces! I'm not watching you every goddamn second you're holed up on the porch all hunched over your wires like a Bond villain."

"But James, you *sleep* with me."

"And I fuck you."

"Right, you sleep with me and you fuck me and you would do that with a person you think is building a dangerously destructive homemade weapon? You're tripping."

"Maybe I like the danger."

"How dangerous is it to want a hot cup of coffee first thing in the morning that is conveniently *delivered* on an elegant system of tracks to my bedside table? Tell me how—?"

James howls, leaning over his board to try and catch his breath from laughing. "Oh my God," he pants. "You're something else."

Sydney huffs, crossing his arms. "You could've told me you were fucking yanking my chain. And also you don't need to remind me again *that* quickly."

James shoots him one last smile, his own laughter slowly fading from his chest, and before he can even realize it, the moment turns thick and crackling, Sydney waiting tense and frozen on his board in light of what James had originally started to say.

James blinks hard, taking a second to order his thoughts, and when he does speak, his voice is surprisingly calm and gentle, rolling across the smooth water. "How long have you been really looking for her?" he asks.

Sydney shrugs halfheartedly, looking down at his board like he's ashamed. "Not that long," he says to the space between his legs. "Lahela mentioned something in her letter a few weeks back—a detail I hadn't known that my father must have offhand mentioned to her. Don't think he knows she's been writing to me, yet. It just got me thinking . . ."

James takes pity on him and reaches over to run his palm across Sydney's forearm, inwardly thrilling when Sydney turns his palm over to catch James' hand in his, entwining their fingers again.

"Why didn't you tell me?" James asks.

Sydney squeezes his hand once and breathes slow and deep for a long moment, and James waits patiently in the silence, bobbing slowly up and down on their boards as the waves rush and hum in the distance behind them.

Finally, Sydney speaks, his voice thin and halting. "I didn't mean to," he says. "I just . . . it all happened so fast, in the beginning. Didn't even seem like much. I still don't have much to go on even now. But, you've been so . . . you've been happy. And it didn't seem fair."

James frowns. "What didn't seem fair?"

Sydney looks up at him, eyes hot and confused. "This whole thing," he says, flicking his hand out towards the horizon. "It didn't . . . I feel bad, James. I mean, I have Lahela, sort of. In some way. And I have you. And now I'm trying to look for my momma, too." He sighs, gripping James' hand, and James' chest clenches at the emotion on Sydney's face. "You don't have anyone to look for," Sydney finishes.

"Oh, love . . ."

James brings Sydney's hand up to his mouth and kisses it, holding the warm skin against his face. "Sydney, I don't need to look for anyone," he says in a choked voice. "You *are* my family. I have you."

"It's not like you aren't enough for me—"

"I know that. God, I know that. Especially after today."

Sydney sighs, then slips his hand from James' fingers to rub it over his face. "I just need to know," he whispers. "If she's still out there . . . I—she was everything to me. Back then. And maybe, to her, I'm still . . . I just need to know. I need to try."

James feels like the ocean could rise up to caress them from the deep, holding them aloft in a large, gentle hug away from the rest of the world. The words come to him easily, settling comfortably on his tongue as he watches Sydney's chest rapidly breathing in the late and hazy sunlight. "I'll go with you," James says.

"You—what?"

James tries to hold back his smile as Sydney slowly processes what he said. James pats his thigh. "I'm sure there's only so much you can do all the way out here," he says. "So if you go looking for her—if you go back to the mainland. If everything works out and you go to meet her. You know that I'll go with you."

The moment settles around them, warm and velvet against their skin. James wonders if the Oahu skyline became magically more beautiful since they said their vows that afternoon. If the sea and sky really did witness them up on the cliff and dressed up just to celebrate with them.

Sydney swallows hard and runs a hand through his hair. He slowly shakes his head. "You are a marvel," he says.

James reaches out and kisses Sydney's hand again before letting it go, chest expanding hotly under his skin. He looks at the man before him, an incredulous smile still painted across his lips. He looks and he tries to match him to the man he'd seen that day on the beach, a crowd of onlookers at their backs, and the buzzing roar of the competition, and the impenetrable, black sunglasses thrown over Sydney's eyes.

He can't.

The man now before him is the endless sea, open and rolling and surrounding James so thoroughly he can't find a part of himself that isn't covered in saltwater, caressed and warmed by the froth. Held by Sydney Moore.

Sydney looks over at him and nods over James' shoulder to the waves rushing into shore behind their backs, filling the air with the rolling crash of trembling, salt-covered foam.

"Nice set about to come in," he says with a gleam in his eye. "You should take it."

"Sure you don't wanna show off first?"

Sydney's drying curls blow into his eyes. "I'd rather watch you."

James drinks in the sight of Sydney sitting in the rippling sun, strong and calm and beautiful on the blue velvet water. Then he sets his jaw, nods once, and throws himself down to start paddling out to the breaking point, feeling Sydney's eyes warmly fixed onto his back. The water rushes against his skin in the familiar salty kiss, sliding across his muscles and rippling through his hair as a delicious ache spreads through his arms and shoulders, racing against the silken hum of the waves.

Just when James reaches the breaking point and chooses which wave he'll take, he hears a voice travel out to him, rolling across the sea on the evening breeze. It mixes and churns with the salt spray in the air, hovering over his skin and holding him together, settling straight down in his bones with a sweet sigh.

The voice sounds like whipped-cream and Sydney and home.

The voice calls out, "Surf like hell, James Campbell."

# About the Author

    C. L. Beaumont received her B.A. in South Asian Linguistics and Art History from the University of California, Berkeley, and now serves coffee in the wee hours of the morning until she can race home each day to dive into her true love: writing. When she isn't hiking or checking another National Park off her list, she enjoys devouring crime fiction, cooking new vegetarian recipes, and trying to complete jigsaw puzzles while she slowly works her way through Rupert Graves' entire filmography. C. L. Beaumont lives near the Washington mountains with her gorgeous forest ranger partner and their child—er, poodle.

# About Carnation Books

Carnation Books is a fandom-powered publisher of the best in inclusive fiction. Founded in 2016, Carnation Books is at the forefront of new author discovery. Visit CarnationBooks.com to learn more, and to sign up for our story-filled newsletter!